SPIRIT GATE

He set his right foot on the glittering pavement, then his left. Nothing happened.

She let out all her breath

He turned and spoke to her. She saw his mouth working, but the wind – or the magic of the Guardians – tore his words away.

'Joss!' she cried, but he turned away and with measured paces worked his way in on the tortuous branched path. All her worst fears choked her because with each step he seemed to recede, although he wasn't really getting any farther away from her: he was only *fading*. It was as if a veil thickened around him, as if mist seeped up from marshland to conceal the landscape. There was nothing quite seen, nothing tangible, but it obscured him nonetheless. Marit had never unduly feared the dangers of her task as a reeve, although she had walked into a hundred different knife's-edge situations with only her eagle, her weapons, and most of all her good instincts to guide her. But fear paralyzed her now.

We've broken the boundaries. We'll be punished.

He faded more as he walked deeper into the labyrinth, never coming closer or back toward her even when the path turned that way. The eagles neither moved or called; the silence daunted them. The ghost of his form, scarcely more than a shadow, reached the center.

He vanished. Just like that: a blink, a shimmer of light – and he was gone.

KATE ELLIOTT

SPIRIT GATE

BOOK ONE OF
CROSSROADS

www.orbitbooks.net

ORBIT

First published in the United States in 2007 by Tor,
Tom Doherty Associates, LLC
First published in Great Britain in 2007 by Orbit
This paperback edition published in 2007
Reprinted 2008 (three times), 2009 (twice), 2010, 2011, 2012

A CIP catalogue record for this book
is available from the British Library.

ISBN 978-1-84149-274-2

Typeset in Sabon by M Rules
Printed and bound by CPI Group (UK) Ltd, Croydon, CR0 4YY

Papers used by Orbit are from well-managed forests
and other responsible sources.

Orbit
An imprint of
Little, Brown Book Group
100 Victoria Embankment
London EC4Y 0DY

An Hachette UK Company
www.hachette.co.uk

www.orbitbooks.net

This novel is lovingly dedicated to my sister Sonja who, during the same year I was writing this book, tackled three major life changes very like those in the story.

ACKNOWLEDGEMENTS

I would like to thank my beta-test readers, all of whom offered exceedingly useful comments: Jay Silverstein, Gerald Rasmussen, Sigrid Rasmussen, Sherwood Smith, Edana Mackenzie, Karen Williams, and Ann Marie Rasmussen. My children, as always, gave me feedback when I asked for it, and sometimes when I didn't.

David B. Coe and Meriday Beth Komor kindly took time to give me advice on wildlife behaviors. However, any mistakes are my own, and have nothing to do with the excellent observations they proffered.

My thanks to Liz Danforth for taking on the map despite my delays in getting her the material she needed; to Jim Frenkel for making me work so hard that my brain hurt; and to Michelle Sagara West for giving me frank and constructive advice at a crucial juncture – not, of course, that she would ever say anything that was less than frank.

Finally, a big mahalo to the women of the Uttermost West, who kept my head above water when the surf got high.

PART ONE

Shadows

In the Year of the Black Eagle

In the Hundred

1

On a hot summer's day like today Flirt liked to fly straight up along the shoreline of the river, huge wings huffing against the wind. The draft off the running water cooled eagle and reeve, and gave the raptor a chance to get close to any unsuspecting deer come out to drink. This time of day, early afternoon, they didn't see a single creature along the shore except once a man chopping wood who had flung up a hand at the sound, poised, listening. When he saw them he relaxed and went back to his work as Flirt's vast shadow shuddered along the rocks. His brindled hound barked, then hushed, ears flat, cowering, as Flirt answered with a piercing cry of her own. She didn't like challenges.

Marit grinned. The man kept chopping and was soon left behind.

Woodland spread up on both sides of the Liya Pass, hills covered so thickly with beech that Marit couldn't see the ground. Here and there a stand of silver birch glimmered on rockier earth, leaves flashing in the wind. The air was smooth today, a steady wind out of the northeast that blew at crosscurrents to their line of flight, but Marit didn't like the smell. She shifted in the harness and wiped sweat off her brow. There'd been something nasty in the air ever since last winter; she knew it and the other reeves knew it. Anyone knew it, who ever tilted her head back to take a look around; who ever stopped to listen. Probably the woodchopper knew it, which is why he'd been scared for that moment, expecting the worst.

Shadows.

'Lust and greed and fear,' old Marshal Alard of Copper Hall had said at winter feast. 'Mark my words. Blood has been spilled in the wrong places, but we don't know where, not yet. Keep your eyes open. Don't turn your backs.'

Not that reeves ever turned their backs, or kept their eyes closed. The Hundred was a broad land made prosperous by towns and villages and markets, by cultivated fields, wide pasturelands, rich forests, and treasure buried in the earth. Yet there were as many hidey-holes – and forgotten caves and old ruins and secret glades and ravines where dangerous creatures might lurk – as there were laughing children.

Like all reeves, she'd ridden a circuit of the land her first year out of Copper Hall. She knew how wide the land was. She knew how the ocean bounded the Hundred to the north and east and how the Spires and Heaven's Ridge with its Barrens protected the good folk of her land from their enemies to the south and west.

'Our worst enemy has always been the one within, Flirt,' she said to her eagle, but the rushing wind against her face caught her words and flung them into nothing. Not that Flirt could understand her words, only shading and emotion. Smart as pigs, the great eagles were, but no smarter than that no matter what the old legends said.

That was the first thing you learned when you were marked out for a reeve: limits. A reeve could do so much and no more, just like her eagle. In the old days, so the story went, the reeves had had more power and been treated with more respect, but not any longer. Shadows had been creeping over the Hundred for a long time but it was only now they seemed to be gathering strength.

She shook away these dusty and useless thoughts. Today had been good so far: Just after dawn in the hamlet of Disa Falls she'd successfully mediated a dispute over the stones marking the boundary between two fields. She'd allowed the local arkhon to offer a haunch of sheep as a snack for Flirt, enough to keep her going until a real hunt. So it went, a typical start to a reeve's day.

Flirt banked and shifted position as the air currents altered because of a notch in the higher hills up to the east. Below, the woodland frayed into the patchwork of saplings and underbrush stretching between broad swaths of mature beech that betrayed human hands at work. Soon enough she saw a pretty green valley nestled between the hills. It was mostly trees and meadows, but there was a village with a small boat dock built out into the river and a few houses on the far bank beside new fields cut into the forest. The summit road dipped down from the east to run by the village, which had probably grown up as a wayfaring stop for travelers and merchants.

As she flew over, surveying the lay of the land, she was surprised to see a man actually in the act of running a red eagle banner up the message pole set in the village square. She circled Flirt around and with a swell of wings and a thump they landed on the stony beach. She hitched her legs out of the harness and leaped down, absorbing the landing by bending her knees. A dozen villagers and more children had gathered at a prudent distance outside the low stockade that kept woodland predators and pesky deer out of their gardens and homes. She slipped her staff out of the harness and sauntered over. The staff in her hand, the short sword rattling along her right thigh, and the quiver slung over her back weren't nearly as daunting as Flirt. The eagle's amber stare, her massive claws, and her sheer, shocking size – bigger than a surly cart horse and twice as mean – were enough to concern anyone. The eagle fluffed up her feathers, whuffed, and settled down to wait.

'How can I help you folks?' Marit asked.

They weren't scared of *her* at any rate. They stared right at her boldly enough, maybe surprised to see a woman.

'Go get the reeve some ale, and bread and cheese,' said the man who still stood with the rope in one hand. The banner snapped halfway up the pole.

In answer, a girl about ten years of age trotted, backward, toward an inn whose low barracks-like building took up one entire side of the village square. The girl just could not rip her gaze away from the eagle. Naturally, after a few steps, she stumbled and fell flat on her rump.

An older girl yelled, 'Turn round, you ninny! That beast ain't going nowhere yet.'

Others laughed as the girl got up and dusted off her bright red tunic and pantaloons, then bolted through the open door of the inn. The sign creaking over the porch bore fresh paint and the cheerful visages of a quintet of happy, drinking fellows: three men and two women. One of the painted men had an outlander's pale hair caught back in a trident braid, but none of the folk who'd come up to greet her had the look of foreigners. These were good, handsome Hundred folk, dark skin, black hair, brown eyes.

'I'm called Reeve Marit. What's the trouble?' She sorted through the map she carried in her mind. 'This is Merrivale.'

'Indeed it is, Reeve Marit.' The man had a bitter twist to his mouth. Everyone else was looking at him with frowns and whispers. 'I'm called Faron. I own the Merrymakers, there.' He gestured toward the inn. 'It's a lad what works for me has caused the trouble.' He coughed. Several folk scuffed their feet on the dirt, looking away. She noted the way their eyes drifted and their fingers twitched. 'Stole two bolts of silk I'd had brought in. It come all the way from the Sirniakan Empire.'

Marit whistled.

'Indeed. Bought it for my new bride and the wedding. I'm getting married again – first wife died three year back,' he added hastily. 'I miss her, but life goes on.'

'You mourned her longer than was rightful,' said an elderly woman suddenly. She had a wen on her chin and a killing gaze. 'That's what caused the trouble.'

The innkeeper flushed. He fussed with the white ribbon tying off the end of his long braid. Everyone turned to look at Marit.

'How old is the thief?'

Faron blew air out between set lips as he considered. 'Born in the Year of the Wolf, he was. Suspicious and hasty. Very selfish, if you ask me.'

'You would say so, given the circumstances,' muttered the sarcastic old lady, rolling her eyes in a way most often associated with rash and reckless youth.

'So he's celebrated his fifteenth year. Has he a weapon?'

'Of course not! Nothing but his walking stick and a bundle of bread and cheese out of the larder. That's all else we found missing.'

'How long ago?'

'Just this morning. We looked around in his usual haunts—'

'He's vanished before?'

'Just hiding out, mischief, breaking things. Stealing odds and ends. It's only noontide that we found the silk missing. That's serious. That's theft.'

'What would he be wanting with bolts of silk?'

'He's been threatening to run away to make his fortune in Toskala.'

'Over the pass and through Iliyat and past the Wild?'

'Maybe so,' admitted Faron.

The old woman snorted. 'More like he's running up to that temple dedicated to the Merciless One, up at summit. He can buy himself more than a few snogs with that fancy silk.'

'Vatta!' Faron's cheeks flushed purple as anger flooded his expression.

'My apologies,' Vatta muttered, rubbing at her wen, which was dry and crusty. She'd known prosperity in her day, or a generous husband. Her well-worn yellow silk tunic, slit on the sides from knees to hips, and the contrasting twilight blue pantaloons beneath were also of expensive Sirniakan weave. 'But he threatened to do that more than once, too. A boy his age thinks of the Devourer day and night.'

Marit smiled slightly, but she had as little trust for devotees of the Merciless One, the All-Consuming Devourer, mistress of war, death, and desire, as she had for outlanders, although the Merciless One's followers were her own countryfolk. Although she'd caroused in the Merciless One's grip often enough, and would do so again. Hopefully tonight.

'Anything else I need to know?' she asked instead.

Faron shrugged.

He was hiding something, certainly, but she had a fair idea of just what he wasn't willing to tell her. Shame made some men reticent. 'I'll hunt for him, and come back and report come nightfall.'

'My thanks.' Faron wiped his brow. 'Here's ale, if you'll take a drink.'

'With thanks.'

She drank standing and handed the cup back to the waiting girl. No one moved away, although at least they had manners enough not to stare as she ate. The bread was hearty and the cheese nicely ripe with the tang of dill. With such provender to warm her stomach she walked back to Flirt, fastened herself into the harness, and lifted her bone whistle to her lips. A single sharp *skree* was the command to fly.

Up.

The exhilaration never left. Never. Every time was like the first time, when a short, stocky, innocent girl from Farsar sent to hire herself as a laborer in the city – because her family hadn't the wherewithal to marry her or apprentice her out – found herself chosen and set in the harness of the raptor who had done the choosing. Such was the custom out of time immemorial, the way of the reeves. It was not the marshals who picked which of the young hopefuls and guardsmen would be reeves; it was the eagles themselves. In ancient days, the Four Mothers had bound magic into the great eagles, and the Lady of Beasts had harnessed them to their task, and Marit laughed every day, feeling that magic coursing around her, part of her now as she was part of it.

They rose above the tops of the trees. Although Flirt wanted to go back over the river, Marit guided her a short distance east of the river along the lower ridgeline where the road ran, in places carved into the rock itself. The road was older than the Hundred, so it was written in the annals kept by the hierophants who toiled in the service of Sapanasu, the Keeper of Days, the Lantern of the Gods. Who could have built it, back before people came to live here?

So many mysteries. Thank the gods she wasn't the one who had to puzzle them out.

She judged time and speed to a nicety – she'd had ten years of experience, after all – and spotted the youth long before he noticed her coming. He was toiling up the road near the summit along a broad escarpment devoid of trees. Fortune favored her. With him so exposed and no trees to hide behind, the catch would be swift. Flirt's chest muscles rippled as the eagle shifted altitude, narrowing down for the kill. Marit felt the raptor's excitement; it burned in her blood as well.

The two bolts of dazzling green silk were clapped under his right arm as he swung along, left arm pumping with the steady pulse of a highland child accustomed to long hikes up grim inclines. A breath of wind, a whisper from the Lady of Beasts in his ear, good hearing – some hint alerted him. He cast a glance behind, down the road. Flirt huffed and swooped. Too late he looked up. He shrieked and ran, but there was nowhere for him to run because he was stuck out on the road on the rocky flanks of the hills. Flirt loved this; so did Marit. The plunge with the wind rushing, the brief breathless throat-catching sense of abandon as they plummeted.

Flirt caught him in her talons and with her incredible strength cut upward just before they slammed into the dirt. He screamed in terror and piss flooded his legs; Marit smelled it.

'Drop that silk and I'll drop you!' she shouted, laughing.

Flirt yelped her shrill call in answer: Triumphant!

It was harder to turn with the added weight of the boy, who

looked like he weighed at least as much as Marit, so they took a long slow sweep south and southwest and northwest and north until they came round eastward and flew back along the river the way they had come. Flirt struggled a bit because of the extra burden, but the eagles weren't natural creatures, and in any case the raptor had an eagle's pride. So it wasn't much past midafternoon when they came within sight of Merrivale, but it seemed like a long trip, what with Flirt tiring and the youth babbling and moaning and cursing and begging and crying the entire time, although he was smart enough not to struggle. Most folk were.

At the sight of them, the inhabitants of Merrivale came running. Just before landing, Flirt let the boy go. He tumbled, shrieking again, grunting and howling, rolling along the rocks but no more than bruised and banged up, as Flirt rose to get past him and then dropped to the earth.

'Oof,' said Marit, jarred up through her chest. 'That was a thump, girl!'

She loosened her harness and swung out quickly. Faron, at the front of the village swarm, staggered to a stop a stone's toss from her and Flirt. The boy crawled forward, cloth clutched to his chest.

'I'm sorry, I'm sorry,' he babbled. He stank, poor lad, and there was snot all over his face. He cringed like a dog. 'I'm sorry, Pap. I'll never do it again. It's just I didn't want you to marry her, but I know I'm being selfish. It's not like you didn't mourn Mam what was fitting. I'm sorry. I'm sorry. I'll never cause you trouble again. Please let me come home.'

Marit smiled.

Faron wept as he lifted the boy and embraced him. The girl in red grabbed the precious silk bolts and ran them into the safety of the inn.

Once the first commotion subsided they tried to press gifts on her. She refused everything but food and drink to carry with her for her evening's meal. That was the rule. No gifts meant no bribes, and once she made it clear she'd not budge, they respected her wishes.

'You'll not spend the night?' asked Faron. 'You can have my best bed. A reeve can take lodging.'

'Lodging and food,' agreed Marit. 'That's allowed. But I can't stay. I've a fellow reeve to meet at sunset, up near the summit.'

'Beware those Devouring youths,' said an unrepentant Vatta. The old woman had the wicked grin of a soul that hasn't yet done making mischief. 'I should know. I was one of Her hierodules once, before I got married.'

Marit laughed. The boy sniveled, chastened and repentant, and Faron wrung her hand gratefully. Maybe there were a few happy endings still to be had.

Joss was waiting for her at Candle Rock, just as they'd agreed five nights past. The rock was too stony to harbor trees; a few hardy tea willows grew out of deep cracks where water melt pooled, and spiny starflowers straggled along the steep northern slope. Candle Rock provided no cover except the shelter of the craggy overhang where firewood was stowed. No man or woman could reach it without the aid of flying beast, so reeves patrolling over the Liya Pass commonly met here to exchange news and gossip and to haul up wood for the signal fire kept ready in case of emergency.

She saw Joss standing beside the smaller fire pit, which was ringed with white stones like drippings of wax. The fire burned merrily and he already had meat roasting on a spit. The young reeve had his back to the setting sun and was looking east up at the ridge of hill whose familiar profile they called Ammadit's Tit, which despite the name was held by the hierarchs to be sacred to the Lady of Beasts.

Showing off, Flirt made a smooth landing on the height. Joss raised a hand in greeting as Marit slipped out of her harness and walked down to the fire.

'Mmm,' she said, kissing him. 'Eat first, or after?'

He grinned, ducking his head in that way that was *so* fetching; he was still a little shy.

She tousled his black hair. 'Shame you have to keep it cut.'

They kissed a while longer. He was young and tall and slender and a good fit, the best fit she'd ever found in her ten years as a reeve. He wasn't boastful or cocky. Some reeves, puffed up with the gloat of having been chosen by an eagle and granted the authority to patrol, thought that also meant they could lord it over the populace. He wasn't a stiff-chinned and tight-rumped bore, either, stuck on trivial niceties of the law. It was true he had a sharp eye and a sharp tongue and a streak of unexpected recklessness, but he was a competent reeve all the same, with a good instinct for people. Like the one he had now, knowing what she wanted.

Grease sizzled as it fell into the flames. The sun's rim touched the western hills.

'Best see to Flirt,' he said, pulling back. 'I sent Scar out to hunt and there's no telling when he'll get back. You know Flirt's temper.'

She laughed softly. 'Yes, she'll not like him moving in where she's roosting. I'll make sure she's settled.'

Flirt was cleaning herself. With a resignation born of exhaustion, she accepted her demotion to the hollow where Candle Rock dipped to the southwest to make a natural bowl with some protection from the wind. Marit chained her to one of the rings hammered into the rock, hooded and jessed her. Then she skinned her out of her harness, greased the spot it chafed, and, with an old straw broom she found stuck in a crevice, swept droppings out of the bowl.

'You'll eat tomorrow, girl,' she said, but Flirt had already settled into her resting stupor, head dipped under one wing. It was getting dark. Wind died as the sun set.

She hoisted the harness, her pack, her hood, and her rolled-up cloak over her shoulders and trudged up a path cut into the rock, back to the fire. Off to her left the rock face plunged down to where the road cut up toward the summit, seen as a darkening saddle off to the south. Joss was sitting on the white stones, carving up meat onto a wooden platter. She admired the cut of his shoulders and the curve of his neck. The touch of the Devourer teased her, right down to her core. He looked up and grinned again, eyes crinkling tight. She tossed down harness and weapons, pulled the platter out of his hands, set it down, and tumbled him.

'Cloaks,' he muttered when he could get in a word.

'Oh. Yes.'

He'd already spread out his traveling cloak and tossed his blanket down on top of it. It was a warm night without clouds and they really only needed a little padding to protect flesh from stone.

'Mmm,' she said later, when they lay tangled together. He was stroking her breasts and belly absently as he stared up at the brilliant spray of stars. She dragged the platter of meat close up and fed him bits and pieces.

'Do you ever think – ?' he started.

'Not when I see you.'

He chuckled, but he wasn't as much in thrall to the Devourer as she was. Sated, he had a tendency to spin out dreams and idle thoughts, which she never minded because she liked the feel of him lying beside her. He had a good smell, clean sweat but also the bracing perfume of juniper from the soaps his mother sent once a year to Copper Hall. 'Just thinking about what I did today. There was a knife fight at a woodsmen's camp east of summit ridge, out into wild country. Both men stabbed, one like to die.'

'Sorry,' she said, wincing. 'Murders are the worst.'

'I wish it were so,' he said, wisely for one so young.

'What do you mean?' She speared a chunk of meat with his knife, spun it consideringly, then ate. The meat was almost bitter; a coney, maybe, something stringy and rodent-like. 'I've got bread and cheese for the morning. Better than this. Got you no provisions for your pains today?'

'Not a swallow. They were happy to be rid of me. I was wondering if you'd come back with me. A few of them had the debt scar—' He touched the ridge of his brow just to the left of his left eye, where folk who sold their labor into debt servitude were tattooed with a curving line. 'and hair grown out raggedly to cover it.'

'You think some were runaway slaves.'

'Maybe so. It's likely. And then what manner of law-abiding persons would take such men in, I wonder? They made me nervous, like they had knives hidden behind their backs.' He shuddered under her hands.

'I'll come. No use courting trouble. They'll not kick with two eagles staring them down.'

Abruptly he sat up, tilting his head back. 'Ah. There he is.'

A shadow covered them briefly. The big eagle had a deer in his claws. He released it, and the corpse fell hard to the ground at the eastern edge of the rock, landing with a meaty *thunk*. Scar landed with a soft scrape and after a silence tore into his prey. Bones cracked. From across the height Flirt screamed a challenge, but Scar kept at his meat, ignoring her. Flirt yelped twice more, irritated, but she wouldn't be particularly hungry yet. She'd settle and sleep. Marit yawned.

Joss wasn't done worrying over the problem. 'I have to go back in two days to see if the man died, and then what's to do? I'm to conduct a hearing? They've no captain, and the arkhon at the nearest village – Sandy Falls – told me he'll have nothing to do with the matter. Maybe the lord of Iliyat will agree to sit in judgment.'

'That's a long way for Lord Radas's arm to reach. He's young in his position, too. His uncle died just two years ago, and he's still testing his wings. I don't expect this will fall under his authority. We should be able to handle it. Honestly, sweetheart, no matter how ugly a murder is, it won't be the first time two drunk men settled their argument with a knife.'

'I know,' he said a little more desperately than the situation seemed to call for, 'but reeves aren't meant to judge. It's the place of the Guardians to hold assizes to settle such grievances and disputes, those that can't be resolved by local councils.'

'True enough,' she agreed. 'I had to mediate in a boundary dispute this morning. I've shifted a hundred stone markers in the last ten years, and I don't like it any better now than I did the first time. Half of them don't like that I'm a woman, but they'll say nothing with Flirt at my back. Still. No Guardian's been seen for – oh – since my grandfather was a boy. Maybe longer.'

'The Guardians don't exist. They're just a story.'

She gave him a light shove, because his words disturbed her. 'Great Lady! That's nineteen years' bad luck for saying such a thing! Anyway, my grandfather remembered the assizes from back when they were held properly. He saw a Guardian once, who came to preside over the court. Do you think he was lying to me?'

'He was a boy then, you said so yourself. He listened to, and danced, the tales, as we all do. Stories blend with fragmented memories to make new memories. He came to believe as truth what never really happened. No shame in that.'

'Joss! Sheh! For shame! The hierophants preserve in the Lantern's libraries the old scrolls that record the judgments made in those days. Judgments made by Guardians. How do you answer that evidence?'

'What is a name? I could call myself a "Guardian" and my attendance at an assizes court would show in the records that a "Guardian" oversaw that day's proceedings.'

She squeezed him until he grunted, air forced out of his lungs. 'Say so if you must! But my grandfather had the best memory of anyone I have ever known. He could remember the time when he was a lad when the first Silver merchant came through the village, with two roan cart horses and a hitch in his stride as if he'd broken a hip and it had healed wrong. He could remember the names of all his clan cousins, even the ones who had died when he was a lad, and the folk they married and which temple their children were apprenticed to. If we see no Guardians now, that doesn't mean there were never any.'

He sighed as sharply as if he'd gotten a fist in the belly. Twisting, he looked eastward, although it was by now too dark to see anything but stars and the dark shadow of the towering spire that gave Candle Rock its name. 'Ammadit's Tit is a Guardian's altar, it's said. What's to stop us flying up there and looking around?'

'Joss!' Startled and shocked, she sat up. She went cold, all goosebumped, although the wind hadn't gotten any cooler. 'It's forbidden!'

'No Guardian's been seen for seventy winters or more, you said it yourself. What if you're right, and there were Guardians once? Shouldn't we try to find out what happened to them? Maybe we could find clues at their altars. Maybe someone needs to find out why they're gone, and if we can do anything to bring them back. You didn't see the look of those woodsmen. They scared me, Marit. Even with Scar glaring at them, I knew they'd kill me if I took a step into any corner where they didn't want my nose poking. They hadn't even a headman among them, no arkhon, no manner of priest. No Lady's cauldron. No Lantern. No dagger or key or greenstaff or anvil. Not even an offering bowl for the Formless One.'

The crawling jitters prickled up and down her back, a sure sign of danger. 'Maybe this is what Marshal Alard was warning us about. You'd best not go back there. Fly to Copper Hall and give a report. If there's trouble brewing . . . men like that . . . men who would run away from their legal obligation . . . they could do anything if there's nothing to check them.'

'Anything,' he muttered at last. He began to speak again, but choked on the words. He was quiet for a long time, arm around her, head still thrown back as he gazed up at the span of stars and the

Herald's Road whose misty path cut across the heavens. 'Is this what Marshal Alard meant by a shadow?' he whispered. 'It seemed to me there was a shadow in their hearts. Like an illness.'

'Hush,' she said, because he was shivering even though it wasn't cold. 'Hush, sweetheart.'

Marit woke at dawn as the sun's pale glow nosed up to paint rose along Ammadit's Tit. Joss still slept, hips and legs covered by her cloak. A blanket was rolled up under his neck, cradling his head. Sleeping, he looked younger than ever, barely more than a child, although he was twenty. A man might hope to celebrate five feasts in his life; Joss was barely six winters past his Youth's Crown, while in another year she would have to lay aside her Lover's Wreath for the sober if invigorating responsibilities represented by the Chatelaine's Belt. Your thoughts changed as you got older. Your hopes and dreams shifted, transmuted, altered into new shapes.

He cracked open an eye. The early-morning sunlight crept up to spill light over his smooth chest. She saw him examining her warily.

'What are you thinking?' he asked.

'If I'm going to have a baby, I have to have it soon. Would you—' She hadn't known how tightly the wish had knotted up inside her; it unraveled in a rush. 'Would you father it, Joss? No need to hand-fast, if you've no mind to. You're young yet.'

'Do you mean to give up patrol?' he asked unexpectedly.

The pang struck hard. 'Why do you say so?'

'It's unfair,' he mused.

'Which part of life?' she said with a grin, but a sour taste burned in her throat.

He stroked her arm thoughtfully. 'I could father ten children and no one would speak one word about it, or think it made me unfit to patrol. But I've seen how reeves who are women are told in so many ways that they'd best be a reeve only and not think of ever bearing children. It's true that when a baby is nursing, the mother must stick close if she wants to keep her milk running. But after the child is weaned, he's cared for by his older cousins anyway. That's how it was in my village. No one would have dared to tell any of my aunties what they could or could not do with their businesses or their labor, and then pretend it was for their own good.'

'You say the most unexpected things!'

He looked at her, silent, for the longest time, and fear curdled in her stomach as his dark eyes narrowed and with a flick he tossed the blanket aside and gathered up his clothes. 'I'm going up to the altar.'

'Joss!'

His expression was set, almost ugly. He pulled on his trousers while she sat there, still naked, and stared at him. 'Who made all those rules? We don't even know, or why, or when. We just follow them without thinking. We see a fence around our village but we never go out to make sure it's still in good repair. Maybe that's why there are shadows. Maybe that's why the woodsmen live in that camp like beasts. They don't see the point of mouthing the same words their fathers did, so they've cast them aside. And if the fence around your pasture looks sturdy from a distance but is falling down, that's when wolves come in and kill the lambs. I've got to find out.'

'Joss!'

The sun illuminated the curve of his handsome chest, the taut abdomen, his muscular shoulders made strong by two years controlling an eagle, the handsome, angular tattoos – covering his right arm and ringing both wrists – that marked him as a child of the Fire Mother. His chin had a rebellious tilt. He threw his tunic over his head. As he wrestled it down, she shook herself and leaped up, groping for her clothes. She always tossed everything all this way and that in her haste to get undressed but at some point during the night, while she'd slept, he'd recovered it and folded it neatly and laid it on her pack, off the ground. She'd not even woken. He might have lain there for many watches brooding over this madness and she never knowing.

'You're crazy,' she said. 'It's forbidden.'

'You don't have to come with me. I know the risk.'

'Do you?'

'Are you going to report me to Marshal Alard?'

'He'll flog you and throw you out of the reeves, no matter what Scar wants.'

'Go, if you have to. Report if you must. I won't blame you. But I'm going up there.'

She paused, shading her eyes as she squinted toward Ammadit's Tit. The black knob thrusting up at the height of the rounded ridge gave away nothing, although – just there – she thought a flash of light or metal winked as the sun rose just off to the southeast behind it. 'The Guardians guard their secrets. Marshal Alard won't have to punish you. They will.'

'The Guardians are gone. And if they're not gone, then maybe it's time someone kicks them in the butt.' His voice was shaking but his hands were steady as he gathered up his harness. 'I didn't tell you what else, Marit. I couldn't say it when it was dark out, I just couldn't. They had a Devouring girl at that woodsmen's camp. They tried to keep her hidden, but I saw her.' Catching her eye, he held it. His gaze was bleak. 'She was *chained*.'

2

That was what decided it, really. The thought of any man chaining one of the Merciless One's hierodules made her stomach churn, but her heart's courage stiffened with anger. It was blasphemy to chain one who gave freely.

She was trembling as she harnessed Flirt, and the eagle caught her mood and pulled this way and that, fussing and difficult, scratching at the rock with her talons and slashing at her once, although not determinedly enough to connect. Marit thrust the staff up to the eagle's throat and held it there, pulling the hood back over Flirt's eyes. Her heart pounded as she listened for Scar's cry, for Joss departing impatiently, but she held the discipline for the correct thirty-seven count before easing the hold. Flirt gave her no more trouble. They walked to the rim of the bowl, she swung into the harness, and the raptor launched out into the air, plunging, then catching a draft to rise.

Scar and Joss were circling, waiting for them. Before departing, he had doused and raked the fire and split wood for kindling to serve the next reeve who camped out on Candle Rock. Now, seeing her catch the airstream, he rose higher as Scar caught an updraft. She and Flirt followed, up and up, gliding south before turning to come up along the high ridgeline. The mountainous mound of Ammadit's Tit was covered with pine and spruce but the actual black knob – the nipple itself – was as bare as the day the Earth Mother molded stone into mountains. The rock gleamed in the morning light, almost glinting. As she circled in more closely, she saw that it was pitted with crystalline structures – sacred to the Lady of Beasts – shot through the stone. She shivered, although the wind was hot and strong. That knot at the hollow of her ribs burned.

At first glance the knob looked too smooth for any creature as large as they were to find a landing spot. Relief flared, briefly, brutally; then Joss hallooed just out of her sight, and she and Flirt rounded through eddying currents to see him banking in toward a cleft situated below the summit.

'Great Lady, protect us,' she whispered. 'Don't be angry.'

She followed him in.

The cleft was about as wide as the feasting hall in Copper Hall was long: forty strides. It was surrounded by a rim cut into the rock, then dropped an arm's span to a flat floor beneath, open to the air but with a sharply angled slope of rock offering a lean-to of shelter to the north. It was difficult to maneuver Flirt in, especially with Scar already claiming territory, but the raptor landed with a cry of protest, opened her wings to give Scar a look at just how big she was, then settled.

Whoof.

Marit sat in her harness as a chill whisper of air brushed her face, like fingers searching, like a sculptor's probing hands. To her left, the sun shone full on Joss. The floor of the cleft was level but scarred by the glittering path of a labyrinth scored into the rock. The pattern took up half the open space; Flirt's open wingspan brushed the path's outermost edge, but both eagles shied away from actually crossing onto the crystalline markings. The space was otherwise empty, just the ledge and the eddy of air swirling around the knob. The northern face ended in that angled wall that shadowed the deepest part of the cleft.

Joss coughed, then slipped down from his harness. He landed so softly she couldn't hear the slap of his feet. He paced the rim, and back again, as she looked about nervously, but she heard nothing but the bluster of the wind. She saw nothing at all, no offerings, no altar post, no Guardian's silk banner fluttering in the constant blow. He stopped at the curving edge of the labyrinth closest to the rim wall.

The outer shape of the path was an oval. Within those boundaries, the shining pavement twisted and turned and doubled back until it was impossible to know how to reach the center, where the ground dipped into a shallow bowl big enough to hold a man and horse together.

'This is the entrance,' he said.

'Joss!'

He set his right foot on the glittering pavement, then his left.

Nothing happened.

She let out all her breath.

He turned and spoke to her. She saw his mouth working, but the wind – or the magic of the Guardians – tore his words away.

'Joss!' she cried, but he turned away and with measured paces worked his way in on the tortuous branched path. All her worst fears choked her because with each step he seemed to recede, although he wasn't really getting any farther away from her: he was only *fading*. It was as if a veil thickened around him, as if mist seeped up from marshland to conceal the landscape. There was nothing quite seen, nothing tangible, but it obscured him nonetheless. Marit had never unduly feared the dangers of her task as a reeve, although she had walked into a hundred different knife's-edge situations with only her eagle, her weapons, and most of all her good instincts to guide her. But fear paralyzed her now.

We've broken the boundaries. We'll be punished.

The boundaries were all that kept the Hundred safe; every child heard the stories; every festival danced the limits; every temple to one of the seven gods was an icon in miniature, each in its own way, of the ancient laws. The master sergeants and the marshal at the reeve halls made the point ten times a day if they said it once.

He faded more as he walked deeper into the labyrinth, never coming closer or back toward her even when the path turned that way. The eagles neither moved or called; the silence daunted them. The ghost of his form, scarcely more than a shadow, reached the center.

He vanished. Just like that: a blink, a shimmer of light – and he was gone.

A gasp escaped her. She couldn't form words, couldn't cry out, couldn't do anything except stare. Her eyes were wet, her heart turned to dust. A thousand years passed while she gaped, too stunned to act.

'Marit! Marit! Come quick! Follow the path! Bring rope.'

Where in the hells was that coming from? She slipped out of her harness and leaped down, skirted the gleaming path, and ducked into the shadowed throat of the cleft, but she could not find him. His voice carried to her on the wind.

She ran back to Flirt and awkwardly got the eagle up onto the lip as on a perch. Her acrobatic skills had saved her from bad falls more than once. Balancing on the rim with the world plunging away far down to spruce billowing below, she swung into her harness. Flirt opened her wings and fell into the sky. Marit shrieked with glee, forgetting all fears and creeping terrors as the wind pummeled her and the eagle dove and then, with that instinct for risk that had gotten the raptor her name, pulled up just in time, just before they would have slammed into the trees. Flirt caught a draft and they rose. Marit's pulse hammered as she squinted into the sun, up along the knob of rock, seeking, searching—

There he was! He was standing, impossibly, at the top of the rock, poised as on the tip of a giant spear. And indeed, somehow, unseen before but perfectly visible now, a metal post thrust up from the center of the knob with torn and fraying and sun-bleached banners in many colors snapping from the post. To this he held tightly with one hand as he waved frantically at her to get her attention.

'Thank you, Lady,' she breathed, and added a hasty prayer to the Herald, the Opener of Ways, whom Joss had served for a year as a lowly message rider before the day he'd ridden into a reeves' gathering to deliver a summons from the arkhon of Haya, and Scar had changed the course of his life.

She circled, but there was no way to land, so she went back down to the cleft. Scar waited with his head beneath his wing, oddly quiescent. She shed her harness as quickly as she ever had, and grabbed her coil of rope. Knowing better than to stop and think, she jogged to the entrance of the labyrinth and put her right foot on the path, then her left. The pavement seemed pure crystal, as thin as finely thrown ceramic, but so thick, perhaps, that it cut down through the stone to the center of the earth. She took another step, and a fourth, and when she glanced up the world seemed to be slowly spinning around her, picking up speed as she walked in. With each revolution a new landscape flashed into view: surging ocean; a fallen stone tower above a tumble of rocks battered by foaming waves; dense tangled oak forest; a vast flat gleam of water – not the sea – and beyond it the pale endless dunes that she recognized as the western verge of the Barrens; an ice-covered peak shining under a bottomless hard blue sky; a homely village of six cottages set beside a lazily flowing river half overgrown with reeds. The visions made her dizzy. She looked down instead, kept her gaze fixed on the path whose windings confused her, except wherever she had to choose between one turn and another it seemed she could smell the memory of juniper, Joss's scent, and she therefore followed her nose.

A man's voice whispered behind her, questioning, urgent.

'. . . when night falls . . . to Indiyabu but only when the Embers moon sets . . . she betrayed them . . . beware the third blow . . . trust me . . .'

Don't turn your back, Marshal Alard would say, but she was walking on forbidden ground. She dared not look back for fear of what she would see. Indiyabu was the legendary birthplace of the Guardians, but no reeve knew where to find it, and none she knew of had ever dared seek for it.

The path took much longer to walk than it should have; she was sweating freely by the time she stumbled into the center bowl. A man waited for her. His long dark beautiful hair was unbraided, twisting around him in an unseen wind. He looked angry, but he was as handsome a man as she had ever seen, demon-blue out-lander eyes in a brown face, taller than most reeves and with graceful long-fingered hands talking in signs, the secret language of the Guardians.

She walked right through him before she realized he wasn't really there; he was only a vision, like the landscapes. The pavement dipped. She slipped into the central hollow. Where her foot slapped into the ground, pain stabbed up through her heels. Light flared, like a lantern's door opened wide, and she was spun halfway around by an unknown force and staggered.

'Marit!'

Joss grabbed her before she plunged off the side of the knob to her death. They stood at the very height, the sky a vast gulf and the sun glaring. Wind howled, trying to tug her off. She grabbed on to the metal post. Thank the gods it was well set into the rock. It didn't shift at all with her added weight. The silk of frayed banners battered her; she was drowned in their colors: blood-red, black of night, heaven-blue, mist-silver, fiery-gold-sun, death-white, earth-brown, seedling-green, and the rich violet of the twilight sky just before night envelops the last light of day.

'Look!' Joss shouted to be heard above the wind. 'Look there!'

He pointed to a crevice just out of arm's reach along the curve of the rock but because of the wind and their precarious perch too far to get to safely. Something fluttered there, a banner torn off the pole, perhaps. It was hard to identify because it was so white and because there were pale objects jumbled beneath, caught within the crevice.

She was a reeve. She knew what it was with a gut knowledge that slammed down, no question – only a hundred questions. A thousand.

Joss hooked his elbow around the metal post and deftly tied and slipknotted the rope around the post. He'd grown up by the sea; he knew twenty kinds of knots.

'Let's get out of here!' he shouted. He was shaking, gray, frightened.

Bones.

The bones of a Guardian were caught in that crevice. That was the Guardian's death-white cloak caught in the rocks, the cloth sliding and shivering with the purl of the wind as though a snake struggled in its folds. Those were the dead one's long leg bones rattling as the wind shifted them. That was his pelvis, if it had been a man, shattered on one side. Most reeves learned to identify human bones: in the course of seeking out lost shepherds whose remains were discovered beneath spring snowmelt; or runaway wives dead of starvation in forest loam; or miners tumbled under a fall of rocks who couldn't be recovered until the dry season made digging safe. She had exhumed the occasional murder victim buried under the pig trough or beyond the boundaries of a village's orderly fields. That pelvis told her something, even seen from a man's length away. That pelvis had been splintered in a tremendous fall, or by a massive blow.

Guardians couldn't die.

'Give me the rope,' she shouted. 'I'm going to recover the remains. We have to find out what happened, if we can!'

'Marit!' He almost lost his nerve. He clutched his stomach as though he would retch. He squeezed his eyes shut but opened them as quickly, and steadied himself, ready to aid her.

She tied the rope around her waist, fixed it, and turned round to back down over the curve of the rock, to reach the crevice. As Joss paid out the rope, she walked with her feet against the rock and her body straight out over the world below, nothing but air between her back and the trees. The wind sang through her. She was grinning, ready to laugh for the joy of it and almost down to the crevice when, above her, Joss screamed an inarticulate warning cry.

A fog shrouded her, boiling up from underneath to choke her. A roaring like a gale wind thrummed through her. Her bones throbbed, and it seemed her insides would be rattled and twisted until they became her outsides, all as white light smothered her.

I can't hear. I can't see.

I can't breathe.

She fought, and found herself ripping at cloth that had enveloped her, that seemed likely to swallow her.

An axe smashes into her hip, shattering it; the pain engulfs her like white light, like death.

'Go to Indiyabu! Beware the traitor ... mist ... I can't reach her.'

Then she was free, feet still fixed to the rock wall. The wind tore the shining white cloak off her body, and it flew out into the sky rippling like light, spread as wide as a vast wing. The bones clattered down the curving slope of the knob until they reached the sheer cliff, and then they fell and fell, tumbling, and vanished into the forest. The cloak spun higher into the sky and was lost to sight in the sun's glare.

'Shit!' cried Joss.

He hauled her back up. She fell on her stomach over the rampart and lay there panting, trying to catch her breath. The wind screamed around them, tearing at their clothes, at the banners, at their hoods. She was grateful for the rule that forced all reeves to wear their hair short, since there was no braid to catch at her throat, and there were no strands of loose hair to blind her.

'What do we do now?' he asked.

'We've got to get down!' she yelled.

She turned, dead calm now, too stunned to be otherwise, and surveyed the rock face. She'd gone *that way* the first time. In her head, she mapped a new route to take them to the ledge below.

'Follow after I've tugged twice.'

She eased out the rope between her hands, let herself lean backward into the air, and walked backward out over the curve of the rock. Down. She was compact and strong and always had been, her chest and arms made more so by ten years of weapons training, by ten years, especially, of controlling Flirt. Strangely, the wind eased once she was on the cliff, and she made it down to the cleft swiftly. There Flirt and Scar waited, heads down, dozing.

How strange that they should doze when the peculiar nature of their surroundings ought to have made them nervous.

By the time she slipped down hand over hand and dropped the last length, her right hand was bleeding and the left was bright red, rubbed raw from friction. Panting, she tugged twice on the rope. Blew on her hands. Pain stung. It would hurt to handle the harness with her hands like this. She pulled gloves out of one of the pockets sewn into the hem of her tunic, but hesitated, not quite willing to pull them on. The gloves would shroud her hands as snugly as that cloak had wrapped her. She shuddered.

No time to dwell on it. Must get on. Must act.

The rope danced beside her. A moment later Joss slid down, half out of control, and she caught him as he fell the last body length. They stood there, holding tight. He was crying. She'd known him almost two years, but she'd never seen him cry. She'd seen him at his first winter feast in the hall, and happened to be called in to assist when he'd found that poor mutilated girl who'd had her hands amputated by her husband's angry relatives. She'd cried that day, but Joss hadn't. Now he wept noisily.

'What about the rope?' she said finally. 'If we leave it, they'll know we've been here.'

He gulped down tears and spoke in a shaky voice. 'I have to report, even if it means I'm flogged out. They have to know.'

Since he was right, there was no answer.

He sighed heavily, stepped back, and wiped his eyes. He looked ten years older than he had that morning. 'Best go,' he said.

She nodded. 'I haven't forgotten that woodsmen's camp.'

'You can't go in there alone!'

'I won't! I won't, Joss. I won't go to the woodsmen's camp at all. But there's a temple dedicated to the Merciless One up at summit of the Liya Pass. I want to stop there, ask their Hieros if they have any hierodules missing. You fly ahead to Copper Hall.'

'I think it's best if I go straight to Clan Hall.'

She considered, nodded decisively. 'That's right. Take it to the commander. He needs to know first. Once I've stopped at the temple, I'll follow you to Toskala without stopping anywhere else.'

He was in no mood for kissing, though she was. She would have laid him down and loved him there on the stone floor of the forbidden altar, but he was too tense and too preoccupied, wholly absorbed in considering just what it all meant. It seemed that despite his talk he believed in the existence of the Guardians after all. An earthquake would have tilted those foundations less. He was unable to talk or to do anything except prepare to go.

As for her, she couldn't dwell on the horror of that cloak twisting around her, of that instant when she'd thought she would asphyxiate; of that noise; of that pain; of that voice.

She couldn't think about what it meant: A Guardian had died, although the Guardians were immortal and untouchable. Maybe all the Guardians were dead. Maybe the Hundred was thereby doomed to fall beneath an uprising of such evil as sucked dry men's hearts, lust and greed and fear chief among them.

She grimaced as she finally tugged on her gloves, wincing at the pain, at the fear. Joss ran back over to her, kissed her hard, then returned to Scar without a word and swung into his harness. She smiled softly, ran a gloved hand through the soft stubble of her hair, and crossed to Flirt, who blinked as if surprised to see her.

'Let's go, girl.'

No use dwelling on what she couldn't change. Best to concentrate on what she could do. That's what she was best at. That's why she was a good reeve.

Joss headed due west and was lost fairly quickly among the hills, but Marit flew Flirt south up the cut of the road to its summit in the Liya Pass, a saddle between two ridgelines. Just east of the road lay a wide pool worn out of the hills by the tireless spill of a waterfall off the height. On the banks of this isolated vale the acolytes of the Merciless One had erected a small temple to house no more than a score of adepts in training. Obviously, with their holy quarters set in such a remote location, these were not hierodules who served the goddess by trafficking with passersby. Most who dedicated their service to the Devourer served as hierodules for less than a year before returning to life beyond the bounds of the temple; the Merciless One was a cruel and exacting taskmaster. Many of those who remained trained as jaryas, pearls beyond price, the finest musicians and entertainers in the Hundred. As for the few, they served Her darker aspect, and it was rumored they trained as assassins.

This was no jarya school, not up here.

They came to earth at a safe distance, right at the edge of the woods. The waterfall splashed in the distance, but the pool had a glassy sheen beyond the spray, still and silent as if depthless. Three buildings rose out of the meadow of grass and flowering lady's heart: a chicken coop; a long, narrow root cellar with a turf roof; and the temple itself, with its outer enclosure, entrance gate, and 'lotus petal' wings surrounding an inner courtyard.

She waited in her harness, listening. Crickets chirred. Wind tinkled strings of bells hanging from posts set in the earth all around the outer enclosure. It rustled the silk banners draped over and tied to the entrance gate. She heard no voices and no music. Nothing. Flirt showed no nervousness. The vale seemed deserted.

She slipped out of her harness and ventured to the chicken coop. It was empty except for a half-dozen broken eggs, sucked dry, and a single bale of straw. She moved on to the root cellar, a building half buried in the earth. She pushed on the door, which stuck. Shoving, she opened it. Cautiously, she ducked under the lintel and stepped down into the shadowy interior. The stores had been cleaned out. That was suspicious, although at this time of year it was possible that was only because they had used up last winter's surplus and not yet received their tithes to carry them through the coming cold season. With the door open behind her, she knelt in the damp confines. The dirt floor had been raked clean. There were no distinguishing footprints; there was no evidence of passage at all except for the brick resting-cradles for two dozen missing storage barrels. Four barrels remained, rounded shadows at the far end of the cellar, barely discernible in the dimness.

Maybe thieves had stolen everything and covered their tracks. Maybe the Merciless One had abandoned the temple and all her people had left, tidying up behind themselves.

It was impossible to know.

A shadow covered the open door. Too late she realized the crickets had ceased their noise. She jumped farther into the darkness, drawing her short sword as she spun to face the door.

But they had already defeated her. They'd been waiting, as if they'd known she was coming and laid an ambush. A staff hit her from behind alongside her right ear. A second blow caught her in the breastbone, knocking the air out of her. Her legs went from under her. The earth slapped up, and she blinked and gasped and breathed in dirt, flat on her stomach, head scorched with pain. Dazed. Choking on dust.

Damn damn damn. If the Merciless One had abandoned the temple, then her hierodules and kalos would have removed the bells and banners before departing.

'Hurry!'

'Kill her now!'

'No, Milas wants her alive.'

'Hoo! Hoo! Hoo! Bet I know what for!'

A man snickered.

Her sword was trapped under her hips. She began to roll, but knees jabbed into her back and the weight of a second man, maybe a third, held her down as they stripped her of her bow and quiver, her sword, her dagger; her staff had already fallen uselessly. They didn't find the slender knife hidden between the lining and the outer leather of her right boot. They trussed her arms up behind her from wrists to elbows, hoisted her up using the rope until her shoulders screamed and one *popped*. The world spun dizzily as she came up, kicking.

The third blow exploded against the back of her head.

She plunged into darkness.

Came to, muzzy, as she was jostled from side to side in a wheelbarrow, banging first one wooden slat, then the other side. She was blind, a cloth tied tightly over her face, over both mouth and nose so that she choked with the fear she was smothering in white silk. Death silk.

No. Just a plain bleached-white linen cloth, maybe a bandanna of the kind worn by laborers to keep sweat from pouring into their eyes. The cloth sucked in and out with her breath. She heard the squeak of wheels on pine needles. She heard the soft tread of feet and the wind sighing through trees. No one spoke. She felt no sun, so couldn't guess at time of day or how long she had been unconscious.

She took stock of her condition: throbbing head, chest and ribs aching, and one heel stinging as though she'd been bitten. Her shoulders were bruised, but somehow the one that had popped was no longer dislocated. It just hurt like the hells. What hurt worst was her fury at her own stupidity and carelessness. Why hadn't Flirt warned her? Her assailants must have been close by, and those who closed in from outside would surely have been spotted by Flirt, who was trained to give the alert.

Shadows.

Some magic had veiled sight and instinct. She had to be ready. Most likely, she would have only one chance to escape and she had to prepare herself for the worst: rape, any kind of brutality, mutilation. She had to lock down her emotions. Thus were reeves trained to respond in emergencies.

'*Your fears and passions must be set aside, placed in a treasure chest, and locked up tight. If you are ruled by fear or desire, then you will lose. Be an arrow, unencumbered by any but the force that impels it to its target. Do not let the wind blow you off course.*'

She stayed quiet as the barrow lurched and rolled along the forest path. She sorted out footfalls and decided there were at least ten men accompanying her. Because they stayed silent, they betrayed no knowledge of Flirt or her fate. She banished Flirt's fate from her mind. Until she was free, there was nothing she could do about the eagle.

At last she smelled wood smoke and the smoky richness of roasting venison. At a distance she heard the sound of many voices, the clatter of life, the ringing of an axe, the false hoot of an owl raised as a signal. She felt a change in the texture of the air as they came out of trees into a clearing. Silence fell. No one spoke, but she felt the mass of men staring. Her skin prickled. Certainly this must be the woodsmen's camp.

'*Do not fear pain. Fear will kill you.*' So Marshal Alard taught.

A man coughed. Someone giggled with the barest edge of hysteria. Hand slapped skin, and the giggling ceased.

'Put her there,' said a baritone.

The silence was ugly, made more so by the sudden glare of sun on her face so bright she blinked under the cloth. Just as her eyes teared, shadow eased the blinding light. Leaves whispered above her. A dozen thin fingers tickled her chest and face. The wheelbarrow jolted to a stop, and its legs were set down hard. A man cursed right behind her, and she heard him blowing through lips, maybe on blistered hands. He did not speak. The wheelbarrow raised up abruptly and she slid forward, awkwardly, and slithered down to land in a heap.

On a carpet.

Metal rattled softly, then scraped. Footsteps receded. A man hawked and spat, and she flinched, but a delicate finger touched her chin and carefully eased the corner of the cloth up over her mouth and nose. She sucked in air gratefully.

'Hush,' whispered a female voice. 'He'll hear. He's coming.'

'Who are you?'

'No one. Not anymore.' It was a young voice, its spirit strangely deadened.

'Let me see your face. Let me see this place.'

'It was a trap.'

'That's how they captured me?'

'It was a trap. Half of the hierodules had turned their back on the Devourer and given their allegiance to *him*. They gave the rest of us over, but he killed the others. All but me. All but me.' The finger tickled her nose, pushed under the band of cloth, and eased it upward until Marit could – bless the Great Lady – see a bit of her surroundings and the girl beside her.

She was very young; she didn't even wear the earring that marked her Youth's Crown, although she had breasts and curves enough that she was no doubt meant to dance into the Crowning Feast at midwinter with the rest of the youths ready to don their Lover's Wreaths and enter halfway into the adult world. No more than fourteen years, then. The remains of a sleeveless silk shift that once had been gold in color draped her body. Over it she wore an embroidered silk cloak, the kind of elegant accessory jaryas displayed while riding across town to an assignation or performance. It was a spectacular orange, now ripped and grimy; she'd used it to wipe up blood, likely her own. But as shocking as the sight of her was, with her curling black hair unbound and falling in matted tails and strings to her waist, and her arms and legs stained with dirt and blood and worse things, Marit had seen worse; reeves always saw worse.

Yet she'd never seen a girl dressed in the acolyte robes of the Devourer manacled by the ankle. The chain snaked back to the base of a huge tree, where it was fastened around a stake driven into the ground. The trunk was that of a massive death willow, immeasurably ancient. The trunk had grown up around the head of a tumbled statue. Wood encased the stone so that the grainy face peeked out and the crown of the head and the sculpted ripples of its hair were swallowed within the tree. The stone face stared at nothing. Lichen blinded both eyes. Streaks of white – she couldn't tell what they were – mottled the chin. The lips were darkened with the residue of blood or berry juice. An awful stench boiled out of the ground at the base of the trunk, something stinking and rotten.

The willow's green-yellow canopy concealed the sky and shaded both reeve and girl from the sun. Marit lay on a carpet, and when she turned her head she saw the curtain made by the willow's drooping branches, many of which swept the ground. Beyond, out where it was light, figures moved, but although she opened and closed her eyes three times she could get no good look at anything out there, as though magic hazed her sight. Beneath the death willow, they were alone.

'Do you want to be free?' whispered Marit, sensing her chance.

'Please let me go,' the girl whimpered. 'Please. Please.' The words sounded well rehearsed; she'd said them frequently. Her dark eyes, like those of the stone head, had a kind of blindness to them, although she tracked Marit's face and movements well enough.

'Is there another way out of here? What lies beyond the willow, that way?' She indicated direction with a jerk of her chin.

'No one goes that way,' murmured the girl. 'That's where he goes when he comes visiting.'

'Does it lead into the forest?'

The girl stiffened, head thrown back, lips thinning, and she sniffed audibly, taking in the air like a starving man scenting food. 'He's coming.' She scrambled to the base of the trunk and tugged hopelessly at the stake, but it didn't budge. Finally she curled up like a turtle seeking its shell, trembling, arms wrapped around her chest.

Voices reached her from beyond the drooping branches.

'My lord! I did not expect you so soon.'

'Have you accomplished what I asked of you, Milas?'

Marit knew that voice.

The baritone hemmed and hawed in reply. 'Not as we expected, my lord.'

'Leave off your excuses!' The curtain of branches was swept aside, and a man ducked in under the canopy. He looked, first, directly at the stone head and the girl cowering there, rocking back and forth on the balls of her feet, staring at him in terror. Marit got a good look at his face: that of a man in his early twenties, with broad cheekbones, a mustache and beard, and astonishingly long lashes above deep-set eyes. To her shock, she recognized him.

Radas, lord of Iliyat. He held one of the local authorities under whose auspices order was kept in the Hundred, and he was unusual only in that lordships – local chiefs whose right to office passed through a direct bloodline – were rare, an artifact, so the tales sang, of ancient days and even then known almost exclusively in the north.

His gaze flicked down to her. When he saw that the blindfold had been tweaked aside, annoyance narrowed his eyes.

'Have you touched her?' he said to the girl. Although he did not raise his voice, the change in his tone made Marit shiver and the girl quiver and moan.

With a snort of disgust he let the branches fall and vanished back into the light.

'She'll have to be killed,' he said. 'She's seen me.'

'Right away, my lord,' said the baritone.

'Nay, no haste. It would serve my purposes best to let the men do what they will. It's necessary that they understand that reeves aren't to be feared or respected. After that, if she's still breathing – slit her throat.'

'Yes, my lord.'

'Where's the eagle?'

'This way, my lord.'

They moved away. In the camp, the noises of men at their tasks trickled back into life. Evidently the woodsmen feared the lord of Iliyat as much as the girl did – and yet, Marit could not fit the two pieces together. She'd seen Lord Radas at court day in Iliyat, a mild-spoken young man passing judgment and entertaining merchants. Less than a year ago, she'd brought in a criminal to Iliyat's assizes, a thief and his accomplices who had raided two warehouses. The ring-leader had been sold to a man brokering for Sirniakan merchants; he'd be taken out of the Hundred into the distant south, into a life of slavery far from home with no hope of return. No worse fate existed. The accomplices were young and foolish; they'd been given eight-year contracts to serve as indentured servants, slaves of the debt they had created through their crime. It was a merciful sentence.

She could not reconcile that man and this one, yet they were clearly the same.

'Hsst. Girl.'

The girl looked up. Her eyes were dry but her expression was that of a child who has given up crying because she knows comfort will never ever come. Her eyes were bruised with shadows; her cheeks were hollow, and her complexion more gray than brown.

'Come closer.'

She shook her head. 'I shouldn't have touched you. Now he'll punish me. He likes to punish me.'

'What's your name?'

'I don't have a name anymore.'

A stubborn one. 'I'm called Marit. Reeve Marit. If I can free you, will you help me?'

'We are all slaves to the will of the Merciless One. There is only one road to freedom.'

There wasn't time to be subtle.

'There's a knife hidden in my right boot. I can't reach it, but you can. Then you can free me.' Marit wiggled her shoulders and hips and rolled onto her left side to display her bound arms. Her shoulders were aching badly, but that was the least of her worries. She knew better than to think about the problem posed by that chain and that stake. When she won free, she had to alert the reeve halls to this blasphemy and Lord Radas's treason. She wouldn't have time to struggle with the stake. It was a cruel decision, but necessary.

'A knife!' The girl crawled forward. Her expression changed, but the disquiet raised in Marit's throat by Lord Radas's frown tightened, and she had to cough out a breath as the girl tugged off Marit's right boot and swiftly, with strangely practiced hands, probed the lining. Faster than should have been possible her nimble fingers extracted the knife. It was a slender blade, meant for emergencies.

'The Merciless One has smiled on us.' The girl kissed the blade. 'She'll grant us freedom!'

'Quick! They could come at any moment.'

Indeed, she heard a buzz of noise out beyond the willow's canopy as though a mob gathered, with stamping and hollering and wild laughter brought on by waste wine and khaif: men working up their nerve to indulge themselves in their worst nature; men being worked up by a chieftain or overlord as music is coaxed out of an instrument by a skilled musician.

As the captain's wife said in the Tale of Fortune: *Make them ashamed of themselves and they will not betray you, because they will know they have stepped outside the boundaries and made themselves outcast by their deeds.*

The girl mouthed a prayer of thanksgiving, then sidled closer, right up against Marit's torso. She spun the blade with the skill of an expert trained to handle knives and touched the point against the cloth of Marit's tunic. It rested just below the reeve's breastbone, nudging up the thick leather strap of her walking harness.

'We'll be free. They won't be able to touch us.'

The prick of the blade bit Marit's skin. The reeve fell onto her back, startled and frantically reassessing as she stared up at the girl.

I've miscalculated.

That face was so young and so innocent, ravished by her brutal treatment, that Marit had overlooked what stared her right in the face. The girl's gaze had the fixed fanaticism of the Merciless One's most devoted followers, who did not separate war, death, and desire.

She's insane!

She pushed with her legs, scooting away on her back. 'Wait! Cut the rope – !'

The thrust punctured skin and gristle with a smooth, strong, angled stroke.

She's done this before.

Right into the heart. There was no pain.

The last thing Marit saw, as the blood drained from her heart, as the white cloak of death descended out of the sky to smother her in its wings, was the implacable face of the girl who was in that instant the Merciless One Herself. Beyond, a lifetime away, men shouted and came running. The girl spun the blade, plunged it up underneath her own ribs and, with a gloating smile, died.

PART TWO

Survivors

In the Year of the Silver Fox

(nineteen years later)

In the Hundred

joss was drinking hard and had sitting on his lap a comely girl who served wine, cordial, and, if you were generous enough and to her liking, certain of her favors. A tremendous shout had risen up from the nearby playing ground, and the boy had just run in from the back to announce the current score on the game – dammit if his team wasn't losing again – when the door of the Pig's Bladder banged open. Light assaulted him. He shut his eyes, but opened them when the girl leaped to her feet. She grabbed her tray as a pair of swarthy men in reeve's leathers charged up to confront him.

'Commander wants you *right now*,' said the first, a slender, nimble fellow as mean as a crate of starving snakes. He grinned mockingly at the young woman, who gave him a scowl in reply. 'Not as handsome as him, am I?' he asked her. 'Even though he is old enough to be your dad.'

She flushed. 'There are Devouring girls at the temple who make it a special holy duty to service men made ugly by the gods' mercy. Or like you, by spite.' She tipped back her pretty chin and sashayed back to the bar.

Joss watched her hips sway as she walked away. The hells! He'd just spent the better part of the afternoon coaxing her away from the attentions of a much younger suitor. He downed the rest of his cup and slammed it down. 'The Commander can stick it up—'

The barmaid glanced back at him, winked with a further, suggestive twitch of her ass, and turned to set her empty tray on the bar. There came the younger suitor, gods curse him, sidling up to her with a smile on his callow face.

Joss glared at the two reeves. 'I agreed to work the entire festival in exchange for the first four days of the new year off. Ghost Festival ended three days ago. That means I'm still off duty for two more days. Free and clear. That was the agreement.'

'She won't be free, a merchant like her, doing it for coin,' said the Snake, nodding toward the bar. 'But I hear Sadit has a thing for you and will give you a roll for nothing whenever her husband's not around.'

'Shut up,' said Joss, coming up off the bench with an arm cocked.

'You're drunk,' said Peddo mildly as he pushed the other two men apart. He was by many years the youngest, broadest across the chest, and as placid as a well-fed lion. 'Begging your pardon, Legate Joss. Commander's noticed that you've been drinking more lately. So have some of us others.'

'I hear he has nightmares,' said the Snake. 'Most likely it's some lilu haunting him, for I swear to you that man cannot keep his cock from wandering into every henhouse. I hear he calls out a woman's name in his dreams—'

Joss shook off Peddo's hand and slugged the Snake. The backward stumble, the smash against the bench, the crash: those were good sounds. Peddo sighed, the barmaid laughed, and the Snake spat blood to the floor. Joss tossed a handful of coins on the table to cover the damage and staggered outside into the glare of the awful sun, which had it in for him today. From the direction of the playing field, the crowd roared appreciatively.

There was a neighborhood well in the middle of the humble square. He got his bearings, made it halfway before he realized he was veering off course, corrected three more times to avoid men bent under yoked baskets, and finally closed the gap and grabbed the lip of the well to stop himself falling over.

'Can I help you, ver?' The speaker was a remarkably handsome woman of middle years who had come with three children and eight sturdy wooden buckets slung two by two over stout poles. She had a hierodule's amorous eye and no doubt had served the Devourer in her youth. You could tell it by the way she looked him over with his reeve leathers and whatever else she saw, including the tattoos that circled his wrists and marked him as a child of the Fire Mother.

'Just water,' he said hoarsely, noting the line of scalloped waves tattooed down the length of her right arm, marking *her* as a child of the Water Mother. With his best smile he added, 'I thank you, verea.'

'Oh, it sure is nothing,' she said with amusement as she winched up a full bucket for him.

He upended it over his head. The cold water was better than a slap. She jumped back laughing as the children shrieked with delight and began to ask, clamoring, if they could do the same.

Peddo strode out of the tavern, rubbing his forehead as though to wipe away a headache, and stopped short when he saw Joss dripping. 'Does it help any?'

'The hells! Does that sun have to be so bright?'

'Do you come here often?' the matron asked.

She had a pleasing figure, ample in all the right places and suggested to good effect in the worn but carefully mended taloos wrapped around her curves. The fabric was a soothing sea-green silk that did not hurt his eyes.

'Often enough,' he said.

Peddo caught him by the elbow, made his courtesies, and dragged him off. Because he was still drunk, there was no point in resisting.

'Can you never stop flirting?' demanded Peddo.

It was a stupid question, which Joss did not bother to answer. Anyway, a khaif seller had set up his cart where the afternoon shadows gave the man some respite against the cruel sun. The fellow had a brisk business going, despite the heat. Joss made Peddo stop, and he downed two mugfuls before the buzz hit and he could begin to shake off the wine.

'It's healthier for a man to visit the temple when the Devouring urge takes him,' said Peddo.

'Won't.'

Peddo coughed, looking uncomfortable for the first time. 'Yeh. Er. So I had heard. Sorry.'

Nothing to do with those dreams, thought Joss sourly as the mud cleared and his sight and thoughts clarified. *Neh, it's everything to do with them*. Nineteen years of bad luck, and dreams to remind him of how one rash act in youth could destroy what you cherished most and scar your life forever.

They started off again through the tidy streets of Flag Quarter.

'What in the hells does the Commander want from me, if you don't mind my asking? Considering the Commander was the one who made the agreement that I would get these days off.'

'Don't know,' admitted Peddo cheerfully.

Despite the heat and the hour and the crowd gathered at the playing ground, the streets of Toskala were not at all quiet, not as they

had been a few days ago during the festival, the ghost days that separated the ashes-end of the dead year from the moonrise that
marked the beginning of the new. Everyone was out, eager to get on
with their business after the restrictions of the ghost days. There
were, indeed, more people than usual in the streets because over the
last many months a steady trickle of refugees had filtered in from
neighboring regions: mostly northeastern Haldia, the Haya Gap,
north and west Farhal, and these days a handful from the Aua Gap
and regions around the town of Horn. Come to think of it, that
handsome matron at the well had spoken with a western lilt. Maybe
she, too, was a refugee, fled from the plague of lawlessness that had
engulfed the north.

And yet she had smiled and laughed. How could anyone smile
and laugh who had seen the terrible things he had himself seen, or
heard about? How could anyone smile and laugh who knew what
was coming, everything his nightmares warned him of? Getting
drunk gave him a moment's peace, but that was all.

Aui! The hells! Why shouldn't she laugh, if she wanted to? If it
made her day easier? Folk *would* go about their lives once they had
a measure of peace, even if they guessed that peace might only be
temporary.

'Busy today,' remarked Peddo, surveying the scene as they
walked.

People stepped up onto the covered porches of shops, took off
their sandals, and brushed past the hanging banners whose
ideograms and painted representations advertised the nature of the
shop within: bakery; sandals; bed nets; savory pies; candies; apothe-
cary; milled and unmilled grains. A pair of peddlers trundled past
pushing handcarts piled high with dried fish. The pungent smell hit
Joss hard between the eyes like a kick to the head, but they were
already gone beyond, turning down an alley. A young woman sauntered past. Over her right shoulder she balanced a pole from which
hung unpainted round fans. Her twilight-blue silk taloos was
wrapped tightly around exceedingly shapely breasts.

'Are you still that drunk,' asked Peddo, 'or do you just never
stop?'

'What?' Joss demanded.

Peddo shook his head as they negotiated a path around the clot of servants and slaves that had gathered around an oil seller set up at the corner. Squeezing past, the two reeves swung out onto the main thoroughfare and headed toward the distant towers that marked Justice Square. Banner Street was lined with prosperous shops that wove, painted, and sold banners and flags of all kinds. Various side streets advertised dye merchants, paint merchants, ink merchants, paper makers, and fan makers and painters. Business was brisk. Walkways were crowded with customers ducking in and out of shops. Carts rolled past laden with bags of rice being brought in from the wholesale markets in outlying Fifth Quarter. Ideograms were stamped on the burlap: first-quality white; new-milled; on the stalk; ordinary yellow; first-quality yellow; old rice. A pair of surly chairmen pushed through, their customer concealed by strips of tinkling bells whose muted chiming alerted the people ahead to make way.

A pack of children wearing the undyed tabards common to youngsters attending one of the Lantern's schools sang in unison one of those tiresome learning songs as they padded down the avenue under the supervision of three elderly matrons. *These are the seven treasures! Virtue! Conviction! Listening! Compassion!* The silver-haired woman in the lead had a face to die for, much lived in, lined, and weathered; she possessed an astonishing grace and dignity. She must have stopped traffic in her youth and was doing a pretty good job of it today, too.

Generosity! Discernment! Conscience!

She caught him staring – women who had lived that long didn't miss much – and smiled with reciprocal admiration. She knew how to flatter a man with a look alone.

'By the Lantern!' swore Peddo. 'That's my grandmother!'

Hearing Peddo's voice, she shifted her gaze. 'Peddo!' she called with cheerful surprise, raising a hand to mark that she had seen him, but she did not leave the head of the line. The children's piercing voices – they were very young – cut off any other greeting she might have thrown their way. *These are the eight children: the dragonlings, the firelings, the delvings, the wildings, the lendings . . .*

'That was my *grandmother* you were ogling!' said Peddo, elbowing him to get his attention back as the children marched away down the avenue toward wherever the hells they were going.

Joss laughed. The headache was wavering; perhaps it wouldn't hammer home after all. Banner Street gave onto Battle Square, where about fifty refugees stood in line at one of the city's rice warehouses for their weekly allotment. Youths wearing the badge of the street sweepers' guild worked the margins with their brooms. There were a fair number of militia standing at guard. Joss gave the square a brief and comprehensive sweep with his gaze.

'Pretty calm,' said Peddo, who had done the same thing. It was reflexive to do so. No reeve survived long who couldn't size up a situation fast.

Not unless the situation was a perfect ambush, impossible to predict or protect against, especially if you had gone in alone, without anyone to back you up.

'You okay?' Peddo asked. 'Got a headache?'

'Just the sun,' said Joss, blinking back the resurgent pain as they headed up Silk Street.

They passed weavers' workshops and drapers and a dozen side streets advertising fine netting, coarse netting, kites, festival streamers, ribbons and tassels, and there a pair of competing bathhouses on opposite corners. A lad was selling hot savory pies from a deep tray steadied by a strap slung around his neck. Next to him a man peddled still-slithering eels out of a pair of wooden buckets.

A line of firefighters tramped out from a side street on their rounds, their commander riding at the rear on a street-smart bay gelding. The men had their fire hooks and pikes resting on their left shoulders. They were sweating in fitted leather coats and brimmed leather helmets.

Now, after all, Peddo gave a couple of the younger, good-looking ones the once-over. 'Whoop,' he muttered under his breath.

'Can't you ever stop?' Joss asked.

Peddo had a sweet grin that gave him a mischievous look at odds with his normally sober expression. 'You're the one with the reputation.'

Silk Street dead-ended into Canal Street, the widest avenue in the city. The canal side of the street was cluttered with quays and modest piers, and there was more traffic on the water than on the paved avenues to either side. At the Silk Street gate, the two reeves cut across to the brick-paved walkway reserved for official business.

Here they were able to stride along briskly. Joss had nothing to say; the headache had slaughtered his words. Peddo pulled the brim of his cap down to shade his eyes against the sun. Across the canal lay Bell Quarter. Orchid Square was visible, swollen with folk decked out in bright silks and cottons. There was some kind of singsong festival going on there, most likely prayers for rain. It was impossible to make out words over the noise of rumbling carts, tramping feet, shouting vendors, arguing shopkeepers, barking dogs, and the nerve-shattering whine of knives being sharpened on a spinning whetstone at the nearest corner.

Nausea engulfed Joss's stomach and throat, suddenly and overwhelmingly. He lurched off the brick path, ducked under the separation rail, shoved rudely through the traffic, and made it to the sewage channel before he was sick.

After he was finished, Peddo handed him a scrap of cloth to wipe his mouth. Folk had paused to point and stare, seeing him in his reeve's leathers, but Peddo had a pleasant way of smiling that caused them to disperse rapidly. Joss eased to his feet, tested his balance, and groaned.

'Better?' asked Peddo.

'I suppose.'

'There are those among us who just never do seem to learn that wine and khaif do not mix.'

'We're always hopeful,' said Joss with a faint smile, 'that this time will be different.'

There was, after all, a water seller just a few paces away. Joss pulled a pair of vey off his string of cash and got two dipperfuls of water to cleanse his mouth.

'Come on,' said Peddo. 'The Commander didn't just ask for you. The Commander's *waiting* on you.'

That didn't sound good. It didn't look any better when they reached Guardian Bridge at the base of the rocky promontory that marked the confluence of the Istri and its tributary. The approach to the bridge lay in the open space where Bell Quarter, Flag Quarter, and the canal running between them ended at the locks. Guardian Bridge spanned the central spillway pool and the deeply cut locks. As usual, there was a crowd waiting to get on the bridge, but reeves had free passage along a separate narrow corridor roped off over

the high arch of the bridge. They could move quickly while everyone else waited.

Out on the spur, they climbed steps carved into the rock to the
north-northwest corner entrance onto the wide-open ground of
Justice Square, the largest open space within the five official quarters of Toskala. From here you couldn't see the river to either side
because the view was blocked by four built-up complexes. Past
Assizes Tower and the militia barracks to the southeast could be
glimpsed the high prow of the promontory with its bright banners
and the humble thatched-roof shelter that shielded Law Rock from
the elements. When you were standing out there on that prow of
high rock, ready to lift, it was like sailing, with the two rivers joining in a swirl of currents below.

Peddo turned left and entered through the gate into Clan Hall
with its skeletal watchtowers, two vast lofts, and parade ground
within. The reeve standing watch had a broken arm dressed up in a
sling. Seeing the pair, he grinned, displaying a missing tooth.

'Commander is waiting for you, Legate Joss. I'm thinking you're
in up to your neck.'

'What's changed, then?' asked Joss, getting a chuckle from the
other man.

Peddo shook his head with a frown.

These days Clan Hall stood mostly empty, with the overburdened
and thin-stretched forces of reeves out on constant patrol of the
beleaguered countryside. There was only one reeve and his eagle on
watch up in White Tower, but when Joss shaded his eyes and stared
up he saw an eagle spiraling in the updraft far above the promontory.

A young and quite attractive reeve was having trouble with her
bating eagle out in the parade ground. Joss would have paused to
help, but the hall loft master, standing back to advise with arms
crossed and an amused expression, seemed to have the situation in
hand. The young one wore long leather gloves wrapped up past her
elbows, but she was wearing her sleeveless leather vest with no shirt
beneath, laced up tightly over a slender but muscular frame. She
glanced their way, tracking their movement until the squawk of her
flustered eagle yanked her attention back.

'They do it on purpose to get you to look at them,' said Peddo as they hurried past. 'I don't mean 'you' as in men in general. I mean you in particular.'

'Upset their eagles?'

'No, no! Dress like that.'

'How do you know?'

'I'm the one they talk to,' he said innocently. 'You should hear the things they say.'

'You won't get me to fall for that one.'

The garden court was quiet except for the chatter of the fountain. The doors to the commander's cote stood open. An old reeve, retired from flying duty, sat at his ease cross-legged on the porch studying a half-finished game of kot. He looked up, saw them, and shook his head in wry warning.

They stepped up to the porch, tugged off their boots, and stepped up and over the threshold onto the polished wood floor of the audience chamber.

The Snake had gotten there before them. He was lounging on a padded bench, slouched back with legs stretched out and ankles crossed and resting on a single heel, arms folded over his chest, and a sneering grin on his ugly face. His lip was bruised, and swelling. Joss opened his mouth to comment, but when he saw the commander's grim look, he thought better of it.

The commander nodded at them from behind her low table. Her crutch had been set on the floor parallel to the pillow she sat on, which meant she expected not to get up any time soon. Definitely, yes, she was annoyed at someone, and when she indicated that Peddo was to sit, Joss guessed that Peddo was not the target.

'So nice of you to join us, Legate Joss,' she said so kindly that he winced. 'I've had a complaint.'

Peddo hesitated, then went to sit on the bench beside the Snake. Joss was left standing, an awkward position now that the other four people in the room were seated.

'This is Master Tanesh.'

'I remember your case, ver,' he said politely to the merchant seated cross-legged on a brocade pillow to the right of the commander's desk.

'Considering the trouble you caused me out at my estate in Allauk, I should think you would.' The man wore an overtunic of a florid purple brocade silk, embroidered with silver- and gold-thread flowers in case you were wondering how rich he really was. And if there was still then any doubt, it could be put to rest by admiring the strings of pearls adorning the loops of his threefold braid.

'I simply followed the law, ver. "When a person sells their body into servitude in payment for a debt, that person will serve eight years and in the ninth go free."'

'In the ninth to go free,' agreed the man, raising his forefinger as though he were lecturing an ignorant apprentice, 'but there's nothing said in the law about additional debt run up in the meantime, which must be repaid in coin or in service, which all agree is fair. I was genuinely shocked by the decision. I don't mind saying that I was offended by it as well, bullying my factor as this reeve did, and humiliating him in front of the witnesses just because he could.'

'The law is clear,' said Joss, who was beginning to get irritated all over again although he could not show it. The merchant's factor had possessed just this same manner of self-importance. 'Indeed, we can walk up to Law Rock and see that the law is *carved in stone*.'

'Legate Joss!' The commander rapped the table with her baton.

'You'd think he was wed to a Silver the way he goes on,' added the merchant. 'If it were allowed, that is. And I don't mind saying I am not the only one who has gotten tired of those people putting in their petition every year at the Flowering Festival, although what right such outlanders think they have to change our holy laws I can't imagine.'

'The Ri Amarah clans are not the issue under discussion,' said the commander.

He backed down unctuously. 'No, no, not at all. That's right. Let's stick to the business at hand. It's just one of my grievances that I'm sometimes on about.'

No doubt he had a dozen wagonloads of grievances.

'The matter will go before the Legate's Council next week,' continued the commander, 'and I assure you that you will not be disappointed in the ruling.'

'The law is clear,' objected Joss. 'I found according to the law that the man in question had served his eight years' servitude in payment for his debt and was unlawfully retained against his wishes past the ninth year.'

'In truth, Legate Joss,' said the commander, 'the law doesn't say anything about debt compounding through actions of the slave which accrue further debt during the period of servitude. Master Tanesh, if you will, we'll send you a messenger when the case comes up next week.'

The merchant rose and fussed and bowed. The commander, naturally, did not get up, and so he went on his way expeditiously. When the doors had slid shut behind him and a decent interval had passed in which the old reeve could escort him at least as far as out of the garden court beyond the possibility of overhearing any further conversation, she addressed Joss.

'We're already fighting what appears to be a losing battle, one that is spreading day by day, that might as well be a wildfire burning out of our control. You know that better than any person here, by the names of all the gods.'

'You know he's wrong! These people pad out debts and assign frivolous fines and make arrangements with corrupt clerks to work debt in their favor. That's the beauty of the law. It's simple, and it understands how to get around some people's desire to take more than they ought just because they are greedy—'

'Joss!'

'Is it any wonder there's been a rash of reports of slaves running out on their debts? Why shouldn't they, if they believe the law is being twisted to work against them? Indenture was meant to be a temporary measure, not a permanent one.'

'Legate Joss! You have to fight these battles when there is peace to fight them in.'

'How can there be peace when the shadows have corrupted even the law? Hells, it isn't the shadows that corrupted the law. It's us, who have allowed it to happen by making an exception here, and another there.'

'Certainly it would be easier to abide by the law of the Guardians if there were Guardians left to preside at the assizes. But there aren't. As you know best of any of us.'

In training, you learned how to absorb the force of a blow from a staff by bending to absorb the impact or melting out from under it, but this hit him straight on.

'That's silenced him, thank the gods,' muttered the Snake.

He could not speak, not even to cut that damned snake to pieces. That Peddo was hiding his eyes behind a hand did not blunt the shock.

The commander studied him. There was not a hint of softening, not in her, not even though she had let him into her bed off and on for over a year about twelve years back, before he became a legate and she the commander. Before her injury. She was not a woman swayed by fond memories. She was not sentimental, not as he was. If nightmares haunted her, she gave no sign of it. She was cold and hard and in charge of an impossible situation.

The Guardians are dead and gone.

And the young Joss, that utterly stupid and bullheaded youth who had thought far too much of himself back in those days, was the one who had brought that knowledge back to the reeve halls while abandoning his lover and her eagle to be murdered at the hands of a band of criminals who had never been caught and bound to justice for the deed. Maybe, somehow, by breaking the boundaries, he was the one who had brought it down on their heads.

As if the commander knew the way his thoughts were tending, and because she would not have said those words if she hadn't meant to hurt him, she went on.

'So. That leaves us with a hundred towns, a hundred villages, a hundred arkhons, a hundred captains, a hundred lords and landowners, a hundred local guild masters, a hundred times over, according to the holy tales recorded by Sapanasu's clerks and chanted by the Lady's mendicants. Any of these towns and villages and lords and guilds may be governed by a wise or by a foolish council, according to what fortune or misfortune has befallen their leading clans. Any of these councils may support an indifferent or a useful militia, according to their custom and that of the surrounding clans. That leaves the holy temples, whose authority is unquestioned but diffuse. And that leaves us, the six reeve halls, over whom I stand as Commander. Which position, as you know, gives me no authority except that of suggestion and coordination. Not in the halls, and not in the temples, and not in the Hundred. This is the strength we possess against an enemy who may not even be an enemy, one who cannot be found or grasped.'

'It's part of what's happened in Herelia,' said Peddo suddenly.

'Every village and town asking reeves to depart and never come back. No reeve patrols in Herelia now. The folk there came to hate us because they didn't trust us. Because they feared someone or something else even more. There's a *power* at work in Herelia, everywhere north of Iliyat and the Haya Gap. Yet we can't track it down.'

Her gaze, bent on Peddo, caused him to sit back and grin nervously, as does a boy called out for whispering to his neighbor during recitation drill.

'This is the strength we possess,' she repeated. 'And it is failing us.' She turned that gaze on Joss. He stood his ground, even under her harsh stare. 'I need Master Tanesh. He has supported the city by providing triple rations of grain and meat, although he's under no obligation to increase his tithing, and a doubled complement of young folk to serve their rotation in Toskala's militia.'

'All of which serve to protect his estates and investments.'

'Nevertheless, it ends up protecting all of us as well. I need Master Tanesh's support. And I need you concentrating on the matter at hand.'

'I thought a reeve's work to rule fairly and uncover abuses and bring criminals to justice at the assizes was the matter at hand.'

'You are so damned naive. You know what they call you?'

Joss glanced at Peddo, but the young reeve shrugged to show he hadn't a clue what the commander was going on about.

'The incorruptible,' she said with disgust.

'I take that as a compliment.'

'I suppose it is one given your predilection,' she said.

The Snake snickered. He was enjoying the free show.

'What I do when I am off duty has nothing to do with—'

She lifted a hand. He shut his mouth.

'I'm stripping you of your position as legate.'

'Stripping me— !'

She lifted her baton; she knew how to menace with it, although he wasn't actually within reach. 'I have already sent a messenger to Copper Hall asking Marshal Masar to appoint a new legate to Clan Hall. One who will replace you.'

He cursed under his breath. Had the wall been close enough, he would have slammed his fist through it—

'Never heard of a legate being stripped of his position like that before,' said the Snake. 'That must hurt.'

—Or into the Snake's face for the second time that day. But, thank the gods, the distance between them saved him from that folly. 'This is Master Tanesh's doing, isn't it? You're doing this to placate that bullying, lying, greed-ridden bastard.'

'No,' continued the commander in the manner of the flood tide, unstoppable, 'it's your own doing. You've forgotten that although the law is carved in stone, people are not. People are water, or earth, or fire, or air. They are not fixed and immutable. There must be room to maneuver, especially in an emergency. And this is an emergency.'

'But it's just that kind of thinking that's caused us to lose so much ground—'

She thwacked her baton against her desk, cutting him off. 'Also, bluntly: *You drink too much.* You're becoming unreliable.'

He indicated the Snake, whose stare challenged him. 'Reeves are often unreliable. In many different ways.'

The Snake flicked up a little finger. Peddo, seeing the rude gesture, winced.

The commander either ignored the exchange or did not notice it. 'Neither I nor the six marshals can unmake a reeve. However, I can ask for a legate to be withdrawn and replaced. As I have done. Because legates cannot be unreliable. Now. Do you want to know why I called you in today?'

'This hasn't been enough?'

'I'm hoping for much worse,' muttered the Snake.

'Volias,' said the commander in a tone so genial it seemed threatening. 'Do not tempt me to start in on you and your manifold faults.'

Peddo sucked in a breath, as if in pain. Then, amazingly, he laughed, and somehow his laughter released a bit of the tension in the chamber. Joss wiped his brow, chuckling. Even the Snake cracked a smile.

The commander nodded. 'I have a mission of particular importance. It is customary for the merchants' guild to hold its grand conclave in Toskala at the advent of every Year of the Fox. The fox being a cunning animal beloved of those who take to the merchant's craft. And so the merchants and folk associated with the guild convened at the Guild Hall at the end of this last ibex year. Their meeting is now over. The first topic among them, I am *reliably* informed, was the safety of the roads. Roads are their lifeblood. Without safe passage, a merchant cannot arrange for the transfer of goods.'

Joss's attention began to wander during this schoolroom speech. He noted how sparsely furnished the chamber was. Only last week a low couch had stood in the far corner, but now that space was empty except for a thin mat rolled up and tied with red string. The cupboard with its multitude of cubbyholes and small drawers remained, on the other side, but the fine glazed vase, normally filled with flowers and set atop the cupboard to give the room some color, was missing. A large gold-plated hairpin weighed down papers on the desk. The commander had served the Lantern in her youth; her ability to write and read was one of the reasons she had been elevated to the post. Her pen-and-ink case, lid firmly closed, sat by her right hand. A painted chest sat on the matting behind her, so she need only turn to get into it. An enameled tray had been shoved back, to the left; it held an orangeware ceramic pot suitable for brewing khaif, as well as two thin wooden drinking bowls small enough to cup in the hands. No doubt Master Tanesh had been offered the hospitality of the hall. Where had the couch and vase gone?

'According to the delegation who met with me this morning, the guild council in association with the guild of carters and transport compiled a list of roads along which caravans and wagons have been attacked in the last three years. These are attacks, mind you, in which both the attack and its aftermath were at no time witnessed by or in contact with reeves. The list is extensive, the danger widespread, and moving steadily into the southern regions of the Hundred. More importantly, of these attacks fewer than half were then reported to the local reeve halls, and of those reports, only a hand's count were traced to their origin and the criminals brought to the assizes to face trial. The guild, need I say, is not pleased with the reeves. They feel we are not doing our duty. They want reeves assigned to caravans as permanent escorts.'

The Snake grunted. 'Begging your pardon, Commander, but we're spread so thin patrolling the hinterlands and making sweeps

along the roads and tracks that we can't assign reeves to act as
guards for the merchants. Aren't the local militias responsible for
the safety of the roads within five mey of every town? Can't the
guild hire guards, like they do in the south when they travel over the
pass into the empire? Or are they just too cheap for that?'

'As for hiring guards, I cannot answer for their quality, cost, or
availability. But it seems the worst of the raids are carried out precisely to avoid the local militia, either by means of their speed or via
misdirection.'

'Ospreys,' said Peddo. 'That's what they call such outlaws in the
south. Dive, and snatch.'

Joss shook his head, raising a hand to ask for clarification. 'Are
you saying that the merchants suspect that some of these raids are
carried out in coordination with local militia?'

She shrugged. 'That remains to be seen. As a gesture of good
faith – for I assure you that we must retain the good faith of the
guilds or else the halls will not be able to provision and maintain
themselves – I have agreed to assign you as an escort for those merchants departing the conclave who are traveling the main routes out
of Toskala.'

The Snake chortled. 'Aui! That's a pup's chore, first-year reeve
duty, escort along the roads. You've had your wing feathers
plucked, haven't you?'

'You, and you, and you. All three of you on this escort duty.' The
commander did smile now, and the Snake choked on his laughter.
Her smile was not a pleasant thing, after all. The Snake began to
splutter a protest, but the commander's gaze cut him off. He crossed
his arms over his chest and scowled.

Joss's head was pounding so badly that he could not taste even a
grain of pleasure from the Snake's discomfort.

'How does it happen,' asked Peddo mildly, 'that even the three of
us can be spared just now? Given that we've lost fifteen reeves and
four eagles to ambush and fighting in the last two years alone. Not
counting the twelve reeves who asked to be transferred out of Clan
Hall, and the twenty or thirty who have been recalled to their home
clans by their marshals. Or all those lost in all the halls since it
became clear many years ago that someone was targeting reeves and
their eagles specifically. If you don't mind my asking, Commander?'

Even Peddo was taken aback by the intensity of her cold, frightening smile.

'I don't mind you asking, since we all know how serious the situation is. Or at least, how serious the situation is here in the north. Yet we must concern ourselves with the south, too. We must concern ourselves with this report from the merchants' guild's council, and from the carters' guild. We must work in concert, or we will not survive on our own.'

'You're pandering to them,' said Joss through his headache. 'There are remote villages who rely on us to run their assizes. We provide the only justice they can count on. These guilds can afford to pay for their own protection. We have better things to do. More crucial ones.'

'I'm doing this to placate the merchants' guild and the transport guild, it's true. I've told them you'll patrol as escort for five days out of Toskala, after which you're to return to Clan Hall with your report. I also want you three to range wide, keep your eyes open, and return each night to camp with the company you're assigned to. I want you to listen to what the guild masters are saying among themselves.'

'You don't trust them?' asked Peddo.

Her smile vanished, and she bent her head, eyes narrowing in an expression that did, at last, soften her. The gods knew everyone liked Peddo, and for good reason. He had never stabbed anyone in the back, or gossiped in order to cause harm, or told tales out of turn to get a man in trouble, or intimidated witnesses and pushed around locals just for the kick of feeling his power.

'Oh, Peddo. My dear boy. You're a good lad, and a competent reeve.'

The commander's instinct for trouble was legendary. Indeed, it was the other reason she had risen to her post: She had never gotten caught flat-footed. That instinct had allowed her to escape the hammer, the perfect ambush designed to slaughter her and her eagle which she and the raptor had instead survived. Not like Marit and Flirt. She touched the crutch beside her, without which she no longer could walk. She had survived, but not unscathed.

'No, I'm not feeling very trusting in these days. Nor should you.'

4

They took flight at dawn from the prow of Toskala, riding the updraft high and higher until the city could be glimpsed as a whole below them. In days of old, Toskala had been founded on the promontory below which the muddy yellow-brown waters of River Istri, flowing inexorably down out of the north, met the bluer waters of its tributary, the Lesser Istri, rushing in from the north-western foothills. The city had expanded beyond the original city wall onto the broadening spit of land between the two rivers, and was now protected by an outer wall and earthworks that spanned the ground from the western bank of the Istri to the facing bank of the Lesser Istri. The first ferries of the day had already started their crossings, men turning winches and hauling on rope as the flat vessels strained with the current.

Toskala was known as 'the crossroads' because here a person had the choice of five major roads. Peddo and his eagle, Jabi, banked south, heading out over the Flats. The Snake, and Trouble, followed the Lesser Walk.

Joss was assigned to the fifth and least of the roads, the Ili Cutoff, which speared straight east through cultivated fields and orchards to the town of River's Bend on the River Ili, halfway between Toskala and the valley of Iliyat. He and Scar flew sweeps all morning, routine patterns over cultivated land that revealed nothing except folk out preparing fields for the coming rains.

The heavens shone blue, untouched by cloud. The landscape was open, cut by streams, swales, well-tended orchards, overgrown pastureland, and a few dense tangles of undergrowth and pockets of uncut trees. Fish ponds and small reservoirs dug for irrigation glittered in the hard sunlight, water drained low here at the tail end of the dry season. Twice he flew over the skirts of the Wild, an impenetrable forest so broad that no human had ever been known to traverse it on foot although several forester clans worked its fringes. The day was hot, as it always was in the last weeks before the rains, but not as hot as it had been in previous years. Not as hot as it could be.

At intervals he crossed back over the ridgeward Istri Walk, keeping track of a large guild caravan that had hired an entire cohort of guards for the journey to High Haldia, Seven, and Teriayne. Once, he glimpsed Trouble off to his left, on a sweep. A really beautiful bird, she had an especially golden gleam, which made it all the more annoying that she had chosen the Snake as her reeve nine years back after Barda's awful death.

Midway through the afternoon, as the heat melted over the land, he and Scar glided back over the Ili Cutoff. The caravan was pulling to a stop under the shade of a pair of ancient Ladytrees, a sweet resting spot beside a watering hole. Hirelings and slaves led the parched beasts to drink, and produced food and drink for the masters. Joss left Scar on a high rock towering over the far side of the pond, the kind of place he and his friends would have dived from when they were lads. The eagle settled on this perch and began preening. Joss strolled over to the Ladytrees. Distinct groups had already formed among the company: under the smaller of the Ladytrees gathered the apprentices and hirelings and slaves permitted to take a break while their brethren worked.

The elder Ladytree was, like a vast chamber, sufficient for 'many families to gather in their separate houses under one roof,' as the tale had it. The four Herelian merchants kept to themselves. When they saw him enter under the cloak of the tree, they turned their backs and sought the fringes of the shade offered by the vast superstructure of overhanging branches and boundary shoots rooted and growing thick like a fence.

A foresting master bound for the Wild and the cart master who supervised this train of wagons acknowledged him with a respectful touch of two fingers to the temple: *I recognize you*. He offered the same gesture in return. He would talk to them later.

He bent his path to where the other groups of masters had settled in three distinct clots. The first group was a trio of Iliyat merchants, two women and a man, wearing sturdy but plain traveling gear and deep in conversation. The second group rested apart from the others. Seated on a folding stool, a merchant wearing expensive silks inappropriate for travel was gesticulating as another man, also on a folding stool, listened with head bent and gaze directed toward the ground. This man's rank could be told not by his clothing but by the retainers hovering close by: a pair of armed guards, a servant holding a tray with a capped pitcher and cups, and a young man wearing slave bracelets and wielding a large fan to cool his master.

Joss halted beside the third group, five Haldian merchants seated on a single blanket. 'Greetings of the day to you, Masters. I'm called Joss, out of Clan Hall.'

The commander was the kind of person who kept digging into a wound long after the infection was cut out, just for the sake of probing. He meant to give her no satisfaction today by flinching from that which she guessed would cause him a pang. He nodded at the man he knew among their group of five. 'Master Tanesh.'

'Greetings of the day to you, reeve.' That might have been a gleam of triumph in the merchant's expression, or else he was just perspiring from the heat.

'The journey finds you steady on your feet, I trust?'

'I've not much farther to go. I'll be home within my walls by sunset. But my guild-kin, these here, all live up by the highlands. They've an uncertain journey before them, eight or twelve days more.'

His guild-kin introduced themselves: Alon, Darya, Kasti, Udit. A range of ages, they nevertheless had a tight bond: They were gossiping about the other members of the caravan. Master Tanesh magnanimously offered Joss a bowl of cold melon soup, and invited him to sit with them. Kasti and Udit moved apart to make room on the blanket. Udit, by some years the youngest of the group, measured Joss with the same eye she likely used to peruse goods available in the market. Then she smiled, a swift, inviting grin, and passed him a cup of cordial as a chaser to the soup. Joss sipped, listening as the conversation flowed around him in lowered voices.

'Those Herelians, I don't trust them.'

'Did you see the bolts of silk they offered at the market? That was first-grade Sirniakan silk. How they'd get that, with the roads out of Herelia blockaded, eh? Or so they claim. Yet they got passage down for the conclave.'

'They're shipping it in.'

'Around Storm Cape? Unlikely.'

'Out of the north, maybe.'

'Nah, nah. It would be too dangerous. There's barbarians living in the drylands, beyond Heaven's Ridge, you know.'

'How would you know? You've never been there. That's outside the Hundred. No one lives there.'

'Someone lives there! These pasture men, with their herds, always wandering. The 'Kin,' they call themselves. And other tribes, too, farther out. Real savages those are. I heard there's a tribe out there that cuts up their women's faces, like marking a slave's debt, to show they are married.'

The company hooted and laughed until the speaker, Udit, had to admit this detail was only marketplace gossip heard tenth-hand.

Tanesh shushed them. 'Don't believe every tale you hear, Udit. But that doesn't mean there isn't a grain of truth where there's talk of trade. Even savages can be hired to guard merchant trains.'

'Savages can't be trusted.'

'Who can be trusted, these days?' Joss asked mildly, with a grin to take the sting off the words.

Not even Tanesh took offense at the words. He and his comrades considered them grimly. An aged slave filled their cups with more cordial.

In their silence as they drank, the loud voice of the well-dressed merchant of the second group floated easily under the canopy. 'But I fear that the members of the Lesser Houses will not cooperate. Worse, we suspect they are ready to rebel against—' The man's voice dropped abruptly. The rest of his complaint was too low to hear across the gap.

Udit elbowed Joss. 'I don't know who that merchant is, but the other man, the one with him, that's Lord Radas, lord of Iliyat. He came down with his retinue for the conclave. They say his family comes out of a merchant clan. He rules the guilds of Iliyat with a tight hand, I'll tell you.'

'What manner of tight hand?' Joss knew his region well, all the local rulers, arkhons, captains, and hierarchs with whom he dealt on a regular basis as well as other community leaders, guild masters, and prominent artisans, and various local eccentrics and ne'er-do-wells. The valley of Iliyat was normally under the purview of Copper Hall, but he had flown there a few times in recent years because of the trouble in Herelia. He had seen the lord of Iliyat twice, in passing, but not to speak with. 'He seems a quiet manner of man.'

'Oh, he's as strange as the daffer stork,' said Tanesh. 'Never looks a person in the eye, too shy to talk. You're thinking he rules with the tight hand of an ordinand, sword or spear at the ready, Kotaru's Thunder well in his grip. That's not it. He rules with the hand of an accountant. "Every stalk of rice in and every one out is counted," as it says in the tale.' He sketched the accompanying gestures with a hand, counting and grasping and a reluctance to let go, and the others chuckled. 'He must have served his apprentice year in the temple of the Lantern as a clerk, to be so tight.'

Joss had to admire the graceful efficiency of Tanesh's talking-hand gestures. 'And you served at the Lady's temple, I see,' said Joss. 'That's the real skill you have. The Lady's gift.'

'Aui! So am I found out.' Tanesh was a man who liked praise. All their past differences might be forgiven if Joss only threw fulsome appreciation his way.

'I spoke the truth, that's all,' Joss said curtly. He hadn't the stomach for more. He rose and gave cup and bowl to a slave. 'I thank you for the hospitality.'

He made his courtesies and continued his sweep, hearing Tanesh's company fall immediately back into a buzz of gossip. The three merchants out of Iliyat greeted him courteously and offered him food and drink, the same as they were themselves eating.

'How was your conclave?' he asked them.

Like all merchants, they enjoyed talk. They described Toskala. The two women – dealers in oil and spices – had disliked the city, thinking it too large and loud and crowded and smelly and filthy with refuse. But the young man had found it exciting to wander in so many grand squares and marketplaces, to see such a variety of shops.

'Just to see Flag Quarter – for I buy and sell banners and flags and tent cloth and such manner of working cloth, not clothing, so it's of particular interest to me – where a person might have a shop selling just game banners or just boundary flags or only the ink for printing your mark on the fabric. That was something! I trade in all cloth, all in my one shop!'

'Was it your first time in Toskala, ver?'

'Oh, indeed! My uncle and cousins used to make the trip, but they died last year so I was handed the mantle.' He tugged on his cloak; he wore a pale-blue mantle appropriate to the season, lightest weight cotton and only reaching to his elbows. Its hem was trimmed with the house mark, spades crossed with needles, something to do with digging and sewing.

'How did they die?'

The man dipped his head and sighed. The women shook their heads, frowning at Joss as though to scold him for asking the question.

At length, the older of the women gestured toward Lord Radas. 'Things run smoothly in the Iliyat valley. We're well governed. But I'll tell you that we don't go near the northern border. We keep our distance from the hills and Herelia.'

'Is there much raiding out of the hills or Herelia into Iliyat these days?'

'Oh, we think not,' said the man at last, dabbing at his eyes. 'The roads are blockaded. No one crosses the Liya Pass anymore, though there's a trading post up where the village of Merrivale was before it got burned down. There's plenty of militia to man the borders, even young men hired in from outside. One of my cousin's daughters married a young man who walked all the way from Sund just to get the work. We're well protected.'

'From Herelia?'

The man shrugged. 'My kin were not in Iliyat when they died. They'd taken the Thread north, to Seven. We told them to take the Istri Walk, but they didn't want to take the extra mey, all the way to the river, you know, and then north, not when the Thread is a decent track wide enough to handle sturdy wagons. You never could tell my uncle anything. He had a hasty manner.'

Joss nodded. 'May their spirits have passed through the Gate,' he said reflexively, and they all touched right shoulder, upper lip, and left temple, drawing out the spirit's passage to peace. 'I'm sorry to hear it, but the Thread's a dangerous road these days, up against the highlands as it is. Very rough country, heavily forested. Plenty of places to hide along there. We can't patrol it all.'

'No, it's been seen you reeves can't,' said the older woman, with a bite to her voice that ended the conversation. 'Will have you more rice?'

It was cold and congealed and lumpy, but flavored with a generous mix of spices and a touch of nutty til oil. He ate gratefully. They watched him in a silence heavy with judgment.

They don't trust the reeves any longer. So the circle of distrust widens, grows, like the shadows as the sun sets.

He made his courtesies and walked to the second group. The well-dressed merchant was so intent on the sound of his own voice that he did not notice Joss approaching. 'We of the Greater Houses spent so many hours arguing over it, but in the end we decided we had no choice lest we lose everything our houses had worked for and achieved. Which is why—'

The lord of Iliyat shifted his foot. The merchant glanced up, startled, and saw Joss. He flushed, then wiped at his chin with the back of a hand as though he thought he had a stain there that needed to be rubbed away.

'May I sit down?' asked Joss, stopping beside them.

The merchant coughed harshly. 'I beg your pardon, reeve. I wasn't expecting you. I thought you were keeping your eyes on the road.'

Lord Radas lifted a hand, as consent. His voice was soft, almost inaudible. 'It was good of your Commander to offer us this escort. We've had a great deal of trouble out of Herelia in recent years.' His gaze flashed past Joss, outward, toward the pond. Scar was visible through a gap in the leafy fence of branches. The raptor had spread his wings to sunbathe.

'Yes,' said Joss. 'So you have, Lord Radas. And so have we reeves.' He unclasped his short cloak and spread it on the dirt, then settled down cross-legged upon it. 'I'm called Joss, out of Clan Hall. I admit to some surprise, seeing a man of your inheritance at the guild meeting.'

'Do you so?' asked the lord, with the ghost of smile, although he still kept his gaze fixed on the earth. The lack of eye contact made him seem awkward and ill at ease, or it might have been a vanity, a refusal to grant recognition. Hard to tell. He dressed plainly, loose linen trousers dyed indigo and an undyed tunic tied with cloth loops, nothing more ornamental than the clothing worn by his own servants. His hair was braided back into a single rope; he wore no head covering. His only affectation was a long gold silk cloak, although Joss was frankly shocked to see him sitting on the lower part of it, as though it were an ordinary ground cloth, not highest-quality fabric far too expensive for the everyday householder. 'My family rose out of a merchant branch of our local clan. We still maintain those ties. It was the basis of our wealth and our later authority.'

Joss turned to regard the other man. 'And you, ver?'

'Feden. That's my name.' He lifted an arm to display an ivory bracelet masterfully carved to resemble a series of quartered flowers linked petal-to-petal. 'That's my house mark.'

'You're not from Toskala. I don't recognize your mark.'

'Olossi.'

'It's a long way from Olossi to Toskala,' remarked Joss in a friendly manner, without mentioning that the Ili Cutoff certainly did not lead south.

'Oil,' said Master Feden. 'I'm seeking whale oil from the Bay of Istria. A fine quality oil, bright-burning, and of particular use in the manufacture of leather goods. Fortunately, I was able to bring oil of naya with me, for trade. I was thankful that I reached Toskala in one piece, for I don't mind telling you, reeve, that we in the south are having a great deal of trouble with our roads.' Once started, he scarcely paused for breath, going on in the manner of a man accustomed to having his complaints listened to with exceptional attentiveness. 'A great deal of trouble all around, if you ask me. Trading charters revoked. Terms of sale refused. Agreements that have held for many rounds of years stomped into the dirt just because certain people feel they've been hard used, as if we who are struggling to keep things in order aren't the ones being hard used, I tell you. I see many people in these days who insist on ingratitude.'

He took a sip from the cup he held in his hands, then continued.

'Aui! It's bad times. I don't know who to trust. I hate to think of being close-hearted, for it goes against the Teachings, but there you are. I can't even send my usual factors south into the empire anymore. These past few years I've had to send one of my own slaves down to do what trading he can. That way he can risk his own stake instead of mine. It's a great opportunity for him, naturally, and

I must say it's not every master would be so generous, as many of my colleagues have said to me. But of course I stand to lose even so, if he's killed, for he cost quite a string of coin to purchase and then of course the later investment in his upbringing, feeding, and training, but mind you, speculating with my own coin and goods in a larger venture just isn't worth the risk these days. You would think I could trust my own factors, some of them clansmen, but even some of them have cheated me and my house. I tell you! How can any person believe it's come to this? How can the gods have let this come to pass, I ask you? What can we do? What can we do?'

As he caught his breath to gain strength for the next volley, Joss cut in.

'Where are you headed now, ver? I'd have thought you would be with one of the other companies. There was a group headed west on the Lesser Walk and another traveling south on the Flats. You can't get to Olossi this way, unless you mean to take ship in Arsiya and sail the storms all the way round the Turian Cape and the roil of Messalia. Even then you'd have to put to shore and take some rough paths through the foothills of the Spires to reach Olossi.'

He recognized his mistake at once. He'd thought Master Feden's bluster was born out of obliviousness mixed with arrogance and conceit, so his feint hadn't been subtle enough. The gaze turned on him now measured him shrewdly, eyes narrowed with a dawning distrust. Joss knew that look well. Reeves saw it all the time, though not from the innocent. Master Feden was smarter than he chose to seem.

'Where are any of us headed, in times like these?' mused the merchant. 'We stumble in the dark hoping to find any light that may guide us to a safe haven. We are desperate, truly. Folk are none too careful what well they drink from if they've had no drink at all for many days. That's just how it is.'

'True words,' said Joss, thinking of the commander's agreement with Master Tanesh. He glanced at the lord of Iliyat, but the man made no polite reply to this heartfelt comment. He didn't even look up, as if bare dirt were the most interesting companion a man could have. Joss had an idea that Lord Radas was about his own age, more or less forty, although the lord looked younger. Some men had all the luck, although the lord of Iliyat did not seem to be the kind of man who coaxed women, not with those reticent manners. 'And you, Lord Radas. How do you keep the valley of Iliyat at peace in these troubled times?'

'With a fence,' said the lord curtly. 'A wall at our borders, strong guards, a vigilant eye, and respect for the law. Within Iliyat, we hold to the law.'

There was a passion in the lord's voice that surprised Joss, even pleased him, yet also, and all at the same time, the skin at the base of his neck tingled with an uneasy shiver, the way it did when his instincts warned him that something wasn't right.

'The Hundred is fractious,' the lord went on so softly that Joss strained to hear him. 'Too many fight, too many argue, too many look away because they have it well enough, although others struggle. Alone, each is frail and selfish. Each town, each clan, each hall lies separate, suspicious of the others, clutching tight to their own small field. Some hold to the law while others give themselves leave to do what they wish while justifying their actions by lying to themselves and to others. Some have already stepped into the shadows.' He looked up, and met Joss's gaze.

Hammered as by the sun. A vivid flash of memory: Five years after Marit's death, Joss stands under the humble thatched awning that shelters Law Rock. Drunk, grieving, and angry, he stares at the first lines, hewn long ago into the pillar of granite:

With law shall the land be built.
The law shall be set in stone, as the land rests on stone.
The rock into which the law is bound shall be set aside, in a separate precinct.
A bridge shall guard access to this precinct. Both rock and bridge shall be inviolate.
Here is the truth:
The only companion who follows even after death, is justice.
The Guardians serve justice.
The reeves serve justice.

The reeves serve justice, and so he would. He had nothing else to hold to.

Then Lord Radas's soft voice tore him out of the memory.

'While some, for all their weakness, remain incorruptible.'

Joss blinked, fighting back dizziness. The filtered light cast all things sheltered under the Ladytree in a gentle glow. Feden was sipping at his tea, as though he'd noticed nothing. From all around murmured the sounds of folk at rest, eating, chatting, burping, chortling, while farther out beasts lowed and whuffled, a dog barked, and – there – Scar called out an interrogatory yelp, as if the raptor had been caught in that vision and needed to know Joss was safe.

Lord Radas was staring at the dirt again, eyes half closed, as though he were about to fall asleep. Behind, a youthful slave raised and lowered the large fan like the steady, hypnotic beat of a wing. The air stirred by that fan stung Joss's eyes, raising tears.

Shaken, he made his courtesies. He went out beyond the Ladytree to let Scar see him, then walked aside to take a piss, to collect himself, to breathe the air although the heat was itself a hammer. No wonder he'd gotten dizzy.

At length, he retreated back to the cooling shelter of the Ladytree and approached the forester and cart master with some trepidation. The cart master had a pair of medium-sized dogs who, as Joss walked up, pulled back their lips to display big teeth. Their ominous growl rumbled so low that he barely heard it, although his neck prickled. But when their master made his greetings, the dogs shimmied over at once for a friendly rub. They had expressive ears held at point when they were alert and flopped over when they relaxed, and their short gray-wire coats were unexpectedly soft.

He and the two men visited for a while, sharing rice wine and dry rice cake, all of it musty, the remnants of journey food. The wine was good, and he nibbled at the rice cake for courtesy's sake as they discussed the day, the season, the dead year and the new one, and the lands all around.

'Nah, I haven't seen nothing of raids where I'm from.' The forester had a clipped accent and a strange way of pronouncing some of his words. He was human, though. Not everything that came out of the Wild was. 'My fields are the forest. I keep to my place there in the skirts of the Wild, and the wildings keep to theirs in the heart. I've never gone farther north than Sandalwood Crossing, for that matter. Once a year I do walk down into Toskala to the Guild Hall on behalf of my clansmen in the Wild. We keep a steady harvest of logs coming out of the Wild, according to our charter. We keep to the boundaries, as the gods did order when the world rose out of the sea.'

'I have a hard time thinking that outlaws would shelter in the Wild,' said Joss.

'If they did, they'd not come out again,' said the cart master with a laugh. He patted his dogs. They wagged their tails.

'What about the Ili Cutoff?' Joss asked.

'She's safe enough. I run this route every month. I've not had trouble, not compared to other tales I've heard tell, but I keep my eyes open and you can see also that my good dogs do keep the alert.' He pointed. Two others of the same breed stood guard, almost hidden in the outer branch-roots of the Ladytree, watching over the wagons and the road.

Under the Ladytree, folk dozed as the heat grew more stifling. Joss yawned, and caught a quick nap. Shade Hour drew to a close; the heat lessened as the angle of the sun shifted.

At length, the cart master got to his feet. 'We need to get another mey of journey in before sunset, if we want to make River's Bend in five days.'

Joss drained another cup of wine, made his courtesies, and returned to Scar. A pair of local lads were sitting in the shade of a mulberry tree, watching the eagle from a safe distance. He paused to chat with them; they had more questions than he could answer, and in return they chattered freely about their village and the habitations nearby. Master Tanesh, it transpired, was well known in these parts as a wealthy landholder who treated his hirelings well and his slaves poorly, a man you didn't want to cross who tithed generously at the local temples and had even set aside land for a temple dedicated to Ilu, the Herald, on his own estate.

Behind, the wagons rolled. Joss made his courtesies, and the boys tagged after until Scar, seeing them coming, raised his proud head and stared them down. The boys stopped dead.

'Nah, come on,' said Joss. He whistled Scar down from the rock, then coaxed the boys forward to stroke the raptor's copper plumage. This attention the bird accepted with his usual aloof resignation.

'Best go now,' said Joss, and the boys scampered back to the tree, to watch as Joss fastened into his harness. Scar lifted heavily, beating hard with slow wing-strokes, seeking an up-current. Finding it, the eagle rose swiftly. The ground dropped away.

As the eagle began quartering the ground, Joss's thoughts quartered the afternoon's conversations. Talk refreshed him as much as drink and food and a nap. He turned the words over and over, seeking patterns, seeking hidden meaning, seeking that which was not meant to be said aloud, but he found nothing yet beyond that strange hammer of memory that had briefly shaken him. Anomalies would come clear in time; they usually did. You just had to be patient, let them work free in their own manner.

No one crosses the Liya Pass anymore.

It had become a land of shadows. He'd known that the morning he and the others had found Marit's gear and clothing, the very clothing she'd been wearing when she and Flirt had flown away from him, the last time she'd been seen alive. He'd known that when they'd found the remains of her mutilated eagle, and months later when he'd flown Flirt's sun-bleached bones to Heaven's Ridge and scattered what was left in the valley of silence. Gone altogether. Gods, he'd been so young.

He turned his attention, again, to the lands below.

This region of Low Haldia, still close to Toskala, was well cultivated and closely settled, villages and hamlets strung along trackways. Seen from the height, the many trackways interlaced across the land, reminding him of the nets he'd cast into the sea when he was a lad, living on the coast. Those days seemed dreamlike, seen from the height of his life now, many years later. The cordial made by his aunts had tasted sweeter. His mother's rice porridge had never congealed into lumps. No one had ever gotten hurt, except that time when he and the blacksmith's son had gotten into a fistfight over pretty Rupa. They'd all been – the hells! – just twelve, celebrating their first return to their birth year. Those days sparked so clear and bright in his memory; all days did, until that day he and Marit had met in the Liya Pass and he had talked her into breaking the boundaries. After that, the curse had settled; he knew it for a fact, because his life had become dulled as with a stain, changed, lessened, corrupted, shadowed. Nineteen cursed years. Better he had stayed home and married pretty Rupa, who had been pretty enough but with a decided lack of interest in anything except her clan's fish ponds along the bay. For her, the rest of the Hundred might just as well never have existed. No doubt she was still wading thigh-deep in seawater, with a grandchild tied in a sling to her back.

Gods, he *was* getting old. And inattentive. Scar was circling, waiting for him to make some signal, choose some direction. The commander was right. He'd gotten unreliable. Too much drink. Too much anger. Too much regret.

A company of men marched briskly along a track off to the east. They had weapons enough that the glint of metal gave away their position.

'Come on, old boy.' The eagle took the signal eagerly; he was always keen to go.

They glided on the wind. A man in the company lifted his head and saw them. Others pointed. As they passed over, Joss saw a flag painted with Master Tanesh's mark and, behind it, the master himself, riding a rangy bay gelding. Ahead lay the tidy fields of a splendid estate, ranks of orchard, a tea plantation, dry-field rice being dug for sowing, mulberry trees, flower beds, and a string of ponds like gems surrounding the whole. This was evidently Tanesh's original holding, not one of his satellite estates like Allauk, which lay farther north. The temple dedicated to Ilu, the Herald, was sited in a hillier area, unsuitable for agriculture. Skimming over the temple, Joss spotted apprentices striding across the temple grounds and a few envoys in sky-blue cloaks. Strange, now that he thought on it, that there had been no envoys traveling with this train. Normally every merchant train had an envoy of Ilu alongside, carrying messages according to the ancient charters that designated a holy task to each of the priests of each of the seven gods.

With dusk closing in, he returned to the road and followed it west until he found the company, lanterns lit and the wagons arrayed in a closed square, a fence against the night. Landing, he sprung Scar's harness, examined his feathers, then released him to hunt. The eagle would find his own roost for the night and return at dawn when Joss whistled.

The cart dogs greeted him first, barking happily and pushing in to get pats on the head. The cart master waved to him, but the man was busy with the evening's settling-out, so Joss strolled through the encampment as it set up for the night's rest. Nothing of interest. Folk greeted him, he greeted them, and passed on. There was one face he did not see.

'What happened to that merchant out of the south?' Joss asked the cart master later. 'Feden, his name was.'

'He turned back after Shade Hour. He didn't go any farther than those Ladytrees where we took our rest. Did you not see him go?'

'I did not,' said Joss, taken aback. 'I flew straight east, I admit to you. Then north. I didn't cross back that way except the once, and saw nothing on the road then, but I might easily have missed him. Did he go alone?'

'He had a ten of guards with him. They had the look of ordinands. Disciplined, well-trained lads.'

'He left, just like that? What did he come for? It's a cursed strange thing to travel along all this way, and then turn around without even having reached a market.'

The cart master scratched his chin. 'Well, now, that I don't know. He sealed some bargain with the lord of Iliyat, for as we made ready to leave, he turned right around and announced himself satisfied with the bargain – whatever it was – and was going home. It seems he got what he came for, and so he left.'

At river's bend, reached midway through the fifth day of the journey, a cohort of armed men who had marched down from the valley of Iliyat met Lord Radas to escort him the rest of the way home. After some negotiation, the Herelians paid to accompany them, and Lord Radas allowed it. The cart master had already been hired to go all the way to Iliyat, and he was eager to continue on while there was still daylight. Stopping only to water the dray beasts and purchase provisions, the main portion of the caravan moved on.

Across the river lay the vanguard of the Wild, the towering forest that engulfed all the land to be seen on the other side of the River Ili. Figures on the far shore greeted the forester and his pair of apprentices with a wave, then got back to work lashing together logs for the float downstream. The forester made his courtesies and took the ferry across to join them.

That left Joss with a much smaller company, the four merchants headed north and northwest into western Low Haldia. With the

Iliyat contingent shorn away, the company had a much more vulnerable look, and it was clear that the remaining merchants were nervous. They had a dozen local lads out of Low Haldia to guard them, but any experienced band of thieves could make short work of this crew. In truth, Joss had no obligation to go farther. The commander had ordered him to return after escorting the company safely to River's Bend. But he had come to like the way the foursome gossiped without much malice, just in the way of trading information. They were generous with their food and drink. Udit had been looking him over with increasing interest and making the kind of jokes that indicated she might be willing to indulge in a little night play. He wanted to get a good look at the hinterlands, anyway. He might hope to meet another reeve on patrol, exchange news, trade intelligence. There were many villages and hamlets in these parts that waited patiently for a reeve to fall out of the sky so they might put to that reeve certain complaints and questions that the local officials were unable to deal with.

It was the task he was best at, the one he craved because out there in the isolated hamlets was the one place where he felt he was doing some good.

'I'll travel a bit farther with you,' he told them.

Udit smiled. She had a pleasing figure, if a little thin for his taste. They decided to rest for the night within the safety of the town's palisade rather than risk an extra night on the road. The foursome sat him down in the local inn and plied him with cordial, as their thanks.

Later, after nightfall, the innkeeper in River's Bend gifted him with a soft corner in the hayloft over the stables for his rest. As he stripped off his reeve leathers and lay down on his cloak, his head reeled from the many cups of cordial he had downed with the evening's meal. Strange, now that he thought on it: Master Feden had offered him no hospitality, nothing to drink or eat. Nor had Lord Radas. It was cursed rare for a reeve to be refused hospitality.

The air under the stable roof was stale, and the scent of musty hay tickled his throat. It was entirely black, no light at all even where he could see through the gaps between the boards in the loft. No flame burned, no lamp illuminated the night. He had been in the last group of drinkers, a passel of middle-aged and elderly locals who had done nothing but jaw on about a recent marriage between a local girl and a lad come from Farsar because, he'd said, there was no work to be had in Farsar, no apprenticeships open except binding oneself to the temple past the usual youth's year of service. In the north, he'd heard, you could get work, but the locals considered this statement at length and found it lacking, except that it was true that a young man might hire himself out as a guardsman to a well-to-do clan. That was what the world was coming to. No one to do the real work; all those young men lounging around with spears in their hands, some of them with the debt mark tattooed by their left eye and no proof they'd served out their debt. Meanwhile, they pretended to be ordinands dedicated to Kotaru the Thunderer without taking on the true dedicate's responsibility.

Weren't old men and women always complaining about how much better the old days were? And hadn't they been, truly? Eyelids drooping, body growing heavy, he sank under, sliding into sleep.

The dream always unveils itself in a gray unwinding of mist he has come to dread. He is walking but cannot see any of the countryside around him, only shapes like skeletal trees with leafless limbs and branches – cold-killed, as they call them in the Arro highlands, where, beyond the kill line, the trees wither in the dry season and are reborn when the rains come. In the dream he is dead, yet unable to pass beyond the Spirit Gate. He is a ghost, hoping to awaken from the nightmare nineteen years ago, but the nightmare has already swallowed him.

The mist boils as though churned by a vast intelligence. It is here that the dream twists into the vision that is agony, the reason that even after all these years he cannot let go. The mist will part, and he will see her figure in the unattainable distance, walking along a slope of grass or climbing a rocky escarpment, a place he can and must never reach because he has a duty to those on earth whom he has sworn to serve.

It begins. Wind rips the mist into streamers that billow like cloth, like the white linen and silk banners strung up around Sorrowing Towers where the dead are laid to rest under the open sky. He begins to sweat, waiting for the apparition.

Waiting to see her. Gods spare him this! But the gods never listen.

A shadow moves along the hill. As though harnessed to his eagle, he swoops closer. There she is!

A hand brushes his thigh, turns into a familiar caress.

He shouts in surprise, for he has never before reached her, touched her.

He sat up, startling awake. His forehead slammed into a jaw.

She fell back, thumping onto the planks. 'Eiya! The hells!'

The pain in his forehead lanced deep.

'Shit!' she added. It was Udit. 'That's cut my lip! I'm bleeding!'

His stomach heaved. Barely in time, he flung himself to the corner and threw up all the cordial and that good venison and leek stew. The taste was vile.

'Begging your pardon,' she said coldly, her humor turning fast into disgust. 'You stink!'

He gagged, retched, and coughed up the leavings.

Scrabbling in the dark, she took her leave. Through his pounding headache, he heard her feet scrape on the ladder as she climbed down. He was shaking so hard he could not call after her. Nor did he want to. He groaned, shifting back to his cloak, but the hay poked and irritated him, and the smell of his vomit rose rankly in the closed space, and the throbbing in his temple would not let up enough to let him rest. At length he pulled on trousers and vest, then crept outside where he sat on a bench on the porch of the inn, sliding in and out of a light doze. The Lamp Moon, rising, had just ghosted above the palisade. River's Bend was a prosperous town with six avenues and six cross-alleys to link them. It had a permanent covered market, unusual in a town this size, and an exceptionally fine temple dedicated to Sapanasu, the Lantern.

The inn's porch overlooked the square fronting the main gate. A Ladytree had rooted there; it was a good place for it, just inside the gates, although no one was sleeping there tonight. It was very quiet, not a touch of wind. If there were guards posted in the watchtower, he could not see them from the covered porch because although the palisade was a simple pole structure, the gate itself had a doubled entryway: You had to enter through the outer gate into a small, confined area, where you waited for the inner gate to be opened to admit you to the town. The watchtower spanned the outer gate, and his view of it was in any case half blocked by the lush crown of the Ladytree.

A scuffling sound caught his ear. He banked from drowsy to woken without moving. He watched as a figure sneaked out of a dark street and up to the palisade, right at the edge of the open ground. The figure leaned against the palisade, as though listening, then turned around to scan the entire open area fronting the inner gate. It did not discern Joss in the shadows of the porch. A moment later, a second figure appeared at the top of the wall, heaved itself over, and dropped, landing with a soft thump. A third and fourth followed.

Joss carefully pulled on the leather thong at his neck and got his fingers on the bone whistle. He set it to his lips as a fifth and sixth topped the wall, lowered until they hung by their fingers, then let go.

The bone whistle had three notes: one that hurt human ears, one that the eagles responded to, and one other, that on occasion served reeves well without drawing attention to them. Tapping that highest range, he blew. No human could hear that sound. But, by the gods, the dogs in town surely could. They erupted in a frenzy of barking and howling, coming from all quarters.

The figures at the palisade froze. Although it was too dark to see them as more than shadows against darkness, he saw by their movements that they were drawing weapons. He did not move except to blow a second time on the whistle, to keep those dogs howling. He had not even brought his knife. Shouts rose in reply. Lights flared on porches.

Unexpectedly, the sally door set into the inner gate scraped open, and five of the figures raced out through it. The sixth faded back into the shadows of the nearby buildings just as the sally door was dragged shut, and the first townsmen appeared on the streets, sleepy, annoyed, and carrying lamps and spears and stout staffs. One man brandished a shovel. The innkeeper stumbled out onto the porch. His comic gasp, when the nimbus of light from the lantern he carried caught Joss's still figure, was enough to make Joss chuckle, and then regret it.

'What's this? What's this?'

'I couldn't sleep,' said Joss, rising. 'I saw five figures come over the wall, and a sixth meet them.'

The town arkhon strode up. She was a woman of middle years,

with an expression on her face that would turn wine to vinegar in one breath. 'So you say! Where'd they go then? We can't have missed them, coming so quickly as we did. We knew somewhat was up with the dogs howling.'

The dogs were still clamoring, but the noise had begun to die down.

He walked them over to the spot. 'See. Here it's scuffed.'

'Anyone could have done that,' said the arkhon with disgust. 'You could have done it. Where'd they go, then?'

'The gate was opened, and they ran out.'

Folk muttered and cast him ugly looks.

'Then why didn't they just come in by the gate, if they could open it?' she demanded. 'Here, Ahion, go take a look.'

Everyone followed the innkeeper as he shuffled over, still half asleep and grumbling as well, like a man talking through his dreams. 'Can't trust damn reeves. Make such a fuss. Cursed troublemakers.'

He held his lamp at the gate and studied the clasp with eyes half shut. At that moment the iron handle lifted, and the sally door was opened. A young man with tousled hair looked through. When he spoke, his words were slurred, and he seemed woozy.

'Why are you all out here? What's that clamor?'

'Gods, Teki! Aren't you on guard? Were you asleep again?'

The youth lifted a chin, attempting defiance. Then his lips thinned, seeing those cold and angry faces. He hunched his shoulders defensively. Abruptly, he yelped as if he'd been kicked. A young woman pushed past him, her expression as stormy as the season of Flood Rains. She wore only a robe, loosely belted and ready to slip and reveal all. It already revealed plenty, and she knew it, and expected every man there to stare at her.

'You promised me a quiet night!' She slapped the lad, turned – flashing a ripely rounded breast before she yanked tight the gaping robe – and strode off through the crowd, swearing at anyone who got in her way.

'Sheh! For shame!' exclaimed Ahion. 'That's the last time that'll happen, my lad.'

'I know. I know. I promise. I won't do it again.'

'No,' said the arkhon. 'That's the last time it'll happen, because you're stripped of guard duty. For shame!'

In a town like River's Bend, everyone knew everyone, and all business was the town's business. The folk gathered began to scold and berate the lad, for drinking, for being distracted, for being a cursed fool led by his cock and not what little straw he might have between his ears.

Joss stepped in. 'I beg pardon, but what of the men I saw come over the palisade?'

The young man gaped at him, blinking fast. 'What men? I saw nothing. I was awatch since sunset.'

'You were atilt, more like,' said Ahion with a snort.

'You were asleep, I'd wager,' said Joss.

The boy's breath stank of soured cordial, and in the lamplight, his eyes didn't track properly. Joss pushed past the boy into the small enclosed court, but naturally no one was hiding there and the outer gate was locked tight with a chain drawn through its rings and bolt. Ahion accompanied him to the gatehouse atop the outer gate, but the narrow room was empty except for a lamp, an unrolled mat, and a spilled flask of cordial. Most of the folk hurried back to their beds, but the arkhon and the innkeeper followed him in, pushing the hapless guard before them.

'Where's your night raiders?' the arkhon demanded. 'What in the hells did you think you were seeing, reeve? You rousted us for nothing.'

'What do you think the dogs were barking at?' Joss peered out through the slatted window but naturally he saw no one on the road. 'Folk came over the wall. I saw them!'

'You drank heavy this night,' remarked the innkeeper. 'Not unlike the lad, here. It wouldn't be the first time that a man thought he saw shadows that were only the drink leading him places that don't exist.'

'I'll stand gate watch the rest of the night,' said the arkhon, giving the lad a look that made him flinch and begin to blubber. 'Oh, shut your mouth, you useless clod! Just go home. I can't sleep anyway, now.' She turned a harsh look on Joss, shaking her head. 'To think reeves have come to this!'

Ahion grunted and, taking the light, forced Joss to follow after him to get down the stairs.

'You'll be leaving at dawn, then,' said the innkeeper as they closed the inner sally door and paused on the porch to catch their breath.

'With the company.'

The merchants and a few of the other guests had come out on the porch to inquire over the rumpus. Udit did not look at him. Her upper lip was swollen. As Ahion told the tale, Joss came over looking like a drunken troublemaker. Grumbling, the guests returned to their beds, all but the eldest of the merchants, the one called Kasti. He was a man with scars on his neck and a broken nose long since healed crooked; he'd seen brawls in his younger days. He lingered on the porch, with a lit taper in his hand.

'Do you still claim you saw those figures? And the gate opened, by someone who gained access from the gatehouse, or outside?'

'I do. Here.' Joss led him down the steps and over to the spot along the palisade where the figures had dropped to the ground. Kasti bent, grunting a little – he was also a portly man, well fed – and traced the ground with the light of the candle. The pressure of bare feet on dusty ground was plain, but it was perfectly true that in these last days of Furnace Sky, waiting for the rains, earth might get scuffed up and no wind or rain come for days to erase those traces.

'Look, there,' said Joss quietly. A piece of flotsam had fetched up against the palisade, partly caught where dirt was tamped in between the curve of two logs. He got his fingers round a leather thong and tugged free a flimsy medallion of hammered tin, meant to resemble an oversized coin with the usual square hole through the middle but with an unusual eight-tanged starburst symbol crudely stamped onto the metal.

Kasti whistled under his breath.

'You recognize this?' asked Joss, handing it over.

Kasti examined both sides. 'I've seen this mark before. Just the one time. My house deals in skins and furs. I do a fair bit of traveling up-country, to the Cliffs, to trade with the folk living there. Good hunting in the wild lands, you know. There was a little hamlet, called Clear-river, where lived a family that was well skilled at getting the best-quality hammer-goat pelts off the plateau. Those bring a good price, I'm sure you know. Three years back – no, four years now, for it was the Year of the Brown Ox – I went up there just after the whispering rains did run their course to take my look at their catch. Cursed if the hamlet was burned to the ground and everyone gone. I suppose they must all have been kilt, for we never heard whisper nor shout of them after. I found such a medallion in the ruins of the clan house. Made me wonder, for it seemed to me that it had been dropped atop the cold ashes of what was left, not that it had been in the burning itself.'

'Best we let the arkhon know.'

The merchant nodded. 'Let me do it. She's taken a dislike to you.' He slipped the medallion in his sleeve. Without looking at Joss, he cleared his throat. 'Udit is my cousin's daughter. Nothing wrong with her, mind you, but she's skittish, and can be troublesome.'

Joss sighed. 'Thanks for the words, ver. But I fear I've already chased off that ibex.'

Kasti chortled. 'Heh. That's right. And she's born in the Year of the Red Ibex, to add to the trouble of it. Nah, you're well rid of her attentions. She's quick to fall in that snare, and quick to leap out, if you do take my meaning.'

Quick to leap out, indeed. At dawn, when their company assembled for the last leg of the journey, Udit greeted Joss curtly and then ignored him.

Joss pulled Kasti aside before they moved out. 'What did the arkhon say?'

'I'll tell you, she was curdled from the night's mischief. Seems that lad who was on guard duty and caught with his trousers undone was her own son. Whew! Anyway, I gave her the medallion and told her my tale. That's all I can do.'

Sometimes you just had to go forward, because you'd done all you could do. In the first few years after Marit's death, he had broken the boundaries again and again, seeking out every local tale and hint of Guardian altars, most of which could be reached only if you could fly in. He had eventually found ten, all abandoned, all empty, lost, dead, gone, before old Marshal Alard at Copper Hall had found out what he was doing and called him down so hard he thought he'd never stop falling. He'd been grounded for months, whipped three times, and finally transferred to Clan Hall, where the old hands had treated him with disdain and, even, contempt, for a time. Well, all but a few of the women. They'd come around first, and in time he had earned respect by sticking to his duty and working harder than anyone else. By serving justice, which was all he had to hold to. But it was so cursed hard to keep going when it all seemed to be slipping away no matter what you did.

These thoughts accompanied him as he flew sweeps into up-country Low Haldia, as the company labored along the track called the Thread through increasingly rugged country with ten wagons, their carters, guards, hirelings, and a few slaves to be sold in the up-country markets. It was a difficult region for reeves to patrol. Woodland blocked his view; ravines cut through the hills, all easy to hide in. Where folk had built their homes, handsome settlements spread out with the houses clustered in a central location and fields draped around. Every one of these villages and hamlets had a palisade, recently constructed or recently repaired and reinforced. The fields provided open ground in all directions, so the locals could see who was coming.

Unlike some eagles, Scar was naturally reticent, not at all fond of attention, so the eagle minded not that Joss camped off by himself every evening and went into camp only to consult about the next day's route. After three days, Alon split off. Two days later Darya reached home to great celebration. The road twisted north; to the east rose the Cliffs, the spectacular escarpment running on and off for a hundred mey where the land lifted pretty much straight up to become the northwestern plateau. In two days more they came to prosperous if isolated country, a haven full of fields, orchards, villages, hamlets. In the town of Green-river, along the banks of a stream tumbling down off the plateau, Kasti and Udit made their farewells.

A job well done, Kasti told him.

That was something Joss didn't hear much anymore. He was grateful for the words, and for the sack of provisions Kasti's clan house offered him for the return. He didn't need much. A path on earth that ate twelve days of walking and riding might easily be traversed by a healthy eagle in two or three days at the most, depending on the winds and the weather. He and Scar sailed along parallel to the striking escarpment of the Cliffs, rising on thermals, gliding down, rising and gliding. This mode of travel was effortless for the raptor. At times such as this, Joss scanned the scenery below but counted on Scar to note any small movements out of his weak human range of sight. Scar was an old and experienced eagle. According to hall records, Joss was his fifth reeve. He had courage, combined with a reticent temper, and was intent on his task in a way few younger eagles could be.

Thus, when Joss sensed Scar's restlessness, a series of aborted stoops at some flash of movement in wood or clearing below that Joss could not discern, he thought it best to make an early night's camp. The eagle sensed danger, was hungry, saw prey or some movement that caused him to react, yet Joss never saw a damned thing in the trees and the shadows and the rugged landscape, and he was not going to explore into an ambush without his eagle at his back.

At length, he spotted a quiet village tucked into the shadow of the cliffs, about thirty structures including the distinctive 'knotted walls' and astronomical tower of a small temple to Sapanasu, the Lantern. They skimmed low, then thumped down in the cleared space beyond the village's earthwork, among the rubble of old straw in a field not yet prepared for planting. There was a single fish pond, a straggle of fruit trees, and several empty animal pens. This was a hardscrabble place, one just hanging on because of the presence of the temple, which could accept tithes from neighboring villages.

He unhitched, sighed as he rubbed his joints, and turned to give a quick check to Scar's harness and feathers before approaching the village. Scar lowered his huge head. His head feathers were smooth and flat, his eyes as big as plates with the brow ridge giving him a commanding gaze, and his beak massive. Folk would focus on that head, when it was the talons they ought to fear most.

'You'll need coping soon,' he said, examining the curved beak.

Scar's head went up. He spread his wings, flared his feathers, fanned his tail.

Joss spun.

A trio of armed men had emerged from the village. They strode halfway to their visitors, then halted just out of arrowshot. Scar called out a challenge. The eagle's entire posture had shifted. He expected the worst. Joss caught up his staff and walked over to meet them, scanning the palisade walls, the surrounding fields, but he saw no threatening movements, no flash of hidden bows, no mass of men waiting to strike.

'Greetings of the dusk to you,' he called when he got close enough.

None smiled or offered greetings.

'Go back!' said the spokesman. 'Leave this place. We want no reeves here.'

'I'm just looking for a night's lodging. A place to shelter my head. A quick study of your assizes court, if you've need of an outside eye to look over your cases.'

'No. Just leave us. You know what they'll do to any village that harbors a reeve.'

'What who will do?'

The eldest among them, whose head was shaved in the manner of one of the Lantern's hierophants, croaked out words. 'They promised we would not be harmed if we let no reeve enter our village.'

'Who promised this?'

'By the seven gods, just leave us alone and go your way.'

The sun's lower rim brushed the tops of the trees.

'I'm not your enemy,' said Joss.

They stared at him with closed gazes. They refused to utter another word, despite his calm questions and pleasant manner. So he retraced his steps, never turning his back to them in case they decided to toss those javelins.

That night they camped outdoors, in a rocky clearing. Scar was restless. The trees tossed in a rising wind as Joss sought relief under an overhang. Of course the first kiss of rains blew up from the southeast that night, a brief downpour that soaked him through. By dawn the wet had all dried up, and the humid quality to the air portended another hot day. Knotted by doubt and anger, and with a growing headache, he retraced his flight along the Thread. By midday he saw a telltale spire of smoke far ahead. They glided in.

The town of River's Bend had been burned to the ground.

5

'They were so frightened,' he said. 'I see that now. I didn't recognize it at the time.'

'The folk in River's Bend?' asked the commander.

'No, those three men outside the village that turned me away. They were so frightened.'

'Just like in Herelia,' said the commander, pouring more cordial into Joss's cup. 'That's why we reeves had to leave Herelia, in the end.'

'Their fear? Or the burned villages and murdered villagers?'

'The one made the other. We reeves are not an army to impose our authority by force. There was nothing we could do, and the villagers in Herelia soon learned it. Thus are we cast out. Now, I see, the contagion is spreading out of Herelia. And we are left with the same dilemma. If we do nothing, we blind ourselves and undercut our own authority. If we interfere, the local folk die. This is what comes of the death of the Guardians. Indeed, I expect it is their loss that has seeded the plague.'

Joss toyed with his cup, turning it round and round as the red liquor lapped the rim, never quite spilling over. His left hand was bandaged; he'd cut it badly searching for survivors among the ruins of River's Bend. He'd found none, although it was true he'd not found nearly as many corpses as he ought to have done. People were missing, and as of yet, neither whisper nor shout had been heard of their whereabouts or their remains.

'I thought sure some of the foresters might have witnessed, and survived,' he went on, 'but when one pair of them did venture out of the Wild to get a look, near dusk, they told me it happened at night and not a one of their clan saw anything or heard anything.'

'Think you they were lying?'

He shrugged. 'I couldn't tell. They none of them sleep the night at the river's shore. They all hike into the Wild to their clan houses. That's where they feel safe.'

'Now we see why.'

The entry bell out on the porch rang to announce visitors. The door was slid open, and the legates filed in. Joss began to rise, seeing his meeting was over, but the commander gestured for him to remain seated.

He lifted his hands as a question.

'While you were gone, I received word from Marshal Masar that he is shorthanded and has no one to replace you as legate. It seems I acted in haste when I dismissed you. Allow me to say that I was, on that one occasion, mistaken.'

He almost laughed, but he swallowed his moment of amusement because of the serious expressions worn by the other five legates. They made no comment. All seemed too preoccupied with their own grievances and worries even to have heard her rare joke. Indeed, they had a difficult time paying attention when, as the first order of business, the commander had Joss recount the scene at River's Bend.

'That's all very well,' said Legate Garrard, 'and a terrible thing, as I need not go on about, but I must return to Argent Hall. I've received an urgent message from Marshal Alyon demanding my return. Urgent.'

'On what matter?'

Garrard shook his head. 'We've had trouble, as I've spoken to you about on many occasions these last seasons. Too many troublesome reeves are being allowed to transfer into Argent Hall from the other halls.'

'We're well rid of those who left us,' said the legate of Iron Hall, a stocky man boasting two stark-white scars on his broad, dark face.

'That may be,' said Garrard with heat. 'I don't blame your masters for letting them go. I blame Clan Hall for not blocking all this moving about.'

The commander merely shook her head. 'Clan Hall has no mandate to block transfers that are agreed to by the marshals of the six halls. Marshal Alyon must stop the transfers. Why hasn't he?'

'It's true we're shorthanded, and we need every reeve and every eagle. But Marshal Alyon is old, ill, and easily pressured by certain factions within the hall. It's too much for him, all the territorial squabbles to be resolved, the gossip, the tempers, the fights—'

'Fights?' asked the commander coolly. She beckoned to the old reeve who acted as her chamberlain, and he brought in a tray of cups and poured cordial all around.

Legate Garrard was normally an even-tempered man, with the black coarse hair and creamy brown complexion common in the south. But he was so agitated now that the other legates stared at him. 'He thinks he's being poisoned.'

'Poisoned!' cried the legate from Iron Hall. 'Poisoned? Who in the hells would want to poison that old man? He's as harmless as a mouse. Now, if it were my old marshal, what passed the Gate ten years back, any one of us would've done it, and gladly, for she were the worst-tempered person I ever did meet in my life.'

This comment brought silence. No one laughed. From the parade ground, an eagle screamed a challenge, but there came no answering call.

Taudit, the legate from Horn Hall, stood. 'I'm leaving,' she said. 'My marshal has recalled me, together with all the reeves posted here from Horn Hall. A reeve flew in this morning with the message. We've all been recalled. I'm sorry.'

The commander sipped at her drink. Then she nodded. Joss was stunned. He hadn't seen this coming, but it was obvious from the commander's response that she had not been taken by surprise.

'I'll expect a report, Legate Taudit,' the commander said.

Legate Taudit nodded crisply. She was a dry, reserved, uncommunicative individual, impossible to get to know. 'You'll get one. Trouble in our region. Marshal wants all of us back, to be one group to face it. We're leaving now, while there's still an afternoon's flying to be had. The heavens are clear. No telling when the rains will start getting hard. We'll send a report when we can.' She made brusque courtesies, opened and closed the door, and was gone.

'I must leave, too,' said Garrard. He gazed at the blank door, the unadorned walls, the quiet room, the commander, and the other four legates. His fingers tapped his knees, making him seem quite nervous. 'I am sick in my heart,' he added, more softly. 'There are shadows everywhere, and I am blind. I can't see through this to a time of peace and order.'

'What of your halls?' the commander asked, looking at the other three legates: Iron Hall, Gold Hall, and Bronze Hall.

The proper strength of a reeve hall was six hundred eagles and six hundred reeves, but no hall was ever at full strength. By tradition, each sent a small contingent together with a legate to Clan Hall, switched out at intervals. Eagles departed for months or, in rare cases, years to breed in the unclimbable and vast wilderness of the Heaven's Ridge mountain range, where their nesting territories lay. Reeves too old to fly regular patrol must be accommodated. Old eagles died, and fledglings needed training and the long process of accommodation to the presence of other eagles in overlapping patrol territories. New reeves must train as well, a laborious process in its own right. Eagles must recover from injury, molting, disease. When its reeve died, an eagle would fly off, and none could predict when it would return to choose a new reeve – or if it would return at all.

No hall ever stood at full strength, not even now when full strength was so badly needed. Yet even at full strength, they would not have been able to do everything that was now needed.

'We're holding,' said Bronze Hall's legate. 'We've had little trouble in Mar, I must tell you. But we hear rumors. We're patrolling the coast and our borders, and keeping our eyes fixed. For now, we need not recall our contingent that's here in Clan Hall.' She smiled at Joss. She was a twelve-year younger than he was, another Ox. Two years ago, when she'd first come, they'd spent a lot of time together in bed and out before parting amicably at her request.

Gold Hall's legate shook his head. His hair was cropped almost to the skull, in the style of the delvings, although he himself was human, a short, thin man who was much stronger than he looked. 'Beyond the borderlands of the Arro Mountains we have trouble. Within the mountains, none dare threaten us. Zosteria lies at peace, for the moment, but there have been incidents along the coast and in the hills. Half of Herelia was under our watch and we don't fly there now, so we know how the worst can spread. We remain vigilant. Nothing has changed since my last report.'

Iron Hall's legate was a man who, like Joss, had been made legate to get him out of the hall, in his case – so rumor had it – away from the friction of personal relationships gone sour. 'I've had my orders. Iron Hall will keep a half contingent here, but the rest have to go back.'

'Why?' asked the commander.

'Because they're needed at Iron Hall! You're not the only ones with trouble! We've lost reeves to transfer, or to death. Even a pair who went missing and never returned, them and their eagles both, yet we have had sightings, and we don't think they're dead. Just . . . fled, more like. Run away. Cowards. There's strange goings afoot up on the plateau, although we've had no particular trouble in Teriayne yet. Some trouble in the upper reaches of High Haldia. Outlaw bands thieving and causing other trouble. The worst of it is bands of young men traveling from one place to another, scrambling in groups out of Heaven's Ridge and vanishing up into the plateau, or back again, not whisper or shout to be heard from after. You can't bring a man to trial who's done nothing but walk along the roads seeking work, not if he's caused no trouble and had no complaint brought against him. So – that's that. That's my orders, and my report.'

'Very well,' said the commander. 'Copper Hall has recalled five of its reeves but leaves me the rest. That leaves Clan Hall with—' Like most of those who had served their apprentice year as clerks in one of the temples dedicated to Sapanasu, the Lantern, she could calculate on the page. She freed a scrap of paper from an untidy stack on her table, turned it over to the rough side, and brushed marks to calculate numbers departing, numbers staying, and, it seemed, a few stray reeves actually being sent to Clan Hall.

'Under strength,' she said. 'We'll be able to fill out only three flights, including our retired and our fledgling reeves.'

'Don't look at me!' cried Iron Hall's legate. 'It isn't my fault!'

But of course she wasn't looking at him. She was looking into the unknown, gauging risk, danger, certainty, the angle of the wind, the timbre of the air.

'I do fear,' she said, looking at each legate in turn, 'that we are not yet facing the worst. Oh no. This is only the beginning.'

'Pleasant of her to say so,' said Peddo that evening at the Pig's Bladder after Joss recounted the whole of the meeting.

'You saw nothing unexpected on your escort duty?' Joss asked.

'Eiya! I did indeed. I saw a farmer who had the handsomest chest I have ever done seen, I will admit to you.'

'You're drunk.'

'He rejected me! I need more wine to drown my sorrow. Whoop! Look there!'

A trio of young men with the brawny shoulders and flat caps of the firefighting brigade pushed into the room.

'Can't you ever stop?' Joss asked.

The serving lass brought a pitcher, and poured a new round for the two reeves.

'You're new here,' said Joss with a smile, admiring her fresh youth, her lithe body, her light bearing and pretty eyes.

'So I am, Uncle,' she said, shifting herself just out of range of his hands, not that he was moving a finger.

Peddo snickered, miming an elderly man leaning on a cane.

'Where's Mada?' Joss asked the girl, feeling stung.

She settled the pitcher on her hip, took a good, long look at the young firefighters, then returned her attention politely to Joss. Exactly the way a well-brought-up girl would tactfully oblige a garrulous but boring old uncle.

'You didn't hear? Her parents made a good bargain. She's getting a legal contract, marriage to a lad out of Wolf Quarter, although they won't be living there naturally. His aunts and uncle are in the building trade, roofers. She'll join the business. It's a good bargain for her. If you know her, you might have seen him around. Nothing splendid to look at, I'll grant you, but decent enough, and a good business to work in. That's worth a lot more than looks.'

She went on awhile in this vein while Peddo ogled the firefighters, and Joss sipped at his drink. In honor of the young year, the cordial had been flavored with the dried and crumbled petals of baby's-delight, which made it ever sweeter. Too sweet, really. In the last few days, since he'd crawled through the ruins of River's Bend, he'd lost his craving. The smell of stew bubbling wafted in from the inner court, melding with the eye-watering smoke of pipes, and he blinked back a tear. After a while, the young men called to her, and she sashayed over, a little too obviously, swinging those hips as though to smash errant chairs out of her path. Whew.

'There was one thing, though,' said Peddo, staring with sudden interest into his empty cup. 'I spotted areas that were trampled, as though a company had camped there. But cursed if I ever saw any such groups roaming. Jabi would see things off in the distance, beyond my sight, but by the time we got there – and he's fast, you know how fast he is – there'd be nothing to see. But cover to be had, if you take my meaning. Once I surprised four lads, who were hiding from me in the scrub. Jabi flushed them out, could see them moving, and they got nervous and tried to bolt. But they were only laborers, out looking for work. It puzzled me. I felt there was always something going on just out of my range of vision.'

'Me, too. I felt the same thing. So did Scar. He was restless, stooping as at prey and then giving up on it. I go over and over those days in my mind. I just sense I overlooked something, that I missed the sign spread in my path, but I don't know what it is.' He'd been missing too much. The commander was right: He'd been drowning himself in cordial, rather than doing his duty. He'd lost his edge. He wasn't keen set. But he couldn't say that out loud.

'You know what the tale says,' added Peddo. '"Forest and cavern and mountain and lake and ravine and every village, too, all these hide crime from the reeve." Nothing to be done about it. We find what we can. We do what we can.'

'That's not good enough. The Guardians are dead. We're the guardians now. Who else is there?'

Peddo scratched his head. 'Well. Any person who seeks to do what is right. Neh?'

Joss watched the lass flirting with the firefighters, who were boisterous, vibrant, and so very young, full of wholesome energy, the gift of the gods. They walked about their patrol every day, and when they saw smoke or flames, they ran to meet their trouble. 'I met a southern merchant. You didn't run across him, did you? He called himself Feden.' Wetting a finger, he drew the man's clan mark onto the tabletop.

Peddo burped, considered, shook his head. 'No.'

The heat from the candle dried up the mark. Outside, it began to rain.

'He was from Olossi. He said he sent his factors, and later a slave factor, down into the empire to trade. It just got me thinking. There must be women in the south, just like there's women in the Hundred.'

'Did it hurt that much when the lass called you "Uncle"? That you think you have to go looking for women outside the Hundred? Don't mind her, Joss. She's not that much of an armful. Shame about the other lass, though. She did like you.'

Joss shrugged. 'It's not the worst day of my life. I'll miss Mada, though I'm happy for her good fortune. No, it's just, after a while, you do wonder, don't you?'

Peddo was eyeing one of the firefighters, the one who seemed just ever so slightly to be eyeing Peddo back. 'I always do wonder, but I rarely find out.'

'That's not what I meant! I wonder ... what it's like. I wish I could go south.'

'South? To Olossi? Why can't you? I mean, with the Commander's permission, of course. You'd have to have some patrol in mind, some mission. A message to carry to Argent Hall or—'

'No. I mean south, over the Kandaran Pass or across the Turian Sea.'

'Out of the Hundred? You're crazy, my friend. You can't leave the Hundred. No reeve can. Break those boundaries, and you will be dead.'

'I'm half dead anyway.'

'Aui! Stop being maudlin. What do you know about the south anyway?'

'Nothing more than what the merchants tell me, and they're all liars.'

'So they are.'

'The fields are always green, the fruit is always ripe, the lands are always at peace, and the women are the most beautiful in all creation.'

'You *have* had too much to drink,' said Peddo. He emptied Joss's half-full cup into his own empty one.

'You've downed twice as much as I have. Anyway, I'm sure of it.' Abruptly, taken aback by how badly he wanted it to be true, Joss leaned forward and fixed Peddo with a glare. 'There must be a place where the shadows haven't fallen. Somewhere folk go about their lives in a measure of peace, like they used to here. Don't you think so?'

Peddo sighed. He bent closer, and pinned Joss's wrist to the table with the pressure of his hand. 'You know what it says in the Tale of the Guardians. "Corruption and virtue wax and wane within the heart. Yet it is the dutiful strength and steady hand of those who live and die while about the ordinary tasks of the world that create most of that which we call good and harmonious." If you give up hope, if you give up trying, you'll never find peace. No one will.'

He sat back, released Joss's wrist, and drained his cup. Glancing toward the table by the door, he suddenly sat up straighter. 'Whoop. He's coming this way.'

'You're blushing,' said Joss, unaccountably cheered by the sight, as if Peddo's blush of itself could banish shadows. 'Do you want me to get out of your way?'

'Yes, but stick around long enough to open up the conversation and make me look clever and funny.'

'That won't be easy!'

'Maybe not, but it can't be any harder than tracking down the most beautiful woman in all creation. If such a thing even exists, which I doubt.'

'Best get my practice in, then.' As the young firefighter paused beside their table and offered them a sweet, if tentative, smile, Joss lifted a hand to indicate the bench beside Peddo. 'Greetings of the day to you, ver. Can we buy you a drink?'

PART THREE

Ghosts

In the South: Kartu Town,

on the Golden Road

6

It began with such a small thing. Who could have known?

'I'm thirsty, Mai! My throat is dry dry dry!'

Mai loved her half sister and cousin Ti; she really did. But despite being the same age as Mai, Ti could not sit still for more than five breaths at a time. On the days when Ti came with her to sell produce at the marketplace, it wasn't very restful.

'Go and get a bowl of kama juice, then. We'll share it. Here.' She unhooked the wooden measuring bowl from the handle of the cart. 'But hurry. I can't sell almonds without the bowl.'

Ti grabbed the bowl out of her hand and bounced off into the swirl of the marketplace, all bright awnings, swarming buyers, and gesticulating sellers. Kartu Town's main marketplace was actually one long street that emptied into the main square. Folk brought their carts and set up their stalls on either side of the street most days, raising awnings or parasols depending on the season and time of day to ward off the sun's glare. The marketplace used to be in the square itself, but not anymore, of course. That had all ended twelve years ago.

Kartu's residents had adapted. As Grandmother said, Kartu Town thrived because the townsfolk were reeds, able to bend when the wind blew.

'Ah, Mai'ili, such a fine day!' Mistress Zaldra swept up to Mai's cart with her youngest child in tow and a slave boy carrying her purchases.

'A fine day, indeed, Mistress Zaldra. I hope you are well.'

'I'm not well!'

'I'm sorry to hear it. What troubles you today, Mistress?'

Her catalogue of troubles was lengthy and detailed, but Mai asked her questions each time she paused for breath and it was the widow herself who finally brought her complaints to a close. 'Enough! I have need of peaches, dear.'

'The market rate is one zastra a peach today. That's what everyone is charging.'

'I can't afford that today! Not after the Qin commander took those two bolts of linen at half the price they're worth! I'll give you three zastras for five peaches.'

'Mistress Zaldra, my father would beat me if I came home and told him I'd undersold by such a price. But since you are such a faithful customer, I can offer you five peaches for four zastras.'

She smiled. 'I'm sure I can get a better price farther down, but you have a good heart, Mai'ili. I'll have five, then.' She handed over four zastras and pointed to the fruit she wanted, then turned to the slave boy. 'Don't bruise them, Orphan, or it'll be a beating for you!'

The child limped forward. Mai gently placed each one in the basket he carried and, when he glanced shyly up at her, she smiled at him until she saw a flush darken his cheeks. 'Go on, Havo,' she said in a low voice, calling him by the name he had once had, back when he had had a family. Poor little boy. 'Just walk softly. You'll be fine.'

His lips trembled. He wouldn't be fine, but it didn't hurt to show him kindness.

'Orphan! How slowly must you move?'

He hobbled after his mistress.

Mai watched him go, then greeted another customer. 'Ah, Master Vin. You are well today?'

'Always well when I see your pretty face, Mai'ili. I see you have peaches but I am also needing a melon. What's the market rate?'

'One zastra a peach today. That's what everyone is charging.'

'Okay. What about the melons?'

He took his time choosing, smiled at her, flirted a little although he had a perfectly nice wife who often bought fruit from Mai's cart as well. Still, what harm? He made only the barest effort to haggle, enough not to shame himself, so she always got an excellent price. She was settling his produce into his market basket when Ti returned.

'Why? Why? Why?' Ti swung the empty bowl in a circle. Her cheeks were flushed and her eyes were round with indignation. 'Why do they have to come into the marketplace? Can't they just stay in their fort? Every clan has to deliver supplies there anyway, so why do they have to come out here?'

'Hush, girl!' exclaimed Master Vin, now pale and nervous. 'You know what they do to folk who speak against them!' He grabbed his basket from Mai and hurried away.

'You didn't get any kama juice, Ti?'

'Hu! Those Qin soldiers! Walking through the market like they own the place!'

'The Qin rule us. Of course they can walk anywhere they please.'

'I hate it! Don't you hate it, Mai?'

Mai sighed and rearranged the peaches now that she had lost the ten best off the top of the pile. A different pattern of stacking would display those remaining to better advantage. 'Hating doesn't change things, Ti. Remember what happened to Uncle—'

'Don't say his name! His ghost will haunt us! It'll spit at us when we're not looking!'

Mai finished with the peaches without replying, knowing Ti could not stay still for long.

'If I go around through Spice Alley I can get to Abi's stall without running into them again. I'm so thirsty. If I don't drink something now I'll die die die! Here they come.' Ti flounced off in the other direction as Mai, startled, looked up.

Five soldiers strolled down the middle of the dusty street. They wore the typical dress of the Qin military: knee-length black silk tunics that tied down the front and were slit for riding, belt and sword, baggy trousers, soft boots, and their hair up in a topknot in the back. It was actually kind of amusing to watch. Although the four soldiers and one officer strolled rather than marched, although they paused now and again to survey the contents of a blanket laid out over the ground or to point at bowls or pots or fruit arranged in a handcart or wagon, they did not swagger, much, or shove their way through the market throngs like bulls. Yet folk melted away. Conversations faded to silence. Market women trembled, and one old man offered the Qin captain a melon, which the officer refused.

They were not monsters. In truth, although strict and ruthless, the Qin ruled more fairly, Grandmother often pointed out, than had the corrupt Mariha princes who preceded them. Taxes and more taxes and yet more again! That was all the Mariha princes had wanted.

'A good morning to you, Mai'ili! I see the overlords are come to sniff at the orchid.'

Mai jumped. 'Widow Xania! I didn't see you coming.'

Widow Xania had a grin that was more like a grimace. She meant well, but no one liked her. 'Careful how you look at them, child. They'll notice you. You know what happened to Clan Bishi's daughter, that one that got taken off to the brothel three years ago because she caught a captain's fancy. I don't know why your father displays you in the market like this when there's already talk of a marriage between you and the Gandi-li clan boy. But I suppose men like Master Vin don't haggle much. I imagine you get the best prices in this market! What man can haggle when faced with such beauty?' She cackled.

Mai smiled patiently. 'How can I help you today, Widow Xania? I hope your son is well?'

'Thank you for asking. You seem to be the only person who remembers him! I just received word from him yesterday, by way of some shepherds, out of the Gandi clan, in fact, who had been up to the temple and spoke to him there. The discipline has given him peace.'

'It was very sad about his wife and son.'

'Yes, indeed.' She touched an eye. 'The wind's blown some dust in. There, it's gone. I'll need two melons. Just pick out two for me. I trust your judgment. And some sword-fruit.'

'Green or ripe?'

'Green, for frying. But the melons ripe. My sister's son is coming today, so I have to feed him. I suppose he hopes he'll inherit the house when I'm gone.'

'Surely not!'

'You know what people are! Always grasping. Always wanting more, and not caring how much pain others suffer! If only my daughter hadn't died – if only my daughter-in-law and the baby – well. How much?'

'Twelve for everything.'

'Twelve! No one else in this market would rob me like that!'

'It is the going price, Widow Xania.'

'Surely not! I can't give you more than seven.'

'Seven is very low. My father would beat me—'

'As if your father would ever beat you! You are the flower of his household. Seven!'

'I really can't sell them for seven, but for you because of your recent sorrows I will make an exception and let you have these for eleven.'

'That's robbery! Eight.'

'No less than ten.'

'I'll consider nine if you throw in a peach.'

'With two peaches, for ten.'

'Done.'

Being particular about how things were arranged, Widow Xania always packed her market basket herself. Mai looked past her only to discover that the Qin officer had paused at the vendor beside them. He was standing in front of the blanket where old lady Tirza sold tomatoes and cucumbers, but he was looking right at Mai. His soldiers waited on the street behind him, arms crossed, bored. Widow Xania finished her packing, straightened up, and saw them. The widow's eyes widened and her mouth pouched in a way that would have struck Mai as comical if she wasn't just now thinking of the fate of that Bishi girl. A Qin captain who lusted after that girl had walked right into the women's baths one day and hauled her off to the brothel and done what he wished since there was no one to stop him. The Qin commander had made him pay a handsome price to the family, and no respectable family had suffered such an indignity since, but they all knew it could happen again.

It was only a matter of time.

Widow Xania clutched her basket and tottered away. All around, the market fell silent. Probably every soul in sight of Mai's cart and the handsome parasol that shaded her was recalling the Bishi girl and her stained honor. The Bishi family had lost face as well, and the girl had eventually been hauled away by some merchant or another who had hired her on as a temporary wife along the Golden Road. It was the best a ruined girl could hope for.

But I am not a ruined girl. I am Mai'ili, eldest child and first daughter of the Mei clan. I have no need to cower before these men.

Although it was always wise to be respectful.

She touched her lips to her wolf ring, sigil of the proud Mei clan, as she bent to retrieve a few melons from the box beneath her feet. When she rose she faced the captain, who had moved to stand before her cart. He smiled, just slightly, as she stood there with a melon in each hand. Taking in a firm breath, she arranged them with the others before turning to him. He had a graciously oval face and a pleasingly dark complexion, with deep-set eyes and a light beard, unusual among the Qin, and a mustache. Only his hooked nose seemed out of place, as if it had come from somewhere else. The sun was not brighter than the golden silk of the tabard worn over his black tunic; only officers were allowed to wear that particular intense color.

'How may I help you today, sir? As you can see, I have peaches, melons, sword-fruit, and almonds today.'

He did not look at her wares, but his gaze did skip up above her head.

'That's a distinctive amaranth pattern on your parasol. Does it come from Sirniaka?'

She laughed out of surprise, then touched fingers to lips to stop herself. That would teach her to think so well of herself! 'I'm not sure,' she admitted. 'My father bought it for me last year when I celebrated my sixteenth year. He bought it from a merchant who had come from the east. Isn't Sirniaka a great kingdom in the east, beyond the eastern Mariha cities?'

'The Mariha cities are all under the rule of the Qin var now,' he corrected, 'but otherwise you are right. It's an unusual parasol, quite beautiful. In the Sirniakan Empire, that pattern is reserved for girls of marriageable age. By displaying it, they indicate they are available for an alliance.'

She flushed. Her heart raced. 'An alliance?'

'Marriage. A wedding. You have such customs here, do you not?'

'Of course we do.'

He smiled again. He looked like a man who had seen a fair bit of the world. He was perhaps ten years older than she was, not that that would ever make the slightest bit of difference to her, who was going to marry that boy from the Gandi sheepherders clan whom she'd known all her life and who was a perfectly nice young man about Uncle Shai's age, not more than two or three years older than she was. Perfectly nice.

'Almonds,' he said, as if repeating himself. 'Two bowlsful.' He beckoned to one of his soldiers, who sauntered up with a small leather sack.

'Oh! Yes!' But Ti had taken her measuring bowl to get juice!

'No bowl?' he asked. 'Two handfuls will do as well.'

She scooped, and he held out cupped hands so she had perforce to pour the almonds into his waiting hands, and by one means or another he brushed her, or she him. His skin was cool, although the sun was hot. Yet she hadn't lost her wits. She named as an opening price twice what she would charge to a local.

He paid it without haggling.

7

Shai never spoke much. He didn't see the point of speaking, since no one ever listened to him, and those who did then usually snapped at him for having the temerity to speak. Best to keep your own counsel under those circumstances.

So it was a wonder to him when his niece Ti'ili came running on the path that led from town up the gentle, grassy slope of Dezara Mountain to the base of the spring pasture. Here, beside a copse of very young birch trees he'd planted and watered himself, he had set up his woodworking shed so he could work in peace without four elder brothers and their five meddling wives and the truculent ghost of his sixth brother plaguing him. Ti's black braids flapped as she ran. He set his attention back to the work before him as she pulled up, gasping, under the shade of the open shed.

'Uncle Shai! You've got to come! You've got to speak up for Mai!'

He finished the stroke of his adze and ran his hand along the grain of the pine log he was planing down to make a fine bedstead for the wedding. Good and smooth, ready to cut to length. When he was done, he looked up at Ti.

'But you've *got* to! She's been crying all day. You know it isn't right that they marry her off to a Qin, even if he is an officer!'

He studied the log, the second of two precious trunks his elder brothers had traded three ewes for so that the family wouldn't be embarrassed when it came time to stand up at the law court and seal the marriage. The legs, out of the other log, were already carved and oiled. He was preparing the last of the supports, although he wasn't going to have time to carve as elaborate a frieze into the wood as he would have liked, not with the date already chosen and written into the law court's record. Seventeen days from now.

'He'll beat her! He's buried one wife already. He admitted it himself! We'll never see her again! Never! Never! Never! He'll get tired of her and sell her into slavery and there'll be nothing we can do to stop it! His masters will be overthrown and he'll be killed in battle and then – !'

'Hush!' He stood, casting his gaze about, but his two younger nephews – Ti's cousins – were out of earshot tending to the sheep.

She kicked at wood shavings with her pretty red slippers, knowing she had gone too far. While it was perfectly true that the Qin had ruled Kartu Town for only the last twelve years, and that shifting alliances, a death in the var's family, or an unexpected push from the eastern cities might cause the Qin horsemen to retreat and some other power to take their place, it was still treason to speak of such a thing. Ti was only two years younger than he was. She knew as well as he did what the Qin did to their enemies or even to those who only spoke ill-considered words against them.

She looked back down the path, following his gaze. Kartu Town was not much to look at, a dusty bee's hive of compounds surrounded by an inner wall which was itself surrounded by startlingly green orchards crisscrossed by slender irrigation canals. Beyond the orchards lay a thick mud-brick outer wall studded with watchtowers and guardposts. The wall was wide enough to allow Qin guardsmen to ride their rounds atop it instead of walking. They hated to walk. The citadel, a circular structure of baked brick, rose at the northwestern corner of the inner town. In the square fronting the citadel rose the gallows, and today three posts were decorated with remains. A vulture circled.

Like all of the inhabitants of Kartu Town, he'd learned to look away. In truth, it was not the sight of the citadel and its square that made him climb every day in good weather to the peace of his shed. It was the vista beyond: endless, open, yawning wide to the west, all sky, the rocky plateau of the desert looming on the southern horizon, and the mountains rising heroically to the north. So beautiful. They were all stark lines and pale slopes with the memory of winter in their snowy peaks.

'I hate it up here!' cried Ti. 'Too much air! Too much sky!' Abruptly, she burst into tears. 'I know I shouldn't have said it – but he's Qin. What will happen to Mai? How could Father Mei have agreed?' She sobbed like a tempest.

'He's decent enough,' said Shai finally as this storm began to die down.

'Who is?'

'Captain Anji.'

'How can you say so?' she shrieked. 'A dirty barbarian! You're a Qin-lover!' Then she clapped a hand over her mouth and began sobbing noisily again. He waited until the worst subsided before scooping up a handful of shavings and handing them to her so she could wipe mucus from her upper lip.

'He doesn't have to marry her. He could have just taken her as a concubine. Branded her a pleasure girl and dragged her to the brothel for his use. We couldn't have stopped him.'

She hiccoughed, sucked in a watery breath, and gave a bleating moan as she pounded her belly with a fist as if she were mourning. 'I know it's not as bad as it could have been. But I can't bear to be parted from her! Ei! Ei! Ei!'

'She'll just be across town, at the citadel. You can see her every day.'

'No! No! No! The news just came this morning, by messenger from Captain Anji. The garrison is being pulled out and sent east on the Golden Road. There's something going on there, I don't know what. Maybe there's war on the border. War! They're going east and she'll have to go with them, and we'll never see her again! Ever! Ever! Ever!'

He set down the adze on the bench, considerably startled by this news. 'How soon?'

'In two days! The wedding is tomorrow, not next month! That's why you have to speak to Father Mei. Maybe they'll listen to you. All the other uncles ... you know them! They always do what Father Mei says. Chicken-hearts! All but Uncle Hari. If he was here still, he'd put a stop to it.'

'For shame, Ti!'

'I'm not sorry, even if no one else will talk about Uncle Hari! He was your favorite brother, too! You know it! You know he was the only one tough enough to stand up to Father Mei! He'd tell Father Mei to postpone the wedding. Wait 'til the garrison comes back. But they'll never come back. That's what Captain Anji knows. He knows they're never coming back and he's taking

Mai away forever and ever and ever!' She once again fell to bawling.

Ti's outbursts were usually like cloudbursts in summer – frequent but short in duration, causing brief floods and then getting all that moisture sucked away as soon as the sun came back out – but this time she was truly upset. She and Mai were close as twins, born the same day in the same month in the same year to his eldest brother's first and second wives, who were themselves sisters. The two girls had never been apart in all their seventeen years.

No use trying to get any more work done today. He gathered up his tools into the cedar tool chest.

After a bit, when she could hear him, he said, 'You could go as second wife.'

'He won't take me!' she wailed. 'I already asked, but Captain Anji told Father Mei he can only have one wife. And Father Mei won't let me go as her maid because it would be dishonorable, and anyway, Captain Anji said he won't take me even as a servant.'

He'd be a madman to take you as wife or servant, Shai thought, although in truth he was shocked that Ti would suggest such a thing. A servant! Someday Ti's impulsive and stormy nature would get her, and the family, in big trouble.

A slender shape toiled up the path and resolved into the slave girl everyone called Cornflower, for her blue eyes. Ti saw her and got *that look* all the women in the house did whenever Cornflower appeared in a room. She wiped her eyes and nose before the slave halted twenty steps below them with hands clasped and body bent in a half bow. No need for Cornflower to say anything. Wind tugged at the slave's wool tunic and her trident braids of uncannily white-gold hair. Her bare feet and calves were burned a pinkish brown, but everyone knew she had unusually light skin beneath her clothes, not like that of normal people but more like that of ghosts, and there was something about the way she stood there so quietly, a well of stillness, that made him always think about what it would be like to . . .

'I better go,' said Ti.

Shai started, unaware he'd been wandering. Cornflower served the two senior wives – Ti's mother and aunt – so her presence here was a summons for Ti. Her presence was unwelcome to any young man whose greatest ambition was to be left undisturbed.

'Promise me you'll come right now.' Ti started down the path at a fast clip, Cornflower trotting behind, head lowered. Ti looked three times back over her shoulder, mouthing words, gesturing almost comically, trying to get Shai to hurry up.

He didn't see the point. He was the last person his eldest brother would listen to. But he whistled for his nephews and finished stowing the tools. His flush receded. His thoughts sank back into an orderly flow. The wind tugged at his sleeves, tied back to leave his lower arms bare. It wasn't warm enough to work bare-chested yet, although he preferred it when it was. He hated to go back down to town, back to the family compound, where sleeves had to be tied down to the wrists and any work you did or comment you made was overseen, overheard, and overruled by others.

Mai was fortunate. She was escaping.

Not that she would think of it that way.

His younger nephew came running, looking important and annoyed. 'What is it?'

'I have to go down,' Shai said, gesturing toward town. 'I'll be back this afternoon.'

'You better be. I don't want to sleep out here worrying about thieves!' He scuffed his feet among the wood shavings and sat down hard on the bench.

Not that there were thieves anymore, not since the Qin took over. Still, no one left good tools and precious wood unguarded, even so.

'What do you have to go down for, anyway?' The boy shaded his eyes and squinted toward town. 'Uh!' He grunted and rolled his eyes, seeing his older cousin far down, retreating on the path. Because of Ti's way of walking, she could not be mistaken for anyone else: all bouncing sleeves, a spring like that of an antelope in her step. 'That Ti! Just a big boiling teakettle, that one! It must be about Mai and the wedding, eh?'

Shai shrugged.

'Make sure you're back here soon. No shirking!' His nephew was eldest son of second brother and, therefore, had more clout than his young uncle Shai, but not enough to overrule Ti's request, because she was daughter of Father Mei. If Ti asked, Shai must go.

So Shai left. An ugly scene would no doubt ensue once he reached the compound, but there was no reason to worry about that on the walk down with the day so fine and the sky so merry and blue. The wind skated up from the east, which meant it was clear of dust torn up from the desert. The tips of the mountains to the northwest could be seen, three deep; that was unusual, quite striking. He thought he heard a hawk's piercing call but when he paused and spun slowly he saw no speck in the sky, nothing flying except one wispy cloud spinning out along the ridge of Dezara Mountain. The slopes still had a hint of spring green in them although they were fading to summer gold. The sheep were hidden above in a fold of land, but he heard a second flock bleating off to the right. That would be the Gandi clan's herd. There had been talk about a marriage between Mai and an elder Gandi boy, but of course the attentions of the Qin captain had cut those right off.

Poor Mai. No wonder she was crying. Still, it wasn't really a surprise. Mai had been doomed from the start.

He stared east, into the wind. Because it was so clear, he could see the old road winding along the mountains for an unexpectedly long way before haze and distance cloaked it. No clouds of dust betrayed a merchant train or travelers. All was quiet and at peace. Shai liked things at peace.

It wouldn't last.

He started down again and soon enough was nodding to the guards at the gate – two grizzled veterans of the town militia who had survived the Qin takeover – and crossed into the verdant oasis of the orchard gardens. The noise of the town was audible but muffled by green leaves and the laughter of the orchard workers. He crossed the Merciful Prayer bridge, passed under the arch of the inner wall, and came out into the sun-blasted citadel square, where no one walked at midday. By the commander's quarters, two stocky Qin soldiers rode patrol, their heads covered by felt caps whose tilted brims shaded their eyes.

The gallows and the posts cast almost no shadows. Widow Lae's remains, dangling from the middle post, clattered in the wind. Keeping his head low, Shai twisted his clan ring three times around his middle finger and walked, trying not to look at the strands of black hair fluttering from the widow's skull and the tattered remains of her red silk tunic, her best garment. Most of her flesh had been picked clean by wind and vultures and sun, leaving these strings of tendons that bound together her bones, the last remnants of hair and clothing, and her ghost.

'I did it!' she shrilled. She was a wraith, more mist than form, a handsome young woman of about twenty although she'd been three times that age when she'd died. 'I'll get my reward soon enough! Then you'll all be sorry!'

The entire town had been forced to assemble to see Widow Lac put to death after she insulted a Qin officer, although everyone knew that she'd been condemned for a more serious offense. A foreign merchant had testified that the widow had asked him to smuggle a letter, whose contents betrayed Qin military secrets, to Tars Fort on the eastern border. At least, that was what the merchant had told a drinking companion at the brothel when they were both drunk. When he'd refused to take the letter, the widow had sent one of her grandsons instead. The young man had never been found or seen again nor had anyone managed to trace his trail, and after the execution all the widow's dependents had been sold into slavery and her possessions confiscated by the Qin commander, who had given the merchant a percentage of the profits. Her distant kinfolk weren't even going to be allowed to bury her bones. So shameful!

No wonder her ghost clung stubbornly to her anger, even though that anger chained her ghost to the earth, to this very citadel square where she had died.

Shai often wondered what had been in that message, in part because naturally he was curious and in part because Widow Lae's death had altered the course of Mai's life. On the day of the widow's execution, with every man, woman, and child of Kartu Town assembled in citadel square, Captain Anji had first spoken to Father Mei about marrying his beautiful daughter.

The walls of the town's many residential compounds closed around him as he left the square and its ghost behind. He whistled under his breath. Father Mei's second wife, the younger of the two sisters, the one who was also Ti's mother, hated whistling. He'd learned to amuse himself softly.

Five turns left, past the town baths, two turns right, and one final left turn down an alley brought him to the servants' entrance to his family's compound, just around the corner from the main entrance.

He shook the bell. The peephole opened to reveal two suspicious dark eyes that crinkled up as the unseen mouth smiled.

'Master Shai!'

One Hand let him in and barred the door behind him, the movements smooth with long practice despite the slave's disability.

'Lots of trouble indoors?' Shai asked.

The old man shook his head with a wry smile. 'We are all sad to see the flower leave us, Master. She bears the Merciful One's gentle disposition in her heart, and holds mercy in her hands.'

Shai sighed. No doubt the household slaves would miss the extra food Mai slipped them when she thought no one was looking, and the ointments and infusions she smuggled into their sleeping room when one was sick. It would have been easier to stay up on the mountain than face what lay within. It was tempting to enjoy the sun and the quiet of the courtyard and pretend the rest of the world had gone to sleep.

'Not a lot of people in the streets today,' he said. 'No one out on the Golden Road, either, not as I could see from Dezara Mountain. I wonder if this talk of troubles on the eastern border is scaring people. If merchants won't travel, the markets will suffer.'

'Storm is not going away while you wait out here, Master Shai,' said One Hand.

Shai sighed again, but delaying changed nothing. He crossed the dusty courtyard, pausing twice to savor the shade, once under a peach tree and once under the grape arbor. He went into the house past the whitewashed slave barracks, past the tapestried halls that led to his married brothers' suites of rooms, past the curtained alcove where he and his nephew Younger Mei slept—

He stopped and stuck his head in. Mei had thrown himself down on the bed they shared. He was weeping, trying to mute his noise in his wool tunic, which was wadded up and squashed against his face. Startled, the boy lifted his head. His entire body shook with a gasp of relief.

'It's you! Don't tell Father Mei.'

Shai let the curtain fall and sat down at the end of the bed. The rope base sagged under him, cutting lines into his buttocks; the servants had taken the mattress out to re-stuff it with new straw just this morning.

'I can't believe she's leaving. My dearest sister! We are twin souls! Born together! Now I'll never see her again.'

Since it was probably true, Shai didn't murmur reassurances. He listened for the tread of hard feet, keeping Mei company while he sniveled. Slaves passed twice, but they walked with light footsteps and none were foolish enough to tell tales on the youth who would one day be head of household, should he live so long. Poor Mei. Father Mei and any of Younger Mei's other uncles would whip him for crying if they heard. In a way it was better to be least and superfluous, seventh of seven sons, an unlucky position certainly but one without expectations and demands beyond remaining silent, keeping out of the way, and doing what you were told.

'All right,' said Mei finally. He sat up and wiped his face dry with his tunic. 'I'm ready.' He stood, straightened his knee-length silk coat, and examined his spotless nails. 'They've already gathered in the fountain court.'

The Mei family compound had the same layout as most every family compound in Kartu Town. First you would see the massive outer wall built of earth or bricks. Behind this wall, and usually ringing the inner portion of the compound, lay a buffering outer courtyard where livestock and chickens could be quartered, a garden and fruit trees could grow, and the servants could launder, cook, clean, and take care of the necessary chores that none of the household kin desired to smell or listen to. The inner compound had a barracks built on the eastern end and a maze of rooms for the family, the most recent added on only four years ago. Some compounds in town were smaller, scarcely more than hovels erected within a corral of sticks; others were palatial and boasted marble floors and second stories.

Unmarried men like Mei and Shai slept in alcoves; unmarried daughters slept in their mothers' suites with the other children. At the center of the house lay the fountain court where Father Mei entertained guests or negotiated contracts. Although a painted, windowless corridor led from the main gate to the fountain court so that visitors would not glimpse the secret heart of the family's private life, Shai and Mei took the slaves' hall that wound through the warren of rooms. It let them in behind the hedge-like screen of flowering bitter-heart from which they might first observe before revealing their presence.

Everyone was assembled. Father Mei sat in the black chair, facing the splashing fountain. Grandmother – Shai's mother – sat on Father Mei's left. She was tiny, frail, and half asleep but otherwise quite magnificent in a gold silk woman's coat, the extraordinarily long, square sleeves embroidered with red leaping antelopes. The uncles sat to Father Mei's right, all in a line. The wives stood a step behind them, and there were at least a dozen children kneeling with heads bowed and hands resting on thighs off beyond the uncles. From this angle Shai could only see the top of Mai's head; she was seated on a pillow halfway between Father Mei and the fountain. In this same way he would present a valuable item to be admired and examined before the haggling began.

Captain Anji sat on the fountain bench with spray wetting the back of his gold silk Qin tabard and the peculiar braided topknot that all the Qin officers made of their hair. Remarkably, he had come alone except for two attendants standing with arms crossed back by the gate. The Qin were famous for their arrogance.

Cornflower was offering rice wine to each of the uncles. Someone had put her in a concubine's revealing bedroom silks so that every time she bent at the waist to proffer the cup, a flash of pale hip was revealed. Despite this provocation, Captain Anji kept his gaze fixed on Father Mei. He was a man of powerful control.

Shai could not stop peeking through the bitter-heart. Her braids had a caressing way of sliding to and fro over her shoulders and upper arms. They were fastened at each tip by tiny nets sewn with lazulite beads as blue as her eyes. Shai shut his eyes.

Thank goodness the ceremony of receiving had almost reached its conclusion! The family had been out here for a while, while Shai was dawdling.

The sigh that escaped Younger Mei's lips was as fragile as the ghost of a wind passing through scattered rose leaves. Shai looked at him, squeezed his arm, and lifted his own chin: Hold firm! Mei gave Shai a *look,* like that of a frightened rabbit determined to bite the hawk that has cornered it but not sure it will survive the altercation. Then he stepped out from behind the hedge.

The heir's place, of course, was to stand at his father's right hand.

Mei did so, taking up position smoothly and without a sound. Captain Anji flashed the merest glance Mei's way but did not otherwise betray that anything was amiss or that another man might have taken insult at the heir's belated arrival. Shai waited behind the hedge, partly because he was so aroused by the sight of Cornflower in her bedroom silks but mostly because no one had bothered to place a chair for him with the rest of the uncles and he refused to kneel with the children. Ti was seated first among the children, her hands clenched and her round face streaked with dirty tears. She looked as if she'd rubbed her face in the dust. But she kept her mouth shut.

The last glass was sipped dry. With an annoyed gesture, Father Mei's elder wife Drena sent Cornflower back inside. It hadn't been the choice of the women, then, to see if Captain Anji could be embarrassed by revealing Cornflower's charms.

'I apologize that we must speak in such haste,' said Father Mei, although the ceremony of receiving always took at least an hour and the usual opening negotiating formalities might take an equal amount of time. 'I had thought the negotiations done and the contract sealed, Captain Anji, but now it appears otherwise. What brings you to us?'

Captain Anji had a soldier's bluntness. 'I sent a messenger ahead to inform you of my situation. You already know my predicament. I've received a change of orders. My company rides out in two days. I would like to marry tomorrow so my bride can journey with me. It is the fondest desire of my heart.'

Now he did smile, nodding at Mai. Shai could not see Mai's reaction because he could see only the back of her head, but he thought her shoulders tightened slightly; it was hard to tell because she was so heavily draped in the layers of blue silk appropriate to an affianced bride. Then again, lots of things were hard to tell with Mai. All loved her for her accommodating, placid nature. She was beautiful, but a little stupid.

'It will be a hardship for my clan to hurry the rites. It will cost us to pay the law courts to move the day, and to make room tomorrow in their schedule, and we won't have ready the many fine luxuries we wish to dower her with.'

'I have some resources. I can pay the law court what they need. I ask nothing of you except your daughter, Father Mei.'

How coolly he said those words! Shai was impressed. Father Mei would inflate the costs and keep the difference for the family, but Captain Anji was apparently no merchant or bargainer and thereby, according to the rule of the marketplace, ripe for plucking. Or else he simply did not care. Beauty in women captured men that way sometimes.

'We will sustain a loss by having her torn from the house before her time.'

As if on cue, Younger Mei sniffled, then stiffened, knowing he must show no emotion. Emotion gave the opponent a bargaining chip.

The captain slipped a hand into the folds of one sleeve, searched for something, and withdrew his hand, now cupped. 'I possess nothing to recompense you for your loss, which is extreme. However, two days ago I purchased an item which I think might be of interest to the Mei clan.'

He unfolded his hand to reveal a ring. It was silver, shaped to resemble a running wolf with its mouth biting into its tail. A rare and perfect black pearl was inlaid as the wolf's eye.

Grandmother bolted upright in her chair. Her hands gripped the arms like a hawk's talons. 'Girish, bring it to me!' she said querulously.

The wives whispered, horrified. The uncles coughed and hemmed. Ti giggled nervously. Father Mei's big hands closed, opened, and with his right thumb and middle finger he made the warding sign, but because he did not speak, no one spoke. No one dared correct Grandmother.

Captain Anji raised an eyebrow, puzzled by the exchange.

She seemed to collect herself, and her memory. 'Shai!' she snapped. 'Nothing-good boy! Hu! I don't know why Grandfather thought you so clever! Come quickly. Get it and bring it here.'

He padded forward from behind the hedge. The uncles and wives and children seemed surprised to see him. Father Mei grunted, a sign that he was holding his legendary temper in check. It always exploded afterward. But as soon as Shai got between the captain and his eldest brother, blocking Father Mei's view, Captain Anji winked at Shai as if in sympathy before dropping the ring into his hand.

'Hari,' breathed Shai, not meaning to talk, but the touch of the ring actually hit so hard that he rocked back on his heels and struggled against a wave of dizziness.

It was Hari's ring. No doubt of that.

He took in a breath to steady himself, then walked back to his mother and placed it gently in her right hand. She slapped him hard with her left, the crack stinging and bitter.

He choked back his surge of anger. He'd gotten so good at doing it that it had become reflexive. The bitch would be dead soon, and he wouldn't miss her. Anyway, her slap – her dislike of him – didn't hurt nearly as much as contact with the ring had.

Hari was *dead*.

He'd known it as soon as the ring had touched his skin, just as he knew that no one else would feel it. *Hari was dead*. He'd been wearing the ring when he died; he'd been angry in an amused kind of way – the anger lingered in the ring. But surely Hari's spirit had already fled earth through Spirit Gate. There was nothing to hold him here, after all. Anger and bitterness hadn't chained him in Kartu Town. He'd not waste time lingering on earth as a ghost when there were adventures to face in the afterlife. Not Hari, the boldest and handsomest and most delightful of brothers.

'Fool boy,' muttered his mother sharply. Her hands shook as she struggled to hide her tears, and Father Mei finally took the ring and examined it. As soon as it was out of her hands, she hid her face behind a sleeve.

'This belonged to my younger brother,' Father Mei said. 'Hari marched east as a mercenary with one of your regiments six years ago. We have never heard from him. Where did this come from?'

Shai shuffled to the side, turning, to see Captain Anji shrug.

'Certain peddlers have a license to travel from fort to fort selling small wares, curiosities, such things. I found this yesterday among the goods offered for sale by a man who had come from the east along the Golden Road. He said it came from a place called "the Hundred," which lies north of the Sirniakan Empire. He bought it from a Hundred merchant, traveling in Mariha, who said it was found near a town he called "Horn." There'd been a battle there. Internal matters, lord fighting lord or some such. I'm not sure of the details. The Hundred folk are barbarians, it seems. They've never had a var – a king – to lead them. Scavengers will always pick clean the fields of battle, and it seems it was no different with this ring. I don't know how many hands it passed through to get this far from the place it was found. But I recognized the ring at once. Mai has a ring like it.'

As did every blood member of the Mei clan.

'Does it bring joy or grief to your house?' the captain asked.

'I cannot know,' said Father Mei. 'Is Hari dead, or alive? He cannot rest if his bones do not rest with those of his ancestors. We can never rest, not knowing what became of him.' His lips were thin, a sure sign of anger.

Lots of anger in this house. Shai waited for the blow. It came quickly.

'When my beloved and precious daughter goes with you, she must have servants, familiar ones who have served her for many years.'

'Of course.' Captain Anji nodded.

'She will be alone, who has never been alone. I ask you, Captain Anji, let my young brother Shai accompany her.'

The words struck, shivering like lightning through him. He stood, stunned, as his brother droned on.

'He is still unmarried, so he leaves no obligations behind, and he is almost twenty, old enough to be considered a man. We'll send a slave with him and provisions and traveling gear, so he'll be no burden on you. Once he reaches the eastern border, he can make his way north to this place called the Hundred and look for this battle-field near a town called Horn. If he can find our brother's remains, he can bring them home.'

'A long journey,' mused Captain Anji, 'and far beyond the bound-aries of the lands the Qin claim.'

'Merchants go there. Peddlers go there.'

Anji grinned as at a private joke. From this new angle, Shai could now see Mai's face. She was pretending to look down quiescently at her folded hands but in fact she was studying the captain. Her eyes widened slightly; her lips twitched. Although she and Shai had grown up together, lived in the same compound all their lives – she as the cherished, pampered daughter, and he as the unwanted and despised youngest brother – Shai did not understand her. What did this flash of emotion portend? Impossible to say. Mai was as sweet to him as she was to anyone. She had no hidden depths, no reserves of deep feeling. Most likely she was frightened out of her wits.

But Shai wasn't, not as the first shock faded.

'Merchants travel where soldiers fear to ride,' said the officer. 'Shai is welcome to come, but I cannot guarantee his safety after he leaves my protection.'

'If you set him on the right path, that is all that I ask,' said Father Mei, pompous and condescending as always. 'Then we will be square, our debts equal and canceled. Do we have an agreement?'

'We have an agreement.'

With those simple words, Shai was released. Unchained. He was free.

8

Leave-taking turned out to be a troublesome business. In the last three generations the only person in the Mei clan who had left Kartu Town by any road other than Spirit Gate was Hari. Everyone knew what trouble he had caused.

Ti had left off clinging to Mai indoors and come outdoors, where she was now yanking on Shai's left arm and crying while trying to speak. Her sobs gusted up straight from her belly. Shai admired her capacity; she'd be a natural for one of the touring acting companies that plied the Golden Road.

'Oh! Oh! Oh! You didn't even try to talk him out of it! You just hid! What will become of me, all alone? Hu! Hu! Hu! I can't bear it!'

Captain Anji had arrived at dawn with the same pair of soldiers who had accompanied him last time; his officer's escort were gathered outside the gate. He waited with apparent patience in the shadow of the arbor although it was by now almost noon. The wives had been in an uproar all morning and had repacked Mai's trunk twice even though Mai had packed it herself yesterday with only the aid of her slave Priya. That linen shift isn't nice enough; the yellow of that silk doesn't go well with her complexion; she'll need thread and her embroidery frame; she'll need a prayer silk; she can buy thread at any town market; cooking spices. No! Hairpins! Shai and Younger Mei had retreated to their alcove and huddled there while the storm raged. In the end, a rare vase was thrown and broken, and Father Mei had intervened with slaps and shouting.

Now they stood in the courtyard waiting for Mai to be escorted out by Grandmother. Captain Anji was seated on a stool. He was smoking terig leaf, dried leaves rolled up in paper to make a burning stick whose smoke you sucked into your lungs. Periodically, he handed a stub back to his attendants, who were standing behind him, and they finished it off. Shai had never tried terig leaf because it was one of many things forbidden to those who weren't Qin. The smoke stung in his nostrils, laced with a faintly sweet afterburn. The wisps drifting over to the entrance gate made Girish's ghost even more irritable than usual, and his wraith-like form danced and gibbered by the hanging tree to the right of the gate, so furious that for once Shai couldn't understand what he was saying.

Poor Girish. Mother had spoiled him after Hari's departure, and, as Mai had once said in a moment of startling and unexpected clarity, he had fermented. He'd never forgiven the family for his death, although it had been his own selfishness and cruelty that had gotten him killed. His anger had chained his ghost to the gate for almost a year.

Shai caught Captain Anji's eye. The Qin officer smiled ever so slightly at him, like a conspirator, and all at once, so strongly that the feeling almost knocked Shai right off his feet, the last two days of tempest focused into a single thought.

I'm glad to be rid of Girish! And the rest of them, too!

Glad! Glad! Glad! None of them could peer into Shai's mind. He'd made sure of that ever since he was old enough to think twice about keeping his mouth shut. They'd never know the truth of his impious thoughts.

He was free!

Until he found Hari's bones and had to come back.

The door opened. Father Mei appeared in his best clerk's silk jacket, flowing to the ground and clasped with intricate knots in three places across the chest. Grandmother tottered beside him, leaning on her eldest son, who was ever burdened with the knowledge that he had never been her favorite. Behind them, Younger Mei escorted his twin, Mai. She wore a blue silk robe fit for display but not traveling; her hair was done up in a complicated series of loops and braids festooned with slender gold chains and tiny brass bells.

Younger Mei was a homely boy; the contrast with his twin sister always astounded no matter how many times one saw them together. The round face, thick lashes, exotic eyes, and flawless bronze-dark complexion that made Mai the best-looking girl in Kartu Town had a doughy lack of firmness in Younger Mei, like bread left to rise too long. Tears streaked his face; he'd get a beating once the cavalcade left. Shai had already said his good-byes to his favorite nephew, the only person he would miss. Younger Mei looked at him despairingly. Ti sniveled; an almost inaudible moan escaped her.

They kept silence while Father Mei made a long speech about the Mei clan's honor and the exceptional value of its most precious orchid, Mai'ili. Captain Anji remained seated throughout, which in any man but a Qin officer would have been a deliberate insult. The entire household stood as Father Mei declaimed. Everyone's eyes were red, even the uncles'. They all loved her. Mai was the flower of the clan, and it had shocked them all when the captain had claimed her.

Now they would lose her. They all knew it was unlikely they would ever see her again.

Even Shai would have to leave her once the captain's regiment reached its new garrison posting, wherever that was to be. Mai's expression, as Father Mei wound down his speech, had the placid good nature of a cow's. Her eyes were a tiny bit red, but the only people in the courtyard as composed as she was were her new husband and his stolid attendants.

At last, Father Mei finished. Captain Anji rose while, behind him, one of his attendants folded up the stool and tied it to the back of a packhorse. The girl was handed from one to the other, the contracts, signed yesterday at the law courts, were exchanged, and Ti crumpled to the ground in a dead faint. Mai looked back toward her. Captain Anji, who already held her hand, turned as well, alerted by her movement. There was a pause. Mai's eyes were very wide but as she came up against Captain Anji's grip, she stilled and did not tug.

The officer released her hand. She glanced at him with a look of astonishment, lips parting, then spun and returned the few steps to kneel beside her half sister and kiss her brow. But Shai, beside Ti, saw this out of the corner of his eye; he felt Mai's gesture more than watched her because he was studying Captain Anji. The Qin officer had a peculiar quirk to his lips, unfathomable, as he surveyed the pretty scene of Mai comforting poor Ti, whom grief had silenced. Father Mei began to speak, but caught himself short. Mai was no longer his to scold and discipline.

Ti stirred, regaining consciousness. The girls kissed one last time. As Mai returned to her husband, Ti buried her face in her hands. The captain gestured, the attendant went to the gate, and four slaves entered carrying the palanquin in which she would journey. He twitched the curtain open. Mai ducked inside without a word and without looking over her shoulder, and the curtain slid down before Shai could get a glimpse of the cramped interior. Her chest was hauled away to another packhorse. Mai's slave Priya waited beside the palanquin.

Ready to go!

Shai gestured to Mountain. The middle-aged slave earned zastras by hiring himself out before dawn hauling night soil to the fields for other families, and five years back he had been given the choice between buying his freedom or using his zastras to pay for a marriage contract between him and Priya. He'd chosen Priya. Now he was being sent with Mai into the unknown. As part of his duties he would attend Shai, until Shai left the company. The big man knelt, fastened the carrying strap across his forehead, and rose with Shai's small chest of belongings balanced across his shoulders.

Captain Anji beckoned to one of his attendants, who brought a horse forward.

'Uncle Shai.' He gestured toward the saddle. It was not a request.

Panic struck as an eagle might, plunged straight down and gripped him by the throat. He lost his voice.

Father Mei said, 'But it's forbidden, Captain. You know our people are forbidden to ride horses, by the law of the Qin. It's a hanging offense.'

Captain Anji nodded. 'Among the Qin, only slaves walk. If he does not ride, my soldiers will treat him as a slave. It is up to you, Uncle Shai.'

The formal mode of address calmed Shai. Anji was about ten years older, but he used the honorific appropriate to Shai's station relative to the captain's bride, not to the captain himself. The kindness was similar to that Anji had shown Mai by letting her give Ti a final kiss good-bye. Whatever man Anji was, he was not a simple one. He was not a faceless triumphant conquering overlord grabbing what he most coveted. Or he was playing a very deep game.

'Thank you.' He forced the words out and stepped up to the horse, which was absolutely massive and terrifying, and of course he hadn't the least idea what to do.

The captain leaned close enough to whisper. The terig had a musty, sharp smell, not displeasing. 'Loop the reins around the pommel, that post there. Hold on as well as you can. The horse will follow the rest. Trust me.'

No one else heard. Ti had started to wail again, and all the wives were crying, with the children sniffling and coughing and blowing their noses on their sleeves.

Be a brave man, like Hari. Hari wouldn't have balked! A soldier came forward and gave him a hand up. He had a moment of disorientation, up so high; then Captain Anji left his side and went to his own mount, held by one of his escort.

Father Mei approached. For the first time in his nineteen years, Shai had the satisfaction of seeing his eldest brother look daunted as he walked up beside the horse, which mercifully stood perfectly still. He pulled a suede bag out of his sleeve and handed it up to Shai, who almost overbalanced as he took it. It was heavy, filled with coins and other valuables; he recognized their heft and shape through the pliant leather.

'Take this,' Father Mei said in his softest and most menacing voice, switching daringly to banki, the local language, which they were forbidden from using in front of the Qin. 'But use it only for an emergency. To bring Mai home if things don't go well. If he beats her. If he gets tired of her and tries to sell her into slavery. Use that gold to bring Mai back. If you use it for anything else, knowing she is suffering, then you aren't my brother any longer. I'll turn my face away from you and in this house it will be as if you were never born.'

Shai nodded. If he spoke, he would fall off. It was difficult enough to get the pouch safely into his long left sleeve, and Father Mei had to help him tuck it into the thief-pocket sewn into the lining.

'There is one other thing I am giving you for the journey,' added Father Mei.

Shai's heart skipped and stuttered. Cold fear tightened his gut. Now what?

'For the sake of peace in my house I should have got rid of her earlier, but you know how it is.'

Merciful One! Worse than he had thought!

Father Mei gestured, looking toward his senior wife, Drena. She smiled, victorious at last, and snapped her fingers. Cornflower padded forward out of the crowd of servants and slaves. She wore a sturdy linen knee-length tunic over loose trousers, undyed; slave's clothing, suitable for hard work. She wore her hair, as always, in a trident braid – one by each ear and one running down her back. She did not look up. Shai broke into a sweat more drenching than he had suffered waiting out under the midday sun. He couldn't go against Father Mei's orders. He hadn't been bound legally into another man's jurisdiction; Father Mei remained his head of household.

On the street beyond, the captain's escort was moving out. The slaves hoisted the palanquin and carried it outside, where pack-horses and soldiers fell into line. Captain Anji lifted a hand as a signal and led them forward through the gate, and without any effort on his part Shai moved after them. As they passed the hanging tree, Girish's ghost screamed in fury, knowing he had lost the only family member who could hear his complaints.

'She'll get you, too! She'll kill all of you, just like she killed me! Bad luck! Bad luck!'

As Shai passed under the gate, he heard Father Mei scolding Younger Mei in a loud voice. 'Strong blood! That's what you have inherited. You must keep the family strong, marry the girl we pick for you, and have strong sons and pretty daughters like Grandfather Mei did. Like I did. Remember only: Don't make the overlords angry, don't do anything dishonorable, and don't lose the family's money. None of this simpering. Mai is gone now. We all knew she was too good to keep. That's what comes for girls as pretty and good-natured as she is. Nothing but grief!'

The cavalcade passed out of range, but those last words ran round and round in Shai's head. Although meant for Younger Mei, the force of Father Mei's anger crashed down on him as well, as it always had no matter how carefully he had kept himself separate and silent. He clutched the pommel of the saddle, swaying this way and that. It didn't matter. He was free of him, now. Free.

He ended up with the rear guard, able to survey the entire procession as they kicked up dust on the broad avenue that led out of the town and onto the Golden Road. Captain Anji rode at the head, surrounded by soldiers who had waited outside on the road with the rest of his group. They were laughing and talking, their seats on these impossible animals as casual as if they sat on a bench by the fountain. Mai's palanquin followed behind, and behind that the packhorses attended by mounted men. Cornflower slipped into the group of slaves trudging behind the palanquin; she was easy to see because hers was the only pale head among the six score folk in the captain's company. She glanced back at him, eerie blue gaze unwavering, then pulled a cap over her hair to protect herself from the sun.

Nothing but grief.

9

Mai'ili had learned her most important lesson in life by observing her twin brother Mei and nearly twin half sister and cousin Ti'ili as they thrashed their way through life.

The only place to find happiness is inside.

When she was very young she had once made the mistake of sharing this wise pronouncement with her uncle Girish, the swine, and he had laughed at her, called her stupid and shallow, and told everyone else about her sage comment in such a ridiculing way that they had either chuckled outright without any concern for her feelings or, patting her on the head, patronized her. Alone, she had cried, then wiped her eyes, and after that, for she couldn't have been more than seven, she had set a clear gaze forward and never looked back, not for the last ten years.

Mai wanted to be happy. Not for her Ti's storms or Younger Mei's sulks. She didn't care for Uncle Girish's tantrums and whining, Father Mei's controlling angers, her mother's jealousy and competitiveness, her aunt's scheming, and her grandmother's favoritism. Even quiet Uncle Shai just withdrew and avoided everyone, although it was obvious he was boiling inside. She loved them all, of course, but she didn't always like them very much.

She had measured the extent and firmness of the walls that bounded her and set out to make a little garden within them, the one thing she could control. She knew that in that way she was like her father: He too liked to control things; it was just that he held the lash of life and death over the entire household. Her scope was much smaller, but she was determined to live life in her own way and on her own terms while at the same time not making anyone so mad at her that they disturbed her tranquil sanctuary.

She had done her best, but it hadn't worked. Anger wasn't the only emotion that made people act rashly and tramp in where they weren't wanted.

Seated cross-legged on a plush mattress ringed with a waist-high padded rim to cushion her from unexpected shocks, she fingered the palanquin curtains as the mattress rocked under her. The slave bearers had a remarkably smooth gait, in part because they chanted in a soft rhythm that regulated their pace. Ahead, she heard men talking and laughing. Behind she heard the shuffle of feet and the crunch of wheels on dust as the grooms, slaves, and servants followed with the packhorses and a pair of wagons. Farther back, a blast blew on a horn to signal that this force of soldiers had just left the garrison at Kartu Town. Which meant she too had left, that they had passed the gate and were venturing into unknown country, as in the old song.

Past these gates live ghosts only;
Stay here in my warm embrace.
Past these gates live ghosts only;
Stay here with your chair and lamp.
Past these gates live ghosts only;
Stay here where there are friends and drinking and song.
There is no song out there but that of the demons, shrieking.
There is no drink out there but the drink of one's own tears.

There is no friend out there but the arms of oblivion.
Past these gates live ghosts only.
Do not go, my child, my parent, my lover.

She flipped her long sleeves back up past her elbows, put a hand over her mouth, and let the tears flow.

She didn't fight them, but she did lean forward from the hips far enough that no moisture would stain the expensive blue silk of her bridal gown. The mattress was a wool batting covered with a dark red linen cover, well-made and practical traveling equipment since the wool wouldn't mildew easily and the color of the linen spread would disguise dust and other stains.

She wept silently, not even shaking. After a long while the tears slowed and ceased of their own accord. By not fighting sorrow she allowed it unimpeded passage through her body.

'*Of course we all suffer,*' Priya often told her. '*But if you cling to suffering or fight it then it will hold on like a rat. If you accept its existence and the pain it causes you, then you can release it.*'

When her tears dried, she fished a linen handkerchief out of her sleeve and carefully wiped her cheeks and blew her nose. Scooting forward, she placed her hands on the front wall of the palanquin. The front and back walls were wood from top to bottom; a breeze managed to sneak through the side curtains, cut cleverly to conceal her while not stifling her. A narrow sliding panel was set into the front wall a little below her eye level. She released the lock, pushed it aside, and looked out. Outside seemed much brighter now that her eyes had become accustomed to the interior's dim light. She blinked until her eyes adjusted.

She counted thirty-two riders visible; there were many more out of sight to either side, but she couldn't be sure how many by the amount of dust they kicked up. All were outfitted in similar fashion – the Qin mostly looked alike – but she recognized her husband's back immediately: the set of his head; the blue, white, and gold of the captain's ribbons braided into his topknot; the brilliant gold silk of his tabard.

Husband.

She considered the word. She had observed husbands. Father Mei and two of her uncles were husbands. Husbands like Master Vin

often came by the fruit stall. Although it was slightly shameful for
Father Mei to put his own daughter out in the stall now that he was
a bigger man in town than Grandfather Mei had been, it was still
perfectly normal for an unmarried daughter to spend the long hours
from dawn to dusk sitting in the shade of a parasol or awning while
selling peaches and almonds and melons and other produce. She
made better money at the little stall than anyone else in the family
could. Men rarely bargained with her, and women were always
kind, although shrewder – but why shouldn't they want their
money's worth and get in a good gossip at the same time? Mai herself did not gossip, but she asked harmless questions, so folk liked to
talk to her and, she had discovered, told her many things they never
told anyone else.

People were generally pleasant, and often good and well meaning,
but they certainly did a lot of trivially cruel things while meanwhile
fretting and gnawing at their troubles and their envies and their
annoyances until, in the end, it killed them or turned them sour. Like
Girish, who had gone bad before he died. She pitied Girish a tiny bit,
because he'd been so bitterly unhappy, but he'd done worse to
others than to himself, so in the end she was sorry to think that he
might actually have deserved such an ugly death.

Girish would have made a bad husband, and Father Mei had
known it, which is why he hadn't let Girish marry when he'd turned
twenty, the usual age for men to claim a first wife. He'd bought a
slave for Girish instead, so he wouldn't keep going to the brothels.
Look where that had led!

To Father Mei, honor mattered above all things. He wanted no
dishonor brought down on Clan Mei's head. She fingered the ring on
her left middle finger, the running wolf that was the sigil of their clan.
She, too, had to uphold that honor. So she would. She'd do nothing
to shame the Mei clan, not like her uncles Hari and Girish had done.
She would be a good wife to the Qin officer with whom she had not
exchanged more than twenty words beyond the meaningless pleas-
antries that were the hallmark of trade in the marketplace.

How much for these peaches? A big storm yesterday out of the
desert, wasn't it? That's quite a distinctive amaranth pattern on your
parasol. Does it come from the Sirniakan Empire?

She had never been alone with him, but she would be tonight.

Tears came again. They flowed like a spring stream swollen with snowmelt, just kept coming and coming as she watched the men ride. As she watched her husband ride. He did not once look back toward the palanquin. He didn't need to. He had acquired her as he might a bolt of handsome silk, all signed and sealed with a contract so he couldn't be accused of stealing. At least he had been kind enough to take her as a wife, thereby allowing her certain legal protections not available to slaves or concubines.

Who would have thought there were so many tears? Soon she'd be like Ti, flooding at every word. At last, when the tears had dried, she wiped and blew just like before and felt at peace enough to twitch aside one of the side curtains and stare out at the landscape. She had never been more than an hour's walk out of Kartu Town, up into the hills where the Mei clan had their wet-season pastures. In the interval while she had cried, the familiar silhouette of Dezara Mountain and its companion hills had fallen behind. She wasn't sure she could see them at all. The hills were a mix of shadow and sunlight, almost golden in the westering light, but their jagged slopes had no recognizable peaks or saddles, not from this angle.

Panic swept her. It raced through her skin; she broke out in a sweat and yet her neck felt clammy and cold.

She didn't know where they were going, or what they would find when they got there.

Anything might come next.

Fear rose, like the tempest. She imagined every worst possible thing that could happen: her husband would be cruel to her in the bed and laugh while he hurt her; bandits would sweep out of the hills and kill them all; she would be abandoned and sold into slavery and raped repeatedly; a sandstorm would hurl itself out of the desert and swallow them alive; a ghost would pinch her; rats would eat her toes and fingers and nose; she would eat spoiled meat and throw up until her insides burst, like Girish had, only he had been poisoned; someone would say something hateful and mean to her; she would die and pass through Spirit Gate.

That wasn't so bad, as the rush poured out of her. All those terrible things ended in death, so eventually she would find peace. Only angry ghosts were restless.

She had another handkerchief. As she mopped the sweat from her skin, reached up her sleeves and under her robe and patted herself dry, she wished she had some perfumed talcum powder to sweeten herself. She had packed some, but Aunt Sada had taken it out because, she said, good talcum was expensive and if the Qin officer had so much cash, then he could supply luxuries for his new wife because it could be bought anywhere.

Anywhere but in the middle of the road after you've been sweating and have started to stink! What a way to come to your wedding bed! She let the curtain fall and, carefully, so as not to upset the rhythm of the slave bearers, who surely must be exhausted by now, sidled back to the front panel and stared out at her husband's back.

Was he a good-looking man? Ti thought all the Qin were ugly ugly ugly, but Mai didn't think so. They looked like people, some better-looking than others, some with pleasant faces and some with closed-up, cranky ones. Anyway, Captain Anji didn't quite look exactly like the other Qin. He was a little bit taller and a little bit less stocky, and his hair was wavy, not coarse and straight. He had that interesting nose, which none of the other Qin had; they had blunter, shorter noses, more like those of Kartu people. He *was* rather old. The one thing she'd learned about him was that he was born in the Year of the Deer, which would make him thirteen years older than she was. Still, he had a graceful way of moving even though he was bowlegged like all the Qin soldiers. He had clear, honest eyes, good teeth, and humor in the way his lips would twitch, maybe suppressing a smile, and he had shown her that astounding glimpse of kindness when he'd allowed her to turn back and give a final goodbye kiss to Ti. Was he a kind man? A cruel one? Honest or false? Grasping or open? Brave or a coward?

Suddenly he looked back over his shoulder. That glance struck as might an arrow. He knew she was watching him. She recoiled and fell onto her back, and then felt the slave carrying the right back corner of the palanquin stagger and swiftly right himself.

She couldn't breathe. It hit like a sandstorm, smothering her. He was just like those sloe-eyed princes in the old stories, who rode out of the desert and kidnapped pining dark maidens and took them to palaces built of rosy-colored stone in the midst of a beautiful oasis. Sometimes those stories ended happily and sometimes sadly, but the middle part was always so good and exciting and gratifying.

I am afraid. I am afraid that I want to be able to love him but that he will never love me, not like in the old stories. I'm just a glittering jewel, a prize carried off by a bandit. I've been ripped from my garden. I can never go back.

This time, despite everything, despite all her efforts, she sobbed helplessly and awkwardly until she was hoarse, heedless of her fine silk gown and her running nose. The noise of the cavalcade drowned the betraying sound of her weeping. Only the slaves in attendance the four who carried the palanquin, the five bearers to alternate places as they tired, and the three slaves who had come from Kartu Town and walked alongside could hear her. They would never tell.

10

Because of their late start they had to halt just before sundown at an old ruin that had once been a village. It was a quiet place, so long abandoned there were no ghosts left. Captain Anji argued with his chief of staff, won, then beckoned to Shai, who handed his mount over to the soldier who had helped him dismount.

'We won't make the posting house tonight so we'll camp here. If you will, dine with me. You may prepare, wash, whatever you wish.'

'Of course, Captain. The honor is mine.'

Shai tracked down Mountain among the men already bustling to their tasks, lighting fires, preparing food, digging a trench for waste, and drawing water from the abandoned well.

'Mountain!'

The slave was talking with one of the soldiers, a lowly tailman by the look of him, but he excused himself and hurried over to Shai.

'Set up my tent in whatever place the master of this caravan deems appropriate.'

'Yes, Master Shai.'

'Can you demand help from these other slaves?'

Mountain cleared his throat suggestively. 'Master. Except for the bearers, and we three from Kartu Town, there are no other slaves. These are camp men or grooms. They are part of the army. Most are Qin. Some are respectable free men, hired for the work and well paid, so they tell me. No Qin military company travels with slaves. They say it slows them down.'

Shai studied the movements within the camp. Now, he saw that the soldiers took care of their own horses and tack, and that the grooms and 'camp men' were either youths not quite old enough to be regular army men, men with a minor disability that might prevent them from fighting effectively, or foreign men who tended to their work with the brisk efficiency of those who are proud of what they do. No idling slaves here. No one lounging while others waited on them.

'Oh. Can you do everything yourself, then?'

Mountain gestured toward Cornflower, who waited about twenty paces away, hands clasped and head lowered in perfect submissiveness. 'That one will help me.'

Shai shut his eyes, making a face. 'Hu! What am I supposed to do with her?'

'She is commonly used by Father Mei and the uncles, Master Shai.'

'I *know*. But I am not my brothers. I have not forgotten what happened to Girish.' He spat on the ground for the offense of saying the dead man's name. 'Even if they pretend they have forgotten.'

'Forgive me, Master.'

'Just set up the tent, if you will. I want a blanket. She can start by massaging me. After that, she can sleep outside.'

Mountain unrolled a blanket on the ground and Shai sat down, wincing. No wonder the Qin soldiers were tough, if they had to endure this every day!

'Cornflower, work on my legs. They hurt.'

She came over, slung her pack onto the ground, and pulled a flask of oil out of the pack. He slipped off his trousers and, in only his loincloth, let her massage some of the ache out of his muscles. Her hands were strong and sure. If they only strayed a little farther up . . .

'Enough!' He grabbed for his trousers. With no change of expression, she scooted backward and bowed her head. Mountain scratched his bald head, then fanned himself with his cap.

'If you do not want her, Master Shai, then perhaps I can sell her services to the soldiers. She and Priya are the only females out of a hundred or more men. It would be a way for you to make a few extra zastras on the journey. It never hurts to have a little extra coin. Just in case.'

Shai looked at Cornflower. Like his brothers, Shai found her sexually attractive and utterly fascinating, and it annoyed him. He was stirred by her touch, and it didn't help with her kneeling so submissively a few strides away, with pale skin and ripe breasts concealed beneath her slave's shift, knowing she could not say no if he took her. Indeed, he could do anything to her at all, but he hated to be like his brothers. Mountain's suggestion had merit. It was wise to plan ahead, cultivate a nest egg. Mountain would take a cut, and the rest would fill Shai's sleeves. Just in case.

'Find an out-of-the-way place, then. Charge a reasonable rate, and not too many men any one night.'

Mountain nodded. He was a big, big man, a little stout with middle age, and missing his left eye and two fingers on his left hand. 'Not more than five a day. I hear from Tailman Chaji that it's twenty-five days' or so ride to the border, if we run into no delays. If every man in the company wants a piece of her, they'll each have one try. That'll keep the price high, if any wish to outbid the others for a second chance.'

Shai nodded. After a glance toward the silent Cornflower, he put on trousers and his best silk knee-length jacket and walked over to the awning where Captain Anji sat on a three-legged stool, on a rug, studying a scroll. A low camp table inlaid with alternating strips of ebony wood and ash-blond wood sat before the officer; a narrow, cushioned divan about an arm's length long stood to his right, with two stools folded up and leaning against it. A black flag trimmed with gold streamers fluttered from each corner of the awning. Two soldiers stood to either side, arms folded, surveying the camp. They tracked Shai's arrival with flat gazes as the captain looked up.

'Sit down,' he said. 'My men will bring food.'

One of the men opened up a stool, so Shai sat down. 'Where is Mai?' he asked.

The old village had about a dozen structures remaining, all built out of mud brick and mostly intact except for the roofs. Captain Anji's escort numbered over one hundred soldiers and two dozen grooms and hired men, together with the slaves who accompanied Mai. The soldiers had set up an outer perimeter, with their precious horses clustered in the innermost protected area of the village and the captain's awning and rug beyond that. The old well and two crumbling houses stood directly to his west. Listening, Shai heard Mai speaking to Priya from within the sheltering walls of one of the those houses, where his niece had sought privacy.

Maybe the Qin didn't allow women to eat with men. Better not to ask. He hoped his question hadn't been taken as an insult. The Qin were notoriously easy to insult.

Captain Anji's chief of staff arrived and opened a stool for himself. He was ten or fifteen years older than Anji – well into middle age – and the two men had an easy relationship; even their arguments gave them pleasure.

'I still don't like it, Anjihosh. The road is flat enough and there'll be moonlight late. We could have made it the entire way. Out here – ghosts, bandits, sandstorms, scorpions, demons, witches. Leopards. There could be anything.'

Anji scanned the darkening village with narrowed eyes. 'No ghosts, anyway, Tuvi-lo,' he said so casually that Shai's heart stuttered and seemed to skip a beat. *No ghosts?* 'If we got in late, the horses and bearers wouldn't get a full night's rest. They'll need it at this stage, to get accustomed to the travel. I want them well rested. They'll need strength to manage the worst part of the journey.'

'So you say.' Chief Tuvi rose from his stool abruptly as Mai halted at the edge of the rug. She looked calm and composed. Priya waited behind her.

Anji stood, took Mai's hand in his, and led her to the divan, a queenly seat, certainly, and far more comfortable than the men's utilitarian stools. He released her; she sat; Chief Tuvi whistled, and four young Qin soldiers – tailmen, all – came forward with platters of dried fruit, yoghurt, and strips of sizzling meat just now roasted over a campfire.

Shai waited for the captain to begin the conversation, but they ate in silence until the platters were empty. Only when hot da was handed round in painted bowls did the captain speak.

'You have traveled well, Mai'ili?' he asked.

She nodded, glanced at Shai, and after a sip at the sharp da ventured a few words. 'My heart is the only part of me that is bruised, Captain. It is difficult to leave your family behind.'

'So it is,' he agreed. 'Is it well that your uncle Shai accompanies you?'

'It is well.' She bit her lower lip, took in a breath as she glanced at Chief Tuvi, and tried again. 'Will we always camp like this? What can be expected?'

He had a steady gaze, kept on her but not intrusive and greedy, more watchful. 'Mostly we will stay at posting houses, which have corrals for livestock and some fortification. We should have traveled farther today, but I don't want to push the horses and bearers at this stage. We'll have to take some night journeys once we reach the borderlands.'

Mai laughed suddenly. Her laugh could charm water out of sand. 'I had my chest packed, but my mother and aunts insisted on repacking it. There was nothing I could do. I'm sorry we left so late. I know you came at dawn. Would we have reached a posting station if we'd left earlier?'

Anji exchanged a glance with Chief Tuvi. 'We would have. No matter, Mai. The Qin have a saying: When the river changes its course, get out of the way or drown. This is not the first time my plans did not go exactly as expected.'

Mai blushed abruptly, responding to a certain passionate tremor in his voice, to his ardent gaze, and she looked away from him. No doubt she was afraid.

Shai cleared his throat and groped for a topic of conversation to draw attention off of her. 'Have you made this particular journey many times, Captain Anji? You seem to know the way well.'

'Only once, and that traveling west,' said the captain. 'But every troop such as mine takes scouts. They're soldiers trained to know the routes and water holes and landmarks along every road our armies travel. Chief Tuvi has been this way before.'

'So I have,' said Tuvi, an entire world of implication flowering in three words.

'May we know where we are going?' asked Shai, feeling bolder as the conversation unfolded so amiably. 'Where we are traveling so far?'

'No. Not now.' Anji's tone did not invite further questions on the topic.

There was an awkward silence, broken by Mai. 'How could you

only have traveled once, and that west? The Qin come from the west. You would have to have gone east and come back.'

'Ah,' said the captain with a pleased smile. 'You have caught out the flaw in my story.' He offered the barest nod to Chief Tuvi, whose answering frown seemed resigned and amused.

Mai had a most charming way of looking puzzled, eyebrows drawn together, cherry lips pressed together winsomely. Much of her beauty was her lack of self-consciousness. Other beautiful women could not compare because they arranged their faces to suit the needs of their audience. 'Will you explain it to me, or is it something I'm not meant to know?'

'Not now. Uncle Shai, have you traveled well?'

'I am a little sore,' he said, rubbing his thighs.

'It will be worse tomorrow,' said Chief Tuvi with a laugh. 'But you stuck it out well for a flatfoot.'

'You must learn to ride as well, Mai'ili,' said the captain. 'The palanquin slows us down, but it was expected by your family.'

'Learn to ride? A horse?' She stared at him. 'But that's forbidden! There was a man in Kartu Town who was hanged for riding.'

'So there was, but you and your uncle are under my command now. I need you to learn to ride.'

'Do Qin women ride?' Shai asked.

Anji's smile had a pleasant tilt. He seemed an easygoing man in some ways, and yet Shai did not think he was. 'They do. My mother taught me to ride. It is a mother's duty to teach her children to ride. When we have sons, Mai'ili, you must be the one to teach them, not me.'

She put a hand to her mouth and glanced toward the palanquin, racked across parallel rows of fallen stones to keep it off the ground for the night. The twilight shadowed her expression, but Shai guessed that she was frightened, thinking of what normally passed between man and woman on their wedding night.

'Ah.' Anji raised his forefinger. Chief Tuvi set his da bowl on the table and retreated, strolling out into camp. 'Uncle Shai, stay please.' He rose and went into the dusk.

Priya crept forward and knelt at Mai's feet. Mai clutched her hand and wiped away a tear, and the slave whispered into Mai's ear words Shai couldn't hear.

'Is it wrong of me to be frightened, Shai?' Her voice was so steady, but her hands, gripping Priya's, shook. 'How will he treat me? I'm afraid, but I know I have to endure whatever happens. He is my master now. I will not shame Father Mei and our clan.'

Shai did not know what to say. No one ever asked him for advice.

'Shhh, Mistress,' hissed Priya. 'He returns.'

Her hiss lengthened strangely. From out of the night erupted a shout of alarm and a series of sharp slaps. An arrow skittered over the ground, coming to rest at Shai's feet. He gaped. Mai's eyes widened. Calls and shouts rousted the camp, and men went running out of sight but well within hearing. That whistling hiss was the song of arrows rushing out of the dark, and Qin arrows – white death – streaking outward in reply.

'Down!' Priya pushed Mai down between couch and fire. 'Crawl over to the house! The walls will give protection.'

Captain Anji appeared at the edge of the fire's light. 'Mai! Take shelter!' He tossed a glittering object toward her, and it smacked into the dirt beside her. A knife in a sheath, curved at the tip. Jewels studded the hilt, catching the firelight. 'That's for you, Mai. Shai! Come with me!'

Shai grabbed the arrow and staggered after Captain Anji. His thoughts were disordered; he couldn't think straight. The captain brought him to a mud-brick wall eroded to chest height, where Chief Tuvi oversaw the chaos. Out in the gloom, figures circled on horseback, keeping just at the edge of the distance arrows could reach. At intervals one would ride in, shoot, and turn hard to dash back out again. It was impossible to judge how many there were, but surely there were more than twenty, and less than fifty.

'Can you use a bow?' asked the captain.

'No.'

'A sword?'

'It's forbidden.'

The captain snorted. 'A staff? You shepherds haven't even sparred with your staffs up in the hills where we can't catch you?'

Shai burned with shame and anger. 'It's forbidden, Captain. Men were hanged for weapons training.'

'Sheep!' said Chief Tuvi with a bark of laughter. 'No wonder they were so easy to fleece.'

'Take this spear.' Captain Anji thrust the shaft into Shai's hands. 'Don't disgrace my bride by showing yourself a coward.'

Then he was gone, moving off into the ruined village to direct the fight elsewhere.

Shai found he had moisture enough in his mouth to speak. 'Are they bandits?'

'They're not ghosts, but they might be demons.' Tuvi lifted his bow, tracked one of the circling horsemen, and released the arrow. It flew, its white fletching visible as it streaked through the dusk and buried its point into the breast of one of the riders. The man reeled but did not fall.

Arrows hit all at once around them. Shai ducked down behind the wall as a half-dozen arrows struck the uneven top, flipped end over point, and slid down to land at his feet. Chief Tuvi didn't move but calmly sighted with his bow again and loosed a second arrow. Shaking, Shai rose to his feet in time to see a second man take the impact. This one fell, but his foot caught in the stirrup. His body flopped and dangled from the stirrups as the horse galloped out into the night.

Behind them, on the other side of the village, Captain Anji shouted a command.

His soldiers, all together, cried out: 'Hu! Hu! Hai!'

The shout resounded; it echoed off distant hills. Shai shivered down to his feet. The Qin were the fiercest warriors in the world. They had swept in from the west as a wave of black banners and white death.

Now that shout faded into the night, but surely it had given the bandits a better guess at their numbers. The riders circled once more before vanishing into what was now night. The moon's glamour illuminated the hills and flats, but the shadows swallowed the bandits so quickly that Shai would have doubted whether they had ever been there at all, except for the evidence of the arrows scattered throughout camp.

Captain Anji appeared beside Tuvi, holding a bow and a lantern.

'They hadn't more than thirty men,' said the chief. 'But we'll keep a double watch for the rest of the journey. I'm surprised that group hasn't been tracked down and slaughtered like the wolves they are.'

Anji shook his head. The wind fluttered the ribbons in his hair.

'They weren't bandits. They were demons, pretending to be men. I saw at least ten take hits, but we'll find no bodies in the morning.'

'If they are demons, then why would arrows stop them?' Shai demanded, finding now that he was shaking as relief hit. Still alive! He would see the new dawn! 'How can you tell the difference between men, and demons pretending to be men?'

'Demons fight silently. Sometimes they use bone whittled down for the shafts of their arrows.' He picked up one of the bandits' arrows and twirled it through his fingers with the ease of a man who has long familiarity with weapons. 'But this is common sapwood, a little heavy for arrows but one of the few woods that can be found up in the northern hills. Maybe there were a few men among them.'

'Men ride with demons?'

Anji glanced back toward the tidy row of tents set up as the night's camp. 'Your concubine is demon's get.'

'She's not my concubine!'

Chief Tuvi laughed. 'If not now, she will be soon! Or else what's that stirring in your drawers?'

Nothing to say to that! Why should even talk of Cornflower get him hardening?

'Tuvi-lo,' Anji said gently, 'demons' get are difficult to resist. They have their spells and charms, a perfume to them, that tugs a man even if he doesn't want to go that way. But they're poison in the end. I can have the creature killed, if you like, Shai. Leave the body at the edge of the desert. Her kinfolk will collect her at the full moon.'

It was tempting. Just thinking of how easy it would be to let Captain Anji remove the burr that chafed him made him sweat. But he couldn't do it.

'No. It's not her fault she's demon's get. My brother bought her in the marketplace two years back. Just like any other slave. He even had a holy man cast a seeing over her, and the holy man said she was as human as you or me.'

Chief Tuvi shook his head, exchanging a knowing glance with the captain but addressing Shai. 'These demon get are good at disguise. They look just like humans, but they're not. There's a whole tribe of them who live west of my ancestors' lands. Out there demons rule. No one dare ride past the sunset. No man who rides that way ever returns.'

'What about women?'

Tuvi hesitated, glancing toward Anji, but the captain just nodded his head, giving some kind of permission.

Tuvi shrugged. 'The demons fear human women, but they'll sleep with them just the same and spawn their demon get in their bellies. Some women go that way to capture a lover. Hu! I suppose the demon males pull women by their jewel the same way the demon women catch us men by the cock.'

Shai flushed. To cover his embarrassment, he bent to pick up arrows. Among such men, he would always be at a disadvantage. After a moment he straightened. 'Is it true you would teach me to fight? That I'd not be executed for it?'

Chief Tuvi gave his amused bark.

Captain Anji was distracted, looking toward the main fire, but he turned back now. 'Yes, we'll teach you. Come. Mai will be wondering what has happened.' He gave both bow and lantern to Tuvi and walked away.

Amazingly, Mai was already sitting out by the fire on the divan, hands clasped over the knife in her lap. Shai was taken aback to see spots of color high in her cheeks. Priya stood behind her, touching her mistress on the shoulder as if in warning as the two men approached out of the darkness.

'I have something to say,' said Mai in a cool voice. Only the tension in her hands betrayed her agitation. 'What is the custom of your people, Captain? Am I meant to kill myself with this knife if bandits overtake our party and attempt to rape me?'

Anji raised both eyebrows, pausing a body's length from the divan. His hands betrayed nothing; they hung loose at his thighs. 'No. I gave you the knife so you could kill any man who attacked you. In time you will learn to shoot a bow as well, I hope, if you feel you are willing to try. No need to hide when you can kill your enemies instead.'

She blinked three times, as much surprise as she ever commonly revealed. 'Do Qin women kill their enemies?'

'When they can.'

'What if they can't? What if you'd been killed and those bandits had overrun the camp? Should I kill myself then?'

'Why? A woman as beautiful as you wouldn't be killed. She'd

be taken prisoner and hauled off to become concubine of their prince.'

'Even if he is a demon?' asked Shai boldly.

'Especially if he is a demon. Women have survived rape before and gone on to prosper, or even to regain their freedom.'

'But the shame . . .' said Shai.

Mai waited for Anji to speak.

He shrugged, as Qin often did. 'What shame is it to be taken against your will when you have no power? Those who were meant to protect you are shamed, certainly. You survive if you can, and pray for a merciful death if life and freedom are denied you.'

'There is shame!' Mai rose and tossed the knife at Shai's feet. 'There's shame on the head of the man who attacks a helpless woman. During the fighting I heard noises from the walls next door to the place I was hiding – just there!' She pointed to the dark slope of a wall beyond the irregular outline of the ruined house just behind them. In the silence that followed, with Mai's arm outstretched and her sleeve swept gracefully toward the ground, they all heard huffing and grunting.

'I looked! And there was one of the Qin soldiers raping Cornflower! Right in the middle of the battle, when he should have been fighting. Will there be any punishment for him? Or will you allow your slave to be abused, Shai?'

Anji looked at Shai. 'Uncle Shai?'

Shai had a blinding insight: Anji already knew about the arrangement. Either Mountain had consulted him or the captain had discovered it on his own. But he gave no sign in any wise of his opinion of the matter. No use trying to hide it.

'It wasn't rape, Mai, although I admit I'm surprised Mountain started so quickly and in the middle of the skirmish! It was a business arrangement. There's only the two women with the troop. I agreed to let Mountain hire her out – no more than five men a night – for a little extra money. It's always wise to keep some money in reserve. I don't want her for myself anyway. I didn't ask for her to come along. Father Mei just gave her to me to be rid of her. Your mother's been wanting her out of the compound ever since she came to us.'

She lowered her arm, still looking toward the shadows. The

grunting quickened, then spilled over into a drawn-out gasp and sigh. Mai's expression did not change, but her hands were fists.

'What? Isn't it my turn next?' a man's voice asked. 'Aren't you done yet? How long does it take you, Chaji?'

Mai still would not look at either man. 'Do you think she doesn't cry herself to sleep every night?'

The words were like kicks, slamming into his chest. 'How would you know?' Shai demanded. He was hot everywhere, but not from lust.

Now she did turn to look at him, and he wished she hadn't. Never in his life had he seen such a glare from that normally placid and sweet face. 'Blind men don't have to see what they wish to ignore! I thought you were better than Father Mei and the other uncles, but now I see you are not. Just because you have power over someone doesn't mean you have to use it. I'm ashamed of you!' She spat toward Shai, wiped her mouth with the back of her hand, and with a swirl of silk ran to the palanquin and crawled inside. The curtain slithered down behind her. Priya stood in shocked silence behind the divan.

Shai picked up the knife. The jeweled hilt seemed to burn his fingers. Maybe he should just drive it into his heart and be done with this misery at once. Mai had never spoken like that in her entire life. Never. Never. Never.

'Some miasma from the demons must have gotten into her,' he said, breathless as he hadn't been with arrow fire raining over him. 'That's not Mai!'

Anji laughed. 'Have you and your family been so blind all these years that you don't know what she is?' He raised his voice. 'Mai! Come back.'

'About time, Chaji!' said the man's voice. 'How is she?'

'A little dry. But her peaches are just right – not too soft, not too firm. Ummm!'

The curtain parted. Mai walked back with stately grace, head high and hands hidden in her sleeves. Her expression was as smooth as an untouched pool. Was this the real Mai, so calm and composed? Who was that other person who had spoken through her lips?

She sank to the ground and knelt submissively before Captain Anji, hands on knees, head bent. She said nothing.

Anji crossed her arms and studied her. 'I don't talk to women who are on their knees before me. Stand, or sit, but do not act as a slave must. You are my wife.'

She rose. Her chin trembled, then stilled. A single tear slipped from an eye. 'Forgive me if my behavior has shamed you.'

'It has not dishonored me, nor has it dishonored you. Have you other things you wish to say?'

She was brave enough to meet his gaze. 'Will you put a stop to it?'

'No. Uncle Shai is my companion but not under my command. The slave's life belongs to him.'

'What about your men? Doesn't it shame them?'

'My men visit brothels. I see no difference.'

'I'll buy her from Shai.'

'You will not because I won't have her in my household. There is no argument on this point.'

The look she cast at Shai was meant to murder.

What right had she to stand as judge over him?

'I never knew you were so troublesome, Mai! Now you've shamed me with your meddling.' The rush carried him on as the words spilled out. 'Very well, then. I'll tell Mountain to stop all the arrangements. She can do something to earn her keep, groom horses or dig trenches. No man will touch her again. Is that good enough?'

The hot, provocative words poured out of him because he hadn't control enough to keep them inside. His big brother Hari used to talk like this. That's what had gotten him led off in chains with the other recruits, so they were called, to fight for the Qin. Gone forever. Missing, but never forgotten.

Shai had been about thirteen that day, now six years past. He'd sworn to himself never to talk as much as his bold, bright, brilliant, beautiful, and much admired big brother Hari did. Talking got you noticed. Talking made people angry, it trapped them. And it made people cry, the ones who got left behind.

Now he couldn't stop himself.

'But if there are any problems, we don't have many resources to fall back on. You're not thinking about me, are you? I've got a longer road to travel than you do. You have a husband. You're protected. You've got everything you need. I'll have to leave this company, and then every zastra will count. I don't even know what land I'm going to. I could end up anywhere, dead by bandits, eaten by demons, sucked dry! Will you care then if I'm the one weeping at night?' Panting, he battled himself to a stop, shamed and embarrassed and still burning so hot.

'I'm sorry to have shamed you, Shai,' she said, and because it was Mai saying it, he knew it was sincere. It sounded so. She looked sorry. 'I'm sorry Father Mei and Grandmother never liked you, too, because it made you into a turtle, always hiding. I'm sorry I said you were just like the uncles, because you aren't. Just look, Shai. I know you see what others can't. Just look.'

'I will go now,' said Shai, sweating, furious, and his fingers in claws that he could not get to uncurl. The air made him dizzy; his head reeled. *I know you see what others can't.* In Kartu Town, they burned as witches any person who could see ghosts. Is that what she meant? Was she threatening him?

Captain Anji raised a hand to show he would make no objection to Shai's departure. His gaze seemed sympathetic, but who could tell? People were turning out so different than they first appeared.

Shai stalked away to find Mountain, who was standing beside a small fire next to the ruined house out of which a second man's noisy attentions serenaded them. This one hummed instead of grunted, a melody of rising arousal: Hmm. Heh. Hoo. Heh. Hmm. Mountain had meat on a stick, roasting it to feed the three men waiting their turn.

'That's the end of it, Mountain. No more hiring out Cornflower.'

'But Master Shai! These men have already paid handsomely.' He shook a pouch; it jingled merrily. Leaning closer, he whispered, 'It wouldn't do to anger them.'

Hmm. Hmm! Hoo! Heh! Heh! Hhhhh!

'Enough! No more of this, Mountain. She'll have to earn her keep some other way, but there's to be no more hiring her out. Do you understand?'

Mountain stared at him as if he had turned into a demon. He dropped to one knee and lowered his gaze to stare at Shai's feet. 'No need to shout to make this one's ears burn, Master. I hear what you have said. I can see you have changed your mind. There will be no more of these arrangements.'

'No more!'

It was dark, so he went to his tent and lay down on the blankets Mountain had unrolled. The temperature at night was chilly, but he wasn't cold. Nor could he sleep. As he lay there, his legs began to stiffen up, his thighs felt as though red-hot pokers were pressing in and out to torment him; his buttocks ached and his back was so sore it hurt to shift. It was no better here than it had been in Kartu Town! With a grimace, he got to his knees and crawled to the entrance, pushing aside the flap. The tent opened to the west. It was late. The camp was quiet, bathed by the last light of half moon, which almost touched the western horizon. Did the demons rope the moon every night, as the old stories claimed, and let it escape every morning?

Where were they going, truly? Would Captain Anji deal fairly with them? Or would he rob Shai of his money and abandon Mai in the wilderness?

Will I ever find Hari's remains? And if I do, will I have to go back?

He heard a sound like the tickle of mice scrabbling on dirt. He leaned farther out of the tent. Cornflower had curled up to sleep on the dirt against one side of his tent, huddled there as though the canvas might give her shelter. She had pillowed her head on one arm, and her face happened to be turned toward him. Her eyes were shut. The moonlight spilled across her face, washing it so pale that he knew Captain Anji was right. She was demon's get, no matter what the holy man had said. Obviously the holy man had been mistaken or in the pay of the merchant trying to sell her. No real person had hair that pale gold color, or eyes that blue.

At first he thought she was sleeping because she lay so quietly, but the night-veiled camp was utterly still, the only sound the footfall of a sentry's shifting. The tickling mouse sound was her breathing, almost swallowed within her. The glitter of moonlight on her face came not from magic but from tears.

Did it matter that she wept? Slaves were like ghosts; they didn't count as living people. They had lost their families and their honor. They had lost, and others had claimed their lives. That was the way of the world.

So Father Mei would say.

He crawled back in and lay down on his back, but still he couldn't sleep. He couldn't stop thinking about Cornflower, about her tears. Maybe the demons had won the skirmish after all. Maybe they had only pretended to flee, but their souls had flown into camp and brought with them the wind that sometimes spills down out of Spirit Gate to unsettle the world of the living with the sorrows of the dead.

11

Mai waited in silence. She heard Shai yelling; she heard the discontented muttering of the Qin soldiers as O'eki, which was his real name even though Father Mei had renamed him Mountain, returned their money. Captain Anji listened with no sign of agitation. He seemed ready to stand here all night. A servant came to stoke the fire with two dried dung patties, then retreated. Priya said nothing, but Mai heard her even breathing.

It was all gone, every part of the round of life in Kartu Town to which she had become accustomed and to which she had accustomed herself. It was dead. In a way she had passed through Spirit Gate and gained a new kind of freedom, and although she remained silent, her heart was pounding and her throat was full, her eyes brimming, her cheeks flushed. There was exhilaration, of a kind. She had made a demand, used her authority. But, oh, she feared what might come next.

Finally, as the soldiers settled down for the night and the ring of sentries paced out their places, Anji spoke to her.

'Is there anything I should know about this slave? I am troubled by the disruption she has already brought down on my troop. I wonder if those demons who attacked us came looking for her, knowing she is one of them.'

She gathered her courage. If she did not defend Cornflower, no one would. No one ever had in the Mei compound. 'She's not a demon.'

'Is she not? With that coloring? Have you seen the western demons, Mai? The ones who live in the country beyond the lands ruled by the Qin? Most of these demons are pale-haired and blue-eyed, just like her. That's where she must have come from, out of the west.'

'If they are demons, how can they be taken as slaves?'

'They can be captured. Or, if she's demon's get, then her dam might be human born. Her mother might have sold her, to be rid of the shame. Where did she come from?'

'The marketplace in Kartu Town, about two years ago. My father said he bought her to appease Uncle, the one who is dead now, but he also bought her because he lusted after her himself. All the uncles did, all but Shai. Shai never touched her. Everyone suspected she poisoned my uncle, the one who is dead now. He did die horribly, so all the wives wanted to be rid of her. That, and because they were jealous of her. All of the uncles used her. Some nights they would take turns. They couldn't keep away from her. My mother wanted her out of the house but the men couldn't bear to let her go.'

The captain folded his arms across his chest and stared thoughtfully at the fire. 'It sounds like she's demon's get. They have that pull on men.'

'Do demons weep when they are sad?'

'I don't know.'

'It was cruel of my father to send her with Shai.'

'Why?'

'Because Shai never got anything he wanted but plenty he did not want. Because he's unlucky already, being a seventh son'

'A seventh son?' To Mai's amazement, the captain looked startled, and his startlement gratified her strangely. Warmly. She hadn't thought she could surprise a man like him. 'Does he have the second sight? Can he see ghosts? Seventh sons can always see ghosts.'

'You must ask him yourself. I don't own his secrets, if he has any.'

He smiled, and she realized, startled herself, that he knew she had already answered him. 'The Qin don't usually see ghosts. There aren't many ghosts out in the ancestors' lands. But I see them all along the Golden Road. Do you see ghosts, Mai?'

His comment and question punched all the air from her. She could only mouth the word 'no,' stunned at his casual admission. Shai would never ever admit he saw ghosts. She had figured it out by herself because of certain inconsistencies that cropped up now and again when he spoke.

'It's bad luck to see ghosts,' she murmured. 'In Kartu, people who see ghosts are burned as witches or banished from town, which is the same as being burned, because you'll die anyway.'

'It's bad luck to see a swarm of bandits riding down on your position when they have twice as many armed men as you do, but at least you're forewarned. Since ghosts are there, isn't it better to be able to see them than to wish you were blind?'

'Do the Qin burn witches?'

'There are no witches among the Qin. Some among the clans have power to see into the spirit world. A few have climbed the axis of heaven and returned to tell of it.'

'What is the axis of heaven?'

'It's the center-pole of the world. Just as in a tent.'

'I've never been in a tent.'

'Ah. Of course not. When we set up our wedding tent, I will show you.'

She thought of Cornflower's silence as that Qin soldier had worked at her, hump hump hump. 'When will we set up our wedding tent?'

'I went to get this,' he replied, as if he hadn't heard her. She bit her lower lip, noticed she was doing so, and relaxed her mouth shut as he went on. Be like finest silk, Grandmother had told her, be smooth and without blemish. 'Just before the demons attacked us. It's the custom among the Qin for a man to give his bride a black banner with her clan's sigil on it before they race.'

'Race?'

'Race, on horseback. If he can catch her, then he has earned the right to marry her. He captures her banner. I had this made.'

Mai watched as the captain unfolded cloth. He had a neat, efficient way of moving without being fussy. He was a man at home with himself, not self-conscious but not self-effacing either. Perfectly balanced.

Unfurled, the banner extended from fingertip to fingertip. It was all black silk except for a few odd silver highlights sewn into the cloth, and it took a moment for her to accustom herself to the fire's light and by its glow see that those silver highlights depicted an eye and strands of hair. The banner was embroidered with the sigil of the Mei clan, the running wolf created in precise detail but in black, on black, so the wolf wasn't easily seen. Such a banner couldn't be finished overnight or in one week. Such a banner had to be planned well in advance, and even a Qin officer would pay dearly to hire a master craftsman able to complete it.

When she did not speak, could not speak, he carried on. 'I have wondered why sheepherders chose the wolf as their clan sigil.'

She found all her breath caught in her lungs, and she let it all out in one gust and after that discovered she could talk, at least to answer the implied question. 'Because our fortune rests on sheepherding, we bind the spirits of wolves into rings to protect our herds and make our family prosper.'

'A wise precaution. Here.' He stepped forward. 'Take it, Mai. It's our custom.'

She extended her hands, heart racing as he came closer. Once he draped the banner over her open arms he advanced no further but studied her with a serious gaze, open and clear. He really did have lovely eyes, and lashes any woman would envy.

'You are not a Qin woman, and I am not a Kartu man, so we will have to come to some accommodation.'

'We will?' Her cheeks were so hot! Yet she couldn't stop seeing Cornflower lying there all limp, like a corpse, eyes staring sightlessly at the heavens.

His gaze held hers. She knew better than to look away or shrink back. She had a good instinct for people, honed in the marketplace. This man wanted flirting with his commerce, while this other preferred to be treated with reserve and respect; this woman wanted a friendly ear and this other a spirited and not entirely amiable disagreement over the price of windfall peaches. Captain Anji did not want a wife who cowered before him, so she would not be such a wife. He encouraged her to speak forthrightly, so she did. He hadn't even been angry when she had scolded Shai. He was not like Father Mei at all, and maybe that was what she had feared more than anything else in the world: that she would end up married to a man just like her father.

'I married you not just because you are beautiful, as this was obvious to any man with eyes, but also because of your graceful manner and because you observe beyond the surface of things. And because you overcharged me for those almonds.'

She flushed.

He smiled. 'Since my first wife is now dead, I could suit myself with my second marriage. However, the last thing I promised my mother, fifteen years ago, is that I would take no woman into my bed unless she possessed the rights given to Qin women upon marriage to a man of the Qin. I promised I would treat no woman as my father treated her. For although they were married according to the laws of his land, she had no more rights than a slave concubine. This banner is my promise to you. When you fly that banner, then I will know that I am welcome in the marriage bed. I will not force myself on you, and I do not expect you to invite me until you are ready.'

He flicked a lock of hair away from one eye, and walked away out of the fire's ring of light. A shadow met him; Mai recognized Chief Tuvi's stocky form and sharp gestures. They vanished into the night, heading toward the sentry lines.

Mai stared after him, mouth aflop like that of a fish tossed out of water. He had known market prices! She didn't know whether to laugh or to berate herself for foolishness. She had been complimented many times, even for her skill at bargaining, but no man had ever complimented her for seeing 'beyond the surface of things.' It was one of the ways she had kept up her garden of tranquillity. By learning to see beyond the moods and day-to-day comments of her customers and of her family, she had discovered that most of the anger or envy or sorrow or pain we bleed onto ourselves is just a wound cut into our own selves. The blood of another that splashes onto you can be washed off. You only suffer, as Priya would say, when your own injuries hurt you.

'He is not what I expected,' said Priya softly.

'What did you expect?'

'Women are like silk. The finest cloth is reserved for the noblest man.'

'Or for the Merciful One and Her avatars and temples.'

'How soon will you invite him into the marriage bed, Mistress?'

'Do you think he meant what he said? That I could choose the time?'

'I don't know. Yet why else would he speak so? He can have you when he wants. It is clear he desires you.'

'Does he?'

Priya laughed, a liberty she took only with Mai, certainly never with any of the aunts. 'You are wise but innocent, Mistress. He feels a strong desire toward you. I don't know why he does not take what is now his to possess. Most men would. Perhaps like us he follows the teachings of the Merciful One and understands it is better not to let his desires overmaster him.'

'There was no other reason for him to marry me but desire. The Mei clan is not an important one. We have no particular wealth. We bring him no advantage even if he weren't Qin, but he is, so an alliance with Father Mei brings him nothing at all. He said so himself.'

'Why do you fret so, Mistress?'

'I fret because I don't know where we're going, or what will happen when we get there.'

'It is out of your hands, Mistress. He has given you the banner. Do not wait too long. But do not offer him what he desires too quickly, either.'

'Why must each choice be weighed as in a game of spirals? Is there no honesty to be had between men and women?'

'Honesty is a pearl, Mistress: rare and precious. Walk this path cautiously.'

'Do you remember that song about the bandit prince and the gold merchant's daughter?' She sang the refrain. "Your eyes speak to me of love, but I remain silent. It may be I am in love, but how can I know?" The words always made her cry. She wiped her eyes, wondering how foolish she looked. 'I just want to be happy, Priya.'

But when Mai looked into her face, she thought Priya looked sad, and even a trifle anxious.

The slave rested a hand on Mai's shoulder. 'Be careful, Mistress. The gods may hear your wish and grant it.'

At dawn, Shai refused to speak to her as he tottered to his horse. He was so angry! Yet if he would not comfort her, hold her up when she was frightened, then who would? Priya coaxed her with soothing words. Captain Anji brought her a placid mare, helped her mount, and rode beside her. At the steady pace they took it wasn't so difficult, since she didn't need to do anything but hang on. Midway through the morning, with the sun well up above above the dusty horizon, he kindly suggested she rest in the palanquin.

'You must work up slowly and gain confidence,' he said.

Her thighs and back were already hurting from the saddle, so she agreed, but sitting in the palanquin, isolated, closed off, gave her time to fret. Fear is a demon, and will gnaw. Where were they going? What would they find there? What would happen to her? Over and over, with no respite, not even Priya to chant prayers to the Merciful One that she could then repeat.

By the time they stopped in the worst heat of the day, midafternoon, at the posting station, her stomach ached and her throat burned. As night swept down she became really sick, emptying her stomach and bowels and then panting in silence as Priya sat beside her with a cool cloth to wipe sweat from her face and neck.

'I don't want him to see me,' Mai whispered. 'He won't want me now. He'll abandon me.'

He did come, but only to assure himself that she was resting and that the proper charms were hung around the room. The next day they remained at the posting station. Mai was confined to a cool chamber with immensely thick walls that muffled the world beyond. The room was quite plain, with only four beds and one chest and a dirt floor. Priya spent the hours singing the blessings for health and ease from worry. Captain Anji came by three times but only to speak, outside the door, with Priya. No one else, not even Shai, came to see her. And why should they? She had nothing left in her stomach yet liquids still made her heave. Still, as evening fell, she began to feel less wretched and was able to sleep fitfully.

Before dawn Priya woke her. 'The captain says we must continue on, Mistress. Can you move?'

'I will,' croaked Mai.

Anything was better than being left behind. She got down a little yellow sword-fruit and a sip of spring water brought down from the northern mountains by a party of the captain's soldiers who had gone to look for a missing patrol. Or so Priya said. Mai was still woozy as O'eki helped her into the palanquin. Over in the courtyard, Shai was laughing with Chief Tuvi. Quite at home with the Qin now! She caught a glimpse of Cornflower's pale hair as the company gathered for the march; then the curtains closed around her. With a sigh, she lay down, bracing herself for an uncomfortable day.

She did endure it, and the next day as well as they traveled at the steady pace which was evidently their usual speed, not too fast but eating ground because they never flagged. She was weak, but as long as she ate only bland, boiled foods, and those sparingly, she managed. They stopped the first night in the garrison fort beside a town but on the other nights at posting stations. Most of these were little more than a mud-brick bastion surrounded by a thorn corral within which the men set their tents or simply slept on the dirt. She rested and slept in the palanquin. Shai avoided her. He seemed to spend most of his time with a group of young soldiers who were teaching him to use both sword and spear. She was lonely for Shai's company, but she wouldn't go back on what she said. She saw that awful scene in her mind's eye every single day, every time she noticed Cornflower walking through camp on some errand or chore. Men watched the slave, and almost every one of them licked his lips or scratched his crotch when Cornflower passed by, but no man touched her.

Shai must walk his own road. She had Captain Anji. Each day in the hour between the time they halted and when it became too dark, he read to her from his scroll, which contained the thirty-seven threads of the Merciful One as related to certain teachers commonly known as the Ones Who Unveil the Treasure.

'Can you read?' he asked her.

'No. I can do sums. Only scholars learn to read. Are you a scholar?'

She thought his smile wistful, or cloaked. 'No, I'm an army officer. I can teach you to read if you wish to learn, but you'll have to learn one of the two languages I can read in.'

She leaned closer to him to study the letters on the scroll. 'Are those markings not the language we speak together?'

'They are not. The var forbids his officers to learn the writing of arkinga, which is also the speech used by traders. Everyone speaks it up and down the Golden Road and in the empire. In the old days, there was no writing at all among the Qin. The letters for arkinga were taken from those used by the traders, together with many of their words. Now only the var's court officials are allowed to set down contracts and letters.'

It was true that the holy masters who served the Merciful One in

Kartu Town had memorized the discourses and blessings, and never carried scrolls. It hadn't occurred to Mai to wonder if they could read as did the scholars who ran the var's law courts.

Unexpectedly, the captain looked past her to Priya. 'Can you read this scroll?'

The silence made Mai nervous. She turned to look up at her slave, whom she trusted perhaps more than any other person in the world. That bland, pleasant face had not changed expression, but a single tear slid down Priya's cheek.

'I can read it,' she said quietly.

'How can you?' cried Mai. 'Are you a scholar, Priya? How could you not have told me?'

Priya did not answer. She was as old as Mai's mother, a robust woman of no particular beauty but a core of inner strength and a well of calm that had always seemed bottomless. Mai admired her. It was true that her complexion was so similar to a dark red clay that Father Mei had named her Clay, but Mai's persistent and public use of her real name had won the day in this single case. She was the only slave in the Mei clan called by her free name.

'The holy women of the Yari are taught to read,' said Captain Anji. 'It is part of their worship. They read the thirty-seven discourses and the eighty-nine narratives from dawn to dusk all the way through the cycle and then begin again. Is that not so?'

'It is so,' murmured Priya.

'How are you come here?' he asked.

Mai stared, caught speechless. Mai had picked her off the auction block seven years ago, and in all that time Priya had never revealed any part of her past!

'Raiders came to our holy pavilion,' she said simply. 'They killed some and marched the rest of us away, north over the pass. The mountains are so high that half the slaves driven across the pass died with blood foaming on their lips. We kept marching north until we came to the Golden Road. I was sold in Kartu Town. I survived because of the teachings of the Merciful One. Death is nothing to fear.'

'No,' he agreed. 'We are all dead men.'

'You don't look like a ghost!' cried Mai more strongly than she intended, still stinging from the realization that she didn't know as much as she thought she did. Then she took a breath. How stupid that comment sounded! And bad luck, too, maybe.

As he began to smile, she recalled bitterly how Girish had belittled her and how the family so often patted her head and called her 'little orchid' and 'plum blossom' as though she were no smarter than a flower. He saw the shift, perhaps even the anger, in her expression. She had betrayed herself. His smile faded as his gaze grew more intent. 'I don't mean that I'm dead, only that we will all pass Spirit Gate in time. There is no point in fearing what is inevitable.'

'I feel that I have passed Spirit Gate already,' she said. 'I am not what I was before, nor do I want to be.'

Priya bent and took her hand. 'Any great change is a Spirit Gate, plum blossom,' she said fondly, and in her mouth the pet name did not cloy. 'I crossed through a gate when I was stolen from my land and my people. I am dead now.'

'Would you go back, if you could?' Mai asked, fearing to hear the answer.

Priya looked at Captain Anji, and they seemed to speak to each other in a language Mai did not understand, one that made her feel terribly young and naive. 'The road that passes under Spirit Gate runs in only one direction, Mistress. There is no going back.'

Because there was no going back, she had to go forward never knowing where the path led. By the tenth morning after they had left Kartu Town she was able to mount her horse and ride for half the day before the effort tired her. That night they camped within the ruins of a fortress so old that the wind had sculpted it into a complex beast half buried in the sand. A constant whistle sounded from the many holes where the wind sang through, changing only in pitch and loudness. They set up tents in the middle of the ruin for some relief from the sting of sand. Chief Tuvi made a shelter for himself in one corner and to Mai's surprise brought out a one-stringed musical instrument from a long leather case which she had all along thought contained a hunting bow. Yet the case proved to carry a slender instrument as well, which he used to draw music out of the string. A few of the men carried rattles or bells. With the wind as accompaniment, they played and took turns singing.

The bay mare rode down to me from out of the sky
She rode down to me from out of the sky.
A celestial horse! Best among horses!
The lord wants her for himself.
But I'll keep her for myself.
A celestial horse! Best among horses!
With the bay mare I rode east along the Golden Road.
This is what I saw along the Golden Road.

This particular song went on for a long time, with men adding verses as they pleased, describing sights they had seen in their journeys, north into the dry hills or south into the stone desert, west into demon country or east along the Golden Road. Mai sat on her divan beside Captain Anji on his stool. She sipped at yoghurt.

When she bent toward him, he, alert to her least movement, turned to smile at her.

'Why are you called east?' she asked daringly, aware of how close he was. If she swayed forward, she could kiss him!

He raised an eyebrow, always a sign of amusement in him. 'I can't say.'

'You can't say because you don't know or because you aren't allowed to tell?'

He laughed. She flushed, embarrassed, pleased, excited, too many feelings thrown together. It made her giddy, and she withdrew – just a little – to give herself breathing space.

'Shai,' he said in a louder voice, still looking at her. 'Come here.'

Shai had been outside sparring with his weapons partners. When he appeared, sweating and dirty, he sat on a stool beside the captain. Anji signaled for the music to stop. The men put away their rattles, and Chief Tuvi sealed up his instrument in its case.

'We are come about halfway,' said the captain, 'the easy part of the road. This place was a town once, on an oasis, but the desert creeps close. The demons are hungry. They've eaten many towns that used to stand here, like this one, and even swallowed the old wells. We'll finish filling our water pouches tonight and press on as soon as the moon rises. We'll rest from midday to a hand's breadth before sunset and travel at night and into the morning. You'll be thirsty but must not drink more than your share. Any who fall behind will be left. Beware demons. They hunt here.'

He stood. 'Rest now. You'll hear the chief's whistle when it's time to ride out.'

The men dispersed, but he stopped Mai as she rose. It was the third time he had ever touched her. His fingers on her wrist were cool, his grip light. 'You must ride, Mai'ili. The slaves cannot carry you on this part of the road. We'll break the palanquin down and bring it as baggage as far as we can. But you must ride now. Do you understand?'

She looked at him carefully. His eyes seemed more lovely to her than they had eleven days ago when they had stood at the law court while the proper contracts were signed and sealed. He was, just slightly, breathing to an unsteady beat as he watched her. His lips were parted just enough that she might slip the tip of her little finger between them, and as if he had heard her speak such words, as if she had actually touched him so intimately, he flushed along his dark cheeks but did not release her.

'Will you leave me behind if I falter?' she asked.

A peculiar expression passed swiftly across his face: pain or anger or a smothered laugh. Something deeper and more complicated.

'You hide yourself,' she said, bolder now. 'Let me see you.'

It was gone, fled as if on the wind. He smiled with that mild look of amusement he often wore. 'You need only ask,' he murmured, and she was burning, all a-tumble, overmatched.

Mercifully, he released her.

She slipped inside the palanquin, lay down on the wool batting, one last time. But she could not sleep. He'd not answered her question, and by not answering, he *had* answered.

He will leave me behind, if he must. He does not love me.

Yet her wrist burned where he had touched her. She had seen the light in his face, the flush in his cheeks. The story was still being told. Anything might come next. Was this not the truth of life, that until we pass beyond Spirit Gate we live always on the edge between desire and loss, joy and pain, necessity and regret?

Only as Priya sang to her, rubbing her shoulders and back, did she finally relax and sleep.

12

The company rode on at moonrise.

'The locals call this stretch of wasteland the Wailing Sands,' said Chief Tuvi to Shai. 'Demons roam here. If you hear your relatives calling to you from the desert, don't follow their voices. That's how they trick people into wandering out to where they can eat them.'

Shai laughed bitterly. 'I wouldn't follow my relatives anyway, if they called to me.'

'They treated you badly?' Tuvi was a pragmatic man, entirely devoted to Captain Anji because of kinship ties Shai hadn't yet puzzled out. 'If you aren't loyal to your kinfolk then they won't be loyal to you in return.'

'I'm the youngest. There were plenty of other sons. I was just an extra mouth to feed.'

'An extra mouth? No Qin commander scorns another warrior. Your people aren't fighters but farmers. That might account for it. Only so much land to divide up between you. Lots of quarreling, I expect.'

'Isn't there quarreling among Qin brothers?'

'Why?' He gestured toward the road ahead, tracks cutting across a wide expanse of dry land with little more than tumble brush and rocks strewn across it. The hills rose terrible and dark to the north, and to the south lay the wild lands where the desert demons roamed. 'There's plenty of land where my people come from. Good land, lots of pasture. If brothers quarrel, then the one can pack up his tent and herd his flocks elsewhere. But quarreling brothers are like single arrows, easy to snap in two. It's only when they hold to each other that they are strong.'

'The Qin are strong.'

'We are. The var's father united his clan and his clan united the Qin.'

'What will do you in the east?'

Tuvi smiled without taking his gaze off the road. The moonlight blended with the dusty color of the land to give the night a ghostly feel, as though spirits hovered everywhere except along the sandy track they followed. 'We do what our commander tells us to do.'

'Will you return to Kartu Town?'

'That place? I hope not. We've been promoted, which is no more than Captain Anji deserves, after everything he's been through.'

'What happened to his first wife?'

Chief Tuvi looked at him, then bent his gaze back to the road.

'Sorry,' said Shai hastily.

The chief grunted.

'Have I offended?'

The horses ahead of them kicked up so much dust that Shai had to wipe his eyes, but he was comfortable enough on horseback now that he could ride with reins only, not clutching the saddle to keep from falling off. For a long time Tuvi said nothing, and Shai knew he'd gone too far. The Qin were friendly enough, so it was easy to forget that they could kill him if they wished, simply for one wrong word.

But the chief did nothing, examining the landscape with a gaze that never stopped long on any one landmark. Shai had never seen him get angry, but he'd seen him whip a soldier for taking more than his share of rations.

'You talk a lot,' said Tuvi at last. 'There are troubles in the west. The grass demons keep pushing east into lands we've always used as pasture. We need a strong var, and we need other things in order to fight them. We've horses to trade to the Sirniakan Empire east of here, and to Yari down south, and even the Vidi over the Sky Pass. Hu! A man can't breathe up so high, they say.'

'The merchants say the Sirniakan Empire is as broad as the desert, but rich and green. They make silk there, and that parasol my brother gave to Mai last year. Good spices, too. The merchants who travel that way value our hill-fed wool for trade. They say the empire is the greatest and most powerful of all kingdoms.'

'Any kingdom is only as strong as its king. We'll see. Look there.'

Tuvi had better night vision, so it took Shai a while to realize that the shadow the chief was pointing toward was a post. A skeleton dangled from it. Bones murmured as wind stirred them. Someone had tied it together with wire and string, to give it a haunting look. Skeletons didn't scare him. They were as empty as the stones that littered the land, and this skeleton's ghost had long since passed out of the world. Maybe that man, like Shai, had wandered far from home. He mumbled a blessing to the Merciful One, praying that the dead man's soul had felt the breath of mercy before death.

'That skeleton was here last time I rode this way,' said the chief. 'It marks the edge of the stone lands.'

'Why are they called the stone lands?'

Tuvi smiled.

By dawn, they were riding through the most desolate land imaginable, flat on all sides except where the northern hills rose off to their left, too far away for the heights to bring the relief of wind and in any case obscured by a haze rising off the desert. Already, as the sun pressed up over the horizon, it was hot. The red dust stung eyes and lips. The Qin soldiers wrapped cloth around their faces, leaving only their eyes visible, so Shai followed suit. He rode with the last group of riders, a dozen tailmen including the one called Chaji, who had been first to take up Mountain's offer. Ahead, Cornflower plodded stolidly along with the other slaves, hanging to the back, away from Mountain.

Nothing grew here. There were not even sand dunes; only these stony flats that went on and on. The sun rose higher and baked them. They kept on at a steady pace. Near midday, Chief Tuvi called a halt beside a bold outcropping of rock that thrust right up out of the earth and rose to a height of five or six men standing one atop the next.

The horses were watered. The men waited in line for their own ration of water, poured by Mai's hand. Captain Anji stood beside her but said nothing as the men came forward one by one. Mai's eye was sure and practiced; each bowlful looked exactly the same, no man favored with more or scanted with less. Shai had to wait his turn with the others. He came after the scouts but before the tailmen and the slaves. Mai offered him a sweet smile, like an apology for the scolding she'd given him days earlier, and he tried to speak, to thank her, but his throat was parched. He gulped down the sweet water with a sigh, but it barely cooled his throat.

'Move along,' said Anji. 'More behind you.'

The horses were given what little true shade skirted the northeastern side of the outcropping, while the soldiers made makeshift

tents out of tunics and took relief from the sun in that way.
Mountain made a clever lean-to under which Shai could shelter. He
dozed on a blanket. He dreamed, but all he saw was hills rising and
falling below him as light and shadow shifted over trees, open meadows, a winding river, and trees again, as if he flew above the land
like a bird.

Hari's bold voice haunted his dream.

'I'm of no use to you. Release me. Let me die.'

*'Only when you have tracked down the man wearing the cloak of
sky, and brought him to me.'*

He started awake to find Cornflower staring at him with such a
peculiar expression that he shuddered. Those demon-blue eyes suddenly scared him. He sat up.

'You stay here. I'm going to check on Mai.'

Out of the shade of the lean-to, the sun's light struck. The land
shimmered. It was so hot his lips cracked. Likely they'd be bleeding
by tomorrow if they didn't get more water. He staggered into the
shade cast by the outcropping. Mercifully, there was more shade
now as the afternoon lengthened, but even so soldiers were offering
water to the horses again. Precious water was not to be wasted on
men, who without their mounts would certainly die and who could
in any case drink blood from their horses when necessary.

Mai was asleep right up against the rock, curled on her side,
head pillowed on a rolled-up blanket. Even in sleep she was lovely;
a little thin and pale because of the rigors of the journey, but
unwilted. Captain Anji sat against the rock beside her, not touching her but with a proprietary interest in her presence. His eyes
were closed, and he breathed steadily and slowly as though asleep,
but his eyes snapped open as Shai neared. He put two fingers to his
lips: Silence.

Quietly he rose and gestured for Shai to follow. His faithful attendants, Sengel and Toughid, padded after them, staying at a discreet
distance. They walked to the edge of the shade, a cruel line between
shelter and death.

Anji indicated the camp. 'Is there a problem?'

'No. I was just wondering how Mai is holding up.'

'She is stronger than she looks. It's hard to see because her beauty
blinds, like this sun.'

The sun did blind. The heat made a man light-headed. 'Do you love her?'

'You talk too much.' Anji wiped sweat off his brow with the back of a hand. 'If there is nothing else, I'm going to rest again. I recommend you do as well.' But as he turned away, he paused, squinting south into the dusty haze.

A scout stationed atop the rock whistled thrice. Men scrambled up, weapons drawn, bows ready. Many fell back to stand shoulder-to-shoulder, while others ran for the horses.

'Hold!' cried Anji.

Chief Tuvi echoed him. 'Hold! Hold!'

The wind moaning over the huge rock was the only sound. The horizon along the south glowered, all black.

'Sandstorm,' whispered Shai, washed with a rush of faintness. His legs buckled, but he caught his weight on the rock face beside him.

Tuvi was already giving orders as Anji strode away from the outcropping and, conferring with two scouts, tested the direction and strength of the wind. The soldiers shifted the herd around to the sun side of the rock, opposite the prevailing wind. The horses moved with restless vigor, stamping, neighing, mares nipping as geldings were forced in close. Tents were raised. Spears were thrust deep into the sand as supports for larger windbreaks of silk – as strong as steel, so it was said – and canvas. Some men clambered up into the outcropping itself to take refuge in holes and overhangs. The two wagons were tipped over and arranged in a square with cloth fastened over them, to protect the water and other supplies. Mai knelt, with Priya beside her, and crawled into the shelter of one of the wagons. Farther away, Mountain shepherded the slave bearers into the safety of a tent.

In the lee of the rock the wind wasn't as strong, so Shai circled, staying as close to the rock as he could, until he came to a low ridge, the tail of the outcrop, on which he could lean. He stared toward the south as the haze grew thicker and he began to breathe dust into his lungs. The old stories told of the zaril-dar, the black storm, that swallowed whole cities in a single night. As the wind rose in intensity he heard voices on the wind, calling to him.

'Shai! Shai!'

Ghosts always seemed to know his name.

'I don't know you,' he said into the wind, not fearing to speak out loud since no one was near enough to hear him. 'Why do you call for me? What do you want?'

'I am looking for my husband. Have you seen him?'

'I don't know your husband. I'm sorry.'

'Have you seen my sister? My lover? My child? Can you help me find the one who poisoned me . . . who abandoned me . . . who betrayed me . . . so I can get my revenge?'

'I can't help you,' he said to each in turn. 'You're dead.'

Their voices laughed and wept. They knew they were dead, but they were so angry; they just couldn't rest.

The wind had loosened his covering veil. He tightened it, but sand leaked in nevertheless. The light dimmed, died. He could barely see the outlines of the camp behind him, horses and men hiding behind cloth and inside wagons, hunkered down in the hope that the storm would not bury them. He was the only man visible.

'How bad is the storm?' he called as the ghosts swirled past him on the wind. 'Will it kill us, too?'

Some were kind. 'The heart of the storm lies south of here, where the demons walk. It's moving east and south, not north.'

Most laughed cruelly, pale forms teasing him as they flashed past. 'Dead! Dead! Dead!' they cried, as if in mockery of Ti. 'It will crawl right over you and eat you all! Hai! Hai! Hai! Unless you have magic to shift it. To survive, you must offer a sacrifice to the demons!'

So many ghosts! Had they all died out in this wasteland, like that skeleton hung from the post to mark the boundary of the Wailing Lands? Did spirits congregate here because of some innate quality in the land? Or were they, like he, only passing through?

Who was lying and who telling the truth?

'Shai! Can you hear me?' The old familiar, beloved voice came from so close, just at his shoulder.

'*Hari?*' He clutched at rock, almost falling. 'Hari! I can't see you!'

'Help me, Shai.' It moved away into the storm.

'You're dead.'

'Help me! Find my bones, Shai. Release me from this torment. Bring me home. I can't rest.'

He staggered along the ridge of rock, having to use it for support because of the battering wind. He could barely see an arm's length in front of his face. Wind pummeled him as he stumbled after it. 'Hari! Wait!'

Out of the storm, a solid figure emerged, and grabbed him. 'Shai!'

He'd not realized the wind screamed so loud that another's voice, even shouting, might sound like a whisper. This was no ghost, whose voices need not compete against earthly noise, but rather Captain Anji, materialized like a spirit out of the howling storm.

'Back to camp! If you wander out here, you'll die.'

'But I heard Hari – I've got to go—'

'Demons ride this wind. They're the ones tempting you. Come back!'

Shai was not weak. He had found solace in carpentry since he was a child whittling scraps into fantastic animals, and he fought now, breaking free of that grasp.

A white-skinned figure walked out there, moving into the black storm, unbowed by the terrible wind. The wind pressed her clothing hard against her front, revealing a woman's form. Her pale-gold, shining hair streamed like a banner, unbound, and it seemed that she had wings with the silver gossamer fineness of a moth's, dazzling as they rippled. Nay, those were not wings. That was cloth, a vast cloak driven by the wind, enveloping the pale figure, swallowing her, before he could see her face. He stepped toward her, drawn by a malevolent yearning.

'Wait!' he cried. 'Who are you?'

'Shai!' A hand caught his belt and tugged him backward. He strained for an instant against that grip, but Anji's will subdued him, as did the abrupt realization that he was half choking on all the sand filtered through the folds of cloth wound around his head. He stumbled in Anji's wake. The vision was lost. Demons walked abroad, beautiful and deadly. His heart was hollow, sucked dry.

Anji shoved him into the shelter of the wagons and crawled in after him. Within, the air was stifling, thick with dust but breathable. Men coughed. One lit a lamp.

'Ah, there you are, Captain,' shouted Chief Tuvi, who was holding the tiny lamp cupped in one palm. The light shrouded the cramped cavern made from carts and cloth. Wind thrummed in the canvas, rumbling like thunder.

Mai reached out, eyes wide. 'Shai. *Anji!*'

Anji crawled over to her. Before he could quite arrange himself cross-legged beside her, she threw her arms around him and buried her face in his chest, shaken but not weeping. Priya sat quietly, head bowed, lips moving in her singsong prayers, but if she was singing out loud the wind's howl drowned melody and words. Anji encircled Mai with one arm, leaving the other free near his knife. He shut his eyes, seeming content to endure the storm and even death in this pleasing manner.

Tuvi blew out the light.

The wind increased in pitch until the sound of it hurt. The spray of sand and dust and rocks was louder than a driving rain, obliterating everything until they huddled in a netherworld in which all substance was caught betwixt and between, neither air nor earth, neither day nor night, neither living nor dead. Shai couldn't even hear the ghosts, or perhaps the storm had scattered them.

The demons screamed, but silk was proof against their kind.

It was too hot and frightening to sleep although now and again he dozed off, only to jolt awake as whispers throttled him.

'*Beware the third blow . . . I betrayed her, but only after she betrayed the others. She betrayed all of us. And I aided her, out of fear. I cannot bear my shame any longer. Let the wind take me. Let this burden pass on to another . . .*'

Yet it was only the heat and sand stifling him, after all, and the close-packed bodies, and his parched throat.

In time the wind lessened and, at last, hours or days later, ceased.

When they dug themselves out and Chief Tuvi called roll, they had lost not one man or horse, although a few were having trouble breathing, and it was clear they would need more water and that soon.

'Not so bad,' said Chief Tuvi. 'The heart of the storm didn't pass over us. It stayed to the south.'

But Cornflower was gone, vanished entirely. Mountain had thought she had taken refuge with Priya and Mai; Priya had thought she was with Mountain and the nine bearers. Shai hadn't thought of her at all.

Captain Anji shaded his eyes to examine the red haze that blanketed the southwest. The sun was setting, although it couldn't be seen through the retreating storm. 'The demons took her,' he said.

Shai hid his tears.

13

All that next morning as they pushed eastward across the dusty flats, Mai thought obsessively of the feel of Anji's arm around her as the storm had raged. She had turned to him without thinking. He had the experience and foresight to shelter all of his people, and somehow that made their intimacy more precious by contrast. Her heart outraced her head. He was so strong. He was clever and imperturbable. He wasn't like anyone in the Mei clan, not at all. He had chosen *her*, out of all people.

Surely the heroine in the old songs had thought as many ridiculous things about the bandit prince she fell in love with!

She laughed and he, hearing her, turned with eyebrows raised as their horses plodded along. She blushed. How much more intense this feeling was even than the sun's punishing light! The old songs were silly and sentimental, but that didn't mean there wasn't a grain of diamond truth hidden in the sand.

By midday it was too hot to ride. Ahead of them the way was cut by rugged ground, and Chief Tuvi led them into a ravine formed by a dry riverbed. There was no surface water but there was shade to be had right up against the cliff face. The slaves set to work digging, but by the time they had got down a man's height, two of the slaves had fainted and there was still no water and not even muddy sludge. A third slave lay in the shade, clutching his stomach and moaning.

'May I go see what I can do, Mistress?' Priya asked. 'They will leave them behind if they're too weak to talk. It would be a terrible way to die. At least in a storm you die quickly.'

'Do you think so?' asked Mai. 'Do you think Cornflower is dead?'

'I hope so.'

Mai shuddered. Swallowed by sand, flesh scoured from bone by the screaming wind. Yet how much more terrible to be snatched and tormented by demons. 'She was so unhappy. Do you think she wanted to die?'

Priya's mouth twitched. Compassion, perhaps, might cause the lips to form that particular angle. 'You are the only one of your family who would ask that question, Mistress.'

The words made her uncomfortable; she was no champion of Cornflower. She'd turned her gaze away, just as the rest had. 'Go help those men.' The words came out more sharply than she'd intended, but Priya bowed and hurried away to the sick man.

Mai sat on a pillow in the shade of the cliff, sweating and tired but not exhausted. She hadn't had to walk, or dig. Down the ravine, soldiers offered their mounts water from cupped palms. Nearby, Anji and Tuvi consulted a pair of scouts.

'How bad is the road?' Anji was asking. 'Can we negotiate it in darkness?'

'We'll have a bit of moonlight. There's hills and dunes for the next two days or so before we get back to flatter country near to Mariha. That's if we don't lose the trail, and if that storm didn't wipe away the caravan markers.'

'How much of a risk?'

'Better to ride it during the day. But if we delay too long here and can't get more water, we'll lose horses first and then men.'

'Let me think on it.'

Anji walked over to stand beside her in the shade. For a while he thought, and she waited. In the marketplace, one learned patience. She felt comfortable with him and, indeed, relieved to be alive. The storm had shaken her. Truly, demons haunted the wilderness; that was why folk kept to their towns and didn't wander. Anji offered her a swig from a finely tooled leather bottle. The slap of rice wine, gone a little vinegary, burned her mouth and soared straight to her head.

'Hu!' She giggled. 'That makes me even more thirsty.'

'Thirst is a powerful goad,' he agreed, smiling. He had a particular way of looking sideways at her that made her shiver with anticipatory pleasure, but when she shivered like that she always, the next instant, thought of Cornflower's blank expression. Hump hump hump.

Enough of that! Cornflower was gone. Yet the image wouldn't flee and refused to be chased away.

'What are you thinking?' he asked abruptly. He'd never asked such a question before. Husbands didn't care what their wives thought. They didn't need to, so her mother and the aunts often told her.

She was taken aback, caught off guard. Lie, or be truthful?

She shook her head, impatient with herself. She had often held her tongue, but she'd never outright lied to anyone. 'I'm thinking of Cornflower. I—' After all, she could not go on. It was too intimate; it was too humiliating. He might misunderstand, or he might understand, which could be worse. Her cheeks were hot. She gritted her teeth, trying to untangle her thoughts and her tongue.

Sand pattered on the ground as the wind eddied, then died. It was a clear day, without haze, and the sky was as blue as Cornflower's eyes and as empty of joy.

'Her death, or her life?' he asked.

'Aren't they the same? She must have run out into the storm seeking her freedom. That would be her death. Her life . . .'

'You think she did not live well in your father's household?'

'How could anyone do so?' she asked bitterly. 'Used like that?'

'Was she beaten?'

'Not after Uncle, the one whose name we don't say, not since he died. The aunts wouldn't touch her. That was the strange thing. They wanted to be rid of her but they didn't hate her even though she had bewitched all the men.' None of the women had hated Cornflower. It was peculiar, when you thought of it. You expected women to be jealous in such a situation, but instead they had all pitied her while just as strongly wanting her gone. Their silence was their shame. 'They didn't hate her even though the men couldn't leave her alone. But she didn't bewitch *you*.' She wasn't sure how he would respond. It was a risky comment.

Anji wasn't a man who frowned much. He did so now, causing lines to crease his brow. 'No. She didn't bewitch me. I've seen demons face-to-face before. I know what they're capable of. Mai . . .'

He looked away from her, studying the red-brown horizon to the south, as if seeking storms. He wasn't shy, just considering his next words. He rubbed at his lower lip with a dirty thumb. Like all of them, he was astoundingly filthy, hands and face coated with grime, officer's tunic gone to a color that could not be described. She rubbed at her own hands as she waited, but the stuff was caked on.

She could feel sand in every most intimate crevice, and every time she blinked, her eyes stung from the residue.

'No,' he said firmly, to himself. And to her: 'It was nothing.'

'It was something.' She stared at her hands and then, with as much courage as she could muster, she looked at him, and stumbled on heedlessly. 'I saw her face when that man was on her. She just lay there. She looked like she was dead, all limp. There was nothing in her eyes or her expression. Nothing! Nothing! Nothing!' She burst into tears.

His mouth had become an 'o' of surprise. He rocked back on his heels as if struck. For ten gulped sobs – her sobs – he stared at her. It took him that long to collect himself, and maybe it was his surprise that soothed her crying, because she could suddenly swallow the rest of her tears and dry her eyes. Her cheeks were slimy with dirt and moisture.

'I need a bath,' she finished, and hiccoughed once.

He handed her the leather bottle, and she drained its contents in one slug and braced herself for the jolt as the alcohol hit.

'Mai.' The captain took one of her hands and looked at her closely. 'I am not those men. I never wanted Cornflower more than I wanted you. Never never never.' He had Ti's diction down perfectly.

She laughed, and hiccoughed again, and he released her hand and strode away toward Chief Tuvi. She wondered if it was better that he misunderstood her after all. She wondered what it was like to take a bath with a naked man, and if a man and woman might wash each other in all their secret places and be pleased to do so, for of course she and Ti had peeked at a certain book kept in one of the drawers of Father Mei's desk that had contained all kinds of drawings depicting what a man and a woman might do with each other. The uncles had looked at that book a lot, and then afterward padded down the hall to the slave barracks.

She wondered why Cornflower had vanished during that terrible storm. Could demons die? And if so, what awaited them beyond Spirit Gate?

'Mistress?' Priya returned, O'eki limping beside her.

'I hope you are not hurt?' Panic flared.

'Just sore, Mistress.' The big man slipped a hand inside one sleeve and drew out three small items, which he offered to her.

She took them without thinking and studied them with confusion: three tiny beaded nets, the kind of gaudy cheap ornament women used to tie off the ends of braids. 'What are these? They're very colorful.'

'Cornflower wore them,' said Priya. 'She always wore her hair in a trident braid. These were hers, the only thing she possessed.'

Mai shivered, wondering if ghosts could reach out through the material goods they had left behind to throttle those they had hated during their lifetime. Yet if that were so, all of Uncle Girish's little treasures would long since have poisoned the Mei clan, which still prospered. She looked up at O'eki. He had a broad face and dark eyes, no different from anyone else; it was only his unusual stature that set him apart. He'd come from the southwest, from an area conquered by the Mariha princes when he was a boy. He'd spent most of his life as a slave to the Mei clan, bought by Grandfather because of his size and placidity. But he wasn't stupid.

'How do you have these?'

'I found them. At dawn, just before we left that cursed place.'

'Where?' She glanced toward Captain Anji, but he was exploring the ravine, involved in an intense conversation with Chief Tuvi and the scouts. Tuvi was gesturing with expansive circles; Anji had his arms crossed, a skeptical frown on his face.

'Right up by the big rock where we were camping when the storm hit, Mistress. Just lying there, like she'd torn them off. Or they'd been torn off her.'

She closed her hand around them. The mystery of Cornflower's disappearance troubled her, and the evidence she held in her hand suggested that the story might be more complicated than it had at first seemed.

'What will you do with them, Mistress?' asked O'eki. 'I can sell them, if you please, at the next market.'

'No. I'll return them to Shai. What she had belongs to him.' She slid them into the pocket sewn into her sleeves. The expensive blue silk gown she had worn so proudly at leave-taking was soiled beyond repair. She had left her other silks closed in the chest in the hope they would survive the journey without being ruined. Unlike linen and wool, silk fought sand better. It might become dirty, wet, and stained, but sand could be shaken out because it couldn't get as much purchase in the smooth, tight weave.

The men had walked close enough that she could overhear them.

'It's too risky to ride this path at night!' Tuvi exclaimed, voice rising as his hands dropped to his side.

'If you're afraid, don't do it,' said Anji. 'But if you do it, don't be afraid. I'm more concerned about water and the heat than the road. We have lamps, and moonlight for part of the night. We'll depart a hand's span before sunset. I won't sit and wait for events to overtake me. There might be another storm. Best to move on. It always is.'

'So you would say!' said Tuvi with a laugh, but he made no more protests.

In late afternoon they made ready to leave. About a hand's span before sunset, they headed up the twisting path, riding swiftly until the light faded. Then, with the moon already in the sky, they dismounted and walked along the trail, such as it was, with Chief Tuvi and the scouts in the lead bearing lanterns.

'You can ride,' Anji said to Mai. 'I'll lead your horse.'

'No. I'll walk with the others.'

'Very well.' It was difficult to see his expression, whether he was pleased or irritated, and she didn't know him well enough to interpret his tone. 'But if you feel yourself tiring, you must ride.'

'Yes.'

They walked on, east – always east. It was slow going. The way was dim and the world shadowed, and she had no idea where they were or where they were going. Yet as long as she kept her gaze fixed on Captain Anji's straight back, as long as she glanced frequently at the track, gleaming slightly in the moonlight, she managed. They reached the crest of a barren hill and paused to survey the vast wilderness and the impossibly depthless sky. The stars burned each one as brightly as the chief's lamp. The heavens were a field of dense flames, each one the shard of a soul released from its earthly suffering, so the Merciful One taught. So many, without counting. The land on all sides was a ghost land, intangible under moonlight, like gauze and darkness. Only in the north was there any solidity, and that because the far horizon was black where mountains rose.

It was as if she had wandered into the landscape known in song, a place present on no map, reached by no true road, where the daily round of life had no meaning. She shivered.

'Are you cold?' Anji asked softly.

'No,' she whispered, afraid to speak in a normal voice. 'It's beautiful.'

'Ah.' Nothing more than his sigh.

Her cheeks blazed with heat. She reached and found his hand, surprising him as she twined her fingers between his. He did not speak, but his breathing shifted and quickened, as did hers.

Chief Tuvi whistled the advance.

'Oh!' she murmured, annoyed.

Anji chuckled, brought her hand up to his lips, turned it over, and kissed the inside of her wrist, then let go and set off again. She followed him, but with that brief kiss the night had come alive. The curl of wind teased her. The movement of his shoulders as he walked drew her on. Once he looked back over his shoulder and grinned, and she burned burned burned. They walked across the land in silence broken only by the jingle of harness, the fall of hooves and feet, and the occasional mutter of one of the soldiers to a comrade; broken by the many soft noises made by the desert, which seemed dead but was alive in a hundred hidden ways. The path was rugged, and twice they had to backtrack when the trail Tuvi picked led them into a dead end up a gulch, but they never faltered nor did any horse take a fall or man stumble.

As the moon set and it became too dark to keep moving, the chief picked out a sheltered overhang for a temporary camp.

'We'll rest here until just before dawn,' he told the soldiers. 'We'll move on again before dawn, and rest again during the heat of the day, and leave again before dusk. Any man who violates rations will be killed.'

They watered the horses and each drank his measured allotment before lying down to rest, careful not to disturb tufts of vegetation and scatters of rock that might shelter poisonous slumbering creatures. Shai sat with head on knees, arms wrapped around bent legs. She was still angry with him for the way he had treated Cornflower. Maybe if he had been nicer, the girl wouldn't have run into the storm. And yet, why cling to anger? There was no way to change what had happened. Poor Shai looked so miserable.

Mai went over. 'How are you holding up, Shai?'

He looked up. All she could see of his face was pallor. His voice scraped, dry and anguished. 'Will we ever come free of this place? Or will we be carried off by the demons as well?'

She touched him gently on the shoulder. 'Captain Anji knows what he's doing.'

'Does he?'

'Of course he does! How can you doubt him?'

'We've not been told where we're going. They tell us nothing at all. You're not scared? Not at all?'

'No,' she said. Then thought about it, hard, closely. No poisonous worm ate away at her insides. Her hands didn't tremble. She shook her head. 'No, I'm not afraid. We can trust Anji.'

The simple words, like a torch, led her footsteps to the long-awaited destination. She left Shai and found Priya settling down to sleep on stony ground. She knelt beside her. 'Priya! Hsst! Where's my chest?'

The slave sighed sleepily. 'The chest, Mistress? O'eki took it off the packhorse, over there, you see where the luggage is stacked. Mistress?'

'Go back to sleep.'

She found it more by feel than by sight, opened the mechanism that locked the clasp shut, and had just tipped up the lid a hand's span and reached inside when she heard him walk up behind her.

'Mai? You should be resting.'

Her breath caught in her chest. Her heart hammered. The silk slipped smoothly under her hands, cool and lovely. She caught hold of one edge and eased the banner out of the chest. It unfolded as it emerged, draping over her knees. Even in darkness, with only the stars to light them, the silver threads picking out the eye and mane of the black wolf shone, perfectly visible although there was no reason they ought to be.

There is never any reason for happiness. Yet it exists. It shines.

For an eternity he did not move: not to touch her, not to speak, not to glance around the camp and the soldiers and slaves and horses who surrounded them. At last, she let the lid close and the clasp catch. Its *snick* jolted him. He caught her hand and drew her upright with the banner caught under her left arm. Quickly, he led her through camp, pausing only to fish a rolled-up length of heavy cloth from his saddlebags.

'Captain?'

'Keep the camp quiet, Chief.'

'Hu!' said Tuvi, but he didn't laugh. Sengel and Toughid faded back toward camp, and Tuvi's form receded into the night, vanishing in the shadows that were everywhere, except in her heart.

They climbed out of sight of the camp to a bare swell of ground mounded among the many hidden clefts and river washes. The brilliant heavens were their roof, and the unrolled tent their bed. They were both filthy, and their kisses tasted of grit, but desire and the night wind cleansed them. The immensity of the empty lands sheltered them, who were alone in the whole wide world, no one else, not even ghosts or scorpions, daring to disturb them, they two, who were now one.

Such a small thing, really, to mean so much.

14

Two qualities Shai possessed in plenty: He had endurance, and a high tolerance for physical pain. Father Mei had never been able to beat the stubborn anger out of him. One quality he sorely lacked: He'd never gathered enough courage to stand up to his elder brothers. Not as Hari had. Bold Hari, best of brothers.

In the early-morning twilight as he trudged along at the rear of the company among the silent tailmen, his thoughts returned doggedly to the subjects he didn't want to think about: We're out of water. We're all going to die if we don't find water soon. Dead like Cornflower. No. Nothing to be done about that. If Hari is dead, then why didn't he pass Spirit Gate? Why is he still chained to earth?

With a stumble and a quiet, sad whuffling noise, a horse collapsed. The company halted. The grooms examined the horse, shook their heads. While life still breathed in it, they opened a vein in its shoulder and drained its blood. It was a salty brew, invigorating. Everyone got a swallow, even the slaves. When Mai drank, the blood stained her lips with red, like a cosmetic meant to beautify.

As the beast failed, and died, they made ready to move out.

'Aren't we going to butcher it?' Shai croaked. 'For the flesh?'

'Take too long, need water more, oasis ahead,' said Chaji, his voice cracked and ragged. Then he cackled. 'You can stay, fight the vultures and demons, if you want.'

His feet must rise and fall, rise and fall, but he was by no means the weakest. They all struggled. The bearers were strong men, but at length some were aided by the others; they refused to let any of their number falter and fall behind. Mai walked alongside Anji. Everyone walked, to spare the horses, who suffered most. Over the course of that morning, two more horses failed, and the blood of those horses gave strength to the living. Thus, Shai supposed, did demons feast on their victims, sucking the spirit out of them. Was that what had happened to Hari?

The sun rose higher, but the air changed. He felt it as a kiss on his cheeks, as an ache, an exhilaration, in his chest. Long before they could see it, the horses smelled it and pulled eagerly, anxious to move faster. The people inhaled its promise through nostrils and parched mouths.

Water.

Discipline held. They marched in good order into an isolated oasis guarded by a surly group of twenty Qin tailmen.

'How long will you stay here?' the chief of the garrison asked them as they filed in.

'Two days,' said Anji. 'We all need a rest and the horses must be well watered. There are a couple too weak to go on so we'll slaughter them and feast tonight. If you send a few men back on our trail, you'll find two dead horses, not too far, to add to the feast.' He walked away to where Mai was seated, washing her hands and face in water Priya had brought from the pond.

'At least we don't have to feed your men, just the horses,' grumbled the garrison chief. 'You don't know how hard it is keeping supplies out here!'

'The worst assignment,' laughed Tuvi, slapping the man on the shoulder. 'When I was a young lad just come to the army, I had a posting like this.'

'Did you?' replied the chief, whose frown curved upward at this companionable talk. 'We've enough to eat and drink. I think it's the boredom that kills you. All this rock and sand! No women and no pasture to admire!'

'Let me tell you about a posting that near did me in!'

The two men walked away, taking turns sucking at a pouch of an alcoholic brew, to make a circuit of the low fortifications that surrounded the well, the pool, and the scattering of vividly green trees and vegetation.

Shai waited his turn to drink with the rest of the men. The horses went first and so sullied the pool that what he drank tasted more like mud than water, but like the rest he made no complaint. Water was life. Life was better than death. He lay down in the shade of a frond tree and fell asleep at once.

'*Shai. Shai.*' Would Hari's ghost never leave him alone? It had been weeks since the day Anji had given Hari's wolf's-head ring to Father Mei, since Shai had touched that ring and sensed Hari's fate. Now it seemed that Hari, like Girish, meant to plague the only person who could still hear him.

'Shai. Wake up.'

The hand pressing against his chest had weight. It was insistent, plucking at his clothing.

'Eh. What? Mai!'

'Hush. Shh.' She displayed a yellow globe of fruit, twisted it so it split open, and showed him how to scoop out the seeds so he could eat the succulent flesh. As he ate, the juices dripping down his chin, she whispered, 'I'm still very angry about Cornflower. You treated her badly. But Shai, you're my uncle. We're kin. We can't fight like this. We have to hold together, don't you think?'

Hu! Who could resist Mai when she was in this mood? He could!

'I'm riding with the tailmen. Cornflower was my slave. You had no right to interfere.'

'Don't be so stubborn!'

'You don't want me anyway. Look at you, flying that Qin banner now. Don't think the others don't talk around me just because I'm not Qin. I know what it means.'

The blush on her cheeks brightened her. Even worn and exhausted, she had a shine that made the world a more pleasing place. No one could stay mad at her.

'Are you happy?' he muttered.

'Oh. Shai.'

She was happy.

He sighed. He grasped her hand with one of his own, now sticky with juice. 'We won't fight.'

'Good.' The plum-blossom softness vanished, and she bent close, fixing him with a gaze as sharp as that of any merchant bargaining hard in the marketplace. 'Listen, Shai. I may only have this one chance to tell you this. Do not breathe a word. Now that – well – now that – well—' She flushed. She hid a smile behind a hand. She giggled, shut her eyes, sighed heavily, smiled again, and finally sucked in a deep breath and fixed him with a remarkable glare. 'I asked. And he told me.'

'What?'

'What! Where we're going! It's because we're past the desert now. We can't possibly go back, or tell anyone.'

Or he offered knowledge as payment, thought Shai, but he said nothing.

'Anji is to be a general. He's been promoted. We're riding all the way to Tars Fort, on the eastern border between Mariha and the Sirniakan Empire. Anji will command the fort and an entire border garrison, an army, much larger than this small company. What do you think?'

The muddy water and sweet fruit churned uneasily in his stomach. He felt a little sick. 'Isn't the border a dangerous place to be? Now that the Qin have conquered the Mariha princedoms, that border lies right up against the most powerful and largest empire known. What if there's a war?'

'Why would there be a war?'

'Mai! Don't be stupid. Why do the Qin need an army and garrisons along the border if they don't think there'll be a fight? I would bet that the Mariha princes didn't think there was going to be a war twenty years ago, when the first Qin rode out of the west. The Mariha princes are all dead now.'

'The Qin can defeat the empire if they want to. Don't you think?'

'Now you are being stupid.'

Defending her husband, she looked positively fierce. 'It's no more than Anji deserves!'

'No. No. Of course not.' Indeed, Tuvi had told him as much, in almost the same words, although he thought it better not to mention this to Mai. 'He must be an important man, to be promoted to such an important position.'

Her anger faded, and she looked thoughtful instead. 'Yes. I suppose he must. I wonder who his kinfolk are. He's never told me.'

Shai squeezed her hand in warning. 'Be cautious of asking. Don't ask too much, too quickly.'

In that moment, as their gazes met, understanding flashed. She smiled, and a knot that had been tangling in his heart, eased.

'I'm not stupid, Shai.'

That connection still flowed between them. He glimpsed, then, how much it bothered her to be thought of that way. 'No, of course not. Of course not, Mai.' He saw, then, that he and the rest of the family might never have understood her at all, that he didn't know her, not really. She was a mystery. She had hidden herself well.

A shout interrupted them. 'Hai! Hai! Rider sighted!'

'I'd better go.' Mai let go of his hand and walked swiftly away.

Shai got up. A soldier waved his banner at the top of the watchtower. The tower was set about one hundred strides out from the old stone-built livestock wall that surrounded the oasis and its stone-built houses. The villagers had long since fled or been driven out, and now the tiny Qin garrison used the houses to store grain for scouts and long-distance travelers. A dusty rider trotted in toward the oasis from the east. Shai wasn't sure how long he had slept. Checking the angle of the sun, he noted that the sun's position hadn't changed appreciably; it still rode high overhead. Over with the other slaves, Mountain raised his big shoulders up and looked toward the gate. Priya lay beside her husband, head pillowed on arms, sleeping.

He looked around. Mai had joined Captain Anji and walked with him to the wall. Anji had a hand cupped under her elbow. Best not to disturb that pair. Instead, he trotted over to Chief Tuvi, who was reeling from the strong drink he'd shared with the other chief.

'Hu! Is that two men or one riding in?'

'Just one, Chief. Do you need an arm to lean on?'

'Pah! You can't keep up with me!'

Shai hurried after him. They got to the gate at the same moment the rider did. The man swung down before the captain, shedding dust as his feet hit the ground. He was a typical Qin, stocky, mustache but no beard, with a handsome grin and a cheerful laugh.

'Hu! Glad to see this place. It's dry as bleached bone out that way.' He gestured toward the east, red dry flat desert country all the way to the horizon. 'I'm called Tohon.'

'I'm Captain Anji. Are you a message rider? How can I help you?'

'Anything good to drink?'

Chief Tuvi offered him what remained of the stuff he'd been drinking, and the man gulped it down, then wiped his mouth. 'Whew! That's done, then. I've come from Commander Beje, and I'm looking for *you*, Captain Anji. An important message. Most important, so Commander says. More important than anything else.'

'Commander Beje!' Captain Anji looked stunned.

'Oof!' said Tuvi.

'You know him yourself?' asked the rider.

'Who is Commander Beje?' The words leaped out of Shai's throat before he knew he meant to say them. Curiosity had got him by the throat. He had never seen the imperturbable Anji taken by surprise.

Anji wiped sweat off his brow and shook droplets off his hand. He glanced at Mai. 'My first wife's father. My father by marriage, back then. What message?'

The rider tugged off his cap and fanned himself with it. 'Whoof! Hot today! A strange message, truly, Captain. You're not to go on to Tars Fort. I'm to lead you northeast in a circuit around Mariha City and up into the hills, where you'll meet with Commander Beje in private. He said this: Your life depends on no man or woman knowing where you've gone, or that you've gone. And this, too: Any troops you meet take with you, even if you leave a posting abandoned.'

'Ah,' said Anji. No more than that. Only his narrowed eyes revealed the whirl of his thoughts. The wind kicked up, rustling in the fronds, but it said no more than the captain did, not really.

*

They left at dawn, absorbing into their troop the twenty tailmen who had been garrisoned at the oasis. In fact, now that Shai took the trouble to really start measuring, he began to think that Anji's retinue was two score or more men greater in number than it had been when they left Kartu Town. But he'd been preoccupied then. He hadn't actually counted everyone. He was probably mistaken. It had been a confused time.

Mai rode beside Captain Anji and the scout, Tohon, at the van. Shai crept his mount forward through the irregular ranks – the Qin were disciplined but not rigid – until he moved up alongside Chief Tuvi, who noted his arrival with a sour burp.

'Hu! My stomach just won't settle after all that drinking and eating last night!'

'Where are we headed?'

'To see Commander Beje!'

'Was he really Captain Anji's father by marriage?'

'That he was.' He patted his stomach. 'Whew! Not so hot today, eh?'

It was possible that today's sun was not as baleful as yesterday's, but Shai doubted it. He knew when he was being told to shut up, however, and so he dropped back to the rear guard and rode in silence until the noon break. Tohon knew the route well. He led them off the main trail to a scatter of rocks where they found shade in which to rest through the hot hours. In late afternoon, they started on their way again and rode into the night before breaking. Four more days they traveled at this ground-eating pace. On the fifth, midmorning, they spotted dust in the east.

'Soldiers,' said Tohon, shading his eyes. 'We'll cut north now.'

'Aren't those Qin?' asked Anji.

'Qin, yes.'

'But no one we want to meet.'

'Not according to my orders, Captain.'

'Is there war in the east?'

'No war. Not yet. But there might be, once the weather is cooler. So we've heard. I don't know the truth of that rumor.' Tohon grinned. He was a man of mature years, a tough veteran who hadn't lost his sense of humor. 'Rumor is like a pretty girl flirting with ten different men. You never know which one she really prefers.'

'Are the Qin going to war against the empire?' Mai asked softly.

Anji shrugged, meeting her gaze. 'Commander Beje will tell me what I need to know.'

The smiles Mai and Anji exchanged excluded Shai and, indeed, everyone else. This demon was jealousy, gnawing at his gut. He fought against it, but he couldn't stop himself. Mai looked radiant and strong, but he felt weak because he was lonely. All he could do was tag along after Chief Tuvi and play at weapons with the tailmen, who respected him for his strength but ridiculed his awkward attempts to shoot a bow; they could hit a marmot from horseback. He was a little better with a staff, not hopeless at any rate, so they let him carry a spear as he rode to get accustomed to its heft and length.

The Golden Road was not actually a single trail leading west to east. It had many paths and roads, some preferable in winter while others suited summer or autumn travel. Tohon led their troop on a northeast spur at a steady clip for the rest of that day, halting at intervals to rest, water, and feed the horses. The beasts were almost as tough as their masters.

They camped that night at a water hole. In the morning they rode east until midday and then pushed north again into the foothills until sundown, when they halted by a dry streambed.

Shai was sore and nervous. Mai was laughing at something Anji had just said to her.

I hate happy people, thought Shai. Mai had confided in him, but he hadn't the strength to return the favor. He watched Mountain and the other slaves digging into the streambed. They struck water about an arm's length down and widened the hole to accommodate as many horses as possible.

All at once, Mai walked up beside him, hands cupped before her. She opened her hands to reveal three tiny beaded nets. 'O'eki found these. I forgot to give them to you before.'

'Who is O'eki? That's not a Qin name.'

'It's Mountain's name, as you should know,' she said tartly. 'He found them. Here. They belong to you.' Anji called to her. She pressed the objects into his hand and walked away.

Cornflower had tied off the ends of her braids with these tiny beaded nets. He had wondered often enough what it must feel like to touch her hair, as these once had, to feel the texture of those fine strands as a caress on the skin. He shut his eyes and listened, wondering if he could hear her ghost in the objects once worn by her.

She had not been dead when these had come off her. They'd been discarded, like ruined clothing. Her pale gold hair had been unbound, just like that of the figure he'd seen taken by the storm.

With a groan, he cast them onto the ground, then picked them up and tucked them into the lining in his long sleeves next to Father Mei's gold. What good was he, who was no better than his brothers, all but Hari? He had lusted after her just as they had, and it hadn't been kindness that had stayed him from pressing his body onto hers. It had been simple stubbornness; he didn't want to be like them. He didn't want to follow in their dreary footsteps and do the predictable things they did. He didn't want to want what they wanted. So he'd pretended not to want her, and by ignoring her, had left her waiting under the lean-to, easy prey for the storm and the demons that rode it.

Nothing-good boy. That's what his mother had always called him.

'Hu!' Chief Tuvi strolled up to him. 'That's some good-tasting water once the dirt is filtered out of it! There's a hand of daylight left, Shai. You want to see if you can hit anyone with that spear? We'll make a soldier of you yet. You're a challenge, sure enough, but we're not afraid of anything, not even your clumsiness!'

His particular companions were waiting – Jagi, Pil, Seren, Tam, and Umar – with their usual hearty grins, calling him names as they taunted him to come over and get the wits beaten out of him.

What a fool he'd been, moping all those years for the reward he'd never get, his family's love and respect. A better prize lay within his grasp. These soldiers teased only when they liked you.

He was one of them now. He found his staff and joined them. He got the wits beaten out of him, and enjoyed it even as they mocked his clumsiness.

Only later did it occur to him to wonder where Mountain had found the bead nets and, once he'd asked him, how unsatisfactory Mountain's answer was.

'Right up by the big rock where we were camping when the storm hit, Master Shai. Just lying there, like she'd torn them off. Or they'd been torn off her.'

15

Midmorning the next day they rode out onto an escarpment from which they could view the spectacular Mariha Valley sprawled below. Irrigation canals cut the land into a bright patchwork beyond which the lush colors faded quickly to a dull yellow-brown. The old city was a vast honeycomb seen from above, ringed by stout walls and graced by a lake at the center where, Tohon said, priests had once worshiped their ancient god and now the Qin watered their horses. There was a holy tower dedicated to the Merciful One, recognizable by its tiered rings, and a second monumental building concealing a courtyard within a courtyard which Anji told her was a temple for the worship of the god Beltak, one of the manifold names given to the Lord of Lords, King of Kings, the Shining One Who Rules Alone. Next to the Beltak temple lay another palatial structure.

'Is that a second temple?' Mai asked. 'It has two courtyards, too, but they're separate, side by side, not one nested inside the next.'

'That's the royal palace, built in the Sirniakan style,' said Anji. 'The larger courtyard is where men congregate and the separate smaller courtyard is for the prince's women.'

'How strange,' said Mai. 'Do you actually mean to say that women cannot go where the men congregate, and men cannot walk in the women's courtyard?'

'I mean to say that in Sirniaka, the palace women – a dozen wives, a hundred concubines, and all their serving women and slaves – are sequestered, kept completely apart. Only the master, his sons, and his slaves can visit the women's quarters. Any other man who tries to walk there would be killed. Executed.'

Mai laughed. 'That's a good story! It's quite a big palace, though. There must be lots of people living there in order to need two courtyards that big.'

'You don't believe me?' Anji raised an eyebrow in that sweet way he had of showing amusement. He was so handsome!

'How could people live that way? Women kept apart! And so

many that they need a place that big! How could one man keep so many women? Two wives is plenty, as the old song goes.'

'You don't believe me,' repeated Anji, shaking his head. 'It seems strange to me now, I admit, because I've lived among the Qin for so many years, but it didn't seem strange at all when I was a child.'

His words caught her up short. She'd been about to laugh again, but he was perfectly serious. He was, briefly, a stranger, looking at her through eyes whose glance had recently become so very intimate.

Tohon whistled. 'Captain! Best keep going. I think we're being followed.'

'They'll see our dust.'

'True, and our tracks. We need only reach Commander Beje's posting before they reach us.'

Anji signaled. Chief Tuvi whistled, and they set off again, riding at a bruising gait that jarred her up through her teeth. Now and again they would reach a vantage point from which they could get a good look behind them, and always there rose that telltale haze of dust, moving as they moved, hard on their trail.

In midafternoon they rode down into a green vale watered by three streams trickling down from the heights. An old stone watch-tower on one slope had been abandoned and replaced with a fortified villa on lower ground. It was a one-story compound sur-rounded by a small orchard, a garden, a single field of grain, and an inner wall of stone and outer palisade of logs ringed by a ditch. Sheep grazed between the two walls. A black Qin banner flew from the gate. They crossed a narrow bridge, single-file, and the gate was closed after them by a silent guardsman.

'This way.' Tohon led them across the pasture and through a second gate, guarded by stone dragons.

Inside lay a stableyard, dirt raked in neat lines. Captain Anji dis-mounted and gave his reins to Sengel.

'Come,' he said to Mai. 'Bring Priya.'

No one else – not even Sengel and Toughid, who shadowed Anji everywhere he went – was invited to accompany them. There were guards on the walls and a score of soldiers lounging in the stable-yard, all armed. The captain's troop dismounted but did not otherwise disperse, as if they expected to have to leave at a moment's notice.

'Are we safe?' she whispered to Anji as Tohon led them into the shade of a long porch. 'Who do you think is following us?'

He paused before entering. The terrace was floored with sandstone, recently swept, but the pillars, eaves, and roof of the porch were all of well-polished wood. A youth knelt at the far end of the porch, not even looking up as their footsteps tapped on stone; he rubbed at one of the pillars with a linen cloth.

'We are safe with Commander Beje,' Anji said. 'Look. There are faces in the pillars.'

The subtle faces of guardian animals peered out from the wood. They leered or snarled or smiled, each according to its nature, and as they crossed the porch and entered the interior, Mai had a fancy that one of the guardian beasts winked at her. Inside they crossed an empty room to a wall of screens that, when slid aside, revealed a quiet courtyard. Their shoes crackled on gravel. Like the first room, the courtyard lay empty except for a quartet of low benches surrounding a dry fountain shaped like a tree with bells hanging from the branches. No wind disturbed the bells. It was utterly silent. A sliding door led them into the dim interior of another immaculate room with wood floors and no furniture whatsoever. All the windows were shuttered, filtering the light through white rice paper. The air smelled faintly of cloves.

Tohon slid a screen to one side, and they emerged under an arbor roofed by vines and surrounded by a net of trees, some flowering and some boasting the small green bulbs of early fruit. A multicolored carpet had been thrown down over flagstones, and in the shade a stout man sat on a camp stool, his back to them, whittling. He set knife and carving on the carpet before rising to face Captain Anji.

He was a good ten years older than Father Mei, a robust man with a face red from too much drinking, and the typical Qin smile, generous and quick. 'Anjihosh!' He wore slippers of gold silk embroidered with red poppies. On these he padded forward to slap the captain on either shoulder. Anji placed his right hand atop his left and bowed respectfully.

'Good you came.' The commander's arkinga was a little different from Anji's. He voiced some of the words in a new way and sometimes used a phrase Mai had never heard before. 'Who is this lovely orchid?'

'My wife, Mai'ili.'

'Not concubine? She's not Qin.'

'No. She is my wife.'

Beje studied Mai for what seemed an interminable time. He had black eyes, and laugh lines that betrayed humor, but he looked her over in the same way a discriminating buyer handles peaches and melons, knowing which are ripe and which not ready for sale. She did not flinch, although she was desperately uncomfortable.

The father of Anji's first wife, of whom she knew nothing except that the woman was dead. Some of the aunts had speculated the Anji had beaten his first wife to death because the Qin were known for their violent temper as well as their hearty laugh, but if that were the case she couldn't understand how the father of that woman could greet Anji so affectionately.

'She can stay, then. If she's your wife, I'll treat her as if she were my daughter.' He pointed to Priya. 'No wife, this one. Why is she here?'

'She is educated. She can read and write.'

'A woman of value! Bring khaif for everyone, Sheyshi.'

The young woman stood so still within the curtain made by drooping vines that Mai actually didn't notice her until Beje said her name and she padded away through the trees on a white gravel path.

'Is she your concubine?' asked Anji, looking amused.

Beje looked confused. 'Concubine? Sheyshi? No, just a slave. I don't like these Marihan girls. They smell funny, but Cherfa likes to be surrounded by pretty things, birds and kits and so on, and she likes pretty slave girls, too. She may sleep with them. I don't!'

'Who is Cherfa?' asked Mai.

'My chief wife. A good woman. She takes care of me. You take care of Anjihosh here, and he'll make you a good husband for all your days.'

'Yes, sir,' she said automatically, because he was the kind of man you addressed with respect. Then she flushed, thinking of love-making.

He chuckled, but turned somber as Tohon brought stools, unfolded them, and they all sat down. There was still no wind, and the air was warm but not unpleasantly sticky. It was so quiet that Mai could not even hear the noise of Anji's troop.

Beje sighed as he settled his bulk on the stool. 'I'm sorry, Son. I'm still ashamed. You could have shamed my whole clan and harmed our position in the var's eyes, but you did not.'

'It was not your fault,' said Anji. 'There was nothing you could have done.'

'Maybe so. Maybe not. She was a headstrong girl.'

Anji's smile ghosted, and vanished. 'Precisely her charm.' He glanced at Mai but said nothing more.

Beje looked at Mai, too, and nodded as if in answer to an unspoken question. 'Truly, this one is a beautiful woman. I have seen many handsome women in my time, but this one I can see has been kissed by the Merciful One with grace of spirit. Still, no need to have married her as she is not Qin.'

'A man may keep a knife hidden in his boot in case he falls onto hard times and needs to defend himself when attack is least expected. She is my knife.'

Mai flushed again as Beje examined her, frowning.

'Is she? Hmm.' They sat in silence.

How odd that it should be so very quiet, as if a spell veiled them. Mai kept her hands folded in her lap and examined first her husband and then the old commander, who after a bit picked up his knife and began to whittle. The *whit whit* of the knife strokes sounded like a bird's cry, heard from a distance. She couldn't tell what shape was emerging from the wood. Anji sat so still that she would have thought him asleep except his eyes were open, though he didn't precisely seem to be looking at anything. Lost in memory, perhaps. Surely he was thinking of his first wife, whoever or whatever she had been.

Headstrong. She had shamed her family.

That didn't sound promising.

I will never shame him or the Mei clan.

A bug *tick tick*ed. Leaves rustled. Beje set down his carving just as Sheyshi reappeared, bearing a tray with four painted bowls on it. Now Mai got a better look at her. Her complexion had a richer brown color than that of Kartu people, whom the creator of all had admixed with the clay and sandstone of the desert, and she had a more prominent nose, in some manner resembling Anji's. She had pretty eyes and pretty ways and a pretty smile as she offered Mai a pretty little bowl filled with steaming khaif, a real luxury, which Mai had only ever tasted once in her life at Grandmother's double-double anniversary four years ago, when she had counted four rounds of twelve years. Even Priya was handed a bowl, out of respect for her learning.

They sipped as the servant girl waited, kneeling, by the sliding door. Priya nodded appreciatively, but said nothing.

When they had each emptied their bowl and the heady aroma and flavor had quite gone to Mai's head, making the world seem large and pleasant indeed, Sheyshi collected the bowls and departed through the trees.

'So,' said Beje. 'So, Anjihosh, you are wondering.'

'I am.'

'Do you know why you were sent east?'

'Yes. To take over command of the garrison and army at Tars Fort.'

'A lot of transfers, troops being moved along the border, and to the border.'

'Yes. I have wondered about that also. The var is too wise to attack the empire. We can't defeat them.'

'It seems unlikely. I can now tell you that all this movement is part of a larger plan, one the var has only recently unveiled to his regional commanders. We are massing an army along the border to ride to the aid of the emperor.'

Anji blinked but otherwise revealed no emotion. 'Why would the Qin act as servants, as hired soldiers, for the emperor?'

'The var wishes to maintain stability. No way to trade with the empire, or collect tribute from their outlying towns, if they're torn apart by civil war, is there?'

'Why would the empire have civil war? Emperor Farutanihosh is a strong administrator. The empire is at peace, and well run.'

Beje reached inside his blue silk tunic – only Qin commanders were allowed to wear that particular shade of heaven blue – and withdrew a pristine folded-rice-paper message sealed with the stylized horse-stamp sigil that every merchant recognized because it represented the authority of the Qin var. Only the var's officials carried such seals. With a manifest bearing that seal, any officer could requisition a family's entire stock of grain or their best ram or bolts of silk hidden away for weddings and prayer offerings.

He held it up now. 'Emperor Farutanihosh is dead.'

Anji paled. The words struck him hard, but he said nothing.

'The emperor's eldest son Farazadihosh has become emperor. However, another claimant seeks the throne. There is dispute, and there is fighting in the southern provinces. The var has offered to help Emperor Farazadihosh put down his rival in exchange for the Qin receiving certain trading privileges. The new emperor has, it seems, not as many troops as the claimant, who seeks to oust him.'

Anji seemed struck dumb. Mai stared. She had never seen him at a loss. Never. Never.

'The new emperor is interested in the var's offer. Of course. He'll lose without our support. Even a fool can see it. But he has one demand. Just one, before he allows our troops into the empire. He wants proof of your death.' He waved the message. 'This message, here in my hand, is an order. For your head. By order of the var himself.'

'Ah.' The sound escaped Anji on an exhale.

Beje waited, but the captain said nothing more. His hands were in fists, his gaze sightless, and he did not move.

'Why does the new emperor, this one called Farazadihosh, want you dead, Anjihosh?'

Mai had gone hot, arms tingling, as though fire burned nearby. She held her breath, waiting.

Anji found his breath, and she breathed again as he spoke, his voice so low she strained to hear him. 'Because I'm his younger brother.'

Beje waved the message dismissively. 'I know you're the new emperor's brother. Why does he want you dead?'

'Ah. Ah, well.' Slowly, he recovered himself, like a man pulling himself by rope out of flooding waters: hand over hand. 'It is the custom of the emperor to kill all his half brothers when he ascends to the throne. Usually his full brothers as well, if he has any.'

'Half? Full? What does this mean?'

'The same man sired us. We had different mothers.'

'But surely your father the Emperor Farutanihosh had a chief wife. Her sons would always take precedence over sons by secondary wives and concubines.'

'No. The emperor may elevate any of his wives or concubines at any time he pleases. He may disinherit, or give preference to, whichever son is his favorite, or the favorite of whichever wife grips his staff most firmly.'

'Tss! That's no way to be strong. Brothers should support one another.'

'Not in the royal court of the Sirniakan Empire. Azadihosh's mother tried to have me murdered once my mother fell out of favor. That's when my mother had me smuggled west to the Qin.'

Beje scratched an ear. 'To her brother, the var. Then if princes are so ruthless in the empire, how comes there to be a claimant to rise against the new emperor?'

'My father the Emperor Farutanihosh has always been a canny and ruthless administrator. No one contests – contested – that. No one who contested that survived. But the noble clans consider – considered – him to be a softhearted, weak man, because at the request of his mother he left alive his younger full brother, Ufarihosh. He even let him marry and govern the southern provinces. The brothers were on good terms, if royal brothers can ever be said to be on good terms in the empire. Azadihosh and his mother must not have been able to murder Ufarihosh's sons before a claimant rose out of their ranks.'

'Yet these would be the nephews of the emperor, not the sons of the emperor. Surely that would damage their claim.'

'Perhaps. The southern provinces are populous, and traditional, old-fashioned. The son of an emperor known to be weakhearted, like Farutanihosh, might not receive their support if a better claimant raised his spear. Anything could happen there. I don't know. My mother hoped to keep me out of palace politics by sending me away to her own people, to the Qin, where it would never matter what happened to me. I would be an exile. I would be dead to the court. But now they've come to find me, just as she feared. She meant to keep secret what had become of me. Do you know how my brother found out where I was?'

'I do not.'

'Hu. A mystery, then.' He kept his gaze on Beje, each man watching the other intently, as if waiting for a knife to be drawn. 'What do you mean to do, Commander?'

Beje tucked the message back inside his tunic. He scratched one ear again, pulling on the lobe. Mai remembered to breathe. Anji nodded at her to show he hadn't forgotten her, before looking back at the commander.

'It's too bad that you never arrived here,' said Beje. 'After that terrible storm in the desert some days ago, I sent out a scout. We found dead horses, dead men, and your banner, torn and dirty, but recognizable. Your ring, too, that gold lion given to you by the var when you were twelve and first come to court. A shame! The storm must have caught your troop unprepared.'

'It never would! That's a slur on my competence!'

The commander smiled sharply. 'You must choose between incompetence or death, Anjihosh. This is the chance I will give you, because I am shocked that my cousin the var would betray his own nephew to the Sirniakans. But then, this is the same man who gave his sister to their emperor as a plaything. It's like spitting at the gods to treat a woman of our people in such a way. I hold to the old ways.'

'None better,' said Anji with a brief smile.

'None better! But shamed anyway, because of my daughter.' He picked up the carving and tossed it to Anji, who caught it deftly. 'You'll have to take all your men. Those who won't go with you I will kill. I can't take any chances.'

Anji glanced at Priya. 'They'll all go with me.'

'Any men who know you came to me will have to go with you as well, including Tohon. He's the best scout I have. You can trust him. Your wife can take the Mariha girl as an attendant. I don't know what use she is except for pouring khaif.'

Anji had an amused smile back on his face. 'Where am I to go, Commander? If my uncle the var will not have me, then I cannot ride west. I cannot ride east into Sirniaka. South lies desert and, beyond that, mountains whose passes are so high that travelers die with their own blood boiling on their lips.'

'North,' said Mai. 'You said yourself there's a place that merchants speak of, like that one who found Uncle Hari's ring. Shai is going there anyway. We'll go with him.'

Anji laughed.

'There is one pass running north, through high mountains, to this land of a hundred lords,' said Beje. 'But it's said the land there protects its own with ancient magic. That any folk who travel that way with malice in their hearts cannot survive the journey. The road vanishes. Blizzards drown them.'

'Merchants go there,' insisted Mai.

'Merchants travel where soldiers fear to ride,' said Beje with a laugh that sounded uncannily like Anji's: amused, resigned, ironical.

'Merchants travel, but every merchant travels with a guard,' said Anji. 'Mai is right, of course. We'll go north, if you can put us on the proper road. We can hire ourselves out as a guard to some merchant caravan heading over the pass.'

'These Sirniakans are fiends for official chits and seals. I hear they arrest any person who hasn't a pass to account for his whereabouts. Heh! Even their dead must have a permission chit for their ghosts to depart for the other life!'

'I still have the palace warrant my mother gave me. We'll go swiftly.'

'That you must. You'll have to ride into the northern reaches of the empire, but I think you'll be safe if you move fast, before anyone suspects the truth.'

'We can leave at once.'

'No baths?' Mai asked, feeling all her dirt, every grain of it.

Anji chuckled. He met her gaze, and she laughed, suddenly not caring. Dirt was the least of it. Dirt was nothing, not if he loved her. 'I promise you a bath. When it is safe.'

'Why not now?' asked Beje, eyeing her with the glint of lechery in his expression, nothing she hadn't seen a thousand times in the marketplace. She smiled, in the way she'd learned to acknowledge men without encouraging them, and he laughed and slapped his thigh.

Anji rose, sobering. 'There was a troop of riders on our trail.'

'It's true you'll need to leave before they see you,' said Beje, 'but you need have no fear of them. They are the men who came from the desert, the ones who found your remains. I'll need your officer's tunic, your banner, and your ring.'

'Once I give you the banner and the ring I am no longer Qin.'

'Yes,' agreed Beje. 'You are a dead man now, Anjihosh. Try to stay alive, if you can.'

PART FOUR

Travelers

16

After they climbed out of the Mariha Valley, they traveled east and north for ten, twenty, forty, sixty and more days along the eastern slopes of the spine of the world, that interlocking chain of mountains and massifs that formed the northern boundary of the world Shai knew. The southern and western deserts – Kartu Town itself – lay three or more months' journey behind them. Dusty trails led them along grassy hills and through sparse woodland. This late in the year, well into the dry season, the streams falling out of the highlands were running low, although there was still enough water for horses and soldiers alike. In Kartu Town, where water came from a trio of precious springs, water cost a tidy price. Here in the wilderness, water was free.

Tohon took Shai under his wing, as an uncle might. They rode forward to scout every day.

'You're not skilled enough to be a tailman,' the soldier explained to Shai, 'but you're cousin to captain's wife, so the men humor you. Better learn a few things.'

'My friends are teaching me to fight,' said Shai, embarrassed by this talk.

'They're just having fun, beating you up. I'll teach you a few tricks. Then they'll respect you.'

Had they been making fun of him all along, in the guise of friendship? Was he that great of a fool, just like his mother and elder brothers – all but Hari – had always said? Had he mistaken all the signs?

'Herdsmen,' said Tohon, pointing toward distant slopes.

Shai saw nothing. Escarpments limned the sky, although there were never any mighty peaks to be seen glittering on high. But the landscape kept no secrets from the scout.

'That cliff. Track, down. Here, now, follow my hand. Those aren't a field of stone. Those are sheep. Captain will send Chief Tuvi up there to trade. We'll eat mutton tomorrow night. You try that throw I taught you on Jagi and Pil. You'll see.'

The Qin loved to wrestle. When Shai threw Jagi the next night, catching his ankle behind a heel and upending him flat on his rump, the soldiers hooted and hollered in a way that shamed and pleased Shai.

'Didn't think you could do that,' said Chief Tuvi. 'We'll make a tailman of you after all.'

Having bet on the outcome, Tohon won a cupful of millet, which he shared in halves with Shai. 'Not much of this left,' he said. They washed the thick porridge down with pungent fermented mare's milk. He seemed unconcerned that the field rations they'd been issued by Commander Beje were, at long last and after being carefully rationed, running out. Mostly, they ate meat killed on the march.

They were camped beside a stream. Mai, with Priya and Sheyshi in attendance, had gone a little ways upstream. Shai could see her scrubbing at her arms and face, although the water was snowmelt, gaspingly cold. In the last light, men set snares, and one of the foreign camp men netted for fish. Anji was seated cross-legged, repairing a harness while chatting with a pair of veterans as easily as if they were family.

'Why are you teaching me?' Shai asked Tohon.

'Eh? Because we Qin respect a man who can fight.'

'No. I meant, why are you willing to teach me?' *If it's true that the others were doing nothing but beating me up.* But he didn't want to speak that thought aloud.

'You're tough. You don't complain. You have the hands of a man who works, not like those soft-handed Mariha princelings. Anyway, I miss my sons.'

'What happened to them?'

'One is dead. Another is a soldier. The youngest tends the herds in the range given to my clan by the ancestor gods. Anyway, these here are Itay men. I'm Vasay.'

'I don't know what you mean.'

'The ancestors. It's an old feud between two clans. I give glory to my Vasay mother by teaching you to win a few rounds and get their respect.'

The next day Tohon paused to eye a pair of hawks hanging on the winds above the long ridgeline to their west. Although this land was tough and dry, it was still handsomely fertile with tall grass and copses of birch, pine, pipe, and thorn-brush trees. Game animals were plentiful.

'Deer. See. There.'

With Shai hanging back, out of the way, Tohon went after the herd, and killed three before the rest scattered out of range. Shai retrieved a few of the arrows that had missed their targets. He'd been given a knife big enough and sharp enough to butcher with, and he set to work as Tohon studied the eastern horizon.

'Smoke,' said Tohon now, but although Shai squinted, he saw nothing except tender wisps of high cloud strung along the reach of sky above the endless rolling hills. The wind was pushing up out of the southeast, and it eddied here where the higher ridge fell away into the broken hills through which they rode. 'Must be coming into empire's territory. You can see how the line of trees begins to break into denser growth. That means the land falls away pretty quickly up ahead, into some kind of valley. There's another pair of hawks riding the wind where the secondary ridge falls away.'

Shai didn't see them, but he nodded.

'You ride back. Let captain know. It's a decent-sized place up there, forty hearths at least. He'll want warning. Decide our tactics.'

'Who lives out here? There's been no one for days. Except those herdsmen.'

'We've stayed in the wild lands for a reason. Any farther east, and we'd be in the empire. Now, the mountains are pushing us there, so we have to go.'

'Do the Sirniakans think of the Qin as enemies, or as friends?'

'Best hope the official who rules the lands out here got the news that the Qin are allies now. Maybe he didn't. Anyway, even if they treat us as friends, they'll have orders to kill Captain Anji. If they can catch him. If they figure out who he is. Go on. Send Jagi up to finish the butchering.'

The hooves of Shai's horse kicked up dust as he rode back the way they had come. Captain Anji deployed many layers of scouts. Soon enough Shai hailed the second rank forward, and sent Jagi ahead to join Tohon while Pil headed off the path to signal the two men riding singleton as rangers, one to either side. As he rode up to the main company, he saw Chief Tuvi call a halt. It was an impressive group that made a lot of dust with a big herd of horses and over two hundred mounted men, Mai, and the slaves: Mai's two female attendants, Mountain, the nine bearers, and a youth who had seen them at Beje's villa and been given a choice between death or exile.

'What news?' asked Anji as Shai came in.

Mai bent close to listen. Her cheeks and forehead were powdered with dust, and she had wound a cloth tight around her hair to keep it as clean as anything could be in these conditions.

Shai repeated Tohon's words. There came after this a silence as the captain considered.

'Avoid, or confront?' asked Chief Tuvi.

Anji shaded his eyes. He was scanning the heavens. His gaze had caught on the same pair of hawks that had gotten Tohon's attention. Shai could see them now. 'No choice, I think. The highlands will pinch off these high trails and leave us stranded. We have to dip into the lower lands to reach the road that leads north into the Hundred. There will be some smaller towns, but we aim for the market town of Sarida. That's where we'll find our caravan.'

'How do you know this?' All looked at Shai, who had rudely interrupted the considerations of the captain.

'You talk too much,' remarked Chief Tuvi.

Anji replied with no change in expression, watchful as he examined the raptors. 'A boy in the palace is trained in an exacting manner. The palace priests command a map room with every temple and way station marked on a vast table sculpted in the manner of a model of the land itself. Every mother of a royal son would whip her boy if he answered a question wrong.'

'Were you whipped?' asked Mai with a laugh. She was the only person bold enough to ask, and not be scolded for asking.

Anji did not smile. He did not frown. The hawks interested him more than the question. 'Never,' he said, absently. 'Never would I have given my mother any reason to be disappointed in me. Tuvi. Pull in the scouts. Mai. You must play a part.'

'Yes.' She agreed without asking what part she must play.

Shai envied the trust and loyalty she granted her husband. Yet what choice had any of them? They were riding into the enemy's country now, and Anji was the only one among them who knew the lay, and the law, of the land.

17

In the Sirniakan Empire, women of rank did not appear in public.

For weeks now Mai had ridden in the open air, and she had come to feel comfortable on horseback, breathing the wind. The palanquin had been carefully broken down into pieces and loaded onto packhorses. The bearers, now accustomed to riding rather than bearing, must regain the strength to carry the palanquin all day without faltering.

As soon as they entered the empire, Mai became blind and soft. Off came the sturdy trousers and calf-length felt coat worn by the Qin. In silks and pillows, she became a royal concubine being sent to the north for unspecified reasons and escorted by a band of slave mercenaries from the palace guard who carried a palace warrant. All this she heard secondhand, or strained to hear through beaded curtains at the many toll stations where Anji's credentials were challenged and, inevitably, accepted.

She listened to the empire and heard many things: the bark of military commands at each checkpoint; the rattle of wheels on stone as they passed carts and wagons; the pounding of hooves and the slap of feet on dirt; the lowing of cows and the bleat of sheep. Water wheels slurped and spat; hammers beat in passing rhythms; laboring men sang working songs in gangs whose melodies rose and fell in volume as she came closer and then was carried away. Towns, she recognized for the clatter of stone beneath them, and because of the incessant clamor of male voices. It was loud even in the market district where an inn could be bespoke for a midday rest or a night's sleep. According to Priya, they never went in through the inner gates of any town they passed. The royal warrant bought all, yet Mai saw nothing except the inside of the women's quarters. These consisted most often of a courtyard surrounded by whitewashed walls and paved with polished white pebbles. Here the palanquin would be set down, and a simple room prepared, stripped of all furniture and its rice-paper-covered windows nailed shut.

'You must not be seen,' Anji had said to her before they left the ridge trails and rode down into inhabited country to set foot on the imperial roads. 'Not even by the Sirniakan women who will serve you. They must deal only with your slaves. You must use only your own utensils and bedding. No royal concubine would touch any item handled by commoners.'

White rooms and white courtyards, and herbs whose perfume leavened the stark gardens; scent was all that relieved the monotony of her days. The food was simple, tinted red and green and yellow with spices she had no name for and whose aroma made her queasy. Usually they had for their drink only a hard wine that left a bitter aftertaste in her mouth and a sour feeling in her stomach, but sometimes there was also a sweet juice, the best thing she had ever tasted and which she could never get enough of. More rarely, she was offered a comforting cup of khaif.

Anji did not come to her. He was merely a captain assigned to escort her, and they could not chance that someone might suspect that the truth was different than the tale he spun. Spies were everywhere: children giggling behind unseen peepholes; female voices murmuring on the other side of closed doors; more distantly the shouting and arguments of men and often the boisterous song of drunken men out on the streets just after sunset, following by the ringing of bells and the profound silence of night's rest. Priya and Sheyshi went about with heads and necks and mouths and noses covered, only their eyes left to them. Otherwise they were hidden in vast shawls that covered them to the ankles.

'The most beautiful silks,' Priya reported. 'Inside the home, the women are most beautiful and dressed as richly as queens. Loose silk trousers and long silk jackets that reach almost to the floor and are clasped with braid across the torso. I wish you could admire the fashion here.'

'No one will ever believe I am a royal concubine if I am not dressed in the proper manner. These jackets and robes from Kartu are well enough for a woman of the Mei clan. Yet I wonder if they would seem poor to a royal concubine. You must say we met with some manner of trouble on the way, my wagons lost in a ford when we crossed. When we come to a town with a proper marketplace, it will be necessary for me to replenish my wardrobe.'

Through Priya she sent this message to Anji, and soon thereafter, at each stop, silks arrived, gifts from local lords and magistrates hoping to curry favor.

Here were colors to delight her – marigold yellows as intense as sunlight, coral reds and blood reds and rust reds, joyous oranges and plangent blue-greens – and patterns to astonish, blossoms and vines and bulbs and leaves, every manner of floral gaudery both woven and embroidered in the style proper to a woman of rank.

'I will die of boredom in this seclusion,' she said one evening to Sheyshi as they sat in a narrow room whose white walls and papered windows oppressed her. 'How soon will we come free of the empire?'

'I do not know, Mistress.' The Mariha girl was combing Mai's hair in long strokes. She seemed content enough. Mai thought it possible the girl was a little stupid. No fault of the girl's, of course. Sometimes things just worked out that way.

'When does Priya return with our supper?'

'I do not know, Mistress.'

'It seemed to me this might be a larger town than the others we've come to,' she added, because the rumble of traffic had been so loud together with the rattle and shrill of pots and laughter, the barking of dogs and the cackle of fowl, and the drone of myriad voices. As she had rocked along the thoroughfare, she had heard the scrape of carpenters' adzes and had smelled wood shavings, as if they passed through a carpentry district. She thought of Shai, who loved to work wood, and wondered what he thought of all this. Had Uncle Hari seen similar scenes when he was marched north out of the empire with whatever doomed troop he had fallen in with in the end?

A door slammed shut with a sharp report. Footsteps drummed erratically on wood. A woman shrieked a protest.

The door into her seclusion opened with the same quick spasm as of a gasp drawn inward in surprise. Two men pushed in. One held a long knife. The other drew his sword. Sheyshi screamed and fell flat to the floor, covered her eyes with her hands.

Mai stared at them for a thousand years, it seemed, although in that space of time they did not move more than one step each. They had complexions not darker but different from Kartu folk, and they had also sharper faces, while Kartu folk had broader cheeks and gentler eyes.

They are coming to kill me.

She had been kneeling on her pillow, but smoothly she rose, and faced them. It was her training, honed in the market. Even in her early days, no customer had ever torn her façade, not even the ones who had surprised her.

'Who are you?' she said in the cool voice she might use to a matron who offered a deliberately insulting price for her wares.

They faltered. Sheyshi moaned in fear at Mai's feet. The two men exchanged a glance, speaking without words. Their smell, like everything in this country, hit her strongly: straw and stables and leather and a hint of piss and a spice that made her nose itch. Her instincts were good. Even in this extremity, she could see into them, men determined but not subtle.

They are surprised by what they find. This is not the face and form and reaction they expect.

The man on the left raised his sword. The other one tightened his grip on the knife hilt. So slowly it all transpired: they took another step, while she considered the strength of the walls behind her and whether it was likely she could smash through them.

A rush of footfalls swept up the corridor. Chief Tuvi burst into the room with Anji behind him as the assassins turned to meet them, but those who wished to protect her had a kind of rare fury to aid them. With a few strokes the men were cut down. They fell to the floor, and they bled and bled, croaking and gasping, until Tuvi cut their throats.

Anji looked at her from the other side of the corpses. 'Can you speak? Can you move?'

'Yes, but Sheyshi is having hysterics.'

'We're leaving now. If she does not get up, then Tuvi will kill her and leave her with these.' He paused, cocked his head as he listened, and dashed out of the room. On the heels of his exit, Priya ran in, tears on her face.

'Mistress!'

'I'm unharmed.'

Priya knelt, gathered up cup, pillows, bedding, and carried these out into the corridor. Mai took in a breath, aware suddenly that she had not breathed for forever. She knelt beside the sobbing Sheyshi.

'We must go now. Now. Do you hear? Come. Stand up.'

The girl pulled her hands from her face, saw a trail of blood oozing toward her, and wailed. She rolled backward to get away from it.

Mai took hold of her shoulder. 'Close your eyes. Do it. Close your eyes and get up.'

'Leave her,' said Tuvi. 'I'll kill her after you're gone. Not worth dying for, that one.'

'Sheyshi! Close your eyes. I'll lead you.'

Tuvi leaped over the corpses. The stink of fresh blood became overpowering, and Sheyshi began to retch, although nothing came up.

'It's very bad, Mistress,' Tuvi said reasonably. 'Some local agent has guessed the truth. We are a day's ride from Sarida. We must get there before those who suspect the captain's identity get news back down the line to a commander who can do something about it. Leave this one. Go!'

'Sheyshi!' Mai was angry now. It was so stupid to die this way. 'Come now, or I'll have to leave you. Come now!' She hooked a hand under the girl's armpit, and tugged, and at last, spitting and groaning, the slave staggered to her feet. Limp and passive, eyes squeezed shut, she allowed Mai to lead her along the wall and out of the room, across the corridor, through the women's courtyard where a huddle of women crouched on the ground under the guard of four of Anji's men. Mai could not see their faces. They had thrown their colorful shawls up over their heads to cover themselves. A toddling boy crouched between two of them, bawling, until one of the women slapped him, and then he bawled louder and was wrestled under the tent of her outer shawl, where his cries were choked off.

The gate that led out of the women's courtyard stood open. Hesitantly, she stepped through. The late-afternoon shadows stretched across the large inn courtyard, but despite the late hour, Anji's men went about their purposeful business, saddling horses, tying on packs. The palanquin stood to one side, sliding door open, interior stripped and empty. Anji led a horse to her.

'You'll wrap yourself as Priya shows you, covering your face.' He did not look at her; already he scanned the wide gates that let onto the thoroughfare. Despite the imposing blockade of a dozen of his soldiers, passersby had gathered to gawk and point and comment. Some, seeing Mai, gave up a shout, and Anji called, and his soldiers pushed into the street by laying their whips about them viciously.

'Aren't we making a stir?' she asked, looking toward the palanquin.

'Too late now,' he said. 'One of the red hounds got away. We must outrun them. Cover your face.'

He thrust the reins into her hands and strode off. Priya ran up and wrapped a shawl tightly around Mai's head and neck and shoulders, twisted it, knotted it, tucked it; gave Mai a pair of hands to boost her into the saddle. The first rank of mounted soldiers pressed forward through the gate. Chief Tuvi came up beside Mai.

'You stick with me, Mistress,' he said. 'You're never to leave my sight.'

Fear clenched like a fist in her stomach. Priya had tied the shawl so tight that the cloth flattened her nose, making it hard to take in a full breath, but Mai was afraid to adjust anything in case it fell off. Already they were moving; the transition occurred without her awareness, only that her muscles tensed as her mount trotted forward alongside Chief Tuvi. She looked for Shai over the heads of the men around her, but she could not see him.

As they pushed through the gate she saw, in the distance, a flower of smoke blooming in the hard bright sky. A high-toned bell began to ring, joined by a second and a third. The noise of crowds of men in a panic swelled like the boom of gusting wind in a storm. A racket of clattering sounds – like sticks striking stone – echoed from out of the streets. She smelled smoke, and turned in the saddle with the shawl almost blinding her, cloth rucked around her eyes. Flames leaped from the steep roof of the inn where she had just sheltered. She stared, unable to comprehend it, because the roof was formed of planks of wood. No one had that much wood, to waste it on roofing! Runnels of fire coursed along the pitch. Smoke poured out from under the eaves.

They turned a corner and, riding fast, hit the outskirts of the town along a series of tenements and hovels fenced into corral-like compounds by waist-high plastered walls. Open fields stretched ahead. Farther out, terraces heavy with crops and, above them, wooded slopes marked the limits of the valley. They turned north, whipping the horses into a jolting run. The road was paved but the roadway itself was much wider than the central stone corridor, which was paralleled on either side by dirt tracks fuzzed at their verge by wisps of grass and weeds. Men straightened from their labor in the fields to stare. Workers toiling over stinking tanning vats leaped up in surprise as the troop raced past them. Folk trudging in toward town with burdens balanced in baskets on their heads or slung along their backs fell backward to get off the road. Glossy orange and red fruit spilled and rolled and was trampled under hoof. Uncannily, no one screamed imprecations after the troop as they scrambled to get out of the way. Theirs was the silence of obedience. Only dogs yipped and chased them. Behind, more bells joined the clamor.

Mai's eyes stung with tears. She gripped the pommel to keep herself steady, although in truth the Qin saddles were built to keep the rider stable, able to stay on the horse while handling bow or spear or sword. They rode at a draining pace through a countryside whose lands were in fields out to every available cranny and corner. Compounds plastered to a gleaming white stood in the midst of grain fields.

Soon it grew too dark to observe the surrounding landscape. Torches were lit, and tailmen took them up, riding at stages within the troop, lighting their way. Naturally, their pace slowed, but the road was smooth and level, nothing like the haphazard tracks whose intertwining threads made up the Golden Road, the route along which trade flowed east and west along the northern shore of the vast desert.

The stars made a brilliant ornament above them. The moon rose, adding its handsome light as they pushed on into the night. Very late, they stopped where an irrigation canal cut close to the road. Here Anji allowed the horses to be watered while the soldiers switched mounts, saddling up those horses that hadn't borne weight on this first leg. They worked in a disciplined silence. Now and again a murmured comment surfaced and was tersely answered.

'This strap has broken.'

'Here's a cord to replace it.'

'This mare is blown.'

'Cut her loose. She'll follow if she can.'

'Let me use your knife.'

'Lost yours?'

'Stuck in bone. Didn't have time to get it out.'

'Huh. Clumsy of you. Chief'll send you back to be a tailman!'

The horses were tough, and the men showed no sign of strain, but she was weary and her thighs hurt and her hands ached. O'eki brought fresh horses. Sheyshi crouched on the ground, rocking obsessively. Priya stood beside Mai, saying nothing, watchful and alert, although the darkness around her eyes betrayed her exhaustion and fear.

'Where are the bearers?' Mai asked. 'Where is Shai?'

'I don't know,' Priya whispered. 'There were fires. Fighting in the rear guard.'

'I heard it too,' Mai said, recalling now the rhythm of the clattering sounds she had thought were sticks.

A short distance away, Chief Tuvi was conferring with Anji. Horses stamped. A soldier jerked a gelding away from the water, where it had been drinking too long. Mai wanted to go looking for Shai, but the urgency of their flight pinned her to this one place, even though she had to pee. If she wasn't ready to go, they would leave without her. Shaking, she reached under the long silk jacket, undid her loose trousers, and squatted right there while Priya swiftly unwound the shawl that covered her head and torso and held it up to shield her.

'This is so hard,' Mai whispered when she was done, and standing again. 'What happened?'

'Some kind of agents from the palace,' said Priya. 'I have seen many strange things in these few days, Mistress. Everything in this land is done one way only. The gates are locked at night and unlocked in the morning. Women live in one place and men in another. Each town has fields laid out in the same pattern, allowing for differences in the lay of the land. Each town looks alike. There is a temple in the center of each town, but the women told me that women are not allowed to go there. They were shocked I should think so. I! Who served the Merciful One as an honored acolyte! That's not all. There are spies everywhere, that is what Captain Anji said. He told us to keep watch for them, and for their scat. He calls them the red hounds. I think they must be like the demon dogs who chased the Merciful One across the bone desert. Their eyes are red with blood and their bodies are feathered with dust and iron shavings.'

'It was men who tried to kill me.'

'They can appear in any guise. They are not earthly creatures like you and me. They are born out of sparks of anger and despair. The whirlwind twists them into a material form.' Priya shuddered. 'You were very brave, Mistress. You stood up to them.'

The memory of that moment did not disturb Mai. It was sealed as in glass, separate from her. But she was still shaking from the rush of the ride, and the stench of smoke in her nostrils. Had those women crouching in the courtyard, with their hidden faces, gotten out of the burning courtyard in time?

'I didn't see,' said Priya. 'We left too quickly. But it would be better for them if they did die.'

'How can you say that?'

'The red hounds will question anyone who survives the fire. It would be better to be dead than to suffer their questions.'

'What about Shai?' she asked Priya. 'I don't see him. What of the bearers?' Where were the nine slaves who had borne her so faithfully for so long?

Priya cupped her hands in emulation of the Merciful One's offering bowl, and dipped her face toward her hands, to show the spilling of sorrow, tears unwept. 'They guarded the entrance to your suite of rooms. The red hounds slaughtered them. That's how we first knew something was wrong.'

Tears unwept, Mai heard the call to mount. She touched Priya's hand, to give comfort, to get comfort. O'eki returned, leading four horses, and without further speech – for what was there left to say? – they rode on.

18

'With me,' said Tohon, jerking Shai's attention away from the open shopfronts where carpenters worked. The street was lined with workshops. The smell of wood shavings brought a sense of peace, the memory of honest industry on the slopes of Dezara Mountain, but Tohon was already riding off and Shai had to follow.

Tohon balanced two sealed jars on his thighs. A pair of tailmen – Jagi and Tam – came with them, Tam leading a packhorse with six or eight jars bound in netting and slung over the beast and Jagi with a bundle of greasy sticks clutched under his left arm and a slow-burning torch held in his right. Down the main avenue they rode. Men paused to watch them pass, curious or suspicious, then turned away with a passivity in the face of the unusual that made Shai feel both safe and queasy. In Kartu Town, folk treated the Qin that way, too, looking away because to question brought punishment. Now he was one of them. Not above the law, but holding the law with the sword in his hand.

This town like all towns in the empire was laid out in an orderly octagon. Fields and orchards gave way to stockyards, tanning yards, construction yards, threshing yards, smithing yards, any kind of activity whose stench or fire danger or need to sprawl made it inappropriate to the orderly and narrow lanes. Next came compounds of humble dwellings with plastered walls surrounding each one and a single gate for entry. Then they came into the market, where they always halted for the night at a compound flying the orange banner stamped with an unreadable blot of lines and circles that, Shai had worked out, denoted an inn. They were not allowed to ride farther in, to the larger residential compounds with their higher walls, the military garrison, and the spires marking the precincts of the holy temple.

Turning right and right again on the narrowing streets, Tohon cupped a hand under one of the jars and flung it into the air. It fell in a long arc and broke, smashing on the roof of a carpenter's compound. Potsherds skittered into pipewood gutters. Oil glided down over the plank roof.

Shai stared, then urged his horse after Tohon. A man shouted in protest. A bright flare flashed behind him, and he turned in the saddle. Behind, Jagi had lit one of the sticks on fire. He tossed it onto the roof.

Spilled oil exploded into flame. They turned right again, rode on, turned left. Tohon flung another jar while Tam, with the skill of a born horseman, extricated a third jar from the netting on the back of the packhorse. Tohon drew his sword and nodded at Shai, a signal to draw his as well. How strange it was to push through the streets with death in your hand. Always, before, he had stepped out of the path of passing soldiers. Now folk fled from *him*. He grinned, although the expression fit his face strangely. Their fear gratified him, but the pounding of his heart and the flush of excitement along his skin made him uneasy. Should he like this so much? When he looked at his comrades, they looked like men about their everyday business, nothing thrilling or horrifying about it, just doing their job.

They moved through the outer streets, tossing jars and flaming sticks. Bells began to ring an alarm. By the time they circled back to where they'd started, the inn was on fire, roaring and snapping with sheets of heat pouring off it. Tohon rode past without stopping, making for the countryside. Shai slowed down as they passed the open gates. Corpses sprawled in the courtyard, but the smoke made his eyes water, hid their faces from view. He thought some might be Mai's slave bearers. Some were women. Wisps of ghostly fabric were only now oozing from the bodies, cowering over the severed flesh. They were not yet aware that they were dead.

The streets were mobbed with men running in a panic, some hauling buckets, others desperate to save anything they could from the fires. A child screamed. The distinctive incense of cedar and sandalwood burning penetrated the acrid taint of smoke. Then they pushed out beyond the streets and turned north on the road, following the trail of the main troop. Behind, the southern quarter of town was going up in flames, serenaded by the clangor of the alarm bells.

They rode hard to catch up with the others, rode at intervals all night, rested in the hour before daybreak when the moon had gone down, and as soon as it was light moved on. The road pushed upward at a steady incline, enough to really strain the horses. Five more were blown and their blood drained into cups to strengthen the men, but the rest pushed on with the same placid tough-mindedness as their riders. Maybe the horses knew what fate awaited them if they faltered. Although Shai did not know the details, they had lost two tailmen, a young groom, and all nine of the slave bearers in the conflagration. No one spoke of the dead men.

The valley broadened but the heights beyond grew higher and more rugged. They came at midday to a spectacular overlook. Beyond, the valley split into three forks, each one plunging into the most impressive highlands Shai had ever seen, steep hillsides so green that the color burned the eye. Slopes blazed under the hot blue sky. Terraces of ripening grain stair-stepped down steep hillsides. Streams coursed down from every height. He glimpsed waterfalls like hidden ribbons caught among the crags.

Below, the road split, like the valley, into three distinct paths. Just north of this crossroads lay a startlingly blue lake and beside it a town.

'Sarida,' said Captain Anji.

Mai was haggard and tense, with her head wrapped in a shawl to leave only her face exposed.

The town had the usual octagon shape but fewer spires in its central temple and an untidy growth on its southern walls: a mass of wagons and livestock seemingly disgorged from the market quarter but not in motion. Any person who lived on the Golden Road could recognize, even from a distance, the caravan quarter. It was the lifeblood of a town, where merchants, carters, drovers, and guardsmen seeking a hire met, mingled, and made mutually advantageous bargains. No one traveled any distance alone.

'It may be that fortune favors us today,' Anji went on. He pointed. 'There's a caravan gathering in Sarida's caravan market. A large one. Let's hope it's traveling north toward the Hundred, and not south back into the heart of the empire.' He conferred with Chief Tuvi, Tohon, and a pair of older men. The three women were directed to change into Qin clothing. Behind a blanket, they did so. When they emerged, they had tucked their hair tightly away under cloth bindings. Tuvi gave the signal to move. Mai pulled an end of cloth to cover her mouth and nose, as against dust, with only her beautiful eyes exposed.

Tohon move up alongside to Shai. 'You stay with me, lad.'

They rode on.

'Empire towns have walls, but they are not fortresses,' Tohon explained as they followed in the dust of the main troop, riding rear guard with six tailmen behind them to sound the warning should the emperor's red hounds catch up. The busier Tohon was scanning the landscape to either side, the likelier he was to get to talking. 'They're not built to repel an army. We hit one once. That was many years ago, before the first treaty was signed between them and us, the one that sent the captain's mother to the Sirniakan court to become the emperor's concubine. I was just a groom, not yet old enough to ride as a tailman.'

'I thought the new treaty with this new emperor made the Sirniakans and the Qin allies. Why did they need that, then? If they were allies before?'

'There was trouble, fighting and raids, along the border after the var's sister – that is, the captain's mother – lost favor in the imperial household. Now there's this new treaty.'

'Then are they building walls in case of war?'

'No. They build walls because their god tells them to. He likes things orderly. Some things inside, some things outside, these things here and those things there. All I know is, never talk to one of their priests. They'll chop off your head just for a wrong word. And, never put a foot into their temple grounds. They'll do worse.'

'What can they do worse than chop off your head?'

Tohon chuckled. 'Tss! You're young!'

'What do their priests look like, so I'll know not to talk to one?'

'I don't know. I never saw one.'

The hillsides were covered with terraces. Men moved barefoot through those small plots, but the work they stooped to in those wet fields made little sense to Shai, who had grown up among the wood shavings and pastureland of his ancestors' holdings. Tohon seemed to take it in with the same interest he would take in the flights of birds and the venture of animals through the grass: only that which might threaten him interested him.

The road came down onto the valley floor among fenced pastures and orchards in strict ranks. They rode in and out of morning shade. Four towers could be seen in the distance, though trees hid the rest of Sarida. Clouds had piled up along the northern horizon, hiding the mountains. Above them, the sky was clear, and the sun growing hot. Bees buzzed where flowers bloomed in parallel rows beyond the roadside paths. A little girl wearing a long blue dress and a gold apron, with her hair tied up in a gold scarf, stood among the golden flowers with a mass of flowers heaped in her arms. She stared as they passed. A man wearing a leather apron and a dirty tunic knelt beside a wheelbarrow half filled with fruit. He shouted at the girl. Hastily, she dropped to her knees and bent her head. A bird sang a five-note song; red wings flashed in the trees. Tohon scratched his nose, sniffing as if he smelled smoke.

Where the road curved past a bristling hedge, they broke free of the ranks of orchard to find themselves right up against the outlying districts of Sarida. Fenced gardens growing herbs, vegetables, or flowers competed for space with stinking tanning yards and the beaten ground around smoking kilns. Off to the right Shai saw a spectacular lumberyard, all kinds and sizes of stacked logs, but Tohon slapped him on the elbow to get his attention as they rode up to the outskirts of the outermost district: the caravan market, where merchants and strangers were permitted to bide.

The caravan market had overflowed its corral-like wall, and the town guards were too busy trying to keep order to prevent the entry of a troop of soldiers bearing a palace warrant. Many wagons had gathered on the field beyond the corral. Drovers and servants loitered there, holding just about anything over their heads to get some shade as the sun rose toward the zenith. Qin grooms held the main herd tightly grouped out beyond the low walls, but the rest of the troop pushed in past the gates to an open plot of ground where the men who ran the market took their tolls and taxes. As Shai rode in at the rear, beside Tohon, local men gave way: porters bearing sacks of meal or carters pushing barrels that smelled of oil; slaves clad in little more than a loincloth, with scars lacing their bare backs; merchants borne in chairs, who shouted at their bearers as they lurched to one side; a pair of dogs with ears and tails down; a pack of boys in short tunics, hair pulled back into braided horsetails, who slunk away after the dogs.

The men who ran the market conducted their business on a raised plank deck sheltered by a plank roof. Anji rode right up onto that deck, the hooves of his horse a hollow thunder on the wood. He had his whip in his hand, but no sword. The market officials rose, outraged, but in the face of about two hundred armed and dangerous men, they did not speak hard words. Many glanced elsewhere, as if seeking reinforcements, someone else to draw the soldiers' attention. Mai was lost among the centermost knot of the troop, while the rest of the riders had fanned out to cover the open ground. Shai pushed forward with Tohon.

'Is there a caravan headed north today?' Anji's voice carried easily. 'We've come with special instructions from Dalilasah, from the Compassionate Magistrate of the Fourth Army, and the Eleventh Warden of the Eighth Pack out of the Glorious Red Hounds. We are to ride north and clear the North Road and the pass of the recent infestation of robbers and heretics.'

'We've heard no such tales, of robbers and heretics!' objected one of the local officials. The man blanched as Anji turned a stony gaze on him and drew the whip through the fingers of his opposite hand as tenderly as he might caress the hair of a woman.

'Surely you have not heard any idle talk of heretics,' said Anji in a voice that made every man there cringe. Other officials stepped away from the fool who had spoken up. 'We do not speak of such things openly, except in deadly times, such as these. Heresy is a plague that kills swiftly. Be wary. Be alert. Meanwhile, I ride with a special dispensation, a warrant from the palace. We leave at midday, after we've watered our horses. Any caravan master looking for protection may journey with us. But they must make ready at once. We do not wait.'

It seemed unlikely to Shai that any merchant would ask for the protection of such a threatening crew. No one spoke up, but a whisper passed through the assembly. At the verge, the crowd melted away in the manner of boys and dogs.

Anji turned his men aside. They set to the task of watering the horses and stealing – they called it commandeering – grain, portable foodstuffs, da, and terig leaf from the storehouses. They provisioned themselves with a dispatch that Shai admired, considering how hungry he was. He himself pilfered sacks of oranges and dates, and slung a pair of these sacks over the withers of his own horse, with the other sacks over a spare pony. Jagi and Pil made fun of him; they didn't know what dates were, and the oranges, they said, would be mashed to pulp after one day on the road.

As the sun kissed the zenith, the troop assembled outside the gates of the caravan market. Astoundingly, a long line of wagons, slaves bound by rope, outriders, and peddlers pushing handcarts waited in marching order. The caravan master presented a hastily drawn-up manifest of merchants and goods to Captain Anji. They were ready to go, and eager, it seemed, to travel under the protection of such a menacing company.

'I can't believe they're agreeing to the captain's terms, just like that,' muttered Shai to Tohon. 'Aren't they suspicious? They have no idea if he's really what he claims to be.'

Tohon chuckled. 'A piece of advice, lad. When you talk, people hear that you don't understand what you see. Best to keep your eyes open, and your mouth closed. Look at them. They're scared. Fear tramples prudence. The captain tells them to obey, and they want to believe that if they obey they'll be safe, so they obey.' He grinned in the friendliest manner possible, twisting the wispy strands at his chin that were all he had of a beard. That smile almost took the sting out of the words. 'Are you any different?'

Chief Tuvi lifted the banner that signaled departure. Shouts and cries rose from among the merchants and wagon drivers. The vanguard pushed out, and the front of the caravan lurched after them as men and slaves all along the line braced themselves, getting ready to move.

North, to the Hundred. There, surely, they would find a safe haven.

19

'I'm sure we're not yet facing the worst,' said Peddo with a rare look of disgust.

'That's what you said yesterday.'

Joss had climbed up a stunted pine tree, scraping his hands in the process, and now angled his body out over the edge of the drop-off. Yes, indeed, the pack of men who had started shooting arrows at the two reeves yesterday at dusk had tracked them down and assembled at the base of the rock on which Peddo and Joss and their eagles had taken refuge for the night. The company below had rope, axes, and plenty of arrows. They had torches and, here in the tail end of the dry season, more than enough parched vegetation to get a conflagration going.

'I said it yesterday,' said Peddo. 'And I was right, wasn't I? But I was only thinking of what the Commander said – when was that? The hells! That was almost a year ago. Do you remember it? We had to do that escort duty along the roads for the first time, and then the town of River's Bend was burned down. "Not yet facing the worst." Truer words were never spoken.'

Joss shinnied back, scraping his hands again on the bark, and jumped down beside Peddo. 'Good thing they didn't find us while it was still night, or we'd be smoked with no way to fly out. Anyway, you weren't at that meeting. That was for legates only. How do you know she said that?'

Peddo had lost weight over the course of the Year of the Silver Fox. He looked hunted, harried, and worn, but when he grinned, you just had to grin with him. 'I got you drunk and you spilled every word said in the meeting.'

'You didn't get me drunk.'

'That's true. You talked without being drunk. It must be part of your charm. Not that I can see it, mind you.'

The first soft tendrils of smoke rose on the updrafts swirling around the huge rock formation. Peddo shaded his eyes and scanned the heavens, east against the rising sun, north, west, and south, but neither raptor – perched well away from each other at opposite ends of the highest spur – had seen anything in the hard blue sky, so that meant no reeves from Iron Hall could possibly be within human sight.

'What do you think?' Peddo asked more softly. 'Those Iron Hall reeves swore to meet us near this landmark. Think they ran into an accident? I fear me—' He hesitated, rubbing his left shoulder where he'd taken an arrow wound two months ago. Glancing toward the edge, he did not attempt to look over at their assailants. 'I fear me that they might have.'

'Best move out, and fly upland. See if we can spot them, or they us.'

'How far?'

Joss shrugged. 'All the way to Iron Hall, if we must.'

'Eagles are getting touchy. We might be attacked by one of our own for flying into their territory.'

'We have to try. Anyway, that accident – four months ago, was it? – with that Copper Hall eagle was completely unexpected. That's the first time in years one eagle has attacked another for flying through its territory. Everyone – reeve and eagle alike – we're all agitated. We have to try, Peddo. We haven't had a messenger out of Iron Hall for a month.'

And they'd been too overwhelmed to send a messenger of their own, just to trade reports, get up to date on the worsening situation across Haldia and the lowlands. Not enough reeves, and far too much violence.

We're helpless, but we have to try.

Below, enough brush had caught that the sound of fire crackling could be easily heard. The two raptors were getting anxious. Scar yelped. Jabi shifted restlessly, and as soon as Peddo fastened into the harness, the eagle thrust upward, beating hard. Arrows spat up from the ground below. Joss unhooded Scar, but then stepped away to the opposite side of the rock, to the lip where it tumbled straight down. He scanned the landscape, splendid to survey but pitted with traps for the unwary eagle: copses in which folk could hide, gulches into which a man could duck, clearings in which archers could raise their bows, sight, and loose, as they were doing now, knowing they had the shelter of trees nearby. There were many more men out there than he had first imagined. He sucked in smoke, coughed, but held his place, watching as arrows sped up from the ground in the wake of Jabi's flight. Jabi had served through three reeves; he was smart enough to gauge his distance, and keep clear, but those men would keep shooting and it was obvious to Joss that there were at least a hundred men scattered within eyeshot of the outcropping.

Scar kekked. Joss spun just as a scrape and rattle of stone betrayed the man scrambling up and over onto the height. Some damn fool had climbed, risking everything for the chance to kill a reeve.

Scar was a big bird. But that didn't mean he couldn't move fast.

The man shrieked, seeing that massive form as it struck. He stumbled backward. Scar's foremost talons raked over the thigh, hung in the flesh. Then, as the man slipped, flailing, into the gulf of air, the flesh ripped free, and he was gone over the edge, screaming.

'The hells!' swore Joss.

He heard the crash of the body as it smashed into rock and rolled over dry brush, and then a shout from wherever the fallen man had come to rest. A yammer rose from the men below like that of hungry dogs circling in for the kill. It was definitely time to go.

Scar was furious, head lowered, feathers raised along the back of his neck. He was twittering angrily, and although the sound seemed incongruous, coming from such a huge bird, Joss knew what it meant: A blooded eagle who had lost his prey was a bad-tempered eagle, roused and dangerous.

But the smoke was getting thicker. Others would climb, or were climbing. He had to act. He put the bone whistle to his lips, and blew the command meant to rouse any eagle to return to its reeve.

Scar lifted his head and opened his wings. Joss fastened into the harness. *Up!* Arrows rose, like rain falling upward, sheets of them, but Scar had grabbed an updraft with the first beat of his wings and kept rising, out of range. Far above, Jabi circled. Below, men scattered into hiding places, making it impossible to get an estimate of their numbers. Scar spiraled up on a thermal. Below, the fire began to spread. Joss and Peddo, keeping their distance, traded flag signals, then flew north in parallel tracks, within human visual range of each other. Gliding and spiraling, gliding and spiraling, the effortless flight of the healthy eagle. For a long time they could see black smoke from the fire, spreading as the blaze got out of control. No doubt, thought Joss sourly, the men who had started it would flee with no concern for what damage the fire would cause. But then, the Year of the Silver Fox had lived up to its worst characteristics: a contentious, difficult, dangerous year colored by ashes and gloom and death, one setback after the next.

As the day rose, they passed over empty tracks and roadways, flew above villages and hamlets where folk turned their fields or trimmed their trees and field shrubs to ready them for the rains due to arrive next month, after the turn of the year. What folk they saw who were out or abroad stuck close by the often pathetic palisades thrown up around every habitation; in many cases, people were raising or repairing walls.

They'd been aloft most of the morning when Jabi screamed an alert. Scar answered him. Both sets of raptor eyes fixed on a sight beyond human range. Soon enough Joss – and Peddo – saw it, too: another eagle and its reeve, circling high, riding a thermal but not really going anywhere. Plumes of smoke cut up from the land. Had they somehow swung around and were returning to the out-cropping they'd started from? Or, the hells, was this a new conflagration?

They had flown well north into the uplands of Haldia. The River Istri, no larger than a stand of blue-green ribbon, snaked along the ground off to the west. The foothills of Heaven's Ridge swept the north and northwest; the upland plains to the east were lost in heat haze, although at this height the high plateau could be guessed, even at a distance of tens of mey, by the yellow shimmer smearing the eastern horizon. Just a few mey ahead lay the city of High Haldia, one of the Thirteen Bannered Cities in the Hundred. And it was the city, surely, that the smoke surrounded. As they flew closer, he caught sight of a second eagle, then counted four. Ten! More like vultures than eagles, circling as if waiting for the death throes to cease.

Whenever Scar shifted his wings, the movement of the raptor's breast muscles bunched and eased against Joss's back. After so many years, Joss could anticipate the changes. The muscles tensed, Scar dipped, then pulled up; Joss scanned the ground to see what Scar had seen and brought to his notice.

Files of men, everywhere.

Sometimes, when you were on patrol, the sights you observed hanging in harness at the breast of your eagle seemed absurd, unreal, a tale unfolding in the movements of tiny carved toys on a rumpled blanket. A mob was converging on High Haldia, whose attendant villages and fields were abandoned and whose gates were shut. Ants might swarm toward a nest of sweets in this same manner. Men were coming from all directions, grouped in compa-nies and ranked by banners to mark their leaders and cadres. Every village claimed a rough and ready militia of thirty-six able adults; every town boasted a militia and guard of one hundred and eight who would run to serve if needs must. Every Bannered City paid a permanent guard to patrol its walls and streets and in addition organized a militia of folk able to stand up with weapons if they were called for, a full six companies if they could manage it or more in the largest population centers like Nessumara and Toskala. But such massed armed forces had become rare in recent times, in the days of Joss's mother and grandmothers. Even in the north, in Herelia, Iliyat, and Vess, where the ancient custom of lordship still held sway, a lord ruler could rarely afford to house and feed more than a single company of one hundred and eight.

There was a name, rarely used, for the creature pulling its net tight around the fields and walled precincts of High Haldia: *an army*.

An eagle dropped down to their elevation and sheared off toward the southwest. Joss flagged Peddo, and they both banked, and followed the Iron Hall reeve ten mey at least, an unexpected distance. The reeve brought the eagle down on a narrow ridge, the last outthrust of a bank of hills. The River Istri churned below, forced to bend sharply here on its seaward course. A ferry banner marked a crossing point below the stretch of whitewater, but no one was out on the river or waiting at the shelter. The Istri Walk, that wide road that ran the length of the River Istri from Nessumara to Seven, was entirely deserted; at this time of day it ought to be alive with the flow of traffic. As Joss and Peddo circled in, testing the air currents, the Iron Hall reeve hooded the eagle and trudged to the far end of the ridge to wait.

'The hells!' cried Peddo when he'd landed a safe distance from the other two eagles, and unhitched. Joss beckoned, and together they walked over to the Iron Hall reeve.

'The hells!' said Peddo again, as they came up to a tall, rangy woman with shadowed eyes, a chin scarred and twisted as though it had been broken but healed crooked, and silver streaking her black hair. 'What's going on? How can it be Clan Hall has heard nothing of this?'

The reeve's expression tightened. A muffled chirp came from the other end of the ridge, her eagle sensing trouble. It was a big, big female, the kind who could cause a lot of damage.

Peddo barreled on. 'Why aren't you reeves doing anything but riding the winds and just cursed watching it all happen?'

She raised a fist. Joss stepped forward before she could slug Peddo.

'I'm Joss, out of Clan Hall. This is Peddo. Mine's Scar, and his is Jabi. Greetings of the day to you. I don't mind saying this looks like a rough one.'

She lowered her hand.

'Sorry,' muttered Peddo.

She relaxed infinitesimally. Not that she looked like she remembered how to relax. 'I'm Veda, out of Iron Hall. Mine's Hunter, there. Give her a wide berth. They gave me the duty of calling you Clan Hall reeves off, when you came. So now I've done. Best you go back to Toskala and tell the Commander—' Her voice, on that word, came edged with scorn, but Joss wasn't sure who or what she was aiming at. '—that the council at High Haldia has sworn to hold out against the attack for as long as they can. How long that will be, I couldn't say. But they've dug in. They're expecting to be besieged. They're as scared as any folk might be. They've heard the stories of villages burned and folk murdered or disappeared. High Haldia is a fine prize for a ruthless thief to grab.'

Peddo opened his mouth, but Joss pressed a hand to Peddo's elbow to shut him down.

'This is all a shock to me, I'll tell you,' Joss said, careful to mix geniality and genuine outrage. 'Where did all those armed men come from?'

'Where did they come from? Out from under our noses, that's where! The first cadre came marching down out of Heaven's Ridge two weeks ago. Then the floodgates opened.'

'They'd been hiding there and you never spotted them?' demanded Peddo. 'That's a lot of men to hide.'

'Where the hells are you from, boy?' snapped Veda. 'Do you know those mountains? That's a lot of mountain to hide in, all the way from where the Fingers clutch at the northern seas down to the south where the Barrens kiss the Spires. Hundreds of mey, and with caves and crevices and overhangs and box valleys and scarred heights aplenty. There's a reason they call it the graveyard of runaway slaves. That's a lot of cursed mountains to hide in! And die in. Not that you and your cursed eagle could likely fly that far!' Her voice rose on the words.

Joss had heard men turn hysterical in just this same way.

'That's right,' he interjected hastily. 'That territory is far too much ground to cover, and impossible to track given all the places a man could hide himself away.'

Given rope, she kept hauling. 'We're shorthanded. We've had to concentrate on settled areas. People demand protection. Arkhons demand protection. Councils demand protection. The cursed guilds demand protection. They want the fields patrolled, the roads patrolled, their stinking outhouses patrolled. And then when an attack like this comes, they're after us for not having spent enough time searching the wilderness for signs of trouble!'

'Neh, neh, don't think we're criticizing you. We're in no better order. Clan Hall is down to three flights, including the retired and fledglings.'

Her wild look eased slightly, although tears had begun to flow. 'Three flights,' she muttered. 'Not that you have much area to cover.'

'We know what you're up against. The town of River's Bend was burned at the beginning of the year. That was just the beginning. We've lost control of the upland reaches of Low Haldia. Almost all trade has ceased with the valley of Iliyat. Oh, I could go on, but I won't. Tell me what's happened at High Haldia. Who is attacking? What do they want?'

She sucked in air between gritted teeth, then wiped tears from her cheeks. 'That's the question,' she said. The wind whined, here at the height of ridge. Reeves became accustomed to the incessant growl, moan, howl, whine, flutter, and roar of wind, but for some reason the way this wind whistled over and through the rocks grated on Joss's nerves. His headache was back.

'What's the question?' said Peddo, looking ready to pop with frustration.

She glared at him, the only target she'd had in days, maybe. 'The question we can't answer. We have captured a couple of stragglers. Did you think we hadn't done even that much? Some had debt marks and no accounts bundle to prove they bought their freedom under the law. Others were free men, the usual scum. Anyway, those who would talk under pressure spouted nothing but nonsense: any desire may be had in exchange for pledging loyalty to the cause; all the bad things done to them would be avenged. They would babble on so about the gaze that burns and the shadow flung down from the sky. Then would come stories of proving themselves worthy, such cruel and nasty things they claimed to have done as would turn your stomach. I don't know how much of them were true. As likely understand the barking of dogs as learn anything from their gabble. They have this medallion they wear like an amulet, to protect them from evil, but it's a flimsy thing, hammered tin. I could fold it with my own hands—' She mimed the action with her hands, front back front back. '—until it snapped in two.'

Joss grunted. 'A tin medallion? By any chance, an eight-tanged starburst?'

'That's right! You've come across it as well.'

'Only in the ruins of burned villages. What of the other men, the ones who wouldn't talk under pressure?'

'They didn't talk, did they? Tough bastards, I'll give them that. They died, rather than talk.'

Dropping down over Toskala, skimming over the rooftops, Joss saw the truth that could no longer be ignored. Within the five quarters of Toskala, in every neighborhood, every courtyard and spare arm's span of space in and around the warehouses or along back alleys was woven with a network of ropes over which were slung heavy canvas roofs and walls to build makeshift shelters. The neighborhood watches patrolled a tight web, working the streets and alleys to stop problems before they spread and to control garbage and pick up night soil. There were a lot of scared people here, torn out of their homes.

The reeves were helpless against this threat.

Everyone knew it. That's why they were all building walls and running to walls. It was the only thing left to hide behind.

'We can see now that River's Bend was simply the opening attack in a careful strategy,' said the commander. 'They're encircling us.'

Like all reeve halls, Clan Hall's architecture included a small amphitheater. In this case, the curved tiers were cut from the rock at the edge of the promontory, and offered a view beyond the proscenium to the river flowing past below, the wide Istri Walk on the far shore, and fields and orchards opening out to the horizon. The commander was seated on a chair, on the proscenium. Reeves sat in the lower tiers; in a former time, they would have filled the tiers, but not now. Joss sat in the front row with the other three legates who remained. Peddo had slipped in beside him. The rest of Clan Hall's reeves who could be spared from patrol or who weren't fit for patrol held the other seats. Their tension was a presence of itself, a huge beast, waiting to rip them apart. Fear is its own challenge, the first battle that must be won. And after that, the war on despair.

Naturally, on top of all that, he had a pounding headache.

'In the eleven months since the burning of River's Bend, we can see the pattern emerging.'

At the base of the curve of seats lay a huge rectangular low-sided box in which was molded a large map of the Hundred as seen with an eagle's sight, from the air. Normally covered, it sat glittering in the sun with canvas rolled up to either side. With a half-length field staff, her baton, the commander pointed here, and there, showing the growth of the rot as it crept out over the land.

'At first I thought our situation was the same as that in Herelia, fifteen years ago, when isolated villages began throwing out any reeves who came to stand at their assizes. There were targeted attacks to disrupt trade and disturb normal patterns of interaction between settlements. Both Copper Hall and Gold Hall had to withdraw their reeves from one area after another when it became clear that if they continued to interfere, then hamlets would be razed and innocent folk murdered. Well. They're moving more quickly now. And it seems we now know why.'

She looked up, noting first Joss and then Peddo in her audience. 'They have more forces at hand than they did fifteen years ago. That is how they've spread so quickly this past year. That is how they've increased their attacks on reeves such that we've had to combine patrols, send out two reeves as a unit, which limits how much territory we can cover. It limits the ability of the halls to communicate with each other, since we are each one of us so overwhelmed by local problems. These are not random attacks, a spasm of angry young men casting stones where they may. These attacks are carried out with a clear understanding of the limitations of eagles and the reeves. They hide in deep cover during the day and move, or attack, at night. The only calm periods come at the days of the Lamp Moon, when certain eagles are able and willing to patrol even at night if the skies are clear. Yet now, with the new year coming and the rainy season bound hard upon it, the cloud cover will leave us helpless always at night, even when the moon is at his brightest.'

Like the wide Istri, she poured on relentlessly. With one metal-capped tip of her staff, she indicated the location of each of the six halls.

'Copper Hall's territory has shrunk. Gold Hall has confined its patrols to the Arro Mountains and the central Zosteria Plain. As we speak, Iron Hall contends with a siege on High Haldia, and the northern reaches of Haldia are in chaos. The northern plateaus remain silent, difficult to patrol in the best of years and as good as closed to us now. Herelia and Vess and the northern coast, as we know, we lost years ago. Of the southern halls, Bronze Hall and Horn Hall remain in communication. We trade a messenger with Bronze Hall twice a month. Mar has suffered no incursions, but in the last four months they've dealt with some troublesome elements pushing down out of the Beacons. Marshal Dessara at Horn Hall sends a messenger at the first and the middle of the month, always the same report: No change in our circumstances; we can spare no legate or reeves for Clan Hall at this time. I admit, however, that their latest messenger is four days overdue. As for Argent Hall, Legate Garrard departed eleven months ago, at the advent of the Whisper Rains. At first we received regular messages from him regarding his concerns about the health of Marshal Alyon and the difficulties besetting Argent Hall and the southern roads, but we've heard nothing in six months. The one reeve I sent south to the Olo'o Sea did not return. I've not had the luxury to send another, under similar risk.'

She raised her head and studied the faces of her reeves, one by one. Joss nodded, to acknowledge her, but she merely touched on him and moved on along the row of legates, the experienced reeves, the cripples and retirees and fledglings. Clan Hall had a higher percentage than other halls of reeves who could no longer fly, men and women who transferred in to help with the recordkeeping, map-making, and other administrative chores with which Clan Hall was burdened. Gods! And there sat that rancid spot of pus, the Snake, whispering in Sadit's shapely ear. Sadit caught Joss looking, and

flushed, and grimaced with anger, and looked away, which movement caused the Snake to note her action and glance Joss's way.
With a smirk, the Snake rudely flicked a finger.

Joss's whole body went rigid, ready to smash that slithering sack
of shit's nose down into his ass . . . and then he thought of the
reeve – Veda – who had lashed out at Peddo only because she had
no one else to be angry with. Volias was a snake, all right, and Joss
had seen him at his poisonous worst, but this situation was not
Volias's fault. He rubbed his head, but the pain did not go away. It
was always worst in the season of Furnace Sky, in the last month
before the rains brought relief.

The commander smacked her staff on stone. The crack resonated
in his skull, making him wince. Her voice was sharp, cold, and flat.
'They're tightening the net, and drawing it closed around us. And
we don't even know who they are, or what they want.'

She stared for a long time at the map of the Hundred. It was a
crude thing, really, once you had flown over the land with all its glorious variation, viewed it aloft from the vantage of the eagle: a prize
beyond any other. Once chosen as a reeve, you were, in a way, a
slave to the halls. No reeve could turn away from the eagles. The
eagles did not allow it.

Yet for all that, he craved no other life. Not even the quiet routine
of the Haya fish ponds.

'So,' the commander finished. 'What do we do now?'

Joss stood immediately. A man snickered; certainly that was
Volias, but he refused to notice him. 'I have said for months that we
need to investigate the situation at Argent Hall.'

'So you have,' said the commander in her kindest and thus most
dangerous voice. 'That's why I sent Evo south. Evo never returned,
and is presumed lost, and dead.'

Joss sat heavily. The Snake coughed like a man trying not to
vomit. Others whispered, scratched their heads, shuffled their feet
on stone; someone was crying softly. The river rushed on. The late-
afternoon sun dragged shadows across them, a mercy in this heat.

'But.' The commander's voice cut through their restlessness, their
uncertainty. 'The siege of High Haldia has changed all this. All my
accounting must alter. If High Haldia falls, and in the face of such
numbers I cannot imagine it will survive for long, then everything

changes. The nature of what we are up against changes. The power that works against us has chosen to move out into the open. We are helpless to act as we have done. We reeves must find another way, or we will be destroyed, for that is surely their plan. The Guardians are dead. And the reeve halls, indeed the very sanctity of the laws and the Hundred, are under attack.'

Such a beautiful, hot, clear day, to hear such bitter words.

'I've selected three reeves to fly south, to investigate the situation at Horn Hall and at Argent Hall. Joss.'

'Of course,' muttered some wit in the audience. 'They always choose him.'

'Peddo. And Volias.'

'The hells!' cried the Snake.

Peddo scratched his chin thoughtfully, then patted Joss's knee in a brotherly fashion. 'This doesn't sound good,' he said in a low voice.

But Joss smiled. His headache had vanished, and for the first time in years, he felt an upsurge of recklessness overwhelm the long slide of despair. Exhilaration tugged at his heart as it had not done since the old days.

'I'm ready to go,' he said.

The commander nodded. She'd known that was what he would say.

20

They took flight at dawn from the prow of Toskala. Folk were already at work along the outer wall and earthworks, strengthening the defenses. There were reeves on patrol out in the countryside where villages and estates lay vulnerable to attack. For a person with keen eyesight, they appeared as specks circling in the sky.

People were moving on the roads and paths, headed out to their fields or pulling out carts laden with night soil. The road commonly called the Flats, which struck south into the lush farmlands of the Istrian Plain, was crowded. But traffic thinned out where the wide road known as the ridgeward Istri Walk pushed into the north alongside the great river. When the three reeves banked to head downstream along the great river for the first part of the journey, Joss noted how quickly traffic turned sparse on the seaward Istri Walk as well.

No one wanted to be far from the safety of the walls.

At length they gained enough height that they were ready to turn more or less due south onto the plain, the eagles gliding and losing altitude until they found another thermal radiating up from the ground as the earth warmed under the morning sun. Fields, hamlets, and villages dotted the plain. This time of year, stubble dried to yellow on harvested fields, in places already mulched and turned into the earth. Here and there dense white smoke rose up from fields being burned clean in preparation for the coming new year's rains. Farmers repaired irrigation ditches, mended fences, and restored the embankments that protected against flooding. Artisans gathered around smoking kilns or arranged bricks in ranks to dry in the sun. Everywhere folk worked on fortifications, digging out and raising earthworks or fragile brick walls around the ten and thousand villages of Istria that had for as long as anyone remembered lived in relative peace.

Now and again a person looked upward and lifted a hand in greeting. No red eagle banners were raised on signal poles. All across the plain it seemed that today might be a calm day, and yet perhaps their good fortune came at the expense of the folk living in High Haldia.

Wind rushed past Joss's face. Scar's wings flapped as the big eagle caught the hint of a shift in the airflow and cut left to find a better current. Strapped in the harness, Joss felt the breathing of the raptor as his own. After twenty-two years together, they communicated in ways that at some times seemed like mystery to Joss and at others no different from the simple understanding granted to two creatures who knew each other very very well and trusted each other absolutely.

He scanned the landscape as the regular pattern of village and fields shifted, and the ground itself changed character. This is what had altered the current: They had reached the Ascent, the slow uplift that marked the end of the Istrian Plain. Hills like bubbles broke the surface; streams cut gullies like lacework through the soil;

stands of uncut trees gave way to woodland and then forest. By noon they met up with the main road, still known as the Flats although here it pushed steadily upward through pine, beech, and sour-sap trees. This was also good farming country. Here in clearings bloomed a thousand tiny reservoirs, although the water levels had sunk low. The berms surrounding the reservoirs were planted with mulberry trees. Cows rested in the shade. Terraces stairstepped down steeper slopes into broad cotton fields or into tea plantations and fenced vegetable gardens. There was no traffic on the road except, once, a caravan of ten wagons with an escort of about thirty men armed with what looked like staves and spears and wearing round leather caps.

To the southwest, the rocky peak of Mount Aua thrust up through the heat haze. The western spur of the Ossu Hills painted a yellow-brown line to the east of the mountain. Between these highland escarpments lay the high, wide saddle of the Aua Gap, entry to the high plains grassland of the south.

It was really getting hot as the afternoon dragged on. Joss was itching with sweat under his leathers. He was sorry he'd worn his short cloak. Usually it was much cooler up high, with the winds tearing at you. Overland, of course, it normally took anywhere from six to ten days to travel from Toskala to Horn, but the eagles, pushed hard, could make it in one day. Joss was just mulling over whether it would be best to set down for the day before the eagles got too hot when a flash caught his peripheral vision. He looked west to see Peddo, who was flying on the west flank of their formation, waving the 'Alert!' flag. Out to the east, the Snake swept wide in a larger circuit so as to scout the greatest amount of ground.

Joss banked, and flew over the road where it worked its way up through soft-shouldered slopes not quite rounded enough to be hills. Ahead, Peddo circled a thin thread of smoke. Joss was soon close enough to identify a hamlet of no more than a dozen structures set beside a stream. The fields lay a short distance away, in stubble this late in the year, but there was also tea and mulberry and the bright gold of jabi bushes. Two altars tucked up one end of the hamlet: a neat, square hut to honor the Thunderer, and an open-sided altar with green tiles on the steep roof and painted green corner posts that held up that roof.

A mob had gathered by the Witherer's altar, twenty men or more, no women in sight, no children. A pair of men had been trussed up against one of the corner posts, arms tied back so you couldn't see their hands. A blade flashed. Peddo swooped low, and a shout burst from the crowd, many voices raised in surprise as they pointed and shouted.

Joss pulled Scar down. While the mob was staring at Peddo's antics as the reeve circled back, Joss landed in the middle of one of the fields and slipped out of the harness. Scar yelped his booming call to draw attention. Joss walked forward, tapping his baton against a palm.

It wasn't a mob, after all, because they fell back into a reasonably disciplined unit, shy of Scar's fearsome gaze and the really intimidating span of his wings as he fluffed up to show his size. There were over thirty, a full cadre, a surly-looking bunch of men wearing the plain costume of laborers but holding real weapons: spears, woodsman's axes, long knives, and a single sword in the hand of the man the rest looked to for a response. One man carried a red banner marked with three black waves enclosed in a black circle.

Joss's ears were burning as though they were on fire. Scar scraped a talon against earth, a sound to warn Joss that the eagle sensed danger.

The two men tied to the post were unconscious, or dead. One had the gray hair of an elderly fellow; the other was probably about Joss's own age, a mature householder. He smelled a tincture of blood and the harsher stink of excrement and urine, but there wasn't any sign of a wound on their tunics, though their leggings were stained. Dead, then; they had voided their bowels, and the ground was moist beneath them, buzzing with flies, so it seemed likely they had been alive when they'd been bound.

He wondered what had killed them. And who had chosen to desecrate the Witherer's altar with the act, and the display. *No one shall defile a temple.*

'A good afternoon to you,' said Joss in his kindest voice, the one that put Scar on heightened alert. 'We couldn't help noticing that you have a bit of trouble here.'

'You're not wearing the badge of Horn Hall,' said the man with the sword. He wasn't any older than the others, but he had that kind of flat look to his eyes that reminded Joss of men who have killed and gotten a taste for it.

'So I'm not,' agreed Joss in his most amiable tone, one that made most of the other men shift uncomfortably. He noted those who did not. 'We're out of Clan Hall.'

'This is out of your territory,' said the swordsman.

Joss halted about thirty steps from the group and, with his baton resting lightly and at the ready on his forearm, scanned the scene. This was a reasonably prosperous farm. There was a shelter for the family cart, and a storehouse set up on posts, as well as a few smaller huts and an outdoor fire pit where the last flare of a dying fire smoked out, a signal fire, maybe. A path led upstream through trees to the nearby pond, visible as a wink of water just above the jabi bushes. A pair of cottages were backed by a tidy vegetable garden fenced in with latticework. The dirt yard between the two cottages had recently been raked and was disturbed now by a single set of child-sized footprints.

All the doors were closed and windows slid shut, but although folk might have been hiding within, he knew they were not. The place was deserted. Emptied.

'In fact, Clan Hall supervises the six eagle clans,' Joss said. 'In the manner of a commander supervising her marshals, if you take my meaning.'

The swordsman had a thin smile. His hair was shaved down tight against the skull, almost in the manner of one of the Lantern's hierophants but with a thicker nap, yet still not enough to grab hold of in a fight. He wore lime-whitened horsetail ornaments dangling from his shoulders, like a badge of rank that made up for his shorn head. The rest dressed their hair in various lengths: horsetails streaked with yellow or red; short beaded braids; rich men's loops woven with bright ribbon. None possessed leather caps or boiled-leather helmets, as militia would have. None wore even the leather coats that protected city firemen from flames and sparks. Some wore silks, and the rest wore cotton tunics or long local-silk jackets over kilts, or loose trousers, or bare legs; every one wore sandals or boots, though, which was unusual. They all seemed to be wearing a similar medallion at their necks, but he wasn't close enough to see if it was marked with the starburst. Most had a

crude copy of the red and black banner pattern sewn onto their
clothing.

'Think of us as a cadre of sworn brothers, then,' the swordsman
said. 'Bound to our clan father. I didn't think you were out of Horn
Hall.'

Joss gestured toward the dead men. 'What's this?'

'Just what we were asking ourselves. We have a foot patrol we
run out here along the Flats, because of the trouble there has been.
This is what we found.' He gestured. 'This hamlet, deserted. These
two men, dead.'

There was no single word, or cough, or movement from those
assembled, as though they were all holding their breath to see how
he reacted. Peddo circled overhead again; he had his bow ready, its
length tucked against his side, hard to see unless you knew to look
for it. The Snake was nowhere to be seen.

They were lying.

The reeves were well trained and well armed, but they could not
fight a pitched battle.

A powerful cry split the air. All of the men leaped and startled as
Trouble swooped in low. The Snake had his orange flag in his hand:
Danger. It was time to retreat.

Aui! How it burned to have to do so. The dead men were farmers, likely grandfather and adult son. This was their place, for all he
knew. But Volias, while a snake and bastard of the first water,
would not give the signal to retreat lightly.

'We're on our way to Horn Hall now, as it happens,' said Joss,
stalling as he gave the gesture with his baton that would call Scar up
behind him. He knew better than to fall back; that might provoke
a burst of frenzied bravado from the men, who were strung tight
enough already, quivering with it. 'What's your name, ver, so I
might mention it to the marshal at Horn Hall when I bring her a
report of this crime?'

'*Him*, as it happens,' said the swordsman. 'It seems you're a bit
behind the weather, reeve. What's your name?'

The assembled men shied back a few steps as Scar walked right
up behind Joss. The harness brushed his back, and he hooked in
one-handed. The swordsman lifted the tip of his sword. A pair of
men in the crowd fumbled with bows.

Jabi stooped, pulling up so late that most of the men hit the dirt. The Snake pulled a wicked fast turn to get back around to give cover, passing over low, as Joss blew one blast on his whistle and Scar thrust. The draft from Scar's wings actually beat down some of the other men. Then they were up and climbing over the trees. He heard a shout, but no arrows raced after him.

The Snake was pointing with his baton. There, to the southwest and not too far away, a cadre of armed men pushed along on a trail through open woodland. They were in a hurry, sure enough, and as they trotted down the path their banner unfurled. Its colors were red and yellow. The Snake had tucked his flag away already, and with hand gestures Joss indicated that they should move on back to the road, continue their journey toward Horn Hall. They had no possible way to make a good outcome in the middle of that: either this new group were allies to the others, or they were enemies, and no matter which it was, three reeves were too few.

Too few, as always. It was a nightmare.

Behind, smoke billowed upward; a larger fire had been set. How he hated this, every effort twisted until it came out the opposite of what the gods intended as justice. Maybe those men had just set fire to the Witherer's altar. Any terrible deed was possible, in these days. He had seen it all, and more, and worse.

When he spotted a rocky hilltop suitable for landing, with a pair of streams coursing along lower ground below, he flagged a halt. The high ground was set above a steep defile, difficult to climb but wide enough in the trough that the eagles could come and go easily. He released Scar, and the Snake released Trouble, but Peddo hooded Jabi as the other two eagles circled down to a spot where the stream widened, for a cooling bath. Trouble was not only an exceptionally beautiful bird but the best-natured eagle Joss had ever encountered, never ill-tempered, never a bully, never needlessly aggressive. Entirely unlike her reeve.

'Why are we stopping?' asked the Snake irritably. 'There's still time to make Horn Hall today, if we push. I don't see a soft bed on this rock.'

Joss arranged sticks in a crevice, wondering if it was worth risking a fire. 'I don't want the eagles blown when we come in.'

'You think there will be trouble?' Peddo was standing on the edge of the cliff with his back to them, a hand raised to shade his eyes from the sun. He was gazing north-northwest, but if he was looking for the column of smoke, they had long since lost it in the hollows and rises of the land.

'Just a feeling that it would be prudent to be able to leave quickly if the need arises.'

The Snake, remarkably, remained silent. He set down his pack in the shade of a gaggle of pine and settled cross-legged atop his folded cloak.

'I can hear that Volias agrees with you,' said Peddo with a laugh, turning back to survey the way the other two reeves had placed a goodly distance between themselves. 'How do you mean to proceed tomorrow, when we come to Horn Hall?'

'Cautiously,' said Joss.

The Snake took a swig from his wine sack.

'Who do you think killed those two men?' said Peddo, wiping grit off his hands. 'The folk who lived in that hamlet? The men who were there when we got there? Or some other group altogether?'

Joss broke a few sticks over his knee. It felt good to snap something, but he had already decided against lighting a fire. They didn't need fire except to boil water for tea.

'Most likely, we'll never know.'

The dream always unveils itself in a gray unwinding of mist he has come to dread. He is walking but cannot see any of the countryside around him, only shapes like skeletal trees with leafless limbs and branches – cold-killed, as they call them in the Arro Highlands, where, beyond the kill line, the trees wither in the dry season and are reborn when the rains come. In the dream he is dead, awaiting rebirth. He is a ghost, hoping to wake up from the nightmare twenty years ago, but the dream has swallowed him.

The mist boils as though churned by a vast intelligence. It is here that the dream twists into nightmare. The mist will part, and he will see her in the unattainable distance, walking along a slope of grass or climbing a rocky escarpment, a place he can and must never reach because he has a duty to those on earth whom he has sworn to serve.

It begins. Wind rips the mist into streamers that blow and billow like cloth, like the white linen and silk banners strung up around Sorrowing Towers where the dead are laid to rest under the open sky. He begins to sweat, waiting for the apparition. For Marit.

A foot scuffs on pebbles.

He jerked awake, rolled, grabbed his baton, and came up to find the Snake crouched beside him with his knife out.

'So it's true,' said the Snake in a murmur. 'You do have nightmares. You do murmur a woman's name in your sleep, only not the one you're sleeping with.'

The stars were brilliant, filling the heavens like a ripe field of glittering grain. Peddo was snoring softly, and the wind was loud in the trees.

'What—?' began Joss angrily.

The Snake touched his shoulder to hush him. 'Someone is climbing up the ridge.'

Joss couldn't hear anything over the shurr of wind among branches. Even the eagles were silent at their rest, all three hooded. It was long past the middle of the night, coming toward dawn if he measured the position of the constellations correctly: The Weeping Boy was falling out of the zenith toward the west, and the Peacock with his spangled tail was rising in tandem with a quartering Embers Moon.

Volias uncurled gracefully to stand. He cocked his head to one side, the motion visible against the faint backlight of the night sky. And there, just there, as the wind died off for a moment, Joss heard a scuff off to the right where the slope dropped steeply away. Then a gust rattled leaves, and the sound vanished.

He rolled up to his knees and drew his knife. Volias nudged Peddo gently with a foot, and damned if the waking reeve didn't cough and snort and startle like a drunkard.

'Eh? Whazzit?'

The noise might as well have been drums and bells and horns, because after all that, although they stood watch in the interval until dawn, there came no further sound, nothing at all. In the morning when it was light enough to see and they explored a bit down the steep slope and afterward flew a pair of full rings around the area, they saw nothing and no one. No one at all.

21

Horn Hall was eldest of the eagle clans, thus 'horn' for the first substance turned into tools, according to the Tale of Fortune. Its eyrie had been built into the rugged cliffs at the rim of the Aua Gap, about three mey from the town of Horn that sat athwart the juncture of three major roads: the Flats, West Track, and East Track. From its high vantage, Horn Hall's reeves were well placed to patrol north onto the Istrian Plain, south into the high plains grassland, or east and west into hill country. The place was impossible to storm on foot or horseback because it was cut into a daunting escarpment, and laid out atop the windswept height, which no person could reach unless she could fly.

So they came circling first at a polite distance, waiting to be marked by the watchers on the towers. When no reeves flew out to inspect them, they tightened their circle until at last Joss signaled the others to remain in the air while he went in.

Reeves got used to the wind, but this buffeting swirl of updrafts and eddies and cross-currents made landing tricky, so he shied away from the broad ledge just below the lip of the cliff, which let onto caves, and set down instead on the wide and windy open space along the top of the ridge. Here watchtowers creaked under the onslaught of shifting gusts, and hydra-headed wind vanes spun. This was the parade ground, the whole damned ridgetop. There were a couple of lofts suitable for housing travelers out of other clans, but the constant noise of the wind battering those walls would drive any reeve crazy. A pair of open-sided shelters with sturdy roofs provided shade. Latrines had been built over a crevice split into the rock. Many stone cairns were piled up at the edge as well as a dozen squat perches fixed at intervals along the parade ground, all places for eagles to land. A huge hole gaped in the rock, off to one side; it was roped off so a person wouldn't accidentally fall in.

The place was deserted. Scar shifted, head up, looking around without any of the hackling or flaring he would have displayed were there unmet eagles nearby. The wind vanes slowed, halted to point west-southwest as the wind steadied. Grit skittered along the rock. A moan came from the forward watchtower as the wind found a voice within the framework.

Joss left Scar on a perch, with his beak to the wind. He walked a circuit, checking first the open shelters and then the lofts. They weren't stripped bare. Each of the shelters housed a pair of benches pinned down with screws into the rock so they wouldn't blow loose. The lofts included a dozen perches as well as tiny sojourning rooms, each tidily set to rights with a rope bed, a low table, hooks to hang clothes and harness, and the closets with their doors neatly slid closed and, inside, containing one folded mattress, a sitting mat and thin sitting pillow, and a bronze pitcher and bowl for washing up. He wiped a finger through dust, and judged that no one had stayed here for a while.

Like most reeves who had survived twenty years, he had a finely honed sense for trouble, for unseen watchers, an instinct for ambush, the things that made the back of his neck prickle, but the flavor here was all dead. He returned to the open space and signaled to Peddo and Volias to hold their positions. They signaled back the all-clear.

A stairway, cut into the side of the cliff, led to the wide ledge beneath. There was no railing, and despite his head for heights he got dizzy descending the stairs. He kept his hand on the rock to steady himself. He didn't look down. He could have flown down, of course, but he just didn't like the situation. He didn't want Scar on that ledge with those tricky winds; best risk only himself, because Scar would chose another reeve, although preferably someone with a better personality than the Snake.

The ledge was itself as long and wide as the parade ground in Clan Hall, the shape of a huge oval. A rock wall, rimmed with perches, ringed the outer edge. According to the Tale of Struggle, this rock eyrie had always been here, but he wondered how such a thing had been hewn out of hard rock, and especially how the work could be done so high off the ground. His footfalls clapped on the ground; there was some kind of echo off the cliff face, subtle and confusing.

The place looked recently swept. At any instant, he expected a reeve or hireling or hall slave to walk out of one of the five gaping cave mouths, the entries to the eyrie within. But no one did.

He walked to the wall and stood with hands on the grainy surface. Morning shadows darkened most of the ledge, but the rising sun was now high enough that it kissed the leading edge. Soon the whole place would be flooded by sun, and by midafternoon in this season, Furnace Sky, it must be hot enough to bake flatbread out here.

The view was tremendous. Only the east was closed to him by the cliff at his back and, of course, the Ossu Range behind that, running east all the long mey to the Istrian Bay and the ocean. Here at Horn Hall, facing west-northwest, he looked across the broad saddle of the Aua Gap to the magnificent face of Mount Aua some ten or fifteen mey distant, visible this morning in the clear, bright air. South onto the high plains there was already a haze, but a couple of mey to the north under the shadow of the last spur of the Ossu Range lay the whitewashed walls of the city of Horn, barely visible from this angle.

Peddo dipped down, flying past through the gulf of air; it was a drop of at least a hundred batons to the scree-laden slope that marked the base of the cliff. Off to either side the ridge fell into folds and ravines, just as deadly. To the south, out on the rolling grasslands, grazed a herd of beasts, hundreds of them, but from this distance he couldn't mark what kind they were or if they were being shepherded by human agency.

Joss turned away from the view and walked in through the highest mouth, into the high hall where he had jessed and hooded Scar years ago on a visit to Horn Hall, then busy with reeves and eagles and hirelings going to and fro. The big hole on the height opened into this chamber, flooding it with light; he'd forgotten about that. He walked on into adjoining passages, all carved out of the rock by hands that must have labored for endless years. Most likely they'd been delved; no one else could do this manner of work. In a nearby chamber, a vast space lit by arrows of light that shot down through slits cut into the air-facing wall, the reeves and their guests had taken their feast. There were lofts for the eagles, quiet and dim. There were three chambers linked into a row given over to the care and manufacture of tack and harness. Next to them, with its own entrance onto a smaller ledge actually on the other side of the ridge, lay the kitchens. The hearths were cold. The pots were stacked neatly. No one had cooked here this morning.

He explored down a corridor lit by cunningly angled shafts along which lay rooms for Horn Hall's reeves. Every one had a blanket folded at the end of the bed, and a table with a lamp or whittling knife or spoon or cup set on it, or the other little things that marked something of the character or habits of the reeve who slept here: a half-sewn glove; a set of ceramic bowls painted with scenes of acrobats; a leather vest hung from a hook, stained at the underarms and with a musty smell; a basket covered with a striped cloth, beneath which he discovered a cache of handsome dolls gotten up to represent each of the fourteen guilds; a set of dancer's wristlets and anklets tucked beneath the two wool blankets folded at the end of the bed; a whip, left right out in the middle of the floor; a forgotten loaf of bread tucked in the back of one of the freestanding storage closets, quite desiccated now and almost as hard as stone.

It was as if they'd all grabbed their traveling cloaks, packs, and weapons, and left at dawn, for there wasn't any dust to speak of. Horn Hall was well kept and well supervised. Even the sliding doors on the closets moved effortlessly, recently oiled. He felt like a ghoul, desecrating the body of the dead.

The master's cote had a separate entrance, but it was a place so bare of any personal touch – there wasn't even a change of clothes in the tiny closet – that he could make no guess as to what kind of woman, or man, it was who was now marshal at Horn Hall. If that swordsman hadn't been lying about that, too.

Farther back lay storerooms and the stairs that led down into the depths of the cistern, but it got dark too quickly and he'd left his lantern tied to the harness. A cursory search did not turn up the halls' store of candles, rushlights, or oil lamps. The air moved softly through hidden vents, and the whole place breathed an uneasy peace, the calm of a spot where the storm has just passed, maybe, and has swept everyone away, or one where the folk have abandoned their home to escape the storm they know is coming.

Gone altogether beyond.

That line from the Tale of Struggle, in the episode of the cunning outlander, had always stuck with him. He had no idea what it meant – or at least, what the cunning outlander had meant by using it – but he felt now that he understood it in a way meaningful to him, at this moment. Maybe he was crazy, and probably he was, but it seemed to him stepping at last back out onto the ledge, now half covered in blinding sunlight, that the soul of Horn Hall had fled together with its inhabitants.

This time Volias and Peddo were both circling within sight of the ledge, watching for him. He gave them a wave and trudged back up the stairs. This time, the lack of a railing did not bother him. He could have tumbled forever into the gulf of air, and then he would have sprouted wings, and come safely home.

'There's something altogether strange here,' he said after the other two landed on the parade ground. 'It's deserted.'

'All gone out on patrol?' asked Peddo. 'That doesn't fit protocol. There should be three duty reeves left on hall at all times.'

'Best we ask at the town,' said the Snake.

'Best we do,' said Joss.

Horn was named after the hall, or the hall after the town. No one was sure.

This was sure: The folk working in the fields ducked and scattered when the three reeves approached overhead, and the militia standing at guard on those whitewashed walls took up their bows and loosed warning arrows.

No arrows came close, but the shock of having arrows shot after them at all hit Joss so hard that he spent some wasted time circling high over Horn's sturdy walls and knotted streets trying to sort it out into any pattern except the obvious one: The people of Horn did not trust reeves. And how in the hells had that come about?

At last he set a course out to the crossroads where the Flats, West Track, and East Track met, not more than half a mey from Horn's gates, and circled there over the wreckage of a line of wagons that, by the look of them, had been burned and upended recently. Folk in the nearby fields retreated, bunching into groups for safety or grabbing their tools and running back toward the gates.

He wanted to investigate, to see if he could estimate how long ago those wagons had burned, but they were still visible to the militia's watchful eye since the town lay upslope with no woodland to break the line of sight. Instead, he turned south with Peddo and Volias off to either side, and they flew along the empty road and fields that, out of eyeshot of the walls, had been left fallow. This was a landscape of smooth ridges and hollows that rolled like sea swells out beyond the breakers. They had flown for not more than a mey when they crossed over a tumble of old boulders and outcrops where the soil had worn down to expose ancient seams of rock. Peddo's whistle blasted within moments of the Snake flagging an alert.

Among the rocks lay scattered remains, skulls and leg bones and scraps of cloth visible. A dark shape moved within a shadowed crevice, difficult to make out from this height. They circled low. The remains spread beyond the outcrop into mixed grass and scrub woodland. Where a stream wound along somewhat upslope, another dense scatter of remains lay strewn along the bank.

It was a battlefield, easy to read: the first engagement had taken place where the stream afforded cover, and then the losing side had retreated in a straggle through heavy growth to the greater defensive position offered by the rocks. It was by no means clear who had won, and who had lost. Wind, rain, and animals at work among the dead had taken their toll of the evidence.

As had human agency: Four figures picked their way along the stream's bank, overturning skulls, using a spade to pry loose rib cages overgrown by grass. They were so intent on their task that they didn't notice the eagles passing overhead.

Peddo stayed aloft. Joss sent Scar down. The eagle fanned his tail and threw his legs forward. They thumped home. Trouble came down right beside him, and both reeves were out of their harness and scrambling as the children – for they were children – gawped up at them with their scavenger's tools hanging forgotten in grubby hands.

The eldest among them, a girl, began to cry without audible weeping, just a smudging trickle on dirty cheeks. She was that scared. The littlest was a scrap of a thing, and it took off only to be grabbed by the Snake and slung roughly back to stand with the other three. There it cowered, hiding its left arm behind its back. Looking them over, Joss saw that one of the middle children was lacking an ear and the other had a twisted hand broken somehow and healed all wrong. The younger two had swollen bellies, and all four had various sores on crusted lips, swollen red-rimmed eyes, flies buzzing around pus-ridden blisters on their bare arms and legs, and besides all that an unhealthy stink in addition to the obvious stink of children who haven't been taken to the baths in months.

They stood in the midst of tumbled remains, which were scoured until nothing but bone and scraps of decaying cloth was left. He was surprised that none of the Lady's wandering mendicants had gathered the bones and burned them in order to properly complete the rites to placate the restless dead.

'What you going to do, ver?' asked the eldest. She had a squint that made her look defiant, but in fact it came from a cut at one eye that had scarred and pulled her lid tight. Like the others, she was as thin as if she'd been constructed out of sticks, with a hollow face and deep-set eyes.

'I'm Reeve Joss,' he said gently. 'What are your names?'

She looked at him as if he were crazy, and did not answer.

He tried again. 'Where is your family? Kinfolk? Parents?' But he knew what the answer would be before he heard it.

She shrugged. 'Gone,' she said as her hand dropped down to brush the shoulder of the earless one. With her good hand, Broken Hand took hold of the elbow of Littlest.

'How came that about?'

She shrugged.

'What of other kin? Aunties and uncles? Anyone to take you in?'

She shrugged. The others stood stock-still with well-practiced silence. They had been alone long enough that they knew the routine.

'The temples take in such as these little criminals,' said the Snake.

'We're not going there!' she said fiercely. 'They just make slaves of us, and split us apart. City folk are that way, willing to make slaves of themselves, that's what my dad says. But our people don't do that. We're doing okay. We're doing good enough.'

The Snake chuffed a laugh. 'Doesn't look that way to me.'

'What are you doing out here?' Joss asked before he lost her, for he knew how some clammed right up when faced with scorn.

She indicated the rib cage she'd been trying to pry up. 'There was a battle here, oh I don't know, a year or two ago so they say.'

'White Lion year,' chirped Broken Hand. 'During the Flower Rains.'

'That's right,' said Eldest. 'We got rights just like anyone to come see what we may find, ver.'

'Looters!' said the Snake with his habitual sneer. 'Grave robbers.'

'Shut it!' snapped Joss. He looked back at the girl, who appraised this exchange with a raised eyebrow and a nudge of the foot to Earless. 'Looks like this field is well scavenged already. As it would be, since it's coming on three years since the battle happened. What are you finding?'

'You going to try to take it from us, ver?' she asked, not with any sort of challenge.

'If I was, I wouldn't say so at first, would I?'

He thought to crack a smile from her, but she just looked at him and considered what he had said with the flat stare of a child who has long since hunkered down to the serious business of survival and is doubtful she will make it. She might have gotten on better without the littler ones, but people often made that choice because they could make no other. Sometimes they even made it because it was the just thing to do.

'You're reeves,' she said.

'So we are, as I said.'

'Those reeves out of Horn Hall, they don't come around no more. You from Horn Hall?'

'We're not.'

'Didn't think so.' She shrugged again, as though ridding herself of a weight. 'We none of us know why – that they stopped coming round, I mean. It just is that way now, and were that way from before.'

'From before what?'

'Before we come to Horn.'

'Where did you come from?'

The Snake moved off upwind, wrinkling his nose against the stink, but Joss held his position despite the strength of their sickly sweet-sour smell.

She looked away from him, blinking rapidly. 'Dunesk Valley, up in the Ossu. We come from there. Can't live there now.'

'What happened?'

She shrugged.

'Where do you live now?'

'Horn. At least, the folk mostly leave us alone if we bide in the alleys and bother no one. If we find something or other, maybe we can sell it.'

'Found a ring,' piped Littlest proudly. 'I did!'

'Hush,' said Broken Hand, pinching Littlest's skin until it whimpered.

'That was last month,' said Eldest hastily. 'Lest you're thinking it was just now.'

Which, by the nervous set of their chins and the way her gaze flicked toward Earless, made him understand that in fact they had found something *just now*. In fact, they believed that two reeves might likely steal what they had. That's what they thought of reeves. It made him want to shout in frustration.

'You need to tell me what happened in Dunesk Valley,' he said instead, because understanding a thing was often the only way to solve it. 'I need to know, because I'm a reeve. You know it's our job to set things right.'

'That's what we used to think, but them at Horn Hall just stopped coming.'

'When was that?'

For a long while she was silent. Earless let go her hand and edged a few steps away, crouched down at the bank, and ladled some water into his mouth. The Snake had backed up and was staring toward the distant boulders. Peddo was nowhere in sight.

Then she started talking in a voice as flat as her gaze, as if all emotion had long since been crushed out of her. 'Dunesk's about a day's walk, by the trail, and one time we come down to Horn a few years back—'

'Snake year it was,' said Broken Hand.

'—that's right, just after that one made his second year.' She pointed to the littlest.

'Four years ago,' Joss said.

She nodded. 'We came down because Dad and Uncle had hides to trade. But then the raiders came. There was all kinds of things they were doing, so our dad he sent us into town because it isn't safe up there no more. We sleep on the street. Mostly folk leave us alone, not always.'

That *not always* made him wince. She was old enough, if a man

had a fancy for veal, which he did not, and anyway any child was
old enough for those who had a taste for that manner of cruelty.

He asked, 'What of your dad? Or your uncle? Are they still
living?'

She choked. 'I hope so.'

'It sounds awful, living in Horn as you do. You ever thought of
going back home?'

She would not meet his eye. 'Awful is what they do in the villages,
if they catch you.'

'What do they do?'

She shuddered and would not speak, and when finally he offered
some dry flatbread out of his pouch, she pointed at Littlest, who
lifted his left arm out from behind his back to display a scarred and
seamed stump. For a moment Joss couldn't figure why he was doing
it.

Volias said, with real revulsion, 'Lady's Tit! They cut off the little
wight's hand!'

Earless scrambled back from the stream's edge, and Eldest broke
the bread into four pieces. They inhaled it, so it seemed, because it
vanished in a blink.

'Look there!' said Volias, pointing to a spot behind Joss's back.

On occasion Joss found himself confused by the way the ground
changed when you were standing on it as opposed to when you
were flying above it. Angles of sight shifted; blind in one place, you
found you could see in the other; unexpected vistas revealed themselves because of the curve and elevation of the ground or when
mist hid from the sky what, with feet on the earth, you could see
perfectly well.

The woodland scrub had seemed, from the air, to separate the
rocky ground from the stream, but in fact the land sloped down into
a hollow where the densest growth took advantage of damper
ground to flourish, and rose again to the stony ground. Seen from
the ground, the rock formations were taller than they had seemed
from the air, with a hundred hiding places and defensive posts.
Seemingly oblivious of the reeves, their eagles, and the four children,
a person bent, rose, walked the ground, bent and rose again. The
figure was dressed in some manner of loose, black robe. From this
distance, Joss thought it must be a woman, but he couldn't be sure.

'That's another like us,' said Eldest, seeing how they were looking that way.

'You've seen that person before?'

'Yes, ver. So we have.'

'She's a scavenger, like you?'

'So she must be, ver. We come out here all the time. We saw her first time a few month back'

'It was Fox Month,' said Broken Hand. 'It was so cold at night, beginning of Shiver Sky. That's the first time we saw her out here.'

'That's right,' said Eldest. 'We see her now and again. Not all the time.'

'You ever talk to her? Have any trouble with her?'

'Nah, she don't talk, except one time she stopped us and asked us if we saw any strange thing that had an outland look to it. She's looking for some dead person, maybe her lover or her son. I don't know and wasn't thinking to ask.'

'Someone she got to missing,' said Earless abruptly in the hoarse voice of a boy about to break into manhood. 'Someone she want desperately to find.'

'How often do you come here?' Joss asked.

'As often as we need to,' said Eldest, who was relaxing a little. 'Gleaning is all we got, you see. No law against it!' she added hastily, looking at the Snake, but he had a frown on his ugly mug and wasn't looking at the children at all. He was tracking the movements of that other person up among the rocks.

'Then you sell what you've found.'

She shrugged. 'We pretty much found everything I expect there is to be found. Sometimes a hand got cut off and rolled into a crevice. That's how—' She almost said a name, but bit her tongue. 'That's how that one found the ring.' She nodded toward Littlest.

'Those dark holes could have snakes and biting things in them,' said Joss uneasily.

She rolled her eyes and said nothing. Snakes and biting things, obviously, did not concern her much compared with her other troubles.

'What'll you kids do now?' he asked.

'What you think?' she demanded. 'We told you all. Can we go now?'

They were skittish, and Littlest kept wiping away the green snot leaking from his nose.

'Have you nowhere else to go?' asked Volias suddenly.

'You ain't been listening,' said Eldest. 'Or you would have heard. You going to take us somewhere on those eagles? And then who will take us in? We got to wait here by Horn until Dad come to get us. That's what he said. When it was safe again. That's what he said.'

Joss shook his head. 'You go on. You've got a long walk back to Horn.'

They lit out as if fire had been kindled beneath them.

Volias settled onto his haunches beside the rib cage, studying it without touching. 'Is that it?' he demanded, glaring at Joss. 'They cut off that kid's hand!'

'What else can we do for them?'

'That's why we keep running from fights? Because we can't do anything else for them? What about those two dead men at that farm? Seems we reeves do a lot of looking, and a lot of squeezing available women, but we don't do any fighting anymore.'

'You're right,' said Joss.

The words took the Snake so off guard that he rocked back, lost his balance, and sat, kicking out reflexively. His foot jostled the rib cage, ripping it half out of the covering of debris that had begun to bury it. The mat of debris beneath it included decaying hempen cloth dyed a clay-red color that the Snake shied away from touching.

'This must be some manner of outlander,' said the Snake. 'Wearing death cloth like regular clothes. Look here. His belt's still in good shape.' He peeled the strip of leather out of the soil, whipping it away from the rib cage. A heavier object went flying to land on the nearby grass with a thud.

'Best we go talk to that woman,' said Joss.

'Why for, if we mean to do nothing about any of it?'

'Listen, *Volias*. The rot's set in deep. We can get ourselves killed, or we can find the source of the rot and kill it. I don't see any other way. But of ourselves, just us three, out here where we've no allies apparently and no idea who is our enemy and who regards us as enemy, what are we three to do? Or did you want to take on two cadres of armed men?'

The Snake ignored him, most likely because there was no answer. Joss trudged down into the hollow, pushing through brush, noting the way the battle had whirled and eddied into clumps of fighting, marked by collections of disturbed bones, and then streamed out again over open ground as one group fled toward the rocks while the other group, presumably, pursued. Why in the hells had a group of outlanders ridden into the Hundred? Who would have hired them? The other reeves ought to have passed along to Clan Hall news of such an unusual occurrence, but they hadn't. Clan Hall had never heard about any battle fought in the Year of the White Lion near the city of Horn.

And it really was strange that the dead had been left out here, stripped and looted, just because no one could be bothered to carry the corpses to Horn's Sorrowing Tower. Outlanders, bandits, clanless orphans might be abandoned in death. Just like those kids who, if they died in the fields beyond Horn, would no doubt be left lying with no one but that missing dad and uncle to care if their bodies ever received godly treatment. Yet it went against the law, not to mention simple decency.

The kites and vultures and bugs would scour them all to bone in the end, in any case. There were worse fates. In a way, to be left dead upon the earth was to be left on the gods' most ancient Sorrowing Tower, because the rock that was the scaffolding of the earth had been erected long before the gods' towers.

Just as Joss reached the outermost stretch of rock poking up out of a gaggle of thorn-flower bushes, the woman came around the pile of weathered boulders. She stopped, although she did not seem surprised to see him.

'I was just looking for you,' he said with his best smile. 'I saw you from over there.'

She was dressed for riding in stiff trousers, light shirt, and sleeveless jacket, with a dark cloak of an almost weightless fabric curling down from her shoulders and wrapped over one arm. In one hand, she held an old spear that she used as a walking staff on the uneven ground. She wore a grave expression on a pleasant face whose years were difficult to count; she was probably his age, or older. Yet she did not look him over the way many women did, with an appreciative eye. She didn't frown either. She wasn't unfriendly. She looked past him, shading her eyes. 'You're a reeve.'

'So I am, verea. I was wondering what brought a respectable householder like you out to search a battlefield.'

That twitch of her lips was not as much a smile as a secret. 'I was looking for something.'

'Did you find it?'

'As it happens, I just did. Who is that following you?'

He looked back over his shoulder to see the Snake scrambling over the rugged ground to catch up to him. 'My comrade.'

'There are three of you,' she said, tilting her head back to survey the sky.

'These days, it's best to travel in the company of those you trust.'

Her gaze slipped to his, and away as quickly, but even so that glance caught him off guard. Funny, when you thought of it, how difficult it could be to know why you trusted some folk and not others. He trusted Peddo. He thought of how much he disliked the Snake, who was a bully, who made suspects cry for the fun of it, who liked to push around locals to see them cringe; who had lied more than once; who had ratted him out when he was trying to woo that merchant's daughter, just because he was jealous. It wasn't his fault that the Snake had no luck with women. The man ought to look to his own behavior to answer for that lack. And yet, Joss knew Volias would cover his back in a tight spot. Aui! He himself was the one who couldn't be trusted. He'd gone wild after Marit's death. He'd been reckless, crazy, defiant, impossible, even dangerous to himself and others. He'd fanned the flames until they got too hot. No wonder Marshal Masar had tossed him out of Copper Hall. He'd been named legate later to keep him away, not from any worthiness on his part, even if people had given him that nickname, calling him incorruptible when really it was only about doing your duty as you had agreed the day the eagle chose you, just trying to make right everything that had gone wrong.

How had the sun gotten so bright all of a sudden? He was staring right into the glare, eyes watering.

'Hey! Look here!' Volias walked panting up the slope and stopped beside him. 'It's a belt buckle.' He had wiped away some of the dirt encrusted in the wrinkles and crevices of the thing. When he held it up, metal caught sun and winked. 'Good quality. A wolf's head, I think. Never seen this manner of pattern before. What were outlanders doing here, do you think?'

'Come to fight, I suppose,' said Joss, looking around for the woman.

'Then they got what they come for. Unlike us.'

'Where'd she go?'

'Where'd who go?'

'I was talking to that woman, the one we saw.'

'You're always talking to women.'

'Didn't you see her?'

'I did, but it seems she took fright of your ugly face and crept off while I was coming up from behind those rocks. I lost sight of you for a bit. Serves you right! You're not used to them rejecting you, are you?'

For once, the Snake's taunting did not disturb him. Wind skirled through the rocks and spit dust at them. They tramped through the maze of outcrops and boulders, stuck their heads into shadowed overhangs, and poked their batons into deep crevices. Birds flitted around them, anxious at their presence, and various animals – rats, mice, rabbits, coneys, a veritable feast – scurried in the undergrowth or down into slits and cracks where they could not reach. Once, Joss saw a fox's clever face peering at him out of a thicket, but when he blinked, it was gone. There were bones aplenty; Joss estimated that hundreds of people had died here, but the remains really were stripped out and there was nothing except skeletal remains and bits and pieces of useless scrap.

They found no sign of the woman.

At length, Joss scrambled to the top of the highest boulder, where he stood at a sheer edge about three body's lengths off the ground. Searching the sky, he saw Peddo and Jabi approaching from the south. That was strange, too. Hadn't Peddo been out of sight, too far away to mark as anything except an unidentified bird? How had the woman known he was there?

He set his whistle to his lips and called Scar, and signaled with the flag for Peddo to come down, but instead Peddo flew low overhead and, banking tight, blew the three short blasts on his whistle that made Joss's whole body jolt just as a fire bell would, heard clanging within the city's vulnerable streets.

Emergency.

He and Scar leaped aloft, Volias and Trouble not far behind. There was a slight updraft over the rocks, but the raptors strained, pushing hard, for they recognized the whistle call as well as their reeves did. Jabi flapped past, pushing hard back the way he had come, and Peddo whipped his flag in the up-and-down motion for *crime in progress.*

By the hells, it would be good to be able to act for a change.

He looked back over the outcrop as they lifted, but he still saw no sign of that woman. She could not have walked away so fast. She must have heard them, and hidden in the rock in some hidey-hole they had not noticed. How had the people of this region come to fear and hate reeves?

He did see the four children walking across abandoned fields in the direction of Horn. They hadn't gotten far. They even looked up and one pointed their way while the others paused to stare.

Peddo glided alongside as close as any of them dared get to the other, and shouted across the gap. 'Osprey attack! Merchant banners. On West Track. Looks bad!'

They found thermals and rose, and from the height the eagles immediately spotted movement a mey or more ahead of them on the road.

Scar and Jabi and Trouble put out a burst of speed. Only as they got closer could Joss make sense of the scene: a pair of wagons flying household banners marking them as respectable merchants, a dozen plunging horses, and men on the road striving mightily against a larger attacking group mostly on foot and directed by a pair of riders hanging back at the rear out of danger. One of those captains was carrying so much gear on his horse that the baggage distorted the animal's frame, making it seem bulkier about the body than a normal horse. The other captain wore lime-whitened horse-tail shoulder crests, and carried a banner strung with four narrow yellow and red flags.

For those on the road, who couldn't have counted more than fifteen or so, it was clearly a losing battle against attackers who boasted over twice that number. Already about half of the merchants and their armed escort had fallen, while the others gave way until they were backed against one of the wagons.

This time he wasn't going to walk away.

The eagles glided in silence and, when the angle was right, they stooped.

You never got jaded to this. The air screamed past; the ground leaped up at you, ready to punch you in the face and then flatten you. And yet your eagle would put on the brakes at just the right instant. Scar came down with wings wide and talons extended. The laden horse was already bolting with its rider clinging to its back, but the other man and horse did not react as quickly. Scar knocked him right off the saddle, and the horse reared back in a panic, shied, backed up, and broke for safety, following the other horse, which was already racing north along the road.

Joss unhooked his harness and jumped free, hitting the ground with legs bent to absorb the impact. He had his short sword drawn. Peddo punched back a pair of men with his spear's stout haft while Jabi went at a clot of bandits who had pushed the beleaguered merchants up against their wagons. The raucous kek-kek of the huge eagle was a terrifying thing, wings beating and talons ripping. The bandits shrieked and cried out and scattered.

Where was Volias?

Scar yelped. Joss shied sideways, an instant before the blow hit him. His shoulder took most of it, but the tip caught him just behind his right ear. Then the man coming at him fell forward onto his own face, and Volias yanked his short sword out of the man's back and shoved the body aside.

'Thanks,' grunted Joss, stung and shocked as he struggled to his feet.

'Doesn't mean I like you any better,' said the Snake.

The fallen man was writhing spastically, blood spitting from his mouth. Joss's head throbbed as a swell of nausea clogged his throat, but he gulped down the bile and tried not to blink, which made the pain worse. Volias yelled, but Joss's ears were ringing and he couldn't sort out the words. Then Scar was there, tearing into a man who had somehow gotten right in front of him. The eagle's talons punctured the flesh, and the man screamed and screamed. Volias, glancing past them, got an awful look on his face and ran as if demon-ridden toward the mess by the wagon.

A pair of men leaped past Joss, having crept up from the left, and swung with halberds at Scar, but Joss spun up and met them blade-to-blade, holding them off until Scar pounced. Their fear killed them, because they hesitated. Scar tore the head off one while Joss stabbed another. The hot scent of death and blood flooded him, and the ache in his head, in that instant, cleared.

He swept the scene with a quick look to identify the danger spots. The last eddy of fighting had caught around the wagon. Peddo was on the ground curled up as into a ball with eyes forced wide by pain. Volias battered back the last two men standing, the ones who wouldn't give up and run. A furious Jabi struck and struck and struck into the torso of one of the men, whose hideous shrieks hurt the ears. The other bolted, but Volias grabbed him from behind, jerked him back, and stabbed him, then shoved him away.

Joss ran, and dropped down beside Peddo. 'Heya! Heya! Peddo! Let's see it. Come on, now. It can't be that bad.'

Volias appeared, his shadow giving them a brief respite from the sudden impossible weight of the heat. The sun was dizzying.

'Ah, the hells.' Volias stalked away to see if anyone was left alive.

'Eh! Eh! Eh!' gasped Peddo, trying to speak, trying not to cry out.

'The hells,' said Joss. 'Just scream, damn you. Let me see it.' Jabi was circling; he hackled, and opened his wings impatiently. He was so damned big, a hundred times more intimidating than any twenty men and their weapons because of his ferocity and high courage. 'He's going to bate, Peddo. He's scared for you. Don't let me face that alone. He'll rip my head clean off.'

Peddo set his jaw and with a roar flopped back. Blood pumped from the cut that had sliced just above his hip and down into his groin. Joss slit the leathers, pulled strips of linen and silk from his own rig, and set to bind it as tightly as he could, to stem the bleeding. All the while keeping up an idiot flow of commentary.

'Damn it but that was a close one, Peddo. Lucky thing that blade didn't just whack your good friend there right off. Else you'd have no reason to visit the Devourer again, but then, I don't suppose that would have bothered you any.'

'Peh. Uh. At least I'm choosy about where my friend takes his festival. Ayuh!' Without warning, Peddo passed out. Jabi settled, crouching over his reeve and spreading his wings to shelter him.

Volias came back. 'Not good. We didn't get here in time. Cursed wolves got them all. There's one merchant who can still talk, but his gut's laid open. No mendicants in sight, so I don't see how we can save him. The rest are dead or unconscious, and the wolves are already circling. They're gathering out beyond range, but they won't stay out there long. We're badly outnumbered, despite the ones we killed.'

Joss rose to survey the scene. The two wagons were rigged to run rugged and fast. The horses had bolted; a few were already being rounded up by those bandits who had fled off to a safe distance. The other two eagles were hackling, strung tight, ready to go at it again.

'Get Peddo in his harness,' he said to Volias.

The dead littered the ground, merchants and bandits alike. Some were still alive, but in that passing way, blood bubbling from their lips or dribbling from puncture wounds in the torso that could not be healed, not even by the Lady's mendicants had there been any here along the road. A couple of the bandits were whimpering, lost in pain, all bloody and torn enough to make you wince until you remembered that they had attacked. The fortunate ones were unconscious and dying, or already dead. One of the merchants had dragged himself into a half-sitting position, propped up on the body of another man. His head was wrapped in cloth, in a turban. A strip of that cloth had come loose, and the entire elaborate structure of the headdress looked likely to unravel. His arms glinted under the weight of a sheath of silver bracelets. His silk jacket was cut through and, as the Snake had said, his gut had been laid horribly open to expose the glistening insides. It was a terrible wound made worse because it did not kill quickly.

'Will he live?' Volias asked.

Joss began to shake his head, and realized that Volias was asking about Peddo. 'If we get him back to Clan Hall before he bleeds to death, and if there's no infection, he just might. That man there, he's a Silver.'

'Yeh. I didn't touch him. He's the only one of that kind in the group.'

'Strange. Usually they travel together with their own kind.'

Joss tossed an extra coil of rope to Volias, then strode over. The wounded man saw the movement and tracked him with his gaze. He even tried to smile as Joss knelt beside him.

'Ah – ah – thought no one would come.'

'We did, but it didn't help much.'

'It is enough,' whispered the Silver valiantly. His face was sheened with sweat, and his lips were losing color. A stink roiled out of his exposed guts. Behind, Peddo's whistle shrilled as Volias blew it to get Jabi to settle and come in.

'Must get the message through,' croaked the Silver.

Joss took one of the Silver's hands between his own. The man's skin was cool, and getting colder as the life drained from him. 'What message?'

'Shefen sen Haf Gi Ri. My house – sent me with these others. The four of us. Sons of the Lesser Houses – in Olossi. And these eight guardsmen – brave men.'

Joss looked the man in the eye to aid him in keeping his focus as he struggled for words. He did not interrupt. The dying man didn't have much time. Nor did the reeves. Out beyond the watchful eagles, the wolves were circling.

'Dissent, disagreement, in the council. The Greater walks hard upon the Lesser, although there are more of us – among the Lesser. We should be heard. Trade to the north has stopped. The Greater Houses say – to be patient – but we – the others of us – the Lesser Houses – we wonder – what is going on. So we sent this group – we four to carry the message. Nokki from Three Rings. Myself. Two from the guilds, Kavess and Aden. Also the eight guardsmen, brave men.' Like the wolves, he was circling, back to words he had already spoken.

'What is your message?' Joss prompted. In this moment, the world was dead to him, all emotion fled and the wind and the smell of battle fading away because he must hear the words that this man was trying so desperately to speak.

'Two. There are two messages. Why has trade stopped? Where are our caravans sent north last year? Why does no trade come out of the north? Show us support.'

'Have you asked the reeves of Argent Hall to help you?'

'They can't hear us,' said the Silver cryptically, and he went on so quickly that Joss dared not stop him to ask that he explain himself. 'Two – the second message. Emergency! There are ospreys hunting on the Kandaran Pass, and along West Spur. Attacking caravans, this season. Now. Right now. Captain Beron of the border guards is no help. He claims he needs more guardsmen. He claims . . . he needs support of Olossi council, of Argent Hall. We of the Lesser Houses . . . we would give aid, more guardsmen, pay for it . . . but the Greater Houses remain silent. They refuse to listen to our voice. They no longer trust us. The wolves are circling, cutting us off at both ends. They mean to choke us. Who?'

His hand clenched Joss's hard, as though a jolt had passed through him, as though he had found his strength and might actually live. 'Who wants to choke us? Who will help them? Who will help us?'

The hells!

The effort of speaking had sucked the man dry. He went limp as the breath of life fled. His destiny, his fortune, to end here, on the West Track, about five mey from safety. If the town of Horn would have offered these men a safe haven.

And the wolves were closing in, damn them all to the hells.

Joss released his hand, tucked in the fraying ends of the man's headdress, and twisted the bracelets off both arms. He cut a length of silk off the man's jacket and wrapped the bracelets up with a twist knot. Rising, he checked the positions of his allies and his enemies.

Jabi had his wings spread wide, and he wasn't happy, but he held still as all the eagles were trained to do when their reeves were wounded. Volias hooked Peddo into the harness and tied him in tightly with Joss's rope, checked the bandage, all with a remarkable lack of concern about that vicious beak and those talons a mere kiss away from his head.

The wolves were circling, getting bolder, and one man seemed to be lining up a trio of archers far enough away that they could pester the reeves with arrows. Joss counted his dead and dying: all twelve of the Olossi men, and fourteen scruffy outlaws. He searched through the corpses for the guildsmen and the other merchant, who would wear an identifying mark on their clothing.

'Joss!' called Volias.

'Go on!' called Joss to him. 'Take Peddo north to Clan Hall.'

'We've got to get back to Clan Hall!' yelled Volias. 'Now. Those damned wolves are going to come after us in about three breaths.'

Joss lifted both hands. 'We've got to follow this up. Bandits on the Kandaran Pass. The West Track unsafe for merchants. Something's definitely wrong at Argent Hall. I'm flying south to see what I can see. Tell the Commander to send a flight south to meet me at Olossi.'

'Stupid shithead,' said Volias. 'Don't you get tired of it?'

'Tired of what?'

'Always having to be the one who goes in first. Ah, the hells! Never mind.' He let Jabi go, and leaped back. The big eagle lifted with a shriek. Volias gave a call with his own whistle and, when Trouble fluttered over to him, hooked into his own harness.

'You got a good haul off that Silver!' he called, as a parting shot. 'The dead will make you rich!'

'Go devour yourself,' shouted Joss, 'since no one else will!'

There, at the end, with the nub of their dislike spoken baldly, Volias actually laughed. 'I hate men like you, so easy with the women!' He said something more, but the words were lost as Trouble lifted in a gust of wings.

An arrow skittered over the ground. The wolves were testing their range. Joss counted ten that he could see, one limping. Five had bows, always the greatest danger to the eagles. Joss stuck his bone whistle to his lips, and the blast of sound shuddered over the carnage as if it might shiver all those ghosts to rest. Scar, already strung tight by the presence of the lurking bandits, by the fight, and by hunger, flew straight at him, leaving Joss barely enough time to turn his back as the eagle landed with a massive thump just behind him. One-handed, he fastened into the harness, and then they were up, Scar beating with powerful strokes until he found a thermal and caught it.

Up and up they rose. Below, the scatter of wagons and dead and dying men looked like a child's toys thrown carelessly about. The wolves dashed in to ransack the wagons and the dead men. After them would come the vultures; a pair glided past, already on the hunt for fresh carrion. Tomorrow or the next day, perhaps, those four children would come to glean through what remained.

The other two eagles were already high above, slipping into a northward glide. Far off to the west, Joss spotted another creature in the sky. At first he thought it must be a vulture, but it moved with the wrong motion. It was not even flying as an eagle did, rising and gliding, but beating steadily. Scar kekked, seeking direction.

Joss considered the distant flyer, already fading from sight. Scar took no heed of it, and Joss hadn't time to investigate a bird that Scar deemed unworthy of notice. Anyway, he had to keep his attention on the urgent matter at hand.

'South,' he said to himself, and signaled with the jess.

They left the battle scene behind, quickly out of sight within the rolling, golden landscape, the high plains grasslands that stretched to the southern horizon. That was the way of a reeve's life. You had to leave it behind. If you did not, it ate you up from the inside out.

HE IS WALKING but instead of skeletal trees he sees the long rise and fall of the slopes that make up the grassland countryside where he and the eagle bedded down that night. Grass rolls away on all sides. There is no horizon. Mist boils up out of the ground as though the earth itself has exhaled. He strains to see through it into the veiled distance. Are those merely shadows on the slope ahead of him or is that a figure climbing toward the crest? Those fingers on the back of his neck are the wind. He tries to move forward, to chase it down, but he cannot shift.

Then, on the wind, he hears her voice as faintly as if she is speaking to him across a vast distance, or in a whisper just behind his head.

'The ospreys raid on the West Spur. Their leader is Beron, captain of the border guard. Break them first, before they take the treasure that the Hundred needs most. The carters and merchants will help you, for they suffer the worst depredations. Hurry. The shadows are spreading. Beware!'

'Marit!' he cried, sitting bolt upright.

It was dawn, and he was sweating, and after all he was awake and there was nothing to see except the dregs of his campfire, his pack and weapons set on the ground beside the bedroll on which he had slept, and Scar rousing himself with the rising of the light. He buried the last embers, and made ready. The sky was cloudless, utterly clear, bound to the flat eastern horizon and still purpling dark where it met the distant Soha Hills to the west. His thoughts, too, were clear, sharp, naked. He thought of murdered reeves and mutilated eagles, of River's Bend burned to the ground, of High Haldia under attack, of farmers tied to the posts of the Witherer's altar, of Horn Hall abandoned, of the four children, of the dying Silver and his murdered companions. He thought of the voice in his dream.

You had to leave it behind, because if you did not, it ate you up from the inside out.

But not this time. This time he wouldn't walk away. He would fix something, serve justice somehow, or by the hells he would die trying.

22

The road north toward the Hundred ran long, and through steep, impossibly high mountains. Shai listened to the chatter of merchants and hired men as he rode through the ranks of the caravan.

'I knew it were not good, the way that other caravan did racket out yesterday.'

'What caravan? I didn't get to the market that early.'

'It were at Sarida before us, you know, readying to go. A smaller group of Hundred merchants they were, anxious to get home. They did bolt at dawn whilst we were still bargaining with the caravan master for places. I bet they did hear something of these bandits and heretics, and hoped to outrace the troubles.'

'The market magistrate said there's been no caravan come south from the Hundred for two months. Not a one, not since our company came five months back before the really cold weather.'

'Might still be snow up on the pass.'

'No. I'm sure it must be these troubles. I hadn't finished with my last trades, I had a few deals to make, but I let them go. Better safe than dead, I'm thinking. I'm that glad we lucked into these strong guards.'

'May the gods watch over us.'

'Hush! No talk of the gods in the empire. You'll get us killed!'

The Hundred merchants had a strange way of talking; many of

the words were the same as the language spoken up and down the Golden Road and in the empire, but they shaped the sounds differently. They had also a peculiar manner of dressing, men wearing loose robes that left their calves bare, or knee-length tunics and sleeveless jackets over baggy trousers. Instead of heavy jackets to protect against the cold, they wore lengths of cloth, cloaks voluminous enough to wrap around their bodies, falling down to their ankles and fastened in place at the shoulder. The complexion and arrangement of features on their faces weren't like anything Shai had seen in Kartu Town, either, where one saw a variety of folk passing through as merchants or soldiers or priests or slaves. They hadn't the red-brown clay coloring of Kartu people, or the dusty brown complexion of the Mariha and desert people, or the mulch-brown features of many of the Sirniakan people, nor the richly brown-black skin of Priya, who came from far to the south past desert and heaven-high mountains both, close to the sun. Most of these northern men had a complexion with a golden-brown shine, black hair more commonly curly than the coarse straight black hair known in the rest of the world, and the brown eyes that marked all human folk.

Not like Cornflower's demon-blue eyes.

Why must he still think of her? Those memories made him flush, made him itch. They shamed him. Chief Tuvi rode through, casting orders as to the winds, and in his wake Tohon dragged Shai away to ride point.

Out ahead of the rest, they pushed their faces into the wind that ran down off the tremendous height piled up before them. Tohon rode in a concentrated silence, his gaze roaming over the unfolding road and the narrowing vista of the land, but Shai sucked in the flavor of the wind and mumbled to himself in a low voice. By breathing in air that tasted of far places and unknown destinations, he hoped to thrust her ghost out of his mind, because she would not stop haunting him. Yet she ought to stop, here in a land where women were not permitted to walk abroad alone and uncovered. She ought to stop, because there were no ghosts in the Sirniakan Empire. Not one.

'Tohon, the Qin soldiers and that groom who died. What happens to them? To their bodies and spirits?'

'To die in battle is a good death. The gods take the dead man's spirit into the heavens, and their flesh is scattered by the animals, returning to the earth.'

'But don't you keep their bones with the ancestors?'

Tohon burst out laughing. 'Hu! You folk with your feet stuck in the bricks of your cities. I've seen those tombs where you bury the bones of your ancestors. How are we Qin to carry so many bones with us? I've my weapons, my saddle, my string of horses, my field rations. Back in my home country, my son tends the family herds. I'd a daughter once, but she died, and my good wife died of grief at the losing of her. It was a bad death. The girl drowned. When the water takes you, the demons capture your soul.' He shook his head, face creased with a frown. Shai had never seen him look so downcast.

'I – I'm sorry to hear such a sad tale. May the merciful heart of the Holy One ease your burden.'

'Huh. That's why I rode east with Commander Beje. I'd done my years in the army, I could have stayed in the home pastures and raised my grandchildren, but the burden was too great. My daughter's ghost haunted me. I wonder in what land my bones will be scattered. This north land, this Hundred land, perhaps.'

'You don't just leave everyone behind, do you? Like those men who died. We just left them behind. Isn't there shame in having no remains to bury with the ancestors? Is there nothing their family has of them, in the end?'

'How is a person to stop in a battle, or on the trail? You talk too much, Shai. I told you before. Once the spirit is fled, the body is just meat. The spirit can be born again and again, and travel on the winds. You can meet them in another life.'

'Not once they've passed Spirit Gate. The Merciful One teaches that once you pass Spirit Gate, you can be free of the world, free of suffering, gone altogether beyond.'

'Why would you want to be free of the world?' asked Tohon. 'I'll never understand you people.'

'What happens when folk die, here in the empire?' Shai asked Anji that night as the captain waited for his tent and awning to be set up. They were standing by a freshly kindled fire. In the hills, there was plenty of wood to burn.

Anji considered, as if searching the question for traps. Finally, he shrugged. 'The Sirniakan magistrates investigate every death and determine its cause. The guilty are punished. Those responsible for the corpse pay the death price. Afterward, the body is taken to the temple and burned. The ashes are plowed into special fields to nourish the living. Everything is always tidy in the empire. Not like in the rest of the world. Ghosts dare not trouble the priests of Beltak, Lord of Lords and King of Kings, the Shining One Who Rules Alone.'

Shai flushed as though the fire had washed over him. Why would Anji mention ghosts? Had he betrayed himself somehow? He had tried so hard to keep his secret. Maybe Mai had whispered the truth to Anji, as pillow talk. Best he not talk about the dead at all, lest folk got to wondering how he knew so much about ghosts.

'Who is Beltak?' he asked, hoping to throw down fresh scent to muddy the trail.

'That's the short name of the god. He has a longer one, but it takes an hour to say it all.' The shifting dance of the flames played on his face. The world was an inconstant place, so the flames might have told him. Anji was a man who appreciated irony, and gave away little else.

'What of the Merciful One?'

'The priests of the Merciful One are executed if they're caught. Or any of their worshipers. Hamstrung, and burned alive.'

Shai shuddered. The awning was settled. A lantern was lit, and a carpet unrolled. Shai excused himself, claiming he had to take a piss, but he was simply too nervous to sit. He walked a circuit of the campsite.

Six fires burned to shelter this consortium of thirty-one anxious merchants, ranging in grandness from long-distance solo peddlers pushing handcarts piled with silks and spices to one grand entrepreneur and his managers shepherding ten wagons of fine goods and forty or more healthy young slaves destined for the markets of the Hundred. No one sang or chattered. They watched the darkness, waiting for bandits or heretics to strike.

One man dressed purely in white sat alone, on a mat, with only an oil lamp for company. He held a wooden bowl in front of him and murmured words as he touched water from the bowl to his forehead. The Sirniakan carters and drovers knelt on the ground behind this man, mimicking his movement with bowls and water of their own.

Shai paused to watch. After a moment, a slender man of mature years slipped in beside Shai. The man wore a voluminous cloak, dark pantaloons whose color could not be distinguished, and a tunic that in the moonlight appeared as pale as butter.

After a moment, the man touched him lightly on the elbow. 'Best not to stand watching, they don't allow it,' he whispered. He flashed a kindly smile, then strode away, cloak swirling around his legs.

Startled, Shai moved on. As he continued his circuit, the Qin sentries nodded at him. These days they seemed polite more than friendly. He had taken their politeness for companionship before, having known so little companionship in Kartu. Now that he understood them better, he recognized that they were bred, or honed, to a manner with a sheen of smoothness that rarely betrayed extremes of emotion. Tohon was asleep, rolled up in a blanket and snoring, his weathered face as peaceful as a baby's.

The sentry closest to the forest's edge whistled sharply. Men leaped up. Torches were lit. The merchants scattered to their wagons and carts. Out in the night, branches snapped and whipped as unseen stalkers scurried to get out of the way. Qin soldiers dashed after them and, in the distance and hidden by darkness, a melee exploded. It settled quickly, fading into a few shouts and a cheery laugh.

The man in white appeared at the edge of camp, holding his oil lamp in his left hand and his bowl in his right. The soldiers reappeared, mocking the tailman who limped in. They dragged a body, a ragged creature who once might have been a man, although he was filthy, skinny, and quite dead now. Shai watched from a distance. It was difficult to see threat in the dead man, but the merchants were as ecstatic as if they had been saved from a marauding army.

A wisp of ghost substance spun out of the man; a face of bitter regret and pain began to form its familiar cry. The man in white lifted lamp and bowl, chanting words under his breath like a prayer over the dead. As he spoke, the ghost substance was pulled and pulled like thread unraveling, and drawn inexorably into that simple wooden bowl, sucked clean into it, until it was all gone.

All gone. Given no chance to pass through Spirit Gate. Trapped in the bowl.

No one else noticed. No one else saw.

Shai broke into a sweat. His hands were shaking as he turned away. The man in white – whatever he was – must not suspect what Shai had seen.

Hamstrung and burned alive.

No talk of the gods in the empire. You'll get us killed!

The man in white moved away. The body was searched and afterward dumped into the bushes like so much garbage. The camp fell quiet again. It took him a long time, but he fought to breathe evenly. Once he thought he could speak without stammering, he circled back around to where he had started, at a spot overlooking the captain's awning.

By the light of a lantern, under the sole awning erected for the night, Anji had settled in to confer with Master Iad, the caravan master, a keen and cunning man for whom no detail was too small to ignore. Together they examined a knife that had been taken from the body of the dead man.

Mai appeared beside him, as if she had been waiting for him to show up. 'What's wrong, Shai? You look worried.'

'There is a man, dressed in white, who travels with the caravan. The drovers and carters mimic him. What is he?'

'He is a priest of Beltak. That's what Anji says. Every caravan traveling through the empire must employ a priest to guard.'

'To guard what?'

'I don't know. To guard against evil, I suppose. I think they're sorcerers. Do not speak to him. He'll leave us and go back into the empire, once we reach the borderlands.'

The caravan master glanced up, seeing Mai, and away again with guilty swiftness.

'He knows you're not a boy,' said Shai. 'Do you think the merchants suspect the captain lied to them?'

'Wasn't Anji magnificent at Sarida? He told them what they most feared to hear, so they believed him.'

'That's not an answer.'

'I don't think they care,' she said coolly, 'not as long as they're safe.'

'Are we ever safe?'

She shuddered.

'What is it?' he asked. 'What's wrong, Mai?'

Shaking herself, she touched his hand. 'I didn't see how it happened, in Sarida. How we lost all the bearers, who walked so faithfully all this time, never complaining. And that poor lad forced to leave Commander Beje's villa only because he saw us on the porch. He's dead, too. And poor Cornflower, lost in the storm. How can we be safe when we never know who we're going to lose?' Her voice dropped to a whisper. 'What if Anji is killed? Then what happens to us? We've been on the road for four months. We're so far from home we can never go back.'

Footsteps crunched on dirt. Mountain's hulking shape appeared out of the night bearing wash water. 'Mistress? Priya says she has your wash ready.'

She forced a smile before hurrying away.

Why should the merchants care that Mai was not a boy, as long as they were safe? If the caravan master had his suspicions, he did not confide them to Beltak's priest. No doubt he'd be twice a fool to protest now, and a dead fool at that. They were all far from home; best not to take chances.

Their company pushed higher and higher into the mountains. The few weak souls in the merchant train who couldn't keep up were left behind. At the order of the priest, one female slave was executed for an unspecified crime. A young slave gone lame was granted clemency and allowed to ride on the back of a wagon until he could walk again. None of the merchants complained about the grueling pace. Possibly this was because they were to all intents and purposes now at the mercy of their guards. Possibly it was because they were eager to push beyond the range of the Beltak priest's absolute power. Or possibly they were happy to have to pay so little, nothing more than feed and provisions, for this magnificent captain and his wolf pack of soldiers who quietly and efficiently guarded the merchants and peddlers and their laden wagons and chained slaves.

At a tiny walled village high in the mountains, at the last registered toll station, the Beltak priest turned aside with no word to anyone and walked away south, downhill. Yet even though his departure brought a certain sense of relief, the most difficult part of the crossing lay ahead. For days, they passed no other villages or indeed any sign of habitation except for a few isolated shepherd's shacks. On several occasions they observed men along the ridge-lines, following and observing their march, but no one approached them.

In time, they had to dismount and lead the horses because of the steady upward incline of the road. Anji pulled the scouts in, and guarded the caravan before and behind with ranks of his most experienced men. In these high reaches, they saw only birds and rodents and deer. At length, in the mountains with white-capped peaks towering above, it became difficult to suck in quite enough air as one trudged along. They were walking in a no-man's-land where only clouds and rain held sway. They had truly left behind the grip of the empire and its priests.

Shai knew it for sure because one morning he saw a ghost, a wisp caught among rocks where a slide had half obliterated an old sod shack. The ghost was beckoning to them, its substance bent in a passionate *come come come,* and its mouth opening and closing with exaggerated desperation.

What did it want? It was too far away for Shai to hear what it was saying.

Seeing the remains of the shack, a peddler called cheerfully to one of his fellows, 'See, there! That's the old way station, where that orange priest used to take alms and offer up that holy water of his. Not far now to the border! Only two or three more days, though most of it downhill! Whew! Downhill is the hard part!'

'What became of him?' huffed his companion, whose legs were as stout as tree trunks from years of pushing a loaded handcart up and down these steep trails. 'That orange priest, I mean.'

'Eh, who knows, up here. Anything could happen.'

They both caught breath, then called out to a slender man of mature years who was striding past them, the very same man who had warned Shai off watching the Beltak priest. In daylight, Shai could admire the extremely bright, even gaudy, colors of the man's clothing: a voluminous cloak of peacock blue, wine-red pantaloons, and a tunic of an intense saffron yellow hue.

'Greetings of the day, holy one. Greetings of the day.'

'Greetings of the day to you, friend. And to you. Almost home, neh?'

'Almost home! The gods be praised! You in a hurry there, Your Holiness?'

'I hear there's another caravan a half day's journey ahead of us. Thought I would catch up to them, get the news.' He kept walking, making for the front of the caravan. Amazingly, the peddlers did not guffaw at this astounding statement. Indeed, the man's stride seemed tireless; as far as Shai could see, he wasn't even breathing hard despite the thin air and a bundle slung over one shoulder.

Shai trudged alongside the peddlers for a bit, watching the other man's bright blue cloak recede up the road. When, in the happenstance of moving along, he caught the eye of one of the peddlers, he spoke up.

'What manner of holy man is he?'

The two men looked him over, measuring him, and then nodded at each other as if to agree that they could speak freely.

'That one? Can't you tell by the sky cloak? That's an envoy of Ilu. Though what he was doing walking down into the empire I can't imagine. They kill priests there.'

'Silk,' said the other peddler wisely, nodding toward the well-wrapped goods in his own hardcart. 'Sometimes the temples send a holy one south to buy silk for the temple. A dangerous task, mind you. Like a test of their courage and wit. Or to see if they're ready to move up in the temple hierarchy. I'll wager he's got silk in that bundle, two bolts of highest-grade quality. Not anything I could afford.'

The holy man reached the van and just kept going, advancing past the forward guard and along the road until he was lost from sight. No one tried to stop him, a traveler moving into the unknown. Would he return home unscathed? Would something terrible happen to him?

But after all, Shai realized, he was really only wondering those things about himself.

PART FIVE

Slaves

23

Just before sunset a man appeared on the road, entirely alone, walking up out of the south. He was a holy man, and he wore the gaudy colors of an envoy of Ilu: a voluminous cloak of peacock blue, wine-red pantaloons, and a tunic dyed the intense yellow gotten only from cloth dyed with that dearest of herbs, saffron, whose value in the markets of the Hundred Keshad knew down to the last vey. Along with the rest of the small merchant company, Kesh stared as the man strode to the spot they were settling in for their night's camp, cheerfully greeted the caravan master, and began chatting as though he'd been traveling with them all along. The envoys of Ilu were known to be insane, not mad in their minds but willing to endure hardships and risk dangers that no ordinary person would get near. This certainly proved it.

But Keshad had his own business to attend to, a wagon, mules, driver, and most crucially the goods he was transporting north over the Kandaran Pass to the Hundred. He had a very particular and complicated routine he must follow at night to keep his goods safe. So he dismissed the envoy of Ilu from his thoughts, and did no more than glance his way once or twice, until midway through the next day when the envoy, pacing the caravan, drew up alongside Kesh where he walked at the front of the line.

'Greetings of the day, nephew.'

'Greetings of the day, Holy One.'

As the two men walked along the ancient trading road, they talked. It was a good way to pass the time. Their feet scuffed up dust with each step. The rumble of cart wheels and the clop of pack animals and the laughter of a quartet of guards striding out in front serenaded them. Behind, the rest of the caravan clattered along. That ensemble of noises always seemed to Keshad the most reassuring of sounds when he was out on the road. If safety could be found in the world, then surely it was found where folk banded together to protect themselves from predators.

'In ancient days,' the envoy was saying, 'the Four Mothers created the land known as the Hundred with its doubled prow thrust east and north into ocean and two great mountain ranges to the south and the west to protect the inhabitants from their enemies. The Mothers joined themselves with the land, and in that transformation seven gods emerged from the maelstrom to create order.'

Keshad shrugged. 'So the story goes, at any rate.'

'Ah. You're clearly born and bred in the Hundred.' The man touched his own left eye, as if to bring to Kesh's attention that he had noticed the debt scar on Kesh's face. 'Yet you don't believe the Tale of Beginning?'

'I believed it when I was a child.'

'You've gone over to the Silvers' way of believing?'

'The Silvers? No, I don't know anything about that.'

The envoy was old enough to be Kesh's father, had Kesh still had a father; a man beyond his prime but not yet elderly.

'Something else, then. Hmm. Keshad is your given name, so you say. That means you were dedicated to the Air Mother at birth. Too much thinking. That's often a problem with Air-touched children. In what year were you born?'

Kesh brushed his elbow, where his tattoo was. 'Year of the Goat.'

'Even worse then! Goats are inconstant and unstable, prone to change their thinking, especially if they're Air-touched and liable to think too much. Still, they can survive anything. Look at you, a young man, in the prime of your strength, good-looking, all your teeth – oh, no! missing one, probably from a fight.'

'That's right. But the other man lost more! And he started it!'

'Happy is Ilu when he hears of those who gain justice!' The envoy grinned, and Kesh laughed. 'Good eyes, not bloodshot or yellow or infected. Strong limbs, open stride. Health in order. It must be your Goat's heart that is distracting your Air-touched mind.'

Kesh rolled his eyes, but he did not want to insult a holy envoy, who was a nice enough fellow, cheerful, lean, strong, and with an amazing set of white teeth that made his grin contagious. Obviously, the man was crazy.

'So, then, lad, you are born to be skeptical. How do you think the world came into being, if you don't believe my tale?'

'I hadn't given it much thought. I'm too busy wondering if we'll be attacked on the road, and if the guards we hired will protect us. Or run.'

'That's always a distraction,' agreed the envoy amiably.

Still, as the small merchant train and its armed escort trudged down the hip-jarring slope of the Kandaran Pass, Keshad studied the terrain of the rugged foothills where bandits lurked. He cast his gaze up at the spires themselves, shining in the afternoon sun. Light splintered off the snowy peaks. Clouds spun off into threads where they caught on summits and pinnacles. It was easy to imagine the fiery eye of a god glaring those formidable mountains into being as a warning to mortal man: *Do not cross me.*

'The way I see it,' Keshad continued, 'it doesn't matter how the world came to be. It matters what path a man takes as he walks through the world.'

'A fine philosophy! Did you serve your apprenticeship to Ilu, perhaps? You sound like a Herald's clansman.'

'No.'

'One of the Thunderer's ordinands, perhaps? I see you carry a short sword and a bow. That's not common among merchants.'

'I am not,' he said curtly, and was then sorry at his sour tone. The envoy had treated him with good humor and deserved as much in return. 'I have spent a lot of time thinking about journeys, because of my own. For instance, a merchant has a choice of three paths to reach the markets of the Hundred.'

'Three paths? I would have thought only one.' The envoy indicated the road on which they walked, but his sharp gaze never left Kesh's face.

'He can brave the seas—'

'And their treacherous currents! The roil of Messalia! Reefs and shoals!'

'That's right. Or the desert crossing to the west over Heaven's Ridge.'

'And thereby across the Barrens! There's a reason they're called that, you know!'

'That's so. But it can be done, and folk do it.'

'True enough.' The man coughed. 'So I hear.'

'Or he can pass this way, as we're doing. Paying a tax to the empire for right-of-way on the Kandaran Pass, because it's the only route leading over the Spires that we know of.'

The envoy's steady gait did not falter, but his eyebrows rose in surprise and his voice changed timbre. 'That we know of? You think there's another way over the Spires?'

'If there was, and you knew about it, wouldn't you keep it hidden?'

The envoy snorted and lifted his walking staff, letting its crest of silk ribbons flutter as he waved the staff toward the heavens. 'That I would, lad! If I were a merchant, and prized profit above all things. Or one of the Lady's mendicants, desiring secrecy. How comes it that you know so much about traveling into and out of the Hundred, if you're not heart-sworn to Ilu the Herald, as I am?'

'I'm a merchant, and therefore I prize profit, so I've tried all three in my time—'

'Ah. As well you might, being an Air-touched Goat. Still, you're yet a sprout. Young to be so well traveled!'

'Not so very young!'

'Three and twenty seems young to a man of my years!'

Kesh laughed. 'Do you want to hear what I've concluded about the three paths?'

The envoy's expression was full with laughter, although he did not laugh, and for some reason Kesh could not explain, the holy man's amusement was not condescending but warm and sympathetic. 'I've heard a great deal about you so far! Why stop here? Go on!'

'Well, then. I've concluded that while Death might find tax collectors amusing, She doesn't often masquerade as one. Therefore: I choose taxes.'

'Taxes?'

'Best to risk taxes now, and death later.'

'As they say, both are certain. Still, I can't help but think they're gouging us.'

'Who is? Death's wolves?'

That grin flashed again. 'Death's wolves aren't greedy. They only eat when they're hungry, not like the wolves among men. I mean the Sirniakan toll collectors, the ones we've left behind. Double and triple toll they charged me! Even a man such as myself who is only carrying two bolts of silk. Just because I'm a foreigner in their lands.'

'It's true their tolls cut down on profits, but taxes are still preferable to death. A man can't work if he's dead.'

'So it's said. Is that all life is for you? Work?'

Kesh looked back at his cargo. He'd rented the wagon, mules, and driver at great expense in the south, and spent yet more to rig up scaffolding and waxed canvas so his treasure would be concealed from the eyes of men, although naturally every person in the wagon train believed they knew what he had purchased. If he listened closely, he heard the two chests shifting and knocking together and the two girls whispering as the wagon juddered along. Otherwise, his cargo was silent and seemingly ignored by merchants and guardsmen and travelers alike, but he saw the way they glanced at his campsite in the evenings, every man of them. Wondering.

The envoy said nothing, waiting him out.

Kesh discovered he'd tightened his hand on the hilt of his own staff so hard his fingers hurt. He shifted the staff to his other hand and opened and closed his fingers to ease the ache.

'Work is the road I must take to reach the destination I seek,' he said finally, knowing the ache would never ease.

'Ah.' Again, the envoy brushed a finger alongside his own unscarred left temple. If he wanted to question Kesh about the debt mark, he kept his curiosity politely to himself.

'What of you, holy envoy? That's a long way to walk just to buy silk, when you can buy Sirniakan silk in the markets of the Hundred. Had you no other purpose? Sightseeing?'

'As if any priest would wish to risk execution in the south just to see the fabled eight-walled city,' replied the envoy with a chuckle, easily falling in with Kesh's change of subject. 'Silk, it's true, can be bought anywhere, but I was looking for a particular . . . grade and pattern.' His frown was startling for being so swift and so dark, but it passed quickly, and Kesh wondered if he'd mistaken it. 'I did not find what I was looking for. Did you?'

The riposte took him off guard. 'I'll only know when we reach Olossi.'

'Who will you sell the girls to?'

'Girls?'

'The two girls.'

Keshad smiled nervously. 'Whichever man will pay the most.'

The envoy glanced back at the wagon. His gaze burned; for an instant, Kesh thought the man could actually see through the canopy and mark the treasure Kesh had hidden all this way by using the time-honored method of illusionists: distract the gaze with the things that don't matter so that your audience doesn't notice the one thing that does. Ilu's envoys were notorious, seekers and finders who noticed *everything* in their service to Ilu, the Herald, the Opener of Ways. They were always gathering news and carrying messages; the temples even sold information to support themselves.

Still, this was none of Ilu's business. Kesh had come by this treasure as honestly as any man could. It was his to sell and profit by, his to use to get what he needed most. After so many years toiling, this trip promised to be the one that would at last bring him what he had worked for, over twelve long years.

It hurt to think of it, because he wanted it so much: *Freedom*.

'Look there.' Perhaps the envoy meant the distraction kindly, seeing Kesh's distress, but even if this were so, it was just as obvious that the sight relieved him. 'The first mey post. We have reached the Hundred at last.'

The white post had carved on it the number one, being the first mey of the road. Above that was engraved the name of the road, written in the old writing, more picture than letter, and recently repainted in the grooves with black ink: WEST SPUR.

The envoy padded to the side of the road to cover the top of the post with his palm. The mey post stood chest height. It was square at base and top but tapered so that the base was larger than the squared-off top where, in time of peril, the base of a wayfarer's lamp could be fixed into a finger's-width hole drilled deep down into the wood. At first the envoy stared north along the road, which began here its most precipitous drop out of the mountains. Then he shut his eyes and bowed his head in prayer as the seventeen carts and wagons of the merchant train trundled closer. When he looked up, he gazed toward the nearest prominence. A rugged mountain rose just off to the east with forested slopes and a bare summit surrounded on all sides by bare cliffs. Keshad thought he saw light winking up there, as if caught in a mirror, but when he blinked, the illusion vanished.

'Home,' said the envoy with satisfaction. He removed his hand and began walking again to keep ahead of the wagons. Kesh hurried after him. 'And hope of a dram of cordial at the Southmost.'

Brakes grated against wheels as wagons hit the incline. Kesh looked back. The black mey marking, which had numbered one viewed from the south, numbered sixty-four seen from this direction: the distance of the road called 'West Spur' from founding post to founding post. The other end of the West Spur lay a few mey outside the market city of Olossi, their destination. For him, this was the last road he would walk as the man he was now.

He felt sick with determination, with hope, with memory.

'I will let no obstacle bar my path,' he muttered.

'What? Eh? Forgive me, I didn't hear.'

'It was nothing. Just thinking out loud.'

'Like the winds, to whom voice is thought, and thought voice.'

'No, more like a mumbling madman who doesn't know when to shut up. There's the border gate.'

Stone walls stretched east and west as far as Kesh could see, with miniature towers anchoring each side of the road. Armed men leaned on those narrow parapets, eyeing the approaching caravan. Below, by the log barrier, a pair of young ordinands lounged against the fence, laughing as they traded stories with those of the caravan's guards who'd been walking point.

'Heya! Heya!' shouted their captain from the east tower. 'Get you, and you, to your posts!'

The ordinands scampered back across the ditch on a plank bridge to take up their places at the second fence, this one gated and closed.

'The guard force has doubled since last time I came through here,' commented the envoy.

'Are they expecting trouble?'

'It's always wise to expect trouble in border country.'

Kesh grunted in reply as he dug into his travel sack for his permission chits, his ledger, and the tax tokens he had received from the Sirniakan toll stations they had passed.

'If you'll excuse me, holy envoy. I must see to my cargo. If you would be so kind as to share a cordial with me at the Southmost, I would be honored.'

'Indeed! I thank you. I'll drink with pleasure!'

The envoy strode ahead. His staff, tattoo, and colors were chit and ledger enough. In the Hundred, the servants of Ilu could wander as they, and the god, willed. Only Atiratu's mendicants had as much freedom. Kesh certainly did not. He dropped back. The forward wagons creaked and squealed as drivers fought against brakes, beasts, the weight of their cargos, and the steepening pitch of the road. It was a good location for a border gate. Any wagon that did not slow to a stop would crash into the ditch, and charging horsemen who cut off the road to avoid fences and ditch would shatter themselves against the stone walls.

Farther back, a wheel, stressed to its limit by the wear of the brake, wrenched sideways and broke off its axle amid curses and shouting. The wagon tipped sideways and with a crack and a shudder blocked a third of the road.

'Out of the way! Out of the way!'

'You cursed fool!'

Kesh jumped back as his hired driver, Tebedir, barely swung past the wreck; then Kesh got a toe on the boards and leaped up beside him.

'I replace wheels before they is too weak to take the strain,' said the driver without looking at Keshad as the wagon rocked with the shift in weight. 'No savings in scanting on repair, if you ask me.'

'It's why I hired you,' said Kesh, 'despite the cost.'

'No savings by hiring cheap.'

They jolted to a stop behind the third wagon, to wait their turn. Ahead, a pair of Silver brothers or cousins – identifiable by their pale complexions, slant eyes, turbaned heads, and the silver bracelets jangling from wrist to elbow on their arms – were arguing with the clerks checking off their ledger. Kesh chewed on his lower lip. Tebedir chewed a cylinder of pipe leaf, spat it out, thumbed a new leaf from the lip of his travel sack, and rolled it deftly before slipping it between parted lips. His teeth were stained brown, but he had a nice grin.

After a while, rubbing his stubble of black hair, Tebedir said, 'Slow today.'

Kesh wiped sweat from his forehead, although it wasn't unusually hot. 'The guards are expecting trouble.'

'Rumor in camp tells it no merchant can travel north past a town the Hundred folk call Horn.'

'It's hard to imagine, although I've heard those tales, too. That would mean the markets of Nessumara and Toskala are closed to every merchant trading out of Olossi.'

'Still, young master, we are only going this far as Olossi. It is no matter to us.'

'That's right. No matter to us.'

As the second wagon moved through, Tebedir gave the reins to Kesh and clambered down to take the beasts and guide them over the plank bridge. Kesh didn't like heights – they made him dizzy so he didn't look over the edge and down into the ditch, although he'd heard that the ordinands cultivated adders in that trench. It always seemed when he crossed that he heard hissing, but that might have been the wind scraping through the pines and tollyrakes that grew in the highlands around them.

No, that *was* hissing. Aui! Had she taken it into her head to waken now? He turned. One of the girls was peeking through a gap in the canvas sheeting tied over the scaffolding.

'Tsst! No! Not allowed!'

She saw him. One dark eye, all he could see, flared as she startled back. The cloth was pinched shut. A voice murmured, too soft for him to hear syllables. Anyway, they didn't speak a language he knew, nor had he taught them words beyond the most basic commands. That way they couldn't talk to anyone.

Tebedir pulled the wagon to a stop where the guards waved him down. Keshad tugged his sleeves down to conceal his bronze bracelets. The captain strolled up, examined Kesh's face, and held out a hand.

'Let's see your ledger, ver,' he said in a friendly way which suggested he preferred cooperation to belligerence.

And why not? A captain at this border station could turn back any man to whom he took a dislike. The Silvers' wagon had been released and was rumbling down the road toward the village that waited two mey farther along. Where the dust settled, the envoy walked along briskly in its wake, his arms swinging. He seemed to be singing, but he was too far ahead for Kesh to hear. The second wagon, piled high with bolts of silk wrapped in burlap, was under assault by a pair of shaven-headed clerks who laboriously matched each bolt to what was written in the merchant's accounts book.

'How slow they are,' said Tebedir, indicating the clerks. 'Why you Hundred people allow women perform the work belonging to men?'

'No use arguing against the gods of the Hundred,' said Kesh.

Tebedir merely grunted in reply, then led the beasts off to a generous patch of shade, beneath trees planted long ago for this purpose. He sat down on a log placed there for drivers, sipped from his ale pouch, and settled back to wait as Kesh handed the ledger over to the captain. The man paged through it. Naturally he couldn't read, but a man in his position knew the old ideograms well enough to mark if everything was in its proper place. As his arm moved, Kesh glimpsed the tattoo on his wrist: the Crane, resting between the clean squares and angles that marked an Earth-born child.

'Looks in order,' he said to Kesh, handing the ledger back, 'but the clerks will have to set their stamp. What's this?' Kesh offered him the tangle of chits, and he plucked the rare one out of the group and dangled it. 'Two ordinary, one exalted. What have you got in there?'

'I call on the law of Sapanasu,' said Kesh, 'to ask for the veil of secrecy. You check yourself, Captain, and see that all is in order. I've no contraband, no weapons, no goods not accounted for in my ledger. I'll pay extra for the veil. It's my right.'

'It's not cheap.'

'I've these tax tokens to prove I've paid the worth of my cargo all the way north out of Sirniaka.'

'I see it. This ledger is stamped with Merchant Feden's seal. We know his mark here. I'll accept your call for the veil. Now let me look.'

Kesh gave his two-note whistle and called, 'Moy. Tay.'

The curtain at the back of the cart parted, switched sideways by a brown hand, and the older girl peeked out. The captain eyed her as she unfolded the step and cautiously descended to the ground. She was small but well formed, if too slender for the taste of most men. The younger followed her out, keeping her gaze lowered. She was plumper but not quite ripe. Under Kesh's gaze, they lifted out the two chests and opened them to display their contents.

'Sisters or cousins,' said Kesh.

'Umm,' agreed the captain. 'Too skinny. Might not be bad, though, with a few more years and more flesh. Where are they from?'

'I picked them up in eastern Mariha, along the border country there. I was hoping to sell them to one of the jarya houses in Toskala or Nessumara, but I hear it's not safe to travel so far.'

'It's true. You've been out of the Hundred for some months?'

'Yes.'

'Roads north out of Olossi aren't safe. That's the word. It would be a shame to lose a good cargo like that to a pack of filthy bandits. But what's this veil you're wanting?' He picked carelessly through the contents of the two chests. 'I see nothing unusual here. Vials of saffron, clove oil, mirrors, a basket of shell dice, ivory combs – very handsome! – and so on. You're not even carrying silk.'

'Go in, if you will. Here come the clerks.'

The captain paused with a foot on the step.

'This one next, Captain Beron?' asked the male clerk.

'Yes.'

Moy and Tay kept their gazes fixed on the ground as the clerks moved in with their charcoal pencils, carved wood stamps, and ink. The clerks wore the nondescript, undyed robes common to those who labored for the Lantern of the Gods, Sapanasu. Like most of Her hierophants, they had shaved their heads, and their brown skin had a pleasing gleam from being oiled. They poked and prodded the girls delicately, and in their efficient way tallied each least item in the two chests and checked it against his account. They were so tidy that they packed everything back in just as they had found it, not a corner's fold of fabric out of place.

The captain ducked inside the wagon, which rocked under his

weight. Tebedir dozed. A fly crawled on one of the driver's eyelids, and without seeming to wake he lifted a hand to brush it away.

'All accounted for.' The female clerk dipped a stamp in ink and pressed it to the appropriate line in the ledger while the male clerk copied down figures in the record book he carried. 'Or was there something else? What's this chit for?'

She held up the rare oblong, carved out of shell into the shape of a leopard.

The curtain trembled. The captain pushed out, wiping his brow, then the back of his neck. He stumbled as he came down that one step. He was flushed and sweating, and looking a little ashamed and yet at the same time a little amused at his own shame, but only a little.

'Tsst! Where'd you get such a thing?'

'I found it. Unclaimed. Mine by finder's right. You know the law.'

He took a long look at Kesh. What passed in his mind was unfathomable.

'Anything we must know, Captain Beron?' asked the female clerk.

'No, set him his tariff and let him go on. He's invoked the veil.'

'Very well.' She and her fellow clerk consulted. They were no older than Kesh, but experienced and swift. They named the tariff. Kesh sorted through his coins, paid them into the locked coffer, and got his border chits to add to his collection. He was now almost broke, except for his trade goods, and paying for food and water would take the rest of his coin over the sixty-four mey of West Spur. It all depended on the price he could obtain for his trade goods once he reached Olossi. Everything depended on that.

'I've seen you before, last year,' said the male clerk. 'You're out of Merchant Feden's household, aren't you?'

'I am.'

'Come on, Denni!' called the female clerk, who had already moved on to the next wagon. 'The envoy said there was a bigger caravan coming up behind this one. We'll be stuck here all week if we stand gawking.'

'Aui!' The male clerk looked Kesh over with a sneer. Boldly, he grabbed Kesh's elbow and rudely twitched back a sleeve to reveal a bronze bracelet. 'Pretending to be what you aren't, as if you'd already bought your accounts bundle and cleared your debt! Don't think we can't see what's marked by your eye.' He let go, and went after his companion.

The captain raised his eyebrows. 'Isn't there a law against you slaves wearing sleeves that cover your wrists?' Recalling the ledger, he added ten to ten, as merchants did, and got twenty. 'You're Feden's slave, aren't you?'

'I am.' He felt how his ears burned, how his cheeks burned. How the shame took him, but also the anger and hope, because he was so close. 'Do you know him?'

'You look like a good Hundred boy to me. What happened?'

Keshad wanted to say 'none of your business,' but the first rule of merchants, and slaves, was never to insult those who might have the means to harm you, or help you, later.

'Family debt. I was a boy. I never knew the details, only the amount.'

'Eiya! If anything should clear your slate, young man, then this cargo should do it.'

Kesh made the traditional gesture, hands to chest, the formal bow of not more than thirty degrees' inclination to show respect rather than submission, and turned to go.

'Whsst! In!' he said to the girls.

They clapped the chests shut and loaded them into the back while Tebedir yawned and got to his feet, stretching, flexing his big hands, clucking as he got the beasts out of their stupor.

'Coming up, Master?'

'I'll walk,' said Kesh.

'If you ask me, a man can wear his feet out, walking too much. Women walk.'

'I'll walk.'

The captain watched them go, his gaze as sharp as the touch of a blade to Keshad's back, but in the end one of his men called to him and he went back to his task. He hadn't even demanded a bribe, but there were men like that. 'Beron' was an Earth-touched name, and he'd worn the Earth Mother's tattoos. No doubt the envoy of Ilu would have a few words to say about the honesty of a man born in the Year of the Crane, dedicated to the Earth Mother at birth, and serving Kotaru, the Thunderer, as one of his holy soldiers, his ordinands.

24

By the time Keshad paid a half leya as toll to pass the palisade gate and walked beside his wagon into the village of Dast Korumbos, the envoy was already seated and drinking at the inn called Southmost. The village's eight rectangular houses were sturdily constructed of halved logs, and in the manner of the southern Hundred were not whitewashed. Chimes tinkled from every eave. The inn's shutters were open under the peaked roof to air out the loft. In the fenced forecourt, a trio of locals sat on stools around the envoy's bench, laughing as he told a story.

'So he said, "No one wants to live so far south, right up into the mountains where anything might happen. But where else will folk pay double price for my sour cordial?"'

The innkeeper trotted out, cast a sour glance at his customers, and went back inside the house. The courtyard boasted two awnings and a grape arbor that also provided shade. The kitchen smoked out back. A chicken wandered past the benches, scratching and pecking. A dark-haired child stuck its head out of the loft where Kesh had slept once on a straw bed, the one time he had had Merchant Feden's coin to pay for lodging. The other times in Dastko he had slept on the ground beside the village well, under the branches of the Ladytree, where no one was allowed to charge rent.

The envoy saw him and lifted a hand in greeting. Kesh handed five vey to Tebedir. 'For the well,' he said. 'See they drink deeply.'

'If you ask me, they overcharge.'

'That they do. You come have a drink, and we'll see what the inn is offering at a reasonable price for supper.'

'We stay here tonight?'

Ahead, the wagon with the two Silvers trundled on through the far gate, headed down West Spur into the north, but the second wagon had already pulled up along the commons. Kesh squinted at the sky with its lacing of clouds and a peculiar purpling blue to the east, what could be seen of that horizon with the hills piled so high and the mountains crowded so close behind.

'It's a half day's journey to Far Umbos. We can't make it by dusk.'

'That wagon goes on.'

'Silvers have some kind of sorcery that protects them. Me, I don't want to sleep out under the trees tonight with any wild beast coming to eat us up. For free!'

'Lot of cold road here in the north,' remarked Tebedir as he got down and hooked the leads onto the beasts' harness. 'Lot of cold road and only wild forest and demon beast on every side. Not like in the empire. In the empire, there's always some person or village in spitting distance. Don't know how you folk stand it.'

'I might say otherwise, wondering how you southern folk can stand to live all crowded together.'

'Not crowded at all!' he retorted with a chuckle. 'Lonely. Brrr.' He shuddered as though troubled by a chill wind, gave a flip to the reins, and guided the team toward the well at the northeastern corner of the palisade.

The Ladytree was an old one, situated to the left of the well between the high outer palisade and the lower ring of stone wall that protected the well. A waist-high corral marked the limit of the Lady's generosity. The top of each post was carved into a representation of her sigil, the double axe, so no one could mistake this for anything but holy ground, but also to provide a hitching post for a traveler's mounts, dogs, or livestock. The Lady was practical in that way. The branches had grown out over the fence and had been twined in with it, and in spots he noted white scars where they'd been hacked back in defiance of the law.

Children loitered by the narrow entrance to the encircled well. Several sat on the high posts that jutted up from the wall. One man and one woman waited by the well gate to exact toll from anyone who needed to water a team. Keshad hoped Tebedir would not kick up a fuss about the woman wanting to take coin out of his hand, but the Sirniakan driver had worked the Kandaran Pass into the Hundred before; he knew the custom here. The wagon came to a halt under the sanctuary of the Ladytree. Tebedir unhitched the beasts with practiced skill and led them around the curve of the inner wall to the gate. The man put his hand out, not the woman. No doubt they'd seen plenty of Sirniakan drivers come through.

'Keshad!' The envoy beckoned. 'Come sit, nephew. My friends here have already bought me a drink in exchange for news from the south.'

The locals moved aside to let Kesh sit beside the envoy on the log bench. As a draught of cordial was placed before him by the smiling innkeeper, he glanced back toward the well, but Tebedir and the animals had vanished behind the inner palisade. One boy stood up on one of the high posts and, balanced there like a bird sentry, turned to watch what was going on at the trough, which was not visible from outside the little palisade.

'What about you, lad?' asked the locals. 'What news from the south?'

Kesh shrugged. 'Not much news you haven't already heard. The old emperor died. It's whispered there's a rebellion brewing in the south against the new emperor. A cousin thinks he has more right to sit on the throne, so there might be fighting.'

'Oom. Hem,' muttered the locals, nodding wisely. 'That bodes poorly for custom, don't it?'

'It might,' said Kesh, 'if fighting reaches so far north no one dares trade from the Hundred into the empire. As for the western markets, the Mariha princes have fallen to an army from farther west, barbarians called "Kin."'

'You traveled that far west?' asked the envoy, surprised. 'All the way to Mariha lands?'

'I did. That's where I got the two girls. It was strange, though. Not one merchant I spoke to complained about their new overlords except that they have a habit of hanging thieves as well as murderers.'

'That can't be all bad,' said the older local, twisting greasy fingers in his beard. 'Good riddance.'

'Unless they call thieves and murderers those they want to hang, even if they didn't steal or kill!' said the younger as he rubbed a scab on his nose.

The trio talked for a while of their own expeditions into the south, though Kesh soon wondered whether these men had stirred more than a half day's walk from Dast Korumbos in their entire lives. Their stories sounded like such a tangle of tales that he suspected they might have heard them from others, and they could never verify details, but the envoy merely smiled at their stories, and nodded at Kesh as if to warn him that there was no harm in letting them spin their fantasies as long as they wished. Other wagons trundled in at erratic intervals. After two marks the traffic ceased. This late in the day, no one else continued north. By arriving early, the first wagons had gotten the prime spots under the Ladytree, up against the net of branches that, having grown into the fence, gave them a second wall of sorts at their backs. Other wagons had to pay for space on the commons or along the outer palisade, and soon most of the open space in the village was littered with a confusing maze of wagons and carts and a few tents being raised.

Tebedir took his time watering the beasts and getting things settled to his liking. After he hobbled the pair beside their wagon, he sauntered over to see about drink and taking a meal. The locals squinted at the driver, sketched hasty fare-thee-wells, and departed.

'I hear tell there's another caravan coming up behind this one,' said the innkeeper as he brought Tebedir a cordial and all of them a pot of lovingly spiced barsh, a green mash of rice, chopped onion, and liver liberally sprinkled with pepper and sharp kursi, which was grown in the eastern marshlands.

'What's this?' Tebedir asked, making a face at the pungent barsh.

The envoy took in a deep breath and smiled broadly. With two fingers he dipped into the mash and tasted it. 'Ah! A better flavor than your cordial, Master Innkeeper. Very good!'

The man grunted, both irritated and gratified. 'The berries were sour this year. I can't afford to throw it out and buy elsewhere. No one wants to live on the pass, right up into the mountains where anything might happen. Heya! I was born here, and here I'll stay, but we have to pay rent and food to the ordinands who patrol the wall and control the gate, and to the clerks who account the trade and taxes. *And* it's a high toll ourselves to bring in any goods we want that we can't grow here. I don't like serving sour cordial, I'm proud of my inn and my service, but sour cordial's all I've got this year.'

'Heya! Innkeeper!' a merchant called from another bench.

He sketched a gesture of leave-taking and hurried away. Kesh hitched the tripod holding the pot of barsh closer to the bench. They set to it eagerly.

Tebedir ate more slowly than the other two and was first to break the silence. 'Not that tasty, if you ask me.'

'What of your girls?' asked the envoy.

Embarrassed to be be taken to task in public, Kesh called the innkeeper over. 'I want two tey of your second-grade rice, and a tey of beans – whatever kind – mixed in. I'll bring the bowl back when they're done.'

'That's a lot of food for two young girls,' said the envoy. He stared toward the Ladytree. Clouds had crept westward, making the late afternoon hazy. The wagon was half lost in the shadows under the spreading branches, but the envoy's gaze had a piercing quality that made Kesh nervous. What if the man *could* see through cloth?

Kesh forced a grin to his lips. 'They're my merchandise. I'll get a better price for them if they're healthy and plump. No profit to me if the girls get sick or starve on the way to the block, is it?'

'No, certainly not. Nor is it any shame to hire folk who worship He Who Rules Alone when there are no good Hundred folk who can make the journey.'

'The Shining One Who Rules Alone,' corrected Tebedir genially. 'King of Kings, Lord of Lords. You Hundred folk will all burn in the fire if you don't change your ungodly ways like Keshad here did.'

The envoy raised an eyebrow but said nothing, and Kesh winced, thinking it would have been better had the envoy spoken his thoughts out loud. Anything would be better than that measured gaze turned on him now that seemed to eat him alive.

'Have you turned your back on your clansmen?' asked the envoy curiously, although no hint of anger tarnished his voice.

'They turned their back on me! Sold me into slavery to pay their debts!' He touched the crudely worked debt mark, more scar than tattoo, curving from his left brow and around the outside of his left eye.

'A sad tale heard all too often in the Hundred, I grant you. But under the rule of Beltak, once a slave you are a slave forever.' He turned to the driver. 'Is that not true?'

'Of course! No man become slave by the law of the Exalted One if he do not fall into disgrace.' He nodded toward Keshad without embarrassment. 'Is different here in the north. Tsst! First become slave, then buy free, and so on. But that is your way. Maybe it will change when Beltak's priests come.'

'Maybe,' agreed the envoy politely, 'but in the Hundred, the gods and the land are as one, not to be separated.' He looked closely again at Kesh as if trying to tease the strand of memory out of Kesh's mind that would explain to him why a good Hundred boy would betray his gods.

Kesh scratched the back of his neck, wondering how he could excuse himself without insulting the envoy. Whatever pleasure he'd taken in the day had vanished. Fortunately one of the innkeeper's lads bustled up with the boiled rice and beans.

'Best get the girls fed and settled down for the night,' he said as he took the big bowl. 'We rise before dawn. Get a brisk start to the day. Olossi Town beckons.'

He tossed enough vey on the table to pay for everything.

'I thank you, nephew.' The envoy smiled. 'Rest well.'

'Crazy priests,' muttered Tebedir as they walked back to the wagon. 'Best they all die in the burnings. Better for your people to worship the Exalted One and not these wrong things they call gods.'

'Leave it, if you will,' said Kesh sharply. The conversation had rattled him. He handed the rice inside.

After the girls had eaten, he returned the bowl to the inn, paid a pair of vey to empty their waste bucket in the inn's latrines, and returned to his little camp. Yet as he knelt in the shadow of the wagon, set a bowl of water before his knees, and said his evening prayers with palms turned upward to face the heavens, he found the words meaningless.

'Rid us of all that is evil. Rid us of demons. Rid us of hate. Rid us of envy. Rid us of heretics and liars. Rid us of wolves and of armies stained with the blood of the pure.' He dipped a thumb in the water and traced that cool touch across his forehead. 'Increase all that is good. Increase life. Increase wealth. Increase the strength of your devoted. Increase the power of your holy emperor, beloved among men.' He dipped his little finger in the water and traced a line on each cheek. 'Teach me to hate darkness and battle evil. Teach me the Truth, Exalted One, King of Kings, Lord of Lords. You are Beltak, the Shining One Who Rules Alone. Peace. Peace. Peace.'

Wind shushed in the branches of the Ladytree, as if the Lady

Atiratu Herself overheard him and muttered Her displeasure among the leaves. His thoughts wound away like the wind, seeking north. The town of Olossi beckoned, sixty-two mey from Dast Korumbos, more or less eight or ten days' journey depending on weather, road conditions, the state of the wagon, and the likelihood of accidents or obstacles as yet unknown.

Nine days! It seemed both far too many and so blindingly few. He could feel the taste of freedom on his tongue, as sharp as the blend of kursi and pepper that had spiced the barsh. His freedom. Her freedom. *Both of us, soon to be free.*

'Hei! Hei!'

The slap of feet on the ground startled him so badly he knocked over the blessing bowl. Water stained the dirt. He jumped up, but his view beyond the Ladytree was obscured by branches. A commotion roiled the commons. A youth came running from the direction of the southern gate with his broad sleeves fluttering back like bird's wings.

'Hei! Hei! 'Ware! 'Ware! Ospreys comin – !' He stumbled forward and plunged headlong into the ground. An arrow stuck out of his back. His arms jiggled crazily as he tried to crawl but could not make his legs work.

'Osprey?' Tebedir had heard the words but from his angle closer to the trunk of tree had not seen the lad fall. 'What is that?'

'Trail robbers. Named for birds – what swoop down and grab their prey. But they never attack into a town . . .'

'Robbers!' exclaimed Tebedir.

'Close the gate! Close the gate!' rang the frantic call.

Already out in the commons, a hand of men in guard tunics ran toward the southern gate. A pair of guards leaped on horses and headed toward the northern gate. A crowd converged on the inn, each man, and they were all men, yelling and gesticulating as they cried for protection, for news, for safety. Kesh grabbed his sword and slung it over his back, then buckled his quiver over it and with a quick tug and pop strung his bow. His stomach had fallen into a pit so deep he couldn't measure it.

'Tebedir, you can run, or stick with me, whatever you will, but if you run now I can't pay you your delivery share and you'll be taking your chances with robbers out among the trees.'

He backed up until he pressed into one corner of the wagon, scanning with each step, and called out to Tebedir again, but the driver had vanished as if consumed by a stroke of lightning. Even the driver's blessing bowl was gone.

There were four vehicles under the Ladytree, crammed to fit: three wagons and one handcart. A sleepy lad draped along the driver's bench of the second wagon raised his head and stared around without comprehension. The others had been abandoned by men gone over to their supper who had, no doubt, paid their companion's lad to stand watch over all. Another merchant, less trusting, leaned against his handcart waggling his hands in fear as he stared at Keshad and his weapons.

'What to do? What to do? That boy just fell down with an arrow in his back! Ospreys never dive into a walled village! Everyone knows that!'

'Run for safety,' advised Kesh roughly.

'And leave my cart? That's all my clan's savings tied up in silk—'

A bell jangled, twice, three times, and then the alarm was cut off by a shrill scream that went on for so long that Kesh realized it wasn't a dying man making that horrible noise but a living one. It was a battle cry.

The other merchant bolted out from under the Ladytree's canopy, but the fool ran for the mob gone into hysterics at the inn rather than seeking the sanctuary offered by the well. The two horses gone north returned at a gallop. One was riderless. The other, shot in the hindquarters, dragged its rider behind, but the fellow was dead or unconscious, his body turning and tumbling as the pain-blinded horse tried to shake him loose.

How could this be happening? How, when he was so close? Were the gods punishing him for turning his back on them? Yet he'd done that years ago and walked unmolested in the Hundred enough times that they'd had plenty of time to dissolve him with the blast of their angry gaze if that was their intent. No, no, it must be now, when he was so close that the taste of freedom had made him at last admit his hunger. The gods were cruel, that was it, and delighted in mocking his hopes.

He reached back and slipped an arrow free, set it against the string. 'Curse you all,' he muttered. 'I won't lose all this now!'

'*Kei? Kei?*' It was the older girl, peering out from between the walls of cloth. 'What go, Master? What go?'

'Down!' he snapped. 'On the bed of the wagon. Down flat!' He heard them rustling, but he hadn't the leisure to look inside to make sure they obeyed. Just what he needed! A stray arrow piercing that precious neck and robbing him of all he'd worked for, for so many years. God, he was so furious at those damned robbers he could kill them and eat their hearts and savor the tang.

'Whass going on?' asked the lad.

'Robbers, you thick skull!'

The lad whistled. He was, it appeared, thick in understanding. He scratched his shaved head and wiped his nose. 'Now what?'

'Run to the well. That's refuge.'

'Can't leave the wagon. Boss said so.'

'If they catch you, they'll kill you.'

'Boss said so. Stick by, he said. Watch these other two, not just ours. Gotta do what Boss said. Plus there's a sticky bun in it for me. When we get to Old Fort. He promised.'

'Hide under the wagon. You've got good position back here with me. Hard to come through these back branches, like a wall—' He pointed with the bow, and the lad nodded wisely. It was obvious that the boy didn't comprehend the danger they were in. 'There's the cart, and that other wagon there, on the other side where it's more open. That's like wall, too. A bit of safety. The Lady's palisade, they call it.'

'Eh,' said the lad, squinting. 'Eh! See there!' He pointed with his elbow, not that Kesh hadn't already seen and felt his insides go from falling to twisting into a tight, tight knot.

Where the caravan guards had got to he did not know, but the men now riding into the commons from both north and south were no raggle-taggle bunch but two dozen men armed with bows, spears, and swords and dressed in good silk. Not the best quality. He had a finely honed eye, and even from this distance he recognized that the shades of crimson, apricot, and azure were decent but second-rate. This was the kind of silk a well-to-do crofter might buy his young bride for her wedding price, or a rich merchant might clothe her servants in for a festival party to impress her rivals.

Behind, branches rustled. He spun. Tebedir pushed through the wall of hanging branches, holding an unlit torch in one hand and a shovel in the other.

'Tsst!' the driver hissed in disgust. 'No robber in my land. God keep order!' He had tied his blessing bowl back onto his belt but now set down shovel and torch and set to work with flint and tinder to start a fire in the bowl. 'Fire scare evil ones,' he explained. 'Burn them.'

'My thanks for coming back,' said Kesh, heartened by his reappearance.

'Never left. I swear my time of service according to the Exalted One. To break a swear – an oath – makes a man a slave! In my country, Master,' he added. 'Not yours. No such honor in yours.'

Kesh grinned wryly but kept his gaze fixed on the way the robbers were closing in around the inn. A few of the merchants bore walking staffs or droving whips, but those that held them aloft did so more as if to say they were ready to surrender. The innkeeper emerged from the inn on his knees, hands clapped to his forehead, palms facing outward in the traditional gesture of submission.

'Mercy!' The man's voice carried easily over the commons. 'By the mercy granted us by the Witherer's Kiss, take what you will and go on your way.'

'Think they'll see us?' whispered Tebedir.

A strong voice called out from among the robbers.

'Move swift! Hurry! Find the treasure, and ride!'

They wheeled, scattering like a flock of chickens after thrown grain. One jumped his mount over the fence surrounding the inn and rode through, whip flashing to either side as men screamed and stumbled out of his way. Another cantered back toward the northern gate and a third toward the southern. Six dismounted and began to tear through the wagons parked all through the commons as that same voice called, 'No, you slackabeds! A wagon with canvas walls! Yes, like that!'

The man giving the orders remained in the road, surveying the chaos, watching avidly as a wagon surmounted by a canvas cabin had its walls slit by spear point. The leader's mouth and nose were masked by a black scarf tied up behind his ears. His dark hair was short, like a laborer's, and streaked with enough gray that Kesh could make out the speckling from here. Two men turned their horses and trotted toward the Ladytree.

Streamers of colored ribbons broke out of the innyard as the envoy used his staff to help himself vault the fence. He cleared it easily and landed with remarkable agility for a man of his advanced years. He trotted through the chaos with a peculiar lack of concern, following on the trail of the two riders moving in on the Ladytree.

'Not much chance fighting these odds,' said Tebedir. 'If you ask me.'

'I'm not asking you! You're free to escape, if you wish.'

'Seems to me Hundred folk like killing southern folk. As good odds here as out on my own. I stick.'

'With my thanks, then. If we survive this, I'll give you a bonus.'

'Hei!' cried the lad, pointing toward the two riders.

Tebedir jammed the base of the torch into the dirt, held the shovel between his knees, and flicked open his tinderbox. Keshad sighed, nocked an arrow, and took aim. Once the first arrow went, he'd be marked and doomed. He could still surrender. The two riders closed. The envoy gained ground behind them, darting through the chaos. Kesh noted him grimly. Was it the envoy who had betrayed them to the bandits?

He loosed his arrow. It missed so wildly that in truth the two riders didn't even notice it, so intent were they on looking back over their shoulders at the fortunate men now looting the wagons out on the commons where merchants sobbed and slaves cowered.

The torch flared beside him, a wash of unexpected heat. Tebedir hoisted the shovel in two hands and gave it a test swing as Keshad set another arrow to the string. He loosed it, only to see it veer wide yet again. Beltak had cursed him, or the gods had chosen to punish him for his apostasy now that he was back walking in their Hundred.

The lad had come up with a bow from somewhere. With a blinking look of confusion, he drew and aimed and shot and the lead rider of the pair toppled off his horse with an arrow buried deep in his belly.

''Eir! 'Eir!' cried the second, waving and hollering until he got the attention of the leader. He drew his sword. 'Got trouble over here.'

The leader gestured. Three more riders turned to ride that way as the second rider bent low in his saddle, letting his mount's neck cover him. The lad fumbled for a second arrow. Keshad swore under his breath and made ready.

The envoy fell to his knees as though hit, but more likely he was only cowering as the new riders swept up beside him, ignoring an unarmed man dressed in the colors of a god. His arms shifted, and without warning he stuck his staff parallel an arm's span above the ground, right in the path of one of the horses. The creature tripped and tumbled and screamed as it went down with all that weight, slamming hard. The rider spilled forward over the horse's neck, hitting head and shoulder on the earth, and lay there like a dead man, although the horse struggled up at once.

'Beware!' said Tebedir in a sharp voice at Keshad's left ear.

Kesh stepped back, and loosed an arrow into the face of the first rider, who was just now ducking under the Ladytree. The man screamed and flailed as his horse swung sharply back the way they'd come to get out from under the branches. The turn and the scrape of branches toppled him from the horse, and he lay writhing in the dirt and moaning and bleating and clawing at his face. The horse trotted away.

Two riders still pounded toward them. Tebedir dashed forward to the cover of another wagon, holding both torch and shovel. The lad had strung another arrow, but the sight of the wounded man struggling and bleeding in the dirt distracted him as did the cries and shouts from the commons and the inn.

The envoy dashed after the riders, toward the Ladytree, only to stumble and fall. An arrow stuck out of his back.

Kesh loosed his arrow as the pair of bandits ducked beneath the tree, but it missed. The lad was still staring at the injured man and the arrow stuck in his eye with blood and matter smearing his cheek.

'Heya! Heya!' shouted Kesh, but the lad turned too late as the lead rider stuck him through the belly with a spear. Choking, the boy collapsed and was then spun sideways as the rider yanked his spear clean. Tebedir thrust the smoking torch into the face of the second horse, and as it shied back he swung hard with the shovel. Its edge cut deep into the second rider's ribs. The man shrieked and grunted; his sword caught Tebedir in the thigh, but only because he was already falling. He staggered as the rider landed at his feet, then battered the man's face with the shovel, cursing as he swung his arms. Blood stained the fabric of his leggings.

Keshad leaped back as the other rider advanced. The man's arm was cocked back with the bloody spear dripping and pointed straight at him. Kesh's hands shook so badly he could not get an arrow free from the quiver, and when his back slammed up against his cart he dropped the bow and drew his short sword, however stupid and hopeless that was. The bandit tried a thrust, but Kesh slapped it aside desperately. Beyond, more riders approached. Tebedir shifted to get a better position in the shelter of the foremost wagon.

'Here! Here!' shouted the lead man, keeping his distance now that he'd seen Kesh would fight back. 'I've got them! Two armed, one wounded. The wagon's here!'

Although trapped against his wagon, Kesh could still see a portion of the commons. The bandit's captain raised his voice, and all heads turned toward the Ladytree. Every man of them reined their horses aside; they had seen their quarry and now moved, like ospreys, for the swift catch.

'It's all over,' called the rider, sneering. 'Throw down your sword and we'll kill you quick. Keep it, and we'll take longer.'

'Is that meant to persuade me?' answered Kesh. 'Can't you do better? Offer me a share in your company? Compliment my skills to your captain? Promise to lay waste to my clan house if I don't cooperate? Neh! You can't even finish me off before the rest of them get here to back you up! You probably need them to help you swive the goats, too—'

He expected the thrust, caught the haft on his blade and shoved it aside. While the man was recovering his balance, Kesh jumped up against the horse's withers, grabbed the rider's belt, and yanked him off the horse.

'Tebedir! Back to me!' he called as he skipped sideways. The rider hit his head hard enough to wind him, and Kesh stuck him up under the ribs with no more mercy than the man had shown to the poor lad, who was still gurgling.

'Not looking good,' said Tebedir as he limped over, leaning heavily on the shovel.

A dozen men trotted over the limp body of the envoy as more came up from behind, converging on the Ladytree.

'You can give yourself up and beg for mercy. I won't mind.'

Tebedir's breathing had gone raspy with pain. 'Better to die with honor than surrender as a woman. I give my word to drive, to keep silence, to bring you and the cargo to Olossi. I keep my word.'

A wind stirred the branches, as though the Lady were whispering. A strange prickling charge made Keshad's skin tingle. He looked around, expecting to see the Lady's servants leap out of the air to protect those who sheltered under her sacred boughs, but it was only the wind and a distant ripple of thunder, a change in the weather.

Too late for him. Too late for *her*.

'Now would be a good time for Beltak to show His power,' muttered Kesh angrily, feeling tears sting and a vast crashing wave of despair and fury and hopelessness. From behind the canvas walls of the shelter he heard one of the girls sobbing with fear. He, too, wanted to weep, but he'd be damned if he would give in.

The thunder grew louder, and the riders toward the back of the group turned their heads to look south. He could not see their expressions, precisely, but he saw their postures alter. Elbows were raised, pointing, and then came an explosion of shouting and curses as they tried to shift direction.

Too late for them. They could not move quickly enough, having been too intent on the fish beneath the waters. A tide of black-clad riders swept through them, scattering them, cutting them down. What fine horsemen! This new company turned sharply and with ease and took from behind those who had been spared the first assault. It was a slaughter. Not one of the bandits, not even the captain, survived.

Tebedir took his shovel and beat in the heads of the men still moaning, until they stopped. He halted beside the lad, whose eyes were open and whose face was white with agony and terror. 'Kill him?' he asked.

'No. No.' Kesh could barely grip his sword's hilt, he was trembling so hard. Saved! Just as he had asked! 'There may be a real healer here. Praise the righteous ruler of all! Who are those men?'

Unexpectedly, horses neighed shrilly, and some reared, only to be ruthlessly reined down and held hard by their riders. Those horses who had no riders scattered in a panic. At the command of their captain, the mounted company withdrew from open ground, back among the wagons. Merchants and slaves pointed overhead, yelling and exclaiming, and most sprinted for the inn as though a squall was about to hit. All this movement cleared a space in the commons beyond the tangle of wagons and carts.

Whoof!

The beast came down fast, body almost at the vertical and wings in a wide curve, and yet with such beauty that Kesh shouted aloud and Tebedir swore in the name of the god. It was a huge eagle with a gruesome healed scar above its piercingly bright right eye. The man hanging in the harness unhooked himself with a speed born of long practice and leaped out with reeve's baton raised and cloak swirling dashingly at his back. But as he surveyed the scene, he relaxed, then grinned, then lifted the baton toward the waiting horsemen as a salute. He turned to the eagle, spoke a word, and stepped back as it fanned out its wings with primary feathers and tail raising. With unnatural power, it thrust with its legs and lifted with its wings and took to the air again. Its wake fanned the air, and lifted the ends of the reeve's cloak. A man actually shrieked in fear, followed by a chorus of anxious laughter and a sudden gabble as all the merchants swarmed the reeve.

Tebedir grunted and sat gingerly on the tongue of the cart.

'Let me see that wound,' said Kesh, but the driver waved him away.

'Best go, first. Talk and see. I not die with this cut.'

'But without you . . . you stuck with me, beyond everything . . . I can't repay you—'

'Oath is worth more than coin. No believing man go against his oath.' Tebedir meant what he said; it was no use arguing.

Kesh sheathed his sword, picked up bow and quiver and slung them over his back, then headed out to the mob. It was true what Tebedir said: As a believing man, a true follower of Beltak, the Shining One Who Rules Alone, he could not forswear his oath to see the task through to its end. Of course, not every Sirniakan who claimed to be a believing man really was one, but in this case fortune had favored Kesh, and he murmured a prayer of thanks.

25

There was a lot to take in besides the twenty or so corpses, the stray horses, and the baggage that had been strewn on the ground around the carts as they were ransacked. Merchants and servants hurried to gather up those wares not spoiled or broken in the assault. One wept over a roll of golden silk that had been trampled, but surely the idiot could see that silk, at least, could be cleaned and repaired and sold at a reasonable discount; it was better than being dead. Other merchants crowded around the reeve, demanding aid or explanation or simply pouring out their fear and anger, but Kesh remained mindful of the force of men that waited off to one side. He estimated their number at about one hundred, all wearing black gear. They showed remarkable discipline, lined up in tidy ranks with a trio of men, their leaders, in front. They appeared foreign in both dress and facial features. He had never seen anyone who looked quite like them, except in Mariha.

He elbowed into the mob surrounding the reeve and, finding the innkeeper, grabbed him by the arm. 'Heya! Heya! Pay attention! We need to bring in wounded men, maybe a dead one. An envoy of Ilu needs our help! Quick!'

Kesh's fierce words cowed the man, and the reeve looked his way with the calm expression of a man completely in his element.

'Go on,' said the reeve to the innkeeper. 'You heard what he said. Bring in any wounded at once. Find that envoy! If there are any innocent folk these ospreys killed, I'll need their name and clan, so we can make an accounting and see that any death tithe is offered correctly.'

Kesh tugged the innkeeper after him. The reeve, meanwhile, gestured to the others to move back to their wagons. Afterward he walked to the black-clad guardsmen. Kesh saw the envoy's bright blue cloak on the ground and he broke away from the innkeeper and ran to kneel beside him. The arrow had an ugly look to it. The shaft had broken four times and it was clear that the envoy had been tumbled when the horses were ridden over him.

'Is there a healer here?' he asked the innkeeper.

The man gave a groan of despair and shook his head. 'Nay! Nay! It's many days' walk to the closest temple devoted to the Lady! We haven't seen a mendicant in weeks.'

'What about the Merciless One? Sometimes there are healers there.'

'The closest temple is all the way north by Olossi.'

'I know that place,' said Kesh grimly.

'Eiya! Horrible!' wailed the innkeeper as he stared at the body. 'To have it known that an envoy of Ilu died here! No one will want to bide here or sup and drink at my inn. It's an ill omen! We're ruined!'

'Get a flat board – a tabletop – a door – something! We must carry him inside.' He looked up at the sky. 'It might rain, and it will soon be dark.'

The innkeeper needed no greater encouragement. He bolted back the way they had come. Kesh pressed a hand gently to the envoy's neck. He breathed still, if shallowly. Life pulsed in his body. The breath of the gods had not yet left him.

Kesh curled his hand around the arrow as close against the envoy's back as he could and tested its grip by slowly twisting it. To his surprise, it slid free easily. Amazingly, the point had not pierced the fabric of the cloak but only driven it deep into the body. He cast the arrow away and swiftly pushed the cloak to one side as blood gushed up through the yellow silk of the tunic. He got out his knife and slit open the back of the tunic to expose the wound. The tumbling by the horses had done the most damage by disturbing the point, but it was remarkable how the silk had not torn despite the speed and force of the missile. He pressed the heel of one hand on the wound to stem the flow of blood and closed his eyes, trying to sense the pattern of the body's humors beneath the skin, as it was said true healers might do who could breathe and smell and even hear the whispering complaints of illness or injury.

'Ssa!' came the whisper. 'Sshuu!' And then, 'Where did they come from? Who set them on us?'

Kesh opened his eyes to see that the envoy's eyes were open. One of them, anyway. He couldn't see the other since the man's face was turned to one side because he was laid out on his stomach.

'Please lie still,' said Kesh. 'Don't talk. I got the arrow out. Hang on. We'll get you to the inn. You'll rest there.'

The first winds heralding dusk sighed down off the mountains, and the cloak rose and sunk into ridges and hollows as if something living were moving inside it. The envoy did not reply, but perhaps he had passed out again. His left arm lay at an awkward angle, and bruises were purpling all along his back where hooves had struck him.

'How badly hurt?' The reeve crouched beside Kesh. He was younger than the envoy but a fair bit older than Kesh, a good-looking fellow with short black hair teased by a few strands of white. He stood at medium height, lean but very fit, and he moved with the strength of a man who has confidence in his ability to stick it out in a brawl. A dangerous man, in his own way, and not unlike his eagle in the way he examined the envoy with a keen gaze, without actually touching him, as predators seek from above the sign of their prey by studying the ripples in grass and the flash of sudden movement along the ground.

Kesh eased the heel of his hand off the wound. Blood oozed, but the gushing had stopped. He pushed the envoy's cloak off the body and into a heap at one side, then slit the tunic from neck to base and opened it like wings.

'Trampled and shot,' mused the reeve, 'but still breathing. Good thing those ospreys are all dead, as it's more merciful than the death they'd receive for killing a holy man.'

'He's still breathing! He spoke to me.'

The reeve grunted and glanced over his shoulder. Kesh looked, too, and saw that the black-clad guards had dismounted and spread out, and were hauling the corpses of the bandits into rows the better to tally, identify, and dispose of them. Locals and servants hovered close by, hoping to strip the bodies of second-rate but still precious silk.

'That's one band,' remarked the reeve, more to himself than to Keshad, 'but it won't be the end of it.'

'The end of what?'

'These attacks along the roads. I came south from Clan Hall to investigate.'

'I heard there's been trouble. I've been south some months. You'd think Argent Hall would have been patrolling.'

'So you would think. Worst, it turns out it's the captain in charge who has made common pact with these ospreys.'

'The captain? The one in charge of the border post? Captain Beron?'

'The same,' said the reeve. 'How do you know him?'

'I heard the clerks speak his name as I passed through earlier today. He seemed a decent man.'

But the thought struck him hard enough that he fell silent: *It was my treasure the ospreys sought. He saw it, and let me pass, and sent these men after.*

He said nothing, although the reeve waited, as if sensing that Kesh clutched a secret to his heart.

'Beron?' The envoy stirred. His voice had the hoarse gurgle of a man talking past blood. 'Dedicated to the Earth Mother at birth. Crane-born – did you see his Crane mark? Sworn to Kotaru the Thunderer. Well. It's no wonder.' That wheeze was, perhaps, meant to be a laugh, but it sounded more like a death rattle.

The reeve regarded the envoy with a look of mild amazement.

'What's no wonder?' demanded Kesh. 'Yet if you would be silent, uncle, we might save you!'

'Cranes are orderly … Thunderer likes discipline … Earth Mother arranges all things but … can be rigid. Overturn these …' He gargled on blood as he tried to suck in air.

'Overturn these,' said the reeve softly, 'and you have chaos.'

'It is easy to subvert a man … who is in all parts desiring order … imposed from without. Eh! Eh! Any envoy of Ilu would have advised against … dedicating this child … to Kotaru.'

'Uncle! Keep still! You must spare yourself.'

The reeve looked fixedly at Kesh as the innkeeper trotted up, gasping and grunting and leading a pair of men who carried a table-top on which to bear the wounded man. The envoy closed his eyes. They shifted him over and hurried off, but Kesh grabbed the innkeeper by the sleeve.

'There's a pair under the Ladytree. A poor brave lad who I fear is dead. And my driver, who needs his wound washed and bound with a salve. If you have any starflower or soldier's friend, they are good for such injuries. Or Bright Blue, which stems bleeding – nay, it's too far south for that.'

The innkeeper gave him a fearful grimace and tore away, shouting at a pair of untidy lads loitering by the gate to come and give a hand, and he lumbered off toward the inn after the envoy while his servants, or slaves, ran toward the Ladytree.

'You know something of the healing properties of plants,' said the reeve, who had not once taken his gaze from Keshad during this exchange. He rose, brushing the dust from his knees, and when Keshad looked past him at the black-clad foreigners tidying the field, he looked, too, to see what caught Kesh's interest.

'Where did those come from?' asked Kesh. 'Were they patrolling? I've never seen such a company of guardsmen in Olossi.'

'No. They're the hired guard for another caravan. It was running about half a day behind yours. I saw them coming down the pass. As a reeve, I have the power to deputize folk when I need their aid.'

'They're not Sirniakan.'

'Are they not?' The reeve sat back on his heels with a look of pleased interest. 'What are they, then?'

'I'm not sure, but I think they're Kin. *Qin*. I can't say it right. Grass eaters. That's what they're called in Mariha.'

'Mariha?'

'That's a princedom west of the empire. They were ruled by five princes for a long time, so I was told, and none were happy except those who ruled. Then these *Qin* people came out of the west and killed the ruling princes. Now the Qin rule in Mariha.'

He was about to say more, but he faltered, seeing too late that the reeve's pleasant interrogation had been meant to draw him out.

'Beyond the western edge of the Sirniakan Empire?' mused the reeve. 'Well, I've seen no maps nor have I patrolled those lands, so I can't say I understand it. These men and their captain claim to be mercenaries. They hired themselves to the caravan as guards.'

For a while that seemed drawn out far too long, the reeve smiled at Kesh as Kesh squirmed, shifting his feet and berating himself in his thoughts. This reeve was a truly dangerous man, for all his cordiality. He must start to wonder why the ospreys had attacked in such numbers and into the village rather than waiting and raiding along the road. He must start to wonder what it was they were after so urgently.

'I'd like to talk to you further,' said the reeve.

'I have to leave at dawn.'

'As must I. Come see me in the inn later, when you've a chance. Don't forget your accounts book and tallies.' He said the words with such a benevolent smile that Keshad knew he absolutely would be rounded up by those grim-faced guardsmen and marched before the reeve as before the assizes if he did not present himself before the man this very night. When a reeve said such words, in that tone of voice, a man had to obey.

'It's getting dark,' he said, to escape.

He fled to the Ladytree to find Tebedir arguing with the lads from the inn. The driver had already poured a dram of his potent brew onto the cut and bound it with a strip of linen, and he refused any other aid.

'Best see to the boy,' he said.

'He must be carried,' said Kesh to the lads, who bent to grab the youth by ankles and wrists. 'Nay, not like that, you fools. His guts will fall out.'

'What matter?' asked the shorter lad. 'He's dead, this one. Just not yet.'

'Wish he'd stop squealing,' said the taller one. 'Makes a lot of noise for a dying man, don't you think?'

'No one can survive a plug to the guts. Gah! He smells!'

'Go get something to carry him on!' shouted Kesh.

They fled as Kesh cursed after them.

The lad was whimpering and keening, and the sound did grate the ears, but Kesh felt pity for him, and anyway the lad had probably saved Kesh's cargo with his stalwart defense of his master's wagon. He crouched and smoothed the lad's forehead and talked to him as he would talk to an injured dog, letting the sound of his voice act as a focus as the lad's breathing caught, ceased . . . and gasped again as he fought back to life.

Tebedir offered a bowl of water and a cloth to Kesh, who wiped the lad's brow as he mewled and cried for his mother. Flies gathered on the dead ospreys, and flies buzzed around the lad's ghastly wound, all pink and gray with oozing blood draining his life as it dribbled onto the ground. Wind whispered in the Ladytree, and between one breath and the next the lad escaped into the air, slipped away on the breeze, his breath following the shadow path toward home. A sprawled hand lay open; the mark of the Ox decorated his wrist.

Tebedir murmured a prayer. Kesh sank back on his heels as the pair of lads trotted up empty-handed. A stout man wearing a stained merchant's coat labored along behind them. When he saw the dead boy, he slapped a hand to his forehead.

'Not under the Ladytree! Now I'll have to pay the death offering to the Lady, too!'

Tebedir raised an eyebrow and looked at Kesh.

'This boy saved your cargo,' said Kesh sharply. 'He defended your wagon with selfless courage. I can't say the same for you.'

'This is none of your business! Move aside! Oh, by the Witherer's Kiss, you fools!' he shouted at the lads. 'You should have dragged him out from under the tree! Now I'm stuck with the cursed Lady tithe.'

Kesh rose and turned to Tebedir. 'Watch the cart, if you will. If I have to stand and listen to this any longer, I'll hit him.'

'Please hit,' said Tebedir. 'That boy fought like brave man.'

'Pissing foreigners!' snarled the merchant. 'Get out of my way!'

Kesh lifted a fist, and such a tide of loathing swept him that he hauled back – the merchant shrieked – and from the cart a female voice said words in a language Kesh had never heard before. It was like a bucketful of icy spring water splashed over him. He recovered; he remembered: Hit a man beneath a Ladytree, violating the Lady's law, and you paid a fine to her mendicants. They always knew; you could never get around it. Pay a fine, and it was that much coin thrown away. He could afford to lose none of his profit, not now, not this time. Not because he was disgusted by a self-important, selfish jackal of a man who paid his lackwit servant in sticky buns since the poor boy was too ignorant and too stupid and now too dead to demand better pay.

Shaking, he lowered his hand, gave the bowl and cloth to Tebedir, grabbed his ledger and pouch, and strode away. The merchant began yapping after him, but Kesh walked fast and didn't listen.

Dusk lay heavily over the commons. A cheerful fire burned in the outdoor hearth of the inn's courtyard, and men gathered there, drinking, but no songs warmed the twilight and the talk looked intense but muted. No one laughed. Other merchants hunkered down beside their carts. A half-dozen hirelings prowled around the ranks of corpses, but a quartet of black-clad mercenaries guarded the dead men, and Kesh guessed that no one would strip those bodies, not tonight, not without permission from the mercenary captain or the reeve. He paused by the gate to look over the mercenaries from a safe distance, not so close that they might feel he was challenging them. A few were setting up crude tents, canvas stretched out as a lean-to over bare ground to provide shelter against rain and wind. A pair rode off toward the south gate. Others moved among the horses, unsaddling some and stringing their spare mounts along a line for the night. They watched the movement of merchants and hirelings and slaves in the commons in the same way that wolves study the behavior of deer in a clearing. They ignored the corpses, though Kesh could not. The souls of dead folk begged for release, and the longer they lingered here, the more likely they would get up to some mischief.

He touched fingers to forehead and lips, and patted his chest twice, remembering the words of the Shining One Who Rules Alone: *Death is liberation*.

'There are no ghosts,' he said, as if saying it would make it true.

Too late he noticed a young man coming up to the gate carrying a full kettle of steaming barsh. He halted and stared at Kesh strangely, as if he'd heard the comment. Kesh opened the gate for him, and the young man nodded in thanks and hurried toward the mercenaries, looking back once. He was dressed differently, in loose trousers and a short kirtle bound at the waist with a sash. His red-clay coloring and pleasant features reminded Keshad more of his two Mariha slave girls than of the stocky riders with their flat, broad cheekbones, sparse mustaches, and predator's gaze.

Inside the inn, the reeve had set up court. He had drawn up a table parallel to one end of the long room. Here he sat, stripped out of cloak and sleeveless vest and down to shirtsleeves, on a bench between table and wall, and seated beside him the man who must be the mercenary captain. The contrast between the two men made Kesh pause beside the door as he tried to decide whether to get in line with the other merchants being interviewed by the reeve, or grab a drink first to fortify himself against the coming interrogation.

The reeve had an easy way of talking to the merchants who laid out their ledgers and tallied their chits in response to his smiling questions. His manner suggested this was merely an inconvenience between friends. The other man was a stranger, reserved, removed, but aware of every action within the smoky interior. He glanced at Kesh, noting his scrutiny, and marked him with a nod before looking elsewhere. That he understood the words flying back and forth Kesh guessed by the way he would cock his head at intervals and glance sideways so as not to seem to be paying too much attention to the talk of cargoes and tallies. He had much the look of the Qin soldiers, but a striking nose and the shape of his eyes gave him the look of a man who has been twisted out of different clay. Kesh wasn't sure which man made him more nervous: the genial eagle or the silent wolf.

The innkeeper sidled past, on his way to the door, and Kesh caught his sleeve and tugged him to a stop.

'Here, now, you old toad. Those two lads you sent were useless. There's a boy dead beneath the Ladytree—'

'Thank goodness!' wheezed the innkeeper, trying to pry his sleeve out of Kesh's grasp. 'That's none of my trouble, then. I have enough as it is!'

'As sour as your cordial! Where is the envoy?'

'Lying as peaceful as he can, out on the shade porch.' He recoiled, although Kesh did nothing but give him a disgusted look. 'He's under a shelter! If he dies under my roof it'll cost me half my season's profit for the purification ritual. I am not a cruel man, ver, but it will not help me or my family if I lose everything we have, will it?'

Kesh scanned the room. An elderly man was filling wooden mugs. A lad not more than ten was cleaning the floor where someone had sicked up. The rest of the staff, evidently, was outside clearing up from the attack.

'Can't get good help, anyway,' continued the innkeeper as he weaseled his sleeve out of Kesh's grip. 'Used to be my good wife and a niece and daughter helped me instead of these cursed useless hired louts, but after the midnight raids of four year back we moved all the women down road by Old Fort. I was lucky. I know a man lost both his strong daughters that summer to the raids. The gods alone know what became of them, poor lasses. Something awful. If you'll kindly let me get to my business, ver, I'll see you get a cup of cordial.'

Kesh let him go as the reeve caught his eye and gestured, smiling as if they were old friends just now reunited. The innkeeper scurried away. Kesh pushed past a trio of grousing merchants and came up to the table as another man gathered up his ledger and chits, thanked the reeve profusely and, with an innocent man's flush of honest relief, headed for the door with a mug of cordial in one hand.

'I forgot your name, ver,' said the reeve. 'Sit down.'

'You never asked it.'

'In the heat of the moment, courtesy gets lost in the fire. I'm called Joss.'

'Fire-touched,' said Kesh, thinking of the envoy as he noticed the mark on Joss's wrist: like the dead boy under the Ladytree, the reeve was born in the Year of the Ox. Kesh's ken for numbers figured it up, unbidden. While the lad must be sixteen, this reeve was likely two cycles older, so he was forty.

Joss smiled. '"A Fire-kissed Ox! You'll drive me to drink, lad!" That's what any one of my dear aunties always said. I don't think I was *that* wild. This is Captain Anji, who commands the guard of the caravan that was traveling behind you on the road. We're all fortunate they happened to be close enough to help us out. I'm sorry. I didn't catch your name again.'

'I'm called Keshad.' It was best to set all his chits on the table immediately. He opened the ledger to the current page. 'I'm a debt slave bound to Master Feden of Olossi.'

'Master Feden of Olossi,' murmured the reeve, gaze fixing on the tabletop as though to seek answers there, or to remember a thing he had forgotten. 'Feden.'

'Do you know him? He's a member of the Greater Council of Olossi. One of the most prosperous and influential merchants in Olossi, in fact.'

The reeve blinked, as though shaking awake, and he looked hard at Kesh. 'How long have you been debt-bound to him?'

'Twelve years now.'

'*Twelve* years? Did you know that on Law Rock it states that "When a person sells their body into servitude in payment for a debt, that person will serve eight years and in the ninth go free.'''

He shrugged. 'Everyone knows that covers only the original debt. Not any debts accrued in the interval.'

'Is that what your master tells you?' asked the reeve in a tone Kesh couldn't interpret.

'That's the usual way. Have you heard different? Is it different in the north?'

The hard look on the reeve's face made Kesh nervous, but the man shook it off quickly.

'No, I don't suppose it is.' He ran a finger down the neat column of the ledger, turning back a page or three. Kesh doubted he could read, but any educated person knew the ideograms for common market goods, the directions, numbers, and so on. 'A trusted slave, I see, running your own trip south and even into lands where Hundred folk don't normally trade. Like Mariha.'

'I like to find goods that will make a profit.'

'For your master?'

'I must clear a certain amount for each trip. After that, I keep the rest of the profit for myself.'

The reeve glanced up at him, then touched each of the chits. 'Getting close?'

'Yes.'

'After twelve years.' He was clean-shaven like a lot of the men north of the Aua Gap: Toskala-chinned, people called it. He rubbed his smooth Toskala chin against an arm, sighed, and scooped up the rare chit. 'The Sirniakans call this an *exalted* token.' He tapped the last line of the ledger. 'I see you invoked Sapanasu's veil for your cargo. Care to tell me anything about that?'

'No.'

The reeve drew his finger up to the top of the page. 'Whatever it is, it seems to have come your way in Mariha together with—' He clicked his tongue, studying the writing. 'Females – two, young, unmarried. What's this?'

'Saffron.'

'Ah. Oil . . .'

'Clove oil.'

'These here – mirrors. I don't know what that is—'

'Shell dice. This one is ivory combs – thirty-two in number.'

'No silk! That's unusual.' His finger slid back to the last line. 'Isn't that the mark for a bouquet of flowers? Or herbs of some kind?'

Kesh did not look at either of them. He kept his hands open, and was able to speak normally. 'An aphrodisiac.'

The reeve nodded, with a hearty grin and chuckle that suddenly struck Kesh as so entirely false that he shuddered and found he'd curled one hand into a fist. All this time, the mercenary captain had watched and listened and made no sound or reaction, like one of those stone monuments so old that any distinguishing marks have long since been worn off its face. This time he raised an eyebrow and said, in a cool, elegant accent, 'Have the men of the Hundred need for such medicine?'

'We haven't any women as beautiful as your wife, Captain,' said Joss, 'or we should never want for desire.'

The captain smiled blandly to accept the compliment. He did not deny it.

'Where are you come from, Captain?' Kesh asked.

'I have come from the south. I hire my company out as caravan guard. This is our first trip to the Hundred.' Anji looked sidelong at Joss. 'Maybe Hundred folk need guards to hire.'

Joss shrugged. 'Maybe so. Times are hard.'

'I hear things are very bad in the north,' said Kesh, happy to see the conversation flow into safer channels.

'So they are,' said Joss with the merest flicker of his eyelids as he considered the north and what it meant to him.

'Maybe you know folk who are looking for honest men seeking employment,' said the captain.

Joss let the chit fall to the table and regarded the captain. The two men had level gazes, and the ability to look each at the other without it becoming a contest. They were different men, with different authority, not rivals.

'It's come to this,' said the reeve, 'that merchants moving goods along all roads in the Hundred need caravan guards. I'll see what introductions I can make for you, in Olossi, in exchange for the good turn you've done me.'

'One, in exchange for another.' The captain extended an arm, and the men grasped, each with his hand to the other's elbow: So were bargains sealed in the marketplace, where the worth of a man's word was soon known to everyone.

'May I go?' Kesh asked.

'Certainly,' said the reeve as though he thought Kesh had left hours ago. 'Just one thing.'

Kesh waited.

Pleasant expressions were traps for the unwary. The reeve wore one now. 'An envoy of Ilu is dying out on the back porch. It's a bad thing in any event, that a holy man is murdered in this way, and I take it more personally because I was dedicated for my year to the Herald, so it's like one of my kinsmen breathing out his spirit a few paces from me. Here I was come too late to prevent it. That's a thing that really burns me hard, coming too late.' His entire aspect shaded to an emotion so dark that Kesh took a step back, and that made the reeve take notice and that friendly smile crawl back onto his lips just as if he hadn't a moment before looked furious enough to rip someone's head right off. 'Tell me, Keshad, did you witness the killing? Can you tell me what you saw? Leave out no detail. Mention everything you noticed.'

'There wasn't much to notice. I retreated under the Ladytree to defend my wagon and cargo.' The best defense was a good offense; he remembered that now. 'You can imagine that I didn't want to lose what I'd bought in Mariha. I'm close – very close – to buying back my freedom, so you can imagine—' Even so, he choked on it.

The reeve nodded compassionately and took a slug of cordial while Kesh caught his breath and thought through his strategy. The captain did not drink.

'I stood there under the Ladytree hoping we wouldn't be noticed because of the boughs. Or that ospreys wouldn't blood sanctuary ground – scant chance of that! Anyway, men came riding our way, and that envoy just ran out toward us. At first I thought maybe he was in league with them, but he used his staff to bring down one of the horses and its rider, and then someone – I don't know who – shot him in the back as he was running, and after that he was run over at least once by a pair of horses. I was busy by then. I didn't see anything more.'

The reeve asked, 'Where do you think the envoy was running?'

'I thought toward the Ladytree, seeing as it is sanctuary

ground . . .' He timed his hesitation perfectly. 'He couldn't be sure the ospreys would grant him safe passage. But he may have been running elsewhere. I don't know. I had my own troubles. We were attacked. My driver got wounded. That lad was killed. I should put in a complaint to you, now that I think on it, because the merchant who hired him looks like to shirk the burying tithe, and I'll wager he's got no interest in seeing the boy's family gets any death tax due them. He was a brave lad, a little weak in the mind, if you take my meaning, but he stuck his ground as brave as any guardsman I've seen, not that he had a chance against the ospreys.'

Captain Anji had a little secret smile on his face that made Kesh turn cold inside. But the reeve said nothing, only stared into the depths of his cordial as if seeking the tiny stems that weren't quite all strained out.

'Did you know his name?' the reeve asked.

'His name? Whose name?'

'The envoy's name?'

'He never said, now that I think on it. They rarely do. I never thought—'

'Yes?'

'Just . . . it all came so fast, the attack, all of that. I really thought we were safe once we crossed the border.' He wiped his brow and found that his hands were trembling. 'Can I go now? Is there anything else you want to ask me?'

The reeve shook his head. 'No. You can go.' His smile was so cheerful that it was almost possible to believe they were two good friends parting after a sweet drink to chase down the day's travel. 'If I think of anything else, though, be sure I'll ask.'

'I'm leaving at dawn.'

'So are we all. I believe your two caravans will be joining forces for the rest of the journey. I'll be patrolling the West Spur as you go, so I can always drop in if I have any more questions.'

'I'll go, then.' He nodded at both men and moved away, swearing under his breath, until he caught the innkeeper coming in from outside. 'What about that cordial you promised me?' He glanced over his shoulder to see the reeve and the captain with heads bent together. The reeve glanced up at the same moment, saw him looking, and waved at him with the kind of bright, deceitful smile that cheating merchants paraded every day of their cheating lives. It reminded him of Master Feden.

'You're hurting my arm,' whispered the innkeeper.

'Never mind the cordial. I'd like to see the envoy.'

There wasn't much to see. The dying man had been carried out behind the main structure, and laid out on a table set up on a raised porch covered by a solid roof constructed of lashed-together pipe stalks and thatch-tree fronds, the kind of place where people congregated in the heat of the day to escape the sun. A single tarry lamp burned, suspended from a hook in the cross quarter beam. Its smell gave him a headache, but the glower of its light offered enough illumination to see. The envoy lay on his stomach with his blue cape bunched along his left side to make him more comfortable. Kesh crouched beside him. He gave no sign of life beyond the infinitesimal movement of one eye below its closed eyelid, as though he were dreaming.

'He'll be dead by midnight,' whispered the innkeeper, too loudly, and – startled – Kesh fell on his butt, and put his head in his hands, and after a moment roused himself to get up.

'Has any effort been made to stem the bleeding?' he asked.

'Bleeding's stopped. Just a bubble of air coming out. See it pop – there! I mark that means it hit his lungs. That'll end him, no doubt.' He gestured toward the smoke swirling up from the tarry lamp. 'That stink'll fetch any mendicant close by, but if there is none of them near, then there's nothing we can do.'

'You've no starflower? Soldier's friend?'

'Wouldn't know it if I saw it. Just herbs for flavoring food and the cordial spices, that's all we've got here.'

Gingerly, Kesh traced a finger around the wound. It was deep and almost perfectly round, rimed with blood but barely oozing. Bruises were blooming all over the envoy's bare back. The bright saffron-yellow tunic lay in pieces, discarded to one side.

'It's the trampling that done him,' said the innkeeper. 'I've seen men run over by horses who got up and walked in for a drink as easy as you please only to die in the nighttime after with no warning. Something gets broken inside. No way to heal that.'

'No,' said Kesh quietly, 'no way to heal the things that are broken on the inside.' He touched the envoy's grizzled hair, as much silver as black. 'Is there a Sorrowing Tower here?'

'Nay, none here. He'll have to be carted to Far Umbos. Another expense!'

'He had two bolts of finest quality silk with him,' said Kesh bitterly. 'That should cover your costs.'

The bartender called from the back door. The innkeeper excused himself and hurried indoors.

Kesh was overcome by such a wave of exhaustion that for a moment he thought the blue cloak was slithering like a snake, as though something trapped inside it was alive. He dozed off. When he started awake, he remembered that the innkeeper was gone, leaving only him and the silent body. The envoy still breathed, slow and shallow. Something about the pale moon exposed in an inky sky and the harsh scent of the tarry lamp made Kesh shiver.

On the breeze he heard the sound of wagons rumbling in, and a few shouts of greeting.

'Farewell, uncle,' he murmured.

In the commons, the second caravan had arrived at last, led in by a pair of scouts. It was a bigger company than the one Kesh had traveled with, about thirty wagons and carts in all although it was too dark to get an accurate count even with hirelings and slaves trudging alongside with torches. There was even one heavily guarded wagon, a tiny cote on wheels rather like his own, but he could not be sure what treasure, or prisoner, was held within. There were another hundred of those black-clad guardsmen riding in attendance. Captain Anji led a substantial troop.

Kesh walked back to the Ladytree and his own wagon, where Tebedir kept watch. He dismissed the driver to get what rest he could. After emptying the girls' waste pail out beyond the Ladytree's boundaries and returning it to them, he stretched out on the ground. There he dozed, restlessly, waking at intervals to stare hard into the darkness.

He had to stay alert. Someone was looking for the treasure he was hiding. A thousand needles could not have pricked so hard. But there was nobody there, and all around him in Dast Korumbos the survivors and the newcomers slept the sleep of the justly rescued. If any ghosts walked, he at least, thank Beltak, could not see them.

26

'We keep our heads down,' Keshad said to Tebedir that dawn in Dast Korumbos as they harnessed the beasts and stowed the gear. 'Stay away from the reeve. Don't let that foreign captain or his wolves notice us. Heads down. Tails down. Walk quietly. Draw no attention to ourselves. Keep in the middle of the group.'

As soon as they left Dast Korumbos, a pattern developed: Each night the caravan halted where the reeve met them on the road, and each night Kesh built his fire, fed his slaves, and kept his head down, watching and listening but never venturing farther than he had to from his wagon. He heard the rumor that the faithless border captain, Beron, was being held as a prisoner, hauled along to face justice at the assizes in Olossi, but no one was allowed near that closed wagon, guarded as it was by a shield of grim wolves. Kesh had no desire to investigate. Best not to draw attention to himself. He was pleased to find himself assigned to the last third of the procession. They'd eat dust back here, but were perfectly placed to remain anonymous as the cavalcade lurched down the West Spur, moving north and east.

He looked for signs of that Silvers' wagon that had gone on ahead, alone, out of Dast Korumbos, but he saw no wreckage, no sign of them at all. Either they'd got away free, or they and their wagon had been hauled off into the trees, never to be seen again.

At length the caravan rumbled down the long slope out of the foothills where the high mountain pine and tollyrake forest gave way to an open, grass-grown, and rather dry landscape with few trees. They came to Old Fort, a low hill where the remains of an ancient monument thrust up into the sky, looking rather like the mast of a vast, buried ship. A palisade ringed the community at New Fort, rising beneath the gaze of the old ruin. The Olo'o Sea shimmered in the afternoon sun. The southern hills and eastern upland plains rimmed the waters of the Olo'o, but west and north the inland sea ran all the way to the horizon. Dogs lapped at the water and, finding it salty, shied back. Along the shore, fires burned merrily where families of fisherfolk smoked their catch beside reed boats coated with pitch to make them waterproof.

At Old Fort, the reeve left them and flew north. The merchants, bickering and complaining, found places in the camping ground built just beyond the palisade and its double stone watchtowers. Those merchants who had spent days walking in the rear of the cavalcade brought their grievance to the two caravan masters, and Kesh decided that he, too, had to demand a forward place lest folk wonder why he was content to skulk in the back. Others complained more loudly; he was quickly forgotten as the arguments ebbed and flowed. He waited at the back of the assembly. A man brought a complaint against a guardsman – not one of the Qin – who, the merchant claimed, had had sexual congress with one of his slave girls; three merchants carting oil of naya and barrels of pitch from the west shore of the sea begged leave to join the caravan; a dispute had arisen over payment for a driver and his teams. As soon as Master Iad handed out new places in the line of march, Kesh left. At the camping ground, the fisherfolk were glad to sell their catch at an inflated price. For his party, Kesh cooked rice, with one fish shared between them.

He sat on the steps of his wagon to watch the sun set. Red spilled along the waters, painting a gods' road where no mortal could walk. Much of the company settled down for the night, though a fair number felt safe enough to get drunk and sing.

Kesh was too restless to sleep. He sat late, marking the slow wheeling of the stars. The sigh of the water on the flat shore nagged at him all night, like his doubts and fears. Twice, he thought he heard the soft sound of weeping from inside the wagon, and twice, it ceased as soon as he rose, thinking to look inside. Shadows crawled along the shoreline. He saw a dark figure striding knee-deep far out in the quiet waters, a death-bright white cloak billowing out behind as though caught in a gale. He blinked, and it was after all only the light of the rising moon spilling along the sea. It wasn't even windy.

In the morning, the caravan pushed north along the road, which took the upland route, always within sight of the Olo'o Sea. This good road, which he had walked before, was packed earth. The sights were familiar and comforting, the glassy stretch of sea to his left and the long rolling swells of the grassland to his right, shimmering under a wind out of the east. It was nice to walk in the front for a change. Each of the next five days, he marked the remaining four of the five fixed landmarks of the West Spur: Silence Cliff; the Scar; Rope Tree; the intersection with the Old Stone Road that led to the Three Brothers, the intersection that was the terminus of West Spur, the last mey post.

An hour after dawn, they passed the alabaster gates of the Old Stone Road. Other folk were also on the road and its attendant paths this early, most carting goods toward town: a girl drove a flock of sheep alongside the road; a dog trotted beside a lone traveler with pouches and loose packs hung from his shoulders and belt; a cripple seated on a ragged blanket was selling oranges, but no one stopped to buy.

Kesh stepped aside from the line of march and walked over to touch the mey post that marked the intersection. The gesture made him think of the envoy of Ilu. It was strange how a brief acquaintance could haunt a man, even a man like himself who kept all those who wished to call him 'friend' at arm's length. He watched as the point of the caravan turned southwest onto West Track. It had taken nine days to travel the West Spur from Dast Korumbos. Now the three noble towers of Olossi shone in the distance, where the land sloped down to the wide river that snaked along the lowland plain.

Tebedir, making the turn, waved at him, and he left the mey post and hurried after.

On the long slow descent down the gradual incline, they maintained an excellent view of the mouth of the River Olo and its environs. The alternating colors of the patternwork of agricultural fields, cut into sections by irrigation canals, faded into the hazy distance to the north and west on the Olo Plain. The town itself lay upstream. The walled inner city was nestled on a swell of bedrock almost entirely surrounded by a stupendous oxbow bend in the river. There were walls of a sort even around the sprawling outer districts, but although Sapanasu's clerks and Atiratu's poets related stories of sieges and attacks fended off by the impressive inner wall works in days long past, the outer wall was little more than a palisade thrown up in stages to mark the slow outward crawl as Olossi 'let out her skirts.'

'A disorderly town,' remarked Tebedir. 'In the empire, all is laid in a double square. Every door and gate has a number and name.'

'With the Shining One's aid, I will leave that place by tomorrow, and never return,' Kesh said reflexively. Olossi's shortcomings did not interest him.

His gaze followed the winding river downstream to where the delta glistened with a dozen slender channels. Tiny fishing boats worked the estuary, sliding in and out of view among great stands of reeds. Even from this distance he saw the rocky island in the delta crowned with a compound of whitewashed buildings. The temple had high walls, four courtyards, and three piers: one for supplies, one for those coming to worship at the altar of the Merciless One, and one for those departing sated or scarred.

He was then and for a long time as he trudged beside the wagon almost delirious with fear and hope. He was sick and dizzy. To keep his balance he had to clutch one of the stout posts that held up the taut canvas cover that tented the wagon's bed. He silently wept with longing, and fixed his gaze on the ground to watch his feet hit, one after the other and again and again. That repetition soothed him as he tramped along. The steady plodding impact of his feet, like the post, was something to cling to as he cut away his fears and hopes and ruthlessly consigned them to the furnace, where they burned; to the cold ice, where they grew a sheen of frost. He set them aside. He must not be weak. Not now.

A pair of horses moved alongside him, riding from the front toward the rear, and one rider turned to keep pace with his wagon.

'Are you well, merchant?'

The clear voice made him startle, and he looked up into the gaze of the young woman who was the wife of Captain Anji. Once or twice on West Spur he'd seen her studying his little camp, as though Moy and Tay – when he let them out – interested her. But she'd never spoken to him before. Her husband watched as wolves did who have recently eaten: curious but not ready to attack.

'A long, weary journey, Mistress,' he said with a forced smile. He let go of the pole and wiped his sweating brow.

Her smile had the strengthening effect of a cool draught of water. 'Close now, I see. Is Olossi your home?'

'No, Mistress. But it is my destination.'

She glanced at his wagon. He had never been this close to her before. She was stunningly lovely, and dressed in a magnificently rich Sirniakan silk robe cut away for riding, with the sleeves sewn so long they covered most of the hand. These were the sleeves of a woman rich enough that she was not obliged to perform manual labor. Her long nails were perfectly kept, painted in astonishing detail with tiny golden dragons curled against a blue sky.

She caught him looking, nodded with a look both polite and reserved, and moved on. He turned to watch her go. No man had the power to resist a second look: She had features not so much perfectly proportioned as entirely captivating, marked by an exotic touch around the eyes, which had a narrowing slant rather like the slantwise eye folds of the Silvers, now that he thought of it. Certainly, she was beautiful, the kind of woman a man must marry if he could. But he possessed a treasure much more valuable. As the pair moved back along the line the captain looked back over his shoulder, and Kesh smiled, finding strength in the thought.

Much more valuable.

He would succeed. He had to.

Some manner of accident – a broken axle – held up the rear portion of the train, but by midmorning the forward half of the caravan clattered through Crow's Gate in the outer wall to the sprawl of Merchants' Walk, the way station, clearinghouse, and bazaar for traders who came from all parts of the Hundred and from over the Kandaran Pass out of the south, and for that trickle who walked the Barrens Road out of the dry and deadly west. Wide, dusty avenues were lined with warehouses and auction blocks. Behind them, alleys plunged in and out of warrens where the lesser merchants and peddlers and cartmen lodged in narrow boardinghouses. Sapanasu's clerks kept two temples here, alive at all hours with bargaining, recordkeeping, and argument.

At the Crow's Gate temple, shaven-headed clerks stood sweating under the shade of a colonnade as they settled accounts. Kesh stood in line with the rest to pay his portion of the guards' fee, and after signing off and paying up he was free of his obligation to the caravan and free to continue into Merchants' Walk. He handed over the last of his leya. Except for a string of twenty-two vey, which was not even enough to fill his leather bottle with cheap wine, he had nothing left except his merchandise and his accounts book.

'We haven't much time,' he said to Tebedir. 'Shade Hour is coming. Everything closes down.'

Beyond Crow's Gate Field, the road split into three. Kesh directed Tebedir to drive to the right, and they soon rolled into Gadria's Oval, commonly known as Flesh Alley.

The broad oval, which maintained a surprising bit of grass, was ringed by stately ironwood trees and by the accounts houses and holding pens for merchants who specialized in buying and selling debt, or paupers and criminals destined for slavery. In the middle of the oval rose the stepped marble platform with its spectacular ornamented roof, where at this moment a pair of boys, guarded by bored hirelings, were being offered for sale. The crowd was sparse. Many turned to look at the wagon. It was not an exciting day at the market.

'The house with the mark of three rings,' he said.

The master of the Three Rings offered shade and water gratis to any customers or purveyors arriving by cart or wagon. Kesh got Tebedir settled, then opened the door of the wagon.

'Moy! Tay!'

They ventured out cautiously, staring around with wide eyes. They looked at him, at the accounts house with its open doors, then saw the marble platform and the business going on there. The younger girl whispered fiercely to her sister, and they clutched hands, bent their heads, and waited.

'Come on,' he said, not liking to look at them. It wasn't right to go so meekly. He would have respected them more had they raged and fought against their fate, but they never had. They had come to him obediently, and it seemed they would leave the same way.

He herded them up to an open door and inside. The room was empty except for a two-stepped wooden platform, ringed by a rail, that stood in the middle. There was nothing else, only tall windows open to admit as much light as possible, and the packed earth floor. Kesh closed the door and rang the bell hanging from a hook to the left of the entryway. He led the girls up onto the platform, where they stood holding on to the railing and looking around with frightened expressions. Yet, knowing a bit about them from the long journey, he understood they had long since accepted their fortune. Neither cried. They still held hands.

The spy window opened and, after a moment, closed. Footsteps pattered away within the house. From outside, the patter of the auctioneer wound up and down. A dog barked. Wheels ground along the dirt.

The inner door slid open, and Merchant Calon stepped down into the room.

'Keshad! I knew you would bring me something of value!' He was a tidy man, narrow, neat, and dressed in an austere tunic scarcely more than what an honored slave might wear. He circled the girls, who watched him as mice might eye a stoat. They did not whimper or cry. In their own way, they had courage. 'This looks promising in a month in which I have suffered many disappointments. Quite unique.' Calon called into the house, where a figure stood half in shadow beyond the door. 'Where is Malia?'

'She is coming, exalted.'

'Listen,' said Kesh. 'We have dealt fairly with each other for several years now. I have always brought you the best of what I've found in the south.'

'So you have. I think we have both profited.'

'I know Malia will want to inspect them first, but let me speak bluntly. Offer me a fair price, and I won't haggle.'

Calon paused and, without looking at Kesh, touched first the ivory bracelet on his left wrist, and after this the one on his right.

'I call them Moy and Tay, which means in their language "one" and "two." Tay is not yet in her bleeding. The elder girl is also young, a year or two older. They may be sisters. That wasn't clear to me when I obtained them. They have not given me a moment's trouble on the long journey, nor did they ever try to escape.'

An elderly woman appeared at the door, leaning on a cane of polished ebony. She wore both bronze slave bracelets and the ivory bracelets reserved for those who were free. 'Keshad,' she said in her spider's voice, whispery and tough. Her smile was tenuous. She was not, in Kesh's estimation, a cruel woman, but she was not compassionate either. 'What have you got here? Southern. Look at those complexions. Very fine.'

Calon rang the bell twice. A servant appeared with a trio of silver goblets, each half full of sweet cordial. He offered one to Kesh. The two men turned their backs so Malia could inspect the girls closely. Kesh sipped as cloth rustled and slipped, as each girl spoke a few words and, when Malia sang a phrase, mimicked her. They had voices as sweet and clear as the cordial. Feet and hands and teeth would be examined, and skin and body prodded and stroked.

Malia took her time, most of it in silence. Kesh sipped.

'What news from Master Feden's house?' Calon asked with seeming casualness.

'We just walked in today through Crow's Gate. I came here first.'

Calon grinned. 'I see. Best not to let Feden's fat fist grab the best of your merchandise. He would only find a way to cheat you, him and the other Greater Houses.'

'I never said so.'

Calon nodded. 'Nor can you, so I'll say it for you. Those who sit at the voting table with a majority of votes held to themselves can play the tune the rest of us must dance to. They see only what is good for themselves, while the land falls into ruin around them. They are made shortsighted by their own greed. Eiya! So be it. Those of us in the Lesser Houses are ready – poised – to make a change, whether the Greater Houses will, or no. As are you. Listen, young man, I expect the day comes quickly when you are able to buy yourself free.' With his chin he gestured toward the girls. 'If you've a mind to, I would offer you a position as a junior trader in my house, for it seems, alas, that I may have an opening. You've a good head, a clear mind, and a cool heart. Consider it.'

Kesh met his gaze, respect for respect. 'If I meant to stay in Olossi, I would consider it, Master Calon. You're the only merchant here I respect enough to work for.'

'I'll take that as thanks, then. Malia? A fair price.'

She circled around once more before standing in silence for a time, calculating. She had never been a beauty; intelligence and ruthlessness had bought her freedom. Kesh smelled the lemon water in which she washed, a bracing and cooling scent even on such a hot day.

'A good investment,' she said. 'They are young enough to learn. They are healthy. They have clear voices. I think they can be trained as jaryas, if it so happens that they are also intelligent. If not, they can be trained to sing what others compose. Although they're not great beauties they have an unusual coloring that will attract notice. Three hundred leya apiece. Six hundred, altogether.'

Kesh pressed teeth into his lower lip, so he wouldn't yelp with triumph and thus betray himself. *Ten cheyt!* Ten gold pieces was the best haul he had ever made. And he would need every vey.

'A fair price?' Calon asked.

'More than I expected,' said Kesh.

Calon grinned. 'Malia is never wrong. I'm of a mind to have them trained in my own house. That younger one, now . . . in a few years, if she has the talent, she might hope to marry one of Olossi's old merchants who has lost his first pair of wives from childbearing or the swamp fever. I can expect to sell her for ten times what I paid. So you're getting no bargain, Keshad. Do not think I am sentimental.'

'I am satisfied it is a fair price. You'll have to train and feed them. Let us seal it.'

Malia led the girls away. They did not look back as they vanished through the inner door into their new life.

Master Feden lived in the inner city, but his clearinghouse, like those of the other sixteen Greater Houses, stood in the outer city along Stone Field, the rectangular plaza at the heart of Merchants' Walk. Paving stones rumbled beneath the wheels of Tebedir's cart, an oddly comforting sound after months squeaking along packed-earth roads. With afternoon settling over the day, traffic in the plaza was thinning out. Shade Hour beckoned. Olossi was slipping into its daily drowse.

Feden's clearinghouse wore a banner of green and orange silk, ghastly colors pieced together in a quartered flower. Its front had seven gates, doors built to a doubled height and width, but only the servants' entrance remained open at this hour. They drove through the open doors, nodding to the yawning guard, who recognized Keshad and passed him through with an uninterested wave. The wagon rattled down a high arched corridor built of stone and into the dusty, treeless courtyard where Master Feden's hired men and slaves hauled water from the cistern, laded handcarts for transport into town, and loitered in the shade offered by rooftops.

'It's Kesh!'

The slaves sweating at their labors set aside their tasks and came over to gather beside the wagon. They looked, but did not touch.

'How'd the run go?' asked old Sushad, wiping sweat from the drooping side of his mouth.

Kesh nodded, too full to speak, and the others, who had been whispering and eager, fell silent and moved away to let Tebedir drive the wagon into a bay at Kesh's direction. Tebedir unhitched the horses and led them to a trough built against the outermost wall of the courtyard. Kesh counted up costs in his head. Feden would charge him for water and feed and stabling, so he had to work quickly and reach the master before it came time to raise the Shade Hour flag.

Footsteps slapped the dirt. He turned.

Nasia slipped into the shaded cover of the cargo bay. She wore a short linen tunic. Her legs and feet were bare, dusty from the court-yard, and she had a smudge of whiting powder on her nose, a smear of oil across her knuckles, and a fresh bruise on her cheek.

'Is it true?' she asked in her soft voice. She didn't touch him. Her slave bracelets glimmered as she raised her hands, and dropped them again. 'They're saying in the halls that you've earned enough to buy your freedom.'

'Maybe so.'

She waited, but he shook his head.

'I told you already,' he went on. 'I told you honestly. I'm going for Bai.'

Her face would never be beautiful, but she had eyes as lovely and expressive as a doe's, wide and almost black. 'You can't,' she said, trembling. 'You can't possibly be able to buy her free from the temple.'

'A treasure fell in my lap. It's now, or never.'

She choked down tears, but he did not comfort her. He had told her the truth all along, and probably she had never believed him. Hope is a cruel master.

'Master Feden hoped we might tie the binding,' she whispered. 'He gave permission.'

'And give him our children's labor to fatten his purse, and more debt for us to pay off? No.'

'If you can hope to go for – her – you could buy off my debt instead. You could.'

'I don't have time for this.'

'Did you ever love me, Kesh?'

'I never told you I did. I like you, that's all.'

'I got – I got—' She pressed a hand to her abdomen. 'They made me drink the herbs. I lost a baby.'

Eiya! Nasia had gotten pregnant. Maybe with his child. Or maybe with the child of one of Master Feden's customers. No matter.

'A child born to a slave is better off not being born,' he said. 'Would you want that? To begin a child's life when it's in debt already? It was for the best. You'll see that, in time. Anyway, this is the end of it, Nasia. You're a good girl. If I can ever help you, I will, but now I have to hurry. I can't afford to pay a whole day's stabling charge.'

She began to cry, but silently, as slaves learned to do. Old Sushad slid into view from around the corner. He said nothing to Kesh, just a look with that half-frozen face and his little finger flicked up. Kesh turned his back. He counted the water skins and satchels hanging along the wagon on either side. He took two days' worth of the remaining flatbread and smoked meat, not at all tasty. The rest he left for Tebedir, who must make a return journey south over the pass to the empire, a good long way even if he got a hire. By the time he looked around, Nasia and Sushad had vanished away into the courtyard, where the ordinary noises of folk at their labor sounded again. Not one person, people he had known many years, came to greet him. Nasia was better-loved than he would ever be. No doubt they hated him for her sake, but he did not care.

By the time Tebedir returned, Kesh had unloaded the two chests, leaving only the treasure inside. Tebedir remained behind to guard the wagon, and Kesh hauled the chests to the wing door. It was a struggle to get them inside, as the door had been weighted so it easily swung shut if not being held. His fellow slaves passed him, going in and out. Not one stopped to help. No one looked him in the eye; not one person said a single word to him.

Aui! News of Nasia had traveled quickly.

But they were only bodies, moving in the monotonous dance of servitude. Their feet shuffled along a wood floor smoothed by generations of barefoot slaves walking quietly, as they must. They grunted, or coughed, or cleared their throats, and if they wept, they wept silently, as Nasia had. The men walked with heads bent. They went mostly bearded, trimmed tight along the jaw, and in general without the luxury of a mustache. Their hair was cut close to the head, easy to care for, nothing to get in the way of work. The women, depending on their station and age and what labor they were set, wore their hair shorn or pulled back in a ring and bound with slender iron chains so that the length of captive hair swayed along their back and buttocks.

He was well rid of them all.

He dragged the chests, one with each hand, and halted panting beside the rear door into the lesser exchange room, the only one he was permitted to enter without permission. He propped open the door and got the chests in, closed and locked himself in, and unrolled a colorless silk viewing cloth over the larger table. Dust motes spun where light poured through windows not yet closed for Shade Hour. It was hot, and getting hotter, but Master Feden would not quite be done for the day, not if his routine had remained unaltered in the last many months. Not if these windows were still open.

On the silk he arranged combs and mirrors and oil and saffron and shell dice, the handsome little items that he had picked up in southern markets on his journey. When he had all arranged to his liking, he rang the bell three times, twice two, and thrice again.

He was too unsettled to sit. He paced, wiped his brow, and rearranged the combs, liking the new pattern better, liking how it set off the richest among the lesser. Feden would want the best for his own family, to show off their long, glossy black hair, the pride of every man and woman who was neither hireling nor slave.

The master's door opened, and the man himself walked through with a shaven-headed clerk in attendance. He was a man made powerful by wealth, stout but not flabby, with his uncut hair braided and looped back in a man's threefold at his neck and shoulders.

Master Feden made no greeting, but walked slowly around the table while the clerk made a running tally and checked it against Keshad's accounts book. The pen scraped in the silence. Outside, the sun's light baked the stone plaza, seen beyond the thick posts where, soon, the slaves would unroll the cloth awnings over the wooden porch. So had Keshad done twelve years ago, when he was a lad sold into Master Feden's service. Unroll the awnings; close the windows; haul water; beat carpets; sweep and rake and look away when some clumsy soul got a hard cuff on the cheek for moving too slowly or simply for looking at a customer the wrong way or any way. Watch the massage girl you fancied be traded away for a mare. Listen as your young friend cried when he discovered he had missed the debt payment and was indentured for another year, during which new debts for food, drink, oil, pallet space, training costs, and interest would accrue, with more added on if you got sick or injured and a healer had to be brought in from the temple.

Pride, swallowed so many times, became a rock in the chest, and it had filled him with stone.

'Impressive,' said Master Feden, with a contemptuous smile that made Kesh want to slap him because Feden never began his haggling with a compliment. 'I congratulate you, Keshad. You have the gift. We need only set a price.'

'As I carried all my possessions with me, no holding space was required for my goods while I was gone, which means the debt set against my freedom in addition to interest accruing on the regulated basis during my absence stands at five hundred and eighty-seven leya,' said Kesh immediately. 'Am I correct?'

Master Feden nodded at the clerk.

She tallied. 'Yes, that's right.'

'The goods you see before you are easily worth twice that on the market. But I offer them, to you, in exchange for the rest of my debt. Which is a bargain for you, Master Feden.'

The master picked up a comb studded with whitestone and walked to the windows to peer at the subtle wash of colors that, Kesh knew, played beneath the surface of the stones. With his broad back to Kesh, he spoke. 'I'm surprised you act in such haste. I wish to offer you a post in my firm.'

The clerk actually gasped.

'You have promise. You've shown it time and again. I'll free the massage girl – what is her name? – the one you show particular attention to, although we had to have the herb woman in a month or two after you left to rid her of what she caught in her belly. I've been thinking of trading her debt to Mistress Bettia, who has a pair of fine embroidered couches my dear wife has been coveting, but I'll reconsider if you'll take her in marriage – both of you free – and sign a contract to trade for my firm – fifty-fifty percentages, we'll say – for ten years.'

The clerk's mouth had dropped open, and this time she looked at Kesh and then at the master's back. She ceased writing, waiting for his response.

He rested his hands on the rim of the table. All that restless energy fell away. He was clear and sharp and clean and perfect in his clarity.

'The rest of my debt. Which is a bargain for you, Master Feden.'

'Stubborn until the end.' He returned to the table. He had fleshy hands and sausage fingers, but a delicate touch as he set the comb down into its nest of silk. 'Very well. Settled.'

The clerk stood stunned, gaping at Kesh as though he had been revealed as a deadly lilu.

'Record it!' Feden snapped with a burst of impatient fury that made the poor clerk flinch. 'I have a meeting to attend. I must leave now!'

She spattered ink, blotted it up, and began scratching with her head bent in concentration and her shoulders hunched in case a blow came. But she was Sapanasu's hierophant, not Feden's slave. If he hit her, he would have to pay a fine to the temple.

Kesh lowered his hands to his side and tried not to twitch. Outside, a pair of lads stumped past; the awning creaked and dropped as they unrolled it. At once, the light through the windows muted to a less intense gold.

The clerk set down the accounts book. Feden glanced over the final entry, then made his mark. She turned it, and Kesh counted up the merchandise, saw that everything displayed on the table was accounted for, and with the pen marked the quartered moon that served as his seal.

'Sapanasu gives her blessing,' said the clerk. 'And her curse to any who turn their backs on what they have sworn in her name. Let it be marked and sealed.'

'Let it be marked and sealed,' said Feden with a smirk.

'Let it be marked and sealed.' Keshad extended a hand. 'My accounts book. It's mine now, free and clear.'

Feden lifted a hand, still smirking. He had rosy lips almost hidden within his luxuriant growth of beard and mustache. 'We have other business. There's a wagon and pair in one of my bays, and water taken from my trough. Stabling costs must be paid. With coin, or in labor.' He chortled.

Out in the hall, a door slammed.

What a fool he was! Kesh discovered his hands in fists and his skin flushed with heat. The clerk, seeing his expression, fell back a step. But he refused to move. He had meant to specify that the stabling charges be included in the final reckoning. Haste is its own trap. He had fixed the bait and walked into it himself. Damn damn damn.

After taking four breaths as Feden watched with intense amusement, he spoke in a flat voice. 'The usual stabling fee in Olossi includes hay, grain according to the nature of the beast, and twice watering. For one night, one leya or a day's labor in exchange. I have not been in this yard one night, nor has the pair under hire taken more than one watering. But I'll accept one leya as a fair charge.'

'I am not a public stableyard. Nor do I charge piecemeal, but only by the night. My premises are more secure, indeed, you have now invaded them as an outsider, someone not of my clan or family and with no other claim or right for biding within my clearing-house, so that will cost extra. And you know my policy about those cursed Southerners. I hate them, the thick-witted fanatics that they are, keeping women like sheep and slaves like pigs. I hear they say that once a man becomes a slave it's the god's doing, and he and any children or grandchildren he may ever quicken through his loins are marked forever with the slave's brand and can never again or any they marry become free men. So because of my distaste for such a person, and the cleaning I'll have to have my servants do after he's left the yard to wash away any stink he's left, I'll have to charge triple my usual fee. He comes under your hire, I believe. Nine leya. Or eighteen days' labor out of you, at the going rate, plus of course I'll have to charge you lodging and for your food for that time if you remain here to do the labor. And you'll have to stay here – you're obligated to do so – in case you choose to run to escape your debt. Three leya a day for lodging and food, to accrue while you work, unless you want to eat more than once a day, in which case a fourth leya for the second meal.'

'It's true,' said the clerk with a kind of dazed fascination, watching the exchange. 'Sapanasu's law supports Master Feden's claim against you, on both counts.'

'You cheating dog,' said Keshad softly. 'Nine leya is an outrage. As is three leya a day for costs.'

'Not in my house. I do not run a roadside shelter offering a plank floor to sleep on and nai porridge for supper. Do not think I gloat over your mistake, Keshad. I am a man of business. I must protect myself and my house.'

'You want me back. But I'm no longer your slave.'

'Do you expect me to believe you have any coin left after that trip? Have you paid up that southern driver? All your expenses? And yet you cast your throw so carelessly. I trained you better than that.'

Kesh let Feden keep talking. Indeed, he savored it, for the man did love to talk and did always believe himself to know more than others could.

'Sign on with me, and the stabling charge will be placed on your first accounts book as a junior partner. I'll still throw in the girl. For nothing. As a gesture of good faith. Otherwise, I fear me, Keshad, you'll be falling behind again. And if I choose not to allow you another trading venture, I am not one bit sure how you will overcome the debt.'

Kesh smiled. For the first time, Feden faltered, mouth pursing with doubt. Kesh slid a hand into the pouch sewn into his sleeve, careful to hide how much coin he had on his strings. He drew off nine precious leya, weighed them in his hand, and placed them each, individually, with a snap on the table. Feden's eyes widened.

'One night, two waterings, hay and grain,' Kesh said politely to the clerk. It was hard not to gloat, even if he was furious at himself for losing these leya through carelessness. He had better uses for the money. 'I'd like to get this settled. I have other business to attend to.'

'Where did you get that?' demanded the outraged merchant.

Kesh waited a few breaths, letting the other man stew. In his head, he tallied up the coin he owed Tebedir, a goodly amount. Everything now hinged on the treasure.

'Well?' Feden looked ready to burst.

With an exaggerated sigh, Kesh bent to close the chests, then straightened, fussing with his sleeves. 'This is not the only merchandise I brought out of the south. You didn't bother to look into my accounts book because you were in such haste to cheat me. But we have already sealed that these items settle my debt price.'

The clerk stared at the coins, which Feden had not touched.

Feden laughed. 'Twice cursed, you are,' he said to Kesh. 'None of your aunts or uncles made the least effort to hold you after the death of your parents. Did I ever tell you that? They were eager to take the money and sell you flat, whatever they could get for a boy of twelve. They couldn't even be bothered to pay the temple for a legitimate debt mark, but only that botched tattoo from a back-alley vendor. That scar can never be altered, the mark of their dislike for you. What makes you think they'll want you back?'

'What makes you think I'm going back to them?'

'But you must!' The stout man looked genuinely alarmed. 'Every man must cleave to his family and his clan. So the gods have set down.'

'Settle the stabling debt,' said Kesh to the clerk.

She did not look to Feden for permission. Kesh was a free man, now. She acted at his orders. She wrote; Feden fumed; Kesh wiped his brow, thinking that he ought to be sweating but he was cool, collected, wrung dry. He was free.

As soon as she was done writing, and marks made and seal set, she handed him the accounts book, the mark of his freedom. He tucked it into the lining of a sleeve, offered her a half leya as a tithe, which she took. Then he twisted the bronze slave bracelets off his wrists. Their weight, in his palm, seemed so heavy that he did not comprehend how he had borne it all these years. Deliberately, looking directly at Feden, meeting his gaze, Kesh placed the bracelets on the table. Feden turned away.

It was done.

Kesh left by the customers' door, which he had never once used in all the twelve years he had lived in this house. He did not look back.

*

'Where we go?' Tebedir asked as they rolled out into the plaza. The heat made the beasts slow, and Kesh's throat was already parched. 'Here, we roast, like fowl in the oven.'

One slave trudged across the plaza, wearing sandals to protect his feet against the hot stones. He wasn't carrying anything visible, but his shoulders were bowed nonetheless. Gates were closed and awnings furled along the long porches of the clearinghouses. Beyond the flat plain of Merchants' Walk rose the inner city on its rocky bed, buildings pressed shoulder-to-shoulder. Tile roofs and white walls baked; heat shimmered off them. The sun made the air a furnace. Only a wisp of pale cloud floated off above the eastern high plains, where, in the Lending, the grassland herders might have hope of a spatter of cooling rain.

Kesh was sweating, and dizzy. *I'm free. But she isn't.*

'We'll go now to Crow's Gate Field. I'll pay off the remainder of your contract.'

'As agreed, the remainder, it is one hundred, eighty, and seven of leya. As agreed, in addition, my costs to stable at the hiring ground, for five days. There I seek hire for journey back to empire.'

'That's right,' said Kesh absently, because his thoughts were already plunging ahead. 'I'll ask around and see who is hiring to go south before the end of the year and the rains. There'll be a caravan south within the week, I would wager. There's a particular chit I can see you get, so merchants know you're an honest and loyal hire. I can never thank you enough for standing beside me at Dast Korumbos . . .'

Tebedir nodded. 'The Shining One rewards his faithful worshipers. Do not despair unless your heart is dishonest. Do not despair unless you have broken the vows you make in the name of the King of King and Lord of Lords.'

Kesh barely heard him. Whatever calm had sustained him in Feden's house evaporated out here under the sun. His ears roared with the tumult inside him; sweat dripped from his fingers as his heart raced. *Do not despair.* He had stumbled onto the two Mariha girls in a frontier town and purchased them for a desperately cheap price, and for a while he had played the numbers in his head: Should he hire a drover and two donkeys to convey them with the other, smaller goods? Should he let them walk the entire months-long road to the Hundred, carrying the chests themselves, knowing that the journey might kill them but that he would save coin? Alone, they could not gain him what he wished, and indeed, they had brought him a greater profit than he had expected, enough to more than cover the expense of hiring a driver and wagon for the long haul once he had stumbled upon the treasure. They had enabled him to travel in what was, for him, relative comfort with his chests of carefully chosen luxury goods.

He had made his choices. He had bought his own freedom.

That night he slept on the hiring ground, under the wagon, with his strings of leya tucked against his chest.

In the morning, he bespoke a pair of bearers and their covered litter, nothing fancy but its cloth walls opaque and tied tight. Once he concluded his business and his contract with Tebedir and paid him the bonus he had promised, he had cleared all of his debts.

Only one thing remained: It was time to cast his last and most desperate throw.

27

The path out to the village of Dast Olo led along a raised stone causeway that ran first through grain fields, then through the pond-like dari fields, and finally into the tangle of reed flats and minnow channels that marked the edge of the navigable delta waters. Kesh walked briskly, but for all his travels he had trouble keeping pace with the two bearers who carried the curtained litter.

'Yah, so,' said the talkative one, who walked at the front rails. 'Brother and I, you know, it is the tradition out there in the Barrens border country, the village sends lads in to the green lands to work three years, and bring home coin and salt and silk. Maybe a wife, but that's hard to come by considering green-land women don't like the Barrens.'

They were short, with broad shoulders and torsos and powerful hands. Talker wasn't even out of breath, and while Kesh had already broken a sweat under the clear early-morning sky, these two had not bothered with a drink from their leather bottles.

'Probably we'll marry Lariada, from out by Falls.'

Silent grinned appreciatively.

'Yah, so, she's a strong girl, and more important a smart one who apprenticed to the Lantern, so she can keep accounts which is a powerful skill to have, to my way of thinking, if a pair of brothers are thinking to tenure good pastureland and build up a herd of cattle like our father and uncles never could do because of the drought back in the Year of the Goat, that would be the Gold Goat before either of us were birthed, not this last one. They lost everything but for the one heifer and the one dray.'

'They didn't lose the goats,' said Silent.

'Maybe not, but those goats'll survive anything, and grand mam said their milk was sour for two year after.'

'How's the caravan trade going up the Barrens Road these days?' asked Kesh, wiping another waterfall of sweat off his brow. He carried a slight enough burden, a satchel slung over his back with nothing more than a change of clothes, his accounts bundle, and the detritus of traveling life: knife, spoon, eating bowl, worship bowl, a pair of wax candles, flint and steel to light them, one day's worth of food, a leather bottle full of cheap wine. His weapons. The coin tied into his sleeves. It weighed like bricks already, because it was everything he owned.

They got within sight of Dast Olo before Talker got through with his description of the last twelve-year of caravan stories, and given that no more than a pair or three of caravans braved the Barrens Road every year, he took a long time telling an awful lot about not much.

'So the strangest part of it all, after the last caravan left and the girl paid her fine to the Witherer's altar – and you can be sure that the arkhon had a long talking to old Silk Ears— !'

Silent snickered.

'—then we in the village were thinking it would be all the travelers until the flood rains passed, and we two were leaving anyway to come down here Olossi green land way for our three year, and what do we see as we start out the walk? Heya!'

Kesh barely had time to open his mouth for the polite reply before Talker rushed on.

'We go passing an envoy of Ilu, walking up the long west-facing slope as cheerful as a redbird and him walking west on the Barrens Road he told us because we did stop and ask thinking he was headed for the village or maybe Falls or maybe Dritavu, because you know that everyone knows there's a Guardian altar up past Dritavu way that is forbidden but sometimes we see a light up there.'

'He talked as much as you do!' said Silent with another appreciative grin, although this one had no lascivious edge to it.

'I do not! That envoy, he'd have talked all five seasons from then until now if that reeve hadn't flown patrolling overhead and scared the donkey! So we must run after, and the envoy must go on his way west over the Barrens Road. I wonder if he's still alive, or come back to the Hundred as a living man, or only his bones! Say. Did I remember to tell you how we came to get that donkey?'

'We're here,' said Kesh with relief.

Dast Olo rested on a huge platform that some said was a natural escarpment of rugged rock but which Sapanasu's clerks and the Lady's mendicants claimed was the base of an ancient fortress whose pillars and roof and walls had long ago been obliterated by wind and rain and the passing of years. The high ground kept the feet of the village out of the waters, even during a ten-year flood. Dast Olo boasted also a lucky five-set of inns catering to pilgrims.

'Straight to the pier,' he said as they paused at the base of the wagon ramp. 'I'll give you vey for beer at the inn once we get back from the island. In addition to your hire.'

'Seeing so much water makes a man thirsty,' agreed Talker as they trotted up the ramp, not even panting. They had a funny way of loping that made the litter skim smoothly over the ground, never jarring. Their legs looked as thick as pillars. Kesh's legs had begun to sweat freely. He was glad he'd stripped down to a simple knee-length tunic and leather sandals, with nothing to chafe as he walked.

Dast Olo's villagers were farmers, fishers, or marketers catering to the flow of pilgrims. The village was already awake. Most of the fishing boats were long since out on the waters.

'Only a city man sleeps abed after the sun is risen!' proclaimed Talker cheerfully as they trotted through the streets to the pilgrim's pier.

Used to everything and anything, none of the folk out on their errands gave the curtained litter a second glance. The transaction at the pier – the price of a half leya per person was fixed by the temple – went swiftly. He handed two leya to an uninterested man with a flat-bottomed scow. The boatman tucked the coin in his sleeve and waited as Talker and Silent hoisted the litter in and settled themselves cross-legged in the rear with practiced ease, barely rocking the boat. Kesh had an ungainly time of it. He was shaking. Every surface seemed slick under his hands. Once the boat stopped rocking, the boater sighed, then poled away from the stone pier, and pushed along the channel toward the temple island. The closest pier flew the silk lotus banner that marked every temple to the Merciless One. Red petals on white linen: passion and death. Kesh shut his eyes as if by keeping them open he might force the island to recede by dint of the intensity of his desire. The boatman hummed a tuneless melody. Talker said nothing. The wind hummed at Kesh's ears in descant to the boatman's song. Once, they hissed through a stand of reeds. He hung a hand over the side and let it trail through the water, which was gaspingly cold except where they passed through a warmer, saltier eddy.

At last, the boat nudged up against Banner Pier. Kesh scrambled out as soon as the boatman tied up the scow. From here, he could not see Leave-taking Pier. The Devourer told no secrets. Those on their way to worship were shielded from the sight of those departing, in the same manner that those departing could expect to skim home without being seen by every arriving pilgrim.

As Talker and Silent got the litter onto the pier, a bare-chested, dark-haired lad dressed in a novice's kilt walked up to Kesh. He was yawning as he rubbed the sleep out of his eyes.

'You're early.' He grinned skittishly, as if he had just recalled that hierodules dedicated to the Merciless One cast no judgment and made no comment. He gave Keshad the once-over up and down, nodded genially to Talker and Silent as if they came here all the time either as bearers or supplicants, and finally looked over the featureless curtains that concealed the interior of the litter. 'My old aunt spent five years as a Devouring girl before she married,' he added, 'and she used to say that no person comes concealed for any good purpose. "Who is ashamed to be touched by the Devourer's lips"?'

'It's nothing to do with *shame*,' said Kesh, a tide of heat and anger swelling over him. His head throbbed, and he wanted it all to be done with and him walking away with what he had come for.

'Eiya! No harm meant! Which house is yours?'

'I'm here to see the Hieros.'

The lad's mouth formed a circle.

A raucous cry split the air. Keshad actually jumped because he was already so on edge, but the others only tipped back their heads as folk always did to mark a reeve passing over along the northern edge of the delta and circling in toward Olossi.

'Uncle Idan says there were more of them reeves back when he was a lad,' said Talker. 'Bad days, since that drought. It just goes to show that when folk don't keep order in their own houses, pretty soon the land begins to suffer. So the gods teach us.'

'Bad luck on them who deserves it,' muttered the lad under his breath, making the cross-fingers sign against ill fortune close against his body, as if he didn't want the others to see. He saw Kesh watching him, flushed, and turned his attention to the two bearers. 'If you will wait in the outer court, I'd much appreciate it.'

'I need the litter brought with me,' said Kesh. 'Then they can go and wait wherever you wish.'

'Are you sure?'

'That I need the litter brought with me?'

'That you want an audience with the Hieros. No one ever asks for that. If you knew her, you'd know' He flicked hair out of his eyes and sidestepped away. 'No one in sight. Not a soul come so early, and there's none to leave.'

'Damn all,' said the boatman. 'First come in the morning means a long wait, or a return trip made empty. My old arms!'

'Sorry, old man,' said the lad. 'It wasn't a lantern night, last night. You know the rules.'

'I won't be long,' said Kesh, 'as I'm not here to worship the Devourer, just to conduct a bit of business. If you'll wait at Leave-taking Pier, I'll pay you passage back, same as came here.'

The boatman grinned, showing brown teeth and gaps between. 'Over there, then. Same number as coming. That's fair.'

The lad hopped from one foot to the other. It was evident he wanted to ask what was going on, but novices did not ask about the

business or predilections or desires or identities, if veiled, of pilgrims. It was against the rules.

'The Devourer eats secrets,' he said at last, with a hopeful glance
at Kesh, as if encouraging him to confide a pair or three of mysteries.

'I'm ready to go,' said Kesh.

Unlit lanterns hung from the parallel ranks of posts that marked
the path up to the outer court. To one side of the posts, the ground
sloped down to the water's edge and a thin strand of pebble beach.
To the other side, rockier ground had been manicured into a pleasing arrangement of rock, moss, and pruned miniature trees, these
islands separated by raked sand. A big ginny lizard – one of the
Devourer's acolytes, as they were called – perched on top of a rock,
sunning itself. As they strode past, it cracked open its mouth just
enough to show teeth.

A tall lattice fence grown thick with herboria and red and yellow
falls of patience marked the beginning of the outer court. They
passed through a gap in the lattice fence and walked toward the
great gates between rows of benches. The outer court filled the wide
space between the workshop wing and the long kitchen hall, which
had a thatched roof but no walls. A dozen men and women
chopped vegetables at tables, or sweated over hearths and grills.
Halfway down to Tradesmen's Pier, a big rounded bread oven was
being cleaned out. The smell of that fresh bread made Kesh's mouth
water.

The lad beckoned them through the gates. 'Heya!' he called to a
pair of youths loitering in the shade. 'Get down to the pier. You
were already supposed to be there.'

They walked into the Heart Garden, a square courtyard surrounded by blank walls. Three closed inner gates beckoned, one
painted golden yellow and one the pale silver of moonlight. The
third, opposite the bronze-colored outer court gates, was painted as
white as the walls and in fact was rather difficult to discern against
the white walls. The lad motioned to benches placed within pools of
shade cast by a dozen vine-covered arbors and surrounded by beds
of bright yellow-bells, blood roses, and blue and violet stardrops.
This time of day it was quiet, and the scent of the flowers, particularly the glorious stardrops, was piquant and heady, like a drug.

They sat in the shade and waited while the lad vanished through the white gates.

At intervals, Talker and Silent glanced at the litter. They knew its weight and balance, but they asked no questions. Kesh rubbed his hands as if washing them. He had never been as anxious in his life as he was at this threshold, not even when he had faced down Master Feden. A hush had fallen. Somewhere unseen, a door scraped open and slid shut. He jumped up when one of the white doors slid open. An elderly woman appeared. She beckoned.

'Bring the litter,' he said.

The procession arrived at the white gate. The old woman was tiny, with chains of delicate dancer's bells circling her wrists and ankles. Her long hair was gone to silver and bound back into a braid brightened with moss-green ribbons.

'Set your burden down just inside and then return out here,' she said to the bearers in a high, light voice. 'We'll call you when you're needed.' To Kesh she said nothing.

Past the white gate, a screen blocked their view of the courtyard beyond. Talker and Silent set down the litter, and as soon as they retreated the lad appeared; he closed the doors by going out after them, leaving Kesh alone with the old woman. She wore blue silk, and smelled of sweet ginger.

She moved away around the screen without looking back at him and with a remarkable and agile haste. He followed the chime of her bells into a court grown so lush with vines and hedges and carefully pruned trees that the scent of green watered growing things made the air almost too thick to breathe. Around every corner of the labyrinthine pathway a new and different tiny glade was revealed, soft and shadowed and usually ornamented by some cunning, tiny waterfall trickling along a sculpture shaped out of rock or pipewood. At length his steps led him to a graveled open space at the center. A fountain splashed, water caressing the flanks of a statue depicting a man and a woman in the grip of the Devourer.

'Crude, but it was placed here long before my tenure. I would never have chosen something so unsophisticated.' The voice was low, harsh, and female.

He turned all the way around. He was alone, although the dense foliage offered a hundred hiding places.

'With what desire do you come to worship at the altar of the Merciless One?' the voice asked.

'I do not come to worship. I come to complete a transaction begun ten years ago. Where is Zubaidit?'

'She's not available right now. You can't see her.'

'I'm not here to see her. I'm here to buy out her debt.'

At a distance, a bell jangled. Nearby, he heard a hissed breath, the scrape of a shod foot on rock, and the whisper of dancing bells. The old woman, too, must be spying on him.

'She won't go! She is a true hierodule of the Devourer. Our best student and most devoted worshiper.'

He heard her words with a contempt that made him snarl. 'That's not true.'

It can't be true!

'I know who you are. It has been two years since you have seen her. Many things can change in that time. She thinks you've given up on her, and she's turned her heart entirely to the goddess. She doesn't want to speak to you again.'

Perhaps it was all for nothing. All those weary mey trudged; all the deals, the bargaining, the cold nights and hungry days and the endless hells of Master Feden's house that he had endured for twelve years because each morning upon waking he could take in a breath that was a promise, that he would be free. And that she would be free.

'That's what you say! I'll hear it from her own lips, not yours.' He stooped, picked up a handful of pebbles, and cast them wildly toward a concealing thicket. They spattered. She mocked him with a laugh that made him grit his teeth. He fixed his gaze on the pour of the water as it coursed down the deep valleys made by the mingling of limbs, woman to man.

'You know the law,' he said at last. 'I've come, as the gods of the Hundred give me the right to do. You must accept my payment if the hierodule agrees.'

Her voice hissed out of the shadows. 'Spare yourself this humiliation. She won't leave the temple.'

'Then she can live here freely, *after* I've spoken with her. She must tell me herself with her own voice. Unless you've cut out her tongue! But your hierodules need their tongues, don't they?'

'Impious scrat! The Devourer will eat your testicles!'

'I'll take my chances.'

Branches rattled as if a rat scrambled away through the under-growth. As he waited, he became convinced someone was staring at him. Scanning the undergrowth, he saw nothing at first, but then, as his gaze picked out shapes, he distinguished the snout of a ginny lizard, shadowed under drooping striped-firecanth leaves. The crea-ture stared intently down at him, from a branch higher than his own head. It bobbed its head at him but did not otherwise move; it watched him as if it were a sentry. A second head joined the first, an arm's length away, and this one bent first one eye at him and then the other, head turning almost flirtatiously.

Footsteps scraped on earth. He turned. A woman walked into view from underneath a tunnel woven of interlaced leaves. Of middle years, she had a bountiful figure wrapped in a patterned taloos covered by an undyed work shirt. But she only looked Keshad up and down with a measuring smile in a manner very like that of the second ginny lizard, and stood at the edge of the clearing to wait. Others appeared, exactly like loitering shoppers who can-vass the market with no intention of buying. About twenty people filtered into the courtyard, strung around the clearing like so many jewels about an old granite-skinned widow's neck. He sensed a few standing concealed within the drowsy growth. A young pair saun-tered up to lean on the sun-warmed stone rim of the fountain. Arms crossed, the lanky girl with luxurious hair and a lazy smile looked him over in a way that made him shiver. The youth, wearing only a kilted wrap around his hips, settled beside her; he nudged her foot with his and whispered into her ear. She narrowed one eye almost to a wink as if promising Keshad his heart's desire. When she shifted her buttocks on the rim, her long tunic, cut high, slipped to reveal a sleek flank. He flushed, and her companion snickered, but after so long in the south he had almost forgotten that Hundred women were the most beautiful of all, dark and lovely, although this one could have used a little extra flesh to round her curves.

Hundred women were the most beautiful of all – except perhaps for the captain's wife – and he looked down to hide his face so none of these, vultures all, could feed on any scrap of truth his expression might reveal. A steady step crunched on rock. When he looked up, there was Zubaidit striding barefoot around the curve of the fountain. She had grown since he last saw her, and even then she had been tall. She wore a tight, sleeveless, short jacket and a knee-length wrap of plain linen kilted low around her hips, leaving her brown belly bare. A jewel gleamed in her navel. She was well muscled, like an acrobat, and her skin glistened with oil and sweat, just as if she had come from exercise.

She saw him, and halted. Her eyes flared with surprise, while her left hand curled into a fist. A purpled bruise mottled her left cheek. Aui! Had they been *beating* her?

When she did not acknowledge him, he said nothing, and when he said nothing, she shrugged a shoulder and twisted to look behind her. Everyone swiveled heads as the tiny silver-haired woman who had let him into the inner court glided into view. She walked with a pitter-pat step that made her seem dainty, but her shoulders had the square stubborn cant of a swordsman's.

The lanky girl coughed, and her friend smirked.

'Are you the Hieros?' Kesh asked without preamble.

'I am,' said the old woman.

'I am here to pay off the debt of Zubaidit.'

Bai looked at him, gaze dark and intense, and her eyelids flickered as if she were sending him a message.

'By what right do you claim the right to act in her favor?' demanded the Hieros.

'Blood right.'

The statement was a formality, so she dismissed it and went on. 'Show the tally bundle.' A young woman in an orange taloos unrolled a bundle of sewn-together sheets. Holding each end of the scroll, oldest to newest, forced her to open her arms wide.

'A tremendous debt,' remarked the Hieros with a caustic smile. 'Her purchase price, and the usual debits for lodging, drink and food, clothing, training as a hierodule.' She ran a finger from top to bottom of each flat tally stick as she traced the account of Zubaidit's service at the temple. 'Set against these debits, and in addition to the favor she accrued through her regular duties, she earned favor by comforting the gods-favored worshipers. Against this, additional training costs to the temple.'

"When a person sells their body into servitude in payment for a

debt, that person will serve eight years and in the ninth go free.'
That's what it says on Law Rock.'

She raised an eyebrow. 'No assizes will rule in your favor, not
when legitimate debt has accrued on an account.'

He had known she would say it, but the distraction had allowed
him a moment to calm himself, to ask the necessary question. 'What
is the tally?'

The Hieros grinned exultantly. Indeed, her smile was almost
ecstatic, and he supposed she had long years of practice, as old as
she was. 'Thirty cheyt, seventy-one leya, and nineteen vey.'

One thousand eight hundred and seventy-one leya.

The number dizzied Kesh. He stumbled to the fountain, sat down
on the rim, and rested his head on a hand. When had he gotten so
tired?

The lanky girl whistled appreciatively.

Her friend chortled, nudging her foot again. 'I heard that one of
the merchants of the Greater Council bought her only son the best
stallion from the best herd off the grasslands and fitted it out with
bridle and saddle trimmed with silver and gold – that was the price!
Thirty cheyt! For a horse and gear! Can you imagine? And then it
threw the fool, and broke his neck!'

'You've cheated me!' said Bai with a kind of parched hoarseness,
as though her throat had been rubbed raw. Kesh looked up. She'd
fisted her hands, as if ready to punch back.

He was genuinely shocked by the debt – he'd expected a similar
price to his own, maybe a little more – but he'd known something
like this might be coming. But what matter if the temple was cheating Bai? He raised a hand, thumb and three fingers curled and
touching his little finger to his lips. Obedient to their childhood
code, Bai subsided, turning her back on the Hieros.

'That's a staggering amount,' he said to the Hieros. 'Is that the
full measure? Are there any other costs you aren't telling me, or that
you mean to add on afterward?'

As her face relaxed, he glimpsed how she might look in the
moments after satiation: a true devotee of the Merciless One, content only with the complete surrender of her victim.

'That is the measure in full, as of this meeting between us, now,'
she said graciously. 'We'll set whatever coin you can offer today

against her account. Next year, you can pay another installment.'
And another and another, she meant, an endless procession of hopeless payments that would never catch up to the galloping pace of
debits.

'No, Kesh,' said Bai urgently. 'Keep whatever you have as seed
coin. Come back when you have the whole thing. Don't waste it out
like this. I know what it means, that you've come today. You must
use it as we spoke of before.'

At her words, he bent, splashed water on his face, and stood. The
dizziness had fled. It was a relief, in a way, knowing that the sale of
the Mariha girls would not have come close to covering the whole
no matter what. The temple was cheating Bai, that was obvious, but
it was also true she had no legal recourse given her circumstances,
and neither did he, no matter what that reeve, Joss, had said.
Knowing it had come to this, knowing he had made the right
choices all along, made it easier to give up the treasure to free Bai.

He met Bai's gaze. She lifted her chin defiantly as he crossed his
forearms at his chest, wanting to crow in triumph.

All done now! Finished. He had won that which he had sworn to
do years back.

He nodded at the Hieros. For the first time, doubt flickered
across her proud face. 'By the gate you'll find a litter,' he said. 'Have
it brought here.'

'Rudely spoken, to command me as though I am your slave,' she
said, but she believed herself safe and so she remained amused. At
her command, four young bodies hurtled away. Another dozen
people pushed to the edge of the clearing, come to watch. Probably
the news was all over the temple by now.

Bai looked down at the ground for all the world like a shy bride,
yet her stance betrayed a body honed and strengthened by hard
exercise. It disturbed him. She had changed utterly since the day
she'd been sold away from him, little sister and older brother on the
auction block of Flesh Alley with aunts and uncle looking on dis-
passionately as they mouthed each rising tally, as the bidding went
higher. Bai had been a thin stick of a thing, first clinging to him,
then sobbing and wailing as the servants of the Hieros dragged her
away. Twelve years ago.

He had lost the desire to revenge himself on his aunts and uncle.

They were meaningless; like the old ruins to be found along every road, they mattered nothing to the caravan of life that must proceed on its way to its next destination. He was so close to success that he felt tears, and gulped them down, and shook as with a palsy. He knew suddenly and with complete conviction that the litter would be gone or the treasure vanished. How could he have left it alone? Had he really been that stupid?

But after all here it came, swaying raggedly with four bearers off-step and ungainly as they crunched over the gravel to set the litter down in the midst of the open space, about halfway between the edge of greenery and the centerpiece fountain. As Kesh approached, everyone except Bai and the Hieros backed away.

'The payment.' He hooked back the curtain, reached in, and grasped the first thing his hand came to, which was a braid. He tugged.

She came unresisting, as she had all along, and stepped out into full sun. She raised no hand to shade her eyes. Her body was hidden beneath her only piece of clothing, a voluminous cloak woven of a silverine cloth. She blinked several times as the light struck; that was all.

Breaths were caught short, or taken in hard. Several people skipped back, and one voice whimpered in fear.

'A ghost!' whispered the Hieros, crossing her forearms away from her chest to ward off the ill omen.

'Touch her. She is no ghost.'

He pulled the cloak back, each wing over one of her shoulders, and heard their moans of fear and gasps of surprise – and their sighs – as her body was revealed, as pallid as marble, as smooth as goat's milk and as creamy. Her hair both above and below was as pale as a field of harvest-ripe grain. Her eyes were not natural eyes. They were cornflower-blue. Demon-blue.

'What I offer, you must accept,' he finished.

Bai grinned in a way that terrified him suddenly. She leaped across the clearing like a cat, halting in front of the Hieros. With a laugh, she slapped her, a crack across that old face.

'Bitch! I've been waiting to do that for twelve years!'

No one moved.

Without lashing out in her turn or even losing her temper, the

Hieros spoke. 'Do what impulse tells you, Zubaidit, but it will make no difference in the end. You are meant for the Devourer. You will see.'

Bai spat onto the pebbles. Grinning with a vicious glee, she tugged her slave bracelets from her wrists and dropped them on the ground.

'I'll meet you at Leave-taking Pier,' she said to Kesh. She dashed away into the greenery under an arched lacework of flowering vines. In her wake, the two ginny lizards rattled away into the undergrowth.

No one spoke, and no one moved, all in thrall to the vision standing among them, no stunning beauty, not like Captain Anji's wife – nothing so pallid could truly be deemed beautiful – but a thing of horrible and irresistible fascination. A whirlpool into which all are dragged and can never fight their way out. She was an evil thing, and Keshad knew it, but he did not care. He was rid of her, and by this means had gained everything he cared about in the wide world: his freedom, and his sister's freedom. The temple could take care of itself.

The Hieros shook out of her stupor. She glided up to them and circled the slave as she would circle a poisonous snake. She hitched the cloak up and looked over the slave's backside, and after a long moment she reached a hand and, after the merest hesitation, brushed her fingers over a forearm. The slave did not even flinch, only stared unseeing toward the green tangle of a witch hedge.

'Where did you get her?' the Hieros asked.

'At the edge of a desert so vast you cannot imagine it.'

'I can imagine a lot of things,' said the lanky girl, giving a lazy and lustful hum.

'Shut up!' hissed her companion. He was not laughing, but staring at the slave as if a hammer had hit him.

'A desert of stone and red sand. She was wandering, lost, as mute and blank as you see her now.'

'Insane!' The Hieros ventured to pinch the lean curve of that hip. If the girl felt the pull of those fingers, she showed no sign.

'But compliant!' he said hastily. That she might be insane had often occurred to him over the course of the journey. It was the only reasonable explanation.

'How do you know she is compliant? Did you go into her yourself?'

As Bai had, he spat on the pebbles, and the Hieros flinched away from him with a look of such anger that he shivered. *She will seek revenge.*

So he smiled, to taunt her. 'You know what they say. It's bad luck to spit in your own trading goods. Men – and women – will come to see if they can bestir her. And even if they can't stir her, if she remains as limp as a puppet in their arms, they'll still come.'

'Oh, yes. I can see it.' She rubbed her hands, but he couldn't tell if it was the thought of caressing that white flesh that bestirred her, or the thought of so many worshipers waiting at the gates for the chance to gaze on – or touch – this living ghost with her demon-blue eyes. 'Better than any aphrodisiac, indeed. I acknowledge that this covers her debts.'

'I want Bai's accounts bundle, properly sealed and marked off.'

The Hieros stepped back to face Keshad. She was truly a devotee of the Merciless One. He could see it in the set of her face, cold and cruel and passionate, devoured by the goddess until not even her soul was her own.

'You have earned an enemy today,' she said as if these were the kindest words she had ever spoken, 'and you will come to regret it, but you are correct that this payment cannot be refused. Take what you have paid for. All will be sealed legally.' She smiled gently, but her eyes were like stones in that handsome old face. 'Be sure that if I ever have a chance to repay you for taking from me my most valuable hierodule, I will do so swiftly and with pleasure.'

'Do what you must.' Kesh's limbs were loose, his jaw relaxed, and his heart calm, now that it was over. 'As I did.'

PART SIX

Wolves

28

They had left Kartu Town and the desert far behind. They had escaped the Sirniakan Empire. Now, after many days traveling over the high Kandaran Pass, the caravan halted at a wall and border crossing guarding the road into the Hundred. In the Hundred, they would find good fortune, or disaster. Shai just didn't expect things to happen so quickly.

At the border crossing, a huge eagle carrying a man landed in their midst, frightening the horses and astonishing even the Qin soldiers who could not, Shai thought, be astonished by anything. After consulting with the eagle rider, Captain Anji commanded his troop to take control of the border crossing. The fight that ensued blew over quickly when the border guards realized it was their own captain who was corrupt. They surrendered to the authority of the eagle rider and handed over their captain at spearpoint. After this, in accordance with an agreement reached between Anji and the eagle rider, half the Qin company galloped north along the road to a tiny way-station village where, so they were told, a smaller caravan had come under assault by bandits. Shai rode with them, under Tohon's supervision.

The Qin slaughtered the bandits with the efficiency of a wolf pack cutting out and bringing down the weakest deer. Two men suffered slight wounds, and were roundly ridiculed for their lack of skill.

'They'll ride as tailmen tomorrow!' said Chief Tuvi, laughing.

The soldiers dragged the dead bodies into rows, clearing the commons so the big caravan coming up behind would have space to settle in for the night.

None of this amused the new-made ghosts of the slaughtered bandits. They were angry, all right; no one liked suffering violent death. At dawn they were still angry, milling around the commons shaking their fists and cursing and weeping, and pissing on the living, not that ghosts could actually piss, but the gesture both comforted and infuriated them – an impotent defiance. They clustered in great numbers around the wagon where the prisoner –

their co-conspirator who once called himself a captain – was kept under guard, but since ghosts are fixed to the earth, they had no way to reach him, who was concealed within the bed of a covered wagon, raised up on wheels.

As Shai went to get a drink of water at the rain barrel, well away from stacked bodies, he pretended not to see the commotion the ghosts made. Thwarted of their prey, the ghosts churned through the open ground and wandered among the merchants, servants, and slaves they had so recently terrorized, but this unworthy audience was oblivious of the wisps haunting them. Captain Anji prowled the caravan as the two caravan masters argued over who should take precedence and in what order wagons and carts should be shifted into a new line of march. Now and again Anji sidestepped to avoid a misty stream of ghostly rancor. Crude men, these Hundred folk. Civilized ghosts had better manners, although their language was just as bad. The corpse of a youth lay beneath the huge tree growing on one side of the open ground, but his spirit had fled, leaving the husk. At least someone was at peace today.

On a cleared space of ground, the eagle rider set a bone whistle to his lips and blew a shrill blast. Shai slurped from the ladle, saw Mai watching the reeve. Seeing Shai, she came over. North of the border, she walked openly as a woman.

'What do they say?' She took the ladle from his hand, dipped, and drank neatly.

'What do who say?'

She hung up the ladle from its hook. A pair of drops stretched off the curve of the cup, parted, and fell onto the glassy surface. Drip. Drop. 'The ghosts.'

'What are you talking about?'

'These bandits. Are their ghosts saying anything?'

'How would I know?'

She looked at him. He hated that look. She had changed since they departed Kartu Town and she became a married woman. He had always been her trusted older uncle – even if only by a few years – yet now he felt he was the younger one. 'I know you see ghosts, Shai. Anji knows it, too. You admitted as much to him out in the desert. Anyway, you're a seventh son.'

'What does that have to do with it?'

'Seventh sons see ghosts.'

'What about seventh daughters?'

'Who ever has seven daughters? Just tell me! We're not in Kartu Town anymore. You aren't a witch here.'

'How do you know? Maybe they'll burn me alive like they do in the empire. Or hang me, or tie me to a post and shoot me full of arrows, or poke me with spears until I'm all full of holes. You don't know anything about this place!'

'You shouldn't be afraid. Anji isn't.'

'Then why don't you ask him what the ghosts are saying?' he snapped.

This revelation did not disturb her. Of course she already knew Anji saw ghosts! She considered him with a placid expression, but he guessed from the tilt of her chin that she was annoyed. 'He doesn't hear ghosts. He only sees them. What you hear might help us.'

When he only looked at her, she continued as she would to a particularly slow slave child who needed each least task explained at length several times over. 'Help us. From the ghosts you can learn of any danger that might be ahead . . . learn the customs of the Hundred . . . Shai! The ghosts can teach us, warn us, even if they don't mean to. If we know more, we'll do better in our new life, don't you think?'

'You don't understand ghosts, Mai. They only talk about the past. What lies in the future no longer exists. That's why they're ghosts.'

Which was why ghosts were often boring, as these were, bawling and bleating like so many discontented sheep:

Captain Beron! You betrayed us, you sheep-tupping son of a bitch!

I didn't mean to eat that rabbit. It isn't fair I was exiled for such a little thing! Forced to live the osprey life. I never wanted it! Why won't you forgive me? Why can't I go home?

I hate you! I hate all of you! Piss on you all!

'One thing, though,' he said, because he found it so curious that he had to share with Mai. 'You know how the arkinga here sounds so strange.'

'They speak it wrong,' she agreed. 'Sometimes I can't understand them.'

'I don't notice it so much with the ghosts.'

'Maybe ghosts only speak the language of the dead. What are they saying?'

The only way to be rid of her questions was for the company to start moving, and the caravan wasn't ready. He'd never seen people slower to get moving in his life! The Qin stood beside their horses, not by a whisker betraying they might be impatient to go.

'Some person named Captain Beron betrayed them. Don't eat rabbit meat – it'll get you exiled. Now I don't want to talk about it anymore. How can I know it's safe here? In the empire, they burn those who believe in the Merciful One. What would they do with me?' When he spoke of the empire, he remembered how that Beltak priest had imprisoned the essence of a ghost, trapping it forever within a simple wooden bowl.

She touched his arm. 'Are you all right, Shai? You're pale.'

He looked around to make sure no one was within earshot. Mai's slave women were busying themselves by the cart Mai had obtained south of the pass through some clever trading of silks and woolens given to her as a wedding gift by Commander Beje.

'Can't you see? I've seen so many ghosts. I don't want to become one myself by speaking when I should have remained silent!'

Her expression softened. 'I'm sorry. Of course you've had to keep it secret all your life in Kartu. I can see why you would still be anxious.'

It was almost worse when she gazed at him with sincere concern. 'How do we really know it's safe here?' he demanded. 'Captain Anji made common cause with that eagle rider awfully quickly.'

She shrugged. 'Sometimes you have to know when to leap. Anyway, he liked him.'

Abruptly, many of the horses whinnied and startled and shied. The big eagle landed with a whomp in the clear zone. The reeve fastened himself into his harness, and the eagle launched itself skyward with a mighty thrust of legs and wings whose strength and majesty brought tears of admiration to Shai's eyes. Mai touched fingers to heart, her gaze open with awe. They both followed the raptor's flight until it vanished away over the trees.

Chief Tuvi called out and, when he had their attention, waved merrily at them and signaled toward the horses.

'We're leaving!' Shai said with relief. He wiped his eyes and went to join the ranks.

The angry ghosts did not follow as the caravan trundled out the northern gate. But they hadn't ridden more than a few lengths when Shai saw an almost transparent wisp trudging along the road, a whipcord man-shape who had such an antique look about him – as though he had lingered in this spot for a hundred years – that Shai actually stared, wondering who this ghost was and where it came from. He had a strange idea that he had seen that face recently, but he couldn't place it. The ghost did not even look at him. As he turned in the saddle to watch it fall behind, it reached a broad stone placed beside the road like a marker, and vanished.

29

For the first three days after leaving Dast Korumbos, they traveled through heavily wooded hills, and although the road bent here to the left and there to the right and at intervals hit steep upward inclines as they climbed out of a valley, on the whole they headed northeast and downslope until Mai thought her tailbone would never stop aching. The Qin never tired or ached, so she refused to complain and had Priya massage her in the evening.

'Sheyshi should massage you, and you should massage Sheyshi.' She lay on her stomach, with her head turned sideways so she could see with one eye. Her hair was caught up against her head, tendrils fallen free along her neck. 'You must ache, too.'

Priya smiled as she rubbed Mai's buttocks. 'This is an easy life, compared to what came before.'

'I wish I was a horse,' Sheyshi whispered. She only ever whispered.

'Why do you wish you were a horse?' Mai asked. 'Oh. Ah! Yes, right there!'

Sheyshi did not answer. She was the most reserved person Mai had ever met, closemouthed, not at all confiding.

'Horses are free,' said Priya.

'Sheyshi, do you wish you were free?' Mai asked. 'When we have found a place to live, I'll make sure you can earn extra zastras – or whatever they use here – to earn money toward your manumission. That's perfectly fair. Commander Beje gave me your bill of sale. That amount is what you must earn to buy your freedom.'

The girl colored, stared at her hands, then lifted her gaze to look at Mai as daringly as she ever had. 'I would like to be free,' she whispered. 'But that isn't what I meant. I dream sometimes about things. I dreamed I was a horse, running over the grass. It felt – it felt' But after all, that was too much confiding! Sheyshi squeezed shut her mouth, twisted her hands and, to make herself busy, offered Priya more oil for the massage even though Priya's hands were moist and Mai's flanks smoothly coated.

Priya chuckled. 'Were you a mare, or a stallion? I've wondered, sometimes, how it might feel to be a stallion – man or horse – and have such a—'

'Oh, stop teasing her!' Mai scolded, because the girl looked miserable. Or maybe not. Commander Beje had implied that the girl slept in the bed with his chief wife and that there was play between them. 'Are you lonely, Sheyshi?'

Sheyshi wore a green silk cap from which hung shoulder-length streamers, some of green silk, some of gold and white beads, and one woven out of supple wire. Normally the arrangement left her face exposed, but with her head bowed the streamers concealed her expression.

'Hard to come by right now,' said Priya as she rubbed, 'but I can make sheaths out of sheep gut if you're wanting comfort with a man without catching a child in your sack.'

Mai chuckled. 'You made me no such offer, Priya! A sheep-gut sheath for a man's sword!'

'You are freeborn, and now a wife. You must get a child as soon as you can.' She paused with a hand resting on the gentle curve of Mai's lower back. 'Perhaps . . .'

'It's too early,' said Mai, suddenly frightened. 'Don't say anything.'

Priya began kneading again as if nothing had been said. 'I will pray to the Merciful One that you are blessed with seven sons, and three daughters.'

It was good to change the subject. 'How can it be, if there are always seven sons but only three daughters, that all the sons can get married? In Kartu, the clan banner goes only to the eldest son. But all my uncles got wives – well, except for Uncle Shai, and Uncle Hari, and Uncle Girish.' She shuddered, remembering Girish. He'd paved his own path to the deepest hell.

'Priests and soldiers need not marry,' said Priya. 'This way we always have plenty of them.'

'Ow! Ow! No, don't stop! Right there!' She groaned in blissful pain. 'Yes, right there! It hurts!' Priya worked in silence while Mai kept her eyes shut and breathed into the knot of pain to try to loosen it.

Sheyshi shuffled around; there came footsteps, an opening and closing of the flap of the tent. Feet shushed along the carpet, and just before Mai opened her eyes to see what was going on, hands began massaging her again. These hands were firm and strong and callused, and no less knowing.

'Anji.' She smiled as she opened her eyes.

He kept kneading with one hand and with the other slipped free the tortoiseshell comb that bound up her hair, uncoiling it and raking it out over her back. 'I am the most fortunate of men,' he murmured.

'I am the most flattered of women.'

He laughed. 'It is not flattery if it is true. Not one man among this company does not honor your beauty and good nature, Mai.'

She rolled out from his hand, onto her side, and propped her head up on a bent elbow. 'Is that what you seek? The envy of other men?'

He considered the comment, but his gaze roamed along her body and his hands twitched, although he did not – yet – touch her. 'It is easy to be gratified by the envy of others, directed at what you yourself possess. But it weakens you. Half the secret of your beauty, plum blossom, is that you do not covet it or use it.' Then he smiled. 'Except in the marketplace, to drive a harder bargain.'

'You will never let me forget that.'

'I must know the measure of those I hold closest. Any commander must measure his troops in this manner.'

'I am no different than your troops?'

He said nothing, and she understood abruptly that it would be foolish to press the conversation any further in this direction.

She groped for and found the scraper Priya would have used to clean the oil off her body. 'When do I get my bath?'

He relaxed. 'Soon.' He took the scraper and worked methodically, but somehow by the time he had finished he was also undressed and she was warm and almost delirious with pleasure.

'Soon,' he repeated, kissing her.

She wrapped her limbs around him and took what she wanted.

Do not fear happiness.

Is it dangerous to become too happy? To get what you want, and be blessed with good fortune? A kind husband. A missed bleeding. As Grandmother Mei used to say, in her querulous way, 'Why do you think you'll get a drink from my cup just because I gave you one yesterday?'

She pondered this question at dawn as she rolled up the blankets and the sleeping carpets while, outside, Priya and O'eki released the tent ropes. She crawled out as the walls collapsed. Sheyshi collected the bedding and secured it to one of the packhorses. Anji stood beside the sentry fire talking with the man who rode that huge and intimidating eagle. Anji had an easy way of conversing with other men. He had a natural precision of movement, and he took up space in a way that made him noticeable without diminishing those in his company. He glanced her way, saw her, and without smiling – just a certain way of narrowing his eyes and the barest curve to his lips – made her flush.

Grandmother had not approved of happiness. She said it led to carelessness and trouble, or perhaps she had meant that happiness led you to carelessness, which in turn took your hand and walked you into trouble. Good fortune was fickle. You must never count on it.

Her hair was already pulled back in a mare's tail swishing down her back to her hips. She twisted it up deftly, and Priya thrust the tortoise comb through the mass of gathered hair to keep it in place. Mai walked over to the men.

'A good morning,' said Joss appreciatively. He was the kind of man who smiles his admiration but shows restraint in the way he doesn't draw too close. She liked him. He was good-looking in the northern way, but pretty old. As old as her father, probably, although his coloring was so different that it was hard to tell. Father

Mei walked old and talked old and frowned old and sighed old, but the reeve had the lively aura of a man who plunges through life because he wants to be happy.

It hit her all at once.

'You're an Ox,' she said.

'Mai?' said Anji in a tone that almost crossed into a warning.

Joss laughed. 'How did you know?'

'So am I. The Ox is hardworking and pragmatic, with a dreamer hidden inside.'

'What gave me away?' He was still smiling, his eyes handsomely crinkled with amusement, and she gave in to the temptation to flirt, even though she knew she should not.

'"The Ox walks with its feet in the clay, but its heart leaps to the heavens where it seeks the soul which fulfills it. The Ox desires happiness, which is a heavenly gift, but it accepts its burden of service on earth even if it knows that happiness has flown out of its grasp." And anyway, the Ox is always beautiful.'

She was aware at once of Anji's boots shifting on the dirt as a complicated expression altered the reeve's face before he found a harmless smile again. 'Does it say somewhere that the Ox is a shrewd judge of character? Or did you serve your apprenticeship to Ilu as I did?'

'I don't know what "Ilu" is.'

He glanced at Anji and made his own judgment. 'We'd best begin our trek. It's still five or six days' journey from here to Olossi. I won't rest easily until these two caravans are delivered to the safety of the market there.'

Anji nodded, and the reeve left.

'He's been called handsome before,' said Anji once the other man was out of earshot. 'He's accustomed to the admiration of women. It was the talk of happiness that made him uncomfortable.'

She looked at him closely. 'You're a little mad at me.'

'This is not the marketplace, Mai, and you are not selling peaches and almonds to unsuspecting men who will be stunned into paying full price by one glance from your beautiful eyes.'

She raised a hand to her cheek, where Father Mei would have slapped her. 'Forgive me,' she said in a low voice, but she kept her gaze fixed to his.

He did not smile to soften his words. His voice was low and even. 'Do not dishonor me.'

'I will never dishonor you! Because I will never dishonor myself!'

Now he smiled. 'I am rebuked.'

Her cheeks were hot, and her heart was hotter. She was still not quite sure what threat she faced because in most ways Anji was still a mystery. Father Mei would have hit her, and her mother and aunt would have pinched her arms and ears until she cried. It had been easier to fit herself into the walls they shaped than to endure slaps and pinches, but she had passed through the gate and survived the ghost lands. She was not the same person any longer. She refused to go back.

'I want to be trusted,' she said softly, 'because it dishonors me if I am not trusted.'

His gaze remained level. He was no longer angry, but rather measuring and perhaps a little curious, intrigued yet not at all amused. 'Honor is all we have. You are right, Mai. I must trust you.'

She nodded in reply. That was as far as she could go. She could not trust her voice, and turned aside gratefully as O'eki brought the horses forward.

Late in the afternoon, the wagons rolled into a meadow already fitted for encampments. A covered cistern opened through a series of cunning traps into a trough suitable for watering stock. A spacious corral built out of logs allowed them to turn out many of the beasts. Posts offered traction for lead lines where horses could be tethered. Pits rimmed with stones marked off six fire circles, all of which had iron stakes set in place to hang kettles or cauldrons over flames. Hired men and slaves set to work to raise camp and get food ready.

She made her way on a dirt path that cut through a thick stand of pipe-brush and under an airy grove of swallow trees to the crude pits set back against a ravine. Some kind soul had woven screens out of young pipe-brush stalks and pounded and nailed arm braces against the steep slope for ease of use. There was a great deal of coming and going and, remarkably, a stone basin cooled by trickling water flowing down through an old, halved stalk of mature pipe-brush. As she washed her hands, she noticed a small structure off to one side that almost blended into the foliage. She walked over, Priya and Sheyshi trailing after, but thought better of mounting the steps when she saw it was a shrine. She had been raised in the path taught by the Merciful One. In the empire, she knew, the priests served Beltak, calling him the Shining One Who Rules Alone even though he was only a harsher aspect of the holy one all folk worshiped.

This altar had no walls, only green poles with the shapes of leaves carved into them, a tile roof painted green, and a green rug laid over a plank floor. The rug was woven of thick, stiff grass-like blades as long as her arm, and it had begun to wear away where folk had trodden on it. A walking staff stood within, propped at an angle, so tall that it fit inside the peaked roof. A stubby log sat on its end in one corner, with a bouquet of withered flowers discarded on top.

'I'm surprised the flowers haven't blown away, or been replaced with something fresh,' she murmured to Priya. 'Is there no bell or lamp?'

'This is no altar for the Merciful One,' said Priya.

'I don't think it's a Beltak temple, either,' said Mai.

'I see no god,' whispered Sheyshi. With head bent, she eyed the shrine as she might a twisting snake whose dance can cause women to fall into a charmed and deadly sleep.

Folk were looking their way, faces obscured by twilight.

'Perhaps we're not meant to stand here,' said Mai. 'Let's go back.'

Anji had staked out the central fire pit, and he stood near its flickering light speaking to the reeve as Mai walked up behind them. They were laughing, and did not see her.

'You are a lucky man, did you know that?' Joss was saying.

'It would be impolite to reply to such a question. If I knew, and said so, then it would seem I am boasting. If I did not, it would seem I am foolish.'

The reeve laughed. 'I am answered!' He turned, alert even before Anji was, and Anji turned, and saw Mai. Sheyshi scuttled away to help O'eki, who was wrestling with a steaming haunch of venison. Priya paused just outside the circle of firelight.

'Surely you are a fortunate man as well,' said Mai, coming forward.

His smile remained easy, but his gaze retreated into itself, as though he were staring down a long straight track into a twilit distance whose landscape was forever veiled from mortal sight. 'I am not married.'

Day seemed to shift into night with the swiftness of a child whose mood can swing from joy to tears in an instant. She halted beside Anji, but she could not look away from the reeve.

'You have a shadow in your eyes,' she said to the reeve.

He looked at Anji, and she looked at Anji, and the captain nodded, and the reeve spoke in a low voice as around them the camp settled into its evening routine of drinking, eating, song, and sleep.

'I gave up telling the tale years ago. It came at the beginning, when the shadows first began to reach into the land, in the north. She was the first one – the first reeve – slaughtered. That was on the Liya Pass. Twenty years ago. Where it all began, when outlaws and cursed greedy lords began hunting down the eagle clans. I still dream about her. I shouldn't have let her go alone. If I'd gone with her . . .' But he shook his head.

'What then?' she asked.

Anji remained silent, watching.

He shrugged, and offered her a wry smile that made her want to cry for his pain. 'Most likely we'd both be dead. Her eagle was found. Not just dead, but mutilated.'

She had a nasty, prickling feeling along her back, as if someone drew cold fingers laced with slivers of glass up and down her skin. 'What of her?'

He shifted his gaze to the leaping flames, his head canted and jaw tight, and continued speaking. 'Her body was never found, but we found her clothes, her boots, a belt buckle, her knife, items she carried in her pack . . .' The fire sparked as a soldier shoved a pair of branches into the flames. The reeve winced back from the flare, then caught himself and went on, although his voice seemed flatter and more distant. He might have been reciting from a scroll. 'Her boot knife was found on a girl, one of the Devourer's hierodules. The girl had been stabbed in the heart. That girl's corpse lay there with the rest of the discarded gear. It was only *her* body we did not find, nor them who did it, as they had all abandoned the camp.'

'She might not have been taken away with those who killed the other one?' Anji asked.

'We searched, but there was never any sign of her. No, she's dead. I knew it as soon as I saw what remained of Flirt – that was her eagle. A reeve doesn't survive her eagle's death. An eagle can survive through the lives of four or five reeves if it's particularly long lived, like my good Scar, but for the other way, no. Better dead than no longer a reeve, so we say.' His smile was a ghost's smile, without life, but he struggled with it and shook his head and said, 'It still hurts. A few years later, bones were found in an unmarked grave up beyond that abandoned camp. Perhaps that was her, hidden because they feared our revenge. I try to leave it behind.' He blew breath out through his lips and shook himself in the manner of a duck shedding water. 'I keep thinking I have.'

'I'm so sorry,' said Mai, wiping away a tear. 'What was her name?'

'Reeve Joss!' A voice hailed him from the darkness. 'Best come see this!'

'Excuse me.' Joss left.

'Every young man loses his first love,' remarked Anji to Mai, 'but most get back in the saddle and keep riding. He's tethered to one post.'

'Is it fair to say so? You don't know what he's done in the years since, only that speaking the tale makes him sad. The storytellers in the marketplace would make a song out of it, like in the tale of the Rose Princess and the Fourteen Silk Ribbons. She ran off with her lover, and he left her by the riverside while he went into town to buy her silk ribbons, and she was eaten by a lion that had been sent to earth by a demon jealous of her beauty. Afterward he wore her bloodstained rags and went on pilgrimage to the fourteen holy temples, one for each ribbon he had bought for her, but he could not calm his heart and after all he turned back to seek revenge, but the demon seduced him and made him steal back the ribbons from each temple and . . . It's a terribly sad tale!' she finished indignantly, seeing that he was trying not to laugh. 'He dishonored himself! What could be worse? There is a song, but it always makes me cry.'

'I would gladly hear the song. You sing with sincerity and a true voice.'

'Maybe not such a strong one,' she muttered. 'But the tone is good, so I am told.'

'You are still angry. I do not laugh at you, dearest Mai. I just have no taste for such tales. To me, they seem ridiculous.'

'How are the tales ridiculous?'

He laughed. 'Any man knows better than to leave a beautiful woman alone by the riverside in the middle of wilderness! Wild beasts and demons stalk everywhere, and not least among them the sort of bandits we drove away in Dast Korumbos. No, I have no patience for those stories.'

'Mistress.' Sheyshi came out of the dark carrying a copper basin filled with water. 'Here is warmed water, if you want to wash your hair and face.'

'Captain!' The reeve reappeared, barely visible in the gloom, and waved a hand. 'If you will. There's something I would like you to see.'

Anji nodded at her and went after Joss. Mai watched them fade into the twilight. She scanned the clearing and the trees but could see nothing exceptional, only merchants fussing at their wagons, soldiers grooming horses, and a dog slinking under the wheels of a cart. Guards ringed the prisoner's wagon, but they showed no sign of alarm as they maintained their vigil.

Movement beside one wagon attracted her gaze. Canvas had been stretched by means of an internal scaffolding to make a cabin over the bed, and two young women knelt beside a small fire, feeding sticks into it and stirring in a pot that hung on an iron tripod over the flames.

'Look there,' said Mai to Priya. 'I've noticed them before. They look a little like Sheyshi, don't they?'

'Slaves,' said Priya. 'See the bracelets and anklets, hung with bells so they cannot run away without alerting their master. Someone means to sell them here in the north. So it happened to me.'

Mai took the other woman's arm, looking for the mark of shackles. 'You have never worn such bracelets, Priya!'

'It is not the custom in Kartu. They were taken off me before I came to your father's house.'

'Still.' Mai scratched a forearm carelessly. 'There's something about those two – or that wagon, anyway – that makes me itch. I don't know what. Like that time keder oil spilled on Ti's hand and made it blister. There's something hidden, but I don't know what.'

A young man appeared by the fire, speaking to the girls, and he looked up as if he felt Mai's gaze. She had seen him before, among the merchants. He was young, with thick, curly black hair, and vivid with a kind of hunger of the spirit, a thing which gnaws at the underbelly and never lets up. He noted her, as men always did, but looked away quickly as if to say, 'You cannot feed me, so I have no interest in you!'

'Find out his name,' said Mai to Priya.

Priya brushed her fingers across Mai's knuckles. 'You shouldn't stare at young men. Best we go on. Your water is ready.'

She followed Sheyshi behind a canvas screen set up for privacy and, with the aid of her two slaves, stripped and had them pour the water over her just for the feel of it. It wasn't a true bath, with a scrub and afterward a hot soak, but she rubbed and soaped and afterward Sheyshi brought two more basins and rinsed her, and anyway it was better than the constant smear of dirt on her skin. She had dried and dressed and was sitting on a stool, sipping at this nasty drink called *cordial* while Priya combed out her hair, when Anji returned, accepted a cup from Sheyshi, and drained it without even a grimace at the sour taste.

'What was it?' she asked him.

'Just in the trees, a man found two skulls, bones scattered. Wild beasts got into them, but it isn't clear if the dead men were murdered or just died from some other cause – starvation, illness. Or where they came from or why, nothing but the bones, not even scraps of clothing, pieces of gear, nothing.'

'It doesn't seem likely that naked people would go wandering in the forest. Unless these Hundred folk have strange customs.'

He smiled, but sobered immediately. 'The reeve tells me they have no holy followers of the Merciful One at all.'

'No followers of the Merciful One? How can that be? We saw a shrine to the god, but it contained no statue, nothing but withered flowers.'

'He kept thinking I was saying the Merciless One. It took us a while to sort it out. He had never heard of the Merciful One.'

'You might as well say you have never heard of the color blue, or the sun and the moon!' she protested. 'Surely all creatures know the Merciful One.'

He smiled. 'Not in Sirniaka, where Beltak, the King of Kings, Lord of Lords, the Shining One, rules alone.'

'Everyone knows that this Shining One is only one aspect of the Merciful One.'

'You would be burned alive for saying so.'

'Then I am glad we did not have to stay in Sirniaka!'

He touched her hand, and cradled it between his. 'Not even for another amaranth parasol?'

'I only needed one!' She laid her other hand atop his, thinking of the flash of jealousy he had displayed. Of course it was gratifying, but it scared her, too. 'I only need one,' she added, and his hand tightened on hers and he looked at her intently in a way that made her both bold and nervous, as though she stood in the court of judgment knowing she had done nothing to dishonor herself.

'Well,' he said, releasing her hand and rising, breaking the gaze. Her shoulders relaxed. 'They'll be given a proper funeral, however they do that kind of thing here. Still, it makes a man wonder.'

'How they came to die?'

'How much trouble the Hundred folk are having in their lands, to find border guards working in league with bandits and bones abandoned in the forest. Another thing I wonder at.' He paused, and she watched him as he regarded the starry heavens with a thoughtful gaze. His profile was a noble one, given a patina of unworldliness by night and stars and the fitful illumination of firelight. So might a man out of legend appear as he considers his destiny, because it is the duty of night to mask his thoughts and lend glamour to his fortitude.

She waited – she had always been good at waiting – and at length he continued.

'Their ghosts were still there. Where men die violently, there remains a whirlpool of rage and fear where the spirit was cut from the body. I had Shai come over. Do you know what he told me?'

'Poor Shai. He's so afraid of being burned for seeing ghosts.'

He frowned. 'It's true you Kartu folk have odd ideas, which we Qin often remarked on. Among the Qin, the few men and women who can see ghosts are honored. It's a rare gift. In the empire, a boy who sees ghosts is given to the priests and becomes a powerful man. It's also true, though, that a woman in the empire who saw ghosts would be executed. So, after all, on all counts, you're better off with me, Mai.'

'Did I ever suggest otherwise?'

'You did not. But, hear this and wonder, as I do. Those ghosts claim to have been reeves, so Shai tells me. They were murdered, although they cannot say who killed them. Yet where are the bones of their eagles? How comes it that our good ally Reeve Joss had no inkling of these deaths? Are these reeves not soldiers together in one unit? Does a crime that assaults one not lash the rest into action? Why is he here alone? Where are those who must stand at his shoulder?'

'What are you saying? That he is a rogue? Or a liar?'

'I think he is an honorable man. But what of other reeves? Are they as honorable as he is?'

'Did you ask him? Maybe he had heard of the deaths but not thought to tell you.'

'He said there is a fort – a *hall*, he called it – of reeves a few days' journey from here. He'll leave us tomorrow at a place he calls Old Fort, and fly to that place to meet with these other reeves, to see what they have heard of this situation. I am thinking he wonders why they have not acted, when all these crimes take place within the lands they are responsible to patrol.'

'He can ask them if they are missing two reeves.'

Anji shook his head. 'I did not tell him what the ghosts told us. I am mindful of the laws of Kartu. Before we let these Hundred folk know that both Shai and I have ghost-touched sight, best we know whether they'll wish to burn us alive.'

She put her hands to her cheeks, wishing that fear did not make her skin burn so.

'We must keep our eyes open,' he went on. 'Reeve Joss promises to meet us in Olossi, to help us in our request for settlement privileges. Mai, there is a part for you to play as well. You are my negotiator. When we reach this city, Olossi, you must speak innocently, and listen well.'

'You want me to be a spy.'

'A merchant, darling Mai. Merchants make the best scouts of all.

Anyway, men speak freely with you in a way they will not with other men. Your beauty and clarity are like wine, loosening their tongues. We have ridden into a strange land. If we are to survive here, we must know what we are up against.'

30

From Old Fort, Joss and Scar flew east-northeast along the ridge that separated the narrow coastal fringe from the upland plateau. They glided from updraft to updraft, making good time. The southern mountains were marked with icy tips. South lay the golden brown grasslands, blurring into the horizon. Just to the north, the Olo'o Sea was fringed with white frills where salt encrusted the shoreline. Seen from above, the sea had the silky luster of a rare gem, and the intense blue of its waters matched the color of the sky.

For two days they paused to feed and rest at one of the abandoned bastions that guarded West Spur, but although Scar could have used another day or two to really recover his full vigor, Joss pushed on. On the day that they passed the last of the bastions, a circular ruin of stone sitting on a bluff and overlooking road and sea, Joss turned Scar north over the sea itself, cutting across the estuarine bay which he had been told was known locally as Fisherman's Delight.

Below, a swirl of currents and contrasting colors marked the outflow from the River Olo, a cooler layer of water borne down from frigid springs and northern hills that had not yet mixed into the warmer sea. Joss no longer hoped that the hidden currents ripping through the reeve halls would be so easy to discern.

Late in the day he glimpsed an eagle off to the north, a speck seen flying above the dark border of the distant shore. Soon he could see the broad Olo Plain with its stripes and squares of fields measured by the straight lines of ditches and orchard rows. From this height, the rocky escarpment of the city was a mere smudge in the east, many mey distant, with the ribbon of the river no more than a wink as the light of the lowering sun caught in its majestic curves. Best to tackle the reeves first, before they had news of his coming. He had a few days before the caravan would reach Olossi.

Argent Hall had built its headquarters right at the coastline, in the midst of rice fields and sheep pasture, making it impossible to sneak up from any side. The huge rectangular compound was elevated on a massive earth platform and lapped by the sea on one side and by a murky moat on the other three. The steep banks of the earthen platform were reinforced along the base with stone, and grown green with mown grass. Sturdy stone corner towers offered a vantage to survey the surrounding fields and the open sea. Skeletal watchtowers suitable for eyries rose at intervals along the long walls. As he came in, two eagles rose on a coastal updraft and circled to fall in behind him.

So he would do, placing an escort on an approaching visitor, if he thought trouble was coming. Apparently Marshal Alyon thought trouble was coming, even in the person of another reeve. Joss considered this bleakly as Scar took the turn in toward the chalk-lightened parade ground and the cart-sized perches, painted white, where they could land. Before the shadows, the reeves from different clans had trusted each other, but that trust had eroded. Sometimes he felt he was himself to blame, since in the first years after the murders of Marit and Flirt he had broken the boundaries multiple times, had invaded the Guardian altars even knowing they were forbidden.

Yet this was not the fault of one young, foolish, reckless reeve.

He had to shake it off, but the dreams kept coming.

Scar pulled vertical, wing and tail feathers fanning out and his false wings standing up as he slowed, and landed. Then he spread his wings to show his size before settling. A kind of flurry of wings and fluffed-up feathers flowed around those few eagles visible from the parade ground and up on the watchtowers. Heads swiveled to stare.

Joss slipped out of his harness and dropped to the net, then swung down to the ground. He bound up his harness out of the way and tied the leash onto the perch's swivel ring.

Folk gathered, most in reeve leathers but a few in loose tunics or in the kilted skirts commonly worn for exercise. He strolled out into the center of the vast parade ground, where he could be seen and examined from all sides.

'I've come to see Marshal Alyon,' he said, and added, unnecessarily, 'I hail from Clan Hall.'

A younger reeve with a scar on his chin and a beady, suspicious gaze answered him without stepping forward to take charge. 'Marshal Alyon's corpse was laid on Sorrowing Tower months ago. We've had a new marshal since the Whisper Rains.'

He let the shock of that bald statement rake through his body without betraying by frown or blink that it stunned him. 'I'm sorry to hear it. We had no word of it at Clan Hall.' He took a breath and let it out. 'We were wondering, too, what became of Legate Garrard and the duty reeves who were called back and never replaced. That was almost a full year ago. Clan Hall sent a reeve called Evo down here as well, some months ago, but he never returned. I've come to see if there's any news of his whereabouts.'

The younger man stared but said nothing. They all stared, a dozen reeves and, by now, twice that many stewards and artificers, and even a few slaves ghosting in the shadow of the lofts as they craned necks to watch the showdown, although Joss wasn't sure who his opponent was. He had faced sullen silences before, only not from his fellow reeves. They were supposed to be allies.

Clan Hall should have had word of Marshal Alyon's death if the marshal had died during the Whisper Rains. That was months ago. These folk knew it as well as he did. And if they knew what happened to Evo, they should have sent word. But no one here was talking.

Shadows stretched over the dusty parade ground. A pair of eagles braked in to land on open watchtowers. Scar fluffed up his feathers. A spike of nerves thrilled up along Joss's spine, but the old eagle held his position, and fixed his amber gaze on his reeve.

Two reeves, the ones who had just landed, clambered down the watchtower ladders. But the attention of the gathering shifted when a young woman strode out of the open door of the west loft. A frown creased her dark face. Her hair was pulled tightly back along the high curve of her skull and braided in a single rope. Folk gave way to let her through, keeping their distance. She wore an exercise kilt, tied up very short, while not much more than a band of linen wrapped her breasts. The rest of her was exposed, and there was a lot of her to see, because she was tall for a woman: smooth brown legs, taut abdomen, muscular shoulders, arms glistening with sweat and oil. She wore sandals, and her feet were clean. She stopped a body's length from him, looked him up and down in the way she might measure a horse, and smiled with a soft whistle of approval that made his ears burn. Turning, she cast a pair of words over her shoulder at him, not in the least flirtatious.

'Come on.'

He appreciated her curves and her brisk walk and the scalloped wave of tattoos running up the back of her shapely legs, and let her get a little ahead of him before he followed, just to get the all of her in his view. Her braid didn't reach much farther than the middle of her back. Those gathered took her departure as a signal to move away in silence, all but the man with the scarred chin whose gaze looked ready to sear both hen and rooster.

As Joss passed close by him, the man hissed between his teeth and said, in a murmur that could not have reached beyond the two of them, 'The shadow of lust and greed rules here. Watch your back.' Then he, too, turned away and, with a noticeable hitch in his stride, favoring his right leg, headed for the east loft.

The woman paused in the alley between the braceworks and the high wall of the west loft, in the shadowed cleft midway between light and light, right where a double-wide door, slid back, opened onto a storehouse built into the outer wall. Ranks of ceramic vessels filled the long chamber: the tall amphorae for groundnut oil; smaller pots marked with the ideograms for sesame and chili oils; the elaborately decorated and stoppered vessels containing the most expensive cosmetic oils; an especially plentiful supply of the distinctive round, sealed pots holding precious oil of naya. Argent Hall had a remarkably well stocked storehouse, any merchant's dream.

'Are you always this slow?' she asked as he halted beside her and gave her his full attention.

He grinned. 'Only when I want to be.'

She snorted. 'Men say so, but they have no stamina.'

'Spoken like one of the Devourer's hierodules.'

'Do you think so?'

'You have the look of it.'

Her fingers, brushing his wrist, were like a wasp's tickling walk along skin. 'Do you want to find out?'

He bent toward her, lips to her ear, not quite touching. 'You'll find me far more at ease once my business here is concluded.'

As she started forward, she said something under her breath that he couldn't quite catch, or maybe it was something he had heard before, lying in the arms of the Merciless One. She devoured the ground with her stride. An impatient woman. She sizzled with a pent-up anger, but he didn't know enough to figure it out.

The alley gave way to the garden court with a narrow reflection pool flanked by fruit and nut trees, a pair of hexagonal fountains spilling water over blue tile, and wide corner terraces heavily planted with a variety of herbs, veil of mercy, and hundred-petaled butter-bright, so yellow that the petals seemed smeared with grease. The marshal's cote was a humble-seeming pavilion built at the far end of the pool. The intricate woodwork in the overhanging eaves and around the closed doors and white-papered windows, and the lacing vines of veil of mercy and climbing stars twining the poles and lattices of the wraparound porch, betrayed that skilled workmanship had gone into both its construction and its ornamentation.

Their footfalls on gravel surely warned the man waiting within. She indicated the steps. As Joss mounted the first one, the door slid open and a retired reeve shuffled out onto the covered porch and stood aside. Joss unlaced his boots, stepped out of them, and crossed up and over the threshold onto the raised floor.

The cote was not a large building. The front room stretched its length, while a single door, currently shut, suggested that a private chamber waited in back. The marshal sat on a pillow at a writing desk, at his ease with a quill in one hand and an ink knife in the other. Such a slender thing, that knife. Joss watched carefully as the marshal toyed with this knife, gaze fixed on the blank paper lying on the desk. He must have been cold, for he was wearing a cloak indoors, although it seemed plenty warm to Joss.

Finally, the marshal set down the knife next to a silver handbell, and looked up. He was young enough that his youth came as a surprise: a man with an unpretentious face and a diffident manner. He was no one Joss had ever seen before, that he recalled, and he had seen plenty of reeves in his time.

'I'm Legate Joss out of Clan Hall.'

'I know who you are. Why are you come here?' The man had a child's plain way of speaking.

'I hear Marshal Alyon is dead.'

'So he is.'

As the pause drew out, Joss understood that no further information was forthcoming. The outer door slid shut behind them, and the woman sashayed in, crossed to the inner door, opened it, stepped through into a narrow chamber made dim with shadows because all its shutters were shut, and closed the door behind her. Outside, someone began sweeping the porch.

'How did he die?' Joss asked.

'In the manner of all creatures. His time on this earth ended, and the gods plucked his soul from the husk to give it a new life in another being.'

Joss had always found these sorts of platitudes irritating, and that fueled his rash streak. 'We'd heard no news at Clan Hall of his passing.'

The marshal blinked.

'We'd wondered about Legate Garrard, and the dozen duty reeves who were withdrawn from Clan Hall at the beginning of the year. No news, and no legate to replace him, and no roster of duty reeves. Clan Hall also sent a reeve this way at the beginning of the Flood Rains. Evo, his name is. Do you have news of him?'

The marshal moved his quill to a different spot on the work table.

It seemed to be all the answer Joss was going to get. He had dealt with uncooperative witnesses many times, but there was something about the hushed room, the lack of pillows on which a visitor might settle to make friendly conversation, the rhythmic stroke of the broom outside, and the memory of that darkened inner chamber that unsettled him as few things did. Even dealing with the ospreys and their corrupt ally had not made his skin creep, not like this.

At last, the marshal replied in that innocuous voice. 'You're come into Argent Hall's territories. Why?'

'I was sent here at the order of the Commander at Clan Hall to find out why Legate Garrard was never replaced, and why we've had no word from Reeve Evo. Nor received any news from Argent

Hall in almost a year.' When the marshal made no effort to reply, Joss went on. 'As it happens, I've also heard complaints from merchants that there is trouble both on West Track and on the Kandaran Pass. They claimed that border guards on the Kandaran Pass were in league with ospreys.'

The marshal smiled as does a child who is told a ridiculous story. 'Do you believe that?'

'I have proof of it.'

Such a guileless face. 'Proof? How can I believe that?'

'I have a man in custody, an ordinand who was in league with the ospreys. Who admits to the crime.'

'Is he with you here?'

'No.'

'Where, then? It's a serious charge. The Thunderer's ordinands are the gods' holy soldiers, famous for their devotion to duty and the straight path. It's a hard thing to imagine one of them casting aside his oath to hunt with ospreys.'

'He'll come before the Olossi town assizes. Had Argent Hall no word of these attacks?'

'Who told you of this?'

'Some among Olossi's merchants tried' He broke off, and reconsidered. 'Word reached Clan Hall of the council's concerns.'

The marshal touched the quill, but picked up the bell instead and rang it. As in answer, a deeper bell rang twice, breathed twice, rang twice, breathed twice, and rang twice again.

'We'll speak tomorrow,' said the marshal. 'At the parting of day, we take our supper.'

Joss considered gain and loss, and decided he had no choice but to stay. He took leave to tend to Scar, to get the eagle settled for a night in the guesting loft. Scar was the only eagle present in the space. For the first time in his life as a reeve quartering in a reeve hall, Joss did not properly leash the eagle. He wasn't sure how quickly he would need to leave.

A fawkner's assistant wearing a slave's bracelets came by to offer a huge haunch of mutton, but Joss fed Scar lightly and sent the rest away. He remained in the semidarkness talking to the eagle about nothing in particular, just that soothing, mellow chatter necessary to allow the old eagle to adjust to the new surroundings, although all guest lofts were built exactly the same in every hall. But Scar had the patience and calm of a veteran and, when the second bell came, took the hood without fuss.

The same slave who had brought the mutton waited outside the door. They crossed the parade ground, skirted the west loft by an alley running along the sea side of the compound, and moved directly into the hall where the reeves and their community ate together every night under the eye of their marshal. He did not see the young man with scarred chin whose strange warning had raised so many alarms. A place on a bench awaited Joss, but not at the marshal's table. The marshal ate alone, still in his outdoor clothing. He was served by the old reeve, who had a habit, Joss noted, of tasting each dish before ladling out a portion onto his master's trencher.

Joss sat at the second-rank table among a flight of experienced reeves, stolid, laconic men and one woman who said nothing, apparently because it was now the custom at Argent Hall to listen to a reading while the meal was taken. A middle-aged woman read in a clear alto from a book of children's poetry about the origins and functions of the fourteen guilds, known to Joss from his schooling days when he'd been set the whole to memorize. It was as nourishing as straw.

> Hew! The forester, strong and stern,
> Swings with the axe the blacksmith forged.
> Soon comes carter to haul the logs
> To the shop where woodwright plies his turn.

Gods, how had he endured it then? Well, he had not, and had been caned on the hands more than once for his tricks when he got bored.

The mention of the carters got him thinking again about his dreams. Strange that he had folded the dying Silver's words into a dream and given them Marit's voice, as if to give himself an excuse to fly south straight into the fray rather than return with the wounded Peddo. For twenty years, hers was the only death he had never been able to leave behind.

The poem droned on and on.

Even bramble, healer uses
To give to dyer for handsome blues

Ghastly! He kept himself busy by sampling every dish, although he was careful to eat lightly, to avoid getting too full and thus too heavy. Argent Hall ate well: boiled fish covered with a spicy red chili sauce, rice cake, fried vegetables, nai porridge smothered in butter. Steamed spine-flower petals, heated just until their edges began to curl, were strewn over lamb basted in sharp ginger. The ubiquitous flatbread and mounds of rice rounded out the meal.

Trenchers were cleared away and cups of wine brought. A cluster of giggling youths dressed in short, sleeveless tunics scurried into the hall. In the pause while this unprepossessing entertainment readied itself, his companions ventured a few comments.

'Clan Hall, is it?' asked the youngest of these veterans. He had a nose once broken but long since healed with a bump and a twist.

'It is,' agreed Joss pleasantly.

They stared at him as though he had grown a second head. The man with the broken nose scratched an elbow.

'Toskala is besieged,' said the woman. 'How goes it there if foodstuffs can't come in or out?'

'Tss! What are you thinking?' demanded Broken Nose as two of the grizzled elders hissed through tight lips. She paled, shaking her head.

'Besieged?' Joss asked, startled and troubled by the comment. 'Beleaguered, truly, but Toskala is not under siege. A strange turn that would be!'

'Beleaguered,' said Broken Nose, elbowing the woman.

'That's right. That's what I heard.' She wasn't a good liar.

Broken Nose continued. 'That's what we heard. Refugees. Food shortages. Fighting in the hills. Fields laid waste in the night. What news have you heard, there in the north? What of the regions north of you? Heard you anything?'

Joss wanted to ask them why no one from Argent Hall had sent any manner of communication to Clan Hall this entire year, but the prickling along the back of his neck kept him quiet on this subject. He shrugged instead. 'The north is lost to us. Few reeves dare patrol there now. The reeves of Gold Hall and Copper Hall say the same, of their territories that touch anywhere along the borders of Herelia and Vess. No news at all from the high vales, so I've heard. But that's only hearsay. The worst news – this I saw myself – is that High Haldia has come under attack. Under siege. Perhaps that's what you were thinking of.'

Six of the seven youths fell into the familiar 'talking line,' and the seventh raised a stick and mirror-drum and commenced to beat out the pulse. As the storytellers fluttered their hands and stamped their feet, it took him a bit to start picking out the phrases from their gestures, because they were not accomplished: 'bird flies to mountain' 'the wind of ice weights its wings' 'falling! falling!' 'a cave' 'the spring fountains, an overflowing wine cup carved into the stone' 'caught in the current!' 'the tumbling water spills into the hidden valley' . . .

This was the familiar Tale of Indiyabu, but he had never seen it performed so crudely. And at such length! Every hamlet and village had a girl or boy who had been trained in the Lady's garden and could entertain visiting dignitaries with a more graceful rendition; any member of the guild of entertainers would be shocked by this display. He yawned, caught himself, and forced a cough. Two of the older reeves were snoring softly. The woman watched her hands; her fingers twitched, as though they knew the gestures and wished to speak. Broken Nose stared at the marshal as if awaiting a signal, but if expressions were anything to go by, there was no love lost between him and the hall's master. Joss scanned the tables again, but the young man with the scarred chin remained absent. No one made a move to leave. Indeed, the audience seemed lulled into a stupor. By the Herald's Gate! Now they meant to repeat the entire thing for a third time!

It was a relief when the drumbeat ended, the marshal rose, and the company was allowed to depart. A row of tiny cells lined the southern exterior of the guest loft. Each cell had a sliding window built into the wall above the pallet to let the reeve check on his eagle at any time during the night. A slave indicated the cell he was meant to inhabit. The rest were obviously empty, doors ajar, pallets bare of mattresses, even. It appeared no visitors had stayed here in many months.

He made his last check of Scar for the night, finished his own ablutions, and paced out the cell to get his bearings in the wavering light of a small oil lamp. Four strides from door to pallet; four strides diagonal to the corner to the right of the door where a square chest, hip-high, could hold baggage and, with its lid closed, might also serve as a writing table; side to side the cell was three strides wide. There was a double shelf at the base of the pallet and some hooks set into the wall on which to hang clothing and gear. He slid the window open. The loft was dark and silent. Scar would alert him if anyone came through that way. Still wearing his leathers, he took off his boots, placed his quiver and staff on the floor just to the left of the pallet, and tucked his short sword between him and the wall. He hung the lamp from a hook and blew out the flame. Then he lay down, resting his head on his rolled-up cloak.

Maybe the food had been contaminated with sleeping herbs. Once he closed his eyes, he dropped so fast into slumber that he had a moment of disorientation before he was inexorably dragged under.

The dream unveiled itself in the gray unwinding of mist he has come to dread. He is walking within a forest of skeletal trees, and by this knows he is dead, awaiting rebirth. He is a ghost, hoping to wake up from the nightmare twenty years ago, but the dream has swallowed him and he walks in a world both sleeping and waking that has no Marit in it.

Foolish. Foolish. Let her pass through Spirit Gate so she can rest. But he cannot let her go any more than he can unbind the harness that ties him to Scar. The Ox's heart seeks in the heavens that soul which fulfills it. He has romanced, enjoyed, liked, and parted with many women – probably too many – in the second half of his life, but he has never loved any of them.

The mist boils as though churned by a vast intelligence. Here the dream twists into nightmare. As the mist parts, he will see her in the unattainable distance, walking along a slope of grass or climbing a rocky escarpment, a place he can and must never reach because he has a duty to those on earth whom he has sworn to serve.

The door opened.

Out of the darkness a woman's figure emerges into what is not light but a supernatural glamour. Marit pauses on the threshold. She is so close to him! She is dressed in an undyed linen wide-sleeved jacket whose front panels overlap and are tied off along one side seam. Her trousers are of the kind that herdsmen wear, loose and comfortable, stained at the knees. Her hands and feet are bare, yet as if it is cold, she wears a death-white cape flung back from her broad shoulders. Her gorgeous black hair is braided into a single widow's spine almost as thick as his arm.

It hurts to look at her.

She does not move forward. She cannot. She cannot speak or act, because she is only a spirit that he dreams as part of his torment. She is not even a ghost, only a shadow to mark his desire.

'Be warned, sweetheart,' she says. 'You are in danger. Beware the third blow.'

His heart lurches. It is her voice, her very own, never forgotten! He tries to sit up, but he is paralyzed in truth, sleeping and awake at the same time, unable to shift his limbs.

'Marit!'

'I have broken my oath once already to warn you. Wake now!'

He jolted awake, jarringly alert even though only his eyes opened as the barest sound scuffed the matted floor. He grabbed his sword and sat up so fast that the shadow froze.

'Who's there?' he said in a low voice.

A cough gave him distance and placement, two strides forward from the door and one to the side.

'I had to come see.' She was taller than Marit. 'If it was true what you said.'

'What did I say?' He eased the sword onto his thighs, hilt toward the room and point toward the wall, holding it underhanded in his left hand.

'That you were slow only when you wanted to be. A woman can look a long time before she finds a man who can really take his time.'

Her voice had that drawling tone that teases a man and causes him all manner of comfortable distress. She changed position, and he saw suddenly that she was naked from the waist up, wearing only that short kilted wrap around her hips. She was all suggestive curves. He felt a stirring through skin and flesh, and in that instant of distraction, because men can be so easily distracted, she struck.

She was fast, but he was wide awake and ready. He ducked under her lunge and extended his arm in one stroke, catching her under the arm with a sharp blow from the hilt. That was enough to stagger her, and he looped his lower arm around and over and slapped her hard on the side of the head, catching her cheek with the flat of the blade.

She collapsed onto the floor with a grunt. Her weapon rattled against the pallet and rolled onto her body. He scooped it up by the handle, rolled it in his fingers, tried its weight. It was light, slender, deadly, an assassin's knife. He knew it as surely as he breathed.

He fished for the chain at his neck and drew up the two treasures that hung there. His fingers brushed the whistle, and for an instant he considered blowing it, to alert Scar, but the pitch would wake other eagles as well. Now was not the time.

Instead, he untied the tiny bag in which he carried his flint. Striking and nursing a spark with the flint, he lit the lamp. Her body was sweetly formed, enticing him. Her braid was wrapped tight and pinned atop her head. Her eyes were closed, and she was breathing shallowly, full breasts rising and falling . . . He forced himself to look away, to examine the knife. A sigil was carved into the handle, the four-petaled mark of Ushara, the Merciless One, the Devourer, mistress of life, death, and desire. They had found a similar tattoo on the body of that Devouring girl, twenty years ago.

The Devourer eats women and men both, and both women and men serve her, but only women served in her innermost sanctum. There, it was rumored, assassins might be bought who had trained in Ushara's courtyards, equally adept at seduction or murder, but even a reeve of long standing like Joss had never been able to fix the blame for any mysterious killing on the Merciless One's secretive hierodules. He had never been able to *prove* anything.

He sawed off a length of her wrap, rolled up the knife in the cloth, and shoved it into his kit bag. Quickly, he pulled on his boots, strapped on his gear, and left Argent Hall's guest rooms behind. Scar was already awake and alert, strangely calm, as though he had been warned. Quickly, and in silence, Joss readied the eagle, then shoved open the great door and walked him outside into the empty courtyard. A single lantern burned at the night watch's tower, overlooking the land side of the compound.

Joss was shaking as he gestured Scar up on the launching post and fastened himself into the harness. A shout rang out from the tower. A second lamp flashed. Scar raised wings and tail and thrust with his legs. No male eagle had a more powerful downstroke than Scar, and he was lifting and moving forward with such strength that he was past the compound's wall before the sentry got his eagle off the watchtower. Joss got a glimpse of him as they flew past, gaining altitude, seeking an updraft. It was the young man with the scar. He set his eagle after anyway, rising into the night and stroking after Joss.

Sweat poured freely down Joss's neck and forehead, although the night's wind off the sea was cool. The heavens were clear, and the stars blazed. Far to the east, the Peacock rose. He turned Scar south-southeast toward Olossi.

As a youth, he had served his year's apprenticeship with Ilu the Herald. He had a seeking mind that did not veer away from the unknown or inexplicable. Now his heart hammered and his thoughts skipped. He could not think through the troubling things he had seen and experienced at Argent Hall. He could make no sense of the day at all, or even the impossible dream of Marit stepping out of the mist where she had long wandered in the unreachable distance. Of Marit speaking. He ought to think of her, but he could not because he kept seeing that dead Devouring girl from twenty years ago. Although pierced to the heart, she had lost little blood, and her face had worn a rictus grin that had disturbed him ever after. So might the Merciless One smile when she suffers death's consummatory kiss.

This night, such a knife had been meant for him.

Sweat stung his eyes, and he wiped his forehead and tilted his face to let the wind pour over eyes and nose and mouth. Scar found an updraft, and they rose and rose and rose as the land fell away below them, as dark and still as a sleeping beast. The sea gleamed, reflecting stars.

The reeve from Argent Hall was still pacing him, neither falling behind nor trying to catch up. Eagles were creatures of day, and flew at night only under duress. Scar was already angry, kekking and making his displeasure known with little stabbing motions of that huge beak. Joss didn't want to put down, but he had enough of a head start out of Argent Hall that he figured it was better to risk the stop rather than let the other man follow.

He and Scar circled down in an open field of rice stubble not yet turned under, a pale expanse where it was unlikely they'd stumble onto any unexpected holes or rills or ditches. It was a risk, but one that paid off as the other reeve landed at the far end of the field, a gap carefully judged to allow an approach without seeming threatening.

Scar flared and spread his wings, disturbed by the difficulty of the night landing, the lack of a roost, and the presence of the other eagle, but after a command from Joss, he tucked his head under his wing and settled in to wait.

Joss unhooked from his harness, hooked the unlit lantern to his belt, and kicked through the stubble. The other man met him halfway. He had kept his traveling cloak on, a signal that he didn't expect a fight. Both raised their staves out in front into 'holding.'

'Why did you come after me?' asked Joss.

'You're really from Clan Hall?'

'So I am.'

'Legate Garrard is dead.'

'How do you know?'

Wind rustled in the dry stalks. Insects chirruped. He smelled a trace of hearth fire, drifting from an unseen farmhouse. A line of mulberry trees rimmed the sea break of the field. It grew suddenly cool, as though the weather had turned back several months to the season of Shiver Sky, but maybe that was just his instinct for trouble shivering to life.

The young man cleared his throat. 'Once I speak, I cannot return to Argent Hall. They'll kill me.'

'They'll kill you anyway, if it has come to that. They'll never trust you, knowing you came after me. Tell me what you know. Afterward it's best you fly to Clan Hall to report to the Commander. Do you know the way?'

'I was there one time, my first year.'

So were they all. It was part of their training.

'I think I can find it,' he added, but he didn't sound sure of himself. He lowered his staff to 'resting,' as a measure of trust, but Joss only spotted the tip of his own against the earth, ready to strike if this proved to be an ambush.

'What's your name?'

'I'm Pari. That's Killer.'

'*Killer?*' He peered through the curtain of night, but the eagle seemed smaller than average and already asleep, head tucked.

'She's very calm,' said the young man with a hoarse laugh. 'Kind of lethargic, actually. I think her first reeve gave it to her as a hope name.'

'Well, then, Pari, I'm Legate Joss, out of Clan Hall. That's Scar. Why did you come after me?'

The other man was breathing harshly, and he caught back what sounded like a sob. 'Ai, where to start? You know, they tell you that the reeves are incorruptible. It's what they teach you the day you step into the circle. Reeves are incorruptible because the eagles can't be corrupted. The hells! What a stupid thing to believe!'

'Don't take it too hard,' said Joss softly. 'It's true about the eagles, anyway.'

'Oh. Sure!' He was aggrieved as only the young can be, when the still waters in which they have gazed all this time are shattered by a tossed stone. 'But a dog can no more cleanse his master's shadowed heart than a child can stop its father from drinking away the wages his family needs for food, or drag its den-crawling mother from clouds of sweet-smoke where she drowns while her children bawl outside.'

'A sight seen too often,' Joss agreed. 'What happened at Argent Hall?'

'I'm three years in, and I never knew that reeves did come and go so much. Folk transferred out, and transferred in. Why, I think a hundred reeves come in just in these last three years, and there was already a big turnover before that, so the old ones tell me. And no new reeves chosen for over two years now. That's even though there's more than forty eagles who've lost their reeves and flown off in the last few years, and never returned.'

Joss shook his head. 'I've never heard of that happening before. No new reeves chosen at all?'

'Only one who came after me. She's dead, now, and her eagle flown.'

A nasty feeling was gnawing at his gut, like a lilu turned from tempting woman to its natural form right in the middle of its grazing. 'Clan Hall is aware of the transfers, but in truth there's nothing can be done by the Commander. She has only a supervisory position. But everyone knows it's disruptive to the eagles to transfer them. It's done only if necessary.'

'Yeah, it was plenty disruptive here, or so they say, as I've never known anything but trouble in Argent Hall. All the ones who had a bad temper, or weren't getting along in their other hall. Reeves who had hit someone too hard, or drank too much, and one woman who's addicted to the sweet-smoke, even, though she still flies! One reeve – that would be Horas – they said he murdered a man but nothing came of it when the family tried to get justice. And the reeves at Argent Hall who complained most about the disruption, they were asked to leave and go elsewhere. Or they just left, and weren't seen again.'

'All this done at the order of Master Alyon?'

Once started, Pari spoke so quickly that Joss had a hard time following him. 'I admit Master Alyon was ill, and infirm, there at the end. There were a foursome of veterans who had the running of things. I heard whispers that he was being poisoned. He did get better right toward the end when he brought in that Devouring girl to do his cooking for him and who knows what else besides. That was around the time when he recalled Garrard. Talk was that Marshal Alyon had Garrard in mind for succeeding him. But then comes this man who calls himself Yordenas – not much older than me, mind you! – and first he tells Dovit that he's out of Iron Hall and then he tells Teren that he's out of Copper Hall, so there's some confusion, as you can guess.'

'The eagle would have a band to mark its territory.'

'That's just it. None of us have ever seen Yordenas's eagle.'

'How can that be?'

'He says it's nesting up in the Barrens. But I've never heard tell of an eagle gone on its nesting season for that long.'

'It could be. I've heard tell of a nesting pair gone most of a year's time. But it is odd, that he comes to you as a reeve, and yet has no eagle. So what happened then?'

'Master Alyon just up and died one night, and it all changed. We blink, and overnight this Yordenas is sitting in the marshal's cote and there are more reeves supporting him than opposing him. When Garrard protests, next thing you know Marshal is calling it out as a mutiny and thirty or more are dead and their eagles flown back to the mountains, just like that.'

'Those are the eagles that never came back to choose new reeves?'

'That's right, most of them. Thirty or forty others left then, reeves and eagles both, although I don't know where they went. It just gets worse. Patrol routes changed. Marshal closed the gates to outsiders, any outsiders, even folk come to report on trouble in their village or to ask for help. We got word anyway of ospreys on the Kandaran Pass and along the West Spur, and there come some Olossi merchants to beg for our help one night, so Dovit and Teren went out on patrol without permission, but they never came back. That was a two-month back, I think. Most of them I knew from three years back when I first got chosen are gone, except the ones I never liked at all. The others are dead with Garrard. Or they left.'

At last, he took a breath. He was trembling. The sliver of moon called Embers Moon was rising in the east, heralding dawn.

'Why did you stay?' asked Joss.

His chin tilted back. The faint moonlight seemed to catch and gleam on the white scar of his chin. He was Toskala-chinned, like Joss, recently shaven. He looked very young.

'Someone had to.'

Joss grinned sadly. 'You've courage to have stuck it out.'

Pari shrugged, as if embarrassed or ashamed. 'Didn't do anyone any good.'

'You did what you could. You'll have to go north. Follow the course of the River Hayi. It runs east-west until the Sohayil Gap; a little past that, the river bends northeast. Once to the Aua Gap, continue north. You can't miss the River Istri. Any landholder there can tell you in which direction – seaward or ridgeward – Toskala lies, if you don't recognize the lay of the ground.'

'Where are you going?' asked Pari.

Joss considered. This might be some kind of complicated ploy, and he daren't risk trusting him, although his heart told him that the young man was being honest. It was hard to playact that kind of righteous, helpless pain.

'I've heard tell of this trouble along the West Spur, as I told the marshal. I'm investigating it. What do you know about it?'

'No one confides in me,' he said with a tone very like a child's whine. 'Just that caravans were being attacked. Women kidnapped, although that was before my time. I suppose the merchants in Olossi would know about it. It's their trade that would be hurt.'

'What do you know about the merchants in Olossi? Anything that could help me? Any names? Anything?'

He shrugged. 'I've went to the Devouring temple a few times, but not recently. Marshal likes to hold us close against him these days, those of us he doesn't trust. I see reeves flying out solo, so I suppose they're carrying messages. Maybe to Olossi. I think they have some kind of understanding with the council there, but I don't know. Anyway, I come from Sund. That's the territory I know best. I'm not allowed to patrol out on my old rounds anymore. I suppose no one is patrolling there at all.'

'So Yordenas is the name of this new marshal?'

Pari laughed as at a cruel joke. 'He calls himself Yordenas.'

'When you get to Clan Hall, be sure to tell all of this to the Commander just as you've told it to me. They can check the records, see if such a reeve is recorded.'

'It won't matter,' said Pari.

'Why not?'

'This is the thing. Garrard stabbed him, when they got in that fight. It was ugly, the things they said, and afterward it was worse. But he didn't die. He should have died, but he didn't. A day later he was up and walking like nothing had happened. I think he's a demon, not a person at all.'

'A stab wound can call out a lot of blood, but do little real damage.'

'So you might think. It was a killing blow, I'm telling you.'

Joss whistled softly, under his breath. He could not make sense of this young man and his passion and his anger and his tendency to slip into a child's manner of grievance.

'You don't believe me.'

'I'm not sure what there is to believe.'

Pari cursed in a low voice, then gave a breathy, cackling laugh like that of a man driven past endurance. 'No, you couldn't know, not unless you'd been there. I'm just saying this: Wolves and ospreys stalk the land. And they're winning the battle.'

'I can't argue with that.'

Night turned. The eastern horizon sparked, limned in fire.

'Best be going, friend,' Joss went on. 'Argent Hall will be looking for us. Best if we're well away.'

'They'll find us.' Pari looked back toward Killer, who was shaking herself awake and looking none too eager to face the day given her interrupted night. 'I'm not brave. Mostly, I was afraid to run for fear they'd catch me and do something awful to me. I don't even know what. Marshal Yordenas has something wrong with him, but I don't know what it is. And the rest pant after him like they're dogs and he's the one holding their dinner.'

'So it may be. Best we be going.'

Pari looked him in the eye, a stare both belligerent and frightened, but he shook himself, nodded, and flattened his mouth into a determined grimace. 'Don't trust anyone.'

Joss strode back to Scar, who had the ability to come awake fast and ready to go. They launched first, and he circled twice until Pari finally got up off the ground and headed east-southeast, making for the river, just as he should. Joss pulled south toward the faint glimmer of watch lights still burning on Olossi's watchtower several mey distant. His gaze tracked the distance reflexively. It caught on an anomaly. A pale spot rose in the southeast, like another creature flying, except no eagle had that ghostly color. He blinked, and the spot vanished. It was only a trick of the predawn light.

With the dawn, he closed in on Olossi Town. He had to get Olossi's council to talk. He had to ferret out the ones who had sent that doomed delegation into the north. Where had that Devouring girl come from, and why had she tried to kill him?

Not that there was any proof, only his word against hers beyond the evidence of the knife and Pari's garbled history. No proof, no clues, no evidence, not even an explanation for why things seemed so very wrong at Argent Hall. Marshal Yordenas could always claim that the youth was disaffected, that the woman – the assassin – acted on her own. Nothing to do with me, he would say, how could I know I harbored these vipers in my hall?

Joss circled the town, swinging wide to get a good look at the avenues and surrounding fields. Early-morning traffic was brisk, folk going about their business in the cool hours of the day before the heat really slammed them. Despite the custom that every city must maintain a wide square or court so that reeves could fly in and out of the city's heart, Olossi's inner town lacked any such space. It had long since been built into such a warren of walled gardens, crowded temple grounds, family compounds, and housing blocks raised by merchants, artisans, and other guild families that the only open spaces remaining surrounded the five wells, the three noble towers, and the ancient timber council hall that was popularly supposed to be the oldest extant building in Olossi. There was a large courtyard, with the customary perch, in front of the Assizes Tower, but the angle of the roofs and the awkward slant of the street and walls along the approach made him chary of risking a landing there. He took a long look at the elongated peak of the council hall and finally decided that it was also too risky, although such a landing would certainly impress the locals. Instead, he banked low over Olossi's skirts, that part of the city that had grown up and out, beyond the inner city walls, into a lively patchwork of slums, warehouses, stockyards, tanning yards, and guild yards along the southern bank of the river.

The shine of the river drew his gaze toward the sea. Far off, he saw the white walls of a Devourer's temple sited on a rocky island in the midst of delta channels. It was possible that the woman who had tried to murder him had come from there, and no doubt he would have to go speak to their Hieros. That would be an interview he did not relish.

A shout rang up from the ground. Below, folk gathered at a gate marked by a temple to Sapanasu were pointing up at him. He turned a last time and swung in low as Scar raised his wings and fanned out pin and tail feathers for the landing. They hit in a dusty field a short walk from the gate.

He tested the jesses on Scar's legs, and stepped back while giving the hand signal for flight and return. Scar thrust and beat upward, circling once to mark Joss's position before flying toward the distant bluff that marked the upland and its potential hunting ground. The reeve slung pack and hood across his shoulders. He walked across the field, kicking up dust, and reached a path that met up with a lane that struck into the roadway. He paid a vey as toll to pass through Crow's Gate and passed the colonnade where the clerks of

Sapanasu had already begun their day's accounting. The caravan with Captain Anji had not yet come through; they were likely two or three days out. He had a few days to work before he would have to meet them and the prisoner.

Business moved early in Olossi, especially in the season of Furnace Sky. A woman and her daughter had set up a stall selling fried palm bread and green mango. He bought one of each – the palm bread still hot from the griddle and the mango peeled, sliced to make petals of its flesh, and impaled on a stick – and ate as he walked along the road that led to the inner gate. Wagons lurched and rumbled along the stone. Women walked with baskets balanced atop their heads. A pair of children bent beneath a yoke from which hung buckets stinking of night soil.

Olossi's council guard manned the wide gates that allowed traffic to enter and leave the inner city. The pair on duty saw his reeve's leathers and his dusty boots and immediately called a captain, who delegated a young man to escort him up the winding avenues to the council hall. They crossed the Assizes Court where a line had already formed in front of the timber hall, whose double doors were still closed. Behind the hall, the square Assizes Tower rose.

From here they climbed the hill. Blocks of houses rose around them as they strode up the steady slope of the avenue that spiraled its way to the top. They passed a tricolored, three-layered gateway that marked the entrance to a tiny garden sanctuary dedicated to Ilu the Herald. A slave carried a pair of covered buckets in through the entrance to a large family compound where smoke threaded up from cook fires within. A pair of stone lanterns holy to Sapanasu flanked the narrow opening to one of the Lantern's holy temples. At one corner, he smelled the sweet flavor of pastry-baking. A pair of very young ordinands lounged, yawning, at the open doors of one of Kotaru's forts; the snap and crack of arms training drifted out from the interior. A 'hatched eye' sacred to Taru the Witherer had been painted on a circular door set into high, whitewashed walls; fruit trees flourished in the hidden garden behind, their scent a fleeting perfume in the air, and flowering vines spilled over the top of the wall. A lane branched off the main avenue, flying the gold and silver pennants of gold- and silversmiths. Beyond this, seen floating away over rooftops, lay

Olossi's Sorrowing Tower. Kites spun their slow circles above its pale stone crenellation.

Despite the early hour, Joss was sweating by the time they reached the highest point in Olossi, with its Fortune Square, the rectangular council hall, and the smooth curve of the dark stone watchtower with its open roof and fire cage.

At this hour of the day, a line of supplicants had formed on the steps of the council hall. The guardsman led him past these up onto the sheltered porch where a line of benches sat empty, and through the sliding doors into an entry chamber. This chamber, which stretched the width of the hall, was paneled with screens charmingly painted with the story of the Silk Slippers. Its only inhabitant was a woman with pleasant features who was no longer in the first blush of youth. She wore a loose tunic with a scoop neck that draped low enough for him to see the blue-purple tattoos running up either side of her neck – the wave-scallops marking her as kin of the Water Mother. Safe to flirt with. Like the woman who had tried to kill him. The image of that one, so sensual, so strong, flashed so powerfully in his mind that he was for a moment disoriented.

'Can I help you?'

'Sorry. Change in light made me lose my footing. I'm a reeve sent from Clan Hall in Toskala. Legate Joss. I need urgently to discuss with the council this matter of the recent border disturbances up on the Kandaran Pass, and along West Spur.'

'Yes, we've had a lot of complaints about safety on the roads this year. But I didn't know it was serious enough to call a reeve out of Toskala.' She was some manner of clerk, seated at a table with a sheaf of documents placed at her left elbow, and a quill and ink stand to her right. She wore Sapanasu's lantern on a necklace as a mark of her service. 'The thing is, the council only meets in the evenings. Even so, there's no meeting until Wakened Crane.'

Four days from now.

'A few council members might come by after Shade Hour to take tea,' she added, with a faint flicker of eyelids, not *quite* flirting but surely interested.

'Can I wait and talk to them? If not the council, what of Olossi's militia?'

'No. Every able-bodied man, and any woman who qualifies,

must serve a turn, but the captains are hired and fired by the council. You could go to Argent Hall.'

He considered, and decided to be bold. 'I've been there, but they're not interested. Can you tell me where the carters' guild is located?'

'I can, but it's all the way down and beyond the gates. You're in luck, though, given the day. Usually the guildsmen take a drink up here at sunset, nothing formal, but it's traditional on Wolf days, kind of a thanksgiving for trips survived without incident. Do you want to go all the way down, or do you fancy a rest up here? I can show you to the garden. Or you can sit on one of the benches outside.'

He rested fisted hands on the table and leaned there, with a smile that made her blush. 'Now that I think of that long walk, and my restless night, I guess I fancy a rest in the garden.'

She blushed brighter. Shrugged. Tongue-tied. He was pushing too hard with this one. Possibly she was married, but no red bracelets circled her wrists. He straightened, and she relaxed.

'I do fancy a rest,' he added, 'but in truth I should go down right away, if you're willing to give me the direction.'

At the door, a man stuck his head in, saw them talking, and withdrew.

'My name is Jonit,' she said suddenly, and he guessed, by the shy tremor of a new smile and by the way her eyelids flickered and her lashes dipped to shadow her eyes, that she was definitely not married or allianced. 'I don't have to open until the hour bell. If you want to, you can wash your hands and face and sit down a moment before you take that long walk back down the hill. If you want.'

'That is tempting.'

She licked her lips, seemed by the way she bit at her lower lip to make a decision, and let out a breath. Rising and moving out from behind the table, she revealed a petite figure, winsome and nicely rounded, wrapped in gold and pearl-white layers of silk tunic and shawl with deep blue pantaloons. Her feet were bare except for three gold anklet rings. A woman with prosperous connections. It seemed surprising she wasn't married.

She saw him assessing her. She had a teasing smile that made her prettier. 'It's a nice garden. There's even a fountain, but you might miss the entrance if someone doesn't show you where it is.'

She began to walk away. Heavy footfalls pounded on the steps outside. She shifted to look back at him, beckoning, but her eyes widened and mouth dropped open. He turned as five guardsmen pushed into the chamber led by a captain in a stiff leather tunic.

'Yes, that's him,' said the young guardsman, the very same one who had escorted him up. The youth stepped away, disassociating himself from trouble.

'What's this?' asked Jonit.

Their captain stepped forward, hand on his sword. 'I'm Captain Waras, of the Olossi militia, under the authority of the Olossi council. You're under arrest, by order of the council.'

'I am?' asked Jonit, looking bewildered.

'No, this reeve here. You're the one who calls yourself Legate Joss? Who claims to be here under the authority of the Commander of Clan Hall in Toskala?'

'I am,' he said.

'If you will come with us . . .' The polite phrase was meant to intimidate.

'Where do you mean to take me?' He did not move but felt keenly the cool touch of the whistle against his chest, hidden beneath his clothing. Scar could land on the peaked roof, but it would be a difficult climb to get up to him.

'Assizes Tower.'

'What is the charge? You cannot prosecute me until an advocate from Clan Hall is here to witness. This is very serious, accusing a reeve. You know the laws.'

'Murder is a serious charge,' said the captain.

That was the kick, but Joss was already drawn too tightly to flinch. Indeed, he was getting angry. 'Certainly it is. Who am I supposed to have murdered, and where?'

Jonit backed away, staring at him as though he were welted with plague. Shadows lined the porch and moved along the rice paper walls of the sliding doors and windows as folk crowded up outside to listen.

'One of the Thunderer's ordinands. A captain stationed most recently at the border fort at the terminus of West Spur, on the Kandaran Pass. Name of Beron.'

He almost staggered, hit so hard and quickly, but reeves learned to keep their feet under them. 'I just arrested such a man,' he said quietly, 'for conspiring with a band of ospreys to rob caravans coming up from the south over the pass. But he's in transit here, with a caravan, under guard.'

Captain Waras shrugged. 'I hold the order. Nothing more. If you'll come with me, there'll be no trouble.' One of his guards leaned in and whispered, and the captain had the grace to look embarrassed before he held out a hand. 'If you please, give me the whistle they say you carry. The one that will call your eagle to you.'

'I will not! None but a marshal has the right to take that from me.'

'If you're innocent, you've nothing to fear.'

Joss laughed. It was all he could do. He had no idea how far the rot had spread, even now, even here. 'I'll come to Assizes Tower and wait for a witness from Clan Hall, as is my right. I'll agree to bide peacefully until the caravan arrives. They are witness to my operations. But I'll give up nothing, not my weapons, not my whistle, nothing. When the caravan arrives, you'll see this is a false charge.'

He pushed past them and out the door, head held high, praying to the gods but especially to Ilu the Herald, that Captain Anji was an honest man and as clever as he looked. Wheels were spinning within wheels here, and even the Herald might not be able to guide him out of this labyrinth.

The folk gathered on the porch scattered back as he reached the stairs. He started down, and on the third step crossed from shade into the blast of the sun. Blinking, lifting a hand to shade his eyes. A gasp warned him, a woman's choked shriek. A whisper of air chased his ear. The haft of a spear smacked into the side of his head.

He dropped hard, spinning in and out of darkness as consciousness wavered. Images flashed: the assassin striking with her knife; the captain's stabbing accusation; beware the third blow.

He hit the ground, tried to raise himself on a hand, but hadn't the strength.

A man's stocky form loomed above him, blocking the sun. 'Take him to the tower, and lower him into the dungeon. And take that damned whistle off his neck!'

He blacked out.

31

After the reeve left, Anji kept Mai close beside them as they rode. She learned to enjoy the constant movement up and down the line of march. As the days passed, she watched for what interested her, spent a great deal of time finding out what coin and other measures of barter the folk here used, and how much things cost. She also looked for and mentioned things she thought Anji might find of interest: a lame horse; an abandoned doll; a shuttered hut; a carter with sores around his mouth that could be the sign of a corrupting disease. Most of the time he or Chief Tuvi or one of the men had already noticed these things, but not always. Sometimes things troubled her that interested them not at all.

The morning they came into sight of their destination for the first time, they paused to survey the river plain, the distant fields, the delta, and the sprawling town with its inner heart and its outer skirts. Anji and Chief Tuvi pulled their horses off to one side and conferred about lines of entry and exit, visible roads and paths, and their options for escape should they receive a hostile greeting. The caravan rattled past. Mai's gaze drifted to watch the faces of the merchants as they recognized that today – at long last! – they would reach the market they longed for. Such a range of pleasure and enthusiasm, relief and laughter!

Yet one man's brows were wrinkled with anxiety. One man, walking past beside his wagon, was not lightened by the sight. As usual, his cargo remained hidden within the canvas tent that covered his small wagon. Mai knew a mystery when she saw one.

She waited for Anji to finish. When at last they rode forward again, passing the slower-moving wagons as they rode toward the vanguard, she watched for one merchant in particular. She marked him easily; he was almost stumbling, hanging on to the wagon as though he were sick and dizzy. As they came up from behind, she slowed her horse to keep pace with his wagon.

'Are you well, merchant?' she asked him.

Startled, he looked up at her. He paused, forced a smile that did not touch his eyes, and tried out formal words on his tongue. 'A long, weary journey, Mistress.' He let go of the pole and wiped his sweating brow.

She smiled, hoping to reassure him. 'Close now, I see. Is Olossi your home?'

'No, Mistress. But it is my destination.'

Or maybe he was getting sick; sickness was always dangerous. She glanced at the wagon, wondering if the girls were sick, too, but they ate so much she doubted it. This was more likely a sickness in his heart. Anji had gotten ahead of her, so she nodded at him and rode after her husband.

'That man is hiding something,' she said when she caught him.

He smiled. 'We are all hiding something.'

'I am hiding nothing!'

'Your true price. Your father sold you cheaply.'

She colored, not liking to think of herself as merchandise bought and sold, like almonds and peaches, but it was true, and anyway she was happy her father had neglected to drive a harder bargain. Not that she would tell Anji that. 'That's not what I mean. You asked me to use my market eyes and my market ears, and now I am telling you that man – he's called Keshad – is hiding something.'

He looked back over his shoulder at the cart, then back at her. 'What makes you think he's hiding something? Besides the obvious fact that he is a merchant.'

'The closer we come to Olossi the weaker and more nervous he becomes. The whiteness around his eyes betrays fear, and his eyes are inflamed by shed tears.'

'Many men suffer the traveling sickness – exhaustion, loose bowels, sick stomach, sore feet.'

'I thought so too. But in the days we've traveled from the border, his pace has remained steady, and he eats at night.'

'You have been watching him?'

Was that a sharp note in his voice? She chose to ignore it. 'I am curious about the two girls in his wagon. They eat enough for three or four. Maybe they're just very hungry. But a prickling between my shoulder blades alerts me.'

He grunted thoughtfully, surveying their surroundings.

The carts and wagons of the caravan proceeded along the middle portion of the road, with its paving stones, but she and Anji rode on the margin paths, against the main flow of traffic, crushed stone crunching under their horses' hooves. Farther out a skein of footpaths paralleled the road, and along this walked various locals. Some carried burdens: a grandmother limped along with a baby in a sling at her hip; a girl balanced a bulging reed basket atop her head; a trio of women easily handled massive sheaves of grain that obscured their faces and torsos. A pair of sweating, half-naked men hauled a cart piled with rocks. Other men and women ambled or hurried toward distant fields and orchards with hoes and shovels and rakes in hand. A pair of boys ran, giggling, with what appeared to be a writhing snake in the hands of one.

They had such a different look here, a different shape of skull, a rich, golden-brown complexion in a variety of shades nothing like the folk she had grown up among in Kartu Town. Yet here and there among them walked an old woman with a brown-black complexion and round features like Priya's, or a young man with the bronze-red coloring of the eastern desert towns along the Golden Road. These foreigners always wore bronze bracelets. On the whole, the Hundred folk were taller and more robust than the outlanders who had washed up in their lands, although some among the Hundred kind wore slave marks, just like in Kartu Town: brands, belled anklets, iron collars.

'Good silk,' she commented, indicating the bright clothing worn by women moving along the paths. Now and again someone passed by wearing a coarser weave of silk that made the quality of the other stand out in contrast.

'They're wearing a lot of Sirniakan silk,' said Anji. 'I would wager that the homespun is local silk. Nothing as good as the Sirni silk. It's no wonder they prefer silk out of the south. Yet it makes me wonder how far the sword of the emperor reaches.'

Her heart beat faster as she thought of the burning town they had left behind together with three men and nine slaves. 'Will we be safe here?'

'We will find out.' He pointed. 'Look there. A troop of acrobats.'

Beyond the foot trails lay cleared ground where lithe athletes, some quite young and others remarkably old, juggled balls and balanced on rope, turned cartwheels and flips, and then did it all again.

A woman of middle years strode among them, hectoring and gesturing. Mai tried but could not quite hear what she was saying. The troupers, male and female alike, were dressed in short kilts and tight sleeveless jerkins; some of the men wore no top at all. It was shocking to see so much smooth and handsome skin displayed right out in public. At the roped-off edge of the dirt field, a group of children had gathered to watch. There was even a quartet of small dogs who stood on their hind legs and turned in circles, like a dance.

She turned half around in the saddle as the field fell behind. 'I wonder if they'll perform here. If we can attend a show.'

When he didn't answer, she turned back. They rode up to the cluster of Qin soldiers who surrounded the wagon in which the prisoner was confined. Chief Tuvi nodded as his captain fell in beside him.

'All is quiet?' asked Anji.

The chief nodded. 'It is.'

Tuvi called to one of the men riding next to the wagon. The wagon had a scaffolding built over it on which planks had been nailed to form a crude shelter, with a canvas ceiling stretched over the top. The soldier leaned out to release the catch on a plank and lowered it, revealing a window into the inside. Through that gap, Mai saw a slice of the dim interior and a man's face. In that first moment, his gaze was direct, defiant, unashamed, but then he flinched and raised a hand against the light. Tuvi nodded, and the soldier raised the plank and latched it back into place.

'He eats,' said Tuvi. 'He wishes to keep up his strength.'

'I wonder what manner of justice he expects from these *assizes*,' said Anji. 'I have spoken with the caravan masters. It seems a court is assembled of men or women from the town who have a certain respectable standing. They hear evidence, and then make a judgment by casting lots.'

Tuvi tugged at an ear. 'Women? Huh.'

'Women listen and observe better than men do,' said Mai.

'I dare not argue,' said Anji in a way that irritated her.

Chief Tuvi gave her a long, careful look as he scratched at his chin and the straggle of beard growing there. 'Maybe so. In the tribe, women rule on women's matters, which are a thing men cannot judge.'

In Kartu Town, the bureaucrats of the law courts ruled on all matters brought to their attention, but these were public disputes. Within the family, of course, Father Mei was the arbiter of all decisions and the executor of all punishments. His word was the only law.

'I think I will like to see these assizes,' said Mai, 'where women sit together with men on the court. And cast lots. And pass judgment.'

But she had lost them. The gazes of both men, and indeed those of all of the soldiers riding on this side of the road, had strayed to follow a thread unwinding through the foot traffic. It was almost funny to see men up and down the caravan become distracted at the sight of a tall young woman striding along one of the paths toward town, not more than fifteen paces out from the road. She had a man's casual confidence but a woman's eye-catching sway and shift. She wore white, a stark color compared with all the bright oranges, reds, yellows, spring greens, and jewel blues that ornamented the many women out and about their business. The hem of her white kilted skirt did not brush her knees; her white sleeveless jacket was so short that her belly button was exposed. Even the locals glanced at her with interest, the men with that lift of the chin, that pause of a gaze, that measures a woman's attributes. Her hair was pulled back into a single braid falling halfway down her back. One of her cheeks had a purple bruise high along the cheekbone, a smear that almost reached the fine perfect shell of an ear. She was barefoot, just as all those acrobats in the field had been. Oblivious of the world, intent on her own thoughts, she was holding a reed pipe to her mouth. Her fingers pressed patterns on that slim surface, but Mai heard no tune whistling from the pipe above the rumble and creak made by the caravan's passage.

A crack splintered the silence. A shout rose from the last third of the cavalcade. Anji turned around at once and pressed his mount forward with Mai following close behind. Men's voices rose in tones of anger, sharp and ugly. Staffs cracked against wood and steel as blows were traded.

'Chief!' called Anji.

Qin soldiers peeled off to follow their captain. Some lengths back, the steady current had broken into an eddy. A wagon listed to one side. Two barrels had tumbled off. One had caught in the wheels of a handcart. A man sat on the ground holding his foot. Men scuffled like wrestlers, arms to shoulders, straining and kicking, and a length of green silk was twisted in the dust.

The chief drove his horse into the middle of this, and the size and weight of the beast was enough to send men scrambling. A youth grabbed the arm of an older man just before he could punch a retreating merchant. Here were men only; as far as she had seen, no women traveled in the caravans that went down to Sirniaka.

'What! What!' cried Tuvi as Anji waited at an intimidating distance with ten soldiers fanned out to support their chief. 'What trouble is this?'

They cursed at each other, shaking fists as they called out their grievances.

The first man was fat, energetic, and ready to throw blows again. 'This man's wagon has rammed into my cart and damaged my goods and my cart. He should be fined for not keeping his wagon in good repair.'

A lean man, puffing and panting, answered him in a breathless voice. 'My axle pin – gone missing – you see how the other is double-looped so it won't slip free. I've been sabotaged!'

Both were overtaken by a merchant splendid in gold and brown robes who clutched a supple leather pouch the size of two fists and shook it furiously. 'Look here! This is my pouch of saffron. The jewel of spices and most valuable! Where do I find it? In the cart of this thief! He's lifted it right out of my wagon, the criminal!'

The man accused of thievery was young. He gaped like a fish tossed out of the water, too dumbfounded to respond to this charge. But others were eager to voice their protests; and many more crowded forward to watch as Anji commanded a boy to run, run, and fetch the caravan master.

'My best bolt of silk, ruined by these blind oafs! Could you not watch where you are going?'

'Aui! The vessel is broken! That is finest oil of naya. Water-white. How am I to be repaid for my loss?'

'What about – my wheel – can't fix – here on the road.'

'I want this thief taken before the assizes. This is an outrage! My saffron!'

The forward portion of the caravan rolled on, heading for Olossi. A gap opened between the forward wagons and this last third held up by the damaged wagon and the gathering crowd. Those stuck behind the breakdown were beginning to raise a clamor, and it seemed some of the merchants were ready to branch off the main road onto the secondary paths and tracks but were hesitant to move because of the presence of the dour Qin soldiers.

She felt cold, and then hot, and not only because of the cloudless sky and glaring sun. She pushed her mount through the soldiers, who reined aside to allow her to move up beside Anji. He had dismounted beside the man transporting the oil. Wiping his fingers along the crack in the sealed clay vessel, he sniffed at the oily liquid, then licked his fingers to taste it.

'Where does this come from?' he asked the merchant.

'The best seeps rise along the west shore of the Olo'o Sea, ver. Right up against the mountains, where the land cracks into fissures and ravines. In the empire, they call it "king's oil."'

'So they do.' Seeing Mai, Anji walked to her horse. 'What disturbs you?' he asked.

She bent, to speak softly. 'There is something amiss here, but I can't explain it. It's only a feeling I have. I'm uneasy.'

He nodded, and whistled to get Tuvi's attention. 'Take Mai and these soldiers and return to the prisoner. Send Tam to bring up the rear guard to support me. I'll remain here until the caravan master arrives.' He walked back to the merchant.

Mai knew an order when she heard it. She had long since learned when there is a crack and when the gate is firmly shut. She rode away with Chief Tuvi, but after all no further altercations disrupted the journey. They had almost reached the outer wall and a wide gate where all the traffic converged when Anji and the caravan master returned.

'Crow's Gate is for merchants and goods and laborers,' the caravan master was saying. 'Because you have a prisoner bound for the assizes, you'll have to enter at Harrier's Gate. They'll want to quarter your soldiers outside the town as well.'

'I see,' said Anji. 'Do the council members fear we'll cause them trouble?'

Tuvi coughed.

The caravan master shrugged. 'I'll speak in your favor, certainly. You've met your obligation, and been true to your promise. But you have to look at it from their way of seeing. You've a strong force, over two hundred armed men. That's always a threat. And you admit that you spun us a false tale, to get out of Sarida.'

'After all this, I would hate to find my faithful men taken as enemies,' said Anji.

'I'll escort you. My journeyman can shepherd the caravan through, and I'll meet him once you are settled.'

'I thank you for the courtesy,' said Anji gravely.

The caravan master nodded with equal solemnity.

This, Mai saw, would be the first test. They would soon learn whether foreigners like themselves had any hope of a future in the Hundred, or whether they would have to turn tail and run, knowing there was nowhere to run. But because Anji appeared collected and calm, she found her market manners and her market face, and gathered her wagon and her slaves and followed as the Qin company and their prisoner split off from the caravan now filtering wagon by wagon through Crow's Gate.

Shai turned his mount in beside hers, since Anji had ridden ahead. 'Do you think after all we'll find no sanctuary here?' he asked nervously.

'We must wait and see.'

'You've a cold heart, Mai, not to be sweating!'

'Anji will pull us through.'

That made him fall silent, thank goodness!

A secondary road ran parallel to the outer walls, which were to Mai's eye an unimpressive collection of log palisades and barriers crudely stitched together. They rode in the direction of the sea and came at length to the river's shore. Here stood a closed gate, framed by stone and capped by a thick black beam. Two guard towers rose, one on either side, manned by archers who leaned on the rail and examined them with the intense and easygoing interest of men who have been bored beyond measure.

'What's this?' asked the younger.

'Call Captain Waras!' called the older to unseen men behind the wall.

'I'm Master Iad,' called the caravan master. 'Well known here,

although my family home lies in Olo Crossing. I lodge at the Seven
Chukars in town, here. Any of your merchants along Stone Field
will vouch for me.'

'You must speak to Captain Waras,' said the older.

The younger nudged him and pointed at Mai, and the older
pursed his lips as if to whistle, thought better of it, and looked away.

They waited.

'I don't like this,' Shai muttered.

'Hush.'

He gave her a bitter look, dismounted, and led his horse toward
the river. She followed his progress with her gaze.

The field before Harrier's Gate had most recently been used, it
appeared, as pasture, cropped short and still sprinkled here and
there with sheep pellets although no sheep grazed within view.
Reeds and tall grass marked the course of the river, now a broad
gray-blue flow spreading and slowing as it frayed into the dozen
estuarine channels of the delta. Huts stood on the far bank, and a
woman in bright blue silk poled a skiff into those distant reeds. The
sun baked them; in patches, where bare earth showed through heavily cropped grass, the soil showed fine cracks.

Mai twitched her shawl forward to give more shade for her face.

A man came to the rail up on the river-side tower. He waved a
hand. 'I know you, Master Iad,' he said. 'You are well come back to
Olossi Town!'

'Captain Waras! Well met!'

'What are these wolves you've brought to my gate?'

Hearing conversation, Shai hurriedly turned back.

'This company of soldiers has guarded us along the Kandaran
Pass most loyally,' Master Iad continued cheerfully, although there
was an edge of anxiety in his tone. 'Led by this man, Captain
Anji.'

'A good number,' said Captain Waras. 'And foreigners, besides.'
The older guard was, laboriously and rather obviously, trying to
count them all, although he had to start over several times. 'Do they
mean to camp outside the walls tonight and depart in the morning
after they're paid? I hear there's a caravan pointed south, ready to
depart in the morning, although it's hot to be out on the road.'

'Not at all. They hope for a further hire here in the Hundred. I'll lay their proposal out in front of the council as soon as the council meets.'

'It's a good number,' repeated Captain Waras. 'That's a lot of men, there.'

'They've done us a service – every one of us, you and me and all Olossi – when we were attacked by ospreys up in Dast Korumbos. Killed them who meant to rob and kill us. The worst kind of knaves. The ringleader was taken prisoner, an ordinand by the rank of captain and the name of Beron. We've brought him to stand trial at the assizes.'

Captain Waras was a considering man, the kind who wasted your time examining each and every peach before he decided that the one you had placed so carefully on top after all was the one he wanted. 'We've had word of some trouble up West Spur. But we heard that the man in question – named Beron – was murdered.'

'Murdered! Not so. We have him right here.'

Waras gestured, and a guard tossed a rope ladder over the railing. Down this the militia captain descended. He wore a heavy leather jacket cut to hang to his knees, and its stiffness made his descent awkward. Otherwise he wore no armor except a leather cap with a pair of red ribbons laced around the rim and his hair tucked up underneath and, at his belt, a short sword. When he reached the ground, a guard, from above, tossed down a stout stick no longer than elbow to hand; it was painted in alternate stripes of red and black and weighted at one end with a shiny metal ball, like a club.

Anji dismounted. The two men surveyed each other, taking their measure.

'You've a strong force,' said the militia captain. 'Two hundred disciplined, armed soldiers, strangers to our land. You can see we are reluctant to allow you to enter town without some surety that you'll cause no trouble.'

Anji nodded. 'You're right to be cautious. It's what I would do in your place. Let my soldiers camp outside this gate tonight. It's no hardship for them, as long as they can water the horses and buy some manner of food – whatever is available – for their supper. I'll come into the town myself with the prisoner, by your leave. Then I can speak in front of the council as soon as it meets.'

'The full council next meets in three days. Wakened Crane. You'll have to attend alone.'

'Together with a small escort for my wife and her slaves. I would prefer it if she be found a decent place to stay. Some place with baths nearby, if you have such.'

She blushed, but he wasn't looking at her although it seemed to her in that instant that he could *hear* her reaction, because of his slight smile, nothing too blatant. A promise, not forgotten even at this juncture. In response, she twitched the silk shawl back, and Waras got a good look at her face for the first time.

'Eh!' said the captain, forgetting words, and recovering himself with a tincture of grace. He nodded at the caravan master, as though the wordless exclamation had been meant for him, and turned back to Anji so deliberately it was evident he was having trouble not staring. She was pleased to see him shaken even in this small manner. When thrown into the wilderness, one must use every weapon at hand. 'I can't allow any of you to bide within the walls. But a bath seems fair. I'll allow you two men for your own personal guard, ver, and four to escort you, verea.' He nodded at Mai.

'We were to meet a reeve here,' added Anji.

'That reeve was the one who alerted us when we reached the border crossing,' put in Master Iad hastily. 'He came in advance of us. You must have heard the entire story from him already.'

Captain Waras had a certain measure of dignity; he had heft and seriousness. 'Given the severity of the accusations, I'd like to take a look at the prisoner. Get a statement from him, his name and clan. If he's alive, that is. Or did you bring in a dead man?'

Master Iad bristled. 'We brought him in alive, so he could testify. See for yourself!' He unlatched the door, opened it, whipped aside the canvas drape, and stepped away.

Mai had lost track of Shai, but now he stepped into view. He had a clear line of sight into the wagon's interior, and the look of consternation and shock on his face could not have been copied by any traveling performer as they acted out a tale. Within that gloom sat the prisoner, cross-legged on the wagon's bed, chin slumped to chest as if sleeping. There was a sudden cold silence, like an unexpected stirring of icy wind into a hot hot day.

'What is it, Shai?' asked Anji, who stood at an angle from the opening. He could not see inside.

Mai already knew. She knew that look on Shai's face. It was the look he always got when he unexpectedly saw a ghost. Always the same look. Always the same.

"'A dart, a dart in my eye, how it stings!'" murmured Shai.

'He's dead,' Mai whispered.

Captain Waras and his men collected more guards and escorted the Qin troop farther down along the river's shore until they reached a side channel in that area where the river became a delta. They forded a shallow channel and fetched up on a small island. Easy to guard and hard to escape from, Anji said, because easy to hear the sound of horses crossing the sluggish backwater.

In this camp, the men had up their tents and set to work with the single-minded concentration she most admired about them. They had leisure now for a hundred tasks. Horses could be groomed properly, weapons polished, knives sharpened, clothing mended, harnesses repaired, pots polished and scrubbed clean. They set to these tasks with a will, all the while seeming to ignore the guards set around them. Yet she knew they were ready to fight. None strayed farther than an arm's length from his favored sword or bow except when they went, in shifts, to wash themselves in a clear-flowing branch of the river; even then some stood guard while others dunked and splashed.

There was plenty of driftwood for campfires. She washed herself as well as she could, although it was not the same as a proper bath. She mended clothing because she had a neat hand with the needle, especially on the delicate lengths of silk. Anji worked alongside the other men, sharpening his sword and polishing his harness.

In truth, despite the threat hanging over them, she was glad for a pair of days where they weren't moving. At first, her worst problem was bugs. But as the first day passed, and a second came to its close, she found herself made restless by anxiety.

'What will happen?' she asked Anji. It was late in the afternoon of the second day. He was seated beside her, replacing one of the leather straps fixed to his saddle. Stripped of grime, and polished, the silver fittings on the saddle gleamed.

He paused to consider her question, then lifted his head and stared across the shallow channel, the fence that bound them to this islet. He marked the placement of the Olossi militia on the far shore and then looked beyond them toward the distant escarpment that marked the high country to the south. There, Mai could just make out the narrow ribbon of road crawling down the long slope down which they had come two days ago. She had felt so hopeful, then.

"'A dart in my eye,'" he mused.

They had gone over the ghost's words again and again. It was the only phrase Shai had heard before the corpse and the wagon had been hauled off by Captain Waras's men; naturally, they had been given no chance to examine either.

'How did we miss the killing? Who wanted him dead?'

Anji had no answer.

32

Keshad sat on a mat under a Ladytree. Off in the distance he heard the river's lazy voice, and the haunting call of a dusk wren. Yesterday morning he and Zubaidit had walked free, out of Olossi. They had walked relentlessly, neither of them flagging. In two full days, they had trudged more than twenty mey on West Track. It would take a caravan three or four days to cover as much ground.

He stared at the string of coin draped over his palm. 'How could you have had that many debts racked up in town? How often were you allowed to leave the temple? How could any slave spend that much money?'

Bai was sprawled in grass just beyond the farthest reach of the canopy, eyes closed and a smile on her face as a fat golden rumble bug looped lazy circles around her head. For reasons beyond his comprehension, two ginny lizards had accompanied her when she had left the temple. Big enough to be intimidating, they were, fortunately, small enough to be carried. Both had spiky frills along their backs; both, he'd discovered, shifted in color depending on their mood and other less obvious changes. They had disconcertingly alert gazes. At the moment, they basked beside Bai, watching the rumble bug with what appeared to be friendly interest. Neither the ginnies or Bai responded to his voice.

'Bai! We only have eighty-four leya left. Oh. And twenty vey. But we can buy a day's ration of rice with twenty vey. To be split between us!'

She sighed contentedly, without opening her eyes. 'I can earn coin, or a night's lodging. Don't worry, Kesh. You worry too much.'

'I'm not worrying! I'm being realistic! How are we going to establish ourselves in a new town with so little seed money? We can't afford to pay a leya here and another there for lodging and food as we travel. We can't afford a ride in a wagon. We'll have to walk the entire way. Not at the prices these villages charge. That man at Crow's Gate wanted two leya for us to ride in the back of his cart, only as far as Hayi Fork. That's robbery! And in that village we just passed through, they wanted a half leya apiece just to stay the night in their empty council house! Because their own Ladytree was so ill-cared-for that it had blown down in last year's storms. That's why we have to sleep out here under a wild-lands Ladytree like the paupers we're going to become.'

She rolled up to sit. 'I heard most of this same speech last night, didn't I? Anyway, I like "out here."'

She scritched Mischief under her chin and rubbed Magic on one puffy jowl, then rose lithely to her feet. She moved differently; the change was impossible to ignore. His strongest memories of her naturally involved the years they had been little children together, when she had followed him everywhere, cried when she skinned her knee, or asked him for help at any and every least obstacle, whether a barking dog or a splinter in her finger or a shadow that had to be circumnavigated. Now she strolled to the traveler's hearth with a feral glide and poked in the ashy remains with a stout walking stick she had cut for herself yesterday. It looked like she was stabbing a man to make sure he was dead. The ginnies ambled after.

The light deepened, made hazy by the heat. The wayside was quiet. They were the only travelers to stop here beside the road. Every one else was likely relaxing in a tub of hot water at an inn. Certainly they had seen no traffic in the hour since they had left the last village behind.

'Doesn't it seem strange to you?' he said, watching her prowl in ever-greater circles around the hearth, pacing out the roughly oval clearing as she searched for certain plants the ginnies liked to eat. Magic had paused, scanning the tree line as if for trouble. Kesh swatted away a swarm of gnats. A pair of dark shapes glided out of the trees and swooped over him, through the heart of the swarm. He threw himself flat, and Bai, turning, laughed.

'Just senny lizards,' she said. 'And a good thing. Sennies will keep the bugs off us tonight. What seems strange to me?'

'How little traffic is on the road.'

She shrugged, then walked over to stand beside Magic, looking in the same direction as the ginny. 'Everyone says the roads are no longer safe. That no one dares walk into the north, past Horn and the Aua Gap. Maybe we shouldn't have taken West Track at all. Maybe we should have walked into the northwest along the Rice Walk.'

'We already talked this over. There aren't any real towns to the northwest where newcomers can set up in business. You know how villagers are. Close-minded, close-fisted, and they smell, too.'

She looked at him. 'I thought from the way you were talking that you'd been up West Track recently.'

'No. Better profits to be made trading south into the empire.'

She grunted. 'Those empire men – drovers, mostly, and mercenaries guarding the caravans – they would come sometimes to the temple. It isn't the law of the Merciless One to turn any devoured man or woman away, but I tell you, those empire men were dogs. It was just a dirty hump to them, nothing sacred. They would say all kinds of prayers afterward, like they were ashamed of what they'd done! Anyway, they didn't smell good. I don't know how you could stand trading with them.'

'My last drover was a good man. He kept silence for the whole trip, and he saved my life by sticking by me when he could have run.'

'Maybe.' With a shrug, she dismissed him.

'Why don't you believe me? Without Tebedir, you wouldn't be free!'

'Never mind. It doesn't matter, Kesh. What matters is that you're finally free, and I'm with you. For a few days at least.'

'A few days? I don't have any intention of indenturing us out, not when we're free of debt.'

'That's not what I meant.' She paused to look down at the male ginny. Magic gave a slight head-shake, then bobbed his head, as if he were actually communicating with her. She walked back to the cold hearth and set the walking stick on the ground. Both ginnies followed her. The sun had set below the trees, and the entire clearing had turned soft and handsome, like an eager lover glimpsed in shadow. 'Help me walk the boundaries. I want to pray.'

'I won't.'

'I can't do it alone!'

'How can you worship her? After what she did to you?'

'What *she* did to me? The Devourer has kept faith with me. It was that old bitch who runs the temple who cheated me and abused me!' She crossed her forearms out in front of her chest in the warding sign. 'That's what you don't understand, Kesh. They'll try anything to get me back. We're not free of them.'

He patted their packs. 'We have our accounts bundles. It's legal. There's nothing they can do.'

'Don't believe it!'

'Why do they want you back? You're a good-looking girl, Bai, I'm sure, but there were plenty of sexier women there.'

'Like Walla?' she said with an annoying laugh. 'I saw you sizing her up. She's a real devourer, though. You have to be careful of them, they like to chew men up.'

'Why would they want you back, if you're not a "real devourer" like Walla?'

'Because I'm the best.'

'Been sucking up too much sap lately?'

'Don't give me that look. I'm not some vain hierodule who serves the goddess for a year in order to have men drunk on wine and fumes worship her as if she was the Merciless One herself. My redemption price would have been much higher—'

'It was robbery!'

'—would have been much higher. You don't know how hard I worked, the things I agreed to do. Gods, Kesh! You don't know the things I did just in the days right before you arrived. All that, just to pay off the debits that accrued from my training.'

'How could your debt have cost *more* to pay off than it already did?'

That shrug was her way of casting him off, like slipping a cloak when you don't want to wear it anymore. 'Let it go. The faster we walk away from Olossi, the better for us.'

'If we don't starve along the way, or puke out our guts from drinking bad water because we can't afford decent wine.'

She circled back to Kesh. Mischief scuttled alongside, and Magic hesitated only long enough to give one last intense stare toward the trees before hustling after the two females before they got too far away.

Crouching, Bai grabbed Kesh's wrist. Her grip was strong. 'We did it, Kesh. Let that be enough for today. We did what we swore when the aunts and uncle shoved us up on the block and started counting their profit. They had enough, they could have kept us and raised us with their own. I'd like to spit in their faces.'

'It wouldn't be worth it.'

Her jaw was tight. She had braided back her hair so no curl or wisp strayed, and then coiled it up atop her head, out of her way. All of her was like that now, streamlined, efficient, sleek, and without ornament. Her expression was unreadable to him. His little sister's face stared at him, grown up and filled out, with that bruise she wouldn't discuss. Little whiny weepy sweet-hearted Zubaidit had gone through a transformation and he did not know the woman before him.

She released his wrist. 'No, it would be foolish. We'll walk, and leave the old life behind.' She cocked her head to one side. 'About that ghost you brought out of the south . . . or is she a demon?'

'Don't speak of it. Let it go.'

'Why not? She was so . . . so . . .' She raised a shoulder, shifted her hip, scratched her bare knee. 'Seeing her, I just wondered what it would be like—'

'Leave it!'

She rocked back at his tone. Both ginnies hissed at him. They had fierce-looking teeth, and their bite was said to be infectious.

'Heya!' he yelped, taken aback.

'Hush.' She stroked Mischief under the jaw, and the female lifted her chin a little and 'smiled' warmly. Magic got a spot on his forehead rubbed. While they were looking at her, she gestured. 'Go on, then. Brother's just jumpy, that's all.'

Mischief moved off, but Magic looked right at Kesh and bobbed his head decisively, as if to remind him who was in charge.

'Heya,' said Bai with a little more force. Magic moved after Mischief.

'Listen,' said Kesh, surprised at how powerfully his anger had erupted. 'Let's not argue. I'm sorry.'

'No. You're right. Let it all be gone. Leave the aunts and uncle and ghosts and bitches and masters to the dying moon where they belong. Our old life is dead twice over, once on the block, and once in inner court three days back.' She rose from a crouch to the balls of her feet, swaying like a woman drunk on fumes. 'Gone gone gone. Gone altogether.'

Branches rustled. Both ginnies stopped, and looked in that direction, but neither seemed alarmed when an apparition draped in rags stumbled into the clearing.

'Gone. Gone. Gone altogether beyond,' it echoed, spinning entirely around, arms pinwheeling. Its voice was a crazed whisper.

Kesh jumped to his feet and drew his sword, but Bai stepped inside his guard and pressed a palm against his chest.

It faced them, rheumy eyes blinking. It was a very old person, as thin as if built of sticks, with skin weathered from sun and wind and hair turned entirely to silver, not even one strand of black to be seen. Kesh could not tell if it was male or female.

'Walking north,' it said in a voice all raspy, neither high nor low. 'Best not go that way. It's all run to blood.'

'Where's your string?' Bai whispered into Kesh's ear. He had closed the string of coins into his weaponless fist, and she pried his fingers open, slipped off ten half leya, and strode across the grass to the creature. She sank gracefully to both knees – kneeling, she was still almost as tall as that shrunken, wasted body – and held out an open hand.

'An offering, holy one. Go in peace.'

The crabbed hand moved so fast that it was too late for Kesh to protest. It grabbed the silver, and scuttled away. 'A blessing on you, child! Do not kiss ghosts. The twice dead cannot love. Also, a fire gnat has just bitten your left ankle. Don't scratch! It only spreads the poison.'

It staggered out onto the road as Bai reached down and – as if bespelled – scratched at her left ankle, then barked a curse, jumped up, and repeatedly slapped the skin where she had just scratched, as though she could batter the stinging bite into submission.

'Five leya!' cried Kesh. 'No wonder you ran up debts!'

'Are you blind? That was a gods-touched vessel!'

'Some old beggar, you mean. Anyone can wear rags and stumble along the road mumbling well worn phrases. "The twice dead cannot love!" Burn it! Now what do we do?'

'I have a hankering to get ourselves into the trees and hide for the night. Scout ahead at dawn.'

'You don't believe in all that ranting?'

But she did believe. She had been raised in the temple, at the heart of the goddess, if the Merciless One could be said to have a heart.

He touched the blessing bowl at his belt, thought about his evening prayers, and shrugged. 'The woods it is. Must we take turns at watch?'

'No need. The ginnies will warn us if any come close.'

He slept hard, curled on his side, but an animal pushing up against his back made him snort awake.

'Hush,' murmured Bai. He saw her form sitting upright beside him. Her hand touched his hair. 'Don't move.'

To sleep, they had crawled into a thicket situated on a rise that allowed them to see the road with little risk of being seen themselves. One of the ginnies was pressed against his upper back and neck as if trying to hide behind his body. He found himself staring through the patternwork of branches, toward the road. Torches flickered a dull red. Banners tied in fours drooped from poles. People tramped along, too many to count, strung out in a line and jangling with the ring and clatter of armed men. They had many horses, all on leads, but only one man was mounted. He rode in the middle, surrounded by the shield made by the rest. The hood of his long cloak shielded his face and fell in massive, lumpy folds over the body of the horse. Except for the sound of their steps and the occasional soft whuffle of a horse, the group moved without talk, striding briskly as they moved west – Olossiward – along the road.

The light faded away. A night-hatch chirped, answered by a second.

Bai leaned so close against him that her hair tickled his cheek.

Her breath was hot on his ear. 'We'll go just before dawn. Follow after them. See what they're doing.'

'We won't! We'll head east and then north!'

She shifted away, but remained silent. The ginny – he still didn't know which one it was – stuck its head up to look over his neck, then ducked down again, pressed right up against him most uncomfortably. He didn't want to shoo it away because he didn't know if it would bite. It was as uncomfortable as a branch sticking into his back. The dreary hours passed in an agony of slowness, but at length he discovered that the mass of shadow off to the right was dissolving into the discrete twigs and leaves of the vast tranceberry bush that had helped shelter them. It was the wrong time of year for berries, which would, he noted with that part of his mind that never stopped toting things up for their market value, have brought thirty vey for a bucketload.

'Come on!' Bai rose. She slung the rolled-up cloak and jacket over her back. 'Let's go. It's light enough to walk the road.'

'Who do you think they were?'

She was already moving through the brush, pausing at the sloped verge to listen and look. Then she scrambled up, the ginnies surprisingly agile, racing in front of her up the slope. She was already fifty paces ahead before he got on the road, and she glanced back, slowed, and waited, tapping a foot. Birds sang their dawn songs in anticipation of day.

'Come on, come on.'

'What's the hurry? The sun isn't even up.'

'Just a feeling in my bones.'

From Olossi to a short way past the East Riding, West Track ran on an almost due west to east axis, parallel to the River Hayi. Past the East Riding, the river curved to the northeast and the road with it, the river dwindling as it moved upstream toward its source and the road reaching for its terminus at Horn.

Standing on the road, Kesh faced Hornward. Bai faced Olossiward. He began to walk east, not looking back. The idiocy of throwing away coin on a useless old beggar still made him burn. His stomach gnawed at nothing. He was hollow and he was angry. But at least he was free. Even free to walk away from Bai, if need be. From everything and everyone, alone in a way that made a smile tic up on his face every time he bit it down, because if he let that smile hit his face in full he would laugh, or he would cry, and he wasn't sure which.

She padded up beside him. The ginnies were draped over her shoulders like an expensive bit of ornament. She didn't look at him. She said nothing. For a long while – at least a mey – they walked east on the road in a silence that was both at odds and in harmony.

How could anyone be so stupid and pious as to give away coin that recklessly? To rack up debts the way she had?

And yet, did it matter? After all these years of toil, of being separated, they had actually succeeded. They were free, and together, able to walk where they willed and disagree as they wished, and no one to tell them otherwise!

Even the road welcomed them, although it could be said that the road welcomed all travelers. It was the coolest part of the day, and the sweetest. But at last the sun rose above the trees and chased away the shadows that protected them.

'The ginnies smell something that's making them restless,' said Bai. The lizards were raising their crests and kneading their feet into her shoulders, tongues flicking as they tasted the air. 'I didn't like the looks of those men. That looked like an army to me. Three hundred and twelve. Enough to cause serious trouble.'

'Three hundred and twelve?'

'I probably missed a few. Three cadres should have three hundred and twenty-four, plus their sergeants and captain.'

He whistled softly, wondering if she were joking, or if she had really been able to count them all.

Her stride caught a hitch; she skipped a step to catch up with him, grabbed his elbow, tugged him to a staggering halt. 'Look! Crows and vultures.'

North, above the trees, the dark wings circled.

33

On the morning of the third day, the day set for the council meeting, Captain Waras came to their island camp with an invitation to the long-promised baths for Mai, her attendants, and the captain and a pair of men, all that would be allowed to enter the city.

In the inner city, on the low ground near the docks, stood a baths complex fit for a rich man, with one wing for men and another for women. Midmorning, Mai found herself here, seated on a stool in a tiled room while attendants soaped her and scrubbed her and rinsed her with bucket after bucket of lukewarm water, just the right temperature for the hot day. After that, she refused the outdoor soaking pool where, it appeared, men and women sat naked together without the least interest in modesty. Instead, there was a smaller pool hidden in a shaded courtyard with little brightly colored lizards scrambling along the latticework walls, pots of orange and yellow flowers, and a dwarf fruit tree whose ripening bulbs were mottled in greens and pale yellows.

The water was very hot. There were several fires tended and tested by the older woman in charge of this wing which kept the temperature stable and a constant supply of steaming hot water at the ready. Mai was the only customer on the women's side except for Sheyshi and Priya. Sheyshi refused to undress in front of people she did not know, while Priya, after washing, proclaimed the pool water to be too hot to be healthy.

Mai sank onto the submerged bench gratefully. Ah! It had been so long since she had really been clean.

Through the lattice she saw a plain courtyard lined with stone benches and wooden racks on which her laundered clothing had been spread out to dry in the blistering sun. It was already a hot day. There also lay Anji's tunic and leggings, now clean. She leaned back and closed her eyes, imagined him joining her in the pool, the two of them, alone and uninterrupted. This was the lowest tower of heaven, where the song of the Merciful One lulled you and you were always clean and well fed.

'Mai?'

She jolted awake, up to her nose in water. Her unbound hair had made a veil around her, floating on the surface of the water.

'No men on this side! No men on this side!' The attendant had a stick, which she brandished with a well-muscled arm.

Anji, dressed, held Mai's clean and dry clothing draped over an arm. He dropped the clothing on a bench and, grinning as he retreated, slipped out through a gap in the lattice.

'We must leave to walk up to the council chambers, plum blossom,' he called over his shoulder.

She was blushing.

The old woman cackled. 'Good-looking boy, that one! What a smile! Cocky, though, coming right in here.'

'We're strangers here,' said Mai, trying out this bid for sympathy. 'We don't know your customs.'

The old woman spat on the dirt. 'Outlanders! I never trust them.'

Startled, Mai said, 'Why not?'

The old woman sat on the other bench and launched into a complicated tale, only partially understandable, about a southern merchant she had taken a fancy to back in the days when she was young, and how he had treated her badly and broken her heart . . .

When Mai realized that the story was going to go on for some time, she got out of the pool, dried herself, and dressed, punctuating her actions with a murmured 'That can't be!' and 'Then what happened?' By the time Sheyshi and Priya were waiting anxiously for her to go, Mai and the old woman – 'call me Tannadit, dear heart' – were best of friends.

'I mean nothing by it, what I said before. It's only the southern men, you see. I've never seen a woman before you who came up from the south who wasn't a slave.'

'All the men are like that one, who come up from the south?'

'Oh, yes, all of them. I'm sure your man is a good one, though.'

'He is. But I'm anxious.'

'What about, dear heart? Pregnant already?'

She felt herself flush. 'Oh! I don't know. I don't think so. We've been traveling a long way, and . . .'

Tannadit's wrinkled hand clasped hers. She had a milky gaze. She was blind in one eye and the other was clouding, but her hearing was sharp and her attention fixed on Mai. 'How can I help?'

'I just wonder if there's anything we need to know of your customs, so as not to offend you folk. Did you know that in the empire, the priests burn any person who worships another god besides their god? That anyone who speaks out of turn to a priest is put to death?'

'Aui! What monsters!'

'That doesn't happen here?'

'Well! Naturally everyone here worships the seven gods. But if a person wanted to speak her prayers to some other god, that would be on her head, wouldn't it? No one here would take any mind of it. Although why anyone would want to worship that cruel Beltak god, I certainly don't know. Not very kind to women, he is.'

'I'm sorry to be so ignorant. Who are the seven gods? How are we to recognize and respect their holy priests?'

The old woman laughed heartily. 'Why, every soul you meet in the Hundred has apprenticed to one of the seven gods. You might as well respect them all, even those who aren't worth your respect! We all serve a year at one of the temples when we're young. Some serve longer, eight years or more, binding over their labor to the temples. Some serve their entire lives because they are poor or because it is their calling to remain in servitude to the temple.' She flexed her arms; she still had strength in her muscles. 'I served a year as one of the Thunderer's ordinands, for I did enjoy cracking lads over the head with my staff. You, I think . . .'

She considered Mai with her good eye, a look of such seriousness that Mai was taken aback. Yet the measuring quality of that gaze had an odd element of respect in it, as if this woman meant to see Mai for *what she actually was* rather than what people thought she ought to be. 'Some might mistake your beauty for your calling, and send you off to be a hierodule to the Merciless One, but I don't. The mendicant's life in service of the Lady of Beasts is not for you, I am thinking. Nor would you feel comfortable as one of Ilu's envoys. You are one who observes more than she talks, yet I do not see you as one of the Lantern's hierophants. A diakonos of Taru, the Witherer, perhaps? Patron of increase and decrease.'

'Fitting for a merchant!' said Mai with a laugh. 'But that's only six.'

She frowned. The brief shadow in her expression made Mai shiver. 'That leaves only the Formless One. A pilgrim of Hasibal? Perhaps. A difficult path to follow, but the deepest. Few walk that road.'

Mai judged her new friend's mood to a nicety, and plunged in.

'Do any outlanders ever come here to settle? Is that allowed? I mean, besides those brought here as slaves.'

'Well they should want to settle here, if everything I've heard is true of that awful place down south of the pass! There's a merchant house whose grandfather came up out of the empire and never went back. Now I know why! Put to death, indeed! Just for speaking out of turn to a priest! I'd have something to say about that!'

'Who would that be? Who came as an outlander and settled here?'

'Master Calon's house, of course. His grandfather – the one who was born in the empire – had a foreign name, but we all called him Beyar.'

'I wonder if he was a third son,' mused Mai.

'He established the house of Three Rings. They mostly deal in flesh.'

'In flesh?'

'Slaves. You might look to Master Calon for advice. He pays his bills promptly. That's how I measure a decent man. He's on the council this year, although he's not among those whose dogs bring back a bird in the hunt, if you take my meaning.'

'I'm afraid I don't. What do you mean?'

'Dear heart, how young and sweet you are, with that disarming smile. I hope your man appreciates you, and treats you well. There's sixteen houses who call the dance in this town. They don't call themselves the Greater Houses for nothing. But these days the Lesser Houses and the guilds are making a lot of noise. Now, I admit, the Silvers keep quiet because no one trusts them. The others know they don't have enough official votes to change things, yet they also know that if you counted each household's vote, they could take power. You can be sure the Greater Houses like things the way they've always been, because that means they get to keep what they have. They won't give up their power on the council easily.'

'I know how that goes,' said Mai, because she did know. This did not sound promising. She'd heard stories in Kartu's market about disputes in other towns getting murderous. 'What about the land beyond Olossi? How is it there?'

'Beyond Olossi? What would you be wanting to go there for?

Farmers. Fishers. They stink. I hear village folk out in the Barrens take a bath only once a month. Whew!' She waved a hand in front of her nose. 'No wonder everyone leaves them alone.'

'Aren't there other towns in the Hundred?'

'Oh. Yes.' She released Mai's hand and found an outlet for her disdain by sweeping the already spotless pavement. 'But those are in the north. You don't want to go there. It gets cold there after the Whisper Rains. That's why they call it Shiver Sky up there. Brrr! Anyway, everyone knows it isn't safe along up in the north anymore. Nothing but trouble up there. All gone to the hells, if you take my meaning.'

Mai knew all about the nine caves of hells, where demons festered and fed on the souls of those who hadn't the strength to be reborn. 'What about other lands? Are there places north of the Hundred?'

'I suppose there must be. West of Heaven's Ridge they say it's barren country, nothing but dry grass and rolling hills with no end to it, and only beasts and barbarians roaming the land. North of the Hundred lies the sea. I hear there are folk living far away, to the northwest, beyond Heaven's Ridge and the sea, but it's very cold there, so the tale says. People actually die of it being so cold. Imagine that!'

Mai sighed. 'Best we stay in Olossi, then?' But she wondered if Olossi was far enough from Sirniaka. 'Is anywhere safe?' she added plaintively.

Tannadit slapped her on the buttocks. Mai yelped, for the old woman still had a strong arm.

But Tannadit only laughed. 'Don't you worry. A pretty girl like you can always find a man to take her in.'

34

It took Keshad and Zubaidit a while to reach the spot where the crows and vultures had gathered. The road descended into a hollow where debris lay strewn to either side like so much flood wrack. At first it was difficult for Kesh to make sense of what they saw, but shapes came clear as they moved closer. Corpses were beginning to bloat in the sun. An overturned kettle had tumbled off a cart with a broken wheel. A dead dog lay on its back, its legs stiffening. Orange silk fluttered, caught in the claws of a thornberry bush. These were the ruins of a caravan, hit by ospreys, as at Dast Korumbos. It smelled like a latrine.

Bai strode into the carnage as if she were wading into storm-tossed waters: careful to keep her balance. The ginnies seemed to be trying to flatten themselves against her shoulders. There were about a dozen open-bed wagons, at least as many handcarts, and no animals except two hands of dogs, all dead. It was a fresh kill. The bodies hadn't yet started to rot, but they would. Kesh kept to the road, which remained clear except for a pair of wagons tipped off the verge.

The line of march, in trying to escape the slaughter, had spilled onto the cleared ground that lay between the road and the straggling pipe-brush and pine forest. At least twenty vultures had settled to feast. They eyed the intruders irritably, and as Bai explored, all but one flapped away to wait in the branches of the nearby trees.

This was not the same kind of attack that had hit the caravan in Dast Korumbos. Kesh fished for a kerchief in his sleeve and tied it over his nose and mouth. There, arched backward over a mound of thick grass, sprawled a girl not more than ten or twelve years of age. Her hands had been chopped off.

He retched into the kerchief, although nothing came up.

Bai knelt, and lifted a baby, but by the way its delicate limbs dangled, it too was dead. At first he thought it wore dull red silk, and then he saw it was naked, covered in dried blood. The beds of those wagons did not carry merchandise; they carried dead people: an eyeless old woman, her toothless, shrunken mouth pulled back in a death's grimace; a pair of boys, each lacking a right hand; a man with a crutch thrown across him, the angle of a tipped wagon concealing his legs. Baskets had tumbled off carts, spilling grain in heaps and mounds. A bladder of ale had been trampled and punctured, and the smell of its good yeasty brew still brushed the air as the last leaked out into puddles. All the harness for the wagons had been cut. What had become of the beasts once pulling them he could not tell.

All was silent except for the buzzing of flies. Even the wind had died, as if in deference to blood and death. If he did not think, he could move past. His hands were cold, but his face was hot in the sun, and his eyes hurt so badly he thought he would go blind.

Bai circled back to him, her expression serene. The ginnies remained hunkered down against her, gone a dull gray color. She seemed undisturbed, as if this were simply a ghastly mural painted on a wall that one might look at, or away from, as one pleased.

If he did not speak, he would be sick. 'I've never seen . . . They cut off their hands!' He pressed the kerchief to his mouth as bile rose and tears burned in the corners of his eyes.

'No, they didn't. If you look at the stumps, you'll see they're healed. Some better, some worse, some more recent than others. These people had already taken those injuries, days or months ago. Look what they have with them: grain, tools, blankets. These are refugees. I wonder what horror they were fleeing from. Out of the north.'

'I guess it caught them up.' Then the heaves hit, and he doubled over, ripped away the kerchief, and threw up on the road.

She stepped away neatly and waited him out. When he stopped retching, she said, 'What of the village we passed through late yesterday? They'll be in the path of these wolves. And after them, all those other villages we passed. We have to go back. Try to warn them.'

'I don't want to go back,' he gasped. His mouth tasted horrible, although he'd had little except bile to vomit. He was dizzy; he could not get the world to stay still beneath him. 'We'll take what we need from these supplies.' He faltered. She was staring at him as if he had begun in truth to spin. 'This will only go to rot, or be eaten by animals! I'm not a thief. The valuables they can keep, not that they can carry them in death. We have to go on! You must see that. I don't want to go back to Olossi!'

'Neither do I. No need to alert the Olossi militia, or any holy officials to preside over the passing ceremony. No need even to drag the dead to a Sorrowing Tower, for you see' She gestured toward the waiting vultures. 'the acolytes of the Merciless One are already come. They and the beetles and the open air will scour these poor dead bodies properly.'

'You're heartless!'

'I am? You're the one who wants to loot the murdered dead and keep on walking as if nothing happened.'

'We can do nothing for them! If we go back, we risk falling into slavery again. You know that!'

'It's true. It's a risk I'm not sure I'm willing to take. What do you suggest, then, Keshad?'

There was no way to look away from the scattered dead. Even if he closed his eyes, the bitter taste in his mouth and the smell rising in the air reminded him of the death that surrounded them. He wiped his eyes with the heel of a hand and found that core of orderly determination that had kept him going for twelve long years of servitude.

'So. So. We can continue on West Track through the Aua Gap and to Horn.'

'Where all the trouble lies.'

'So we hear. We can walk along West Track another couple of days until we reach the Passage. That road will take us north through the East Riding into Sohayil. Or we can walk south into the Lending.'

'There are no paths in the grasslands.'

'We can retrace our steps to Olossi and take the Rice Walk, maybe walk all the way to Sund or Sardia. Or we can walk south-west, back to Old Fort. At Old Fort, there's a track that leads south along the foothills and eventually comes to the southern coast and West Farro.'

Bai walked to the nearest wagon and nudged a corpse of a woman with the end of her walking stick. The woman's mouth gaped, and flies crawled in and out. She had no left hand, only a scarred stump. Bai was right: these were old wounds, poorly healed. The dead woman had been so poor that she was wearing an undyed hempen-cloth taloos, not even a coarse silk weave. The taloos had been mostly pulled off her, yanked up above her hips, and it was evident by the bloodstains on her thighs and pudenda that she had been raped multiple times before they had slit her throat.

'It seems foolish to go into the north, when that's where all this trouble is coming from.' Bai set down the ginnies. She knelt beside the dead woman and tidied the taloos, pulling it down, straightening it. Then she crumbled the dry leaves of a sprig of lavender onto the corpse's pale lips. The rest of the lavender was wedged where the chin had fallen against the shoulder. 'See, here.' She pinched up a trifle between forefinger and thumb, whispered a prayer, and blew the fragments to the winds. 'I saw lavender sprinkled on the other bodies, too. Some holy person has spoken the ceremonies over the dead, succored their ghosts, and opened a path through Spirit Gate. I suppose it was that Lady's mendicant we saw last night. Aren't you glad, now, that we gave her coin? It would have been blood money, otherwise, us clutching it to ourselves now that we've seen this.'

He sighed, touching his blessing bowl. Now was not the time to tell Bai that he no longer believed in the gods of the Hundred, because they had abandoned him.

Magic hissed, crest flaring, and opened his mouth wide as he turned to face Olossiward, staring intently west along the road. Mischief whipped her tail so fast that she seemed to turn around in a flash; she scuttled off the road and vanished into the brush. Magic looked at Bai, and abruptly Kesh understood the eye, the look, the color, the posture: *Can't we go now? How much longer do I have to stand here to protect you and your idiot brother?*

'Trouble.' Bai scooped up Magic. 'Off the road. Now.'

Numb, he followed her as she wove around the wreckage: the staring eyes that did not see the blue sky; a young child stabbed through the back; women, girls, and boys raped before, or after, they were murdered; an old man with his throat cut so deep, severing his spine, that his head had begun to roll off his shoulder because of the slope of the ground. The horror rang in his skull to the throbbing of his pulse. But he must not think on it. He and Bai had to save themselves. These dead could not be saved.

They pushed into the trees, following Mischief's trail, but the pipe-brush and pine saplings gave little cover here in the month before the wet, when plants turned gold and brown as they withered. Back a way they ran, and shoved at last into a thicket of pipe-brush crowded close enough that they could crouch down in their center and peep out between thick stalks. Mischief was waiting here. As soon as Bai set down Magic, the female ginny pushed in close beside him. Bai scritched them, talking a low, soothing voice. They quieted. All went still.

Feet trampled the earth in a steady rhythm, moving fast but without the erratic thunder of the panicked. Bai put a hand on his shoulder as the first rank appeared, coming from the direction of Olossi and marching Hornward. Reminded by the pressure of her fingers, he stopped himself from crying out. There were about thirty armed wolves and at least that many unarmed youths and children bound by ropes and stumbling along with blank expressions of shock. The wolves pushed past the massacre without a glance to either side. These were hard-faced men, and a few women, most dressed variously in leather coats, or in coats with rings sewn on for added protection, or in lacquered hide coats molded to fit the torso; caps of hide curved around heads, held on with a chin strap. The rest wore short robes woven of hempen cloth and had bare feet and bare heads, hair tied up in knots of linen. All carried either spears or swords except one woman who rested a woodcutter's axe on her left shoulder. A few handled wooden shields, while others held lacquered shields cut from hide. All of the shields had a bright red mark on them, a blurry crescent moon that looked as if it had been smeared there with fresh blood.

They had taken slaves in the ancient way, known in story but since outlawed according to the decree on Law Rock: *No one shall take a slave as a prize in war*. This was obviously part of that group which had passed Kesh and Bai last night, marching Olossiward. Now they marched back Hornward with their prize. What lay in the north, that wolves could bring war-gotten slaves to the hearths of honest, or dishonest, citizens? How far and how deep had the shadows fallen?

He swayed, but Bai leaned against him to steady him. The ginnies were absolutely still. He was the only one whimpering under his breath. The wind had come up without him noticing, and the rustle of leaves hid his faint noises.

A child trotting along raised its eyes and saw the bodies sprawled everywhere. It gasped out a sob. The man walking next to it slapped it without breaking stride, and it hunched its shoulder and bit on a hand while the other young ones stared with wide eyes and bitten lips, and bent their stride to walk faster. Children never walked in so much silence. He looked at Bai, but he could see nothing familiar in her. She was a stranger, maybe not Bai at all but some demon who had taken Bai's shape and now traveled with him on its own errand. Demons weren't necessarily malicious. They simply had their own ways and their own hopes and fears, none of which had anything to do with humanity.

The party of slavers moved out of sight, leaving the dust to settle behind them. The orange silk caught in the thornberry fluttered, one corner twisting up and twisting down as it tried to wriggle free. It too was captive. In the trees, the vultures waited with the patience known to all servants of the gods. More had joined them, their scabrous heads light among the dark branches. The boldest lifted, and flapped awkwardly down to land next to a child's body.

He began to shift, to go out there, but Bai caught his wrist in a fierce grip and stopped him. Magic had opened his mouth wide. Kesh was panting, his throat sour and his stomach heaving, but he swallowed it down until his eyes watered and he thought he would pass out.

The vulture exploded off the ground, taking wing.

They came at a trot, in the wake of the cadre. The two men wore short robes but no armor, and each one carried a bow, with a long knife strapped to his belt. Although the others had tramped past without stopping, these two slowed and paused, drawn at once to the bile Kesh had vomited up. They surveyed the ground; they conferred in low voices; bent over, they scoured the road's dust for signs. Like their comrades, they ignored the bodies and the buzzing flies as easily as if it were a sight they saw everyday, and perhaps it was.

Magic pressed himself against Bai's side as one of the men, on hands and knees, followed the faint trail left by Kesh and Bai's passage down the sloping verge and into the grassy cleared space between road and forest. His companion had an arrow ready, and he scanned the trees with a hard gaze that seemed to pierce right through the foliage.

Bai lifted both ginnies and fixed them on Kesh's shoulders. He stifled a yelp. Mischief's tongue flicked against his ear. Magic grunted, displeased to be dumped on this unappetizing male rival. But they stayed with claws clutching Kesh's robe, gazes rising as Bai rose smoothly to her feet. She unfastened the top two ties on her sleeveless jacket, and pushed out of the thicket of pipe-brush. Once away from him, she made as much noise as she could pushing through branches as she approached the cleared verge.

Kesh was frozen, a coward, too stunned to respond as she placed herself in the open.

'Whew!' she said as the men saw her and the crawling one straightened with a leer on his face that made Kesh shiver with disgust. 'I hate peeing in the woods.'

The way her jacket set on her shoulders changed somehow, its tight curve over her shoulders relaxing away as, he supposed, the front gaped open. The two men dropped their gazes right down to her breasts.

She leaped. She had a knife in her hand. Light winked on the blade. It sank into the chest of the closest man before Kesh could blink. Yet when he did blink, two or three times, as if he had a midge in his eye, afterward he saw a new movement, already begun. The other man had lunged, with hand gripped to the arrow. He thrust the arrow as though the barbed arrowhead were a spear. She sidestepped the thrust, kicked up into his groin so hard that bone snapped, and spun away as he howled and doubled over. Meanwhile, as if he had just realized he was dead, the first man collapsed in a flaccid heap, spirit fled.

A knife blade flashed. Somehow, the other man had unsheathed his own knife. Despite his injuries, he cut at her. She sprang, actually flipped twice – hands feet hands feet – and ended up on the other side of the dead man. With a graceful sweep, she bent low and came up with his sword. Blades clashed as long knife met short sword. She twisted hers, and flipped her wrist. The knife went flying and hit the ground with a thunk. He yelped, stumbled out of range, but went down with his companion's sword buried up to its hilt in his gut. She shoved him onto his back as she let go the sword, scooped up his knife, and straddled him.

Face contorted with fear and pain, he thrashed, begging for mercy: '—pray you, Lady, I pray you—be merciful—'

'So I will be. You will be paid, in the same coin you took.' She cut his throat, jumped back as blood spilled, and tossed his knife onto his twitching body.

Turning, she raised a hand to wave. How strange, thought Kesh, that there was no blood on her palms. 'Come on! Quickly! There may be another set of scouts.'

He rose, but his legs could only be moved in a shuffling stagger. The ginnies weighed heavily on his shoulders. He had to lean on her walking staff to stay upright.

She gave him a look, fastened up her ties, and hit the wreckage like a scavenging dog. She collected six bladders of drink and a basket with shoulder straps which she filled with wedges of cheese, flat bread, rice balls wrapped in se leaves, several precious pouches marked with the ideogram for dried tea leaves, and oilcloth wrapped around what was surely dried fish. His stomach hurt, just looking at it. His gaze skimmed across the open eyes and rictus grins of the dead, elided the splashes of dried blood. All at once, he dropped. The ginnies scrambled off as he heaved again. There was nothing in his stomach to lose.

She came back to him while he was still kneeling at the side of the road with a hand shading his eyes and his stomach clenched, all sharp pain.

'Blood takes people that way sometimes,' she said, setting the basket down by her feet.

Her voice could not be that of his sister. Zubaidit, whom he had once known, would have been screaming with hysterics. It infuriated him that this lilu had taken over Bai's form and done violence with hands that ought to have belonged to gentle little Bai.

'I've never killed a man,' he said accusingly.

'Yet how many out of the empire have you sold into slavery over the years to buy us free from our debt?' she asked him. 'Isn't that a way of killing the life a person once had? Isn't that what happened to us? And at least Hundred folk sell only their labor and have a hope of earning out their time. Those slaves from the south will never go home.'

The bile rising in his throat choked him.

Was it the same? No, not at all. Not at all.

'Where do we go?' he asked. All his determination had fled. The buzzing of the flies had sapped him. He was empty. A vulture, seeing them stay still for so long, sailed down to land beside a corpse, and bent its head to tear.

'We have to go back. Think of that village we came through yesterday in the afternoon.'

'It isn't our fault their Ladytree rotted through and fell three years back and the new one is only a sapling. They ought to have allowed us to shelter for no coin in their empty council hall, instead of wanting to charge us just because they're greedy.'

'It doesn't matter how they treated us. We have to go back because it would be wrong to go on, knowing others will be used in this same way. Come on. I found food enough to last us a few days.'

'Looted from the dead.'

'I picked up forty vey, too, although I must say that these were desperately poor folk, to have so little. Or else the wolves already took their coin. Maybe so.'

The ginnies circled the basket, and she hoisted them to her shoulders. She took a few steps, paused, and turned back.

'Kesh? *Kesh!* Come on!'

Her voice had a bark, like that of a snapping dog. He startled as though struck, shook his shoulders, and rose to his feet. No use crying over what was already spilt.

'At least let's stay off the road,' he said. 'At least that much.'

'What difference will that make? They're west of us and east of us now. We're stuck between sections of their company, and I expect they have scouts moving through the forest. That's what I would do, were I their captain. We'll move faster on the road. The ginnies will warn us.'

Aui! No place was safe. He indicated the weapons carried by the dead men. 'What about these?'

'Leave them. Unless you're skilled with a bow.' She was already moving, her long legs flashing as she strode away from him, heading back toward Olossi, the one place he really did not want to go.

He hesitated. He had paid off all her debts. He was so furious that his anger tempted him to turn and walk away from her, deserting her and her idiot schemes and pious scolding.

He couldn't do it.

The quivers were trapped under the dead men, and he didn't want to touch them. He didn't have the stomach to pull that sword free, but he picked up both bows and tossed away the littler one that was flimsy and had too light a draw. You could always sell a good bow. He grabbed the basket of looted food and drink, slung its straps over his shoulders beside his empty pack, tucked the bow in, and hurried after her. You had to stick by your kin. She was all he had.

She strode ahead, the ginnies' tails hanging down behind like ornaments. He huffed along after her with nothing but a red rage and a flowering confusion in his mind. In his haste he did not even mark the huge shadow that overflew them until she cursed and ducked, although nothing had been thrown at her. The booming shriek of an eagle split the air above them. Now he looked up, but it was already too late. The reeve – for it was a reeve – was circling back.

'He's seen us,' she said unnecessarily. 'The hells. Come on. Best we try to make our escape through the forest. The trees give us an advantage.'

'But that's a reeve.' He waited on the roadway, watching the eagle bank around in a wide curve. 'A reeve could help us.'

'Gods curse you, Keshad. Why are you so stupid?' She shrugged off the wine bladders that were slung over her shoulders. 'Never mind. Maybe you're right. Just follow my lead and keep your mouth shut. Take these.'

He took the sacks of wine, leaving him burdened and her free.

More quickly than he would have thought possible, the eagle swooped low, running straight down between the trees and dropping into the canyon made by the cleared road. It hit the roadway with a solid whomp that made him skip back in fear. The reeve unhooked swiftly and swaggered forward with a baton held at the ready.

'Who are you?' Bai pounced so aggressively into the silence that the reeve actually came to a halt, as if she'd slapped him. 'You're out of Argent Hall, by that badge you're wearing. You look familiar, but it seems to me you were gone for a long time and only recently returned.'

'I know who you are,' said the reeve, clearly surprised. He was an ordinary man of middling years and middling height, slender, fit, with a broken nose long since healed and a vicious scar on one bare, brown shoulder that cut through the triple ring of flame tattoos on his upper arm. 'You're the Devouring girl they brought in to warm up old Marshal Alyon. But he died anyway.'

'So he did.'

'Did you murder him?'

'As it happens, I did not. Was that the rumor?'

The reeve's mouth twisted as he thought this over. His eagle fixed its intimidating stare on them. Keshad felt he would be slaughtered if he so much as took one step sideways. Falling to an eagle would be a very bad way to die. He wasn't quite sure which would be worse: gut punctured by the talons, or head torn off by that wicked beak.

'We hear lots of things,' the reeve said finally, 'so it's hard to know what to believe.'

'I was with the old marshal when he died. He was clean of poison. But he was old and frail and heartbroken. That's what killed him.'

'Huh. Good riddance to him, then.' There it was again. He had a tendency to drawl out a rounded 'oo' and to slurp his 'r's. He was definitely not born and bred on the Olo Plain.

'Were you always at Argent Hall?' she asked, as if she had gleaned Kesh's thoughts. 'Or did you come from elsewhere?'

'None of your business. Why do you ask?'

She shrugged, with an unconcerned smile. 'A habit I got into after Marshal Yordenas took on my contract. Just helping him out.'

The reeve cracked a smile. 'I hope he got more pleasure of it than Marshal Alyon did.'

Oh my. Keshad was not much for women. They were complications, and he had never had time for complications. It wasn't his fault that Nasia had fallen in love with him. Now he watched as Bai gave a certain kind of smile with a certain tilt of her hips that got the reeve roped in tight. This could not be his sweet little baby sister!

'We Devouring girls have our secrets,' she said to the reeve with that offering of a smile. 'We're not allowed to tell. That would be going against our oath to the Merciless One. What man or woman would come to the temple to worship if they thought their dearest secrets and desires were talked about later?'

'Sorry I asked, no offense intended,' he said, stumbling over his tongue as he tried to apologize. 'What are you doing out here, though? If I may ask.'

'Oh, just an errand, like you. There was that border guards captain that I had to kill, for he was breaking the law, as you know, *and* he broke faith with the Thunderer, *and* with the Merciless One, I might add. You don't want to face *her* anger. His death was easier than it might otherwise have been. Now I just have one last loose end to tie up, and my contract is finished at Argent Hall.'

'What's that? I can't figure out how you got behind the strike force. They should have stopped you on the road.'

She glanced at Kesh with an anger that silenced him, not that he had anything to say. His chest was so tight he could scarcely breathe. Even she tensed, one hand squeezing into a fist while the other waved in a casual gesture meant to suggest a carefree lack of worry. It didn't look very convincing to Kesh, but that reeve was almost licking his lips and anyway his interest was flagged by a significant stiffening in those tight leather trousers.

'Getting past the strike force was no problem. They know I've been working for Marshal Yordenas, just as you are. I'm on the track of that reeve – what was his name? – the one who got away from me at Argent Hall.' She touched her bruised cheek. 'I have a personal grudge to settle with that one, I'll tell you.'

'Him?' He sneered. 'Our allies in Olossi threw him in the dungeon.'

'Did they? That makes my job easier, then, because I've been wandering out here on his trail and my feet are sore and I had just about given up. Heya!' Her face changed expression as quickly as sun brightens when it comes out behind cloud. 'I don't suppose you could give me a lift? To Olossi? I think that eagle can carry two for a short way. If it gets too heavy, we can always stop along the way for a, umm, rest.'

'Oh, ah, yes, ah.'

'What's your name? Marshal Yordenas kept me away from the rest of you, and I can see why he'd be worried. I see you're Fireborn. I really like Fire-born men. They have a certain . . . *heat* about them that warms us Water-born.'

'Oh, eh, ah, Horas. My eagle is Tumna. But I'm carrying a message uproad.'

'Really? How far?' She glanced at the sky. It was not yet noon.

'Not sure. Two days if you walked it, so by midafternoon today, since they'll be on the road and easy to spot with all those thousands. It just depends on how far they're running behind the strike force.'

'I'm actually in a lot of trouble for letting that reeve get past me. It would be such a help to me if I went by Olossi straightaway, before getting back to the temple. I'm not usually so clumsy as to let them get away once they're marked.'

'Yes, Yordenas was furious,' he said, snickering. 'That was a sight to see.'

'Aui! He was mad, wasn't he? I was happy to leave his service, I'll tell you. Truly, I wish he'd had as much vigor in his other, um, pursuits.'

This was really too much, but the reeve was swallowing it whole. It was true that lust blinded you. That's why Ushara, the goddess of love, death, and desire, was known as the Merciless One.

She pushed her advantage. 'But a contract is a contract. I'd like to finish off that reeve and be shed of my obligation.'

'Well, uh, then, it wouldn't do any harm to take you along . . . I'm going back downroad to Argent Hall *after* I deliver my message.'

'Oh, yes, your message to *them*. If I went along with you, do you think you can drop me just out of sight of Olossi's walls before nightfall? I would be so very very appreciative.'

'I . . . I should do. I mean, I'm to deliver the message, and return with an answer, if there is one. I'm expected back at Argent Hall tonight in any case. Tumna's a strong girl, it's not too far for her to carry us both.'

'Not many eagles could manage it.'

The reeve preened. 'No, I don't think they could.'

Kesh strangled a cough. He was sweating with the sun beating down on them and not a cloud in the sky, and that eagle's stare grinding into him as though to wipe him into the dirt. He dared not move, or laugh, or speak.

'I'm not sure what to do about my hired man. I don't want him to run into trouble. He's, well, if you take my meaning, he's good for carrying a heavy load and not much else.'

'He hasn't much to say,' agreed the reeve, looking Keshad over and dismissing him as no rival to his evident ambitions. 'I'm not sure I can help you with him, though. Every member of the army wears a special coin around their neck to mark their allegiance to the Star of Life. That medallion would give you safe passage, although if you ask me, it's a bit simpleminded to think you couldn't just steal or loot one and pretend to be what you weren't. Still, no one has been able to stand against them once they set their sights on a town, so it doesn't matter. Olossi will be defeated without much of a fight, more's the pity. I was looking for some fun.'

She sighed extravagantly. 'So was I.'

With a lift of the shoulders, she sauntered over to Kesh and bent close, ostensibly to unwrap one of the wine bladders from his shoulder.

'Go back and grab one of those medallions from the dead men,' she whispered. 'Then head for Olossi, but this time stay off the road, you idiot. And stay away from reeves, in case you haven't figured that out. The Argent Hall reeves are not any friends of ours.'

She turned toward the reeve and raised her voice. 'Will your eagle tolerate my ginnies?'

'They look pretty big. That's a lot of extra weight to add on. Heh. Don't know if she'd fancy them for an appetizer before her supper?'

'That settles it!' she said with a laugh.

She transferred the ginnies to Kesh, where they dug in hard enough that he squeaked.

'Hush, now!' she scolded him, or maybe the ginnies. She dropped her voice to a murmur. 'Magic. Mischief. You're to stay with Brother until I get back. Don't let him get into any trouble.' She kissed their snouts and tickled them under their scaly chins, and they replied with chirps just as if they could understand exactly what she was saying.

To Kesh she said, softly, 'I'll expect to meet you in Olossi at, oh, there's a tavern called the Demon's Whip in an alley within the entertainers' district in Merchants' Walk.'

'You owed him seventy-eight leya – for what I'm not sure! I remember that place!'

'Yes. And it was worth every copper. Tell Autad that I'll work off your bill, if you don't want to spend any more of your precious coin. It won't be a problem anyway, since I'll likely get to Olossi before you do.'

'Bai!' he said, hard, under his breath. He couldn't believe this was happening.

She slapped Kesh, as Master Feden and his wife used to do. 'Do what I say!'

'Trouble?' The reeve had moved closer, trying to overhear.

'Not at all.' She turned her back on Keshad and strolled over to the reeve. 'He's scared of being on his own.' She whistled breathily and seemed by the motion of her head to be looking the reeve up and down. The man actually flushed.

'Too bad about those awkward tight trousers,' she said as she came up to him and pressed her palm against his leather vest. 'I guess you can only get into and out of them while you're standing on earth. I wonder if it would be possible to, you know, do it while you were flying and holding on to each other.' She took one step back and rested that hand atop the swell of her breasts under her tight sleeveless jacket.

The reeve swayed as if he had been hit on the head.

'You haven't been to the temple in a good long time, have you?' she said sympathetically.

He gave a little involuntary groan. 'Not allowed,' he gasped. 'The hieros at the temples aren't sworn allies to the Star of Life. So it's forbidden to go. Yordenas is a real bastard about it. That's why it surprised me to find a Devouring girl working at Argent Hall.'

'You know what they say, the master eats the meat he refuses to his dog.'

Horas sucked in a sharp breath. 'Isn't that right!'

'As for the temple, you know we are bound to accept all worshipers within the walls. As for outside jobs, we take whatever hire comes our way, as long as the customer matches our price. Are you ready?'

'Aui!' He wiped his brow, then licked his lips. 'Surely I am.'

He called the eagle by putting a whistle to trembling lips, but Kesh heard no sound. Bai did not shudder or shrink as that huge creature came up behind him so he could hook in. He even had extra harness to strap her in, tight against him. With a sharp cry, the eagle thrust and lifted. The last Keshad saw, the reeve was working to insinuate a hand inside Bai's jacket as the poor eagle beat hard to get all that weight above the trees, banked low in a wide curve, just skimming over the treetops, and headed Hornward along the West Track.

Kesh stood there like a lack-wit until Magic bit his ear.

'Ouch!'

Were the damned ginnies *laughing* at him? They had bright, knowing stares. He didn't like them, but they seemed to accept him as, well, as their idiot brother. You had to be loyal to family.

He shuddered. He had no choice but to go along with Bai's crazy plan, whatever it was. He trudged back the way they had come and at length and with sweat pouring freely he got back to the stinking massacre site. The vultures considered him such a paltry threat that they merely lifted their heads to observe his appearance before going back to their feeding.

By now he could ignore the scene by pretending it did not exist, by covering his mouth and nose with cloth to mask the odor, and by keeping his gaze fixed on the stony roadbed. Only those puddling bodies existed, those two men that Bai had killed, and they were just corpses, nothing that could harm him. Ghosts couldn't hurt you. They had no substance; they were only emotion and spirit.

He knelt beside the man she had knifed in the chest, because this body was less soaked with fluids. She'd taken her knife; he hadn't noticed that at the time, or had he? The ginnies scrambled down off his back and away from the bodies, not liking the tang. He fumbled at the man's garment, found a leather thong along the hairy neck, and with distaste wangled it over the head and fished it off. It was a medallion, like an oversized coin with the usual square hole through the middle but an unusual eight-tanged starburst symbol stamped into the metal. He sniffed it, and bit it. It was tin, not even silver. Allegiance came cheaply, it seemed. He wondered what else the 'Star of Life' was offering. Or what it was; perhaps some kind of secret society banned by guild and council alike.

None of it made sense.

He rose and, reflexively, dusted off the knees of his trousers, then scooped up the ginnies. Yet he paused, there on the road. Bai was gone off on some fool's errand. He had food, and drink, and a decent string of leya as well as a few items that could be sold to set up in a safe town as a laborer or to hire his labor out to a local merchant somewhere.

Should he really chance going back to Olossi? He could not imagine what Bai thought she was up to, or what all that talk had meant between her and the reeve. He had no loyalty toward Olossi Town, or the temple, or the reeve hall. He wanted to start a new life, while Bai had abandoned him in the service of whatever old-fashioned notion of duty she had imbibed at the breast of the Merciless One. Maybe, after all, it was best if they split up, if he never met her at the Demon's Whip.

Maybe.

For the first time since he had been sold into slavery by his greedy relatives, he had no fixed purpose to guide him. So of course, standing there like the idiot he was, he waited too long. The ginnies hissed, and flattened against him as if they expected him to protect them from a threat he could not see. Crows and vultures deserted their carrion in a chaos of caws and wings.

About twenty mounted men appeared out of the east, from Hornward, blocking the road. They were riding toward Olossi. Each man wore a staff tied up against the back of the thick leather jackets they wore as armor, and on each staff, over their heads, flew four long ribbon-like yellow and red flags rippling in the wind. When they saw Keshad, they all drew their swords.

35

After the last years with his luck turning sour at every chance just to spite him, Horas knew that fortune had finally given him an armful of the very best. He'd been happy to fly messages for Marshal Yordenas these past months since he'd come to Argent Hall. For one thing, it gave him insight into the plots and plans of those who played the pipes to which the rest of them danced. And anyway, it was better flying messages than having to cool his heels at the hall with all manner of restrictions set on him while the master ate the very meat he refused to his dogs.

'Heh,' he said, liking the phrase. He'd gotten his hand inside her vest, and he tweaked a nipple.

'None of that,' she said sharply. 'You've no idea what I can do to you if you make me mad. Aii-ei!' She gave a yelp as Tumna dipped, and pulled sharply up again. Then she laughed as folk do when they are scared and thrilled at the same time.

A hot shiver coursed through him. Her breasts were firm and shapely, and her tight buttocks ground up against him because he had hitched her into the spare harness with her back to his front. He was a little taller, and could see over her, which was a good thing since Tumna was huffing and beating hard trying to get loft. They hadn't found a good updraft yet, no doubt because they were too close to the river, but he didn't care. It had been months since he'd worshiped the Merciless One, not for lack of trying.

'We're forbidden to enter a temple,' he said.

'No one can be forbidden the temple.'

'But he'd know. He killed one reeve for disobeying.'

'I don't remember that! Whoo-ei! How do you get used to this?'

But he was used to flying, the dips and turns, ups and downs, heights and dives. It was the memory of the quick and brutal death that softened him, and she seemed immediately aware of his distress.

'In all that time, there's one thing I never did discover,' she said over her shoulder. 'Where Marshal Yordenas came from.'

'Don't know and don't care.'

'Where do you come from?'

'Haldia.'

'You're a long way from home.'

She shifted. The feel of her body, helpless in his grasp and moving against him, got him going again, burning and full. She sensed it, and twitched her buttocks right up against his groin until he groaned and begged her to stop, or let him land and have done, they could just find a clearing and land and no one would be the wiser.

'Oh. Oh, no,' she said with a laugh as Tumna found a draft and rode it up. 'This is amazing! You know, you can't serve the Merciless One if you're too hasty. How I despise men who are hasty. Surely you aren't going to be one of *those*? I thought you were strong enough to take your time.'

'I'm strong. I've bided my time this long, haven't I?' He was sweating so much that beads ran down to sting in his eyes.

'Bided your time in Argent Hall? It's true, Marshal Yordenas is a slimy worm. I didn't like him, and I'll tell you something in confidence. If you promise not to say.'

Then she did it a second time, and it was killing him with his trousers so tight and nothing to be done up here, and Tumna slipping out of the updraft into a glide over the trees, the first real height the eagle had gotten so he daren't land now and lose all that effort. Best keep his mind on other things.

'I promise not to say. I hate Yordenas. Always have. Arrogant sneering bastard.'

'He really is a worm. He's got a limp prick.'

'Heh! No. Truly?'

'Truly. No milk in him, I'm telling you. What a disappointment! But I can tell you're nothing like that. You're as full a man as I've snuggled up to in a long while. Tell you what.'

It was hard to talk because he was so horribly aroused between the smell and shape of her and knowing he was going to get something Yordenas couldn't have. It was like the sun shining right in your eyes, blinding you. It was agony. 'Ah. Ah. What?'

'Look at that view!'

He could see the view anytime. It was the view of her that was something new.

She went on breathlessly. 'Let's see your message delivered, and us on our way back to Olossi with enough time in the day, and I have an idea about how to get those trousers off you while we're still in the air. Want to try it?'

Just thinking of it was almost enough to push him over the edge. 'The hells. What do you think?'

She laughed. 'Careful, now. You don't want to be spilling your milk too soon, do you? Here, now. Tell me a story.'

'Don't know any stories.'

'Tell me about where you grew up.'

'Nothing to tell.'

'You got to be a reeve. That must be something to tell.'

'Not much. I hated the village I grew up in. It was full of prating, mewling farmers and foresters and carters who would go on and on about what we owed the gods, and good manners, and where I should serve my apprentice year when all I wanted to do was serve the Thunderer, and how a man ought to behave when that wasn't

what I wanted at all and I didn't see what business it was of theirs
to be telling me what to do!'

'They're like that at the temple, too, the old bitches. Always
ordering a person about.'

'Heh. Yeh. Then there was some trouble over the headman's
daughter and the rights to the best parcel of land, but of course they
would all plot against me, so after I – well, anyway, after that I left
and walked all the way to High Haldia. I'd heard a man could get
work in their militia, and I don't mind saying I was strong enough
to do their kind of work. I was good with a staff, always was, ever
since a boy, and good with a bow, did a lot of hunting along the
river when I was a lad. That's all even though they wouldn't let me
serve my apprentice year with Kotaru, but I showed them by thrashing every one of those who did, in all the villages nearby. But
anyway, they didn't take kindly to me in High Haldia, for their captain was jealous of how good I was with the staff, better than any
of his men, although of course he wouldn't admit to it and had to
spew some other such vomit about why I wasn't fit for their puny
little militia. I thought I'd have to work felling trees again, which
wasn't to my liking, I'll tell you, even though a man has to eat, but
it came about that a consortium of merchants was looking for
guardsmen to accompany a caravan upriver to Seven and up the
Steps to Teriayne. That wasn't bad duty, even though the caravan
master was a real prick about everything and let me go as soon as
we reached Seven. I spent a while there doing this and that. One
thing led to another, and next I knew I was sent with a supply train
up to Iron Hall and after that Tumna chose me. That was a surprise!
I showed them, didn't I?'

'You showed who?'

'All those who said I wouldn't amount to anything. But I showed
them!' He was juiced, the words flowing into that sympathetic ear,
and the story of his many grievances at Iron Hall tumbled out as
Tumna labored upriver parallel to West Track. How the arms
master had picked on him, and made fun of him in front of the
others, just because the man didn't like that one time he had gotten
in past his guard and scored a hit to his shoulder. How that hireling
girl had told him off when he'd made her an offer, and damned if
anyone would speak to him that way, but he'd shown her, hadn't

he? You didn't treat a man with so little respect and expect him just
to walk away. How he'd gotten passed over when it came time to
appoint a new wing leader, which ought by rights to have gone to
him but after all the marshal had favored that bitch of a northerner
out of the high country, probably because she was milking him not
because she was anything special as a reeve even if the rest of them
did sing her praises just because she had a creamy way of talking
sweet to them all. And then she'd pretended to be kind and sorry
afterward, the way you would scratch a dog's head when it was
whining, not that he ever whined even when he got cut the short
end of the stick. Anyway, it wasn't his fault that man assaulted him.
You didn't have to take that kind of nasty shit-talk from common
farmers just because you were a reeve and ordained to keep the
peace, as the veterans were always droning on about. Reeves ought
to be treated with respect and not shoved and cursed at and called
rude names. So it wasn't his fault that the man had pushed too far,
and he'd retaliated with perfectly reasonable force. Not his fault at
all, no matter what anyone else said. They were overreacting, just
because the man died when after all it was his own bad temper that
had done him in. You'd think they would have taken that into
account, but it always seemed the marshal – everyone, for that
matter – weighed in against him whenever there was trouble.

'You've an eloquent way of telling your tale,' she said. 'I do feel
I know you better now. How do you like it at Argent Hall?'

'It's a little better,' he said grudgingly. 'There's a good group of
reeves there who have taken a liking to me, but I must say that
Marshal Yordenas is a disappointment. He's weak. Too puffed up
with his own importance. If the lord commander hadn't appointed
him marshal, he'd never have risen so far.'

'The Commander of Clan Hall? Appointed Yordenas as marshal?
I thought reeves elected their own hall marshal – Oh . . . of course,
I'd forgotten about the lord commander's part in all this.'

'Hard to see how you could overlook it, considering this is his
army.' Because he had a sharp gaze honed from years as a reeve, he
gestured to make sure she saw the sight coming into view where
West Track cut across open country. 'There they are. Tumna usually
would cover this distance faster than she did today. That's about
two days' march we've covered just since midday. I don't want you

to think she's like other eagles, she's much better, but the weight slowed her down.'

Her body tensed, but there was nothing sexual about the way she felt against him now.

'What?' he asked suspiciously. 'What's wrong?'

She relaxed, and gave that twitch against his groin that made him suck in breath between clenched teeth, thinking of how hard it was to wait to devour her.

'I just didn't expect so many,' she said.

From the height, it was an impressive sight as Tumna circled in to seek a landing site. It was the only army Horas had ever seen, certainly, although he understood that the northern army being fielded was twice this size, the one they were going to throw against Toskala and Nessumara after they finished off the city of High Haldia. The vanguard was out of sight where woodland concealed the road, but the body of the beast stretched a fair way back with men marching in ranks of six with six abreast, each of these cadres separated from the next by a banner and sergeant, and three such sergeants to a company with its triple banners and captain, and six companies to a cohort, each cohort assigned a marshal and badge according to the taste and whim of their commander. Six cohorts had been sent against Olossi, although the mounted Flying Fours had been split into foraging groups, one of which was riding two days ahead as their strike force while the rest were split into cadres and subcadres roaming up and down the road, scouting or probing out on raids into the nearby countryside.

'I thought . . .' She paused.

'You thought what? I'm not stupid, you know.'

'No, no,' she agreed, resting a hand on his right thigh, right up close to his groin, stroking it just enough to set the flame burning higher. 'That's why I know you can answer me. The one thing I've never understood. What's in it for Olossi's council?'

'The hells. You *are* just a Devouring girl, aren't you? More tits than brains.'

She giggled, and gave another of those killing twitches. 'Is that what they say about us Devouring girls?'

'Not most people. Most people would give me a good scolding for you know how they will blab on about the duty we owe to the gods and how we each serve and how every service maintains the balance and the many streams that flow in the world. But I say, who would serve the Devourer and give for free what they could be getting coin for, if they didn't want a lot of filling up of what's otherwise empty? Eh?'

She laughed, genuinely amused, and for an instant he was furious, thinking she was laughing at him somehow, and then he realized that of course she was agreeing with him.

'A lot of filling up, you like that, don't you?' He pumped against her buttocks, wishing they weren't both clothed although in fact that kilt and vest she was wearing didn't cover much.

'I do like a real man filling me up, that's true. But I so rarely meet one. I guess Olossi's council will be getting the same treatment, eh?'

'Not at all. Heh. They're getting nothing. They just think they're getting a good milk, but they'll just get a stiff shaft and nothing to show for it, which is all they deserve. "Greed makes of men rank fools."'

'So it does. Whoo-ah!' She actually gripped his hips, tensing with fear, as Tumna came down fast to land with a bump and a thump in the grass close beside the road. Then she laughed.

The soldiers kept marching. They had long since learned to ignore the reeves who came and went. Horas ran his hands up and down her lithe body while he still had her hitched against him, but here damn it anyway came a captain wearing the lord commander's colors riding right toward them, on a mission, just as he was. He unhooked her, and she sidled fast out of reach of Tumna's beak, not that the eagle would do anything to her if he didn't command it done. Tumna was strong, and that mattered, but she was balky and slow to obey, and her balkiness had gotten worse over the years, worse luck for Horas, who never seemed to get much good fortune come his way although the Devouring girl stood there waiting to see what he wanted her to do, with a dumb, expectant look on her face that got him all hot and bothered again just as the captain rode up and halted at a prudent distance and looked them over.

'Reeve Horas?'

'Eh, yeh. Captain Mani. Who do I report to today?'

'Who's that?' asked the captain with an ugly frown and a curt tone.

'No need to bark at me like that!'

The captain gave him a look that Horas wanted to scrape right off his face, but he held his temper in while the captain gave the girl a second look. 'Who's that? And why's she here?'

She raised both hands palm-up in the manner of a pilgrim come to worship at the temple. 'I'm the Devouring girl hired on by Marshal Yordenas at Argent Hall. Maybe you heard of me.'

'I didn't,' said the captain.

'It's a long story,' she said with a lazy smile, 'but maybe we can talk about it at length, later.'

'Hey!' objected Horas. 'You're mine!'

She had a way of lifting her eyebrows that made him feel he was already in the saddle. He flushed.

'I belong to the Devourer,' she said.

'I'm not interested,' said Captain Mani. 'Except in what you're doing here.'

She shrugged. 'Marshal Yordenas of Argent Hall set me to kill a reeve out of Clan Hall who came nosing around. But the reeve got away, so I was out on West Track looking for him when Reeve Horas here found me on the road and kindly let me know that the Olossi council had already caught the reeve and put him in their dungeon. So I asked for a lift back to Olossi.'

'To do him in?' asked the captain.

'If need be. I like it said that I finish what I start. Reeve Horas offered me a lift to Olossi, and I took it. Naturally, it meant I had to come on this part of the errand first.'

The captain turned his stare on Horas. 'I suppose you hoped to peel and pound the nai root on the side, eh? On your way back to Argent Hall and Olossi?'

'None of your business what's done in the hand of the Devourer!' How these tight-lipped bastards made him want to slug their sneering faces!

Captain Mani shook his head with a grimace of disgust. 'Keep it in the temple, then. That's where it belongs. Move sharp. The lord commander saw you come in and is wanting your report.'

That shrank him down to size. The lord commander was not a nice man, or a patient one. Not that Horas was afraid of anyone or anything, but still, the lord commander wasn't to be kept waiting.

'All right, then. She can wait here under guard of Tumna.'

'I'd like a drink and a bite to eat if there's anything to be had,' she said, with a sly smile, probably thinking to earn a little coin with a few quick milkings while he was off giving his report.

'She'll come along where I can keep an eye on her,' said the captain. For once, Horas figured this was a man who would keep his hands dry.

'All right,' he said grudgingly. He commanded Tumna to stay. With a downcast gaze, the woman followed as he slogged over sun-bleached, heat-dried grass toward the road, keeping pace with Captain Mani. They didn't speak. A drum rattled out a rhythm, repeated twice, and the beat was echoed in both directions up and down the line. Soldiers faltered, and came to a halt, then set down their weapons and made themselves comfortable on the road. They drank, chewed, lay back to nap, and there a quartet formed a square and began rolling dice. Men did stare at the Devouring girl as they crossed the road and pushed into the forest on the other side. Some even licked their lips. It was good to know men envied you for what you had. He thought of slapping her on the butt where everyone could see, but then Captain Mani gave him such a look that next thing he knew his hand was in a fist and it took all his control not to punch the thin-lipped bastard.

The first rank of trees beyond the road were growth come back after an initial felling, not yet sturdy enough for heavy building. Past this strip of woodland lay open ground stretching all the way to the river's edge, which was here steep because of the way the swift-running current cut under the land. Downstream, a herd of horses had been loosed to graze. Closer, cloth had been strung between trees as a roof, and gauzy curtains hung to make walls that undulated as the breeze groped them.

'Stay out here,' said Captain Mani to the Devouring girl. 'Reeve, go in, as you've been commanded.'

He looked at the woman, but she was staring toward the horses with eyes narrowed and mouth pursed tight just like all those women when they told him to go milk himself. He hated that look. The captain coughed sharply, and he hurried over to the enclosure although it didn't seem there was a door, only places where curtains overlapped, allowing entry if you fingered them aside and slipped between them. The grass here by the river was still moist and green, curling around his knees. The thin curtains curled around him as well, as he pushed the cloth away from his face and found himself in the shade facing the lord commander.

The lord commander was an attractive man with a northern look to him, a light-brown complexion, broad cheekbones, and dark-brown eyes with lashes as long and pretty as a girl's. His beard and mustache had a trim look to them, not a touch of gray, and his black hair was braided in three loops. Mostly, Horas noticed the rich cut of his clothes, the kind of things a reeve could never afford. Best-quality wide trousers were tied over a colorless silk shirt so fine it seemed to shimmer. Over the shirt he wore a sleeveless, knee-length jacket the same dark blue as the trousers and embroidered in the same color thread down the front, the kind of decoration rich men wore to show they had the money to pay a craftsman to do painstaking work that most people would never come close enough to notice. Thrown over all this was a gold cloak so light and fine that he boiled with envy. When would he ever possess such fine things? It wasn't fair.

The lord commander stood beside a table on which a long map had been unrolled, weighted at the edges with cunning ivory carvings the like of which only rich men could afford. He was speaking to four underlings, punctuating his comments by tapping on the map with an arrow.

'The march on Olossi is our first volley into the south. If you deliver the town to us, then we'll see about your reward. But from today, you captains are on your own with this campaign. We have to return to the north by the end of the day. There's too much going on there, more resistance than we expected at High Haldia—'

He broke off as Horas walked into his line of sight. With a sweeping, scornful gaze and a harsh frown, he took the reeve's measure.

'You're from Argent Hall. I expected you sooner. What's your report?'

The lord commander had the kind of power that made you tuck your head even though to be spoken to in that way really made a man want to growl back. Horas hated the way he sounded when he replied, like a squeaking boy caught licking sugar cakes by the meanest of his aunties.

'Matters have not changed since two days ago. Heh. Eh.' He cleared his throat and found a better tone. It wasn't easy to stand up for himself while keeping his gaze slanted off toward the map. 'The most recent caravan up from the empire brought along a mercenary company, two hundred strong. They cleared the roads. Rumor has it that the malcontents on the council will choose this moment to strike. They'll vote to allow this company to stay and continue safeguarding the southern roads. Meanwhile, Marshal Yordenas awaits word from you as to the disposition of his forces. As I understand it, that reeve who was nosing around lies in the dungeon of the Assizes Tower. I've heard it said he's very ill.'

'Why have they not simply killed him and have done with the threat?'

'There were witnesses to his arrest. Questions will be asked.'

'Look at me!'

He met the lord commander's gaze. A stone might have dropped into the pit of his stomach. He was stricken with an intense fear that the cloth walls and ceiling would fall inward, wrap him, choke him, all his breath sucked right out of him by that touch until he was only a dead husk, withering into bones.

He thought he heard a woman's voice speak a single word. The lord commander's gaze shifted away, and Horas dropped hard back into himself. He was sweating, and trembling. The other three men – three dressed in soldier's jackets and short cloaks and one dressed in humbler garb – were staring at their feet. They were afraid, too. Everyone was afraid. Even, strangely, the lord commander, who brushed his chin with the back of a hand and came a step closer, with a gesture as if he meant to thrust the point of the arrow into Horas's eye.

'That's not good enough. Why haven't they killed him?'

'They mean to bring him up on trial at the assizes, that's all,' Horas said in a rush, tripping over the words because if he directed the lord commander's anger elsewhere then the man would not be mad at him. 'They were waiting for that border captain to be dead, so they'd have a charge to lay on the reeve and evidence to go with it. Now that they have the body, the hearing and trial can go through the proper assizes ritual. That's how they plan to discredit the council faction that is trying to take over.'

'It's taking too long.'

'Oh, eh, yeh, of course! Clumsy oafs! No wonder they need a new governor. They're not fit to govern themselves. But I've got the Devouring girl with me, the one that killed the border captain, so she claims. She tried to kill the reeve, but failed. She's saying she'll go back and finish him off. Not much he can do when he's stuck in the pit, eh?'

The lord commander's gaze sharpened. He sniffed, as if taking in a scent. His teeth showed as lips parted, and his tongue flicked out. 'A Devouring girl? Where is she?'

Horas shuddered. Spiders might crawl on his skin so, to make him shrink away in fear. The man had a cruel voice.

'Lord Radas. Enough.'

The words came from beyond an inner wall of gauze. As if in response to that quiet voice, a wind caught the filmy hem of that inner wall and lifted it enough to give him a glimpse into a second chamber hidden away within this temporary shelter. A woman was seated at a low writing table, with her back to him. Just before the curtain fell back into place she raised her left hand and curled her fingers in toward her palm. Then the gauze slid back, and he could not see her.

He hesitated.

'Go on,' said the lord commander, voice tight with suppressed fury.

Horas figured it best to move fast. He had trouble finding the opening. The cloth seemed heavier than it should have, the air so thick it was almost liquid, but he squeezed through and came into a cooler zone. The awning overhead rolled in waves as the wind stroked it. All trace of the outer chamber and the outside world was erased. The isolation made him twitchy.

She sat cross-legged on a pillow, back board-straight, her hair bound in a single thick braid running true down her spine. The blackness of her hair blended with the night-black cloak hanging from her shoulders, its lower portion draped in graceful folds around her hips and legs. She seemed to be sitting on a spear whose haft and point stuck out on either side. A table rested in front of her. Her body blocked his view of the table except for a few items lined up straight, and parallel to the table's edge, to her right side. There lay a common dagger, nothing ornamented or fancy, but it looked serviceable; you could stab a man in the guts with such a dagger if he pushed you too far and it would kill him if you got it in deep enough and in the sweet spot. There was also a sharpened, hollow green stick, recently cut from a stalk of pipe-brush, the kind of thing you could use as a stake or to stab through the flesh of a moonfruit and suck out the juices inside. Closest to her elbow lay a narrow wooden box that contained four writing brushes resting on a silk bed with an empty space where a fifth brush must normally reside. That fifth brush was in her hand. The paper on which she was writing was hidden by her body. There was no one else. Perhaps she was the lord commander's private clerk, his secretary, who took down his decrees and pronouncements and orders.

Without looking at him, she spoke in a pleasant, friendly, warm voice.

'Reeve Horas, I am relieved and pleased you have come so promptly. What is your report?'

He repeated what he had told the lord commander.

For a while she did not reply. He couldn't see her writing hand, but that arm rose, bent, retreated, and shifted forward, as she brushed down words. He shuffled his feet, scratched at a bug bite on his jaw, and, thinking of the Devouring girl, gave a reflexive nudge to his crotch.

'Come around where I can see you.'

How was it that such mild words could dig into a man's worst fears? Hot tears filled his eyes, and he hated the Devouring girl, for she had brought this on him, surely. But he walked around to the front of the table, sure that his legs weren't shaking. He wasn't weak like those men who pissed themselves, or who fell begging to their knees. He hadn't even met this woman before. This was just spillover from being on the ugly end of the lord commander's annoyance, a dangerous thing, truly, but he was a reeve and therefore he had stature no common soldier could possibly gain.

Aui! After all she was a woman not much older than he was, one who had celebrated three feasts but still waited on the fourth and fifth feasts of life. She was ordinary in all ways, with the ample body best suited to a woman of her years, a round face with regular features such as any hardworking and prosperous householder might have, and confident hands. She was obviously no warrior trained, not like the lord commander, whose sword could stab a man through the guts, whose captains would order men strung up by their thumbs or tongues or ears if they displeased the lord.

A writing mat had been rolled out on the table and paper placed upon it, weighted with a stone in each corner. The long stick of ink, carved in the shape of a crane with head bent back as if looking over its shoulder, had not been cut, and the ink basin with its sheen of water was clear. The paper remained blank. The hairs of the brush she held in her hand were dry.

This much he glimpsed before he placed himself directly in front of the table and cast his gaze down because aunties liked young men to stand humbly before them. It was the coin they demanded, if you wanted to eat and be clothed and get work in the village. He clasped his hands behind his back to hide that humiliating tremble.

'Look at me,' she said kindly.

Surprised at the request, he looked up into her steady gaze.

At first he was reminded of the nicer aunties who lived in his village, the ones who swept their porches and weeded their gardens and washed and cooked and spun and tended their silkworms and engaged in their small crafts and gossiped by the well. The ones who said it was best to give a rebellious boy a second chance, because such high spirits might mark the sign of a lad destined for greatness. She was just such a woman, come from a humble background, no different at all.

No different.

Not at first. Not until it seemed you were being twisted inside out and your secrets pulled like fish from water to gasp out their lives at the mercy of the fisher. Her gaze was a hook caught in his head. The world was clear but it was also swallowed in a haze he could not penetrate. He drowned in memories, each one plucked out and set before him like a gem for sale in the marketplace. Forgotten voices roared in his ears, and every spike of fury and prod of lust and cut of greed and claw of envy stormed in his heart *and he was ashamed of it* until he thought he would pass out. But he did not pass out, though he wished he could.

'Assault, rape, murder,' she said with the same matter-of-fact tone an auntie in the market points out which vegetables she wants.

'That is just what lies at the surface. A rough start in your life, Horas.'

'They asked for it!' His hands were stinging, and his heart pounded in his chest so loud it seemed like those drums that had earlier called the army to rest, only he couldn't rest, only stand there, sweating and shaking and as flushed as if he'd been standing in the sun all through the blasting heat of a blazing afternoon.

She looked down at the blank paper and set down the brush. Suddenly it was cool again, and he heard wind in the branches, and the murmur of the captains making their plans with the lord commander, and folk bantering outside. The hells! Some of those dogs were chatting up his girl. Their voices drifted through the gauze.

'Think of me as a dagger,' the Devouring girl was saying in a voice made strong by a laugh bubbling up. 'Watch you don't get pricked.'

'I'd like to prick you,' replied a wit.

'My friend, you'll need to sharpen that dull point of yours if you want to be pricking anything.'

'She's handling them with ease,' said the woman. 'I suppose such dreary banter is the kind of thing hierodules become accustomed to when they venture outside the temple. Within the temple walls, no one dares act with such disrespect. The ceremonies are sung and danced and paced out in their proper order, and with proper respect to law and custom. Those who walk in the hand of the Devourer are holy in the sight of the land. It falls ill with the ones who think only of their own lust and not of the holy act of joining. Isn't that right?'

He slid his gaze sideways so as to avoid hers, but he knew that if she demanded he look at her again, he would have to.

'I believe that Wakened Crane is council day in Olossi,' she continued, without making him look. 'Which is today. Go to Olossi immediately. Speak in private to their leader and tell him that these mercenaries must under no circumstances stay in the Hundred. After this, attend the council as a silent observer. That will be message enough to the council members who may think to disagree with those who rule them. Watch and mark who speaks and what they say. Set the hierodule on her road, to eliminate the imprisoned reeve. Then return afterward to Argent Hall and tell Marshal

Yordenas that I am displeased with him.' Her fingers brushed the hilt of the dagger. 'Just that. Nothing more. He'll know what I speak of. As for you, Horas, know that I will know. I am watching you now. I do not like disrespect toward those who are holy in the sight of the gods.'

She picked up the dagger and turned it in her hands as though it had a message for her. This was his dismissal.

He staggered outside and stood there panting until the world stopped spinning. When no one offered him so much as a drink to cool his parched throat, he cursed the lot of them for selfish bastards, but not out loud.

'Come on,' he said to the Devouring girl.

She looked surprised but followed without asking questions. His thrill in the day, in the catch, in the promise, was ruined. On West Track, the army was being drummed to its feet. Tumna waited in the open ground beyond. He hooked into the harness and hitched her in before him, and she was puzzled but cautious, trying to read his mood.

'We'll go quickly,' he said. 'Get there as fast as we can.'

That was all. They flew to Olossi and though he thought once or twice of the things the Devouring girl had promised to do to him and let him do to her, fear doused his rod. He showed her no disrespect, and without his charm to loosen her tongue, she made no offer.

36

The dream unveiled itself in the gray unwinding of mist, but this time the mist did not end, nor did it part. There was offered both drink and food on a tray lowered down through a hatch in the ceiling. In a haze he gobbled down what was there, but it all came right back up again. Much later, he drank, coughed up some but kept down a little, and after dozed fitfully. He could not remember where he was, only that he was so terribly thirsty.

There it was again, the bowl, and he drank, but the liquid churned in his stomach and he retched it all up. The effort exhausted him. His head was shattered with pain. Through these choppy waves he sank into the depths.

Later, he discovered he had emerged out of deep waters into a kind of waking delirium.

Woozy-headed, he tried to make sense of his surroundings. There was an awful stink, and when he managed to hold up a hand he was after all holding up two hands; both blurred even while he felt he had another arm braced under him. Had he grown a third hand? The effort of thinking and moving made his guts lurch and bowels go loose, and he coughed and heaved and felt the fog overwhelm him once again.

He dreamed, but in fragments: the pain in his head; Scar; a woman inviting him to her bed with a sly smile; a field of rice stubble; sipping from a bowl of water whose pure fragrance drowned him; the deserted temple up in the high hills of the Liya Pass that stank of fear and shame. Here he is wandering. Where has Marit gone? He tries to call after her, but his voice makes no sound. He will never find her.

A click and a scrape woke him.

'For shame!'

He stirred, hearing a voice young and feminine and pleasing.

'Is it right you allow this man to lie in his filth? He looks ill. Is he even conscious?'

'He's a murderer.' That was a man's voice, low and rumbling like sifting through gravel.

'Has he been seen at the assizes yet?'

'No, verea. He has not.'

'Who is he?'

'Not our business to know, verea.'

'If he hasn't been seen at the assizes, then he's only accused. The magistrate hasn't read the sentence. You'd think it best if he came to the court smelling like a decent person. If you won't clean him up, I will.'

'Not allowed, verea. He's not allowed up, nor anyone allowed down.'

He cracked one eye, then the other, but it wasn't easy; some dried substance had crusted them over. The walls – for there were walls all around him – were stone built, and not so very far away.

He was curled up in one corner on stone that was both slicked in patches with a drying stink and elsewhere rimed with a dried coating that crackled under him as he tried to shift up, to sit, to see where those voices were coming from. The walls were plain, with no openings.

'He's waking,' said the young woman's voice. 'Do something, I pray you!'

He gagged and his stomach heaved again, but he had nothing in him. His throat was raw; each swallow was a stab of pain. His head throbbed. His clothes were stiff and nasty, and it became clear to him immediately that he had soiled himself while ill. But at least now he could sit up, blinking in the flickering lantern light. Where was that light coming from?

Ah! It was above.

He squinted up. The movement hurt his neck. Far above, floating in a sea of darkness, was a ceiling constructed of night or, possibly, planks of wood. There was an opening cut within them, and floating in this hatchway the veil of mist.

Yet as he stared, the gray mist hovering over the opening vanished abruptly to be replaced by a man's disinterested face. The light was withdrawn, a lantern hauled up on a rope, and he sat in blackness trying to recall who he was and why he was here. Footsteps cracked away down an unseen corridor above him, quickly swallowed in the echoless stone.

'I like that,' said the gravel voice.

He was answered by a wheedling tenor. 'That the Silver girl who always comes?'

'That one? How should I know? Always got their faces covered, don't they?'

'Heh! But you'd recognize the voice.'

'Yeah, I would do. Same one. Seems nice enough, but you know how it is.'

'Neh, I don't, for I've never stood so close to a Silver before, not even one of the men. Never seen one of their women. I thought they weren't allowed into the light.'

'You're come recently from the country, aren't you!'

'No shame in that!'

'Neh, neh, never meant there was. Those Silvers, the women are so ass-ugly that they daren't show their faces in the light of day where others can see. That's what I hear.'

'You ever seen one of their faces?'

'Not me! It's a curse if you do, for they've certain tricksy magics, you know. Curses and rots and suchlike. Make your cock fall off if you so much as look at them crosswise. They paint their hands with all manner of spells, did you notice that?'

'I thought she had a skin disease on her fingers.'

'Oh, no, those are spells. Not even tattoos. Spells, painted on their hands. It's the only part of them you ever see. Nay, don't mess with them, I tell you.'

'Aui! I won't!'

'She's all right, though, that one. She comes through and brings food for the prisoners whose families have no way to feed them. Else they'd starve, you know.'

'What would make a person go and do that?' asked Tenor. 'If family can't help you, then why would you go and trust a stranger? Probably better to die.'

'Don't know why she does it. They're outlanders, you know. Comes of their peculiar customs, I'd wager.'

'I did hear one thing,' added Tenor cunningly. 'That they pay off those who would make trouble for them. That's why they never come to trouble before the law.'

'Neh, maybe so, but they do trade fairly, you must give them that. My old uncle needed a medicinal for his son who was sick with the flux, and it happened it was the end of the season and there was none to be found except in the end one of the Silver shops had a last vial. I'll tell you, that merchant could have charged him ten or twenty times over, for Uncle was that desperate, and there are some merchants in this town who would have done so, but that Silver charged him market price, same as anyone. It was fairly done. So I don't mind the girl or her escort.'

'Always an escort, those men with her?'

'Always. The Silvers treat their womenfolk like slaves, didn't you know that? Always under guard. Can't walk out on their own, or show their face. Bodies completely covered in those loose robes, which is peculiar, if you think about it.'

'The men do look funny,' agreed Tenor, 'with those pulled eyes and their hair all tied up in cloth like women sometimes do. I hear they have unnatural congress with beasts.'

'And horns, under the cloth! That's why they must cover their heads. They're demon-born, back in their old country. It's why they were run out and come here to the Hundred.'

The Hundred!

Joss found his memory and his voice.

'Enough!' he croaked. Speaking that word made his head ache worse. 'What have the Silvers ever done to you that you should speak of them so cruelly?'

'Eiya!' yelped Tenor. 'It speaks!'

Light wavered before the opening, dropped through, but it was as blinding as the darkness, slamming right into his eyes.

'He does stink,' said Gravel. 'I'll ask Captain if we can wash him up. Whew!'

'He looked harmless enough. Who's been feeding him?'

'That girl brings a ration of rice every day, enough to share out among the destitute. We shove his portion in through the hatch. First day he did take it, but he cast it all back out again a time or two.'

'I can smell that! Eh!'

'Then he was sleeping or sick. I'm no healer! I thought him like to die. But Captain Waras came by and said to let him be, and we must obey the captain.'

'What day is it?' Joss said in his strange, roughened voice.

'Wakened Crane,' said Gravel kindly.

'Council day, isn't it? I have the right to appear before the council.'

Gravel snorted. 'Even if we could let you out, council bell already rang, so by the time you crawled up to Fortune Square it'd be all over for the week!'

They laughed as if this were the best joke they'd heard that day.

'You're too late for this week!' cried Tenor over Gravel's honking laugh.

The lantern was drawn up, and the hatch shuttered with a slam of wood. Their laughter and footfalls faded away, leaving him in unrelieved night. He groped at his chest, but the bone whistle was gone. Of course. There was a slight movement of air in the dungeon through slits set in the walls or ceiling, but no view of the sky. He grimaced, realizing truly how horribly grimy and disgusting he had become, matted in his own dried vomit and feces and urine. His head pounded, but at least he could think.

Gingerly, he lay flat on his back and stretched out with arms over his head. In this position, he easily touched opposite walls. He was no better than a rat trapped in a hole. His foot nudged the rim of an object: It was the food tray with a lump of cold rice and the bowl half full of warmish water that smelled as if it had not been fouled. There weren't too many bugs. He didn't mind the bugs.

He drank, and he ate, and this time he kept it all down.

37

Captain Waras led them on a long, hot, and sweaty walk up through Olossi Town to a place he called 'Fortune Square.' Certainly their fortunes would rise or fall depending on the outcome of this council meeting.

At the council hall, she and Anji were allowed to sit on benches in the outer room while Sengel and Toughid took their usual places a few paces to either side of Anji, watching the occasional entrance and exit, and indeed every movement that flickered into being however brief its life, and marking each least scrape, rattle, and word that flew into the air. Priya was watchful, but Sheyshi had her eyes shut fast as she mumbled a singsong prayer in the voice of a woman near to tears with fear. There was no one else there except Captain Waras's guards, and Mai expected that Sengel and Toughid could make short work of these six callow youths who hadn't the posture of men who have been tested.

Anji listened carefully to her account of her conversation with Tannadit. He made no comment until she was done.

'Sixteen "Greater Houses"? And an untold number of dissatisfied Lesser Houses? "Silvers"? I wonder what they are. Useful, anyway. You learned more than I did. I mostly heard tales of merchants and traders and peddlers who could not bring their goods into the north, past a town called Horn. If goods come up from the south, and cannot be moved elsewhere, it will hurt the merchants in this city.'

'You think you could offer your company as caravan guards on the roads here.'

'It seems possible.'

'Isn't "Horn" the name of the town where my uncle's ring was found?'

'Yes.'

They suffered an interminable and dreary wait through the afternoon while the air grew more turgid and the heat more stifling. She whispered thanks to the Merciful One that here there was no need to cover her face, as there had been in Sirniaka. She whispered thanks that she was allowed to whisper thanks without fear of being burned alive. At last, the doors slid open, and a steadily increasing stream of women and men flowed into the building through the entry chamber and on into the high-raftered hall where the council met.

She studied them as they passed, marking the most curious faces. A man obsessively fingered a fresh scar on his clean-shaven chin; it looked like someone had clawed him with a nail. An old, bent woman needed assistance to walk, closely tended by a pair of younger relatives, who resembled her about the eyes and jaw. A stout woman of middle years swaggered with the assurance of a Qin officer, a servant skulking like a beaten dog at her heels. Most of these folk had gleaming black and brown-black hair caught up in looped braids. Some of the women wore their hair pinned high, with a horse's-tail fall down their back or a cluster of heavily beaded braids that clacked softly as they walked, like gossips. A pair of men came in with their hair entirely wrapped in cloth whose ends were tucked away to make a turban. The younger was a remarkably handsome young man, despite his pale complexion and strange headdress, and he was dressed in a rich marigold-yellow silk knee-length overcoat. His gaze roamed, as if he were looking for someone, and when he saw her, he smiled winningly, but was pulled on his way immediately by the scowling older man who probably was his father if one judged by looks and dress. No other men wore their hair wrapped away in a turban.

The shutters were taken down in the hall to let air move through, although there wasn't much wind. The afternoon shadows had lengthened, and if there wasn't precisely a breeze rising up off the river and delta, there was a softening of the heat. The hall was lined with benches. It was a vast space bridged by huge crossbeams of wood. Trees never grew so large in Kartu, not even on Dezara Mountain where the sacred grove was tended. Already, these Olossi people were bickering, seating themselves in clots and clusters that suggested factions and alliances.

The murmur of their voices was like the whisper of wind in leaves – just like in the poem! Although that tale had a bad ending.

She shifted, feeling anxious. Priya and Sheyshi knelt on the floor. Anji sat utterly still, hands resting on his knees, back straight, expression smooth and pleasing in the manner of silk. She could not guess what he was thinking.

In Kartu, of course, the overlords ran everything, even back in the days of the Mariha princes. The council met only when the rulers of Kartu called in the leading men of the town to inform them of new regulations to be implemented.

The din of competing voices from the council chamber was rising. A young woman hurried past clutching pens and several scrolls; ink stained her fingers. She glanced at Mai and Anji, and her eyes widened in surprise. She dropped a pen. Bending to pick it up, she lost two more. A grand gentleman swept up the steps behind her. He was attended by a surly-looking man with a crooked nose who was wearing a leather vest and leather trousers almost exactly like those worn by Reeve Joss. Reeve leathers, Joss had called them. The clerk cast a frightened glance back as he approached, and scrambled to gather her things and get into the hall.

'Shut the doors,' said the grand gentleman, pausing in the entry chamber with a gaggle of attendants bringing up the rear. He wore a magnificent overrobe of iridescent green silk, embroidered with orange feathers and gold starbursts along the hem and sleeves and neckline. His long hair was braided in three loops, decorated with ribands and beads. If he saw Anji and Mai, he did not deign to notice them, but the man with the broken nose stared rudely at them, gaze dropping down to examine Mai's chest.

A grating and quite high woman's voice shouted for silence in the hall. When it was quiet, the gentleman strode into the chamber with his gaggle trailing him in the manner of nervous goslings.

Attendants shoved the doors shut, screens colliding with other screens in a series of sharp reports like staffs whacking wooden targets.

That nasal soprano rose again, calling the council to order in rapid-fire words Mai had trouble following; at speed, and muffled by the closed doors, the differences in pronunciation and phrasing made it difficult to understand. The long wait and the stifling heat had turned her thoughts to mud. She found it hard to concentrate as words and comments emerged from the council hall.

'. . . never allow outlanders to settle . . . bad luck . . . goes against the gods . . .'

'. . . fools not to hire out a guard for caravans going north . . . '

'. . . we must get the trade going again!'

'. . . no need, the road is still safe . . .'

A burst of furious and disorderly disagreement, shouted down.

'. . . no news from the five-flags caravan that left after the rains . . .'

'. . . no trade out of . . .'

'. . . desperate! . . . need that wood in order to . . .'

'. . . you have stuck your heads in the sand . . . the threat . . .'

'. . . perfectly safe . . . this other is exaggeration . . . heavy rains have washed out the roads . . .'

A loud voice penetrated clearly. 'Rains! Last year's rains, perhaps! How long must we wait while our commerce dies?'

Others took up the call. 'We have lost patience . . .' And were called to order.

'Strange,' said Anji in a soft voice. 'Any merchant of Sirniaka speaks the arkinga, but the holy language of the empire is nothing like the same, although bits of it show up in the trade tongue. We among the Qin have our own speech, but most of the Qin who ride the Golden Road also learn the arkinga. So do the folk in Kartu Town. Yet haven't you an older speech there?'

She was startled. 'The grandmother words, we call them. I knew enough to speak to my old aunt, though she's dead these ten years. They still speak that speech in the temple. The Qin forbade its use in town. Everyone uses the arkinga now.'

'Here, too, it seems they use the arkinga, not just in the marketplace but in their council halls. Maybe it came from here first.'

'Can a language travel?'

'It must, just as folk do.'

Of course that was obvious, once you thought of it. Mai blushed, not liking to look stupid; it was the worst thing people had said of her in Kartu. *Good thing she's pretty. She hasn't otherwise many eggs in that basket. Not much to say!* Not like the chattering of the others, which they kept at all day. Better to keep your mouth shut to keep people guessing than to open it and prove yourself a fool. How glad she was to be rid of her family!

She smiled a little, thinking of it.

He brushed his fingers over her left hand.

'What are you thinking?' he asked her softly.

'Are you nervous?' she asked, surprised he had touched her in public.

'I suppose I am,' he said, savoring the moment of consideration. 'We can't go back.'

It was true. The thought of returning to Kartu Town was like poison. In a way, it was a blessing that they had lit a fire behind them in the empire. They dared not travel back that way. And could not return whence they had come, because Anji's life also was forfeit in Qin territory.

A hush fell abruptly within the hall. On its wings, a door slid open. Captain Waras appeared and beckoned to them. 'You are called.' He surveyed their attendants, and motioned that the slaves and soldiers must stay behind.

Anji rose, waited for her, and strode confidently into the hall. She could not match his stride, so walked with clipped steps, trying to remember how to glide, how to compose her face into an expression both pleasant and unthreatening.

The hall opened above them, crossbeams floating away into shadows; the opened windows fed light mostly onto the floor of the hall. In such a building it was easy to imagine mysteries and secrets and whispered intrigues despite the crowd that jammed the space now. Benches were packed with seated people crammed in leg-to-leg; more folk stood behind them, elbows rubbing the backs of heads, or lined up along the back of the room and along the side aisles against the windows and even up on top of the long strip of bench that ran along each of the long outer walls. Every human emotion was displayed among those faces: a sullen old man; disdain and envy in a pair of elegant women; a bored girl, half sleeping with chin propped on a hand; anger in some faces and bitterness in many; a woman who looked frightened and a man who looked sardonically amused; that handsome young man from the entryway who was now, oblivious of all else, flirting with a pretty young woman dressed in a gorgeous length of gold-white silk wrapped cleverly around her body in the fashion that most of these women wore, a costume both discreet and enticing. Mai looked for the father, but he stood a few steps away from his son and had his attention fixed on the council table. The broken-nosed reeve stood with his back to the far wall, watching with an ugly sneer on his face.

A rectangular platform was built in the center of the hall, crammed between the innermost interior columns. At one end of this platform was a roped-off section; the rest was taken up with an enormously long table that had the center cut out and one end open. Around the table sat – she had the gift of counting quickly – thirty-one council members. The grand gentleman sat at his ease, smirking. The proud lady yawned as if to say that her time was too valuable to waste on such trivia. The ancient woman sat hunched in her chair, with a young attendant whispering into an ear. One at that table could not hide the cloud of anger on his face. He tapped the fingers of his left hand impatiently, repetitively, and with a reckless energy. Some glanced at him with a flash of annoyance in the grimace of their mouths or the narrowing of their eyes; others ignored him; a few looked at him with anxious mouths and then glanced toward the silent reeve, if that's what he was. These were all signals to one trained in the exacting commerce of human interaction. The restless council member didn't matter to the others seated at the council table, she realized. He was the odd man out, and somehow it was the presence of the observant reeve they wondered at, and worried about. Yet time and again, the restless council member glanced into the crowd and met the eye of some attentive soul, like the turbaned older man. Then he would nod, acknowledging that one – or another – or another. He had a huge following in the hall. He did not look once at the reeve.

In the open section where the table had been cut away, at a

minuscule writing desk, sat the harried clerk, pen scratching on paper. Next to and above her stood an elevated platform not much more than a stride's length squared, ringed with a railing that also served as the ladder to get up and down. Here presided a small woman wearing a brilliant peacock-blue robe belted with a wine-red sash. Her hair was mostly hidden by an artfully folded kerchief of an eye-dazzling yellow that did not, in truth, flatter her complexion.

'The suppliants approach,' she cried in the nasal soprano that had opened the proceedings. She bent an arm, gestured, and the caravan master stepped up onto the platform. 'Master Iad, do you give witness that this is the mercenary captain who guarded your caravan from the town called Sarida in the empire and over the Kandaran Pass here to Olossi? That this is the woman he names as his wife and business partner?'

A second attendant scurried over to hand Master Iad a lacquered stick.

Taking it, he spoke. 'I do witness it, in the name of the Holy One, Taru the Witherer, to whom I served my apprentice year.' He looked at Anji, nodded with a flicker of movement in the way his mouth turned down. A message, but Mai could not interpret it.

'Will you state, again, that they misrepresented themselves to you when you first met them at the caravansarai in Sarida.'

His mouth twitched. He rubbed his right eye with his left hand. 'They did, but as I said before, they were completely honorable and discharged their obligation'

'Step down, Master Iad. You are finished.'

Master Iad flinched, and hesitated. Before he could speak again, the attendant snatched the stick out of his hands and scuttled away to stand behind the writing desk. With a shake of the shoulders, the caravan master stepped down. If one could judge by the rush of emotion that softened his taut expression and heightened the color in his cheeks, he was either grateful to be released from cross-examination, or shamed by his own testimony.

'Let the suppliants step forward.'

Anji and Mai stepped up. Out of the back of the hall, from the direction of the handsome young man, burst a flirting whistle. Folk laughed appreciatively. Men eyed her, craning forward to get a better look. Anji raised an eyebrow – just that – and there was a shuffling of feet, and knees needing to be scratched, as any number of gazes dropped away.

The envoy said, 'Master Feden claims the right to speak.'

'Wolves, we call them,' said the grand gentleman into the awkward silence that followed. He spoke in a voice that carried effortlessly to each corner of the hall and even, indeed, into the rafters. He held his right hand with palm up, cupped around a large white stone. 'Men who hire themselves out to fight.'

Belatedly, Mai realized that children crouched up in those rafters, half hidden in the gloom as they peered down from their high perches.

'In the wilderness we walk softly, hoping not to attract their notice. In the fields, we kill them for stalking our sheep. Why then would we open our gates and allow them into our city? Are we all such *fools*?'

The last word he roared. Mai actually started, the force of his voice like a wind battering her. Anji did not move, did not react.

The angry council member leaped to his feet amid a murmur of speculation. 'What of the attack at the border post? The rot infecting the ordinands, some of whom conspired with ospreys to rob merchants? What of the testimony of Master Iad and Master Busrad, both caravan masters of long experience and good character? Do you dismiss all this?'

'Master Calon, do sit and not strain yourself. I still hold the stone.' The grand gentleman pursed a smile in the manner of a discerning customer who finds the bruised peach lurking at the bottom of the basket, the one he supposes you have been attempting to foist upon him. 'The prisoner is dead. These caravan masters might have concocted the story between them. They might be in the pay of this wolf. He's an outlander. We already know he lied to the caravan master in Sarida, in order to get the hire. We can't trust him.'

Anji spoke, startling, clear, cool. The accent of his arkinga made him seem even more out of place, very much a black wolf among brightly plumaged birds. 'What of the reeve? The one from Clan Hall? He journeyed here before us. He came to alert this council to the corruption ripening in the border guards. Where is he?'

A cough came from back by the door, where the guards stood.

Folk shrugged and rubbed their chins. The council members stared at Anji. The man with the broken nose had vanished. Mai had not even seen him go.

'There is no reeve here,' said the grand gentleman. 'Nor were you given permission to speak.'

'Yet there was a reeve,' said Anji. 'Dressed very like that man who just left. He called himself Joss. He came from Clan Hall, from a city he named Toskala.'

'Out of the north,' said the man with a gloating sneer. 'Every manner of villain has crawled north into the shadows. He might have been anyone.'

'Have you many of those great eagles?' asked Anji, with all the appearance of surprised curiosity. 'That 'anyone' might ride one? I confess, I have never seen such an intimidating creature as that raptor.'

'A spy. A traitor. These wolves come bearing tales of a conspiracy between Kotaru's holy ordinands, and unholy ospreys, yet their so-called prisoner is dead and conveniently cannot defend himself against these charges. They might have murdered Captain Beron themselves!'

'If you mean to accuse us,' said Anji, 'then justice decrees we be allowed to defend ourselves.'

'Enough of these interruptions!' The grand gentleman slapped his free hand onto the table, making not a few people jump, and indicated the woman on the platform. 'Envoy, I ask for this point of order: that we conclude, having determined that this wolf and his pack be banished from all the territories surrounding Olossi and with whom we have friendly relations. Red in favor. Black to decline.'

'No!' Master Calon leaped to his feet as many in the crowd rose with angry voices to goad him on. 'You refuse to see the danger. The caravan masters vouch for this man. He and his men acted honorably. We need to strengthen our militia against the rising tide out of the north. Our livelihoods, our very houses, are in danger. Our own messengers sent into the north do not return, yet *you do nothing*. You ignore the reports from the north at your peril! You shrug off this tale of ospreys along West Spur because you are the fools, not us! I demand an open vote, each member to state a choice. I call for an open vote.'

'Open vote! Open vote!' the crowd chanted, while a few remained tight-lipped, hunkered down. The other seated council members stared in stony silence. This was a tangled weave, much more complex than the warp and weft of Father Mei's household and its petty grievances and old grudges.

'Silence! Silence!' cried the woman presiding, although by now Mai realized she was merely a facilitator. She had no more power than a shuttle in the loom, which is directed by the weaver's hand. 'You do not have permission to speak.'

As folk settled down reluctantly, Anji raised his voice again. 'Am I not allowed to speak on my own behalf and on behalf of those people for whom I am responsible?'

They ignored him. Just as Mai had been ignored, in her father's house, when there was business to discuss not considered fit for the ears of a girl who would be married out of the family and thereby no longer have any interest in the matters of the household. The envoy called for an open vote, and the vote went around the table so everyone could see, the council members raising either a red flag or a black one. Now the split came clear to Mai: there were sixteen Greater Houses, but only fifteen votes allotted to the guilds and the Lesser Houses. So they voted exactly on those lines: sixteen red flags and fifteen black. So the Greater Houses won their victory while the crowd seethed with an ugly anger. What held the crowd helpless Mai did not know.

The envoy waited until the clerk scrawled the results and rang a handbell at her left hand.

'Therefore,' said the envoy to the hall at large, 'the decision carries: the suppliants will not be allowed to settle in the Hundred. Master Feden, have you anything more to say?'

The grand gentleman rose to his feet with a weary sigh, hoisting the heavy stone. 'It is late,' he said in tones of kindness, nodding toward Mai. He wore an ivory comb of astonishing beauty in his hair, fixing into place the loop of his middle braid. He wore, as well, a magnanimous aspect. The victor can afford to be generous, and can expect gratitude from the one he has defeated when that loser might otherwise expect a death sentence. 'Too late really to send you on your way at once, although many have urged you be driven out of town immediately. You may camp outside the walls for one more night. As long as you are on your way by the first bell after dawn, we will not trouble you further. You'll ride south. An escort will be provided for the first leg of the journey. As for the rest of you, let the ban of Taru the Witherer be upon any of you who think to conspire with these outlanders. They are hereby called into exile from the town's commerce. Captain Waras, escort them out.'

He sat.

The captain came forward with a doubled guard of soldiers. It was stuffy in the chamber despite the open shutters, and the captain had loosened his outer jacket enough that the chain of the necklace he wore sagged free, and the object fastened there slithered into the open.

The reeve's bone whistle, with which he called his eagle.

38

A stick prodded Keshad awake.

'Ow!' he yelped, but the man at the other end of the spear merely poked him again with the haft.

'Here, now. Your turn on watch.'

'Must you prod me? That hurt!'

'Heh. A lot less than those ginnies would hurt when they bit my hand or ankle if I shook you kindly awake, yeh? I saw what they did to Pehar's hand. Heh! Mean beasts!'

'True enough,' said Kesh, sitting up and rubbing his sore head. The ginnies gaped their mouths to show teeth to the intruder. 'Although it was stupid of Pehar to reach in on them like that. Those ginnies will protect what's mine – what I'm safeguarding for my mistress, that is.'

'Heh! I'd risk their bite for a taste of Devouring right now. Is she good, your mistress?'

Kesh made a face. 'I'm only her hired man.'

The man, who called himself Twist, snorted in disgust. 'Seems you're used to being beaten by her stick. Come on, then.'

Kesh chivvied the ginnies into a makeshift sling. He saw how Twist eyed the pouch that the ginnies had been guarding, then shifted his gaze to Magic. Magic stared right back at him. Kesh had been very careful to hide his remaining string of leya, but every soldier in the cadre suspected he carried coin. Really, the ginnies had protected him. He gathered up the rest of his trifling possessions and spat to get the sour taste of bad wine out of his mouth. 'Where do I go?'

'You can leave your things here.'

'I'll keep them near me and my little guardsmen, if you please.'

'Heh, heh! Come this way. Be careful where you step.'

Twist held a rushlight that steamed off more smoke than flame. The sergeant of their cadre had opened his bedroll in the empty council house in the very village whose inhabitants had – only one night before – sought to overcharge Keshad and Zubaidit for accommodations in those same quarters. The rest of the cadre had lain down to rest on the entry porch, where they could move out quickly if need be.

It was this cadre Kesh had been absorbed into earlier that day when the mounted men had captured him on the road. They'd have killed him if he hadn't possessed that cheap tin medallion, the one he'd looted off the corpse of the man Bai had killed. But he had looted it, and so he was alive. Others weren't so fortunate.

The village was little more than a posting station with buildings strung along the road like beads. Each building was a business with an open front, an awning sheltering an entryway partly floored in earth and partly raised up as a floor of wooden planks. The strike force running ahead of Kesh's cadre had decorated these porches with the corpses of the village folk who had lived and worked within. The sight of these slack forms greeted Kesh as he and Twist trudged toward the west-facing sentry post. There was an innkeeper Kesh remembered, a jovial man who had scoffed at their attempts to secure housing for a lower price; he had been stripped of the fine sea-green scalloped silk robe he had been wearing, and sprawled on his entry porch in nothing more than a sleeveless shift as pale as a death shroud. Here was the kindly seller of rice, an old woman with a bent back now softened and straightened in death. The aura of torchlight revealed more personal details: One had a slashed throat, while the other seemed unmarked but no less dead for all that. He hoped they had died quickly.

Twist had a sickness lodged in his chest, something nagging and snotty, and the man breathed with a rattling intensity and paused now and again to cough up gunk and spit it out. He did not glance at the bodies. To him they were chaff, nothing important. Along with the others in the cadre, he had ransacked the village at sunset, complaining bitterly all the while that the strike force had carried away everything both valuable and portable, although naturally heavy household goods remained, things impossible to haul under these circumstances.

Had these folk been alive, Kesh could have passed them without a moment's thought, but they were horribly dead. Bai's words nagged at him. Was it possible that if they had acted more quickly they could have saved these hapless innocents? No, they would only have been killed as well. Had they slept the night in the council hall, they would be dead, too. These reflections allowed him to walk behind Twist without showing any sign of revulsion. If the others suspected he was not one of them, they would kill him, and he was determined to stay alive.

Laughter came from one of the porches. A group of men were joking, calling out bets. One of the men was stretched out atop a body, humping busily.

'Fifteen! Sixteen! Seventeen!'

'He'll go on twenty!'

'No, on twenty-five!'

'Whoo! Whoo! Twenty-two! Heh! I win!'

With a chorus of laughs and shouts, coin changed hands.

Kesh averted his eyes and kept walking as he whispered thanks that the poor victim was not screaming. Ahead, the village ended in fenced gardens, livestock sheds, and a pair of granaries on stilts. A tent had been raised just outside the last shed, although it was little more than a lean-to of canvas rigged out from the shed's cantilevered roof. A trio of men stood at attention beside a small fire, guarding both tent and shed.

'Who sleeps there?' Kesh whispered.

'Eh! The lord does.'

'The lord?'

'He don't usually stop by us, but there's somewhat afoot. Anyway, he don't like to be disturbed by the likes of us. So, hush!'

It was middle night, more or less. There was no moon. Kesh stumbled more than once before they clambered back on the road 'downstream' of the shed. The road here ran fairly straight, with a long view back into the village and its emptied buildings. In an open meadow lay the ruins of the old Ladytree, fallen into a massive tangle of trunk and branches that no one dared cut up. In the darkness, the new sapling, no more than two years old, wasn't even visible.

They walked a little farther on the pale surface of the road until they came to the road's intersection with a wide gravel path that pushed straight through the woods toward the distant uplands. The path's beginning was marked by one of the three-span gates that marked a temple to Ilu, the Herald, though it was too dark for Kesh to see any buildings in all those trees and brush. Just ahead, the road began to curve. Here in the middle of the roadway stood two sentries.

'Heh! About time!' said one, a burly man with his hair shaved down against his head.

'What was all that noise?' asked the other.

'Just Rabbit,' said Twist, wiping his nose.

The burly man cackled. 'Eh! He wouldn't know what to do with a live one, eh? You ever get to wondering just what he did do to get run out of his village?'

Twist spat. 'Did you ever think I don't want to know? Eh?'

Kesh felt sick, but he said nothing, made no expression, just waited.

Fortunately, the pair headed back for camp without any further discussion. Kesh's companion settled into a comfortable stance, feet shoulders'-width apart and weight canted onto his spear.

The ginnies slept, a heavy burden in their sling. Kesh shifted nervously as he looked back toward the camp, wondering what he ought to do. There were thirty-six in the cadre. He'd counted three times: eighteen mounted and eighteen walking on their own feet; he made the thirty-seventh. A sergeant led them, but who their commanders were Kesh could not tell. In general, the southern towns were council-led, so he wasn't sure how one could tell a 'lord' apart from a well-to-do council member, although there must be signs and customs that spoke of such things. In his travels in the empire, he had dealt with merchants who were agents for lords, of whom they spoke in only the most formal of terms. But lords in the empire were a different beast, set apart, isolated. Nor could he ask Twist to explain it to him, lest Kesh seem too ignorant of things the others took for granted. As the old saying went, better keep one's mouth shut and be thought a fool, than open it and be known as an impostor.

It was so quiet. The horses had been strung up on a line near the council house, visible from here by the distant glimmer of light from a single lantern hung at the porch. The mascot dogs who accompanied the cadre were tranquil beasts, and he supposed they were now sleeping. In truth, it was the look of the men with whom he marched that agitated him.

Like Twist. The man's jaw had been damaged and healed wrong. He was missing two fingers. He had a net of lash scars on his back. He carried himself with the bravado of a man who relishes a fight over nothing.

A figure appeared on the road out of the darkness and loped up to them in that gangling, hopping way he had.

'Eh, there, Rabbit,' said Twist. 'Finally remember you have sentry duty?'

'Heh. Heh. Yah.'

Like this one, who tolerated the others calling him 'Rabbit' and who had a way of grinning at unseen sights that made Kesh think he was unbalanced, and who was capable of the most grotesque acts, things Kesh had not thought anyone could force himself to do. Like what he had just done. All Kesh could think of was that if the woman, or man, was dead, then there wouldn't have been any pain.

'How long have you been on this road?' he asked Rabbit, because the silence was making him twitchy.

Rabbit fished a strip of dried flesh out of his pouch and chewed on it before answering. 'Eh. Since I was kicked out of m'mam's village and forced to take cover up in the hills. There I found some who were more like me than otherwise. Comrades, you might say.' He hawked and spat, then wiped his mouth clean. 'Let me see. That was ten years ago now, I'm thinking.'

Kesh whistled. 'That's a long time. How old are you?'

'Oh, I'm a Goat, sure enough. You work it out.'

'Huh. Same as me.'

'Really?' said Twist. 'You look younger than Rabbit.'

It was true. Rabbit had the wiry strength of a young man but his face was seamed and weathered in the manner of a person who has suffered far beyond his years and lived to tell a noisome tale. He bore a series of parallel white scars on his right forearm, and he kept himself clean-shaven because of the knotted scar along his jaw that prevented him from growing an even beard. No telling what he had done to get run out of his home village, and since this was the second corpse he'd humped since Kesh joined the company this past early afternoon, it was best not to ask and not to know.

'How long, you?' the older man asked Kesh.

'Oh, in the service of that one, since I was twelve,' said Kesh, figuring it better to tell as much of truth as he could.

Rabbit twitched. 'Heh! You ever done it with her? Front or back?'

'Her? No.'

'I bet that reeve done it. That one was carrying her. Heh! He was as ready as a split log to burn. Popping right out of his leathers, near enough. Fancy them dropping down just like that to warn us of you waiting there by our dead comrades just ahead.' Rabbit scratched where Kesh did not want to look. That weird, crazy grin crept up the corners of his mouth. 'Wonder who killed them.'

'I'd like to know,' said Twist. 'I've been camping with Jeden and Ofass for five years now. If I caught that one who did them, I'd open their chest and squeeze their beating heart 'til they told me. And then burst it anyway.'

'Heh. Heh. Just like we did at that place . . . huh . . . it had a name.'

'Reyipa,' said Twist.

Rabbit snickered. 'Then we tossed them from the cliff, four at a time. Heh. Heh. "It's the flying fours for you!" Remember how we called that out? Heh. Pretty clever.'

'Whew! I do have to pee,' said Kesh, not liking the turn of this conversation. 'I'll be right back.'

Trying not to disturb the sleeping ginnies, he picked his way sideways down off the roadbed and gingerly high-stepped along the ground, to the edge of the trees. Made water there, while his thoughts spilled.

If he ran, they would just be on him. This motley group, part of a larger unit that called themselves the Flying Fours, had embraced him into their ranks only because the reeve and his fascinating passenger had dropped down beside their cadre and warned them to 'pick up the lad who is just up the road, and keep him safe.' Or so the sergeant had made sure to tell him. How Bai had managed to persuade them he could not imagine, since he hadn't been there to see, but she seemed at this juncture capable of anything except, he hoped, raping corpses.

He peered into the trees, but it was all darkness beneath the canopy of rustling leaves. The river ran close by, a constant chuckle of amusement, no doubt laughing at his plight. What was he to do? He could race to the shore and throw himself into the water, but he didn't know how to swim, and anyway the ginnies would likely drown. He could hide in the undergrowth, but the dogs would probably find him. In the other direction the woods thinned where the ground began its steady rise toward the high plateau of the Lending. He might have a chance running in that direction, up the path toward the temple at first before veering into the bush, but it seemed foolish to take the chance when Bai had managed to gift him with safe passage. Such as it was. He hated to march with this group back toward Olossi, especially not knowing what they intended. He hadn't quite asked, and they hadn't quite said, but from the way they spoke it seemed they were riding to meet up with the strike force, which was almost a day ahead of them. That strike force had murdered the poor folk in this exceptionally inoffensive village.

Everything had gone wrong. But at least he was still alive.

He heard what was not a sound, felt the shadow although it could not be seen in darkness. A prickling sensation ran from his ears to his neck, and his throat went dry, and he was suddenly horribly, terribly, genuinely scared, so badly that he would have wet himself if he hadn't just peed.

He stepped away from the trees, thinking at first that the threat came from beneath the canopy, but as he set a foot on the slope of the road's underbed, a shape passed low over him. He and the other sentries ducked, covering their heads although nothing came close to hitting them.

On the road behind them, the shape descended sharply. His breath lodged in his throat. The creature made the transition effortlessly from flying to trotting. When those mundane hoof-falls slammed on the road, he choked and gasped, and scrambled up to the road's pavement to stare after it as it moved away from them and toward the tent.

He would have called it a horse with two heads, one equine and one human, each one streaming wings like smoke. But as it came to a halt a little away from the campfire, it separated as its rider dismounted; it was a person wearing a voluminous cloak that had gusted out in the landing. But the horse really did have wings, fanned out at first as it came to earth and then folded in against its body. They swaddled its flanks like a monstrous growth.

'"Rid us of all that is evil,"' he muttered.

'What did you say?' asked Twist.

'What is that thing?'

It was the wrong question to ask. Twist and Rabbit looked at him, chins lowering as might muzzles dip on dogs who are thinking of taking a bite out of you.

'You don't know?' asked Twist.

'Heh,' said Rabbit suspiciously.

'I've never been out of the south,' said Kesh in a choked voice. 'Never saw such a thing before.' He sorted through his choices and opted for belligerency. 'You want to make something of it? I can't help it I'm not well traveled like your sort. I have to go where the mistress tells me, and she doesn't stray far, let me tell you. She works for the temple, and they don't let their hierodules off the leash. If you take my meaning.'

'Heh. Heh.' Rabbit scratched himself. 'Like to see that.'

The creature and its rider vanished inside shed and tent respectively. One of the guardsmen detached himself from the campfire and jogged down to the sentry post.

'Where's the new one?' he called when he was within earshot. It was the sergeant of their company. 'Master wants him to come.'

'Heh,' snickered Rabbit.

'He always interviews the new ones,' said Twist with a sneer. 'Sees right through you, if you take my meaning.'

Kesh did not, but he saw no chance to escape with three armed men beside him and he with only a knife and an unstrung bow for which he had no arrows and no facility. So it would end badly after all, and just in the teeth of his victory. Fortune had turned its back on him, that was clear.

He trudged to the tent with the sergeant beside him.

'Young man come to my company a month back,' remarked the sergeant, 'and didn't take to our way of doing things here. So I had to break all his fingers. I did that, you see, to get him to tell me why he'd come. It seems some folk from Nessumara had sent out a few likely lads to scout the land, see what was up. I just don't like folk who will go tattling tales of me to people who don't like me. But he fessed up pretty quickly after I got to cutting off his fingers.'

'Did he now?' asked Keshad, thinking of the marketplace and how you could never let your true feelings show. 'What happened then?'

'Oh, it seemed a kindness just to slit his throat. I'm not one for drawing it out, although I admit a few of my soldiers asked me to let them have a go. I don't think that's right, once you've gotten what you need. I just killed him. Most likely the vultures ate him, if the Lady was feeling as kindly as I was. Here you go.'

He motioned for Kesh to go through a rigged-up entryway made of hanging cloth and in under the canvas roof. Kesh heard the sounds of the creature moving within the shed. It seemed to be eating or drinking; it made horse-like noises, so that in hearing it one would think it a horse. But horses had wings only in the old stories.

In the stories about the Guardians, who had long since vanished from the Hundred.

If this was a lord's resting place, then it was no better furnished than the hovel of a simple farmer. There was a pallet covered with a thin blanket, a folding table on which stood a bronze ewer and basin, and a small traveler's chest so old its edges were smoothed to a shiny curve and its planks were warped.

The man sat on a stool, still dressed for travel. If he was a lord, then he wore clothes common to every laborer: a long knee-length linen jacket dyed an indeterminate color that the candle flame did nothing to distinguish; wide-legged trousers; knee-high boots that looked well worn and scuffed. His dark cloak pooled around his hips and thighs as if he had scooped it over them to keep himself warm.

He looked up as Kesh halted uneasily before him. He had a strange cast of face, a little broader across the cheekbones, a shade different in complexion, the shape of the eyes more exotic, twisted and pulled. Something about his features seemed passing familiar. He might be an outlander, or else the son of some hidden corner of the Hundred whose folk rarely left their home valley, a person glimpsed once and recalled now in a spin of dizziness. No, Kesh had never seen this man before. His eyes were so brown as to be black, and they were like holes driven into Kesh's heart to lay bare his secrets.

He spoke with a slight drawling accent that Kesh could not place. 'You were picked up by this troop yesterday afternoon, so I hear.'

'Yes.' Kesh kept it short. He didn't know how to address him, or how to stop from breaking down into tears out of fear.

'Before they found you, the troop was met by a reeve who was carrying a hierodule who said you are her slave.'

'So I hear. I didn't witness that meeting myself.'

'Naturally.' Almost, he might be about to smile, but instead the expression made Kesh shiver as if a ghost were breathing on his neck.

The candle burned straight up. There was no wind, nothing to sway that flame. The horse bumped and snuffled within the shed.

'You are not what you claim,' said the man.

Kesh could say nothing, because he was pinned by that stare. The air had grown as hot as the hell where dance those lilu who have not yet found a crack through which to wiggle out onto the mortal world. He was hot and cold together, so frightened he thought he might faint.

'It would matter to the others, although not to me,' said the man cryptically. 'I ask, and you must answer. Do you mean to harm me or mine?'

'No.' The word was forced out of him by a vise gripping and squeezing until only the truth was left. 'I care nothing for you or yours.'

'How can you know, since you have not asked who me or mine are? Yet strange as it seems, you are telling the truth. Very well.' He raised a hand as though the effort taxed him. 'Go. Best if you not come to my attention again.'

Kesh backed out so fast through the curtained entrance that he stumbled as soon as he was outside and fell on his backside hard enough to jostle the ginnies. They hissed at him, and Magic nipped at his wrist as if to warn him to be more careful next time, an 'I told you so.'

He had forgotten about the ginnies! They had lain so still in the sling that the lord had not noticed them at all. Usually they made their feelings known. Not this time. They had chosen to avoid the man's notice.

The sergeant glanced at him, unamused by his pratfall. 'Go back to your post.'

He scrambled up, soothed the ginnies, and hobbled back to the sentry post. Best stick to the routine and do nothing, absolutely nothing, that would bring him to the attention of that man and his horrible stare.

He knows all and everything, all my secrets, all my crimes, all my hopes and all my fears. But he let me go anyway.

'Heh,' said Rabbit, seeing him return.

'Passed muster,' said Twist with a sly, cruel grin.

Kesh grunted a noncommittal reply. Above, the stars shone bright and cold, while the night was warm and the tender breeze a balmy presence. The trees whispered in a mild conversation. A nighthawk kurred. All was quiet.

No, it was only an illusion brought on by the tension of his situation, caught in the midst of an invading force whose soldiers would as easily kill him as spare him. There had been nothing strange about that man, nothing at all. Any clever man might spout truisms like 'you are not what you claim to be' and 'you're not telling the truth' to the kind of twisted, rabbity men willing to join this manner of army, and know he was hitting the mark.

He had certainly imagined the wings on that horse. It was only the play of shadow in the night.

There, now. That was better. The sergeant was a bigger threat. Did he suspect, or had Kesh truly passed muster? He had to glean any useful information before he made his eventual escape. He couldn't think any other way. Never give in to fear.

'What is the lord's name?' he asked, treading softly on this new ground. Each word was like the snap of a finger being pinned back and broken. 'Where does he come from?'

Rabbit shuddered and turned away as the smell of urine spread sharply off him. He had wet himself. He began to weep with small, animal noises. 'They scare me,' he whimpered. 'They scare me. Stop it. Stop asking.'

Twist snarled, and the ginnies hissed in answer, crests rising as they stirred along Kesh's arm.

'Best keep your mouth shut.' Twist's voice rose in pitch until he fought himself and controlled it with a grimace of dismay. 'Best keep it shut and ask no more questions. If you want to stay alive. The lords don't like those who question. That one – he's the kindliest. He only burns you.'

'What do you mean? Like he, uh—' Now that he had set out to say it, he realized the words might make them suspicious again, but it would be worse to break off as though he had something to hide. '—uh, sets people on fire, bound in a cage, like they do in the empire to execute criminals?'

Twist shrugged. 'Eh, I don't know anything about the empire, but that seems a nasty way to go for a poor criminal, nothing quick about it. No. You faced him. You know what I mean.'

So he did. All his doubts roared up as he recalled that deadly gaze. He had been cleaned out, every crevice of him burned down to bedrock. *Rid us of demons*. He needed a plan, any plan, to escape.

'What comes next?' he asked. He could never escape if that 'lord' was always watching over them.

'What comes next?' mused Twist philosophically.

'Heh.' Rabbit looked back toward the village. When Kesh and Bai had walked through that village, it had lived and breathed; now it was dead. 'Heh. Maybe we get a chance ourselves, at some loot. Doesn't seem fair the strike force cleaned this out and left us nothing but their leavings. I'd like to try – heh. Heh.'

'Olossi's pretty big,' continued Twist, who like the rest of them mostly ignored Rabbit. 'Plenty of loot for everyone.'

'Oh, yeh, sure,' stammered Kesh. 'And after that? Then what?'

'How should I know? One campaign at a time, until we're done.'

'Of course. Until we're done.'

'Yeh. Yeh.' Twist scratched the stubble at his chin. 'The armies are on the move. High Haldia first. Olossi set to fall in the next few days. Toskala will go down soon after. Or maybe it's Nessumara next, all the cities and big towns, yeh. It won't be long until all the Hundred is ours, just as the lord commander promised us.'

39

After Anji and his party returned from town with the bad news, the soldiers accepted it with their usual stoic pragmatism. As twilight turned to evening, they settled down to sleep. Why not? No matter what came, it was best to be well rested.

Anji did not sleep, so Mai sat up by the fire watching him as evening turned into night. He did not pace or curse or appear in any way restless, but for the longest time he did sit on a mat with a fist pressed against his mouth, staring at the flames.

After a while, he gathered his advisors: Chief Tuvi; Scout Tohon for his experience; Mai because it was the custom of Qin commanders to consult their wives; Shai because he could hear the words of ghosts; and – curiously – Priya, whom Anji respected because she could read and write the script used in the holy books sacred to the Merciful One. Sengel and Toughid stood a few paces away, at guard as always, but they were never consulted.

'I am not sure we have been betrayed, because I doubt these Great Houses have much interest in us except that we might bite them at an inconvenient time. We are too few in number to truly frighten them. But I am sure that Reeve Joss has been betrayed in some manner. The question is: What are we to do about it?'

At night it was almost cool, with a lazy breeze teasing the dregs of heat. Mai slapped at the midges swarming her face and shifted to get into the draft of smoke off the fire they sat around. She would stink of smoke, but it was better than being bitten raw. That sweet bath seemed ages in the past. It was hard to believe she had luxuriated in those waters only this past morning.

'If we go back to the empire, we will be killed,' said Chief Tuvi.

'If we go back to the Qin, we will be killed,' said Tohon. 'It would be death without honor, like a starving cur who slinks back to the fire though it knows it will be cut down.'

By the light of the fire, Shai was whittling at a scrap of driftwood, shaping it into a spoon whose handle was fashioned as the forelegs and head of a springing antelope. She could see the form come into being under his hands in the same manner she could see thoughts and solutions coming into being and being dismissed as unworkable by the way Anji's expression shifted. But she didn't know what her husband was thinking.

'I have considered every piece of information we know.' Anji sat cross-legged on a square mat woven of reeds, just like the one on which she sat. His hands were now folded in his lap. 'I have turned it, and turned it, but I have no answers. Some manner of conflict boils among the reeves. Guardsmen resort to banditry to prey on the caravans they are meant to safeguard. Discontent simmers within the Lesser Houses of the council in Olossi because their voices go unheard. Rumors of trouble in the north frighten the merchants, who wonder if outright war or some demon's spawn has poisoned the trade routes between these parts and those farther north. The reeve's bone whistle is worn around the neck of a city guardsman. Where is the reeve, then? Living, or dead? If dead, who killed him? If living, why did he lose his eagle's whistle, and why did the council master claim he knew nothing of the reeve?'

'He didn't say he knew nothing of Reeve Joss,' said Mai. 'He said there was no reeve here for us to see, which could mean anything, quite the opposite. That woman suggested the reeve was some manner of villain falsely claiming to be a reeve. They know what's happened to him. There was a man dressed in similar fashion, another reeve, surely, who left before the meeting was over.'

Anji nodded. 'They are not dealing honestly with us.'

'No surprise there,' said Shai morosely.

Mai nudged him with her foot, bent close, and whispered in his ear. 'Say something useful, or keep quiet!'

'Well, then,' said Shai defiantly, 'what of my brother's ring? I've heard talk of this town called Horn. That's where the story said the ring was found.' He held up his own hand to display the family ring: the running wolf biting its own tail, with a black pearl inlaid into silver as its eye.

Her identical ring was hidden by her sleeve, although the quality of her pearl was finer than the one on Shai's ring, because she
was Father Mei's eldest daughter rather than only a seventh, and
excess, son. Everyone knew that six sons were plenty: two to
marry, two to die, one for the priests, and one for spare. That's
how it had been in their house: Father Mei and the second son,
Terti, had married young and given birth so far to many healthy
children. Third son Sendi had gone to the priests, while fourth son
Hari, for spare, had been exiled and marched away by the Qin
army, leaving fifth son Neni to marry unexpectedly in the wake of
Grandmother's grief over Hari. Of course sixth son Girish had died
a spectacular and well-deserved death, shame on her even to think
so, except it was true because he was a nasty man. Shai, poor Shai,
was left over, the unlucky seventh son with the curse of seeing
ghosts that he must hide from his own family as well as every living
soul in Kartu Town lest he be burned and hanged in the town
square, like Widow Lae, although the widow hadn't actually seen
ghosts but had done something just as bad when she had betrayed
her Qin overlords.

'What was in Widow Lae's letter?' she asked. The men looked at
her, Shai with his mouth popping open in a most ridiculous way,
Tohon and Tuvi with puzzlement, but Anji with a faint smile.

'Widow Lae?' Chief Tuvi asked. 'Who is that?'

'She was burned and hanged in Kartu Town square,' said Mai,
looking at Anji. 'I know *you* remember that day.'

'I saw her ghost,' Shai muttered. 'She said she was waiting for her
reward.'

Mai nodded. 'What did she do? The order we heard read in the
citadel square said she had insulted a Qin officer. But the whisper
told us she'd asked a passing merchant to carry a letter to Tars Fort,
in the east. When he wouldn't do it she sent a grandson instead.
That merchant received a share of the proceeds of the sale of her
estate and her kinsfolk, and then he left town by the Golden Road.
What was she really executed for? I always wondered.'

The fire snapped, its bridge of brittle driftwood collapsing into
sparks. Tuvi gestured, and Pil came in from the gloom with an
armful of new branches. The soldier arranged them on the coals and
blew on the lattice until fire caught and flared high, burning

strongly on the dry wood but without enough smoke to smother the horrid midges.

Anji batted a swarm away from his face, scratched his neck, and nodded. 'Widow Lae,' he said, musing over the name. 'I think, Mai, that you have spotted the only blossom on the otherwise barren tree. I had forgotten about Widow Lae.'

A bird's whistle startled out of the brush at the shoreline. The men leaped to their feet. Mai rose and clutched Priya's hand. Sengel strode away toward the sound. But Anji kept talking, as if nothing strange had happened.

'You're right that Widow Lae was not executed for insulting a Qin officer, except in the most general way.'

She waited as he rubbed his chin. He lifted an arm to point. Every head turned to look toward the shore. Inland a tiny light – torch-light – advanced along what must be the main road, heading for Olossi. They watched in silence, because it was such a strange sight to see that pinprick of brightness aflame against the dark.

At length, Tohon muttered, 'A runner, or a rider. Too fast to be walking.'

Anji grunted. 'It's an urgent message,' he said evenly, 'that travels into the night.'

'The Sirniakans have night runners,' said Priya, and she shuddered, releasing Mai's hand. 'Agents of the red hounds.'

'Do you think it could be the red hounds?' whispered Mai.

Anji caught her wrist. 'Enough. We may never know, and it does no good to spin these thoughts when they have nowhere to go.'

'The agents of the red hounds never travel alone,' said Tohon.

Anji turned his head to look, in the most general way, toward the southwest, whence they had come. Out there lay the wide, flat delta, dark under the night sky. The river had a slow, deep voice here as it spilled away into a hundred channels and backwaters. Wind found a voice in the rushes and reeds and bushes growing everywhere. A nightjar clicked.

'I had forgotten until now,' he mused, and for a moment Mai could not remember what they had been speaking about because she had not yet banished the vision of giant slavering red dogs panting and growling as they closed in for the kill. 'She was executed for passing information to an agent of the Sirniakan Empire. To our enemy. To one of the red hounds, perhaps. Certainly a traitor must expect death. But now that I think on it, by the time Widow Lae was passing intelligence to an enemy agent, the var would already have sealed the secret treaty he made with my brother Azadihosh. Emperor Farazadihosh, I should say. Whose position as emperor is so weak that he must seek Qin aid in putting down his rivals. The orders for me to ride east came from my uncle, the var.'

'He was sending you into a trap,' said Tuvi.

'Just so.'

'Did the commander of Kartu Town know of the new treaty?' asked Mai. 'Did he send you east innocently, or did he know he was sending you to your death?'

'I don't know,' said Anji. 'But all the commanders in the eastern part of the Qin territories would have to be told of the treaty because of the major transfer of troops onto the eastern frontier. That means it's likely that the commander of Kartu knew of the treaty, and knew that the emperor was now our ally. If that's true, then I must ask myself, who was the enemy that Widow Lae was found to be passing intelligence to?'

'I never heard a whisper of rebellion in Kartu Town,' said Shai.

Anji smiled softly. 'Nor did I. The people of Kartu Town possess a pragmatic wisdom that has served them well.'

Mai frowned. 'You were an officer. Weren't there rumors in the garrison?'

'All we were told was that the widow was passing information to the enemy. Which we all took to mean that she had tried to pass information to the agents of the Sirniakan emperor. But we were wrong, because by that time, they were our allies, not our enemy. I never heard anything more about it after her execution. I never heard if the grandson – if there was a grandson – was ever found.'

'There was a grandson,' said Shai. 'Everyone knew Widow Lae's grandson. A little older than me, a hard drinker, and he knew how to ride a horse.'

'Huh,' grunted Tuvi, who found this amusing. 'Riding a horse is a capital offense, if you're not Qin!'

Shai grinned. Widow Lae's grandson had been one of those young men that you admired but disliked. 'He vanished before she was arrested. That's why we all knew she was guilty. He was her favorite.'

'What other enemy could there be?' asked Chief Tuvi. 'If not the Sirniakan emperor?'

Mai said, 'Who else was interested in the transaction? Who else might benefit, or take a loss, from any secret treaty signed between the emperor and the var? Who might wish to know of Qin troops moving into the empire? Or of trading privileges reserved for the Qin that might formerly have been available to others?'

'Exactly,' said Anji, without looking at her. 'There may be other agents involved that I am not aware of, merchants of some kind. But common sense suggests that the sons of my uncle Ufarihosh have an interest here. So we must ask ourselves, if she had ties to them, how did she come by those ties, and what message did she send, and did it reach them?'

'How can we possibly find out?' Mai asked. 'Is there a chance the sons of Ufarihosh might give us asylum? If we can reach them?'

Raising two fingers to his lips to enjoin silence, Anji tilted his head back as if looking at the many-souled sky. He shut his eyes. Now she heard, fainter than a splash, the lap of water. He pointed toward the river's edge, away from the slow-moving channel that separated them from the shore. Chief Tuvi drew his sword. Toughid shifted five steps to the left, to cover more ground. Tohon was already gone. Reeds whispered as dark shapes pushed through them, soldiers converging on the bank, which she could not see from here. In the quiet, a horse snorted, and a bird's lazy koo-loo throated along the air.

A shout of surprise cut the silence, startling Mai so badly that she jumped. Priya clasped her hand.

Sengel and Tohon reappeared a few moments later. In their wake walked a dozen soldiers with two prisoners in tow. One was the handsome young man with the head covering whom Mai remembered well enough from the council meeting. The other was the older merchant who had defended them at the meeting, Master Calon.

'Look what we caught,' said Tohon. 'They came by boat. They say they bear a message for you, Captain.'

Firelight lent glamour to the young man's pleasant features. He resembled ordinary people with his black-brown eyes and dark lashes, but there the resemblance ended. Although not ghostly pale in the manner of poor, dead Cornflower, he had a lighter complexion than Mai was used to seeing. And his eyes had a pull to them, stretched at the corners with a fold at the lid. She was herself known for having grandfather eyes, the sloe eyes seen more commonly in Kartu children long ago, so the grandmothers said, tantalizing for seeming exotic, for hinting of a promise as yet unmet. The legend of Dezara Mountain told of the long-ago time when a rotting plague killed all the men in what was then Kartu Village, followed by a terrible storm that had lashed the houses into splinters and burned the trees off the slopes, after which a ragged band of about fifty foreign hunters had walked down off the mountain saying that the wind had blown them far from their homeland. They were men of a handsome burnt-sugar complexion very different from the lovely red-bronze clay color common in that region, and they had handsomely slanted eyes, troubling and exciting to look upon. It was whispered they were demons wearing human form, but they were pleasant company and hard workers, and they kept their hair clean and combed. In the end, they had married the widows and maidens of Kartu Village and bred so many children that the village had grown to become a town.

Now here was a young man who had something of the look she had always supposed those grandfathers to have. If this one was a demon, he hid it well. Maybe the turban on his head was meant to conceal his horns. He grinned at her most flirtatiously, until Master Calon cuffed him with a genial swat.

'Here, now, cub. Show respect. I promised your father you'd not shame him.'

'I am surprised to see you, Master Calon,' said Anji before the young man could reply to Master Calon's scolding.

'You should not be.' The merchant nodded briskly. 'I think by your actions and speech at the council that you're not eager to return to the empire.'

'I am not,' agreed Anji.

'Then there's no sense in waiting through the opening measures before we start the dance. This is how it is.'

He paused as might a man who wants to show his goods in the best light, making the buyer lick his lips before he gets a taste. Anji nodded, showing neither excitement or disdain.

'We have the votes, only we don't have the votes,' broke in the young man, 'because those bastards will always use the old law against us—'

'Hush!' Calon pressed a sandaled foot onto the exposed toes of the young man, who yelped in pain and fell silent.

'The Lesser Houses and the guilds possess only fifteen votes,' said Mai, 'while the Greater Houses hold sixteen.'

'That's right!' said Master Calon with an admiring nod. 'You must be a merchant yourself, verea. That's how they can always outvote us, although we are many more than they are, and with allies among more than just the Lesser Houses and the guilds. For instance, this cub is called Eliar sen Haf Gi Ri.' He paused as if the news ought to astonish, or light a flame of recognition, and when Anji waited, the master glanced at Mai, at the others, and read what he could from their expressions. 'That means nothing to you, then?'

'What does it mean to you?' asked Mai.

He grinned, and she liked him for it. 'His people are outlanders, like you, who come to settle here.'

Eliar waved a hand. Silver bracelets jangled at his wrists. 'Whsst! A hundred years or more ago, my people came here! You can't call me an outlander any more than I can call you an outlander.'

'It's true my folk came from the south not so long ago, but you will always be outlanders to Hundred folk until you cast away your strange way of dressing and naming and come to worship proper gods.'

'Likely not!' said Eliar with a carefully measured sidelong glance at Mai. 'You know that normally my fathers and uncles and kinsmen would never have made this agreement with you. It's a sign of our desperation.'

'Thus you prove my point.' Master Calon turned back to Anji. 'Many among the Lesser Houses and their allies fear the Greater Houses too much to act against them. They will gripe—'

'So they will!' broke in Eliar. 'Gripe! And do nothing about it!' Now she saw real passion furrow the young man's handsome face. His admiration of Mai's beauty came frivolously, no more than skin deep.

Calon nodded. 'We of the Lesser Houses and the guilds and our other allies in town fear that the Greater Houses see only their own profit, this season's coming harvest, without attending to the storms that will come in the seasons beyond. They are blind to the shadows. We of the Lesser Houses, guilds, and other households in Olossi have a made a pact among ourselves. We cannot stand back any longer. If you are desperate enough, we hope you may consider an agreement with us.'

'What manner of agreement?' asked Anji.

'Let me first explain what my allies and I have done to this point. If you will.'

Anji stepped back as Tohon stepped out of the shadows, moved up beside him, and whispered in his ear. Master Calon waited as Anji gestured to Chief Tuvi, who ghosted away into the coarse grass that shielded the land-facing shore of the island.

'Some movement of guards has taken place among those set to watch the ford that links this island to the shore,' said Anji to Calon. 'Have you seen?' He pointed to where that distant torchlight wended its long descent toward Olossi. 'Know you anything of what that light might portend?'

'I do not. Nor of any messenger coming into town this late.' Calon turned to Eliar. 'Think you it's news from Master Nokki and your cousin Shefen?'

Eliar winced. 'Shefen is dead. I fear the others lost as well.'

'You can't know he's dead. There's been no word. How did he die, then?'

Eliar shook his head. 'I can say nothing, and I don't know anyway. This knowing is woman's magic, not the province of men. If they say he's dead, then he's dead. Anyway, it's unlikely they would travel at night.'

Calon sighed and turned to Anji. 'As you saw yourself, we came by the water, hoping to escape detection, so we've had no view of the road until now. I would ask the ones who guard you, but since most of Olossi's militia dance to the tune played by the fiddlers of the Greater Houses, they would only march us straight to Assizes Tower and lower us into the dungeons besides.'

In the distance a splash resounded, but the sound was quickly drowned by the relentless push of the river's current. From their vantage point Mai could see past Anji's head onto the dark reaches of the spreading delta. A light winked on and off, on and off, and her first thought was that this was a firefly bobbing in the curling breeze, but as her gaze adjusted to the distance she realized she was seeing an artificial light turned off and on as though a lantern's protecting veil was being shut and opened.

Someone was signaling, out there on a boat riding the river or hugging the shore of another low-lying island.

'Anji, look,' she said, and he turned, but the light vanished as though her voice had warned it. 'I saw a light blinking, like a signal. Think you it's related to the messenger?'

'That's only a fisherman,' said Master Calon. 'There's a good night catch to be had this time of the moon.'

'Not just fish are caught this time of night,' said Eliar with a laugh. 'There's plenty who smuggle goods across the water so that Sapanasu's clerks can't demand their tithe. Not that I'd know of any such criminal behavior, being a law-abiding citizen.'

'My attention is caught,' said Anji, stepping back to face Calon. Priya set a pair of sticks on the fire, and the flames licked higher as Calon wiped his brow.

'My nose is itching,' agreed Calon. 'Many whispers have tickled my ears these last few nights. Listen!'

Mai listened, but she heard only the night sounds and the crackle of the freshly burning sticks, and when he went on she saw that this was a storyteller's punctuation, readying his audience for the meat of the tale.

'I cannot spin the whole tale to you now, for we haven't the time. But this is how it is.'

'He doesn't even know the lay of the land!' said Eliar impatiently.

'Patience, cub.'

'It's true enough,' said Anji.

'Very well. It's rich country in the north. The two great cities – Nessumara and the crossroads of Toskala – lie in the north, along the River Istri. The fertile fields of Istria and Haldia grow rich crops. To the northeast lie the richer fields of Arro, where the delvings glean gold and iron from the mountain fastness. And many more places besides, all sung in the tales of the Hundred.

'Once we commanded a steady trade along West Track through the Aua Gap and to Horn, that road which leads to the markets of Nessumara and Toskala and the fields of Haldia and Istria, even to the mines of Arro. All this has wasted away these past few years, sucked dry. Merchants rode north, and never returned. We hear terrifying tales of fighting in the north like to the hundred wars of ancient days, before the Guardians came. No caravan has reached Olossi from Nessumara for over a year. Last year there was talk of Horn being overrun, but we never had any direct news. No one dares send their wagons and goods on that route.

'After all, here in the south we can always trade throughout the south and over the pass into the empire, so it never seems as urgent as it ought to be. It's also true that the roads into western Olossi, Sund, and Sardia are still open, although they've become more dangerous as well in recent months. There's some trade also into the far south, places like Farro and Ofria, but that trade passes along foot trails overland through the foothills of the Spires, a path expensive in both trouble and time. A merchant must have safe, open roads to make a living. We have sent many messengers to Argent Hall asking for them to investigate this matter, but we've heard no answer of any kind, only silence.'

'Argent Hall? What manner of place is this?'

'It's the reeve hall with the obligation to patrol and protect this part of the country.'

'You hope they will help you in what manner?'

'Have you no reeves where you come from?' asked Eliar with astonishment.

'They have not,' said Calon. 'There are no reeves outside the boundaries of the Hundred. The Lady tamed the great eagles and gave them to the reeves, so we might protect ourselves, but beyond our lands they cannot stray, for that is the law of the gods.'

'So your priests tell you,' said Eliar stubbornly, 'but how can you know it to be true?'

'I have never seen anything like the reeves and their eagles in the lands I've traveled, nor heard any tale of them until I came here,' said Anji.

'Old Marshal Alyon sat in authority over Argent Hall until a few seasons ago,' said Calon. 'He sent a representative to every one of our council meetings, as has always been customary. Then no representative came for two passes of the moon. After that, we heard that a new marshal sat in authority over Argent Hall, but we have never learned his name. Worse, it's rare to see reeves patrolling around Olossi any longer, although they fly into the Barrens regularly. Now and again we see one pass overhead on an unknown errand. The villages and farms of western Olossi have no one to preside over their monthly assizes, so they come to us to ask for help. That's why we sent so many emissaries to Argent Hall. But we are given no answer at the gates, not even when we beg for aid to patrol the roads against ospreys such as the ones you killed in the pass. I fear the shadows have crept long, and that we here in Olossi are being covered by their stain without our knowing.'

'That's a sobering tale. So tell me, Master Calon, what do you want from us?'

'We, the Lesser Houses and our allies, seek your aid.'

'You want us to overturn the Greater Houses and set you in charge of the council.'

Calon met his gaze squarely. 'We do. Not to harm them, only to force them to share the power they have gathered to themselves. We must be allowed to take our place as our numbers and our judgment warrant. If there's a truly open vote, and all are allowed to vote on council matters who meet the requirement, we will be content. Then if the vote goes against our proposals, we'll accept it.'

'You do not expect that outcome, however. That an open vote will go against you, or your proposals.'

'I do not. But the agreement I offer you comes in two parts. That is the first. The second is this: That once the council is under our control, you accept a commission to ride to Horn, and back. We sent a small group north recently, and have heard no word of them. We fear they're lost. Dead. What we want is a report on the condition of the roads and way stations, on the market in Horn, and on the prospects for travel north into Istria and Haldia and Arro, and east into Mar.'

'Mar, by all means!' said Eliar. 'Our supplies of kursi grow ghastly low, and I fear I shall waste away rather than eat bland food.'

'It's no joking matter, cub,' said Calon. 'I am afraid of what we cannot see, and so should you be.'

'If the bid to overturn the Greater Houses fails, what then?' asked Anji.

'Oh, to us, any manner of thing,' said Calon carelessly. 'They will vote to strip the conspirators – for such they will call us – of our right to run a business and sell goods in the marketplaces of Olossi. They may execute the leaders. As for Eliar and his people, they might exile them.'

'These are serious risks,' said Anji.

'Mostly for young Eliar here, because his people are exiles twice over according to their lore and have nowhere else to go,' said Calon. 'If I escape execution, I can always uproot my house and begin again in Sund, or Ofria.'

Eliar whistled under his breath. 'It's said they're poor as dirt in Ofria, all living in mud huts and eating snails.'

'Little you would know! Snails are a delicacy! Here, now.' Calon untied a purse from his belt and handed it to Anji, who weighed its heft with two hands. 'We are serious folk, despite the manners of this cub, but he is a good lad and an honest broker, and I trust his people even if they don't care for my line of honest trade. I'll have you know his people have wagered the most on this gamble.'

'We've the most to lose,' said Eliar with a crooked smile. 'But I'll not mind saying, anyway, that the Greater Houses are fools to avert their eyes at the dark tidings that stare them right in the face. My people can't afford to turn their backs. We did so once, in the old country, and suffered greatly.'

Anji set the pouch at Mai's feet. It was too heavy for her to pick up, though she was not frail, so she opened it and picked out a pair of bars and a handful of coins, just the uppermost layer. A hoard rested beneath.

'These are cheyt,' she said, 'the full gold coins, not the quartered ones. There's no silver that I see. As for the bars . . .' She bit on the end of one bar. She knew gold's texture. The eldest daughter bred out of a merchant's family had to expect to handle money when she was married into a worthy household. No one wanted a mere ornament as a wife, however much the poets sang of gorgeous flowers whose pleasing scent drew princes and captains.

'Please count it all,' said Calon. 'It matters to me that you see we are serious in every possible way.'

'To overthrow the Greater Houses is a serious undertaking,' said Anji. 'And the expedition to Horn, after everything we have heard, more serious still.'

'True enough. I believe there are deadlier forces at work than any who bide in the Greater Houses care to admit.'

'Unless they are in league with them already,' said Eliar. 'For that's what I believe.'

'In league with whom?' asked Anji.

'No one knows,' said Eliar. 'But the reeves of Argent Hall turn us away, and the Greater Houses ignore every warning sign. How can I not believe they are in league with the shadows? That they are not themselves conspirators? My friends and I—'

'A wild pack of cubs,' interjected Calon softly, 'including my once sweet and pliant nephew.'

'My friends and I went on a scouting expedition two months back. We saw the reeves flying patrols up into the Barrens. They're looking for something, but we don't know what. Of their work – patrolling the roads, settlings disputes, standing in at the assizes, prosecuting criminals – the work that is their duty according to the law of the land, this work the reeves of Argent Hall have given up. They've forsworn their obligation to the people of Olossi and the territory they're meant to oversee.'

'Nothing can be proven,' said Calon. 'What would the Greater Council serve to gain from such plans, in any case? They already hold power over the council.'

'They want more, more even than they have now, more power over the rest of us, and more coin in their coffers. Sometimes greed is answer enough, Master Calon.'

'It just doesn't make sense to me,' the older man retorted.

Mai knelt on the ground beside the woven mat she usually sat on. On the mat's surface Shai tipped out the contents of the pouch. Their visitors fell into a respectful silence as she stacked and counted coins and bars. It was all gold, a prince's ransom.

'Four bars, whose weight and value must be considerable,' she said at last. 'And fifty cheyt.' Fifty gold coins.

Shai hissed an exclamation under his breath. Chief Tuvi grunted, scratching an ear.

'A handsome offer,' Anji said without emotion, 'but a dead man has no use for coin. We are only two hundred men. You're asking too much.'

Eliar gritted his teeth, gasping like a man in pain.

Master Calon raised a hand. 'But—'

'No,' said Anji in a tone that invited no response, a tone that meant he was not negotiating. 'I will not send my men into a battle that cannot be won. No.'

He was done. It was over.

In the silence that followed, Mai rose. 'Wait.'

Every person there was obviously surprised to hear her voice, even Anji. For courage, she touched her lips to her wolf ring, sigil of the proud Mei clan. Then she met Anji's gaze square on. 'I have something to say, and I would prefer to say it between us alone.'

Chief Tuvi raised an eyebrow. Master Calon put a hand to his mouth, clearing his throat as if uncomfortable. Eliar looked at his feet. Shai stood and, when Mai nodded at him, he gestured to Priya and walked away, into the shadows.

At last, with a slight gesture, Anji agreed. Chief Tuvi led the two merchants away, leaving Anji with Mai and, of course, one of his silent but ever-present guards.

He said nothing. He was angry.

She took in a deep breath and considered her words, considered her tone, considered her posture and her expression. All these made a difference in whether you made your sale. 'I am not experienced in the arts of war, nor have I any training in battle. But I am a merchant's daughter, and I know how to listen and how to observe. Also, it is my right as the wife of a Qin man to speak my mind.'

'It is.'

'This is what I have to say: Where will we go next? There may be a refuge for you with your cousin, in the south of the empire, but surely those cousins will also want to kill you, since you have a better claim to the imperial throne than they do. The lands that the Qin control are closed to us. So, to go south back over the pass leads us only to lands where our lives are already forfeit.'

'There are other roads,' he said curtly, as if he had already had this argument with himself and did not want to repeat it with her. 'Northwest. North. East. We haven't seen everything that's out here. This is a fool's choice, Mai. No smart general commits his troops in a situation weighted so heavily against him. He moves elsewhere until circumstances fall to his advantage. The Qin have always fought in this manner.'

'Maybe so, because the Qin do not live in houses, or in towns. The Qin do not till fields and plant vineyards and orchards, which they must then protect. But sometimes you have to fight where you stand.' When he shook his head, she went on. 'Anji, why did your mother send you back to the Qin, when you had as much right as any man to claim the imperial throne?'

'Because my half brother was named as heir. He and his mother meant to see me dead. I was a rival, brighter than him, I admit. Better suited. Better liked by our father. I was my father's favorite son.'

'Yet he chose your brother over you.'

'My brother's mother has powerful political connections, ones my father did not wish to anger. Although he was an excellent administrator, his position was not exactly strong.'

'Even so, why didn't your mother go to the emperor? Ask for his protection for you? Surely he could have done that much for his favorite son.'

'She had already fallen out of favor. He preferred a new wife.'

'Did she not try at all?'

He hesitated. For the first time he looked away from her, toward the fire, whose flames consumed the wood with bright splendor. 'It is not the Qin way to beg for favor.'

'She took the Qin way, Anji. She moved you elsewhere, hoping that circumstances would change. But they did not. And why should we believe they will change now? We have been offered a chance to stand and fight for the thing we need most: a home. It's time to stop running.'

'Death is also a home. One we will find ourselves fallen into very quickly, in this situation.'

She smiled, covered her mouth with a hand to hide the smile, glanced down at the ground, then bent her gaze up to look at him past lowered lids. His eyes narrowed as his interest quickened. 'Surely, Anji, you are capable of finding a way to win this fight.'

He laughed. 'An appeal to my vanity. Mai, you have cut me. But nevertheless, *no*.'

'What if there is no safer haven? In the south our lives are forfeit. In the west lie barren lands. North there is constant trouble, some kind of war. East lies the ocean. Yet we have to go somewhere. Any place we ride now will be a place we've never been before, so we will be placing ourselves in danger nevertheless. We might as well get paid to do it. We may never get another offer, and why should we? Who will welcome a troop of two hundred experienced soldiers? A ruler who wishes to use them to fight, and die. Ordinary folk will fear us, and rightly so. Anyway, we cannot continue journeying endlessly, in the hope that something more to our liking will appear, a peaceful haven, a secret valley where the flowers are always in bloom and all the ewes give birth to twin lambs. You have said I am foolish to listen to the tales, to believe in them, but isn't this just another tale you are telling yourself, that there is a place waiting for us somewhere, in the distance, just beyond where we are now? What if there isn't?'

Flushed and out of breath, surprised at her own vehemence, she broke off.

Frowning, studying the fire, he scratched under his right ear with his left hand. The fire popped, and sparks sprayed and fell. At length, he looked at her. 'That day in the market, in Kartu Town, every other merchant offered me their wares for free. They feared me, as they feared all the Qin and especially the officers. I suppose they thought by giving me for nothing what they normally sold for a price, they would gain my favor, or I would not hurt them. But you charged me double the going price.'

'And you paid it!'

'Because it amused me to do so. Because you surprised me. Because you held your duty, to sell your clan's produce, higher than your fear of the Qin.'

'"If you are afraid, don't do it. But if you do it, don't be afraid." Do you remember saying that?'

He shook his head, shrugging. 'It's a common saying among the Qin.'

'When we were in the desert, and running out of water. After the sandstorm, when you and Chief Tuvi had to decide whether to ride at night through those ravines. A dangerous, difficult passage. You said it then, to him. I took those words into my heart. I tried to live by them. I always thought that I was being strong, in the Mei clan, by bending before the wind, by going along with everything my family wanted, by never disputing with them or raising my voice or causing trouble. Now I see that I was afraid. But there will always be another storm, Anji. There will always be something. If we don't stop now, then it will be because we're still afraid. That's the thing we can't escape by moving elsewhere. It's still traveling with us. We have to do it, and not be afraid.'

He was silent. The night wind murmured in the brush; beneath it, she heard the whispers of men, waiting on this decision.

He stepped up to her, took her hand, laid it on his palm. Without speaking, he twisted the wolf-sigil ring off her hand and slid it onto his little finger.

'There,' he said. 'To remind me. But if we fail, and if we die, you must not reproach me.'

All at once, her words vanished. He was so handsome, a prince in truth, an exile, as she was now. She could never reproach him, not for anything. But she could not speak to tell him so; she was too full, choked with the tales she had grown up on, had loved and recited, had sung and played. Had used as an argument against him. She knew herself to be young and naive, stupid, really: she always had believed those tales, even in the ones where everyone ended up dead. She had always wanted to believe them, because they had seemed so much brighter than her own life within the Mei clan's walls. But they had only been a way of hiding from the truth.

'No,' he added softly, so sweetly. 'I suppose you won't.'

He released her hand and stepped back, then whistled sharply. Chief Tuvi returned with the two merchants, and Shai and Priya walked back into view.

'Master Calon,' said Anji without preamble. 'I am skeptical that you can accomplish your goals in the face of such difficulties. I doubt you can. And I doubt I am willing to risk my men, who rely on me to command them wisely and prudently. But perhaps you can give me a little more information.'

'Go on,' said Calon, with a glance at Mai that revealed nothing except, perhaps, a shiver of curiosity, of hope.

Eliar turned the silver bracelets that ringed his forearms, restless as he shifted from one foot to the other and back again. He seemed like a child who wants to speak but is trying to hold its tongue.

'Three things. First, what manner and number of soldiers serve the council of Olossi? What resistance will we face in helping you overturn the Greater Houses? Second, if we ride north, and return with the information you ask for, where do you advise us to go afterward? Gold is not enough. We wish to settle in a safe region nearby where my men might also find wives and sufficient pasture-land to support herds.'

Eliar coughed, bracelets jangling as he shook his arms impatiently.

Calon nodded with a grim smile. 'We are both desperate men, and dangerous for being desperate. Olossi has lived in peace for a long time and we have gone fat and lazy. Kotaru's ordinands do most of our border guarding these days. You saw what came of that! By custom, any adult in Olossi is expected to lift a spear in defense of the city, but in truth we can call on no more than five hundred militiamen should it come to that. More could be called out of the countryside – many more . . .' He paused. All looked inland, as he did. That torch still stuck its stubborn path along the road, heading for the city. '. . . but most of them untrained and inexperienced. We are sheep, ripe for the slaughter. We can't protect ourselves against a real attack, in force, in numbers. And that's what I fear.' His voice fell to a whisper, and darkened. 'That's what I truly fear. As for the other, were you and your company to ride into the Barrens, and break up into smaller groups, you could find villages that would welcome more hands. It's sparsely settled, especially along the west shore of the Olo'o Sea, in the valley of the River Ireni, and in the West Olo uplands against the mountains of Heaven's Ridge. There's decent pasturing – it's not good for much else – and plenty of land unspoken for in the high reaches. Your men might even find wives there, for I've heard rumors in recent months that young men all around are leaving for the north country to find work and promises of gold, and never come home again. I can't guarantee you'll be welcomed there, but I can guarantee that if you form this alliance with us, the council will give you a legal right to settle in this region. What was the third thing?'

'We met a reeve at the border. He'd heard news of these troubles along West Spur, although he did not tell me how he had come by this information. He asked for our aid in tracking down the bandits, and we helped him. He left us on the road because he wanted to visit Argent Hall. After that, he was supposed to come here to

Olossi ahead of us, to speak in our favor and preside over the arrest of the border captain, the one who died untimely. This reeve called himself Joss.'

'Heya!' cried Eliar.

'Hush, cub! Let him finish!'

Anji's gaze sharpened; he was not accustomed to being interrupted. He coughed, and went on. 'He rode an eagle whose name was Scar. Have you any news of him? Because it seems he has gone missing.'

'Argent Hall, eh?' Calon scratched his chin. 'Maybe he changed his mind and flew back north. People do that, quit themselves of any claim to duty.'

Anji shook his head. 'Perhaps, but he would have left word. He would have let us know the change of plans. He is a man of honor. He said he would meet us at Olossi. He did not.'

Meanwhile, Eliar was rolling his eyes and waggling his hands like a madman, although both of the other men ignored him.

'You're stubborn on this point,' said Calon. 'For you spoke of it in council as well.'

'It's a point of honor.'

'I surely know nothing of this reeve, except for what rumor your comments caused after the council meeting.'

'Let him speak,' said Mai, almost laughing.

Eliar did not wait for permission. 'It's true a reeve did come to Olossi a few days back. Legate Joss was the name he went by.'

'How did you hear of this?' demanded Calon. 'I never did!'

'That clerk who was recently assigned to work in Fortune Square at the council hall—'

'One of your flirts?' asked Calon with a laugh.

'She's a friend to my sister,' he said with an unexpected bite.

'Begging your pardon, cub,' said Calon hastily. 'No offense to your sister intended.'

Eliar fixed his sharp gaze on Anji. 'Before I met up with Master Calon to come out here tonight, I related the events of the council to my sister. This clerk is a friend of hers. My sister told me in strictest confidence that her friend had confided to her that this reeve was arrested and taken to Assizes Tower. The clerk who witnessed his arrest is afraid she'll be imprisoned in Assizes Tower herself if she speaks of what she saw. She's that frightened. There were a number of witnesses to the arrest, folk waiting that morning for council desk to open, but even so, she fears to speak of it, because she heard his name.'

'How long ago?' asked Anji.

Eliar shut his eyes briefly, as if counting, then opened them. 'Five days back. My sister said that her friend said he was a handsome man, I remember that particularly. That she'd been quite taken with him, and thus triply shocked that he'd been hauled away, thinking she'd been fool enough to flirt with a criminal. He was accused of murder.'

'That's him,' said Mai.

'A murderer?' asked Calon.

She flushed. 'No. He's the kind women flirt with on short acquaintance.'

'Who was he accused of murdering?' asked Anji.

Eliar shrugged. 'A captain, she said. A captain guarding the southern border.'

'Captain Beron.' Anji nodded. 'Five days back, Reeve Joss was arrested, it seems. Three days ago, Captain Beron was still alive. Before the dart stung his eye. So tell me, Mai, how could Reeve Joss have been arrested for a murder that hadn't yet been committed?' He extended a hand, gestured, and Mai tossed him a gold coin, which he caught deftly. 'He was arrested for a crime someone else was planning to commit, someone who discovered that Captain Beron's operation was discovered, and that Beron himself had been arrested. Yet no man or woman left our caravan between the border and Olossi, none except Reeve Joss.'

'They betrayed him!' cried Eliar.

'So it seems, and another man besides,' said Anji. 'Captain Beron was alive yesterday morning, and was dead by the time we reached the gate. Who killed him, and why?'

Master Calon shook his head, like a weary ox trying to shake away a pestering swarm of flies. 'This grows deeper and darker,' he muttered.

'Truly,' agreed Anji, 'since this man called Captain Waras was wearing, around his neck, the very bone whistle which we had previously seen in the possession of Reeve Joss. Without it, I think, the reeve has no way to call his eagle. How can a man be freed from Assizes Tower?'

Calon shook his head. 'Assizes Tower was once the responsibility of the Guardians. After they were lost, the reeves came to sit in authority over the courts. Now even that measure of justice is lost. The Greater Council rules at its whim.'

'This reeve is not the only prisoner in Assizes Tower,' said Eliar with a frown. 'All the criminals are taken there. Yet I know – as do you – of a well-respected man who vanished after he claimed that the Greater Houses were involved in a conspiracy, that they'd allied with unnamed villains out of the north. He's not been seen since. He was murdered.'

'Hush, now, cub. That's gossip, nothing proven. He was known to be of an envious, restless nature, an Air-touched Rat, and worse besides, if you take my meaning.'

'You suspect he was murdered, too,' retorted Eliar. 'Who can measure his true crimes now that he has vanished with no chance to speak on his own behalf?'

Talk of prisoners made Mai uncomfortable. The Qin had been able to drag criminals and, indeed, any person at all off to their prison block in Kartu Town, where they held their own manner of court, and the law court of Kartu Town had no authority to stop them or even oversee the hapless prisoners. She began to replace the coins and bars in the bag. It gave her something to do with her hands.

'How can a man be freed from Assizes Tower?' Anji repeated.

'Impossible,' said Calon.

'Necessary,' said Anji. 'First, I have an obligation to him, and my honor to uphold. Second, he knows things we don't. We are grasping in the dark, and he holds a light insofar as he knows which people he talked to, and if he traveled to Argent Hall, and what he saw there.'

'I'll see it's done,' said Eliar.

Calon groaned, clapping a hand to his head in a gesture so very like Ti that Mai expected him to declaim in threes. 'Fool!' he growled. 'You can't get into Assizes Tower.'

'My sister can. My sister was there today. She said there was one man in the deepest pit, untended and filthy. It could have been this reeve.'

'Your sister goes to the Assizes Tower?' Calon asked. 'Whatever for?'

'She brings food to indigent prisoners.'

Calon laughed as though it hurt. 'The hells, yes, you Silvers do go on about your "god rules" in a way that does get to annoying people. Begging your pardon, Eliar.'

The youth gave something like a wink with his right eye. Mai saw at once that he was angered by this comment but didn't want to show it. 'We will be judged at the gate according to the measure of how we walked in the world and showed justice and mercy to poor and rich, innocent and guilty, those with power and those who are helpless, according to the law.'

Calon coughed. 'That was the law in the land you came from. That's why folk will keep calling you outlanders.'

'No, it is the law in all lands, not just the land we came from.'

'Let's not have this argument, cub.'

Eliar turned his back and took several steps away, shoulders heaving, hands in fists up by his mouth.

Anji watched.

Mai said, 'Master Eliar, even if you could get into Assizes Tower, how would you know Reeve Joss if you saw him, and why would he trust you, even if you could speak to him?'

From Eliar came silence.

Master Calon rubbed at his chin with a knuckle, looking thoughtful, and turned to Mai. 'Perhaps you could go with that sister of his, verea.'

'How could I do that?'

'Because the Silver women only appear in public with veils covering their faces. No one need know it was you.'

Maybe this could work after all. Heart pounding, Mai turned to Anji. 'I can't fight. At best I can defend myself at close quarters with my knife, but any competent soldier would overwhelm me. This is something I could do.'

'No,' said Anji. 'What do you trade in, Master Calon?'

'Flesh. In slaves.'

'So. This entire complicated scheme might be nothing more than a plot to rid yourself of my company, which seems dangerous to you, and steal my wife without any risk to yourself. You and I both know she would be worth a great deal of coin on the slave market.'

'I could sell her for twenty cheyt, at the least,' agreed Master Calon with a genial smile.

'I won't have this talk!' cried Eliar, lurching back to the circle. 'Never tell a man of my people that he has stirred his hand in the pot of slavery! Do you mean to insult me?'

'Cub, hold your tongue!' Calon grabbed hold of his arm, but Eliar shook him off.

'Enough.' Anji stepped between the two men, and they both backed off. 'Answer me a few questions, if you will, Eliar sen Haf Gi Ri.' He grabbed a stick out of the fire and held it up. Flames licked down the wood. 'On what fuel does the flame sup?'

'The wood,' said Eliar, looking irritated. 'What is the point of this?'

'And on what food did this wood grow?'

'On water and earth and sun. As any fool knows!'

'And water and earth and sun, where are they grown? What is their origin? Is it not the case that "all things blossom out of the heart of the Hidden One"?'

'I beg you, accept my apologies,' said Eliar in a stricken tone.

Anji tossed the stick on the fire. 'No need. I studied the archives as part of my education at the palace school. Now I know who you are. Your people lived in the empire.'

'Not my clan, but distant cousins out of other clans, yes. After our people crossed the ocean, some of the clans fetched up on the shores of the Sirni Empire. They were driven out because they would not make sacrifices at the temple of the false god.'

'That's not quite how it is written in the histories of the palace.'

Eliar had the grace to blush. 'I suppose it would not be. I intend no offense.'

'You can be sure I take none, as I am not a believer. But you're right. It was a long time ago, four generations. As it happens, the priests of Beltak had a lot to say about your people, as they have a lot to say in all their writings. But I never thought I would meet one of you. They called your people "the servants of the Hidden One, an avatar of the Lord of Lords, King of Kings." They claimed you lived half in light and half in shadow, and in the end the priests insisted that any of you who refused to perform the sacrifice at the temple depart from the empire or be put to death. It is written there were no executions, so I am minded to believe that the priests were merciful in your case.'

Eliar nodded. 'It is said in our lore that some among the clans betrayed our people and sacrificed to the false god in order to stay in the empire. But the rest came north into the Hundred to join their kinsmen. A few sailed farther north even than that, to the lands beyond.'

'Many things were written,' added Anji, 'but I recall in particular that the priests of Beltak were outraged that among these "servants of the Hidden One," slavery was entirely outlawed in all ways and shapes, and in every manner. In the empire, clans and houses are required to provide slaves for service in the temples. This your people refused to do.'

Eliar nodded. 'It is against the will of the Hidden One that any should hold another's life in bondage, or aid in such a transaction.'

'But what of their labor?' asked Calon. 'Labor is separate from life, as it is written in the law of the Hundred. Still.' He smiled as Eliar puffed up, ready to burst into a tirade. 'This is a dispute for another time.'

'Everyone keeps slaves,' said Mai. 'That's just how it is. How can anyone change that?' She looked at Priya, but Priya remained silent.

Anji looked at Eliar, and then at Mai. 'These are desperate times. But tell me, Master Calon, how are we to manage this overthrow, since it will take longer than one night to plan and execute? If we don't depart in the morning, they'll guess something is amiss.'

Calon took in a deep breath, and seemed to have breathed in a midge, because he set to coughing until Chief Tuvi slapped him on the back and dislodged the irritant from his throat.

'Eh. Gah. I thank you.' He wiped his brow. He was sweating, although it wasn't hot any longer. 'Misdirection. In the morning, ride west along West Spur, as if you mean to obey the council's order. After a day or two cut south into the Lending.'

'The Lending?'

'The grasslands. The high plains land south of the Olo'o Sea. With good horses, and if you can hunt, you'll manage. It's a difficult time of year to find water, but the rains will come soon. We're almost to the turn of the new year. Out there, the Greater Houses won't be able to follow you, for despite the power they hold here in Olossi, they don't possess more than the town militia. I guarantee you that the militia won't march out into the Lending in pursuit. They've had trouble out there in the past, but if you're hospitable to the tribes and raise no sword against them, you'll be given free passage. Then you can await word, until we're ready to strike.'

'A great risk, for uncertain gain,' said Anji.

Priya's soft voice startled Mai, although the Qin did not seem surprised to hear her speak. 'The Merciful One teaches that where a river cannot breach hard rock, it will find a softer path to go around.'

'True enough,' agreed Anji. 'This may be the softer path.' He gazed into the darkness toward the distant watch lights burning along the city wall, barely visible from their campfire. 'But a dangerous one, despite that.' He looked at each face illuminated in the circle of light thrown off by the fire before settling on Mai. 'I cannot bring myself to allow you to ride out on such a perilous expedition.'

Calon made a noise, a soft grunt of surprise and pleased assent.

Anji nodded at Calon. '*Should* we agree to your offer, that is. Such a plan would not only put my wife at risk, but her presence on military maneuvers put the rest of us at additional risk because we will need to take additional measures to protect her. Therefore, Master Eliar, I ask you, would you on your honor as a servant of the Hidden One give shelter to my wife? I will pay for her lodging at fair market value—'

'Impossible!' cried Eliar.

Mai stepped back, startled by his vehemence.

Even Anji looked surprised.

'Cub, what are you saying?' demanded Master Calon.

'I mean only – I pray you—' He was flustered. 'She would bide with my family as our guest. We cannot take payment. It goes against the law of hospitality.'

'Then you will have my undying gratitude,' said Anji as smoothly
as if these were the very words he had expected to hear. He turned
to Mai. 'Sending you with them is a risk we must take if we mean
this venture to succeed. For one, you will seek to free Reeve Joss.
Also, the coin will go with you. If something happens to me, you
will have the resources to set up a business for yourself.'

Eliar nodded. 'My people will shelter her as one of our own. And
do what is necessary to aid her, no matter what comes. I do make
my oath on the heart of the Hidden One that she will suffer no
harm nor will she be sold into bondage while in the shelter of our
house, and that she will leave that shelter only upon your return, or
of her own choice if she is widowed.'

'So taken,' said Anji.

'So taken,' said Mai, but the words came roughly, and her eyes
filled with tears. She had talked him into this, and now he would
run the campaign according to his understanding of war even if it
meant she was to be separated from him in this foreign land and
sent to live with strangers. Yet it must be done. If you do it, don't be
afraid.

Priya took her hand in her own.

'A shrewd bargain,' said Master Calon. 'So, Captain. Verea. Do
we have a deal?'

Anji indicated Mai. It went against everything she had learned
and lived in the marketplace to agree to any deal without negotiating for a better offer.

'Double the price. The balance to be paid if we succeed.'

Eliar whistled.

Calon took the bait. 'Impossible. We've already given you everything we have with us.'

'Impossible, indeed, to ask our company to risk so much. Life
cannot be bought by gold. Death cannot be bribed by gold. Double
the price.'

'A third again as much.'

She glanced at Anji. He had his head tipped slightly and appeared
to be looking not at her but at Toughid's boots, with his mouth
pulled tight as if he were trying not to smile. He flicked a finger
against his chin as he sometimes did, to her chin, when they were
alone, and she sucked in a breath to give her a volley of courage.

'Two-thirds again as much.'

'You'd do better to ride back to the place you came.'

'Master Calon, surely you do not expect me to believe you offered us everything you and your consortium possess in your warehouses and stock? No merchant of your undoubted prosperity offers his best price first. Something must always be held in reserve. Yet we are as you see us. We have no reserves, except what this payment will bring us. We are at the mercy of fate. Two-thirds again as much.'

'Half again as much.'

She nodded. 'Agreed.'

Eliar laughed. 'She has bested you, Calon. Take that!'

The merchant shook his head, giving a slow smile. 'I am impressed. And I am also desperate, although it appears to me that while your desperation is equal to my own, you are not undone by it, as I am. I agree, as spokesmen for this consortium, as you term it. The rest of the payment to be delivered upon completion of the tasks.'

Anji stepped forward to shake hands with Master Calon in the traders' manner, each man's right hand grasping the elbow of the other as a seal to their agreement. After a hesitation, Mai stepped forward as well. In Kartu, only widows without husband or son to act for them dealt in public legal contracts. Master Calon grasped her elbow, squeezed, and let go without any surprise or answering hesitation; it seemed he considered her presence perfectly natural in a transaction of this kind.

'Let Sapanasu, the Lantern of the Gods, give Her blessing,' he said in the cadence of a ritual utterance, 'and Her curse to any who turn their back on what they have sworn in Her name. Let it be marked and sealed.'

'Let it be sealed,' repeated Anji.

'Let it be sealed,' said Mai.

Lights scattered and flared along the outer wall as a swarm of torches moved out from the gates to engulf the singleton and escort it toward the walls.

'An irrevocable step for all of us,' said Master Calon. He blew out his breath. 'I need a drink!' He gestured toward the darkened city and the distant torchlight. 'I wonder what *that* is all about.'

40

He was dreaming, walking along the shore near Haya that he knew from his childhood. The strand ran for mey ahead in a curve that faded at length into distant hills whose hieads were shrouded in rain clouds, although here where he walked the sun shone, its light winking on smooth waters. His feet crunched on coarse sand. The rhythmic shush and suck of waves along the shore and the shrill cries of seabirds overhead kept him company.

A mist rose off the surface of the wide bay. It boiled into a silver fog that rolled toward the land like a watery beast shouldering up out of the depths. On the crest of this fog, as on a wave, lifted a rider mounted on a winged horse, and it surely was Marit riding that horse because even at this distance he would know her anywhere. He ran toward the water, to meet her. The foam of the cresting wave broke over the form of rider and horse, obliterating it; he was left behind with wavelets lapping his toes and his hands grasping air.

'Reeve! Reeve Joss!'

The low voice woke him, or possibly he woke himself, moaning aloud. He stirred and sat, and found that he could sit. The bit of rice and water taken earlier had strengthened him. His head ached, but he could blink without wanting to pass out.

After all, he was only hearing things. He could see nothing in the blackness. The air smelled of rotting things and sickness and worse, a foul smell lightened only because it was rather dry, not at all fresh. Thank the gods.

'Reeve Joss!'

The hatch scraped open to reveal a light lowered through to dangle, swaying back and forth on a line. A hand appeared, fingers slender and strong. It fastened the lantern's looped handle to a hook set in the ceiling off to one side, too high for him to reach. He blinked back tears as his eyes adjusted, and when he was able to look up past the light, he saw a face looking down at him through the hatch as hands lowered a rope until its end curled on the floor.

'Hurry up,' she said. 'Are you strong enough to climb?'

The rope had been knotted at intervals to provide footholds and handholds.

'Very thoughtful,' he said, for it took him a moment – he was thinking slowly – to recognize her. 'But I'll take my chances with someone who hasn't already tried to kill me.'

'As usual, you men always jump to conclusions about what we women intend. It's quite tiresome.'

'When I met you last, you tried to kill me.'

'Are you sure?'

'Hmm. Let me think. A naked knife. A mostly naked woman. I admit that part was appealing.'

'Why in the hells would I come to kill you stripped to the waist?'

He chuckled, although it sounded exceedingly like rolling pebbles in his mouth, a trick he had tried when a lad with predictable results. He felt now, too, as though he had swallowed something small and hard that wedged in his throat. There was still a little water left in the cup, and he sipped at it and recovered and could speak.

'I thought it was a clever ploy to distract my attention.'

She laughed as she grinned down at him. The flame of the light gave her complexion a glowing cast, bathing it in gold. Her eyes were very dark, heavily lidded. Her mouth was lush and very red. Delectable.

'Aui! The hells,' he muttered. 'I'm delirious.'

'No doubt. All the better reason to climb that rope and escape your prison.'

'With your help?'

'I'm the one with the rope.'

He lifted a hand and was pleased he had strength enough to gesture in a casual way, reflecting a degree of unconcern he did not, in fact, feel, not with her hanging over him in such a position that he got a look right down her vest to the rounded shadows beneath. He remembered – very well – the curves she had on her.

'I'll pass.'

'You'll wait for the justice of this corrupt council? I think you'd do best to be well shed of them, for they've been colluding with all manner of folk who will be happy to kill you once they have conquered Olossi. Which they are like to do if you can't get a message to the northern reeve halls, which I wish you would do by climbing this rope, calling your eagle, and leaving this place as soon as ever you can.'

'Oh. Slow. I beg you. That was too much and too fast, my sweet.'

'I've not given you permission to call me your "sweet."'

'Maybe not, but you ask me to trust you. That should give me a few privileges, don't you think?'

'Why shouldn't you trust me? You're such an easy target now that had I wished to kill you, you'd be dead already.'

'It is a great comfort, knowing that. Why did you try to kill me before?'

'As I said, you misread the signals.'

'A knife thrust at my guts is a strange way to signal something other than murderous intent.'

'I had to protect myself. I wasn't sure who had sent you. You might have been on the side of our enemies.'

'Who did you think had sent me? Who are your enemies? And who are you?'

She looked away, over her shoulder, then back down at him. 'Best we get you out of here before we're interrupted, then I'll tell the tale.'

'So, again, you're saying I must trust you.'

'Or stay here. Your choice.'

'How did you get here? Where are the guards?'

'Aui!' She had a very attractive way of setting her jaw when she was exasperated. 'You talk too much, after all. Just like other men. Here I hoped you were different.'

'Oh! Eh!' He laughed, although it hurt his head and his ribs to do so. 'Now you've appealed to my vanity. I can't bear to be 'just like other men."

He tried to stand but found he was too weak to do it easily. Setting a hand against the wall and one on the ground, he managed to lever himself up, but he had to lean against the wall lest he collapse. He was cold, and then hot, and then cold again, in waves that made him sweat and shiver. 'Whew. I'm sorry to say, it'll be hard for me to climb that rope.'

She withdrew. A second rope slithered over the lip and its end dropped to the floor. Two bare feet appeared, gripped the rope as she eased her body over the lip. She shinnied down hand over hand at a speed that should have burned her thighs, landed softly, and paused with a hand still on the rope to fetch a tiny globe from her cleavage. It was glass, of a kind. With it balanced in one palm, she blew into it, and it lit with a pretty flame that cast an aura of light before her.

'I'll help you up,' she said.

He stared at her tight sleeveless vest and short kilted wrap. The rig showed her figure to advantage, and she knew it. She smiled, amused by his stare.

From above, a snap like the sound of a door slid hard shut cut the quiet.

Her smile vanished as quickly as it had come. She stepped forward to examine him, and the floor of the cell, under the glow of the globe light. He became aware of what he must look like and how he must reek. For the first time, he got a good look at the coating of dried grime that had slicked the floor, every possible thing he could disgorge from his body: blood, vomit, diarrhea, urine, the worst sort of spume.

She lifted the globe to the level of his eyes. 'Did they try to poison you?'

'I don't know. I ate a little rice earlier. It – stayed down.'

'Follow the light.' She moved it slowly from side to side, but she watched his eyes. 'Did you take a hard blow to the head?'

'That I did.'

'Ah. Sometimes that will make you cast out your stomach. Yes, you've quite a few signs of that illness. You'll want a bath and your clothes washed. We best hurry, for this is taking longer than I had planned for. Can you walk?'

'I don't know.'

By the way she tilted her head just a little to the right and then back a little to the left it seemed she was considering options and discarding them.

She touched the globe to those rich lips. Its light extinguished immediately.

'I'll put it back in its warm setting, my sweet,' he said hopefully.

She looked at him sidelong in a way that would have set him

aflame if he wasn't feeling and smelling and looking like a dead rat well run over and left in the dank to get really ripe. Then she tucked away the globe, slung a strong arm around his waist, and helped him over to the rope. There was nothing seductive in the action. She tied him up in the rope to make it a seat around his hips. He was so dizzy from moving that he couldn't even say what he would like to say about where her hands were working because the words went awhirl and he had enough to do to stay on his feet as she rigged him up and left him standing there. She climbed swiftly up the knotted rope and eased herself gracefully out of the hatch. A moment later, the rope drew tight, strained, and he grasped with all his strength to avoid pitching backward as she hauled him up. He rocked. He shut his eyes, but decided that was worse. His knee rapped the hot surface of the lantern, but not hard enough to shatter anything, by Ilu's mercy.

The room above, which he did not remember, was a holding cell with rings along the far wall where folk could be chained up until ready to be moved. She had used one of these rings as her lever, with the rope pulling over it, and when his head came up past the opening she tied it securely, crossed back to him, and used main force with her arms hooked under his armpits to drag him up and onto the floor. There he sprawled. While he panted, trying not to sway although he wasn't moving, she cut him loose from the rope now tangled around his legs.

'You'll have to walk the next part.' She stepped back and pulled up the lantern.

'Where are the guards?'

She knelt beside him. There was a pleasant smell to her, like jasmine, but under that a scent he recognized with a kind of delayed shock: She smelled of eagles.

'You'll need this.'

Her hands were cool as she lifted his head enough to slip a leather thong over it, settling it at his neck. He groped at his chest, found the bone whistle. He groaned, would have wept had he retained water enough for tears. 'What bell is it?'

'Middle night.'

'I can't use this until daybreak. Once they discover I'm gone, they'll search for me.'

'Which is why we must hurry.' She got an arm under him, and with her help he stood. The whistle gave him strength.

'I can walk on my own.' That he was so helpless, and she so competent, irritated him enough that he nudged her away. 'Where do we go?'

After all, she was not immune. A smile chased across her lips. Her eyelids drooped, and for a moment she had the sleepy look of a woman woken after a night of passion, smug and certain and well pleased. 'Does this mean you trust me now?'

He'd be a fool to try to walk unaided, this close to freedom. He grasped her arm just above the elbow. She had satiny skin, and taut muscle under it.

'I'm Joss, but you already know that. What's your name?'

'Zubaidit.'

'Ah! Such poetry! "Where the axe hewed, the man was stricken."'

Now she was amused. 'Not everyone knows the story of the woodsman's daughter.'

He would have leaned in to speak intimately close beside her ear, had he been clean and sweet-smelling, but he was not, and although she had as yet made no slightest sign of finding him foul in his current state, he didn't care to chance seeing a grimace of disgust cross her face. After all, if he survived this, he would recover his strength, and take a bath, and then she would see what it meant to meet her match.

So he smiled at her, as well as he was able. 'It's one of my favorite stories from the Tale of Fortune. Especially the ending.'

She laughed, a clear sound that she made no effort to muffle or disguise. What in the hells had happened to the guards? But he didn't ask again. It was time to take his chances, and see where this tale of fortune led him.

'You would say so,' she said with a smirk. 'Come, now. We have to go see someone.'

She doused the lantern, led him down the corridor, helped him up a set of stairs and through an open door into a spacious hall swallowed in night but which he recognized by the carved railings at one end as Assizes Hall. She moved smoothly, graceful despite the darkness, and he, leaning on her, was able to stumble alongside creditably. No one was about. It was weird how very quiet it was, all the guards lost. Murdered, maybe. And who in the hells were they going to see?

'It's a strange way to murder me,' he muttered, unable to help himself. 'Or have you some other more convoluted plot in hand?'

'I do, but you'll need all your powers of persuasion to help me. Now, hush.'

They came to the wall of screen doors, all closed. A faint, wavering light could be seen through the papered screens. Nimbly, she slid a door halfway open and eased him onto the wide front porch that ran the length of Assizes Hall. A stocky man carrying a small lantern was waiting at the foot of the steps. Beyond him, Assizes Court was empty, all in shadow, no lamps at all.

'What of the eagle?' she whispered, dropping her voice now that she was outside.

'Without me, he won't fly until it's day. I can't call him until dawn.'

She helped him down the steps. The man who waited was master of a handcart, which was empty except for a cloak bundled in the bottom.

'This is my friend Autad,' she said. 'He owns the Demon's Whip, a tavern in Merchants' Walk. He's agreed to cart you, since I wasn't sure how far you'd be able to walk on your own.'

'You've thought of everything. Where are we going?'

She tilted her head back as if she'd heard something, and sprang up the steps to vanish into the hall, sliding shut the door behind her. She was gone as quickly as if he had only dreamed her.

'Get in, ver,' said the man in a genial voice, pitched low. 'Hurry. I'll cover you with the blanket.' He moved up beside Joss, and even in the night Joss could sense that terrible grimace. 'Whew! Begging your pardon!'

'Where did she go? Where are we going?'

'Where she tells me, ver.'

'Do you trust her that much?'

'She's a true servant of the gods, that one. Very pious.' The man hesitated. 'If you wouldn't mind, ver.' He indicated the cart, coughed, gagged a little. 'Geh. Well. Best if we do this quick. If you don't mind.'

Once in Haya, one summer when he was a lad, he'd been out

swimming with his friends and been grabbed by a rip current that had dragged him out into the sea. But you learned growing up on those shores to let go instead of fighting what you could not resist, because fighting would kill you. Eventually, of course, the rip current had slackened, and he had worked free of it and swum back to land.

'Thanks, ver,' he said to Autad. With the man's help, he clambered into the belly of the cart. Autad flipped the cloak over him. The cloth smelled of hay, but it was a good, honest, clean smell, one he appreciated. The cart rocked beneath him as Autad lifted and pushed and began walking. The wheel rumbled over stone. The movement jostled him.

For a long way Joss just lay there, thinking of nothing, really, too drained to fret or scheme. The streets were quiet around them. Evidently in Olossi people did not commonly walk out at night, while he was accustomed to the streets of central Toskala, which were more or less awake at all hours. Sometimes it seemed they rattled up a hill, and sometimes it seemed they rolled down one, and only once in that journey did Autad speak, in the manner of a man who has been mulling deep thoughts in his mind and finally found words to express them.

'I'd do anything for that girl. I do owe her, for saving the life of my sister. She had that rash that eats the skin. Poor thing, suffering so. Zubaidit spent her own coin to buy the oil of naya, which is the only unguent that cures it. I couldn't afford such a luxury.'

'But—'

'Hush! Now we're coming to where folk are about. I don't want anyone suspecting. I'd lose my license, and be subject to exile. Or worse.'

They moved into a neighborhood where there were, indeed, a few folk out even at this late hour, judging by the sounds of footfalls and soft conversation and the occasional clink or clatter of unseen objects changing position. Joss's hip was bruising where it pressed against the bottom of the cart, and every time they lurched forward his right shoulder knocked against wood. Autad hadn't brought any padding, more's the pity.

Abruptly, the cart rocked to a halt and Autad pulled the blanket off. 'Can you get out?' He stood back, not offering a hand.

Joss got first to his hands and knees, and then awkwardly clambered out by levering his legs out first and following with his body. He was weak, but damned if he would inconvenience the man with his stink, when it was so obvious how appalling it was. They stood in an alley of towering white walls, both ends lost in shadow. A lit lantern hung from a hook protruding from one of the walls above doubled doors. These were broad and high enough to admit wagons, and a smaller 'walking' door for foot traffic was set into the larger door. All around, the cobblestone pavement had been swept clean; there was no trace of litter or noisome debris. Indeed, it was pretty obvious that the only nasty thing in this tidy alley was Joss himself.

'Wait here,' said Autad. He probed in his sleeve, withdrew a ball of rice rolled up in a se leaf, and without *quite* touching Joss gave it into his hands. Joss was so hungry that he ate it at once, trying not to choke on big bites, forcing himself to chew. Autad moved off with the cart while Joss had his mouth full, but when Joss tried to speak, the other man paused, hoisted the cloak, took a whiff, and tossed it at Joss, then with the cart trundled off down the alley until he vanished into the night.

Joss finished the rice, then chewed up the se leaf – beggar's food, as they called it, but despite being stringy and tough, it was edible and it settled lightly in his stomach.

Neither bell nor device adorned the door, by which a man could signal that he stood outside. Any night noises were here muted by the walls and the isolation. He could not even tell how long the alley was, or how far it reached on either side, but he guessed that he stood between two large compounds that were likely either temple establishments or the households of rich men.

For a few breaths he simply stood there to quiet his heart, calm his mind, and consider his options, alone in the dark city with a chance to escape. Definitely his best bet at this point would be to turn and walk away and hope to make it out of the city without being stopped, although it would be tricky to get past the gates of the inner wall.

Without warning, the 'walking' door opened and there stood Zubaidit.

'The hells! Come inside quickly! Anyone might see you out there!'

Since he could think of no clever rejoinder, he followed her into a wide court with trough, cistern, hitching posts, stable, and a small warehouse. Here tradesmen could bring their provender without sullying the main entrance of the rich man's home, for certainly a rich clan's compound was what this was.

'Over here,' she said, indicating the trough. 'Best hurry. There's a change of clothes. He'll never speak with you if you're not cleaned up a bit.'

'Where are the guards?' he asked.

'Right there.' She indicated the opening of the stable, where a trio of men were trussed and gagged, but still alive by the way they twitched their shoulders and waggled their feet to get his attention.

'What game are you playing?'

'There is only one,' she said with a smile, pressing a bag of rice bran into his hand. 'The game of life, death, and desire. We haven't much time.' She turned her back and folded her arms.

Though he was shaking with weakness, and could not trust her, the entire night's adventure had taken on such an air of unreality that he let himself be dragged onward and outward, as into the sea. He stripped, with some difficulty prying himself out of the tight leather trousers, and tossed trousers, jacket, shirt, and cloak to one side. All were unbelievably foul, soaked through, matted, dried, and stiff in spots. A bucket stood beside the trough. He filled it and dumped it over his head, filled and dumped, filled and dumped, until he was soaking. Using handfuls of the bran, he scrubbed himself, working quickly, finding all the worst layers of grime. After, caught by a sense of impending doom, he dressed in the simple shirt and knee-length jacket provided, draped and tied into place with a sash. She did not once turn to look, although he had wondered if she would. He crossed to the cistern, took down the drinking ladle from its hook, dipped, sipped, and hung it back.

'Ready,' he murmured.

'This way.'

He followed her into the warehouse, whose walls in this darkness he could not perceive. If folk slept here, he did not hear or see them.

'This way.'

Behind her, he groped his way up the rungs of a ladder into the attic. Here she lit her tiny globe to reveal a long chamber with a steeply pitched roof on both sides. The low walls were lined with shelves on which rested various boxes and bags neatly filed away according to a system he could not quickly comprehend. She moved to a cabinet, opened it, and gestured. Ducking through after her, he was at once choked with a sense of closeness, weight pressing on him, dust a congestion in his lungs, walls falling at him on either side. But after all he fixed his gaze on her backside, very shapely, as she climbed stairs in what was little more than a narrow tunnel, the ceiling so low that he kept thinking he would slam his head against it and the walls so close that if he leaned any little bit left or right his shoulders brushed the paneling. It was quite dark, although the glow of her light outlined her figure most pleasingly. Hers was an easy target to aim for. He mounted the steps behind her, but she got farther away and he fell behind because the climb exhausted him and she was swift.

She opened a door and passed the threshold. At length, puffing and panting, he got to the top and stepped into a fine chamber ornamented with all manner of luxurious furnishings. Beside an open coin chest rested a reclining couch imported from the south. A set of paintings depicted a crane seen through the six seasons, edges embossed with gold foil to frame each hanging silk scroll. Two greenware ceramic ewers flanked a brass basin worked into the shape of a very rotund peacock with feathers spread high and small mirrors adorning each 'eye,' so a person could catch a glimpse of himself as he washed his face.

It was the kind of chamber where a merchant entertained guests he wanted to impress with his wealth, or where he reclined on his couch in order to entertain himself by counting out his strings of money. It appeared that Zubaidit had arranged a different sort of entertainment for the other person in the room. This grand gentleman wore only an ankle-length night jacket cut from such a fine grade of southern silk that even Joss could appreciate its quality. The precise shade of blue was hard to distinguish because there were only two lamps burning, both set on tripods, one on each side of the chair to which the man was tied. Zubaidit finished untying the gag she had secured around the man's mouth, and with a glance at Joss, she seated herself cross-legged on the couch next to her prisoner and folded her hands in her lap.

'I've met you!' said Joss, staring at the merchant. 'I met you in the north.'

'He stinks!' croaked the man. 'Don't let him sit on my best pillows! Or on my Dayo'e carpet! Aui!'

'You have an overly sensitive nose. Best you be thinking of your life and livelihood and that of this city, rather than your pillows and expensive carpet. Oh, just sit down, Joss.'

He had to. His legs were about to give out. He tried to stay away from the doubled rank of eight pillows with their embroidered scenes depicting that day in ancient times when an orphaned, homeless girl knelt at the shore of the lake sacred to the gods and prayed for peace to return to the land. This set of scenes portrayed the gods's answer: the calling of the Guardians, and the gifts given by each of the gods to those Guardians, to aid them in the burdensome task of restoring peace and establishing justice.

The merchant whimpered as Joss sat, but Zubaidit cut him off. 'Master Feden, I thought perhaps you might be more likely to believe me if I let you speak to Reeve Joss, who hails from Clan Hall.'

'You're lying,' said the man. 'This is some story you've woven to confuse and befuddle me. You came here with Reeve Horas earlier today. You stood beside him as his ally, and swore to him that you would deal with this prisoner. Yet here this man sits, contaminating my good carpet! What have you done to my guards?'

'Nothing as lasting as the death that will greet them if you do not believe me when I tell you the truth. There is a strike force not a day's march from these walls, and an army two or three days' march behind that, many thousand strong, who mean to burn, rape, and plunder this town and set their own governor over what remains. You were a fool to ally with Argent Hall and whatever folk out of the north you have made alliance with. But it is not too late to act, and save yourself and this town.'

'An army?' said Joss. 'On West Track? I saw none when I flew down . . . and yet—'

'Go on,' she said encouragingly. She had yet to move her hands, clasped so easily there between her thighs, as if she were waiting for a cup of tea to be brought so they could sip in cool collusion.

'On our way down here, we came across groups of men, armed

bands. But I never thought ... Could small groups be brought together that quickly, to form an army?'

'If they are well led, certainly. Who is your ally, Master Feden?'

'None of your business. None of the temple's business.'

'Surely it is. If the temple is to be attacked, the temple must be prepared to withstand the assault.'

'Who would attack a temple?' cried Master Feden.

'You have not been listening to the stories that have walked south, have you? Those who serve the Merciless One have become targets, just as reeves have. In the north. Only in the south and in the east have the temples remained immune.'

'Impossible. No one would hurt those in service to the temples.'

'On the Ili Cutoff, you were talking to Lord Radas of Iliyat,' said Joss to Feden. 'It just doesn't make sense. Does Lord Radas know about this army? Who leads it? Where it comes from?'

Feden did not answer.

'I'll tell you this,' said Zubaidit. 'I have seen a thing I thought I would never see, a thing spoken of only in stories.'

She moved smoothly, uncoiling more than rising. Stepping away from the couch, she bent, picked up one of the pillows, and displayed the fine needlework in the spill of lamplight. Folk no doubt lost their eyesight stitching those tiny details. It made Joss's eyes water to look, or perhaps that was the cloying scent steaming off a heated bowl of perfumed water strewn with petals that had been placed on the low side table next to Master Feden's chair. It had the sticky aroma of diluted sweet-smoke. Joss wondered if the man was an addict. Master Feden was twisting his hands, testing the bonds that trussed them, but he was caught fast.

'Look at me!' She shook the pillow. 'You see? Here, the gods offer their gifts.'

Every child knew the Tale of the Guardians by heart, how the orphan had come to Indiyabu to plead with the gods to intervene, to save them.

Joss chanted.

Taru the Witherer wove nine cloaks out of the fabric of the land and the water and the sky, and out of all living things, which

granted the wearer protection against the second death although not
against weariness of soul;

Ilu the Opener of Ways built the altars, so that they might speak
across the vast distances each to the other;

Atiratu the Lady of Beasts formed the winged horses out of the
elements so that they could travel swiftly and across the rivers and
mountains without obstacle;

Sapanasu the Lantern gave them light to banish the shadows;

Kotaru the Thunderer gave them the staff of judgment as their
symbol of authority, with power over life and death;

Ushara the Merciless One gave them a third eye and a second
heart with which to see into and understand the hearts of all;

Hasibal gave an offering bowl.

'I saw two of them,' said Zubaidit.

'Two Guardians?' said Joss, with a thrill of fear and excitement.

'Two orphans?' said Feden with a sneer.

'Two horses, winged.' She threw down the pillow. 'Two horses. Winged. And an army of thousands, too many to count. Although based on the number and formation of their cohorts I would say there were four or five cohorts of about six hundred soldiers in each. Let us estimate three thousand men, three hundred and twelve in the strike force, and more ranging up and down the line as foragers and scouts. That, Master Feden, is the army that marches on Olossi. What did they promise you?'

'There is no such army,' he said, 'and all agree the Guardians have long since vanished from the land, and were anyway only a tale told by our grandparents to school the young ones. You are insane.'

'I'm tempted to agree,' said Joss, but by the look she gave him in response, brows drawn down and mouth scowling, he saw he had truly angered her.

'So be it,' she said. 'I wash my hands of both of you.' She crossed to the coin chest and helped herself to two fat strings of silver leya and one of humble copper vey.

'Thief!'

'Payment for services rendered. Yet the information is true enough. I'll return to the temple to warn them, as is my duty. After that, you are all on your own.'

'You give no proof,' said Master Feden. 'You have no proof. How did you release this reeve? Why didn't you kill him, as you said you meant to do?'

'Marshal Yordenas commanded me to kill him—'

'You *were* trying to kill me!' Joss cried indignantly.

'No. The temple sold my labor to Marshal Alyon, when he requested protection. I stayed on after Marshal Alyon's death because the Hieros ordered me to. She saw that things weren't right at Argent Hall. She thought all the reeves had become corrupt. That's why I was armed when I approached you.'

Joss could not help laughing. 'Armed and naked. A deadly assault.'

'The reeve is wanted for murder,' said Master Feden. 'Murderers deserve death.'

'Murder? Whom is he supposed to have murdered?' she asked scornfully.

'A border captain named Beron, a holy ordinand in the service of the Thunderer.'

'You and your council are fools five times over. I killed that man, on a commission given me from the temple.'

Master Feden, surprisingly, remained silent.

'Captain Beron undertook a commission to assassinate a member of the Lesser Houses,' she continued. 'The Merciless One alone claims the privilege of such action. He crossed the boundaries, took a life in a way forbidden to the Thunderer's ordinands. Therefore, he was marked for death at our hands.'

'The hells!' Joss glanced at Master Feden, but the merchant was now staring at his hands, all tied up tight, and not speaking. 'How did you manage to kill Captain Beron? He was caged, concealed, and guarded by the Qin.'

'I arranged for an axle to break. In the fuss, I meant to make my move. But as it happens, just before the breakdown a window opened, and I took the opportunity.' She smiled, looking Joss up and down in a way that made him wipe his brow. She was laughing: at him, at herself. 'I have many skills.'

'We needed his testimony! He was willing to talk, to tell us who he was working for, who was paying him off.'

'The Merciless One is a jealous mistress. He violated the boundaries. He had to die.'

'Then we'll never know who hired Captain Beron to assassinate a man, and to hunt with ospreys.'

'Master Feden might know.'

'Me? Me!' Feden sucked in a lungful of smoke, and set to coughing. Belowstairs, heard either from down along that hidden stairway or through the closed door into the main part of the house, a clamor rose of many voices calling out the alarm.

'Master Feden! Master Feden!'

A high bell rang to wake the household.

'Heh! Heh! The guards come! You've been discovered! Now you can't escape justice.'

She drew a knife from a sheath tucked up high on her thigh, hidden by the kilt. It was a thin, killing blade exactly like the one he had taken off her in Argent Hall. 'It's all the same to me whether you die now, Master Feden, or die later at the hands of the allies who betrayed you. What did the leaders of this army that is marching on Olossi offer you? Gods! How gullible can a man be? Is it only greed that blinds you? Or are you just that stupid?' She waved the knife toward Joss. 'Go on. Down in the warehouse, turn behind the ladder and find the fourth locker. Open it, and feel with your hands three bricks to the left. There is a stamp on the fourth brick. You can fit your fingers in and lift it, and find a hook beneath. Pull on that, and a door will open. Follow the tunnel out to the street, taking the third turn to the left and the second right. Go swiftly.'

'What tunnel? I know nothing of a tunnel under my warehouse.'

She ignored Feden's spluttering, and instead repeated the directions.

'How will you escape?' Joss asked. Feet pounded on stairs. Soon they would be at the door.

She clenched her jaw. 'Why must men be so stubborn? Just go. Save yourself. I am not clumsy enough to be caught by this manner of men.'

'Heya! Heya!' cried Master Feden. 'Help me! Help me!'

Fists pounded on the far door. 'Master Feden! Master Feden! We've news! Terrible news.'

'He's busy!' she shouted. 'Come back later, when I'm through devouring him.'

But they were desperate. Her reply did not raise a single answering retort, not even a lewd joke. 'Terrible news. You must open up. Villages are being attacked and all the folk in them murdered. A lad escaped. Hurry, Master Feden! We brought him, to tell his tale.'

A new voice joined the chorus. 'Master Feden! It's Captain Waras! Master Feden, open up, by the gods. You must convene the council. What will we do? What will we do? We've been betrayed!'

The merchant had been frightened before, then flushed with rage and doomed triumph as he contemplated being murdered in cold blood by the Devouring woman. Now his complexion faded to a ghastly gray. 'Villages massacred? Can it be true?'

She said nothing. Joss found he could not move his limbs, as if he had fallen into sucking mud and gotten trapped.

Then she moved, too quickly for him to stop her. She unlatched and slid the door open, and behind it unlatched and slid open a second, secured door. Captain Waras strode in, looking first at her, then at Master Feden, and finally at Joss. He was so flustered and shaken that he did not act as a guardsman should, to assess and react to the threat. He waited, hands loose at his sides, sword in its sheath. A pair of guardsmen walked in, supporting a lad of some fourteen years, a slender boy with the wiry legs and arms of an experienced rider. He had the stone-shocked look of a person who has seen something he dares not believe but cannot deny.

Joss rose. 'Give me your report,' he said, finding his reeve's voice. 'Quickly, while we still have time.'

The lad lifted his chin, responding to the command.

'They marched in along West Track, from Hornward.' He spoke in a flat tone, all emotion smothered. 'I was at the Olossiward end of the village, stabling the horse for the night, and then . . . and then . . .' Almost he cracked, but he swallowed and blinked multiple times. He held on. 'I rode away as fast as I could and though they rode after me they could not catch me and I rode all night and I changed horses at the villages and I warned them and some believed and some did not but I got torches and I kept riding through the night, oh the gods have set their hands down on this land, what will we do? Everyone. Everyone who could not run. They were all killed. All dead. Slaughtered like animals.'

His eyes rolled up. He fainted.

The guards stared at the fallen youth, then at each other, waiting for someone to give them an order. Joss crossed to the lad and knelt beside him to be sure he'd not cracked his head; his breathing was even, and the reeve arranged his limbs more comfortably. Zubaidit sheathed her knife and went to the window, leaning out to stare into the darkness.

Feden wheezed out a breath. 'Betrayed,' he muttered, as if trying on the word as he would try on a new jacket, one as finely made as that which slipped around his bare legs now to reveal pudgy knees and ample thighs, a man with plenty to eat and plenty to boastfully display. With plenty to lose.

'We have been betrayed,' said Captain Waras. 'Everything these allies of yours promised the council, Master Feden. Lies. They said no one would be hurt, only that we would get our trade routes back and extra portions and a larger share of the market for those who cooperated with them and a lesser share for those who did not. That they would put down the revolt of the Lesser Houses.'

Feden had long since ceased struggling against the bonds. He sagged, and his chin drooped, and trembled. 'Betrayed,' he said in a strangled voice.

'I must return to Clan Hall with these tidings,' said Joss.

Zubaidit turned back to survey the chamber and the stricken men: merchant, captain, guards, and fallen boy. 'No matter what you choose to do, you can be sure that the reeves of Argent Hall will see everything.'

'What will we do? What will we do?' Feden broke down and wept.

She spun the knife through her fingers, an entertainer's trick that was not at all charming in her hands. When she smiled, Captain Waras took a step away from her.

'I have an idea,' she said, 'but you won't like it.'

41

Shai envied Mai her ability to sleep when his every nerve jangled. She sat back-to-back with Priya near the fire, her head drooping gracefully and her fingers tucked under her belt. Shai had already bundled up his sack of carpentry tools and his meager possessions, leaving them with the neat pile of goods that would go with his niece at dawn, when the man with pulled eyes and turbaned head came to take her away.

Honestly, he was shocked that Captain Anji had let her go so easily. It was all very well for a man to claim that his people and his god abjured slavery. You could say anything, but that didn't make it true.

One of the soldiers appeared out of the night and placed driftwood on the fire, then faded back into the dark. In his wake, Anji came back from the main campsite and beckoned to Shai.

'Come. You'll attend me.'

Together with Sengel and Toughid, Shai walked with Anji to the ford, and there the captain called across the channel to the men on guard.

'I have a request. Is there anyone I can speak with?'

There was a big bonfire illuminating the bank and much of the length of the channel, to make sure no one snuck across. By its light, a man walked through the multitude of sentries and halted at the edge of the water, not so far away, really. His feet were hidden in reeds. The creak of bowstrings sounded faintly from farther back, at the edge of the fire's light, covering him.

'I'm sergeant in command of this cadre. What do you want?'

'You know our situation,' said Anji. 'Since we have to return to the south, we'll have to hire ourselves out as guards again, if we're allowed. Do you think I can go over in the morning and arrange for a hire?'

'Not my decision,' said the sergeant. 'I was told you're to ride straight out.'

'There'd be something in it for you if you could see to it that one or a pair of your men might run into town on my behalf. I saw the makings of another caravan—'

A fellow came up beside the sergeant and spoke to him, too low for Shai to hear.

The sergeant nodded and raised his voice to call to Anji. 'That group rode out two days ago. There's no hire waiting for you. You'll just have to go.'

'In that case, I've need of coin. Are there any merchants in town willing to buy flesh?'

'Buy flesh?'

'Yes. Much as it grieves me, I'll have to sell my concubine.'

It seemed every guardsman on the far bank heard him, for there was a rush of sound that briefly drowned out the bass cry of the river. Their voices rose, and jokes came, laughter in plenty although the words themselves were washed together.

'You can imagine,' said Anji into this so sternly that those men quieted and there was only one last laugh, choked off, 'that I'm unwilling to part with such a valuable flower for anything less than top price. As I said, if you've a man willing to run into town, perhaps a few of your merchants might be willing to come out here at dawn to bargain with me.'

The sergeant whistled. 'You're a cool one. I thought you told the council she was your wife.'

'Slaves can be wives. She lent respectability to my offer, but it wasn't enough. I can purchase ten more just like her in any market in the south. She's too much trouble to me at the moment. She takes two slaves to keep her, and they slow me down.'

'Thought you didn't want to ride back south,' said the sergeant. 'Are you changing your story, eh?'

'It doesn't seem to me I have a choice. Now, are you willing, Sergeant? There'd be something in it for you, as well.'

'How much could I get my hands on?' asked the sergeant with a coarse laugh.

'A bit of coin for your trouble. Anything else you'll have to arrange with the merchant who buys her.'

'Whew! I doubt I can afford it. She'll go to the houses up on the hill, for certain. Well, I'll send a runner in to Flesh Alley, but I can't promise you any of them will be willing to creep out of their comfortable beds before the dawn bell. Best you and your company be ready to leave as soon as the sun is up.'

'We'll do what we're told,' said Anji, 'having no choice in the matter.'

As they walked back to their own campfire, Anji said to Shai, 'Do you think that went too easily?'

'Do you think he was suspicious?' Shai asked.

'I don't know. In the Qin territories, no one would have believed that sorry tale. Not after I'd publicly proclaimed her as my wife. Concubines and slaves may be shed and taken at will, but not wives. Still, in the empire, unless she had powerful relatives I did not dare to offend, no one would remark on it.'

'There was a man in Kartu Town who bought a slave. A year later he took her to the priests to have a scroll written to free her of all claim and to make a marriage contract, since he wished to marry her. And he did, and held a marriage feast, too. Three months later she stole his strongbox and fled from town with a passing caravan.'

'The authorities did not catch her?'

'No. It was during the rule of the Mariha princes. The captain of the guard wanted a bribe to go after her, and the poor man had no coin. He tried to sell his land and his business to raise money to go after her, but my father talked all the merchants in town out of taking advantage of his weakness. It was obvious to everyone he had been possessed by a demon. Later, he recovered, and after that he came to our house and thanked my brother, for by then my father had died and my brother become Father Mei in his place. That was the difference between my father and my brother. My brother would have bought land and business at the bargain price, and been happy to do so.'

Anji shook his head. 'The Qin would have brought her back and executed her as a thief. A crime of that sort weakens all of society. It's no wonder the Mariha princes fell so swiftly. They were already like a wood post that is rotten and soft all the way through. Easy to topple.'

'Do you trust this man? Master Calon? If his Lesser Houses have so many people who support them, then why haven't they already overturned the council?'

'They are frightened. They are shackled by habit. Or they are just now testing their strength, which they have only newly discovered. It may be these problems with the roads have only recently made them desperate enough to act. I can't tell.'

At last, swallowing, Shai asked the question he dreaded asking but must ask. 'Will Mai be safe with these "Hidden Ones"?'

They had come to the fire, where Mai dozed, Sheyshi snored, and Priya watched. Father Mei would have yelled at Shai and struck him for his impertinence in asking such a question, since a younger brother must not question an elder, but Anji rubbed a midge out of his eye instead. His was a thoughtful expression.

'The priests of Beltak, in the empire, hold all men to be as slaves to the god. Those who do not believe are allowed to travel to only a few of the border towns, where they must remain in the markets. Within the empire, if you do not sacrifice to Beltak and pay his tithe, you are executed. Yet they wrote of the servants of the Hidden One with respect. They accounted, especially, any number of instances of their honest dealings. And they complained of their treatment of their womenfolk.'

'How so?' asked Shai, looking at Mai. Fearing for her. She had endured this journey better than he had, if you really counted it all up, but no one could look at her and not think her fragile, even knowing better. 'How do they treat their womenfolk?'

'It seems the servants of the Hidden One allow their women to keep their accounts books. In the empire, women are not allowed to handle money, so you can imagine that this offended and shocked the priests. But the servants of the Hidden One refused to alter their custom, saying it would go against the law of their god. So I am thinking, Shai, that if Mai will be safe anywhere, it will be in the hands of people who let women run their businesses, even if they are hiding away behind a veil. Perhaps especially, for Mai, in a strange land, where her beauty is hidden behind a veil.'

'But how did they know?' asked Shai.

'What do you mean?'

'In the empire, men live separately from women. So you told us. So I saw for myself. How could the priests of Beltak know who kept the accounts?'

Anji laughed, but his laughter ended abruptly when Tohon came out of the brush and began speaking to him. Without answering Shai's question, the captain walked away with Tohon to oversee, Shai supposed, the breaking of camp.

Shai sat down next to the fire and tried to sleep, but he could not calm himself. They were true mercenaries now, taking up another man's fight for coin. If they survived the first test, they would ride into unknown lands, to that town where Hari's ring had been found. At the start of this journey, the idea of actually finding the place where Hari had died had seemed impossible, but now it seemed he might survey the field of battle where, it was supposed, Hari had died. But would this knowledge, his witnessing, bring peace to the Mei clan? These thoughts unsettled him. He sought out Tohon, in the main section of camp. Shelters were already taken down and bundled up. Men made themselves ready. There was nothing for him to do. He was not only extraneous – he was useless. He went back to the fire and watched the lick of flame as it ate up branches. Priya nodded to acknowledge his presence. Mai still slept, and none disturbed her.

The slender crescent moon, the herald of dawn, was rising in the east. A nightjar clicked. A bird whistled, and there came an answering bird song out of the bushes. Out on the water, a few boats appeared, being poled or rowed downstream toward the estuary. Lanterns swayed from their bowsprits, hung on poles out over the water to attract fish. The color of night was fading as the tones of daybreak shaded the world around them and brought life to all those creatures who hid and slept at night, fearing what they could not see.

No different from me. For the first time, he thought longingly of home, of the sere slope of Dezara Mountain, of the tidy orchards and narrow streets, the familiar scents and angles of the town where he had lived his entire life. His brother Hari had left willingly, even eagerly, boasting of lands far off that would welcome him better than he had been welcomed in his father's house all the years of his erratic rebellions and outraged criticisms. But at least Hari had been bold. Shai had been pulled along for the ride, a twig tossed into the flowing stream, nothing done of his own volition but only caught and taken by the current.

A splash sounded in the shallows where a fish leaped. A series of chirrups chased a path through a clump of bushes. A twig snapped under the foot of one of the sentries, who later would be ridiculed for the lapse. Wind gossiped in the leaves, a murmur that never seemed to stop, just as the whispering in Father Mei's house, among the wives and cousins, never seemed to stop. These were his chorus, and after all maybe it was better to be standing here awaiting word of their departure than to be standing in the courtyard once again awaiting whatever crumbs the family would throw him, the seventh and least of sons.

Grandmother Mei had wanted a daughter last of all. That was the traditional way: a daughter to keep at home to care for you in your waning years, since a daughter-in-law, while under your rule, could not be trusted to be as faithful and considerate as a daughter of your own blood and body. But she had gotten Shai instead, and a pair of miscarriages, so he was often reminded, and after that she had withered in the way women do when they grow too old to bear any longer. She had used up the last of her birthing blood on a useless boy.

No, definitely, he was well rid of them all. It was only that he missed the wide vistas and the soft colors, the stormy height of Dezara Mountain and its spacious grazing grounds, and his solitary shelter.

'Look, there!' said Tohon, startling Shai when he appeared suddenly out of the night.

Shai went over to the scout. From this angle, he could see the city walls. A single torch – the second one they had seen that night – reached the city walls and vanished inside. Closer at hand came another splash. Anji came into the light and bent down to gently wake Mai. She woke quickly and without fuss, and was on her feet in a moments, alert and ready.

'Here he comes,' said Anji.

Escorted by Seren and Umar, Iad the caravan master skulked into view. The stocky man looked around nervously as if he hadn't expected to see people's faces, and he retreated to stand in the gloom with his face in shadow.

'I am surprised to see you here,' said Anji, not with anger, simply speaking the truth.

'I'm surprised to be here,' said the man. 'I've been sent as an emissary by the council of Olossi to make a proposal.'

'The council of Olossi?' Not by a hair or a shading of tone or a flickering of the eyes did Anji betray emotion or thought or any reaction at all. 'The Greater Houses?'

'Yes. I'm here at the behest of the Greater Houses.' Iad hesitated, swallowed a gulp of air for courage, and spoke. 'They sent me because you and I have dealt honestly in our crossing out of the empire.'

Anji looked at Mai. As if bothered by a bug, she scratched at

her right ear with her left hand. 'Go on,' said Anji, looking back
to Iad.

Well, now things were getting interesting. Shai moved closer, to
hear better.

'They thought you would trust me where you might not trust
another. They said to tell you first of all that a certain reeve, called
Joss, has been discovered in the assizes prison where he was accidentally placed after a case of mistaken identity. He's now been
released, and taken no harm from his sojourn in the prison.'

'Released? Unharmed?'

In an undertone, Mai murmured a prayer of thanks to the
Merciful One.

'Yes,' said Iad.

'A bold if convenient move.'

'They hope this will show you they are ready to deal' Breaking
off, he wiped his brow nervously. 'The hells! You must know they
did no such thing. I mean, the reeve is free, and has taken no lasting
harm, but it wasn't the council who released him. Someone else rescued him – a hierodule, of all people – and brought him in to
confront Master Feden about this news she had of an army
approaching'

'Hold. Hold.' Anji raised a hand, looked at Mai, then back to the
caravan master. 'An *army*?'

Mai's eyes had gone very wide. An army? Had the empire sent
soldiers after Anji? Shai saw movement in the shadows: the Qin
soldiers, those not on watch, were stirring, coming in close to listen.
Everyone was on edge.

Master Iad swallowed like a man wishing he could eat his words
rather than speak them. 'It's like this. This is the question the council sent me to ask. Can a company of two hundred defeat an army
of three thousand?' Having gotten the words out, he wiped his
mouth as against a foul taste.

'An army of three thousand?' said Chief Tuvi. 'Are you sure of
that number?'

'The hierodule saw the army earlier today, and got a decent
count: about five companies, which would be three thousand men
more or less. Several days' march east of here, Hornward, that is, on
the West Track.'

'How could she have seen that today, and then have rescued the reeve from Olossi's prison this night?' asked Anji. 'If they're several days' march east of here?'

Iad clapped a hand to his forehead. 'She got a ride to Olossi from one of Argent Hall's reeves, but she says the entire hall is corrupt . . . Aui! It's a complicated tale. Then a lad rode in after nightfall, saying his village had been attacked by a strike force and everyone laid to the sword, killing and burning.'

'The torch we saw,' said Anji to Chief Tuvi.

'That would explain it,' agreed the chief.

'The reeve, Joss, confirmed that Argent Hall had been corrupted. And Master Feden confessed that he had made a deal with some villains out of the north who it seems meant to betray him all along, for they said nothing to him of sending an army!'

'So what, precisely, is it that you want?'

'An answer to the question! That's all I agreed to. Can a troop of two hundred defeat an army of three thousand?'

Anji laughed. 'Not in a pitched battle, with mounted forces, such as I command. A company of two hundred would be foolish to attempt it.'

Master Iad relaxed, shoulders sinking and lips going slack. 'Eh. Ah. Exactly. I told them so, but they are so desperate, they insisted I come.'

Mai raised a hand. 'Master Iad. Before you step away from a sale you believe you cannot make, let us hear your entire proposition. You can't simply have been sent to ask a question.'

'I told them it would be impossible,' said Master Iad, 'but they insisted.'

'You treated us fairly, so it is only fair that, in return, we hear you out,' said Anji, and the poor man started, so surprised was he. 'Did you say the Lesser Houses are involved in this transaction? That they knew of it?'

'The Lesser Houses? No, not at all. They knew nothing of it. Even now, only a few know the truth, for it was just laid before Master Feden a short while ago. The Lesser Houses and the guilds may seem numerous to you, but they have no power in the council. I come at the behest of the Greater Houses. Aui! Now that I know what is upon us – an army of three thousand! – I'm cleaning out my warehouse and dependents and leaving at first light, as soon as I get back to the city, unless they've locked me out, which I wouldn't put past them. The Greater Houses have destroyed themselves with their own greed! They brought this calamity down on Olossi, and the rest of us will be ruined with them!'

'Well, Mai,' said Anji, looking at her with an expression Shai could not begin to interpret. The captain raised a hand to his lips. When had he gotten Mai's wolf-sigil ring? He touched it to his lips, then nodded at her, waiting.

'Can you do it?' she asked.

Anji smiled, as Shai imagined a wolf might grin – in a manner of speaking – when it spots a helpless fawn caught in a mire. 'Go on, Master Iad. Now I am interested.'

As dawn rose, the caravan master began to talk.

42

A quartet of guardsmen accompanied Joss to Crow's Gate. Although he had bathed again in the court of Master Feden's compound, and had been given clean clothes in the style of those worn by Olossi's militiamen, he insisted on wearing his leather trousers instead of a clean linen pair. For the moment he regretted it, as they were damp from being rinsed and wiped down, so his legs chafed where they rubbed the saddle. The lingering stench of his captivity caught in his throat.

Crow's Gate was still barred for the night. In the half-light that presages dawn, he watched as another rider approached them. She was riding one horse and leading a packhorse and a spare on a lead.

'You can't have been to the temple and back by now,' he said.

'No. As it happens, I ran into another hierodule in town, a kalos, in fact, a fellow I know and trust. He'll take the message to the temple in my place. That gives me more time to make some distance west. What did you decide?' She indicated the four guardsmen, who had looked her over and then away. She was subdued, and with her hair pulled tightly back and wrapped into a knot at the back of her head and her body concealed in a loose knee-length jacket, she was a woman you wouldn't give a second glance. Not unless you knew what she was.

She smiled, teasing him for staring at her so.

He wasn't usually taken so off guard. 'Oh, eh, yes. These good men here will escort me south to the intersection with the Old Stone Road. I believe it will be safe to call Scar from there.'

'Yes. You're less likely to be seen. I expect a certain reeve from Argent Hall to fly in soon after dawn. It's best he be given no chance to see your eagle.'

'Why?'

'Why shouldn't he see your eagle?' There was something more than teasing in that pull of her lips. She had a way of raising her eyebrows and tilting her chin that was deeply sensual, even triumphant. She was a woman confident of her power and, in that, desperately attractive.

'Why do you think the same reeve will come back?'

'Marshal Yordenas will send someone back to make sure those mercenaries leave. I am pretty sure Horas will volunteer, say he knows the situation best, so best he be the one to supervise. I admit, a lot of the plan depends on it being him who returns. It's a gamble. But we've only got one throw before we're ruined, so we may as well be reckless.'

'I still expect this is all a ploy to catch me off my guard, or capture my eagle.'

'If you say so. Had I known you were so full of yourself, I'd have known I need only wait until you fill up with the poison of self-love and strangle on it.'

Seeing that he had begun to lose her interest made him try harder by shifting ground. 'What do you gain from this gamble?'

Her expression was closed to him. She drew her horses aside as Crow's Gate was opened and the first folk were allowed to pass. Riding away, she spoke a last comment over her shoulder. 'Nothing so different from what's in it for you.'

He was flushed, and bothered. He let all the other traffic go ahead until the early tide of traffic had flowed out. Their party was released to pass Crow's Gate, and they headed out on West Track, riding due south toward the escarpment while the sun rose east over the Olo Plain and the river's meander. For a while they rode in silence. Farmers had set out into their fields. Early-morning peddlers trundled their goods out toward distant villages. Joss wanted to tell them all to turn back, to hide within the safety of the walls, but he could not. The reeves of Argent Hall must not suspect that Olossi's council had learned the truth about their alliance. And so, in the service of their desperate gamble, they sent folk out unsuspecting into the lands where wolves were already on the prowl.

The four guardsmen were likable young men who could not, in fact, stay silent for long. They had the confident bearing of those granted youth and health and strength, but the least of Captain Anji's tailmen could, Joss supposed, take all four out without a great deal of effort. These were not hardened men. They were not honed. They were like a sword made for show, not for fighting, pretty in their dyed linen jackets and loose trousers and bright silk sashes of teal or crimson or sea-foam green.

'Did you see the incomparable Eridit last night?'

'No, she was engaged with another man. I went to the arena to see that new troupe.'

'Were they at the Little or the Big?'

'Oh, at the Little. They came out of Mar. It wasn't much of an audience.'

'It wasn't much of a talking line, I heard.'

'That's true. But there was *one* girl . . . still, you know how they are, they will say they are sworn to purity until their tour is done.'

'They say that if they aren't interested. What they say to a handsomer man is quite another thing.'

'That's not what your sister said.'

'Hey! That's not funny. You know she's getting married at Festival.'

'Stop it, you two! Or I won't cycle you off duty on Festival First Night.'

The chatter changed course into safer channels: the upcoming new year's festival; a jeweler who gave good deals on trinkets suitable for wooing jarya companions; a flower seller who had given good advice about a certain herbal that gave off an arousing perfume; the cockfights and horse races meant to take place on Festival Third Day; the demise of their favorite rice-wine seller in an unexpected fall from the upper story of his warehouse; the preparations of one of their party for his appearance in a talking line on the last night of the festival, which mostly had a great deal to do with properly gathering and sewing together stiff nai leaves to make the traditional bristling wrist guards.

These young men, like all the rest of the early-morning travelers and indeed most of Olossi's population, were ignorant of the magnitude of the threat that stride by stride marched nearer. It seemed Olossi's council really did like to hoard its secrets, even when knowledge might save lives. It did not, on the whole, make him trust them, neither the Greater Houses or the Lesser.

'Look! There!' said the fourth young man, who up until now had said the least.

They had gone a ways up the slope and could look back with enough command of the height that the wide plain and the curves of the river winding through it made a striking scene. Sunlight glittered on the river. The sea was a vast sheet of calm water, bluest beyond the delta's mouth. Over Olossi, a reeve circled, dipped, and descended for a landing.

Joss swung around to look up along the road. A fair stretch ahead of them, where the going got steepest, a rider moved at a leisurely pace. The rider was leading two spare horses, one of which had the bulky outline of an animal laden with supplies. As he watched, she reached the turn where the road bent sharply right to run east parallel below the escarpment.

To his companions he said, 'Let's get moving.'

43

Horas spent a dreary evening stuck in hall while Master Yordenas made him repeat his report twice like a simpleton who couldn't understand two words rubbed together, and while the party of four argued. At length it was agreed that someone really had to go back to Olossi to make sure the mercenaries got the hells out of town and well away from anyplace where they might have a hand in disrupting the larger plan.

'There aren't many of them,' said Horas. 'I don't see why they're such a threat.'

'Ten would be too many,' said Toban. 'You were given strict instructions.'

'We'll have to send a reeve to oversee their departure,' said Weda. 'You ought to go, Horas. You know the Olossi council master better than the rest of us do.'

'You just don't want to stir your fat ass out of here,' he retorted. But he thought of the Devouring girl, and stirred restlessly in his chair. Yet those thoughts drew up from the well of his memory the stark gaze of that woman under the awning, the clerk with her brush and blank scroll. Her gaze had left him raw and shriveled. 'Let someone else go. I'm due a break from running messages.'

He pushed back from the table and took his leave. He thought of checking in on Tumna, but there were loft masters, the hall's chief fawkner and his assistants, to tend to injured birds. Anyway, he was tired and cranky. Before the lamps could burn dry, he retired to his usual cot in the barracks. The musty smell of his mattress, the angle of the wedge propped under his neck, the feel of his beads wrapping his wrists: these brought sleep and chased away bad dreams.

In the morning, he woke with a clear head and a niggling sense of disgust with himself. What a fool he was to have let that Devouring girl get away without paying for her passage! Thinking of her got him stiff all over again. He was no better than a child, flinching at shadows. Indeed, he could not really identify what had gotten into him yesterday. Likely it was sour wine curdled in his stomach whose gassy effusions had made him believe that a gaze from a meek clerk had power beyond what was natural. Strange how a good night's rest and a comfortable meal could set things right.

He rose early and told Toban that it was best for he himself to go back and personally supervise Master Feden and the council. 'I'll even follow the troop for a day, make sure they're really getting gone.'

'No matter to me who goes,' said Toban. 'You might think about giving that eagle of yours some rest, though.'

'Yah. Yah.'

Toban was a withered stick who hadn't any juice left in him. He wouldn't understand about lusting after a woman, the kind you didn't get a chance to gorge on more than once or twice in your life. Tumna was ragged, surly, and slow from the oversized feeding the chief fawkner had stupidly insisted on last night, but she was strong enough for another day of flying.

Ragged the eagle was, and slow, and cranky at being roused early, but the pair took their distance easily and circled over Olossi soon after dawn. Every Assizes Tower was required to maintain a perch for eagles, and space enough for flight in and out, but Olossi's council had always begrudged Argent Hall their due. First he thought of landing outside the walls, but then he'd have to walk. He had made this turnaround and steep approach enough times that he knew how to bank the turn just right and give a last hop of height in the landing, just before the gap of Assizes Court opened below. They made it, even if the landing was hard. He left Tumna hooded on the perch and commandeered a pair of young guards to escort him to Master Feden's compound, always difficult to find in the twisting streets of Olossi.

After a bit of confusion at the compound gate, he was led to a spacious courtyard and seated at a low table shaded by a cloth awning. Platters of fruit and soup and porridge and dried sourfish were brought. A slender slave girl poured khaif and leavened it with a spicy tincture of moro milk. He gave her a good look-over, but she wasn't anything compared with the Devouring girl, hardly worth mentioning. He set to without waiting.

It was a reasonably good feast, not perfect. The sourfish had a proper bite, but the flat cake was bland. The nai porridge was sharp with kursi, but the soup hadn't any cut to it at all and only a pair of trifling leeks when any decent cook would have layered them on to give a morning kick. Still, the fruit was ripe, moist with juices.

'Good to see you enjoying the food, Reeve Horas,' said Master Feden, entering.

'Couldn't eat last night,' said Horas as he pulled the tough strings from a globefruit and gulped down its sweet pulp.

'I'll join you.' Master Feden gave a command, and a small, wiry-haired dog whose coat was a mixture of gray, white, and black settled down, its gaze fixed on its master. Seating himself on the only other pillow, Feden took his khaif without milk or spice and dismissed the girl. 'How can I aid you this morning? Is there a message from Argent Hall?' His hand trembled as he lifted the cup, but after he sipped at the hot khaif, the trembling eased and he set down the cup with a firm hand.

'Uh.' Horas swallowed the last of the luscious globefruit and licked the sticky sap off his lips. 'Just need to make sure the mercenary company departs for the south. Master Yordenas isn't wanting any trouble with them.'

'I shouldn't think they're likely to give any trouble.' Master Feden glanced across the courtyard as he said it, but there wasn't anyone over there except a pair of guardsmen loitering under the arcade, out of the sun. 'Have more khaif?'

'Can't eat too much.' Horas took a good long look at the abundance of food, and levered one more sourfish off the platter. Popping it in his mouth, he savored its bitterness, the sting it brought to the eye. That was good. 'I'll have to catch them up. When did they leave?'

Feden looked startled. He snagged a round of flat cake, cut it in half, cut the halves into quarters, and tossed one of those eighth pieces to the dog, which caught the treat in its mouth and gulped it down without rising. He put a piece to his own lips, but lowered it again.

'The report's not come in yet.' He beckoned, and one of the young guardsmen trotted over. 'Find Captain Waras. I'll need his report.'

'I'll go out myself and look.'

'A strange thing,' said Feden. 'That Devouring girl asked about you, after you'd left.'

That was something to make a man burn brighter, even better than the sourfish. 'Did she, now? How was that?'

'She came back to report to me, rather later in the night, if you take my meaning.'

Thinking of the imprisoned reeve from Clan Hall, Horas nodded.

'It was strange. She must have known you were going, but she asked again if you'd happened to stay the night. Said it was late enough when you left the council hall that maybe you'd had second thoughts about flying back to Argent Hall.' Then the merchant smiled. 'Seems you roped a bit of interest there. She's a little too – whew! – spicy for my taste.'

Horas looked at the pieces of untouched flat cake placed on the master's platter, and made his own judgment about the merchant's tastes. Casually, he dabbled his fingers in the cleansing basin. 'She still around?'

'Nay, she left at dawn with a packhorse and a spare, off to fetch some hired man she mislaid on West Track, so she said. I got to wondering if it was a lover she was going after, she was that eager to get out of town.'

'Hierodules don't take lovers.' But after all, she was out and about, and she had shown an unusual concern for the man she'd left behind on the road. Now he got to thinking about it, maybe she was hiding something from the temple.

'Lots of things we say we don't do, that we do do,' agreed Master Feden with a hearty chuckle.

That got Horas to thinking about what she had promised, and why the hells hadn't he gotten what he wanted when it was offered? Was he crazy? Surely it must have been something he ate, to make him feel all woozy and beaten down yesterday when it was there for the taking, all the sweet juicy flesh, just like the globefruit, only better.

He patted his fingers dry on a cloth and tossed it back on the table, where its edge lapped over his platter and one corner dipped into the unfinished soup.

'That mercenary troop ought to be gone by now. Let me get out to see them.'

'I've some fresh redberry juice. Are you sure you don't want to wait for Captain Waras? He'll know what's up.' He called over the slave, sent her off with a slap on her hindquarters, a good clout that got Horas to biting his lip for it did make him think of what he might get up to with the Devouring girl if only he could catch up to her before she got lost one way or the other, or killed by accident, now that he thought about it, which was the likely outcome if she came across the strike force who would act first and say sorry for it later.

'I'll just head out,' he said.

But after all, the guards who had escorted him to the compound had vanished, and there was some fuss over finding a guide to replace him since Horas was quite sure he would lose his way in the confusing labyrinth of streets. Master Feden jabbered, and there came Captain Waras with a snarl on his face and a surly attitude that would have gotten him whipped in Argent Hall.

'I've got my hands full rousting that mercenary troop,' he informed Master Feden.

'What! What? They were meant to leave at dawn!'

'Seems they're negotiating with some merchants from town, who won't be budged. I don't want a fight on my hands, not if I can avoid one.'

'Negotiating for what?' asked Horas. 'I thought the council ruled they were to leave immediately and without hiring themselves out here.'

'I was just about to send a troop of riders to set them on their way. Would you like to come? Is that redberry juice, Master Feden?'

'So it is. Just uncanted this morning. So sharp you'll cry.'

'Might I—?'

Down the captain sat, right on the carpet, and the slave was sent to bring a third pillow and a third cup. It transpired that the captain was a devout follower of the game of hooks-and-ropes, as Horas had been back at Iron Hall when he had followed league play in Teriayne. Olossi had teams, as did many of the surrounding villages, and there had been a particularly good scandal last season having to do with a hookster and a very cunning bribe, which Waras explained in entertaining detail. They drained the pitcher of redberry juice, and as promised Horas had to wipe tears off his face. His tongue had gone numb.

'Best we go out,' he said as he blinked away the last bitter tear.

After all Master Feden would come, and then there must be a procession, because council masters did get all twisted up if they weren't given a chance to parade before the lesser, as Horas's old grandmother was used to say.

Out they went. Passing through the fields and waste country beyond the outer walls, they met a group of men and slaves returning with a palanquin carried in their midst. The curtains concealed the treasure within. Master Feden cursed roundly at a merchant he recognized in that group, and there was a nasty exchange, more of looks than of words.

When they reached the river's shore where the militia had posted its sentries, they found the mercenary company ready to move out.

Master Feden called the captain over. The fellow was an outlander, with a hooked nose and a closed face, the kind that never gives anything away. He'd been calm enough in the council meeting, even when the vote had gone against him. Horas knew this kind; they would speak softly to your face and knife you in the back when you turned to go.

'I'm sure you remember who I am!' said Master Feden in a stern voice. 'You were told to be gone at dawn.'

The captain had a cold expression. He wasn't a nice man. He was the kind people thought was nice, but Horas had learned in the mountains that a sunny day on the high slopes could turn deadly in the turn of a hat and never care who was left for dead behind the storm.

'Negotiations took longer than expected,' said the captain with a glance at his men. They were a sleek bunch, tough as leather, sharp as a good blade. 'We are leaving now.' He spared a glance for the reeve, dismissed him in the most insulting way, and signaled to his soldiers.

'Negotiations for what?' Mester Feden cried.

The company moved, splashing across the shallows.

'I sold my wife,' he said, over his shoulder.

The council master turned red. Captain Waras whistled beneath his breath.

'Damn him,' said the council master, even redder. 'I'd have thrown in a bid.'

As the company passed, Horas tried to count them, but he gave up after forty. They were nothing, really. The strike force would overrun them, and even if a few scattered into the countryside, the main army would catch them, crush them, and eat them with supper as flavoring, as the saying went.

He was eager to get back to Tumna, but he must wait with Master Feden as the company crossed. A man threw a shoe, and there was some fuss, and a delay, and gods help them all if by the time he trudged back on weary feet into Assizes Court it wasn't noontide with the sun at its worst and the wind struggling to catch any breath in this furnace heat. He rested awhile and took a cooling drink, and in the end it was only the thought of that Devouring girl on the road and marching step by step farther away from him and his chance to get a piece of her that got him going. He shook Tumna out of her sunning stupor.

The mercenary company was moving at a slug's glide. It was easy to get a comprehensive view of their line of march and of the road stretching before and behind them. There was the usual traffic, slowing to a trickle as it moved into the heat of the day. Trust the stupid outlanders to march right into the worst. They trudged along in a torpor. They were pushing in the correct direction, anyway. Maybe the captain was sorry, now, that he'd sold off his pretty wife. That was something to laugh about.

He circled wide, catching an updraft off the escarpment and banking wide to get a view of West Track more or less parallel to the east-flowing length of the wide River Olo. The river looped and curved along the plain, but West Track ran straight as a spear. There were little villages and fields and swales and low ground and hills hidden by old trees too difficult to chop down. The heat had melted the locals. The villages were quiet; the householders seemed early to their afternoon Shade Hour. He saw no one on the road except a pair of peddlers with packs slung over their backs, a single man leading a horse, a trio of women with the jaunty swagger of entertainers, and – yes! – a woman mounted on one horse and leading two others.

He spotted open ground a distance ahead, circled her until he was sure she'd seen him, and flew ahead for an easy landing. Soon enough, she appeared along the empty road, the only creature abroad. He waited in the shade of a massive old oak tree, while Tumna perched in the sun with wings spread. As everyone did, the woman kept her distance from the eagle, but she tethered her horses across the road and sauntered over.

'I thought you had abandoned me yesterday,' she said, raising her chin with a challenge. 'You sure were cold. Out on patrol again?'

The sheen of sweat on her made her glisten. A man could go crazy looking on a woman who looked the way she did, with her vest bound so loose you might glimpse anything through those lacings but never quite did, with her linen kilt sliding along taut thighs. She considered the eagle.

'I wonder what she would do,' she said, 'if I were to tie you up. Would she attack me? I think she could rip my head right off.'

In the Tale of Discovery, the shoemaker had been literally blinded with lust, and Horas suddenly wondered if he was about to undergo the same transformation. The sun was so bright, and the pale colors of the dry landscape filmed away into a haze. He was slick with sweat, and so tight he actually could not get a word up out of his throat. But he could move his arm, giving the hand signal for flight and return. Tumna shook herself and kekked irritably, but she took off with a massive thrust and a storm of wing, and vanished over the woodland to find a more peaceful place to sun.

'I suppose that's my answer,' she said, watching the eagle go. 'Wait here.'

She walked back across the clearing and over the road to where she had tethered her horses, and just to watch that shapely rump sway was enough to make his throat dry and his gaze blur. Into the woods she disappeared, leading the horses, and reappeared a bit later without them. With a faint smile, she returned to him and grasped his wrist. He was choked with desire.

She led him deep into the woodland, close beside the river where there was lots of cover and plenty of twisted trees that made perfect hitching posts, to which she tied him.

After a long time, she asked him if he wanted her to stop, and he gasped, 'No.'

A while after that, she asked him again, and he whimpered, 'No.'

Not that he could have stopped her anyway. Not that he would have wanted to.

Even later, she said she had to go get more water, and he needed a break by that time, because it was hard work, as the Merciless One knew. The slow heat of the afternoon drowsed around him. His hands began to tingle and go numb, but he couldn't relieve the pressure of the rope. He began to lose feeling in his feet. He cooled, and withered.

The colors within the trees changed as shadows drew long under the branches. It was about the time he realized that he was too effectively trussed up to free himself, and too far from the road for his voice to carry the distance, that he also discovered he had lost his bone whistle. Even if it was concealed beneath the pile made by his clothes and gear, he could not reach it.

It was getting dark fast, for night always came quickly.

He heard male voices, laughter, in the trees, but when he called after them, no one answered.

That's when he understood that she wasn't coming back.

44

Keshad was tired of trudging. Mostly he thought about how he was going to get away from Rabbit, Twist, and the rest of his new comrades, all of whom were the kind of people you never ever did business with unless you were already on your way out of town. It was as if someone had swept up the worst criminals into one band, on purpose.

What was he even thinking? That was exactly what had happened.

It was almost dark when they caught up with the strike force, a group of several hundred soldiers. This was the group Bai had counted two nights ago. Three hundred and twelve, she had said, but as he walked into the rough encampment the soldiers were setting up alongside the road, he wondered if there weren't more. Canvas was rigged up along ropes to form shelters. Grooms walked the horse lines. Men piled hay along the rope line, feed filched from village storehouses. Although dusk was falling, no one had lit any fires. Wagons were driven across the road to form barriers before and behind the line of march.

'Heya! Second Company! Over here!' A captain called out their sergeant. 'We'll reach Olossi tomorrow. The last village we came through was already abandoned, so it seems someone had news of our coming. We're covering three watches, not two, tonight. On high alert. Your men will take all the watches. Double your normal numbers.'

'That's not fair!' Twist muttered. 'They always give us the watches, like we're not worth any other duty. Aui! I liked it better when we were on our own.'

Keshad forbore to remind Twist that he'd been complaining all day about not getting first pickings with the rest of the strike force.

How had his luck changed so fast? He had gambled, and won freedom for himself and for Bai, but now he was no better than a captive in enemy hands. They'd as happily cut his throat and rape his corpse as give him a handful of rice, and certainly no rice or even a hank of stale flatbread was forthcoming tonight. Nor dared he try to purchase anything, which would mean he'd reveal his coin. Stomach grumbling, he stuck close by Twist as they found a bit of ground to rest on. When Kesh rolled out his blanket, the others hooted and called him names.

'Very particular!'

'Quite the merchant's son. Southern silks never too good for you!'

'Nah, he's hoping for a bit of company.'

'Rabbit here won't do it. You're too wiggly for his tastes.'

One thing Keshad had learned in the marketplace was not to let your opponent smell blood or weakness. 'I'm wanting a bit of sleep, if you don't mind!'

'Oooh. Isn't he particular!'

The ginnies opened their mouths to display their wicked teeth. The men looked away.

'Just shut up and leave the lad alone,' added Twist. 'And if you don't mind my saying so, I can't sleep with your chatter. So just shut it, all round.'

They settled down, but Keshad could not sleep. As soon as he shut his eyes, he saw that hideous, distorted creature descending out of the night sky and onto the road. Yet when he opened his eyes to banish the vision, there were a dozen snoring men scattered around him, lying on the ground at all angles like a crazy fence, trapping him. There was no way he could escape.

And they all stank.

The air was clear, untainted by smoke or moonlight. He turned onto his back. The ginnies shoved into the gap between his arm and his body. With them pressed against him, he stared at the sky. Each star had a name and a classification in the lore of Beltak, the King of Kings, Lord of Lords, but he did not know more than the two every believer must recognize or be subject to the lash. There: the Royal Road that spans the heavens. There, low and in the north: Iku, the Head of the King, around which the heavens spin.

Older tales whispered in his ears as if the trees were mocking him, reminding him of the Tale of Plenty and the Tale of Fortune. There came the Carter and his barking Dog, rolling slowly up out of the east. In the north, the Sacred Tree had fallen sideways. The Three Footsteps trod west. Tree cover hid the southern sky. But these were Hundred tales. They were all lies.

He dozed off, woke at the sound of hooves, but it was only a man walking a horse along the road. A normally shaped horse. The other vision had been a lie.

Next thing he knew, the butt of a spear slammed into his ribs.

'Eh! Aui!'

Magic clamped his jaws over the shaft.

'I wouldn't have to do it this way if those things didn't bite,' said Twist.

'Let go.'

The ginny let go, and Kesh had to rub him to calm him down. Mischief 'smiled,' as if amused.

'Come on. Up! Our turn at watch.'

Up he dragged himself, sticking close to Twist as they got their assignments.

'Smart of you to bring your bundle with you,' said Twist. 'Someone will steal it, and you'll never know where it's gone.'

'Thanks.'

It wasn't that he trusted Twist, precisely, only that he mistrusted him less than he did the others. They'd been assigned to the rear guard, and fortunately that meant the wagon barrier. He found a comfortable spot to sit, on the driving bench of one of the wagons, and wedged his bundle in beside him. The ginnies draped themselves over the bundle, snugged together, and closed their eyes. He amused himself by whistling under his breath to pass the time, every tune he could think of and then over again. Twist dozed, leaning against a wagon. A pair of other men paced, arguing in low tones about a bet one had lost and the other had won. After a while they fell silent and shared a smoke, off by the edge of the road, huddled close to hide the spark of its burning.

The night wind whispered its tale in the trees. The horses moved restlessly on the rope line. The stars remained silent.

A woman laughed.

He started up, but no one else seemed to have noticed. The pair sucked on their smoke. Its dizzy-sweet smell pricked his nostrils, and he shook himself. That laugh had sounded like Bai. He squirmed around, peering along the stretch of road. The shelters had been strung off the road, along the cleared ground and back under the woodland cover. The horses formed an irregular line of shadow along the river side of West Track, although the river lay too far away from the road in this spot for him to hear its running. He could not see the other barrier. The road had a strange quality in the darkness, the barest hint of a shine that made it possible to travel at night, even during the dark of the moon without lamp or candle or torch to light your way.

He yawned, sucking in a sudden cloud of sweet-smoke that had drifted his way. The flavor punched into his lungs and sent him soaring.

He is aloft. Alone. The wind is a high road under his feet, under the hooves of his mount, which gallops on air as easily as if it were on earth. Its great, slow wings are like bellows pumps, displacing air with each squeeze. The beast nickers, alerted to horses below, dark shapes moving in the night through the trees. 'What's there?' a man's voice mutters. 'Best we go check.' They begin to turn. Shapes scatter along the ground below as the winged beast snorts.

The hells! The nightmare just would not leave him!

Then comes the kick of surprise as the man swears under his breath. 'How can it be? How came Shai here?'

'Hei!' Twist shoved him hard in the ribs with the butt of his spear. 'We'll get whipped if they catch you sleeping! Here they come. Thank the gods! I was ready to doze off myself.'

Keshad looked up at the sky, but nothing disturbed the spread of stars. Nothing flew overhead. Reeves couldn't fly at night anyway. Nothing could, except owls and nighthawks and such creatures. He was just dreaming. Shaking, he clambered off the wagon as their relief walked up rank-smelling and yawning and belching to take their place. There was Rabbit, scratching himself.

'Heh. Heh,' he said by way of greeting, when he saw Twist and Kesh. 'I'm hungry. When we going to eat them lizards?'

Magic bobbed his head aggressively, but Rabbit never noticed. Kesh gathered up his gear, and the ginnies, and followed Twist.

'Did you hear a woman laughing?' Kesh asked as they walked back to their doss.

'Whew! You're dreaming! There's a couple of bitches marching with the strike force, but they'd as soon cut off your cock and cook it for their dinner as pay you any other kind of mind. Best get some rest. If we're lucky, we'll see action tomorrow. Earn some pickings.'

Kesh picked a spot at the edge of the group, outside the sprawled bodies. With some difficulty he convinced the ginnies to curl up inside his cloak, with their heads peeking out one end and tails from the other. He lay on the ground with grass and twigs and stones poking into him. From this uncomfortable bed, he monitored Twist's breathing. After a long while, he rolled to one side and levered up onto a knee, testing the air and the silence. He rose to his feet, tucking his bedroll and pouches under his arm. The ginnies he slung over his back, already trussed up in the cloak. As if they knew what he was about, they remained quiet.

'Any problem?' said the sergeant in a low voice, off to his left.

'Got to piss.' Kesh was surprised at how cool he sounded when for an instant all he could see was a flare of bright red anger, and the shadow of a twisted black fear.

'Need to take your gear with you to piss?'

'Twist says if I don't carry everything with me, it'll be stolen when I get back.'

'Huh. That's true enough. I'll come with you.' The sergeant was a stocky man, almost a head shorter than Kesh, the kind of man you never dared grapple with. The kind who could likely rip your arm from its socket, and would.

'Always a pleasure,' added Kesh, 'to piss in company.'

A Sickle Moon was rising, its fattened curve lightening the eastern sky. A cloaked man walked along the road, leading a horse burdened by panniers. Or maybe those weren't panniers. Maybe those were folded wings. He shuddered. The horse line was still restless, as he was. He grunted in surprise as a hand slapped onto his shoulder.

'You coming?' muttered the sergeant, who paused to survey the road, then turned away in disinterest. For once, Kesh was glad to follow him, to turn his own back on that sight. The wind crackled in branches. The air smelled of the coming dawn, floating a memory of yesterday's heat. A bird whistled its morning tune, but there came no answer to that call. It was still too early for waking.

They pushed a little way into the woods and found a stand of young pipe brush that rattled a friendly chorus as they peed onto them. The sergeant said nothing. He didn't need to. As they finished their business, Kesh wished that for once things could run in his favor. Had he heard Bai's laugh? He'd been separated from Zubaidit for so long that it was more likely he couldn't recognize her laugh at a distance, at night, in strange circumstances when he was wishing more than anything that she would return and get him out of this. Was she even coming back to get him? This means of escape obviously wasn't going to work, but if Bai was in camp searching for him, he had to go back and look for her.

The sergeant grunted. His knees sagged, and he folded over. Kesh blinked. The sergeant crumpled into the stand of pipe-brush, snapping stalks as he went down. Magic stuck his head out of the sling made of the cloak and closed his mouth over Kesh's elbow. The pressure was less than a bite but more than a kiss, enough pain that Kesh dropped to his knees as he hissed out a curse and reached for the lizard's crest to dislodge him.

An arrow passed over his head. He threw himself flat, arms out. The ginnies scrambled out of the cloak and onto his back. With his head twisted to one side, he saw with one eye as their crests flared and they opened their mouths wide to show threat. Mischief's claws poked into his butt. A stone dug into his cheek right below his eye, and Magic, that bastard, raised himself up with his forelegs on Kesh's head, pinching claw cutting hard right over his ear.

A foot slammed down a finger's breadth from his nose. It was a foot shod in leather trimmed and shaped unlike Hundred footware, which was mostly sandals. He'd seen such boots recently. Those Qin mercenaries had worn such boots, sturdy, strong, and indestructible. Too heavy and hot to market in the Hundred.

'If you keep quiet and don't move, Master Keshad,' said a voice as soft as the breeze, 'you'll live through this.'

From this angle, he could see into the length of camp along the road. Fire flashed into life along the horse lines, eating out of the piles of hay. The horses screamed and bolted. They had all been cut loose. He could tell because they broke away from the ropes and stampeded in all directions, frantic to get away from the flames. Arrows whistled out of the night, some tipped with fire. Canvas shelters caught as men stumbled up to the alert. Burning hay spun in the wind. A man fell beneath the hooves of panicked horses. The captain hadn't cried out the 'Beware!,' but sergeants shouted at their men to 'Come alive,' 'Get up!' 'Rise! Rise!' 'Get those beasts under control!'

His sergeant lay dead in the dirt beside him, lifeless fingers inert, just within reach of his left hand.

The boot was gone, the man wearing it vanished into the darkness. Kesh stirred. Magic shoved his head against Kesh's ear, took hold of it, and closed his mouth with the greatest delicacy around the lobe. He didn't bite. Not yet. Kesh didn't dare move.

A man who travels a great deal in troubled times knows himself wise if he has learned enough of the arts of war to defend himself, and enough of the arts of prudence to keep out of fights. Kesh had avoided many a fight in his years trading at Master Feden's behest, but he had also scored a few wins when forced to the wall.

Not today. Today, with the dawn scarce breathing its first light, he lay as flat and still as he could with the pressure of ginny claws on his tender skin. He smelled smoke on the air, tasted floating ash and scorched hay on his tongue as the camp went up in flames.

He listened.

Branches snapped. Arrows sighed. Swords sang a bright rhythm where men fought. Horses thundered past, escaping the tumult and the burning.

Men shouted; they grunted; they screamed. Men ran, heard in their stampeding footsteps. They fell. The blood of the sergeant crept close to his fingers before the earth drank down these scantling rivulets and that spring dried up once and forever.

The course of the battle ebbed and flowed along the road. Twice men sprinted past him into the trees. Once, no more than a stone's toss away, he heard a man gasp as death overtook him, as metal struck to the bone.

The Qin were Death's wolves, ghosting out of the night to devour their foes.

A soft footfall trod the ground behind him. The ginnies chirped in welcome. A slender, sandaled foot pressed down the undergrowth an arm's span from his staring eye.

'Up,' said Zubaidit. 'We're getting out of here.'

The ginnies scrambled off him, but circled her warily, tongues tasting her savor. Rising to hands and knees, he realized belatedly there was light enough to see. Blood spotted her feet and legs. She had blood on her kilt, and a stripe of blood on her face, as though she had forgotten blood was on her hands and tried to wipe something else away.

'Follow close,' she added. 'You'll carry the ginnies. I have to be free to strike if anyone attacks us. They're not all dead, and even the least of them will kill us if they can. And there are other creatures abroad we must avoid.'

'Like what?'

Like the ginnies, she tilted her head and licked. 'Something that tastes very bad,' she murmured, 'and feels very old. We've fulfilled our obligations, yours to your old master, and mine to the temple. They can fight their own battles now. We're getting out of here. And we're never coming back.'

From the road, the sounds of fighting were dying down, and what cries he heard were those of helpless men as their throats were cut. Bai did not flinch, not as he did. Gliding away, she seemed no different from the black wolves who had raced past him earlier.

As he got to his feet and grabbed his gear and chased the ginnies into the sling, he remembered that after all she was born in the Year of the Wolf. Generous to those they love. Loyal to clansmen. Sentimental, uninhibited, forthright, and courageous. Yet a wolf will tear apart any creature that falls into its clutches, even if it is not hungry.

She looked back at him. The blood slashed her skin like shadows. She half blended into the woodland cover.

'Kesh!' she hissed. 'This is no game! Hurry!'

For the first time in his life, he was afraid of her.

45

Before the last march of the night, Chief Tuvi pulled Shai to the back of the line. 'You're too inexperienced. You'll wait back here with the tailmen. Your job is to cut down any stragglers who run this way. Do you understand?'

'I understand.'

'Best thing you could do is get in a kill or three, just to get blooded. You're little use to us otherwise.' Chief Tuvi wasn't as encouraging as Tohon, but Shai hadn't seen Tohon since yesterday before dawn. About eight other men were also missing from the troop, but no one had bothered to tell him where they had gone.

They had left Olossi at about midday and marched as slowly as they possibly could out West Track to the intersection with West Spur. There, they had headed southwest, as if returning to the empire, moving as if led by hobbling ancients and delaying themselves with frequent stops. Late in the afternoon, when given the signal by the captain, they had simply pulled off the road as if to camp. As soon as dusk gave them cover, they had marched at speed through the night, past the crossroads that led down to Olossi and farther yet along the river bottomland east of the city. This was unknown country, but now the missing scouts appeared at intervals to give their reports. Late, as the waxing crescent moon sliced its way out of the house of the dead, the captain called a halt. Shai and a dozen tailmen took up stations along the road. Grooms led their horses into the trees. The rest of the company vanished into the night, hooves muffled by cloth.

For a long while they waited. There was no conversation.

Shai wanted to talk, but he dared not be first to break the silence, and he had a damned good idea that none of these tailmen would utter even one syllable. Every gaze was bent along the road. Shai had never seen such a road before. It shimmered, very faintly, as though a ghostly breath rose off it, like a cloud of breath steaming out of a warm mouth in bitterly cold weather. The other road they had traveled, West Spur, had exuded no such glamour.

A shadow passed overhead. He ducked. The others, those he could see, looked up, but there was nothing to see, only a cloak of stars and night thrown over the world. The wind died suddenly. An insect clik-clik-clikked. One branch scraped another. Strings creaked minutely as bows were readied. Swords whispered out of sheaths.

It caught them from behind, an explosion of wings and hooves and the crack of a staff as it met a hard leather helmet. One of the Qin went down, but the rest, these paltry tailmen, were already rolling, tumbling, jumping out of the way, finding a new position, a new angle. Shai stood there and gaped as a massive horse galloped out of the sky and right at him to trample him under.

Far away, in counterpoint, shouts and screams rent the silence. The noise of a distant battle breaking out jolted him into action. He ducked, stumbled, fell, scrambled out of the way just in time. The beast pounded past him as the tailmen whistled to each other, calls to mark position and choice of attack. The rider billowed like a cloud, only that was a voluminous cloak rising out behind his body as though caught in a gust of wind. The horse slowed to a canter, and it pulled in its vast wings and turned on a right rein, back around to face him.

The horse had wings.

The glamour on the road brightened where the horse's hooves touched it. That unnatural light rose as if with the dawn, but it was not yet dawn. Far away, the battle raged as Captain Anji and his men hit the strike force with their surprise attack. Close at hand, Shai saw clearly the face of the man who rode on the back of that impossible horse. He rose, trembling, and raised a hand to ward off what he knew must be an insubstantial ghost.

'Hari.' His voice choked on the name.

A hiss of arrows answered. The tailmen were the least of the Qin company, but a Qin tailman would stand as an elite in most armies. Five arrows sprouted from the rider's body. A javelin, cast from the side, caught the man in the torso, just above the hip. He grunted in pain, and swayed in the saddle, but he kept his seat.

'Hari!'

The ghost spoke with Hari's voice, urgent and angry. 'Shai! How can it be you've come here?'

'I came to find you.'

'You shouldn't have. Go home before the shadows swallow you as they did me!'

The horse screamed a challenge, tossing its head, and it launched itself down the road as if to assault Shai. He was stupefied, bound, paralyzed. It leaped, and took to the air. One hoof shaved the top of his head, knocking him flat. The tailmen fixed arrows and loosed them after the animal. No arrow touched those gleaming flanks. But the rider was not so fortunate. Those dark slashes fixed in his body, yet he did not fall. His dark cloak billowed, a shadow entwining him.

Jagi whistled the alert. Shai grabbed his sword, which had somehow fallen out of his hand. A dozen or more horses bolted toward them on the road. None bore riders. Not far behind ran twenty or more men on foot, in a disorderly retreat.

'Get off the road,' said Jagi in a calm voice that meant he was irritated.

Shai got off the road by stumbling backward down the ramped earth and falling hard onto his butt. There he sat, too stunned to act, as a trickle of blood, like a tear, slipped down his cheek from the scrape atop his head. Its salty heat caught in the corner of his mouth. The panicked horses swept past. The tailmen coolly picked off their enemies before those hapless men understood they were still under attack.

It wasn't the aftershock of the battle that immobilized him.

The tailmen had seen Hari. They had filled Hari full of arrows. Yet how could they see, much less kill, a man who was already a ghost?

46

Eliar took her from camp about midday, just before Anji and the others rode out. By the time he had escorted her and her slaves up through the city, a tedious and very hot walk, the shops along the streets had begun to close their shutters for their afternoon's slumber. Olossi's avenues twisted and turned; even the main streets shifted position with curves and doglegs and sudden sharp-angled corners. Down the narrow side streets and deeper within alleyways lay walls and gates, the walls washed white so they all looked alike and only the gates painted with symbols and colors to give a hint of what household bided within. They hurried at length down a street where gold- and silversmiths displayed their wares, but by this time scarcely anyone was about to remark on the sight of Eliar, his two male companions who carried their belongings, and the three women. They turned left at a corner where a fountain burbled, then right into a cobbled alleyway wide enough to admit a wagon and swept so clean Mai could distinguish no speck of dust. White walls flanked them. The alley dead-ended in a plain wooden gate, its double segments marked only by yellow trim, a greeting bell hung to one side in an alcove in the wall, and bronze door handles fashioned to resemble deer in full flight, slender legs thrust out before and behind. A small door reinforced with bands of iron was set into the right-hand gate, with a slit-like peephole cut just above the level of Mai's head. High up on the wall, on either side, were set small grated windows.

He rang the bell, and waited.

'Where are we?' Mai asked.

'This is the house of my clan,' he said. The walls were the height of two men, but there was a single building within the compound that towered above the walls, fully three stories high with a balcony ringing the highest floor, its interior screened by latticework.

'Do you need permission to enter your own house?' Mai asked.

'This is the women's entrance. I can't go in and out through here, nor can you use the men's entrance on the other side.'

'If you live separately, then do you keep secrets from each other?'

'Not secrets, no. But I don't know everything that goes on in the women's quarters.'

Anji's mother, a Qin woman, had been sent to a country where women were not allowed to ride. Yet she had contrived to teach her son to ride, according to the custom of her people. The emperor sequestered his women, but clearly, he hadn't known everything that was going on with them.

'Look! Look there!' Eliar cried.

An eagle flew over, but with walls rising high around them, they quickly lost sight of it.

'Is that Reeve Joss?' she asked. 'Or one of the eagles from Argent Hall?'

The metal strip blocking the slit rasped free, drawn away by an unseen hand. In the opening thus revealed appeared dark eyes, narrowed and tucked, rimmed by lovely black eyelashes and outlined with a black cosmetic.

'Enter,' Eliar said to Mai with an expansive smile and a bold gesture of welcome, arm swept in a wide curve. 'Be welcome to the house of the Haf Gi Ri.'

'Sen Eliar!' The woman's voice brought him back to earth. 'What means this?'

'I have sworn to take these women in as guests, under our protection.'

The eyes blinked. The voice said, 'Does anyone else in the family know what you've done, Sen Eliar? Did you ask permission, or warn anyone?'

She answered herself. 'No, of course not. Very well. Get out of here.'

The words were uttered so curtly that Mai could not help but flinch, despite that she had long since trained herself not to show displeasure or fear or anger.

Eliar cupped his hands over his eyes in a gesture very like obeisance, or prayer. The two companions dumped her gear on the ground, and all three men backed up to a safe distance, then turned and strode away down the alley. Shocked by the rejection, Mai shifted to follow them, but Priya grabbed her arm and caught her before she could take more than one step. Whispers teased her. Looking up, she saw movement behind the grating of the two high windows. A giggle floated on the air. On the other side of the gate, bolts were shot and a heavy weight shifted and moved. The inner door set within the doubled gate opened inward on well-oiled hinges.

'Come! Come! That boy! No need, we'll bring in your belongings.'

Sheyshi started to snivel. Mai stood as straight as she could and, with Priya and Sheyshi, walked through into a small if pleasant courtyard the exact width of the alley. In the far right corner stood a dry but very clean fountain. Several planting troughs lined the walls, most of them fallow though one boasted the stalks and spiky leaves of fragrant paradom, not yet in its flowering season. One trellis supported grape vines; another bent under the weight of thickly twining rainflower. Benches offered respite from the sun. Behind her lay the gate through which she had come. Ahead rose the three-storied building, open to the air on its upper stories although she could see only the suggestion of movement behind latticework screens. To her right stood a doubled door, another gate, in a high wall; heavy wagon tracks suggested that, sometimes, wagons were driven in this way. To her left a spacious veranda welcomed her.

'Come in out of the sun,' said the woman, who now appeared to be of middle years, with features similar to Eliar's but no pronounced resemblance. A pair of young women stared at Mai with wide-eyed interest, but at a gesture from the woman they hurried past to fetch the gear left out in the alley.

They must leave their footgear at the step, she showed them, and once they stepped up onto the veranda wear cloth slippers, although the ones available did not quite fit. Indoors lay a suite of rooms furnished with pillows, low couches, a writing desk, brushes and ink, and innumerable cupboards, all immaculate. Finest silk covered those pillows, embroidered with birds and flowers in pleasing designs.

'Rest,' said the woman. 'The girls will bring you something to drink. No one works at this hour. Dinner is eaten at dusk.'

The girls brought their belongings up onto the veranda and then brought cool drinks, and pitchers of cool water so they could wash their hands and faces in a copper basin. After this, they were left alone. Exhausted, Mai dozed, and she was glad of it afterward, thinking that to endure an afternoon of fretting would have been too much. After all, she was the one who had convinced Anji to make the gamble.

Later, toward dusk, the same girls brought trays of food, but this time both of the girls arranged the platters on the low table and sat down to eat with them.

Sheyshi tried to serve, but the older of the girls, a young woman a year or two older than Mai, waited even for the slaves to sit before she would portion out the meal. This task she undertook with an exactitude that Mai, accustomed to measuring out a cupful of

almonds in the marketplace, could appreciate. Then she and the
other girl bent their heads, closed their eyes, and touched fingers to
foreheads, with palms turned inward. What words they said, if they
said any, Mai could not hear. Afterward, they ate together, but no
one spoke.

When Sheyshi made an effort to stand in order to clear the
platters, the other girl stopped her and took everything away. Cupboards, opened, revealed mattresses and bedding to spread in the
back room. Once this was settled, the young woman took her leave
with the regretful smile of a friendly conspirator whose cunning plot
has been thwarted. She left through the far gate, the one that did not
lead into the alley. The guesthouse itself, it seemed, had no entrance
except the veranda. They were, in fact, shut in, betwixt and between:
not on the street and yet not truly within the compound either.

The previous night had been a long, restless one, and this night
transpired no differently because of the heat and the constant spark
of images that flew into her mind's eye and took their time drifting
away again. She had to believe Anji would succeed, that he could
manage anything, but in the dark, in a strange room, that was
sometimes difficult. She would doze, then start awake thinking she
heard voices, or the clatter of hooves on stone, or anguished sobbing. The food sat uneasily in her stomach; often she woke burping,
and this churning discomfort further disturbed her dreams.

Very late, Priya woke also and held her close. 'Rest now,
Mistress. Fretting will not change our course, nor will it alter what
is to come.'

Sheyshi snored.

'Let the peace of the Merciful One embrace you, Mistress.'

'It is hard to find peace,' said Mai in her smallest voice. 'I am
afraid.'

Priya kissed her. Held tight in those arms, Mai was able to sleep.

Not long after dawn, the women of the family took their morning
khaif in the shade of the veranda. A trio of girls came first, bearing
trays, and after them a procession of stern women of various ages:
young, mature, and aged. Mai looked in vain for the friendly young
woman who had brought them dinner last night.

The aroma of paradom melded with the sharp spice of khaif and the scent of freshly baked buns. That combination of spicy khaif and sweetened bread with an even sweeter bean curd core made Mai's heart race uncomfortably, but it was evident by the casual demeanor of the women that this was their accustomed morning feast, the appetizer to their day.

At length, the long silence was broken.

'I trust you rested well?' demanded the wrinkled grandmother over the rim of a very fine, thin ceramic cup.

'Yes, verea. Thank you.'

They had pulled around pillows and couches the better to examine her.

'And the meal brought last night was to your taste?'

'Yes, verea.'

'You didn't eat all of it. You left half of the soup, all of the cabbage, and one dumpling.'

The cabbage had been the nastiest thing Mai had ever tasted, and the sour sting of the soup had made her mouth go numb. She smiled her market smile, and said, 'Concern for my husband left me with little appetite, Mistress. I beg your pardon.'

'Few like the way we pickle our cabbage,' said the old grandmother, 'but you've turned a pretty phrase by way of thanking us for our hospitality.' She had wispy hair, gone to silver and let loose to straggle over her shoulders. No horns peeped through, and there wasn't enough hair to cover horns had they been there, so after all the Ri Amarah were ordinary people, not the children of demons. In a way, Mai was both disappointed and relieved. 'What do you think of these sweet buns? Our baker is the best in the city.'

'I've never tasted anything like them before.'

Several of the women chuckled.

'A truthful statement!' agreed the old grandmother. 'None make them but our own people. Do you cook?'

The question surprised her. 'Even my husband did not ask me that before we wed.'

'He was obviously not looking for a cook,' said the old grandmother tartly. 'As any person can see, looking upon you, a pretty girl, with a pretty smile, and pretty manners. Do you cook?'

'I learned to cook the specialties of our house, as do all the girls raised in the Mei clan. I can embroider a sleeve, although none of my work was considered elegant enough to be worn outside the house on festival days. I can mend. I have some small skill at carving, taught to me by my uncle.'

'Can you brew a cordial or bind a lotion?'

'I was not taught such things. But I know which herbs to blend as teas and simples for remedies for common complaints.'

'Distill and mix perfumes?'

'No.'

'Prepare silk for dyeing?'

'I've scoured wool, and applied the mordant, and thereafter dyed those skeins. We did that commonly. Our clan raised sheep.'

'Can you read?'

'No.'

'Paint figures and images?'

'No.'

'Can you sing?'

'I have been told I have a passable voice.'

'Can you dance the lines?'

'I don't know what that is. The festival dances, certainly. Everyone learns those.'

'Can you reel and spin?'

'I have spun thread, and carded wool.'

'Silk?'

'Silk is not grown where we come from. We buy silk at the market, but only for bedroom clothes and festival garments.'

The women smiled, and one coughed behind a raised hand.

Grandmother was not done. 'Can you weave?'

'Not well. Others in my household showed greater skill, so I was sent to other pursuits. Anyway, most of the weaving was done by our – ah—' Recalling Eliar's impassioned speech against slavery, she chose another word. 'By our hirelings.'

'What *did* you do?'

'I sold produce in the market.'

'With your face uncovered?'

'I beg your pardon?'

'With your face uncovered? It is not the custom of my people for women to walk about in the streets exposed to the world's staring eye.'

'I beg your pardon, verea, but it was not the custom in my country for women to conceal their faces.'

'No need,' said the old grandmother with a pointed smile, 'to bite me, young one. It seems to me that those who set you in the marketplace hoped to gain by displaying your pretty face, as much as their produce. Can you keep an accounts book?'

This was too much! 'Of course I can!'

'I'm finished,' said the grandmother. A woman rose from a bench and took the old woman's cup. Another rose from a padded couch and helped the old grandmother to rise, then led her across the courtyard. None here wore slave bracelets. Mai could not distinguish between servants and family members. They moved off, some gathering up trays and cups and a few moving among the troughs to inspect the dusty soil and the spiky paradom. A pair found brooms and began sweeping the veranda.

A woman of middling years, similar in age to Mai's own mother, knelt beside Mai.

'We've much to do, as you can imagine, verea,' she said with a kind smile. 'There's a great deal of serious business in these preparations, and all must work if we wish Olossi to be ready to withstand what will come. You'll have to remain here. However, now that Grandmother has approved you, my daughter can keep spoken company with you.'

'I thank you,' said Mai. 'I am called Mai, of the Mei clan. I never had a chance to say so.'

Mai saw a resemblance to Eliar in the way the woman narrowed her eyes as she smiled. 'It's not our way to exchange names as one might trade goods or coin in the marketplace. I am the mother of Eliar, who brought you here. Ah! Here she is.'

The young woman who had smiled so sweetly at Mai last night appeared at the inner gate. She hurried across the courtyard. Her nose was red and her cheeks blushed as from steam, and the skin of her arms was damp to the elbows, pink with heat. Like her brother, she had a handsome face, rather square, with heavy eyebrows, a small nose, and eyes as black as ink and sharp as a brushstroke. Her hair was pulled back away from her face and bound atop her head under a beaded net.

She offered a courtesy to her mother, a dip of the knees, a

crossing of the arms before her breast. Then she slid out of the out-door slippers she was wearing and found a pair of indoor slippers from those lined up along the edge of the veranda. Eliar's mother left together with the other women. They left a single tray with a ceramic pot of khaif and six sticky buns, together with saucers, cups, and serving utensils.

Sheyshi rifled through their belongings and, finding a hem to repair, set to work. Priya sat quietly on a pillow at the edge of the veranda, watching the shadows change as the sun rose above the eastern wall. She had her eyes half closed as she did when she fell into the trance through which one rises to the heart of the Merciful One. Mai did not want to disturb her, so she walked out into the courtyard and sat on a bench in the shade of the grape arbor.

Eliar's sister settled beside Mai and, in a bold show of complicity, tucked her hand into Mai's elbow and pulled her close. 'That can't have been fun. Did Grandmother pluck you, one feather at a time?'

'Something like that.'

'Grandmother is nothing but an accounts book, figuring up the worth of everyone and every thing she encounters. You mustn't think she has taken a dislike to you. You're our guest, and she will treat you as such.'

'Your mother said she had approved me.'

'Yes! So she did. It was the cabbage.'

From over the walls Mai heard the shouts and laughter of children, as bright and constant as a waterfall. A faint clacking serenaded them, which she identified as folk working at looms. She heard horses, and smelled their ordure. It seemed the stables lay close by. There rose also a tangy scent as of a sharp brew or cordial, and a whiff of a metallic vapor, like skeins of wool being set in alum.

'You can call me Miravia, by the way.'

'My name is Mai.'

There followed an awkward silence, and tremulous smiles.

'I was up at dawn cooking up a cordial,' said Miravia, by way of making conversation. She displayed her arms. That moist sheen of water was evaporating swiftly in the waxing heat. 'Hot work, I'll tell you! Steam boiling up! But I've been released from my duties for the day to act as your host.'

'I beg your pardon. I do not mean to offend. Am I to stay here?'

'With us? Yes, of course. Eliar offered you guest rights. We are beholden now to meet the obligation.'

'I meant, here.' She indicated the courtyard and the veranda, meaning as well the chambers beyond.

'In the guest court? Yes, certainly. This is where we entertain all of our friends and guests.' Miravia looked around. 'It's nicer after the rains come, when there are flowers. It's rather dusty now. Is there anything else you need? The one thing we can't offer you is a bath beyond washing out of a tub of heated water. But I might be able to ask if you can be given an escort down to one of the bath-houses. There are several that my friends have mentioned as being of special quality. You would be safe there, and your escort would remain close by until you are returned to us here.'

At some command Mai could not hear, the children quieted. Their silence, compared with the raucous activity that had come before it, was unnerving.

She lowered her voice in deference to the hushed children beyond the wall. 'This is a lovely house and courtyard. I am so appreciative. It's just that I'm so restless, wondering what has happened.'

'With your husband and his company? Eliar told me. He's quite wild that he wasn't allowed to ride out with them. I'm sorry for it, that you must wait while the men ride out. I feel the same frustration, although I beg you never to tell anyone and especially Grandmother that I ever said so.'

'I won't. But don't you—your brother said—' Again, she found herself hesitant to speak, not knowing what was permitted and what might, and might not, be known. 'Your brother Eliar mentioned that you visit the prison.'

Miravia laughed. 'Yes, I have managed that much. Because of the obligation. I bring food to those who are so destitute their families cannot feed them.' Her tone had a bittersweet edge. Her smile seemed touched with anger. 'Eliar told me that you and I were meant to rescue that reeve, but now even that small task has been taken away.'

This passionate speech put Mai at ease. She began to feel that she might say anything, and not fear a sharp rejoinder. 'I was surprised, too. It seems the council freed him.'

'Someone did, but I don't think it was the council,' said Miravia with a frown. 'I'm glad for his sake, poor man. It's just . . . I had hoped for my own adventure. I'll have none of those once I am married.'

'Is it already arranged?'

'Oh, it was arranged long ago,' she said dismissively.

'Do you know him?'

'His clan lives in the north, in Toskala. I've never met him, but we correspond.' She sighed. 'He's a scholar. Everyone speaks highly of him. I'm sure he's very nice.'

'You've never met?'

'Why should we? Our families arranged everything. Anyway, the roads are very dangerous these days. No one dares risk the journey. I ought to have been married last year, but they had to put it off. I'm glad of it. Is that bad?'

Mai could not resist a gaze that shared in equal parts a glimpse of disillusionment and the presence of an ability to be amused at one's own selfish, lost hopes. Like her brother, Miravia had charm and also a core of passion that, it seemed, she had learned to disguise.

'I was meant to marry a youth from another clan,' Mai said, 'but it came to nothing after the Qin officer decided he wanted to marry me. Of course my father could not refuse him.'

'Well! That could be a disaster. Or a triumph.'

Mai blushed.

'Just like the Tale of Patience! Love's hopes fulfilled!' Hearing her own voice ring out so clearly, Miravia pressed a hand over her lips and said, through her fingers, 'Don't tell Grandmother I said so. I'm not supposed to know such stories. But I do.'

'I don't know the Tale of Patience,' said Mai. 'Will you tell it to me?'

'You don't know it? Everyone knows it!'

'Not where I come from.'

'If I tell you the Tale of Patience, you must tell me your story, your life in the faraway land, your marriage, your travels. Your adventures.' Like her brother, she had a way of grinning that lit her as with fire from within. 'How I want to hear it all!'

'I'll tell you, gladly. Will you have some khaif? I can get a cup.'

'Oh, I must not.' Seeing Mai's confusion, she added, 'I'm not allowed, of course. Only adults can drink khaif.'

'Surely you're as old as I am. I'm an Ox. When were you born?'

Miravia bent close, lips almost touching Mai's ear. The intimate gesture made Mai shudder with pleasure. 'I was born in the Year of the Deer. But we're not supposed to know about that. The elders call it an ungodly custom, a superstitious way of naming the years instead of numbering them properly. Don't tell anyone. Please.'

Mai grasped her hand between hers. 'Of course I won't! But I still don't understand. If you're two years older than I am, then how am I allowed to drink khaif, while you are not? Is it because I'm a guest?'

'No, because you're an adult.'

Mai shook her head. 'I don't understand.'

'You're married. And pregnant.'

'He-ya! Tay ah en sai!'

The children's voices thundered out in a unison chant, echoed by three unison claps. A woman's powerful voice called a singsong phrase, and the children replied in a penetrating chorus, punctuating each phrase with unison claps. This call and response went on while Mai stared at Miravia and felt as though she had just been overtaken by a sandstorm.

From the veranda, Priya opened her eyes and turned to look toward Mai, a smile blooming on her round, dark face. Sheyshi's head remained bent over her sewing. At length, Mai discovered she still possessed a voice, although it had little enough strength to pierce the roar of the schoolroom chorus beyond the wall.

'What did you say?'

'You didn't know?'

Without warning, a deep clanging resonated out of the earth, so full and heavy that the whole world seemed to vibrate to its call. Mai pressed her hands to the bench. The sound throbbed up through the earth and the stone and into her body. Into her belly. Into her womb.

Could it be true?

Of course it could be true! It was even likely. Probable. Expected.

Yet she could not catch her breath. She could not even think, not with all that noise.

The children's chorus stammered into silence. A little voice began to wail in counterpoint to the shuddering bass roll of the bell.

Miravia rose, face flushed with something other than steam rising off a boiling cauldron. 'There cries the Voice of the Walls. May the Hidden One protect us!'

The bell ceased ringing. The sudden, shocked silence lasted long enough for a breath to be drawn in. Then, on those wings, rose a clamor from all around, within the walls and without, as if every person in Olossi cried out at the same time. That roar was its own storm, battering the heavens.

'What does it mean?' Mai stammered.

'The Voice of the Wall is Olossi's alarm bell. When he sings, any person outside the walls knows to retreat to the safety of the walls. Once a year on Festival First Day, we hear him. Today he cries in truth. There must have come news. Bad news.'

She looked down into Mai's face, and such a look of pity transformed Miravia's features that Mai began to weep. To think of Anji was to gasp in terror, so she must not think of him. She rose to grasp Miravia's hands.

'How can we find out what happened? Will the council meet? I have to go there.'

'We can't. It's forbidden.'

'Look!' cried Priya, pointing at the sky.

Eagles.

There were too many to count in one glance, circling above Olossi and then, on unseen winds, soaring away.

Mai had never possessed a reckless temperament. Always she had said to Ti: 'The price is not worth what you hope to gain.' But Anji had ridden out against impossible odds, because she had counseled the bold choice rather than the cautious one. He might be dead. He might never come back, and she would be alone, pregnant, abandoned in a foreign land, the very thing she had feared most when she left Kartu.

The sound of jangling chimes broke over them. The deep bell took up its tolling cry once again, a reverberation that seemed to crack out of the very roots of the earth. Its voice hammered Mai. Her hands were cold, and her chest had tightened until small shallow breaths were all she could manage.

After all those years tending her sanctuary so she might live with inner peace and no outward trouble, she could not accept waiting any longer.

'I must go to where the council meets. I will walk out those gates and make my way alone if I must, but I will go.'

Miravia stared at her. Tears rolled as if jostled loose by the clangor of the bell. 'I wish I could say so, and do so,' she said in a voice so low Mai could scarcely hear it. 'How I admire you! How I envy you!'

'If you can go to the prison, then why not to the council house?'

'To bring food to the prison and the healers' house is all they allow me, and only because the laws of the Hidden One cannot be twisted to forbid it.'

'Well, then, dear one, I am sorry for it, if it makes you unhappy.'

Miravia was not one to cry. Mai saw by the way she clenched her jaw and sucked in a ragged breath that she was used to swallowing her griefs and troubles, as she did now, but the pain still sat deep in her heart.

'It is nothing, compared to what you face. Wait here. I'll go find Eliar as quickly as I can. He'll know what to do.'

'Does he know the law of the marketplace, in the Hundred?'

'Eliar? Surely he does, for you know, he must know it well in order to flout it. Yet I know it well, too. All the women of my people know it. It is one of our chief studies. Why?'

'I am a merchant, just as your people are.'

The grin brightened her face. She laughed. 'Well, then, my dear friend, let me help you. For there is so little else I am allowed to do.'

Mai took her hands. 'I'll accept your aid gladly. I swear to you I will repay it one day.'

47

At dawn Joss rose with a light heart despite the rough ground he'd slept on and the terrible sights he had seen yesterday afternoon while flying Hornward along West Track. He was exhausted, aching, and still weak, but Scar's presence heartened him as nothing else could. Women might come and go, please themselves and him while they were at it, and that was truly a fine thing, but as long as he lived, he knew that Scar would be his most faithful companion.

Indeed, the eagle had fretted, kept close, brought him a deer. This they had shared in the evening, Joss slicing off a portion to roast over a campfire, while the rest Scar dragged to one side.

In the morning, casting done, Scar bowed to him in greeting and came eagerly to the harness. They had not been aloft for long when the eagle cried a warning. Soon after, Joss saw the first distant eagle, and at once spotted another three, then five more. An entire flight approached out of the east, in a staggered formation with flanks spread wide. It was exceptional to see thirty eagles flying together. They were temperamental and territorial beasts, and on the whole disliked their compatriots. But under the control of their reeves, they would endure most anything. It was part of the magic bred into them in ancient days.

Strung out, of course, they also covered a great deal of ground, seeing most everything that moved over many mey. Joss cast a prayer to the winds, and found a draft on which Scar could rise, the better to allow them a chance at outrunning the flight. But a reeve has good reason to gain familiarity with the creatures he lives beside. He recognized, quickly enough, Volias's sleek and gorgeous Trouble. Gliding down, he and Scar found open ground and landed.

On his tail, Volias came to earth with a pair of reeves flanking him. One was Pari, the Argent Hall reeve. The other was Kesta, young, muscular, shapely and, of course, child of the Fire Mother as he was, so therefore taboo.

'You look like you've been dragged through the hells,' said the Snake as he sauntered forward.

'You look pleased to think it might be so.'

'Only had I been there to enjoy watching you suffer. What happened? Should I bring the others down? Turn them around?'

'By no means. You can't imagine how glad I am to see you.'

Volias laughed. 'That bad, eh?' He was a bastard, but he knew his duty.

'How is Peddo?'

'He'll live.' Volias scanned the sky, then pointed toward Pari. 'The Commander wasn't minded to do anything after Peddo and I got back. She said, let you run on the winds of your nightmares and come back when you'd shed yourself of them. But then this boy arrived at Clan Hall and told us a tale I wouldn't have believed if I hadn't seen Horn Hall. As it was, the Commander was given strong reason to believe his outrageous tale might be true. So she sent me in command of the Third Flight, to bring what aid you might ask for.'

'I applaud the Commander's wisdom. Why did she only send one flight?'

'There's a second flight following behind this one,' said Volias.

Kesta broke in. 'Why did she send any? Why in the hells are we wasting our time out here?' Her glare was almost as intimidating at her eagle's. 'We should turn around and go back right away. In case you hadn't heard,' she added with drawling scorn, 'High Haldia's walls were breached, and the city was burned. Iron Hall's reeves fled to their hall, unable to stop it. Now there's an army of about ten companies – six thousand men! – marching seaward down the Istri Walk. Marching on Toskala. I have seen such things . . . and that we abandoned the countryfolk of Haldia to come stooping after this hare!' Her fury was like steam, almost visible rising off her.

'You'll see those same things here in the south, alas. For there's an army not more than two days out of Olossi, closing fast. About five companies, we estimate. Burning and slaughtering as they march. Desolation in their wake.'

Volias shook his head. 'Two armies, hidden from us for this long. How can we have been so blind?'

'Was there news from Horn Hall?' Joss asked.

Their look was his answer.

Pari had stayed back by his eagle, whose head feathers were flared and wings half opened. An Argent Hall eagle would not feel easy in the proximity of so many unknown raptors.

'He's handling him well,' remarked Joss.

Kesta smiled wickedly. 'He's not bad. A little young, but that fault improves with time.'

'Unlike you,' said Volias to Joss, because he could not stop jabbing. 'So what are we to do? Two flights of reeves can do nothing against an army of three thousand. Iron Hall was helpless at High Haldia. An army won't submit to arrest.'

'I wish they were all lost in the hells and eaten alive by rats!' said Kesta, tossing her head back.

'Best we meet up with Captain Anji.'

'Who is Captain Anji?' demanded Kesta. 'What kind of name is that?'

'An outlander's name. He's our ally, and we're fortunate to have him. Indeed, if he survived the night, he'll be happy to see us sooner than he expected. We thought it would take me days to fly to Clan Hall, persuade the Commander, roust a flight, and return here.'

'There's one other thing,' added Volias. 'This Argent Hall marshal who calls himself Yordenas? The Commander had us hunt in the records. There was mention of a reeve called Yordenas. He was a young man newly come to Iron Hall. He was killed about ten years ago, while trying to stop a skulk of bandits as they were beating and raping and robbing in an isolated village up in the high valleys. The reeve's eagle was mutilated and left for dead, and the man's clothes were found, soaked in blood. But they never found his body.'

'So we don't know he was killed.'

'In the testimony of the villagers, those who survived, they stated quite clearly that he was killed. That he died in the arms of a woman who'd given her apprenticeship to the Lady. She'd seen death before. The reeve who took her testimony felt she knew what she was talking about.'

'What happened to the body, then?'

'That's the mystery. It vanished soon after. No one could say how.'

The flights flew wide of the road, so as not to be spotted, but Joss sent Volias and Kesta to shadow West Track. He'd taken his chances yesterday flying over to observe the army. He didn't want to be spotted, knowing it necessary that Argent Hall and their allies believe, for the time being, that he was dead. But yesterday he had needed to see, and today so did these two, so they could understand as well as he did what they were up against.

He had never in his life seen quite so many people on the move all at the same time. They marched in orderly groups, ranked by cohorts. Their weapons gleamed; blacksmiths had been working for years to produce that supply of swords, spears, halberds, axes, and

arrows. Their wagons trundled along, pulled by draft animals.
Behind them, villages lay emptied. The road stretched, deserted,
before and behind the army's killing path. He had glimpsed a handful of people in the woodland cover, scrambling to hide when they
saw the eagle's shadow: these might be outriders and foragers, or
they might be innocent villagers trying to hide from the wolves. He
had seen fresh mounds of dirt heaped over corpses, an act meant to
demoralize and terrify the country folk, since it was truly an abom-
ination to bury what should be left to the Lady's acolytes to purify
and the Four Mothers to gather into their wombs.

Worse even than all this was the knowledge that the horror was
just beginning, if they could find no way to stop it. No adult in
living memory had seen an army gathered, although armies were
spoken of in the old tales of the civil wars that had almost torn
apart the Hundred. To think there were two such armies made him
want to scream.

Midday came a signal flashed through the flights by flags. Joss
had told Volias what to look for, and they had found it. He shifted
the flights northward to move out over the road and the river plain,
while he flew in over West Track. There, on the road below,
marched a band of some two hundred mounted soldiers, all in
black.

The Qin soldiers moved at a speed Joss could hardly credit, but
they switched off between horses, and all of them – men and horses
alike – had a stubborn toughness that was impressive and even disturbing. Joss took Volias and Kesta down with him and left the rest
aloft, as it took less energy for the eagles to circle high overhead,
rising on drafts and gliding back down to repeat the cycle, than for
all to land and take off again. Anyway, they were safer in the air.
The army was at least a day's march behind them by now, but there
would still be scouts and outriders ranging along the land and
sneaking through the woods.

They landed a short ways out ahead of the Qin. Joss left Scar off
the road and clambered up onto its surface. Where the Qin scouts
hid he could not tell, but they got their message back to the company somehow, because a short while later Anji came galloping up
in front of his troop with six companions, including Chief Tuvi and
his usual dour guardsmen, Sengel and Toughid.

The captain dismounted and strode to Joss, then grasped his arm, hand to elbow, and grinned with genuine pleasure. 'Well met. What news do you bring me?'

'These are Volias and Kesta, reeves out of Clan Hall. They've brought two flights, sixty in all. You can see some of them.'

Anji shaded his eyes with a hand and surveyed the sky.

Joss said, 'The rest are spread out to oversee the land. What of your task?'

The captain dropped his hand. Dried blood spattered the back of his fingers. 'The ambush succeeded. They were lax, and lazy, accustomed to easy pickings. I myself would always put my best soldiers in my strike force, and if that is so, then this army is strong only in numbers. However, I can't be sure their generals act as I would.'

'So the strike force is wiped out.'

'Some escaped. That was to be expected. But as a unified force, they are broken. How far behind is the army? How large is it?'

'A day's march behind. The Devouring woman had it right. About three thousand fighting men, formed into cohorts.'

Anji nodded at Volias and Kesta, to invite their attention and input. 'So, it is as we discussed when the council got the news and came to us begging for our aid. We've accomplished the one commission, the one we agreed with the Greater Houses through Master Iad.'

'What of the greater battle?' Joss asked.

'There are far too many of them for us to hope for a victory in the open field. With the strike force destroyed, we have three choices. We can retreat to Olossi, where the council should already be calling in the townsfolk and preparing for a siege. We can run entirely, and abandon both city and land to the invaders. We can stay outside the walls and harass the army when it invests Olossi with a siege, as we must expect it will do. If the latter course, then we would hope eventually to wear them down, starve them, deny them battle, and make it dangerous for them to move about the land to forage and raid in small bands. To carry out this plan, we must ourselves disperse into bands so we can supply ourselves and appear to be everywhere at once. They must never be able to find and pin us down. But for this choice to work, we must have the advantage of speed and sight. We must be able to cut off all messages running between the army and Argent Hall, and between the army and whatever allies they hold in the north. Otherwise, we have nothing they do not already possess, and, as well, the reeves who cooperate with them can seek out and discover us as we move across the land.'

Kesta was devouring the captain with her gaze, listening as if each utterance was a jewel that must be caught. She seemed smitten.

Joss said, 'I've seen no reeves besides our own today. How did the other part of the plan go? What happened to the reeve from Argent Hall?'

His words cut like an axe. There was a pause, as though he had said something shocking. A horse snorted. A hawk skimmed overhead and shied off, spotting the eagles.

Then all seven of the Qin – stolid, serious men – laughed until they wept.

When he was done, Anji wiped tears from his face. 'Aui! That woman is dangerous. She knows more than one way to kill a man.'

'She murdered the reeve?'

'No. But he got all tied up in his honor.'

Chief Tuvi snorted, and they all chortled again.

Anji finally found his voice. 'He wasn't able to alert Argent Hall. But my own tailmen ran into a man who rode a horse that had wings, and could fly. This man they shot with many arrows, and a javelin, yet he did not fall. My tailmen do not exaggerate. What do you make of it?'

'There are no winged horses,' said Kesta. 'It's a tale for children.'

'What tale?' asked Anji. 'For I can tell you, my men were shocked at the sight of a winged horse. Of a man who would not fall no matter how many arrows he had in him.'

Kesta said, 'The tale is a simple one. The gods brought forth the Guardians to bring justice to the land. They gave them seven gifts, and departed. After that, the Guardians acted as judges at the assizes. But it's only a story. There are no Guardians.'

'It's not a story,' said Joss. 'Many people's grandparents remembered seeing a Guardian when they were children.'

'A little lad may see all manner of things in shadows and in wishful dreams,' retorted Kesta. 'What do you think, Volias?'

Yet Volias, who never on any account liked to agree with Joss, remained thoughtful. 'I think the testimony of this man's soldiers must be taken into account. They aren't the only rumors I've heard in recent months.'

'When folk are frightened, they'll see and say anything,' objected Kesta. 'Not that I blame them. But that doesn't mean what they say and see are true things. Only that they're frightened.'

Joss shook his head. 'Zubaidit saw winged horses, too, when she was in the enemy's camp. So she reported to me, when we met in Olossi. But she saw no Guardians.'

'Could you recognize a Guardian if you saw one?' Kesta asked with a sharp laugh.

'Excuse me, if you will.' Anji shifted to look down the road, back the way he had come. The front rank of his company rode into view. 'We have little enough time. What do I need to know about winged horses, and these creatures you call "guardians"?'

Joss nodded. 'Kesta is right. According to our tales, the nine Guardians served as judges at the assizes for many generations. Then, they vanished. No one alive today has met a Guardian. We have good reason to believe they're all dead. Remains have been found. Bones. I think they're gone. But, according to the tale, among the gifts given them by the gods were winged horses, "formed out of the elements so that they could travel swiftly and across the rivers and mountains without obstacle."'

'A useful skill,' said Anji, indicating the resting eagles. 'As we have seen.'

'We've got a flag,' said Volias suddenly.

Joss looked over his shoulder to see all three eagles staring at the sky, but not at the two reeves circling overhead. After a moment, he saw a speck in the southern sky that quickly grew until he could make out an eagle and reeve moving in fast.

Joss turned to Anji. 'Remember that no eagle can descend on you if you and your men and horses take cover in woods. And at night, eagles are blind.'

Pari and Killer landed at a prudent distance, and the reeve unhooked and ran over to them. He was panting as he came up.

'The eagles are flaring,' he said. 'There's at least two flights approaching out of the north. It must be Argent Hall.'

Joss looked at Volias, and Volias looked at Captain Anji. The Qin troop had halted on the road behind him. They waited in neat ranks, with their remounts and grooms in the center of the marching order.

'If we draw them off,' said Volias, 'these have a hope of getting to Olossi before the army catches up. Or of scattering, without the Argent reeves marking their movement.'

'What will you do?' asked Joss. 'What meeting place will we arrange?'

Anji looked toward Pari. 'This man wears different markings than the others. What does that mean?'

Volias said, 'Pari, back aloft. Alert Ulon that we'll be drawing the Argent Hall reeves off toward the escarpment. We'll meet up with you shortly.'

'Don't you trust me?' demanded Pari. In the distance, Killer gave a twitter of anger, seeing a change in Pari's stance. The feathers were rising on the back of Scar's neck as he swiveled his head to stare at the smaller eagle.

'Best go,' said Joss. 'I don't want a confrontation between those two eagles.'

Pari gave way.

As the young reeve walked off, Anji, rather like the fierce-eyed eagles, watched him go. 'Can you explain that?' he asked.

'He came to us from Argent Hall,' said Joss, 'with troubling stories of their marshal and their activities. He claims to be on our side, and I believe him. But I think it best not to discuss our plans in front of him.'

Anji nodded. 'Best move quickly, then. If you can, let Argent Hall's reeves see us riding for Olossi. Afterward, draw them off and keep them busy. We'll resupply in Olossi this afternoon and scatter at nightfall. By tomorrow, the army will come. It's most likely they will trample the countryside and invest a siege. Were they hauling the makings of siegeworks?'

Joss shrugged. 'How could I tell? There are accounts of sieges in the old tales, but I've never seen such a thing. They had wagons carting supplies.'

'If they believe the gates will be opened from within by their allies within the Greater Houses, they won't be prepared for a drawn-out ordeal. That is what we must hope for.'

Kesta and Volias walked away toward their eagles, but Joss lingered. 'What happened to Zubaidit? I don't see her with you.'

'She took her brother and went her way at dawn. She said she had fulfilled her obligations, and meant to walk her own path.' Anji grinned at Chief Tuvi, and around the group of seven they shared smiles. 'Nor did I think to stop her, fearing she might take her revenge on me someday when I least expect it.'

'If these eagles are come in their numbers from Argent Hall,' said Chief Tuvi, 'then it seems she set free the pig and he went running to his mire!'

Their laughter annoyed Joss, and he did not even know why. As the other eagles took off, Scar called to him, an eager chirp. The raptor knew something was afoot. He didn't want to miss the action. As Joss hustled back to the eagle and hooked in, he worked through what was bothering him so much: that Zubaidit had just run away like that, when he had some things left to say to her. Yet she was free to go and come as she wished. She had no bond to him, no obligation. He might wish otherwise, but he knew when to give up the dance.

There was more to his irritation, hard to point to, subtle but rankling.

The Qin were not demonstrative men. In truth, they had about them a fastidious air of superiority; it was well hidden for the most part, but so pervasive was this quality to the fabric of their personalities that it seemed woven into them. Their laughter had shown no scorn. By any measure, it was clear they admired the Devouring woman, as if they thought her worthy in a way no one else they had met in the Hundred was. Not even Joss.

48

The worst came just after dawn when he heard thrashing in the trees. By then, he could not feel either hands or feet. He could not protect himself. And he looked like such a damned fool idiot. Sometimes death was better than shame.

But, after all, the impulse to live was stronger.

A man beat a path through the woods. He had a knife out, and the remains of a soldier's kit, leather scale coat, empty sword sheath, sturdy boots, baggy trousers sewn of stiff cloth, all torn and bloodied. Seeing Horas, he stopped dead, and like an eagle he gaped, showing his tongue.

'What are you?' he asked.

'A reeve from Argent Hall. Cut me loose.'

The man looked at the trussing, and the clothes, and he scratched his chin in a puzzled way, trying to work it out. He had worn a helm once; a leather strap, sliced clean, dangled where one end had gotten caught in the neck of his coat.

'Cut me loose!'

He shrugged, and cut him down.

Horas collapsed.

The man pawed through the pile. 'No offense, reeve, but I'll be taking this string in exchange for my trouble.' He tucked the string of vey into his sleeve. 'And this knife.'

Horas groaned. Hands and feet came alive with a flaming agony that made him weep. He could do nothing to stop the other man, who finished his theft with a satisfied smile. Back within the trees, a branch snapped, and the man's eyes flared with fear. He cursed under his breath and took a step.

'Wait,' Horas said, his voice a croak. 'Before you run – what happened?'

'We were attacked at dawn. They weren't taking prisoners, I can tell you. I haven't an eagle to fly away like you do, just my own two feet.' He spat on the ground, the old country tradition of expelling bad fortune. Without a spare glance, he took off into the woods.

Horas soon lost track of the crash and rustle of the man's flight. He lay there, teeth gritted and eyes watering. In the end, he crawled to his clothing, and he dressed. In the end, he staggered to a clearing, and set the whistle to his lips. In the end, Tumna came for him. Together they circled until they found the carnage left on the road and saw the company – the very mercenary company that had marched away yesterday! – marching double-time on West Track back toward Olossi. The council had lied to him! They had betrayed their own allies!

That Devouring woman had used him, lured him, shamed him, and then hadn't even had the stomach to kill him afterward.

Furious, fuming, and still hurting like the hells, Horas set his course for Argent Hall.

Midmorning he circled a leaden-winged Tumna over Argent Hall, and landed. Leaving the eagle for the hall's fawkners, he shouted at some stray lagabout to ring the alert before walking to the marshal's cote, where he was refused entry. The alarm bell jangled twice, but quit after that. He was just about to push past the old slave who blocked the steps and shove the door aside himself, when the senior reeves hurried into the garden.

'Are you insane, Horas?' whined Toban. 'You'll get us all punished.'

'Too late. The strike force was attacked at dawn and wiped out.'

'Why didn't you warn them?' demanded Weda. The bitch.

'Nothing I could do,' he said, 'you cursed fool ass-lickers. While you sit here and feast and the marshal pokes his merry pigs, Olossi's council is betraying us. I flew past on my way back here. The whole population is afoot, fleeing into the walls. They know what's coming, and they're making ready to fight.'

The door slid open. Marshal Yordenas appeared, looking weary but composed. His cold gaze made the reeve suddenly wish he were an ant, beneath notice. He wiped sweat from his neck.

'Why did you not return last night?' asked the marshal in that dull, quiet voice.

The lot of them were fools twice over, and all his shame and anger boiled up just thinking of it. 'Captured, that's what! They're a damned sight cleverer than any of you are. It's mere fortunate chance I escaped and got back here to warn you.'

The gang of four watched the marshal carefully. It struck Horas for the first time that they watched the marshal in the same way they would keep their gaze fixed on a poisonous snake.

'Best you gather two flights and rid us of these troublesome gnats.'

'You going to fly with us?' Horas demanded.

Toban gasped, and Weda flinched. They cowered, waiting for the marshal to bite. They were all afraid of him, but he was only an opportunist who had moved in and worked promises and threats to get himself elevated to a position he did not deserve and had not earned.

Those blank eyes were turned on him. 'Did you know, Horas, that I never sleep? I am burdened by such dreams as would drive a sane man into madness.'

Horas stepped back, anything to get farther away from him. For obviously, the dreams had already done their work. Why hadn't he seen that before? Toban grabbed his arm and yanked him another few steps back.

'Nay, make it three flights.'

'Uh, uh.'

'Speak up, Toban. I can't hear you.'

'Marshal, we're sorely understrength. Three flights aloft will leave us only one to cover Argent Hall.'

'Three flights,' said the marshal as if he were discussing the night's menu. 'It will be three flights. Olossi's Greater Houses must not be allowed to betray the agreement they sealed with us. And there is a rumor – she is looking for the one who escaped her – she'll be angry—'

He broke off, and went back into the cote without explaining who 'she' was, who the one who escaped her was, and why she would be angry or her anger matter to anyone.

'Three flights,' said Toban. 'You'll lead them, Horas. Time you had a command.'

He looked at them, who had cosseted and praised him. They were all rotten. They hated him, just as he hated them and everyone.

'Three flights,' he said. Why not? A man with the knack for command could win the loyalty of reeves who might then join him when, as in the Tale of Change, it was time for new leadership.

Three flights took time to launch, and they struggled once in the air to find a formation. The eagles did not like to fly so close together, nor had Master Yordenas flown them in drills as often as he ought, given so many were eagles who had migrated into new territory. He had preferred to send constant small patrols into the Barrens.

Looking for what? For the nest of my missing eagle, he'd said, but also, for signs of habitation in high isolated reaches. Any place, it seemed, a person might hide where only eagles could reach. Maybe what *she* was looking for, the person who had escaped her, whoever *she* was. For some reason, he thought of that mild clerk who had interviewed him at the army camp, of the way her gaze had burned right down to his cringing heart, curse her.

Enough! Circling above Argent Hall, he fixed his attention on the landscape below. He didn't love the sight of the land unrolling beneath, not as many reeves claimed to. The people were too small, reminding him of bugs, and perhaps it was best most folk be squashed for they would be gnawing and biting at him, ill-tempered as they all seemed to be. Paths and roads threaded through dry fields. The irrigation canals were emptied, nothing more than scars scratched into the dirt. Yet there was a smell in the air, a taste like a kiss of spice on a Devouring girl's tongue: the rains were coming soon. The new year would green out of the withered stalks of the one passing away. The Year of the Red Goat was waiting to germinate, bloody and stubborn. Jealous, passionate, fickle, like that damned Devouring girl. If he ever got his hands on her again, she'd not be laughing at him afterward.

At length, his flights were assembled in the air. Flanks stretched far out to either side. With the first flight, he took the lead, striking out for Olossi and West Track. Fields poured away below them. Soon enough he saw people on paths hauling carts and wagons piled high with possessions. From out of the walls rose the clangor of a bell. They had been warned. They were running for the safety of the walls, curse them.

The wind was hot, and the afternoon sun hotter yet. They circled Olossi a pair of times just for the pleasure of seeing so many faces upturned, so many pointing, shouting, weeping. It was good that the crawlers were frightened of reeves. They ought to be.

A flag flashed off to the left south flank, forward of his position. He banked, and the lead flight followed, with the other two keeping a prudent distance. Villagers hurried down the road, all in a jumble, some clots passing others, some resting, some splitting into two while others joined up. These were no threat. The flag whipped its signal again. His gaze caught on a distant group that, like ants, crept along the road in something resembling order. An eagle circled high aloft, watching over that company.

He slipped loose a flag and signaled to the rest to 'stay back.' He beat higher. The company on the road sparkled in their ranks. They were armed with swords and spears, although their dress was dark. What seemed at a height to be creeping was in truth a brisk march, eating up the mey.

As he banked, he got a good look at the reeve who was guarding the troop, and damned if it wasn't the very reeve who should have been dead. Joss, his name was. The other reeve's eagle was a big, old, experienced bird, and Tumna clamped down her feathers, not wanting to approach.

The other raptor pulled in close enough that that damned smug reeve could shout across the distance. 'What do you intend?'

'Go back! Go back! This is our place!' Then he saw what waited to the south.

Two flights of reeves, in tight formation, seen as specks over the escarpment where the thermals were strongest.

'Reeves do not war on other reeves!' called Legate Joss. 'Let us make an alliance.'

Three flights, to the enemy's two.

His bow was strung, clipped to his chest harness. He got it into his hands, pressed to the end of its tether, and nocked an arrow. Swinging wide, he released the arrow, but what would have been a fair shot on the land went astray in the currents and missed wide. The other eagle beat its wings, calling a challenge, and swung talons up as though to close and grapple in midair.

Horas tugged on the upper jesses, and Tumna dove out of the way. They twisted back and returned, flying hard, to their flight.

Reeves had no signal for attack. They were not soldiers. Using two flags, he gave two signals.

Crime in progress.

No quarter.

Perhaps the reeves of Argent Hall had simply been waiting for action. Still, it surprised him how they bent with a will, eagles ready to defend their territory and reeves eager to take out their frustration on Clan Hall's enforcers. Many of the Argent Hall reeves had, like him, been driven from their original places by the spite and envy of others. Now they could get their revenge.

They flew over West Track and, continuing south, grabbed height as they could, but Clan Hall had already taken advantage of the good updrafts along the high ground. As Horas and his flights moved in, Clan Hall's eagles shifted, in disciplined ranks, toward the west. He turned his group to follow, but at once the glare of the westering sun got in their eyes and made it difficult to aim.

Again, he signaled. *No quarter.*

Numbers would tell. Seeing what they were up against, Clan Hall would break and flee.

That's what he would do, in their situation. He wasn't a fool.

The lead flights closed. Some were too high and some too low; all the lines were staggered at irregular intervals. They almost seemed to be flying through each other, as the chanters in talking lines may shift places by weaving in between their comrades. A few arrows flew harmlessly. Some reeves grabbed an updraft, while others stooped to get out of the way.

The escarpment was a jumbled blanket of gray stone outcrops and grass dried almost white by the heat of Furnace Sky. Far to the south, a trickle of dust rose, marking movement, but the high plains were otherwise empty except for the eagles circling here along the spot where the earth thrust up from the river plain.

Horas found himself beyond the fray. He cursed at Tumna and turned her, although she protested. They banked steeply, losing altitude but getting back around where he could see the wheel of raptors in the sky above him in a silent gyre so beautiful that you might believe, for the space of a breath, that the gods had intended it exactly that way.

Then it happened.

An eagle faltered. Bated. Plunged.

It was difficult to imagine that the arrow in the eagle's eye was a carefully aimed shot, but it proved lethal. Everyone watched as the reeve struggled, trying to get his eagle to respond to his frantic pulls on the jesses, but they tumbled regardless. There was no sound when they hit. They merely became a motionless discoloration on the earth.

He wasn't even sure who had fallen, only that the man wore Argent Hall colors. The flanking flights turned wide. The Clan Hall flights split with a remarkable display of coordination, some stooping while others climbed. It was impossible to surround them.

Arrows sped through the air. Reeves shouted curses. A javelin whistled past below Horas's feet, and he twisted in the harness, trying to see who had come so close, but his view was blocked. Someone had gotten behind him, out of his range.

Down. Down. Above, two eagles passed close enough for reeves to jab with their staffs. Tumna labored, found a thermal, and caught it. Rising, Horas tried to grasp the sprawl of the skirmish. As more arrows and javelins were expended, the fight came to the raptors themselves. Their natural instinct to drive any other out of the territory they claimed for their own goaded them. Two eagles would close, and strike with their talons. Another would calculate its distance and dive, but because all possessed an uncanny ability to judge distance and velocity, only once did eagles collide in midair, and that to disaster, for both raptors tore each at the other, one reeve was sliced loose from his harness, and all plunged to earth.

Tumna shifted abruptly, beating out of the thermal. Movement flickered in the corner of Horas's eye.

Talons appeared over the eagle's right shoulder and raked Tumna's side The strike tumbled them. Tumna dropped, and Horas's stomach lurched as they fell. As he struggled with the high jesses, he saw Reeve Joss wheel above.

'Call them off! We have a common enemy!'

Tumna fought, coming around.

'There you go. There you go!' Horas cried to the bird.

With two great beats, the eagle regained control and pulled up far too close to the fatal ground. By the way she was bringing up her talons, Horas could tell she wanted to land, but that of all things the reeve could not permit. On the ground, they were no better than a crippled deer caught in the open when a hungry eagle passes overhead.

An arrow spun end over end and splintered against a spine of rock. A Clan eagle circled toward an outcrop, with an arrow in its wing. Tumna had gained stability, and Horas took a shot as the other eagle fought to control its descent.

He had a good aim, and the bird was moving slowly. His arrow pierced its neck, yet still the eagle maintained control as it broke momentum for the landing and found purchase on a knob of rock.

The reeve unhooked and swung out with bow raised, a standing target.

Too late Horas saw the danger: he was close, and the other reeve, a woman whose face was contorted with rage, drew calmly and fixed him in her sight. But the sun was behind him, and she squinted against it, and the arrow went wide. He pushed over the ridgeline and flew into the grasslands stretching south to the horizon. They skimmed low. Tumna was obviously in difficulty. Each shallow slope of hill was a mountain barely surmounted, talons brushing tips of grass. Shadows pulled long in hollows. At last, he eased Tumna down and they hit hard and he unhooked in

a rush and came down, twisting his ankle. Pain made his eyes sting. The eagle flopped forward, lay there for an instant, then drew herself up, too proud to collapse.

'Oh shit.' Horas searched in his travel pouch for ointment, but the damned fawkners had neglected to replenish his supply. Blood oozed from the wound. When he stepped forward to inspect it, Tumna slashed at him, and he leaped back, cursing.

Shadows raced over the ground. The eagles had followed him, and he was out of arrows. Only, as the first landed on the far rise, did he recognize his own Argent Hall compatriot. Another five landed, and ten more. A second flight passed overhead, seeking shelter. They had followed him.

The exhausted birds sank to earth as the sun set. There came Weda, the bitch, running to him with a cut on her face and her skin gray with fatigue.

'What now?' she demanded. 'Did you see how they were toying with us?'

Tumna flared, feathers rising. She backed away.

'Here, now. Here, now. What's wrong with your eagle, Horas?'

'Injured.' Strange how his voice had been scraped raw, although he'd uttered barely ten words since he started. 'How do you mean, toying with us?'

'They avoided us.'

'Nah. That was just clumsiness, just like us. Reeves don't fight reeves.'

'They do now. What do we do now?'

But it was pointless. Darkness was nearly upon them. She wanted him to make the decision, because if he did, then she could blame him later. It was always like that, his whole life. How he hated them all.

The third flight, almost intact, skated overhead and came to rest in staggered lines as night spilled over the rolling plains and ate the pale wonder of grass and the fading splendor of the sky. The first stars bloomed. As the blindness of night overtook them, the restless, angry, agitated eagles settled, but Horas could not. The fear and fury would gnaw at him all night.

To Weda, he said, 'Nothing we can do now. We'll stick it out here until dawn. Pass the message. We leave at first light.'

'And then what? Keep fighting?'

'No point to it. Neither of us can win. Best we go back and report that Clan Hall is sticking its nose in Olossi's business. Let him figure it out. He's marshal, isn't he!'

'That's what you're going to tell Marshal Yordenas?'

'You that scared of him?'

'You should be. You are.'

'He doesn't even have an eagle. He just says he does, but I think he's been lying all along, pretending his eagle is at nesting all this while. I think his eagle is dead. I don't think he's a proper reeve at all.'

'No reeve can survive the death of their eagle,' she said in an anxious whisper. As though Yordenas could hear them from this distance! 'What do you mean to do? Challenge him? You saw what happened with Garrard. You saw it all, Horas.' Her stance, seen as a deeper shadow within the gathering night, was tense, defiant, and fearful. 'He can't be killed.'

It was true. They'd all seen it.

No person could survive such a wound. But Yordenas had.

'Will you challenge him?' she repeated, but the sneering anger did not hide her terror.

He wanted to cut her yapping mouth off with his knife, but he dared not. She was a bitch, but he had to remember she was one of his few allies. One of the few people who had shown him a measure of casual kindness. She and the rest of the gang of four had approached him, allowed him into their councils, given him a part to play when Marshal Alyon's whimpering, weakling sycophants had made their final attempt to grab power.

'I didn't mean it,' he said. 'I didn't mean it, Weda. I'm mad, and Tumna's hurt.'

'No. No. Of course you didn't mean it. We're the marshal's loyal reeves.'

'As always. We'll go back to Argent Hall in the morning. That's the best thing we can do, like I said. Let him worry at it. Have you any ointment? I lost mine in the battle. Tumna took some scratches.'

She handed over a small leather bottle of salve. Then she walked away to pass the word that they would overnight here in the grass and return to Argent Hall at daybreak. Night swallowed them all. The sky was staggering in its brilliance because there was no evening moon. All around he heard reeves speaking softly to their eagles, calming them after the battle. Reeves had fought reeves.

There were three things you learned your first day in hall, the first day after an eagle had chosen you.

First. If your eagle dies, you die, so tend your eagle well and care for the eagle before you care for yourself, because your life depends on it. If you die, your eagle can claim another reeve, so tend your eagle well and care for the eagle before you care for yourself, because the strength of the halls depends on it.

Second. Serve justice. That is the whole of your duty.

Third. A reeve always comes to the aid of another reeve. To do otherwise is to cut away the heart of the halls.

Tumna refused to let him come near with hood and salve.

He wept.

49

It was the second worst day of Joss's life. Worse than the day he'd learned his mother had died. Worse than the day his baby brother had succumbed to a fever. Or perhaps the emotion of those days, suffered as a child, had worn thin until he didn't truly remember the intensity of his tears.

Today he'd done what needed doing, as awful as it was. Reeves relied on authority and mobility, and on the intimidating presence of the huge eagles who could kill any human and were not themselves easily killed. Reeves did not train as soldiers. Their charter forbade their use as enforcers for any council or captain who might wish to hire their services.

Yet today's skirmish was done, and could not be undone. Clan Hall's flights pursued Argent Hall's fleeing eagles into the grasslands, at a distance, then circled back to set down in the grass for the night. As afternoon faded to dusk, Joss left Volias in command with strict orders to keep watch but not engage, and the Snake, troubled and pallid, accepted the order without even a sarcastic reply.

Kesta was grounded, her eagle badly hurt. The young reeve from Argent Hall, Pari, was dead together with his wonderful eagle. There were at least two more dead eagles as well as other wounded ones, and a pair of dead men from Argent Hall whom Joss could not name, sprawled on the ground while their eagles walked around them.

All this Joss surveyed as Scar ascended on the currents and they turned toward Olossi. The river's lazy curves were visible to the north. There lay the line that was the road. Far to the west gleamed the salt sea, while in the forested lands to the east the river plain rose slowly into the high country of Sohayil, a gradual change in elevation difficult to discern from the ground with the night coming on. They left the southern plateau behind and worked the currents over the escarpment, rising first, and then hitting a high glide perfectly judged by the exhausted Scar to bring them with minimal effort across the mey to Olossi.

The voice of a bass bell rolled out from the walls, crying its alarm across the shimmering waters and the darkening land. All day villagers within sound of the bell had streamed into the city with what belongings they could carry. Stragglers still struggled along the main road, converging on the gates in panicked crowds. Dust floated in clouds; this time of year, there was no moisture or vegetation to hold it down.

He flew low over the outer walls. From below rose the clamor of many folk talking all at once, a roaring similar to the battering of waves on a storm-swept beach. Folk swarmed the paths and streets and alleys like ants poked from their nest. Children cried. Women and men shouted demands and questions. A beggar's chime tinkled faintly, then was overwhelmed. At the gate between outer town and upper town, the throng slowed, crawled, stopped.

'Hurry! Hurry! Move on!' A man's voice spiked above the cacophony. 'We must get inside!'

So many were desperate to push within the security of the inner walls that they had packed together in that open space before the gate until no one could move.

The inner city rose before him as he passed the walls. Children shrieked, pointing at the eagle flying so close overhead. In the courtyard of Assizes Tower, torches had been lit along every wall and even set at intervals to light his way to the perch. As planned, Anji and his troop had reached the city before him.

'Time for one last trick, my friend,' he said, and despite the twilight, and the crowds seething along the avenues, and the tolling of that damned bell, Scar negotiated the approach with ease and pulled up neatly to land on the perch in the courtyard of Assizes Tower.

Here – thank Ilu! – the Qin company waited in tidy ranks while clots of Olossi guardsmen kept their distance. The Qin had their horses with them. It seemed they had just ridden in. The square was slightly sloped, and backed by steeper roads leading down to the gates, with the tower built to overlook that open space and beyond it over the walls to the roofs and fields of the lower city. It was not as good a vantage place as Fortune Square, from which you could see in all directions, but Assizes Tower faced the busy gates through which flowed and ebbed the lifeblood of the town. Although he could see little in this gloom, he felt the presence of many hundreds of people pressed into the streets and avenues branching off Assizes Square. They were crammed shoulder-to-shoulder, held out of the square by the presence of militia, yet all desperate for news.

Joss hooded Scar swiftly and sprang up the steps to the porch that wrapped Assizes Hall. Behind, the old stone tower blocked part of the night sky.

The doors were already open, revealing the timber hall whose far end abutted the old tower. An argument raged in the crowd of council members, guild members, and other notables.

'You got us into this! What promises did you make them?'

'We did nothing except for the good of the city!'

'Liars! Fools!'

'You Lesser Houses stymied us at every turn! You forced us into a desperate bargain!'

'It was your greed that led you on! Now you would abandon the outer city! And I'm sure that is because your goods have all been moved into your compounds up here. What of those of us who have no place within the inner walls to save our goods and livestock?'

'Yes, what of us?'

'All must be saved! Everything!'

A long table stood to the right, under five arched windows. At one end of the table was placed a single chair on which sat the beautiful Ox girl, Mai. She had an almost heavenly shine, a 'moonlit calm' that drew the gaze. Captain Anji was bent over, speaking softly in her ear; when he paused, she replied, lips barely moving.

Midway down the table sat the clerk Joss had flirted with mere days ago, although it seemed like years. *Jonit*. Chief Tuvi and the scout, Tohon, flanked her, and she marked with charcoal on rice paper according to their direction. A young Silver man with hair hidden beneath a fine silk turban and silver bracelets halfway up both forearms stood a few paces away, beneath the middle window. An older Silver man with a full set of bracelets glowered beside the younger, arms crossed as he studied by turns the yammering crowd and the bare-faced women.

Anji straightened, and stepped away from Mai. He held a quirt in his left hand. He marked Joss, nodded, then raised the quirt and brought it down on the table so hard that the slap of its impact made everyone jump. And stop speaking.

'Enough!' He fixed one last chatterer with a stare that shut the man up between one word and the next that never came. 'Enough of this. What happened in the past, or even yesterday, does not matter today. How you sort out your grievances is your own business, to be argued over later. *If* you are alive to argue. I guarantee that if you continue to accuse each other now instead of making ready, then you will fall, and this city will fall, and your grievances will be dust and your children will be slaves.'

Fear settled them. His voice held them.

'Against an army, we cannot protect the outer city. Once we defeat them, you can rebuild, but you cannot rebuild if you are dead. And lest you think that we are outnumbered, then wonder no longer. It is true. This reeve will tell you what he saw, as he told us earlier.'

Joss nodded, but Anji did not wait for him to speak.

'Stout walls give us an advantage, if we can hold them. Captain Waras, what is your report? You already received tasks, which we discussed yesterday. Have they been carried out?'

Waras stepped forward, his color high and his face bruised as from a hard blow to the side of the head. His lower lip was split and still oozing blood. 'I passed out the word that all able bodied folk were to be divided between those who will labor to strengthen the walls and those who can bear arms and fight. But then the council began squabbling this morning about what that meant, and which men would not sully their hands with digging and who did not want their sons risking their lives with swords and spears. That quarreling has gone on all day.'

'If none risk their lives, then I guarantee all will be dead, and my men and I long gone, safely escaped.'

None spoke to answer him. They were already cowed by their fear and their helplessness. So many faces stared at the captain, their expressions as stark as those of a dreamer woken from nightmare to discover it was not after all a dream.

'We haven't much time. Therefore, all who can labor must labor to strengthen the walls. Runners must race *this night* to the villages too far to hear the bell. The watch fire must be lit, if it has not been already. If you have a watch fire, as all wise folk should. Every person, male or female, who is able to bear arms will muster at dawn. Those who can reach the walls will shelter within, in every courtyard and house and alley. Those who cannot reach the walls must hide themselves as they are able in their own village and fields.'

He paused to let these words sink in, but he did not cease thinking and communicating. He gave a signal to Chief Tuvi, who answered with a lift of a hand. He gestured to one of his guardsmen, who took a whispered message and strode out of the hall. He did not look at Mai.

'Master Feden. Master Calon. Mistress Ulara. See that competent people are assigned to oversee these tasks. Best you do so promptly. Get the work begun this night.' As though stunned, they nodded.

Anji beckoned to Joss. 'What report do you bring us, Reeve Joss?'

Jonit looked up, hearing his name, and down again so swiftly that Joss winced. She was sorry to see him, with an expression on her sweet face that suggested there'd be no satisfaction to be found in that quarter. Aui! That was certainly a trivial matter best let fly to the winds!

He addressed the crowd. 'A brief report. Reeve fought reeve this afternoon, a terrible thing brought about by the corruption that has eaten away at our land. Of that, I'll say no more except to tell you that it is one of the three pillars of the eagle halls that "A reeve always comes to the aid of another reeve. To do otherwise is to cut away the heart of the halls." If a reeve cannot trust another reeve, then how can any of us be trusted? So be it. The shadows have been creeping over the Hundred for a long time, and now it seems they mean to overwhelm us.'

'And the battle?' asked Anji mildly.

The pain was of the kind that may bring a twisted smile to the lips. 'Reeves do not train as soldiers. We were clumsy enough that we did ourselves little physical damage, thank the gods. But we did enough.' He shook his head, shook it off. There wasn't time for this. As Marit had once told him: *You think too much.*

'Three flights out of Argent Hall rest in the Lending this night. Two flights out of Clan Hall remain near the Argent Hall flights, to watch them. Our intention is to stay away from the Argent Hall reeves at dawn, not to engage unless we have no choice. As for the next step, that is up to you.'

Anji bit his lower lip, looking thoughtful.

Folk murmured, but no one spoke up. All deferred to the Qin commander.

'How many left, do you think, at Argent Hall?' he asked Joss.

'How many reeves and eagles?' Joss considered poor, dead Pari's report. He considered what he had himself observed. 'Each hall is meant to house six hundred reeves. But there are never six hundred on any given night, or in any given month. Some are assigned to Clan Hall. Some range on sweep patrols. Some eagles have left for their nesting season. A few will have lost their reeves and gone to the mountains for whatever it is they do there to comfort themselves. Some reeves may be on leave to visit their families. Others will be in training. I happen to know that at least fifty reeves abandoned Argent Hall when the new marshal took over the cote. I happen to know that no reeveless eagle has chosen a new rider in many seasons. Some have transferred out to new halls. Three flights sit in the Lending, trapped by darkness.'

'Why trapped?' Anji asked.

Joss shrugged, gesturing toward the lamps that lit the hall. 'Eagles are blind at night. They are essentially helpless. They cannot fly, and it is impossible for them to strike what they cannot see. Their hearing is good, but they live by their eyes.'

Anji nodded. 'They cannot fly. But I can. How many blind eagles remain trapped by darkness at Argent Hall tonight?'

'No more than a hundred. Probably less.'

'What will those three flights out of Argent Hall, the ones out on the Lending, do tomorrow?'

'Most likely a few will fly to the army, while the rest will return to their hall.'

Anji nodded. 'Let none reach the army.'

'To do that, I would have to kill those who try.'

'They will kill you. Best you strike first.'

'If there is war between the reeves, then justice may never again be served in this land. Even if Argent Hall is corrupt, and I believe it must be, we may do worse mischief in trying to cut out this corruption.'

'No choice is not a choice,' said Anji.

Joss saw that the decision was already made. To the Qin captain, the ancient traditions of the Hundred were merely words, no more meaningful than the babble of the arguing council. But then, after all, the man surprised him.

'I do not go against the customs of your land lightly, Joss. Do not think I demean them or think little of them. But if I were you, I would rather choose to live. It's time to attack Argent Hall.'

Joss sighed. Among that crowd, many sighed, hearing that a decision had been made. It was easier that someone else had the courage, the boldness, to set foot on the path all others would avoid, fearing the consequences.

Yet one person was reckless enough to raise her voice, to speak against the captain.

'This will not do,' said Mai, rising from her seat. 'What use to me a husband who is dead? For what will you risk yourself? Why risk yourself and your men at all, when the Greater Houses brought this trouble on themselves? When they thought there was no risk for them, they imprisoned Reeve Joss and lied to all of us about his whereabouts. When they thought they had an alliance with these others, this army and its leaders, they refused our entreaty to grant us nothing more than a place to settle, somewhere out of the way. They exiled us! They only called us back when they were desperate, when they saw they had been betrayed! They did not themselves even release the reeve. A hierodule acting on behalf of the temple freed him, although then the council pretended they had done so to curry favor with us, as a sign of good faith. I don't consider lies to be a sign of good faith! You have done enough, Anji. You have purchased a day for them to prepare themselves. If they have not made use of that day, it is not your fault! I say we ride out with the coin we received from the Greater Houses for last night's commission.'

Master Feden pushed forward. How different he seemed now, to Joss's eye! The big, bossy, imperious man might cow the council, but Joss could only see him as a ridiculous blusterer bound by rope to a chair with his mouth popping like that of a stranded fish. Gods, what he would not do for a glimpse of Zubaidit! But she was gone, utterly gone, and never coming back.

'You can't leave now!' Feden cried. 'You made a bargain with us!'

'We agreed through Master Iad to fight one action only,' said Mai. 'The attack on the strike force, to buy the city time to gather its population inside the gates. That action was completed. Successfully, as we all know.'

Folk murmured, shuffled feet. 'Do something, Feden. Do something!'

'You got us into this!'

One merchant commanded a sizable contingent at his back, and a grim smile on his lips. He wore the badge on his silk jacket marking him as a merchant who trafficked in flesh. Feden, glancing that way, saw that smile and those supporters. He might have been a trapped rat, staring at the dog ready to chomp its neck.

He looked back at Mai. 'But you must help us!'

'I see no reason to bargain with the Greater Houses at this

juncture,' Mai said, 'considering all that has gone before. If we deal, we deal with the whole of Olossi's council, an open vote of all members with a right to sit in on council meetings.'

Joss judged Feden's degree of shock by the heaving way the man panted, as if taking in her words as breath but finding that breath choked him. 'That goes against all our traditions. That way, with so many voting, lies madness. Only the Greater Houses have the wisdom, the stake in security and peace, the many generations building Olossi's fortunes, to make proper decisions!'

The young Silver cried out. 'Let's have a vote, now. A vote to elect our council master. Take the roll!'

Feden could not protest, even though a Haf Gi Ri had raised the issue, even though the Haf Gi Ri could not vote. He and his allies had already lost, and he knew it. Quickly, the roll was read, and votes tallied around the hall from every one of the Greater Houses, the Lesser Houses, and the guilds. Sixteen votes for Feden. All the rest, to Joss's surprise, were for the same man, a merchant named Master Calon.

Yet why should he be surprised? Mai and Ánji were not surprised. Nor was Master Calon. Like the ambush last night, this had obviously been carefully planned.

Beads of sweat left runnels through the powder that gave a smooth color to Master Feden's aging skin. His fingers twitched in spastic patterns. 'This can't be. This is out of order. I won't allow it. You have no right.'

Master Calon stepped smoothly into the open ground, from which he surveyed the assembly with a look of satisfaction. He nodded at Anji, and Feden saw that nod.

'We've been betrayed!' Feden cried. 'Can't you see it? We've been betrayed by these two wolves, acting in concert.'

'Yes, we have,' said Master Calon. 'We've been betrayed by you, Feden. By you, and the Greater Houses, making deals with an enemy out of the north. Wolves, all of you, eating our young. Let this be the end of it.' He acknowledged Mai. 'Verea, our business with you remains unfinished.'

'But – ! But – !' All ignored Feden, even his old allies.

Mai's expression was so bland that, as his aunties might say, one would not know she had already licked the cream.

'Olossi's council seeks our aid to defeat the army that will soon lay in a siege outside your walls. Very well. I'll state our price.' She paused.

Abruptly, Master Calon's smug expression wavered. He blinked. He looked worried.

She went on. 'It is the custom of the Qin to control the taxes and tolls of any territory which lies under their governance. Therefore, we will require a specified grant of land, a designated territory, over which the captain and his family hold the right to exact taxes and tolls as long as heirs of his body unto all generations are alive. This grant of land will contain pasturage sufficient to maintain two hundred households as well as farmlands tenanted by local families. These fields will be taxed at the rate of one part in nine, to be farmed in common. That portion goes to the governor, that is, the captain and his family. According to the custom of the Qin, pasturage sufficient for a household can be measured by the amount of land one man can ride around in one day. Wives will be found for all of the men who desire to settle down in a household and with pasturage of their own. In addition, a single payment will be made in this manner: From each of the houses that make up the Greater Houses, fifty cheyt, for a total of seven hundred and fifty cheyt. From the Lesser Houses and guilds, in common, two hundred and fifty cheyt.'

In the quiet, Joss heard distinctly the intake of breath from those gathered, even Master Calon. Especially Master Calon. Joss was himself dizzied by the amounts so casually falling from her pretty tongue.

Captain Anji had his head tipped slightly and appeared to be looking not at Mai but at Toughid's boots. His mouth was pulled so tight that at first Joss thought he was angry, and then he realized the captain was trying not to smile. The two Silvers, younger and older, *were* smiling, as at an apt pupil or a masterful parry.

She raised both hands, palms up, to signify that no coin had yet changed hands. 'According to the law of the Hundred, each of the members party to the agreement will swear to abide by the agreement as long as the captain or any of his heirs, or the heirs of any of his soldiers, still live in this country. No deliberate harm will be inflicted on any of the parties by any of the others, nor will any of the parties renege on the agreement once the danger is past. For our part, we will abide by the agreement, aid Olossi, and settle peaceably afterward in lands set aside under Qin control. Is the council agreed, Master Calon?'

Master Calon shut his eyes as if gathering strength to reply.

'I don't agree!' sputtered Feden. 'It's too much! You all know it's too much. Land! Coin! Gods and hells! How are you standing for this? A payment, a single payment, a simple bargain of labor in exchange for work done should be'

Mai cut him off. 'Agree to our terms, or find someone else to help you.'

The bell boomed to life, and tolled once, twice, three times. The sound washed like a wave over them and kept moving. At length, its voice died away.

Master Calon opened his eyes. He stepped in front of Feden and put a hand on the other man's chest. 'You and your allies brought this down on us all,' he said coldly. 'You and the other Greater Houses betrayed this town, for what you thought would be your own benefit. Did you not?'

Feden trembled. He looked at the floor. He did not answer. In the crowd, folk shifted away from certain people, isolating them.

Calon swept his gaze over the assembly. Indeed, he seemed overcome by emotion, ready to break down and weep. 'What choice have we? What choice?' He turned back to Mai, held out his hands, palms up, signifying that no coin had yet changed hands. 'Let Sapanasu give Her blessing to those who fulfill the bargains they make, and Her curse to any who turn their backs on what they have sworn in Her name. Let it be marked and sealed.'

'Let it be marked and sealed.' She might have just sold a cupful of almonds in exchange for two vey.

Anji raised his quirt. Many held their breath. A few stepped back, as if to get out of range.

'Let all the people of Olossi do their part,' he said curtly. 'Let the council act wisely. And swiftly.' He took a step back to survey the map being drawn by Jonit under the light of a pair of oil lamps. 'As for myself, I had thought to stay here and order the city's defense, but that task will have to fall to Captain Waras, Master Calon, and the council. It's a shame,' he added, with a frown, 'that the priestess,

Zubaidit, has departed, for I am supposing she would accomplish what I am not entirely sure this council can. Well.' With a cutting motion, he sliced that notion away. 'No use trying to eat food that doesn't exist. I have a different plan now, a better one. Eagles are blind at night, but we are not. I'll need a hundred competent guardsmen who can be ready to ride immediately with my troop.'

The captain looked at the two Silvers, as if to mark a promise they had made to him, then at his wife. She had the most astonishing face, open and fathomless, so lovely to look upon yet hiding her true feelings. He offered to her no fulsome farewells, no touching good-byes, as in the old tales. He had no time for such sentiments. After a moment, she looked down at her hands.

'We ride.' With a gesture, Anji called his men, and the Qin soldiers left the hall.

Joss followed them.

50

They crossed the River Olo on a bridge made of floating barges strung on chains across the current. Later, when Shai looked over his shoulder, the hill that marked Olossi was barely visible as a dark irregularity on the southern horizon. All else lay so flat beyond the raised roadway that the landscape seemed artificial, as if the earth had been planed smooth. Members of the Olossi militia strode alongside, holding lanterns to light their way. These were young men, eager to prove themselves. In the shifting bands of light he saw them grinning, in contrast to the grim Qin soldiers, who had been up for two days and had already fought a battle. But as the company strode along, it was the militiamen who rubbed their aching thighs, who paused to gulp down an extra breath of air or take a slug of bracing spirits.

Shai stumbled as he walked, even though the road was well made and level. Half the time he leaned against his horse for support. How the Qin soldiers and horses endured this relentless pace he could not imagine. About half of the herd had been left behind to recover at Olossi under the stewardship of Mai and the clan that had taken her in. That act alone made Shai understand that Captain Anji had committed to the enterprise in the way a man standing at the top of a cliff takes an irrecoverable step forward into the gulf. No Qin soldier left behind his string of mounts except with clansmen.

The ground on all sides lay dry and dusty. Parched irrigation ditches ran at right angles, black threads trailing off into the darkness. Yet there was water in the soil, more than there ever was in Kartu country, which was fed by no mighty river. Plants grew alongside the ditches, and ranks of trees rose at the shores of shallow ponds. Even the taste of the air had changed. The locals whispered of the rains coming, bringing with them the new year and its festival.

They passed through a village whose houses were slung along either side of the road; the silence that accompanied their march was that of a town abandoned, not sleeping. A single dog yipped at them, then scuttled around a corner. Soon they passed beyond houses and storage sheds built up on logs, past shelters and empty byres, back into the flatlands with rectangular fields scored into a patchwork by irrigation ditches.

They took a turning off the main road, a two-cart road, as the locals called such, and struck out onto a narrower path. This one-cart road was also raised on a berm, so it almost felt as if they were walking on the air like spirits or demons.

On and on they marched, into the night. A breeze rose up off the distant salt sea, whose broad expanse was not yet visible ahead of them. Once a shadow passed overhead, but probably it was Reeve Joss. According to Anji, he alone of the eagle riders was carried by an eagle who trusted his rider so thoroughly that the creature was willing to fly blind. Still, how could any of them be sure, if he did not land?

The stars shimmered in a hard, clear sky. Shai marked the progress of the shadow as it moved west, briefly blotting out individual stars and clusters which reappeared as the blot flew on. At length, he could no longer see it.

Was that really the reeve? Or a man wearing the face and voice of Hari?

The world, like those river barges, seemed to tilt and sway

beneath him. He could not keep his feet when the road would keep shifting, rising and falling with each fresh step. Everything had pitched him off his balance, and he could not find steady footing.

What creature had spoken to him? Hari was dead dead dead. He knew that, because he always knew what was dead and what was living. Hari's wolf ring had spoken with the voice of truth; objects could not lie, not to him, not to anyone. They had not the capacity. Yet it seemed he was wrong, because that had been Hari on the road. He had been solid, angry, passionate; he had scolded Shai, just as he always used to do. Get up, Shai! Speak up, Shai! Run faster, Shai! You can, Shai! You must, Shai! Hari was the best of the brothers, the one who cared, the one who struggled. That was why he had run from the stultifying walls and customs imposed upon the sons of the Mei clan. Yet after being marched away by the Qin, had Hari been sold into slavery, or his services as a mercenary sold to the highest bidder? It was impossible to know, unless Shai could find Hari again. But how could he find Hari again when Hari was dead?

Yet the man he had seen was living, or was living at least at that time when he had first seen him, on the road, riding a winged horse. How anyone could survive such a barrage of arrows, all striking true, and that well-aimed javelin cast, Shai did not know. No person could. So that meant that Hari was dead after all. But if he was a ghost, then the other men shouldn't have been able to see him.

Jagi strode up beside him and bent close.

'Don't let us down,' he said in a low voice. 'The landsmen think you're one of us, but you're staggering like one of them.'

Better to have kicked him and have done with it! Shai stiffened, his only reply a puff of breath between gritted teeth. Jagi faded back to the ranks of the tailmen. So after all Tohon had been right: the tailmen tolerated him, but did not respect him. He belonged to no one, not to the Mei clan, who had been eager to be rid of such an unlucky son, or to the Qin, who tolerated him solely because of his kinship to their captain's wife. He hadn't seen Tohon for three days, and was himself not skilled enough to ride as a scout.

That was the truth of what he was. Tohon felt sorry for him, Mai ignored him, and no one else wanted him. Even Hari had told him to go away. But he wasn't afraid of the shadows. Hari was all he had. So he would find Hari, no matter what.

Thus he found the strength not to falter. He did not want to be compared to the local men. He walked, and the stars rode the wheel high into the heavens and rode the wheel down into the west, as they always did, every night in every land. They were the same stars. It was only people who gave them different names. People might name him anything they wished, but he was what he was, and he would with the aid of the Merciful One accomplish what he had come here for: Find Hari, or Hari's bones, and return them to Kartu.

Very late, with the waxing sickle moon rising, they halted in a wide field where the captain met with the reeve. The land here was very flat but it sloped westward to the Olo'o Sea whose waters stretched like a field of darkness except where the moon's glow traced a glimmering path. At the edge of the sea rose an edifice. Watch fires burned atop towers built at each corner. The wind had been blowing out of the southeast, bringing the promise of rain, but now the wind faltered and died. The late night air grew stifling and close.

Chief Tuvi called the tailmen together. 'This is your part. The walls are of stone. A careful man can climb them. This you will do, kill any you find within, and open the gates. Do it quickly. The reeve will land inside, while you are about your business, and provide distraction. Move too slowly, and he'll die. I need a volunteer to fly in with the reeve. It's the most dangerous job. You'll have only a moment to kill any guards at large before they kill you.'

'I'll do it!' said Shai, stepping forward.

The others laughed. Chief Tuvi smiled in that good-natured way he had, but he chose Pil, who had not even volunteered.

Shai looked away as Pil sauntered off, proud of his chance at glory. Burning with shame, Shai checked his weapons and marched out with the rest of the tailmen, leaving the locals and the elite guard behind. They must walk the last few fields lest their horses be spotted. Across sheep pasture he trudged, and as the others split into pairs and trios, he found himself alone and, it seemed to him, awash in moonlight. Of the rest, he saw no sign or motion; they had vanished as if they had never come.

He cut into a rice field and crept through the stubble, but the rustling of dry stalks shattered the silence, so at length he found a dry irrigation ditch and used its depth to cover his approach. He meant to do something this night, although he wasn't sure whether he was likely to end up living, or dead.

The watch fires burned steadily. Of guards he saw none, but that did not mean they weren't there. The last field he crawled across, grateful for the dry weather. Beyond the field the ground rose into a low ridge. Just below the top he paused, then rolled over and plunged down the slope into the murky, stinking moat. Algae slimed his face and hands as he pushed through the water. It never came up higher than his chest, but the weight of water soaking his clothes made it difficult for him to clamber up the steep wall beyond. The stone wall offered fingerholds, nothing more. Yet years of carpentry had given him strong hands. Hand's-breadth by hand's-breadth he climbed the wall, never looking down. No guard called out. No arrow pierced his back. Nor was the wall so very high, after all; not nearly as tall as the wall of the citadel in Kartu where the town's rulers, whether Mariha princes or Qin commanders, held court. The reeves of Argent Hall did not fear assault so very much, it seemed. Maybe everyone had grown fat and lazy and complacent, thinking nothing would ever change.

His right forefinger began to bleed, but he was almost at the top. The moon scattered its pale beams over the endless flat plain. When he rested, pressing one side of his face against the stone and gazing outward with his uncovered eye, he saw no movement there beyond.

Abruptly, a shadow passed overhead, coming down fast. A man's sharp cry rang out from inside the walls.

'Who goes there?'

'Reeve's shelter!' cried a voice Shai recognized as that of Reeve Joss. 'I claim reeve's shelter. I have terrible news!'

Shai grabbed the topmost battlement and heaved himself up onto his stomach, kicked, scrambled, and swung first one leg and then the other over. Leaped down onto the wall walk. Dropped into a crouch. He was in.

No one had marked him. He spotted a guard off to the left, but the man was looking down into a wide courtyard mostly hidden from Shai's position. Staying low, Shai moved along the walkway in the other direction and found a ladder. Down he went, got lost in several turnings, and found himself in a garden after all, where he hid behind a fountain. No water ran. That lack of noise made him feel vulnerable, because sound was like shadow; it concealed what wished to stay hidden. It was very quiet, but even slight sounds carried in the night: the scrape of a foot on gravel, a distant laugh, the trickle of water from a second, working fountain. An insect whirred.

In the garden stood a cottage. The pair of windows he could see from this side were open; a lamp burned inside, but from this angle he saw no one. He crept along a lattice screened by a fall of vine. He reached the porch, and eased up onto it. Around the corner, a door slid open. Beyond the garden, a man shouted in alarm, and was answered by an eagle's fierce shriek.

A foot fell; a shadow breached the corner of the porch; a man's shape slipped into view.

'Who are you?' he said.

Shai drew, and thrust. The point of his short sword cut into flesh, pushed deep, kept sliding until the hilt slammed up against the body it had impaled. Panting, Shai wrenched it loose, but the blade caught on ribs. He fought with it and shoved the man back and actually got his foot up on the man's thigh and shoved with the foot while tugging on the sword.

All fell free. The man collapsed onto the porch without making a single sound, just a thump. The cloak he wore wrapped around his shoulders shifted, rising as if wind breathed into the fabric. Shai took a step back, then a second, waiting for the man to struggle up and attack him. Waiting for his ghost to rise out of his body, cursing and moaning.

The body did not stir. No misty form shimmered into the air.

Behind him, a man chuckled.

'Well done,' said Tohon, appearing out of the gloom. 'But move fast, now. We go on.'

'He's not dead.'

'Looks dead enough. If not, we finish him later. Follow me.'

A clamor rose from beyond the garden. Cries and calls were punctuated by the clatter of weapons. Tohon set out at a jog, and Shai ran after him, wiping his mouth, which was suddenly moist with saliva. They crunched along a gravel path. The scout seemed uninterested in how much noise they were making. Two corpses sprawled in the garden; their ghosts were caught in an eddy around their bodies, trying, Shai supposed, to figure out what had happened to them.

He and Tohon crossed under a gate and ran down an alley, made a twist and a turn, and sprinted into a wide and dusty court. Reeve Joss's giant eagle walked with wings spread while a pair of hapless men cowered away from his talons. Several bodies had fallen in the court, but in the dim light it was impossible to know what had struck them down. A ghost was weeping beside one corpse, but the other ghosts, strangely, were already tearing away from the flesh, seeking Spirit Gate, through which they would cross into the other world.

Near the fortress's massive gatehouse, a fire burned in a outdoor brick hearth. Here guardsmen might warm a cup of khaif to keep them awake through a night's watch, but tonight the flames illuminated a quartet of tailmen as they set their shoulders to the wheel. With a groan, and a rumble of gears, the gate creaked. Black-clad riders streamed into the fortress.

Anji rode up to Tohon.

'Done,' said the scout. 'But it was the lad who killed the marshal.'

Anji nodded at Shai. 'Well done.'

He signaled. Together with the Olossi militia, the Qin soldiers spread throughout the barracks, stables, chambers, and lofts of Argent Hall. Reeves and servants were caught, bound, gagged, and confined under guard, while the dead were carried into the same high loft where the prisoners were kept and lined up in tidy rows for the living to contemplate.

Living among the reeves were guildsmen called fawkners, men and women whose work was to care for the eagles. They proved most cooperative. As soon as they saw that the hooded eagles under their care were not to be harmed, they seemed, in truth, relieved at the incursion, even though many of the eagles were badly distressed, restless in the darkness.

As soon as every room was accounted for, the troop set to work. Anji and his officers inventoried the contents of the storerooms. The militiamen dressed in the garb of the hall's hired men. The Qin soldiers rolled wagons into position and took their stations. Joss hooded Scar in an empty loft, to rest him. Men napped, hoarding their strength. Shai was too restless to sleep. He walked back through the compound and found the garden and its cottage, where he had stabbed that man. No body lay on the porch, of course, but strangely, no blood stained the boards either. For the longest time, as light rose and the night softened with dawn, he stared at the spot. There was no evidence that anything at all had happened. Inside the cottage, the lamp still burned, but it was guttering on the last of the oil. He moved toward the entry door, thinking to go inside, to blow it out. To look for something he had surely misplaced, only he wasn't sure what it was.

'Hey! Shai!' Jagi waved at him from the shadowed alley. 'Come on! We're supposed to take up position. You're with me.'

He shook himself. To his surprise, his hand was already on the door, which was closed, but he wasn't sure whether he was about to open a closed door, or had just closed an open one. Uneasy, he backed up, then jumped down the stairs and hurried over to Jagi.

As Shai came up to him, Jagi punched him, hard, on the arm. 'Tohon says you struck down the marshal. You didn't let us tailmen down.'

Shai could only grit his teeth so as not to wince in front of his companion. He did not look back at the deserted cottage as they trotted away down the alley. The night's activity seemed like a dream to him, something best left behind. They took up their station on the wall walk where scaffolding gave them protection; they still had a good view over the courtyard. It was very quiet, very still. Jagi readied his bow.

To kill a man, you must be willing to see the ghost he becomes. Such was the curse set upon him. He was not sure he was willing to be a soldier, if he must face, every time, the ghost he had created. Yet releasing ghosts did not seem to bother Anji, and anyway, Shai knew he would never have the courage to ask the captain if it did.

A militiaman rang the first bell as soon as the sun's rim broached the eastern horizon.

'Captain has a new idea,' said Jagi. 'Something to do with the oil he found in the storerooms. He's talking it over with that eagle rider, right now. I wonder, though.'

'You wonder what?' asked Shai. He wondered, too, at the empty courtyard, the abandoned rooms: Argent Hall's ghosts had fled quickly, almost as if they were happy to find release.

'Let's say we survive this. I wonder what kind of wife I can find here. She won't be able to cook the things I like to eat. I tried a bit of their yoghurt and milk. Gah! It had no bite to it! I suppose I'll have to learn to eat what she cooks. That's what my mother would tell me to do.'

He settled down with chin on crossed wrists and bow tucked beside him, dozed off . . .

A bell woke him. Just as he opened his eyes and remembered where he was and who he was with, a whistle called the alert. Jagi tipped from slumping against the wall to a low crouch so fast that one instant he seemed asleep and the next ready to loose an arrow.

Shai peered over the wall. If you looked hard you could see specks in the sky.

Argent Hall's eagles were coming home.

51

At dawn, a wind rose off the Lending as if earth itself exhaled. Grass bent under the blow. The sun rose. One by one, the reeves of Argent Hall took off for home. Although Horas exhorted them to stick in their flights, so that they could ward off Clan Hall should the other reeves attack again, no one listened and many were, of course, too far away to hear him. With his own eagle injured and refusing care, Horas knew he'd lost any respect these arse-faced bastards might ever have had for him, which wasn't much.

He waited until the last were no more than a speck of dust in the sky, and waited yet longer as Tumna kept her gaze turned to follow their flights, for Tumna could see much farther than he could. At length, the eagle swiveled her head and gave Horas a glare that would have peeled the skin off a lesser man. The eagle walked to the crest of the ridge, where there was a bit of a cliff to help her lift. Once there, she looked again at Horas, curled her talons into fists, and settled. All was forgiven.

Horas approached cautiously, and paused when the eagle stood.

Tumna suffered him to hook into the harness. Wings spread, the eagle thrust, and they leaped into the air. The ground sped up beneath Horas's feet, and he sucked in his breath for death's scream, but just before they hit, Tumna beat hard, caught an updraft, and they were up and rising.

Even so, it was a long, slow, difficult flight, managed only because Tumna rode the winds until they were so high that Horas had to shut his eyes lest he weep, and then the raptor angled a slow glide that ate up the mey as they crossed the Olo Plain. The least movement on that injured wing, the better, it seemed.

The road was a faint ribbon seen far below, and on its track Lord Radas's army oozed along like so much sludge, dark and nasty. The army would reach Olossi by midafternoon, Horas judged. But he was so weary he could not care one way or the other. Tumna was wounded, and angry at him. No reeve could live without his eagle. Aui! So the tales went: the glory and the honor and the fine adventure and thrill to ride aloft, to fly into any town or hamlet with such a formidable creature at your back that all folk must acknowledge you. But the tales lied. Everyone lied. He hated them all, and they deserved his hate, for the world was nothing but a smear, a bit of smut, a spat word and a kick in the ribs.

He would have wept again, but he was too ashamed. Fear was a worm in his belly. He knew himself for a coward and hated himself most of all. He had seen the truth in that clerk's gaze. He was ash, muck, nothing but leavings.

All at once, Tumna chirped as though to tell him something. Good news! Good news!

Aui! It was obvious, now he thought on it. The clerk's gaze had lied, too. No sense in believing her, when he had no reason to trust her. He might yet make something of himself, but he guessed, now, that he'd find no comfort at Argent Hall.

'We'll fetch our things and get out,' he said to Tumna, and the eagle chirped, as if in answer to his tone.

No hall would have him. But they needed no hall. He felt no duty to the reeves, not any longer. They'd fly to the Barrens, find a place to live, and hunker down until the shadows passed.

Tumna chirped a third time. The sea glittered ahead, flat and gray. Horas saw eagles circling as they waited to land at Argent

Hall, still too far away for him to quite distinguish. But Tumna was excited. Tumna saw what he could not.

They glided down, and down, and the confusion of eagles circling began to take on a frightening significance. Those pale streaks flashing up from the ground were arrows and javelins. Of the eagles circling, some were trying to land while others were trying to get a lift to move away. Already a quartet of reeves was beating north, fleeing the skirmish.

Above the walls of Argent Hall, an eagle tumbled so suddenly that he thought it was a clot of dirt flung out of the sky, until the poor creature tried to spread its wings and could not. It fell, out of his sight behind the walls, into the sea. With his gaze drawn that way, he saw along the shore coming up from the south more flights of eagles, too many and in too regular a formation to belong to Argent Hall.

He began to tug on the jesses, trying to get Tumna to angle away, to fly north, but the eagle ignored him. Still at a good height, Tumna found a thermal along the shoreline and rode it, and they soared as both reeve and eagle examined the swirl of raptors below. A group of about twenty reeves lost heart and wheeled away in the face of the flights approaching along the shore. But more carried the fight to the invaders, although it seemed strange that they should do so when those on the ground had the better position.

Reeves dangled like dead men in their harness as their eagles kept passing over and over as if seeking a landing. Although a few of the Argent Hall reeves were loosing arrows down into the hall, the arrows streaking up from below had, it seemed, manifold advantages: their archers were good shots, they had stable footing, and all had taken cover behind posts, wagons, and scaffolding. Strangely, certain of the eagles were trying to land within the hall despite the resistance. A dozen or more had taken perches, as many as could come to ground at one time, and either their reeves were already wounded, or the eagles were injured and could not fly; but in any case, those reeves were at the mercy of the people who had taken over Argent Hall. A dozen or more eagles had come to earth outside the walls, and as Horas tugged and tugged at the jesses, trying to get Tumna to move off, he saw a band of horsemen race out of the walls and, keeping their distance, shoot arrow after arrow into reeves trapped because their eagles would not fly.

Horas could bear it no longer. He was helpless. Argent Hall had fallen to what villains he did not know, although he could guess that the Clan Hall reeves had turned against every oath sworn by hall and eagle and with unknown allies betrayed their fellow reeves.

Tumna closed her wings and plummeted. Horas shrieked. With his staff he jabbed the eagle's breast. With an angry call, Tumna pulled up, swooped over the hall, and dropped toward the earth beyond. Horas slapped at the eagle again, aiming for the injured wing, and with his other hand tugged at the jess.

'Up! Up! Damned eagle! We've got to get away from here! North! To the Barrens!'

They hit hard in a dusty rice field. Horas unhooked and stumbled out the harness. Tumna struck at him with her beak. Horas leaped away, shouting. He caught his heel in a hole and fell on his backside. The eagle settled back and, with the greatest dignity and a look of affronted pride, tried to preen at the oozing wound on her wing, which she could not quite reach.

Pissing, stupid eagle!

He scrambled up. Argent Hall stood several fields away. A trio of riders galloped in their direction along a raised path between fields.

His string of oaths did nothing to gain Tumna's attention. He got a good grip on his short staff and marched over to the idiot bird.

'Up! We're getting out of here!' He whacked it alongside the head to get its attention. 'I'm in charge, you stupid arse-wit!'

Wings flashed out. He sucked in a breath to speak, took a single step toward the harness.

Tumna struck.

The weight of her talons pitched him sideways. At first, there was no pain. But when he shifted, thinking to rise, he found himself pinned to the ground. Blood soaked the dirt, and it was still spreading.

'Gah!' he said, as he tried to speak. A shadow covered him. Tumna loomed above.

She wants to be rid of me.

Then the cruel beak came down.

52

At dawn, Eliar's mother came to the guesthouse and, in a gesture offered in the most casual manner imaginable, invited Mai to take khaif with the other adult women in the women's tower. To do this meant entering the family gate.

Sheyshi must be left behind because no unmarried woman not born to the Ri Amarah could ever be allowed within the walls. Priya, offered the gate, told Mai she thought it best to remain behind.

'You will keep your head about you,' she said to Mai. 'But this one may panic if I am not here to calm her down. I will also keep an eye on our possessions.'

'I don't think they're likely to steal what they could have taken at any time,' said Mai, but she did not press the point.

Eliar's mother opened the gate herself; no servant performed this mundane chore for her, as one would have in the Mei clan. Behind the gate lay a brick-walled room, already uncomfortably hot, with slats in the roof and one heavy gate in the opposite wall. She rang a bell, and waited as a series of bolts were shot on the other side.

'You can see,' said Eliar's mother, 'that we guard ourselves well.'

'It is kind of you to admit me.'

Mai had to skip back as the doors opened out. A second set of doors, set right up against the first when closed, had already been opened. They passed through a dim corridor and emerged into a vast rectangular garden with well-tended greenery, benches, and several open shelters for shade. A covered porch stretched along the other three sides. All along the edge of the raised porch were scattered indoor and outdoor slippers in matched, or mismatched, pairs.

The narrow end of the garden opposite their gate abutted a three-storied tower. One long wall opened to living quarters, many sleeping and sitting rooms alive at this hour with children running in and out and along the covered porch. A harassed matron tried to herd them into some manner of hall whose doors were slid open to give light and air. The other wall opened onto kitchens set back from the main buildings.

As Eliar's mother led her along a gravel path the length of the garden, the children were chivvied inside and seated in rows alternating between boys and girls. At some command Mai could not hear, they bowed their heads and cupped hands over mouths and noses. Not one peeped.

At the porch, Mai followed the example of Eliar's mother and exchanged one pair of shoes for a pair of cloth slippers. Inside, the ground floor of the tower was a warren of narrow halls with whitewashed walls and polished plank floors. Where wall and floor met curved an inlaid strip of blond wood minutely carved with vines and flowers. Now and then a plain wooden door banded with iron stood closed. Oddly, these were not normal house doors, but fitted in the same manner as gates in a wall, with hinges, so that they opened inward. Hanging on each door was a chalked board on which were scrawled strange symbols.

'This way,' said Eliar's mother.

Mounting stairs, they passed through a weaving hall with its clatter and chatter just getting started. A second set of stairs took them through the second floor, a spacious chamber open on all sides to a screened balcony and furnished with low tables, cubbyholed shelves, the entire apparatus of a merchant's counting room. This room was empty.

A final flight of stairs took them into the open air. Bright silk awnings, and trellises green with lush vines, offered shelter from the morning sun. The aroma of herbs and flowers growing in troughs of earth melded with the spicy sharp smell of freshly brewed khaif.

The women of the house of the Haf Gi Ri had already gathered for their morning ritual, presided over by the aged grandmother. The pouring proceeded in silence, but although Mai watched carefully she could discern no obvious order in which the women were served, only that the aged grandmother gestured to various women and then, with trembling hands, poured for each one. Mai's turn came last.

She returned to a pillow, beside Eliar's mother. All sipped. Grandmother pronounced it good. Then her intimidating gaze fixed on Mai.

'Certain men of our house attended the council meeting yesterday, as is their habit, and their right as merchants holding a license to trade in Olossi. The head of our delegation spoke admiringly of your bargaining skills when you spoke before the council. He said that you overset the Greater Houses before they realized what you were doing, and further that you then took advantage of this victory to drive a harder bargain than the Lesser Houses and guilds expected. Because these acts are worthy of a kinswoman, it was deemed proper by both house councils that you be treated as a cousin.'

Every eye bent to Mai, a circle of women waiting on her answer. This was more daunting than the council meeting! She did not smile, as she would have were they men.

'I thank you for the honor you show me by allowing me inside your walls. Are cousins allowed to thank their hosts by name?'

Eliar's mother lightly touched Mai's knee: As warning? As admonition? As comfort? As encouragement?

Grandmother's smile discouraged. She gestured, and a young woman offered Mai, first among all, a sticky bun from a platter. The matter of introductions, it seemed, was not to be discussed. They fell to talking about yesterday's council meeting and the preparations of Olossi for the army marching on its gates. Although not one woman had been present at the council meeting, they were remarkably well informed, not speculating and gossiping in a frivolous way but discussing plans, logistics, construction, and financing as if they had been consulted and now needed to work out additional details. They asked Mai specific questions, although none that probed into her own plans and strategies. Some of these questions she could answer: What words had she said, what words had she heard? Who had replied? Some she could not answer because she did not know the people and fashions involved: Which subfactions had been standing together? Were certain persons wearing colors indicative of their allegiance and mood?

At length, the ritual came to an end. Cups, and a platter's worth of uneaten sticky buns, were gathered up. Women rose and took themselves off down the stairs. Eliar's mother found a broom in a corner and began sweeping. Several women began to work in the troughs, among the plants. Miravia appeared on the roof and walked over to Mai.

They clasped hands, and kissed each other on the cheek.

'I thought you were not allowed up here,' said Mai cautiously, 'because you are not an adult.'

'Only for the morning convocation. I am training as an herbalist. It is one of my tasks to care for the garden, here, where we keep some of our rarest and most potent plants. Come. You can help me.'

For a while Mai stood alongside while Miravia told her the names of plants, and they chattered in low voices about the council as Miravia weeded, plucked leaves, tested the moisture of the soil, and examined buds. Master Feden, in disgrace, had nevertheless managed to account for himself a lucrative warehouse lease. Eliar was furious that he hadn't been allowed to ride out with the militia who had gone with the Qin soldiers. The warehouses in the inner city were being filled with refugees. A pair of men had been caught thieving from a closed shop in the outer city. A child had been lost, and a troop of disreputable entertainers accused of her kidnapping.

A bell rang. Both young women looked up in time to see a pair of eagles dropping fast toward Assizes Square. Mai crossed to the opposite side of the roof. She gripped the lattice. Through the interwoven strips, she looked out over the city and the surrounding countryside.

Olossi was built on a substantial swell, with two flattened high points and a saddle of ground between them; below this ridge the hill fell away into the lower ground, in some places steeply and in others more gradually. Avenues curved up the gentle slopes while stairs cut up the steep ones. The Haf Gi Ri compound lay almost opposite Fortune Square, where she and Anji had faced the council. To the northwest, the height of the second hill cut off her view of the delta and the sea. Here and there other three-storied towers blocked a portion of her view, nor could she see the courtyard of Assizes Square because of the angle of buildings and slope. Yet despite this frustration, she nevertheless gazed at a magnificent vista, over the city's rooftops and beyond, where the lower town and fields stretched to the south and west and even into the east. She could just make out a line that must be West Track, so distant, cutting down from the southern escarpment, that it seemed no more than a filament. Walking along the roof, she found a line of sight that allowed her to look over the flat plain lying north of the river.

A raised road struck straight through a tidy patchwork of fallow fields. If there was traffic on that road, a returning company of black-clad riders, she could not see them. She watched for a long time.

'Mai? I'm going down now. Do you want to come?'

Reluctantly, Mai pulled her gaze away from the road and the plain. 'Will you be able to get any news? Of the business of those eagles?'

'It will come to us in time. I'll tell you whatever I can find out.'

'May I stay up here? That way, I can see them.' *If they come.*

Miravia took her hand and smiled softly. 'You will want to stay in the shade. The sun gets very strong this time of year. I'll come as soon as I hear anything. Or with midday soup, if that comes later.'

'I'd like that. What of my sl— my hired women?'

Miravia glanced around, but by this time they were alone on the roof. 'Are they slaves? Eliar told our father they were hired. Else the clan would not have allowed you in!' She seemed about to say something more, but did not.

'I'm sorry.'

'Are you ashamed to own slaves?'

Mai considered her statement for so long that Miravia blushed, and let go of her hand.

'Have I offended you?'

'No. I'm not ashamed. In Kartu, there have always been slaves. That's just how it is. I've never heard of people who don't own slaves. Are there any who own no slaves, besides your people?'

Miravia laughed bitterly. 'Don't let the old ones hear you ask. The truth is, I don't know. How should I? We're not taught such things.'

A lively tenor bell rang three times.

'That's prayer bell. Now I really have to go.' With a kiss, Miravia departed.

It was better to wait alone. It was easier that way to find a place of calm and silence in which to wait. Mai made herself a place to sit in the shade where she could watch the northern road. From this angle, she could not see the river crossing, which she understood was some manner of floating bridge. Nor could she see Argent Hall, which lay too many mey away for the human eye to see, although Miravia had told her that an eagle soaring above Olossi could mark a path to the reeve hall because of its astonishing eyesight. For someone who claimed to know nothing of the outside world, Miravia knew a great deal, although naturally Mai could not be sure all of it was true. She herself knew so little of the Hundred that anyone might tell her a wild tale with enough evidence of sincerity, and she would believe it. In Kartu, they had laughed at her appetite for tales. Now, of course, she was living the adventure she had taught herself to dream of but never expect. Yet, of course, the tales and songs usually ended in tragedy. So she sat, watching the road, as the sun rose to its zenith. She did not weep. Either Anji would die, or he would live. Nothing she did now could alter that.

Sometime later, an eagle beat up from Olossi's walls, then with wings open seemed to stop moving and simply to rise up and up as though lifted by an invisible hand. It flew out along the track of the northern road, and was quickly lost to her sight. Below, the courtyards and kitchens came to life, fires lit and stoked, huge pots hauled out, as if in preparation for a festival feast. No one disturbed her; no one came up the tower at all.

Her life lived within the strictures of the Mei clan had trained her well for this day, out of all days, when she must accept that, right now, there was nothing she could do to alter the course of events she had helped set in motion. There was nothing she could do except wait.

Much later, Miravia brought up a kettle, a pair of bowls, and a dipper. Together, they sat on a bench in the shade and drank their soup. Miravia had pulled her hair back into a scarf.

'Heard you any news?'

'No. I've been too busy. We've been set to a new task, wrapping rags and dry rushes into torches and soaking them in oil.'

'What for? Do they expect to be attacked at night?'

Miravia shrugged. 'I am not an adult. I'm not allowed to know.'

'Is it something I can help with?'

'I'm sorry. If they wanted you, they would send my mother to ask.'

'I suppose I'm best left here, out of the way! It's so hard to wait.

Anything would be easier. Look at you. All of you. It seems you work all the time, at all manner of tasks. I saw your mother sweeping! Do your women do everything? Even if you own no slaves, have you no hired folk?'

'We are all servants of the Hidden One,' said Miravia, surprised at this question. 'The work of the world is our sacred labor.' She touched the lattice screen. Her smile was bitter. 'Although I wish I had as much right to walk freely through the city as does my brother, who runs a shop.'

'You visit the prison.'

'With an escort. Provided grudgingly by my elders, since they cannot think of a way to refuse my request, which I can honestly claim is an obligation.'

Mai sighed. She had no good answer to this. In Kartu, a married woman must be prudent in how she walked about town, lest gossip destroy her reputation. In the empire, the women lived entirely sequestered, although Mai still found this difficult to believe. And Anji had mentioned that the priests of Beltak had given grudging approval to the Ri Amarah because of their customs regarding how they separated their own women from public life.

Abruptly, Miravia pressed a small hand on Mai's forearm. 'Listen!'

There fell a hush, and out of it, as loud as judgment, the Voice of the Walls cried its plangent warning five times before it ceased. A shout rose from the walls as guards called out in a thin echo of the bell. The two girls ran to the other side of the tower. As they stared in the direction of West Track, other women came up the stairs and pushed to get a look until so many were crowded there that the ones pressed against the lattice had to call back the details of what they saw to those waiting behind them.

West Track had begun to move, only it was not the road that had come alive but an army marching upon its surface. Steadily, in their ranks, they closed the distance. The searing heat of the afternoon did not affect their pace. A few stalwarts who had remained in the outer city clamored at the gates, begging to be let in. Around Mai, some women wept while others pressed their lips tight and scurried away to be about useful tasks. She smelled oil boiling. A harsh stench rose out of the kitchens, making her eyes water. It seemed half the kitchens in Olossi were boiling vats and kettles. The air wavered, rippling with a haze. Far away, in the southeast, a line of cloud massed. This mass ran so dark, and lay so low along the horizon, that at first she thought it was another army, but Miravia tugged excitedly on her arm and exclaimed:

'The rains! The rains are coming early, before the new year begins! It's as if they're marching in pursuit of our enemies!'

Midday crept into afternoon. The second eagle and its rider fled town. The first ranks of that dreadful army swarmed down the southern slopes and began to set up in a wide half circle around the outer walls. More came, filling in the gaps.

'Have you ever seen so many soldiers?' cried the women around her.

'Yes,' Mai said. 'When the Qin armies marched through Kartu. One was on its way east, and the other, months later, was marching west. Those were much bigger armies than this one. The one marching east took all day to pass the town, and its rear guard camped within sight of the walls. We saw their watch fires burning all night.'

'Would that such an army marched now, to save us,' said the women.

Mai said, quietly, 'They will.'

Scouts probed the locked gates and crude walls of the outer city. Late in the afternoon, they determined they would meet no resistance. Like a crawling mass of black spiders, the army swarmed into the lower town. She could not bear to watch. She crossed back to the view of the north, but even there rode outriders as well. Olossi was encircled. Trapped. Except for the two eagles, the town might as well be alone.

Yet two eagles had come, and both had departed. She only wished she knew what message they had brought, and what message they had taken away with them. Although she asked several of the women, none would answer her question, and she deemed it unwise to push. The prayer bell rang again. They left her. Later, Miravia came alone and begged her to descend for the evening meal. Twilight crept into the sky. Below, the army was looting the lower city. Fires had begun to burn.

'You have to eat,' said Miravia.

Mai touched her own belly, barely rounded. If the women of the

Ri Amarah had not told her she was pregnant, she would not yet have guessed. She hadn't dared tell Anji, in case they were mistaken. 'I know,' she said. 'Let me go to the others, so they'll know I'm well.'

Miravia took her back to the guesthouse. In the company of Priya and Sheyshi, she ate what she could of spicy cabbage and spicy meat and a bland, dry bread that had to be dipped in broth to be edible.

Miravia brought a lamp.

'Is there any news?' Mai asked her.

'I'm told nothing,' said Miravia angrily. 'Nor will I be, until I am an adult. It seems so unfair, for there are girls younger than I who are married. And you, who have come into our house, you are also left in the dark. Isn't that how the saying goes?'

There was nothing to do but sleep.

Day rose again, after a restless night. Again, Mai was summoned and taken to the rooftop garden for the women's morning convocation of khaif and sticky buns. The ritual did not alter. The old grandmother would have poured the cups in the proper ritual manner, Mai thought, even with marauders pounding up the stairs and threatening to lop off her head. Afterward, the women cleaned up and departed to their tasks.

Standing at the lattice railing, she surveyed the streets and avenues. Wagons and carts rolled in a steady stream down toward Assizes Square, piled with twists of rag or bundles of freshly cut arrows. Along the battlements, guardsmen assembled, and she thought that women stood among them. At least half of those on the wall held bows or crossbows.

The army out of the north spread like a blight around Olossi, dark and cankerous. Flags and banners fluttered as a wind belled up out of the east. Six catapults had been drawn close during the night, and men bent busily around them. At the rear of the army, several large tents stood in a row, like the early arrivals at the quarterly market fair held in Kartu Town when folk walked many days from hill villages and isolated hamlets to purchase what they could not grow or make themselves. Around these central tents the fence of guards made a triple layer. Lines of men marched to reinforce those troops gathering within the outer town.

Out of the army came a crack, and a fine, high whir, and then the splintering thud of impact as a heavy object hit inside the town. Dust wafted up from a house a couple of streets inside the inner walls. Shouts rang out, and folk ran down what streets she could see toward the stricken compound. Looking back at the army, she saw that the great arm of one of the catapults had swung over. Another was being winched back.

By the main gate, a flag was drawn up on the pole.

'Now they will negotiate.'

Mai yelped, because she was so frightened, but it was only Miravia speaking.

Mai grasped her elbow and pulled tight against her. 'I thought we meant to fight them.'

'The council must purchase time,' said Miravia. 'I heard my mother speaking of it to my aunt. Master Feden disgraced himself. Now it is up to him to purchase time. He must delay the assault at any cost. It's said he will sacrifice himself to save the city.'

Mai did not need to ask what Miravia meant. She knew how the story would go. An official is allowed out of the walls to negotiate with the enemy, knowing he may be first to be killed. He is led to the tent of the general, or the prince, and taken inside, where he stands at their mercy. He talks at length, and speaks of the honor due to his ancestors and to the gods or spirits who watch over his town. He may sing a song relating to the founding of the first trading post at the oasis, how a mare led her sand-blinded master to the spring in the midst of a howling storm. For these acts we must be grateful, for there are those whom we cannot see who watch over us. When the ambush, or the counterassault, comes, he will be trapped behind enemy lines, but his act of sacrifice will save the day – or else it will be in vain, if the city is already doomed, since that is as likely an outcome as any other. She knew the tales by heart. In truth, her own father had related to her the actual story of the coming of the Qin army to Kartu Town, and how the Mariha administrator had met an abrupt death while trying to stall for time in the hope of receiving help from the next staging post to the east, where a substantial Mariha garrison was stationed. He had not known, of course, that the next staging post, and its garrison, had already been overrun.

'You're weeping.' Miravia touched soft lips to Mai's damp cheek.

'There's no shame in weeping,' whispered Mai.

'No. Our tears water the garden of life. Or so the poets say. Look. Now there he goes. I think it must be Master Feden, but I can't be sure. He's too far away.'

The Olossians were distrustful. Rather than opening a gate or extending a ladder, they lowered their negotiator down by basket from the inner walls. For a long time after this Mai could make out nothing of what was transpiring, but at length a procession emerged from the outer walls and struck straight for the central, and largest, of the tents. Most of those in the procession were soldiers dressed in the drab leathers of fighting gear. One was a merchant whose bright silks advertised his wealth because of their splendid colors.

'That's a saffron yellow,' said Miravia with the sure tones of one who knows her wares. 'It's said Feden is a man well filled with himself, but I must say it takes courage to march to your likely death dressed in your most expensive cloth. He might have left it for his widow, although everyone says they hate each other. And his heirs, no less. Oh dear. Have I shocked you?'

An attendant pulled aside the curtain that blocked the entrance to the largest tent. Mai shuddered as the merchant vanished within, to whatever fate awaited him. Who would meet him there, inside the tent? What questions would be asked? And how would Master Feden answer?

They watched the distant tent. Miravia's fingers dug into her forearm, but the pressure seemed too distant to be bothered about. Mai caught her breath in, held it. What was going on inside? Was Feden spinning a tale to protect Olossi, or spilling the truth and thus betraying his new allies for the sake of mercy from his old ones? It seemed that the wind died abruptly, that a dead calm enveloped them as a shrouding cloth is thrown over the face of one who has crossed under Spirit Gate and left this world behind. It seemed that the skin along her neck tingled as if kissed by a demon. She felt that a hidden gaze sought to pinion hers, and dig deep into her, but she rejected it, she shoved away that sense that her heart was being probed. She had nothing she was ashamed of! Yet, troubled by that pressure, she stepped back from the lattice barrier, shaking off Miravia's hand, and reflexively rubbed her arm until she realized that the other woman had held her so tightly that her nails had left marks in the skin. Miravia swayed, as if hammered, and Mai caught her under the arms and helped her sit on a nearby bench.

'What was that?' Miravia gasped, although she could barely force the words out. 'I felt as if hands were clawing in my head.'

No sound enlivened the air. Mai's ears seemed stuffed with wool, and her throat was choked as with dust and ash. Olossi was strangling.

Then, the catapults woke. Their arms creaked and swung. Mai sucked in air to cry out a warning but no sound came out of her mouth. Six impacts shook the town. Wood shattered. Stone cracked. Dust burst skyward. Shouts and screams cut the silence, and folk hiding in their houses or standing frozen on the streets all came to life at once with shrieks and calls, the buzzing chatter of fear.

'They know,' said Mai. 'They know we mean to fight them. Maybe he's already dead.'

Supine on the bench, hands lax on her belly, Miravia said, weakly, 'Look.'

A swift shadow darted across the troughs of herbs, succeeded by a second, and a third. Mai flung back her head and stared up into the blue pan of the sky. Four more passed overhead.

Eagles.

The Voice of the Walls boomed its warning cry. Seven times it rang.

Mai ran to look. Along the inner walls, guardsmen and civilians alike were passing bundles of arrows and rags up to the wall walk. At regular intervals, reservoirs of oil were set alight. Smoke uncoiled upward in threads of black and gray.

Beyond, the catapults made a clattering grind as they were winched back. Ranks of archers leaped to position, targeting the eagles as they glided low over the besiegers. An arrow flashed in the air. A stream of arrows was released out of the army, against the approaching eagles, but Mai could not see if any hit their target.

As the first flight of eagles swept past, each one released an egg from its talons. Up the eagles beat, seeking altitude. Down these large eggs tumbled, and when they hit the ground they shattered as ceramic does. It seemed a pointless effort as only one out of thirty struck a man, even if that man dropped as though felled by a hammer blow. The rest broke uselessly on wagons, or on the earth here and there with a splatter.

All along the wall, arrows flared as they were set alight. A volley of burning arrows hissed out from the walls into the outer town, where the army had gathered along the wide roadways. Arrows fell among them, and where the twisting flames met the splatter from the shattered vessels, fire burst with such brilliance that Mai cried out.

Now dropped a second flight of eagles. From below a fierce volley met them. One eagle lurched sideways and began to drop fast. Another released its egg early, so the ceramic vessel fell somewhere within the inner town; this eagle broke away from the rest and with faltering strokes beat a wide turn, trying to get away. Of the rest, some released their pots over the outer town while the rest waited until they were beyond the outer walls and over the encampment of the enemy with its tents and supply wagons neatly laid out as targets. A dozen eagles from that first flight had circled back and, daringly, dropped down into Assizes Square, rising again as quickly, with the reeves holding bronze basins filled with burning rags. Arrows sought them. An eagle plunged into the outer town. Yet the rest made it through, and cast their rags to the earth. Where a pair of burning clouts tumbled into the roof of one of the tents, fire blossomed with bright rage.

Miravia stepped up beside Mai. She leaned on the railing. Far away, men were beating at the flames, but it seemed they could not put them out.

'It's the breath of the mountains,' said Miravia. 'The fire lanterns. Oil of naya. In its crude state, it rises from seeps, particularly along the western shores of the Olo'o Sea, where the earth cracks and bleeds.'

Along Olossi's walls, the archers fired at will as a third flight passed over the encampment outside the walls. Fire and smoke began to obscure portions of the outer town, and where, in the open spaces, it was still possible to make out movement, Mai saw the enemy running away from the deadly flames. One man was burning as he ran, and even when that tiny figure dropped to the ground and rolled back and forth on the earth he did not stop burning. She could not look away. She was overwhelmed with joy, with horror, no space separating these two. A distant wagon, laden with the distinctive round, sealed pots in which oil of naya was carted, caught flame; when the axle was burned through enough to crack, and the wagon fell to one side, the pots rolled free and broke, and then the oil exploded with a roar that briefly drowned out the panicked cries of the enemy and the cheers of Olossi's guards.

Fire raced along the tents. It seemed to leap to any spot – tents, catapults, wagons – where the splatter had touched. Even a taste of flame, a drifting spark, set a new conflagration. Men frantic to escape the burning broke from their ranks and scattered on the road or through dry fields.

The inner gates opened. Olossi's militia ran out in force to drive back the invaders. They pushed forward confidently, cutting down men without mercy. Behind them, townsmen set to with axes to clear a firebreak between the inner wall and those motley houses and hovels built up into the dry-moated forecourt that separated the inner city from the outer sprawl. Bucket brigades lined up, but not even water thrown directly on it killed the flames.

In the encampment, the tents were ablaze. No creature caught in that inferno could live. What would Shai see, if he were standing here? She shaded her eyes; she squinted; she stared; but she saw nothing but the chaos of the living. What did Anji see when he witnessed the rising of the ghosts of those he had killed? Did he fear their vengeance? Or did he know that ghosts are impotent in the world if you do not fear them? Only past Spirit Gate do they gain a measure of power, so the priests said. Yet according to the teaching of the Merciful One, power of the spirit comes to the spirit only by giving up power. According to the teaching of the Merciful One, Spirit Gate leads to peace because beyond the gate lies nothingness. Surely, in such a place, power as soldiers and merchants and princes understand it means nothing. Is nothing.

'Look!' Miravia tugged on Mai's elbow to pull her gaze away from the chaos below.

There! As they fled back along the road, back to the north and east from which they had come, the routed soldiers were hit by a wave of riders who smashed through them, galloped on, turned, returned, swept back through, slashing and cutting, and raced on into fields and woodland, gone as swiftly as they had come.

A second wave of horsemen stormed across the tide of fleeing soldiers. Even in their low numbers, these riders cut a devastating wake, wolves on a summer's night. The army was broken. They could only run, single men, small groups scrambling for safety, while the wolves devoured the stragglers.

The camp burned steadily. In the lower town, every able-bodied adult fought to save the warehouses and shops and living quarters from the fire, smashing some to spare the rest. There was nothing to do but watch as the battle shifted from defeating the army to defeating the fires. More folk poured out of the inner town and down through the gates into the outer town. Smoke boiled upward as flames raged along the outer wall. Ash stung her eyes, and she blinked back tears. From this high eyrie, the battle took on a certain detached fascination: there, a warehouse roof collapsed; there, a gap was cut between one burning house and a neighboring tenement just in time to prevent the fire leaping. The open spaces and squares in the lower town became crowded with folk pausing from their labors to gulp a drink of water; with wagons carrying barrels of water drawn from the river; with piles of goods hauled out of the path of the fire. The eagles did not return. Like the wolves, they pursued the enemy.

'We are on our own,' said Miravia, staring shocked and weeping at the fire. 'Look, there! I think that's Eliar!'

Mai could not recognize him among the throng, except that a contingent of men wearing the distinctive turbans of the Ri Amarah men could be seen bearing buckets alongside Olossi's fire brigade. Ash hissed onto the roof garden, covering everything with a thin layer.

'I hate waiting here,' whispered Miravia with a fierce anger. 'Unable to act! I hate it!'

Mai took her hand, to comfort her. She said nothing. She had trained in a hard school. Hating didn't change things. The world went on regardless, far beyond the feeble lives of humankind. People could change only if they changed what lay in themselves.

If Anji did not return, then she must raise the child alone. She had the will to press forward, because it must be done.

'All will be well,' she said, 'even if it seems otherwise now. Many will lose their homes or goods, and many will suffer, but not as they would have suffered had that army not been driven away. What will come, will come, despite our wishes and dreams. All we can do is see our way clearly. Pay attention.'

A fat drop of rain shattered on Mai's arm. Raindrops splattered across the garden.

'We are saved.' Miravia sank to her knees and sobbed, hands veiling her face.

A cool wind drove up out of the east as the clouds surged in. From this height, Mai watched the rain front approach from the southeast, dark and grim. Horns blew, in celebration. The wind rose in intensity, pulling at her hair, and at last the storm gusted over them and the pounding rain smothered what so many anxious hands could not, after all, put out on their own.

At nightfall, the troop rode up through the half-ruined lower town and in through the inner gates. Mai met them in Assizes Square. She, and everyone in town, stank of ash and burning, but also of the wet. Here, at twilight, the first downpour had slackened to a drizzle. Hooves sloshed in puddles. Feet splashed, or slipped where fallen ash had churned into slick gray mud. The crowd was, for the most part, silent as they waited in the square. Despite their victory, the mood remained subdued. Every adult appeared to be smeared with dirt and ash, or with blood, from the struggle; even many Ri Amarah men, Eliar among them, had taken up axes and staves and fought to save the warehouses. Their turbans were singed, and their linen tunics torn and dirty.

The Qin soldiers split into ranks and, at a hand signal from Chief Tuvi, halted. Anji dismounted and limped to the veranda, where the remaining council members waited. Master Feden was not among them, but Mai was. They had made room for her when she arrived with her escort of elderly male Ri Amarah 'cousins.'

Anji nodded at her as he climbed the three steps up to the porch. His expression was calm; what manner of injury he had taken did not seem to concern him overmuch. The blood staining his clothing might well belong to those he had killed.

'Where is Captain Waras?' he asked.

'Badly injured,' said Master Calon. 'He's not likely to survive the night. He led the first wave out of the gates.'

Anji nodded. 'I bring a message from Argent Hall. It now lies under the temporary control of Reeve Joss and eagles out of Clan Hall. They have returned there to number their dead and wounded, and to await word from their Commander. A new marshal will be chosen.'

These words were met with a silence, broken when Master Calon stepped forward.

'The council of Olossi – both Greater and Lesser – has conferred, and has voted. Captain Anji, it is our wish that you accept the post of commander of the militia of Olossi.'

The rain had faded to spits and kisses. Under the veranda, Mai remained dry, but the weary folk crowded into the square were soaking and shivering as a night wind rose out of the southeast. Only the Qin soldiers remained unmoved. No doubt they had survived much more extreme temperatures in their distant home in the grasslands. Then she saw Shai; he, at least, rubbed his arms as if he were cold. He raised a hand to mark that he had seen her, and she touched a finger to her lips in reply. She wept, just a little, to see him whole and safe.

Anji wiped his forehead with the back of a hand, smearing grime. He had a splash of blood on his right cheek. These ornaments gave him a dangerous look as he surveyed the council members, each in turn, and the sweep of rooftops where Olossi climbed the hill beyond. Lamps were lit along the length of the porch. On the streets above, within closed compounds, lamplight glimmered. At length, he looked at Mai, but she shook her head, and he smiled faintly and turned back to the council.

'I am not moved to alter the bargain already sealed. My men and I will take lands west and north of the Olo'o Sea, in those regions of the Barrens where there is decent pasturage.'

Which lands happened to lie near the seeps and fissures where the fire lanterns burn.

'Is there anything else that cannot wait until tomorrow?' he asked the council. 'I will arrange for guards to be posted, some from my troop and others from the militia. I believe the threat is over, but we must remain cautious.'

'No one could have survived that fire,' said Calon. 'Their leaders surely are dead. Together with Master Feden.'

'He gave his life to save his honor,' said Anji. 'It was a worthy death.'

He stepped forward and took Mai's hand. 'Now, if you will, I desire to rest.'

The council members, too, were stunned by the day's events.

Eliar moved forward before any other could speak. 'If you will, Captain Anji, we offer you guest rights in our house. I'll go ahead to make sure all is ready for you.'

'I accept with gratitude,' said Anji, but he turned his gaze back to examine Mai, searchingly. He bent close, so others could not hear him. 'What is different?' he whispered.

'You are alive.' She made sure her voice did not tremble. She was strong enough to do what must be done, but she was so very very very glad she need not do it alone.

'So I am,' he agreed, 'although twice dead, once to my father's people and once to my mother's people.' Then he smiled, closely, warmly. 'You have a secret.'

Remembering what it was, she smiled in answer. She could not help sounding as if she were boasting. 'We will have a child.'

He was not a man prone to display, but he grasped her other hand and held it tightly. Anyone might guess what they spoke of, merely by looking at his face. 'It seems we have passed through Spirit Gate into a new life.'

And of course, so they had. A parting, a journey, a battle, a new life. A fine tale, truly. There is never any reason for happiness. Yet it exists.

PART SEVEN

RAINS

On the Eve of the Festival

At the Advent of the Year of the Red Goat

53

Hands cupped around a shallow drinking bowl, Joss brooded. He sipped until the bowl was drained dry, then set it down. After pouring a fourth helping of rice wine from the carafe, he placed it back in its basin of hot water and with a sleeve wiped from the table's top the droplets of water left behind by the pouring. But none of it helped, not the ritual of pouring, not the punch of the wine rising to his eyes, not the peace or the quiet. He sat by lamplight in the master's cote of Argent Hall, alone except for the whisper of rains on the roof. The doors to the porch were all slid back so he could see outside, but the garden lay in darkness. At the beginning of the wet season, it was always difficult to adjust to a night sky covered in cloud, with no stars or moon to be seen, or to see by.

So it seemed to him. He was waiting in the dark. He was blind, with nothing to guide him. They had won a victory, but only by going against the code of the halls.

Reeves were meant to enforce the law, not to wage war. He could win the argument within his head, claiming they had been given no choice, and know it was true. He could rejoice in his heart that Olossi had been saved, and feel it as worthwhile, a bold triumph. But in his gut, he knew any more steps taken down this road would lead to a terrible place where he did not want to go. No matter the reason, they had betrayed the reeves of Argent Hall. They had passed through that gate, and they could never go back and pretend it had not happened.

The rains lulled him. The cool air washed over him, dragging him into sleep.

The dream always unveils itself in an unwinding of mist, but this time there is no journey in the wilderness, no distant figure that vanishes as soon as he glimpses it. She walks right out of the darkness and up onto the porch, and she examines him with an expression of regret mingled with amusement. It hurts to look at her, because in his dream she seems so very ordinary and alive.

'You're drunk,' she says.

He raises a hand to acknowledge her with an ironic salute. 'Of course I am. Whenever I think of you, I drink.'

She shakes her head. 'Joss. Do not carry this burden. Do not mourn me. Let it go.'

'I can't. It won't let me go. Oh, Marit. Do you know what we've done?'

'I know. That's why I came to warn you: Beware the outlander.'

He chuckled, because the dream was agony: to hear her, to see her. Why must he torment himself? Why throw these words at himself, as if to blame someone else for a decision he had helped plan and carry out? Or perhaps the gods had chosen his dreams as an entrance into his heart, to scold him, since in sleep he could only listen and speak but not, truly, act.

'What are you?' he asked her. 'Are you real? Or only a dream, as I fear?'

She displayed both hands, palms facing him. Strong and subtle hands, whose touch he recalled too well. 'I am a Guardian now,' she said sadly.

He sighed, feeling the pull of the dream as it slid into impossibility, the place where he was forced to acknowledge that none of it could be real. 'The Guardians are gone . . . or else this is their way of punishing me for walking onto forbidden ground . . .'

Twenty years ago, back when he was young.

And he woke, startling out of sleep at the clop of feet on the porch steps. He rose too quickly, and knocked the bowl onto the floor.

'Marit!' he called.

'Oh, the gods,' said the Snake, who was standing on the porch in the soft morning light together with a half-dozen reeves. 'He's drunk. Again.'

'You bastard,' said Joss, picking up the empty carafe and hefting it. 'This will make a nice sound, shattering on your head.'

'Enough of that!'

Blinking, he saw who had come with Volias and the others. Leaning on her stick, the commander limped into the room. She had already taken off her boots; all of them had, which meant they had stood on the porch for a while watching him sleep, and babble in his sleep, no doubt. He flushed.

'Set that down, Joss,' she added. 'It's a fine piece of porcelain. It would be a waste to throw it away so lightly.'

Still gripping the carafe, he moved aside, and bumped his foot on the bowl as he got out of her way. The wine had soaked the pillow, but she levered herself down regardless and winced as she got her leg turned the best way. Picking up the bowl, she set it back on the table, then extended a hand. After a moment, Joss gave her the carafe. She placed it beside the bowl.

'Tea, if you will, Volias,' she said. 'Send someone, if you would be so kind. All of you, then. Out.'

The Snake smirked. 'That'll be a good dressing-down, if it must be delivered in private.' But he made the words lascivious, and mocking.

'To the hells with you,' snarled Joss.

'Go,' said the commander.

They went. Kesta, at the rear, cast him a look that might have been sympathetic, or gloating, or disgusted; he was just too exhausted to tell the difference.

'This must go quickly,' said the commander. 'Don't sit.'

'My head aches.'

'All the better, for it will ache more after you've heard me out.'

He rubbed his eyes, but the ache – and the commander – did not disappear. They were no dream.

'You may be surprised to see me. After the report I received three days ago of the events here at Argent Hall, and in Olossi, I had to come see for myself.'

'What do you mean to do?' he asked wearily. 'I'll take full responsibility. The other reeves were only following my orders.'

'Yes, I'm aware of that,' she said without smiling, without mercy. Pain had cleansed her of humor. It had been years since he had seen her laugh, and she did not look like she'd be laughing now. 'I fear the worst. You made a terrible choice, one that will haunt us in the days to come.'

'I know.'

On she went, unsparing in her litany. 'In the meantime, Horn Hall's reeves are still missing. The north is still closed to us. Our control over our own hinterlands shrinks every day. High Haldia has fallen in blood and flames. Toskala and the lands along the river lie under immediate threat. Here, Olossi's lower town lies half in ruins. Yet Olossi's council members praise your willingness to act to save them, despite some misunderstanding that, it seems, led you to be imprisoned in a cell beneath their Assizes Tower for several days. This captain they hired, who will be settling in lands to the north and west of here within Argent Hall's territory, speaks most highly of your leadership and levelheadedness. It seems you have led them to believe you are capable and trustworthy.'

'Eiya!' he said, for the words came at him like a dagger's point. 'Did you mean that to prick quite so much?'

'Just to make sure you are awake to hear the rest of it: I'm assigning you to become marshal here at Argent Hall.'

The shock of the statement made him stammer. 'But . . .'

'I am aware that each hall chooses its own marshal from among their own people, although there are exceptions to this custom, which I invoke now. I am aware that Scar will have to uproot for a second time from his accustomed territory, but he is stable enough, and tough enough, to withstand the challenges and make the accommodation to a new territory. Whether *you* are remains to be seen, but I have spoken to the council in Olossi, and I have spoken to the reeves here, and it is obvious to me that, for the present time, you are the only available and acceptable choice.'

'Argent Hall has lost so many of its eagles, and reeves. We believe that Marshal Yordenas was killed, but his body hasn't been located. Many who aren't dead or missing have fled. Less than a quarter of the normal complement remain, although I admit they thanked us for our intervention.'

'It's said the great eagles cannot be corrupted. That they will, in the end, rid themselves of any reeve who turns wholly against the code of the halls.'

'It's true that Yordenas had no eagle anyone ever saw. So we were told by those of Argent Hall's reeves who surrendered into our custody after the battle. He claimed it had gone to the nesting grounds, but maybe it had already abandoned him.'

She nodded. 'Come. Let me show you what flew beside me, at the sun's rising, when I arrived here at dawn.'

For her to sit, knowing she would rise again so soon, made the gesture more pointed. He stepped back deliberately, because he did not want to make the mistake of offering an arm, any aid at all. The struggle was swift, but defeated as surely as it always was. She got her balance, and she hobbled to the porch and, with dexterity born of long practice, got into her boots, which were in any case specially made to ease her condition.

He followed meekly. His head still hurt, but at least the glare of a hostile sun wasn't spiking him between the eyes. The gravel path was darkened by the wet, but the rains had ceased with the rising of the sun. Their progress through the marshal's garden went slowly. A flight of eagles spiraled high above, reveling in the morning's cooling breeze. She said nothing, so he said nothing.

Until they came to the courtyard, long since cleared of the debris of the battle fought five nights back.

All ten perches were taken, bearing unharnessed eagles. When he looked closely at those circling above, he realized that most of them – thirty more, at least – carried no reeve.

'What are all these?' he asked. 'Where have they all come from?'

'Argent's eagles have come home, seeking new reeves,' she said. 'There is much to do, Marshal Joss. And your first task will be to rebuild.'

54

After the seventh bell had rung its closing, the temple of the Merciless One lay quiet. The night's rain had not yet come, and the wind had settled. Only the streaming waters of the river could be heard, all manner of voices melding together in that watery chorus, some deep, some high, some constant and some heard at intervals like complaints. The ginnies slept. A few nocturnal night-reed birds patrolled for flies and midges, and their throaty *ooloo* calmed those who woke with disturbed dreams. There were many such dreamers in these days, who had before slept soundly.

All at once, erupting out of the drowsy night, a dog began its clamor, joined by a second and a third until the whole rude pack of them were howling and yammering the alert. Lanterns and candles flared to life. Folk stumbled sleepily from their beds, rubbing their eyes, cursing under their breath, whispering questions to the other hierodules and kalos as they emerged in ones and twos onto the verandas.

The dogs hushed as abruptly as if they'd all been throttled. The folk standing in their bare feet in the cool air hushed as well, if not quite as quickly. It seemed that half of them saw him immediately, and the other half felt an inchoate fear, enough to slow their chatter until they spotted him for themselves.

A man stood beside the courtyard's fountain. A spray of raindrops and grit swirled around him and settled, as though a wind had eddied through the vegetation, caught up this chaff, and now died.

'How did you get in?' called Walla, boldest of those already awake and present. 'You can't have come through the gate. It's locked for the night. And my good, dear, aged uncle, I just don't see how you could have climbed over the wall!'

Nervous laughter followed this sally, because everyone knew there were bells tied along the wall to discourage amorous young folk from climbing over to seek satisfaction at an inappropriate time of night. The Merciless One offered her favors freely, but on her own terms.

Their visitor remained silent. After Walla's outburst, none of the temple folk spoke. They waited, glancing at intervals toward the sky as if expecting the wind to wash him away. The moon rode high, but it was the many lamps and lanterns brought into the courtyard that illuminated him most clearly. He was a man beyond his prime but not yet elderly. He held a stout staff in his right hand, but he did not need it to lean on because he was so obviously a vigorous, healthy individual. Dressed in the manner of an envoy of Ilu, he wore exceptionally gaudy colors: a voluminous cloak of peacock blue, wine-red pantaloons, and a tunic dyed the intense yellow gotten only from cloth dyed with saffron.

At length, the Hieros appeared on the veranda. She was pinning back her white hair and looking truly irritated, although it could be said that she usually looked that way. When her hair was fixed back with two polished sticks, she strode into the courtyard and halted a prudent distance from the intruder.

'It is late, uncle. Here on the eve of the Ghost Festival that separates the years, we do not accept worshipers, as I'm sure you know.'

He smiled amiably. His voice was clear and courteous and so pleasant that everyone there smiled to hear his apology.

'I am sorry to disturb you. I am not here to worship the Merciless One.'

The old woman, as always, was immune to any person's charm. 'Then what do you want?' she snapped.

He had a friendly grin, yet there was a quality in his face that made a few of the hierodules shudder and others gasp and feel suddenly like succumbing to tears. Even the ginnies, hiding in the shadows, made their lizard bows as to authority. Even the Hieros, most merciless of all except for the goddess Herself, took a step back, although he made no threatening move and spoke in the mildest voice imaginable.

'You have something I've been looking for, for a very long time. I've come to get it.'

The wind sighed through the garden foliage.

She turned to her deputies. 'Go and get her,' she said in a low voice.

They hurried away with scarcely any noise, for they were trained to move about soundlessly.

'The treasure is mine,' she said to the man. 'I paid for it, a fair exchange.'

'You cannot buy what this is,' he said kindly, 'and I am sorry if it came into your hands in any manner which led you to believe you could own it.'

'Who are you?' she asked.

He raised both hands in the opening gesture of the talking line. 'My nose is itching,' he said. 'Many whispers have tickled my ears these last few nights. Listen!'

Acknowledging his right to speak, they listened.

'This is my tale. It is one you all know.'

'Go on,' said the Hieros, but now she seemed afraid, and all those who lived under her care and her rule found that her fear rang like a bell whose resonance made their own fears tremble and wake.

He told the story, punctuated by the most basic of gestures, enough to suggest the tale's outlines.

'Long ago, in the time of chaos, a bitter series of wars, feuds, and reprisals denuded the countryside and impoverished the lords and guildsmen and farmers and artisans of the Hundred. In the worst of days, an orphaned girl knelt at the shore of the lake sacred to the gods and prayed that peace might return to her land.

'A blinding light split the air, and out of the holy island rising in the center of the lake appeared the seven gods in their own presence. The waters boiled, and the sky wept fire, as the gods crossed over the water to the shore where the girl had fallen.

'And they spoke to her.

'"Our children have been given mind, hand, and heart to guide their actions, but they have turned their power against themselves. Why should we help you?"

'"For the sake of justice," she said.

'And they heard her. They said, "Let Guardians walk the lands, in order to establish justice if they can."'

'"Who can be trusted with this burden?" she asked them. "Those with power grasp tightly."

'"Only the dead can be trusted," they said. "Let the ones who have died fighting for justice be given a second chance to restore peace. We will give them gifts to aid them with this burden."

'Taru the Witherer wove nine cloaks out of the fabric of the land and the water and the sky, and out of all living things. These granted the wearer protection against the second death although not against weariness of soul.

'Ilu the Herald, the Opener of Ways, built the altars, so that they might speak across the vast distances each to the other.

'Atiratu the Lady of Beasts formed the winged horses out of the elements so that they could travel swiftly and across the rivers and mountains without obstacle.

'Sapanasu the Lantern gave them light to banish the shadows.

'Kotaru the Thunderer gave them the staff of judgment as their symbol of authority.

'Ushara the Merciless One gave them a third eye and a second heart with which to see into and understand the hearts of all.

'Hasibal gave an offering bowl.

'Now it so happened that the girl had walked as a mendicant in the service of the Lady of Beasts, and when the other gods departed, the Lady of Beasts remained behind.

"'They are content," the Lady said, "but I see with the sight of eagles and I listen with the heart of an ox, and so I know that in the times to come the most beloved among the guardians will betray her companions."

"'Is there no hope, then, for the land and its people?'"

"'One who is an outlander may save them, but I prefer to put my trust in what I know. Therefore, I give to you, my daughter, a second gift, so that ordinary folk who live and die in the natural way can also oversee the law of the land.'"

'And she brought out the eagles, so great in size that they might carry a person.

'The girl asked, "If even the holy guardians can be corrupted, what of ordinary folk?"

'But the Lady of Beasts had already departed.

'Yet Hasibal the Formless One waited half in darkness and half in light, unseen until now.

"'That is the nature of the offering bowl, child, that it can be full, or empty, or partially full, and yet change in an instant from any of these states to another. Thus do corruption and virtue wax and wane within the heart. Yet it is the dutiful strength and steady hand of those who live and die while about the ordinary tasks of the world that creates most of that which we call good and harmonious."

'After this, she was alone.

'So the Guardians came to walk in the Hundred. In this manner also came the reeves and their eagles who, with the blessing of the Guardians, established order in the Hundred one village and one clan at a time.'

The man's voice ceased.

He lowered his hands to his side.

The Hieros said, more humbly, 'Who are you?'

When he did not answer, she said, 'The Guardians are lost. Gone.'

'No,' he said, his voice as calming as the cry of the night-reed. 'They are not gone.'

He stopped abruptly and lifted his chin, tipped forward onto his toes, seeing a thing as it appeared out of the darkness. Those gathered did not need to look to know what it was, but they looked anyway, because they could not help themselves. They had to look at the young woman who had the pallor of a ghost but the heat and solidity of a living person. The moonlight made her pale hair and creamy skin seem even more uncanny and desirable. She wore a sleeveless tunic, cut short for sleeping. Even at night she wore the cloak, her only possession. The moon's light caught in the folds and ridges of the silverine cloth as she was led into the courtyard, more like a sleepwalker than a waking woman. Her escort pushed her into position and turned her to face the man.

After a moment of silence she looked up and saw him. She *saw,* who never took note of anyone or anything. She stared at him, and an expression – like hope, like life – transformed her face. Half the assembled gasped, and the other half sighed, and the man shut his eyes and then opened them.

Her lips parted. No one here had ever heard her voice, but she spoke now in a faint, high voice as hoarse as if she had rusted it by choking down too many tears.

'Who are you?'

He offered both hands, palms up and open. 'You belong with us,' he said. 'If you choose to come with me.'

At a nod from the Hieros, the deputies stepped back. For the first time, the ghost moved of her own accord. She took one step, and a second, and a third, like a woman waking out of a nightmare who is not yet sure it is really over. She halted at arm's length from him and reached out. But she did not touch him.

She said, 'I will come with you.'

She lowered her hand, and waited.

'What of my payment?' demanded the Hieros, but everyone there noted that she did not try to stop the slave girl from leaving or the man from claiming her.

He spoke over the pale head of the slave. 'No Hundred-born person had the right to sell this woman into your keeping, for no one owns what she has become. Seek redress from the one who dealt unfaithfully with you.'

'You can be sure that I will!'

He chuckled, a man at peace with himself, and his good-natured amusement inflamed the Hieros yet more.

'You have not answered my questions! Who are you? How have you come here? Why did you tell us the Tale of the Guardians when all know that the Guardians are long ago lost, and never to be found?'

He smiled sweetly at the girl, but he replied to the Hieros, for all who live in the Hundred must answer the questions set them by the women who speak for the Merciless One. 'The Guardians are not lost. But they were broken long since, sundered each from the other, and distrust and hatred and greed and envy were sown between them. The shadows have spilled out from this broken vessel, and as shadows will, they reach out to swallow the land.'

'This we know!' she said fiercely. 'Just now an army out of the north rode against Olossi. It was a close thing that we escaped blade and fire. For, as the tale says, an outlander saved us. There has been peace until now, but it seems to me that we will have to go to war to defend the heart of the Hundred and the laws which sustain the land.'

'You are right, and you are wrong,' he said.

'Often right, but rarely wrong!' she retorted.

He lifted his staff, and all cried out when a light flashed from its end, no more than a candle's spark, quickly extinguished. A wind rose, and out of the sky roiled two great shadows. The hierodules and kalos shrieked and fell back under the cover of the veranda. Only the Hieros held her ground.

Two horses seemed to leap out of the sky and come to earth in the courtyard. They had vast wings, and delicate legs, and handsomely formed heads. When the girl saw them, her mouth dropped open. She looked at the man, and he nodded. Cautiously, she ventured forward to introduce herself to the beasts with the manners of a person who feels comfortable with horses.

The Hieros touched her fingers to her forehead, in prayer.

At length, she lowered her fingers, then raised her head and looked at him. Her expression was somber. Her tone had changed. 'I will be your ally, if you will trust me.'

The man touched the heel of his hand to his breast in a gesture of respect as he gave a slight bow to the Hieros. 'You are an honest servant, holy one, if a bit hard-hearted. Listen!'

They heard the hiss of the approaching rains over the water, but it was his voice they listened for.

'The Guardians are not lost. For here, now, stand two of us. I, who am old and weary of running and hiding. And this one, who is newly cloaked and awakened, as ignorant of what she is now as I am ignorant of who she was before she came into the Hundred.'

The Hieros staggered, but caught herself on the arm of one of her deputies. The soft night rains swept over the garden, pattering among the leaves, showering a mist over them. Among the hierodules and kalos, many began to weep softly. Hearing their distress, she recovered herself, and nodded, to show he should continue.

'You are right,' he said, 'that we must defend the heart of the Hundred and the laws which sustain the land. But you are wrong in thinking there has been peace until now, that there has been peace in the Hundred these last many years.'

'Go on.' She was no longer afraid.

In his gentle smile rested the weight of long years of struggle. 'The war for the soul of the Guardians has already begun.'

VIRGINIA WOOLF

VIRGINIA WOOLF
NIGEL NICOLSON

WORCESTERSHIRE COUNTY COUNCIL
CULTURAL SERVICES

Weidenfeld & Nicolson
LONDON

First published in Great Britain in 2000 by Weidenfeld & Nicolson

© 2000 Nigel Nicolson

A CIP catalogue record for this book
is available from the British Library.

ISBN 0 297 64620 6

Typeset by Selwood Systems, Midsomer Norton

Set in Minion

Printed in Great Britain by
Butler & Tanner Ltd, Frome and London

Weidenfeld & Nicolson

The Orion Publishing Group Ltd
Orion House
5 Upper Saint Martin's Lane
London, WC2H 9EA

to Joanne Trautmann Banks

By the same author:

Vita and Harold
Portrait of a Marriage
Mary Curzon
Long Life: Memoirs

ILLUSTRATIONS

* Courtesy of the National Portrait Gallery.
All other photographs from the author's collection.

ACKNOWLEDGEMENTS

I wish to thank Ed Victor, my literary agent, for suggesting this book to me and for much other help, and the following for permission to quote from Virginia Woolf's published books, diaries, letters and some unpublished papers:

The Society of Authors, as the Literary Representative of the Estate of Virginia Woolf, and Olivier Bell, the editor of her Diaries.

The Berg Collection of English and American Literature, the New York Public Library (Astor, Lenox and Tilden Foundations).

Quotations from other books listed in the Bibliography are acknowledged in the text, and covered by the 'fair dealing' convention which permits short quotations without specific consent from the authors, to whom I owe my thanks.

I thank Ms Sue Fox for much help and advice.

N.N.

January 2000

I

IN HER CHILDHOOD Virginia Woolf was a keen hunter of butterflies and moths. With her brothers and sister she would smear tree trunks with treacle to attract and capture the insects, and then pin their lifelike corpses to cork boards, their wings outspread. It was an interest that persisted into her adult life, and when she discovered that I too was a bug-hunter, she insisted that we go hunting together in the fields around Long Barn, our house in Kent, two miles from Knole, my mother's birthplace. I was nine years old.

One summer's afternoon when we were sweeping the tall grass with our nets and catching nothing, she suddenly paused, leaning on her bamboo cane as a savage might lean on his assegai, and said to me: 'What's it like to be a child?' I, taken aback, replied, 'Well, Virginia, you know what it's like. You've been a child yourself. I don't know what it's like to be you, because I've never been grown-up.' It was the only occasion when I got the better of her, dialectically.

I believe that her motive was to gather copy for her portrait of James in *To the Lighthouse*, which she was writing at the time, and James was about my own age. She told me that it was not much use thinking back into her own childhood, because little girls are different from little boys. 'But were you happy as a child?', I asked.

I forget what she replied, but now I think I know the answer, since her childhood and youth have been more amply recorded than almost any other. It was not so much unhappy, as troubled. Her mother died when she was thirteen, and her half-sister when she was fifteen. At twenty-two she lost her father, and two years later her brother Thoby. Another half-sister was mentally deranged. Virginia herself, while still quite young, suffered from periods of acute depression and even insanity. She was sexually abused by her half-brothers when she was too young to understand what was happening. It was a string of calamities that could have resulted in a youth that was deeply disturbed. But she was courageous, resilient and enterprising. As her early letters and diaries reveal more convincingly than her later recollections, she developed normally enough, and although she was indifferent to social success, she had a gift for friendship, and very early in her life, an impulse to turn every experience into words. It was on the same occasion as our butterfly hunt that she said to me, 'Nothing has really happened until it has been described. So you must write many letters to your family and friends, and keep a diary.' Pain was relieved, and pleasure doubled, by recording it.

Virginia was born in London on 25 January 1882, the third child of Leslie and Julia Stephen. For both her parents it was a second marriage, and each partner inherited from the other, children born of the first. It is simpler to describe their complex genealogy by a diagram, to which I have added in brackets their ages in 1895, the year when Julia died:

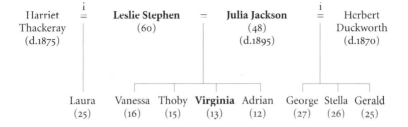

Laura was the mentally unbalanced child, who was treated by her father with scant affection, and after Julia's death was placed by him in a mental home where she lived until she died at the age of seventy-five. Leslie's first wife, a daughter of William Thackeray, the novelist, and Julia's first husband, Herbert Duckworth, a handsome barrister, can have meant little to Virginia apart from the tragedy of their early deaths and the progeny of cousins, chiefly Fishers and Vaughans, which they generated. It was a large family group, from which different members entered Virginia's life with varying degrees of intimacy and persistence. Emma and Madge Vaughan (the original of Sally in *Mrs Dalloway*) were among her earliest friends, but they were not to last long in her affections.

The people who mattered most to her in childhood were her parents, her sister Vanessa and her elder brother Thoby. Julia was the daughter of John Jackson, who spent much of his career as a doctor in Calcutta, and Maria Pattle. Like her mother, Julia was one of the most beautiful women of her age.

In her youth she posed for Watts, Burne-Jones, and her aunt Julia Margaret Cameron, the photographer, who has left

3

an image of her which is distinctly Pre-Raphaelite, often tragic in countenance, and like Virginia, always beautiful but never pretty. What strikes one most about these portraits is the serenity of her gaze, as if life was a constant test of character which she would survive triumphantly, but this impression may be due to the immobility needed for early photography: one cannot hold a smile longer than an instant without it appearing false. In *To the Lighthouse*, where Mrs Ramsay is a close portrait of Julia, Virginia shows us another side of her mother's character – swift, decisive, impatient of stupidity, quick-tempered but incapable of unkindness. In a memoir dated 1907 she wrote of her parents, 'Beautiful often, even to our eyes, were their gestures, their glances of pure and unutterable delight in each other.' Leslie revered Julia, and she controlled him by her submissiveness. In a sense she was the stronger character of the two, quietly dominating. But Leslie was no weakling. Born the son of Sir James Stephen, a senior civil servant and then a Professor of history, he developed from a shy boy into a man who could be formidable, and as a mountaineer, tough. He was ordained a clergyman in his youth but lost his faith and left Cambridge for London, where he earned his living as a literary and political journalist, and became a leading intellectual, the originator and first editor of *The Dictionary of National Biography*, a friend of Meredith, Hardy, Henry James, Tennyson, Matthew Arnold and George Eliot. Virginia's childhood was therefore comfortably upper-middle-class and intellectually stimulating. They lived in a respectable Kensington cul-de-sac, 22 Hyde

Virginia Woolf in 1902, when she was 20. A studio photograph by George Beresford. Like her mother, Julia Stephen, Virginia was 'always beautiful, but never pretty'.

4

Park Gate, where seven servants ran the house under Julia's directions. The weekly journal, *Hyde Park Gate News*, which Virginia and Vanessa began in 1891 and sustained for four years, portrays a lively, talented, funny family, in which tensions were cushioned by mutual affection. The older members supported the younger, and the younger amused their elders. Virginia's talent for fiction developed early. When she was only six or seven, she wrote to her mother (the letter first surfaced in Joanne Trautmann Banks's *Congenial Spirits*):

> Mrs Prinsep says that she will only go in a slow train cos she says all the fast trains have accidents and she told us about an old man of 70 who got his legs caute in the weels of the train and the train began to go on and the old gentleman was draged along till the train caute fire and he called out for somebody to cut off his legs but nobody came he was burnt up. Goodbye. Your loving Virginia.

The legend that Leslie was cantankerous and indifferent to his children is not confirmed by the many references to them in his letters to Julia, now in the Berg Collection, New York Public Library. He called them his ragamice, and Virginia was Ginia: 'Kiss my ragamice and Ginia. There will be no more of that breed.' 'Little Ginia is already an accomplished flirt. I said today that I must go down to my work. She nestled herself down on the sofa by me, squeezed her little self tightly up against me, and then gazed up with her bright eyes through her shock of hair and said, "Don't go, papa". She looked full of mischief all the time. I never saw such a little rogue.' 'My sweet little Ginia. I shall be glad to have her back.' 'My love to all my pets, specially my Ginia. I have been thinking of her all day.' 'Ginia tells me a story every night.' And then this, when Virginia was eleven: 'Yesterday I discussed George III with her. She takes in a great deal, and will really be an author in time.'

Their holidays were spent in Cornwall, at St Ives, where Leslie rented Talland House for thirteen summers until Julia died. It was a curious choice for a man who was not naturally a beachcomber, and was careful with his money. Cornwall was distant from London, and the expense of transporting his large family and several servants was considerable. When they had recovered from the long journey, the children were very happy there, and Leslie showed his kindest side, relaxed and paternal. Two years before her death Virginia wrote, 'St Ives gave me all the pure delight which is before my eyes, even at this moment'. Every day brought an experience which, if not novel, was treated as a novelty – walking on the moors, swimming, boating, shopping, and playing games, indoor and out. A photograph taken in Cornwall when she was about six shows Virginia sturdy, tomboyish, concentrating on her role as wicket-keeper while Adrian batted. Then an incident occurred that was to surface years later in one of her best-loved novels. She recorded it in *Hyde Park Gate News*: 'Master Adrian Stephen was much disappointed at not being allowed to go.' It was the expedition to Godrevy lighthouse in St Ives Bay.

When Julia died, life changed for all of them. They found no consolation in religion. Both Virginia's parents were agnostic. Though their children had 'sponsors', none of them were baptized. Leslie was exhausted by his grief, and by the tide of relations who washed up at Hyde Park Gate to gratify their benevolence and overwhelm him with excessive sympathy. He would groan aloud at meals, and complain every week when Stella, who had taken on her mother's role as housekeeper, presented the weekly bills for payment. 'He went through an extraordinary dramatisation of self-pity', Virginia wrote in recollection. 'He sank into his chair and sat with his head on his breast. At last, after glancing at a book, he would look up and say half-plaintively, "And what are you doing this afternoon, Ginny?" Never have I felt such rage and such frustration.'

He was in danger of losing his children's affection. They felt imprisoned by him. The boys could escape to school, but the girls were housebound. When Stella fell in love with Jack Hills, Leslie's attitude was like that of Mr Woodhouse in *Emma*, thinking only that he would be deprived of her company and help, and when she married, his only consolation was that they took a house across the street. When Stella died, probably of peritonitis, only three months after her wedding, he seemed not particularly to mind. His capacity for grief had been exhausted by Julia's death, and Vanessa could take over the management of the house, which she did, dutifully and reluctantly.

In later life Virginia would sometimes complain that she was denied the education that was given automatically to boys, but her protests were not consistent nor wholly justified. Once, in middle age, she wrote to Vita Sackville-West, who had reproached her for her lack of 'jolly vulgarity', that she had had no chance to acquire it. 'Think how I was brought up! No school; mooning about alone among my father's books; never any chance to pick up all that goes on in schools – throwing balls; ragging; slang; vulgarities; scenes; jealousies!' But would she have become a different, more rounded person if she had experienced all this in company with schoolgirls instead of with her siblings? As for universities, she found academics limp and dull. Visiting Oxford in 1907, when she was twenty-five, she described its atmosphere as 'quite the chilliest and least human known to me. You see brains floating like so many sea-anemones, nor have they shape or colour', and two years later, after another visit, 'There were Regius Professors at dinner, and undergraduates who had won prizes without number and were consequently unable to talk.' In the Oxford chapter of *The Years* she lampooned university life brilliantly. She would have been sucked dry by it. Nor was she denied tuition in her youth. Leslie gave her the run of his extensive library, talked to her about what she read, and encouraged her to write, and on those occasions she felt soothed, stimulated, full of love for this unworldly, distinguished, adorable man. He paid for her to take Greek lessons from Janet Case and Latin from Dr George Warr ('my beloved Warr'). While Vanessa left daily for art college, Virginia remained alone at the top of the house, puzzling over Homer and Sophocles, line by line with a lexicon, naturally studious, and determined to be a writer.

She discovered for herself the pleasure of dipping deep into the treasury of the language to express her exact meaning, partly by writing essays and a diary, but mainly in the form of letters to her family and friends. Often she would write to her brother Thoby at school and later at Cambridge, and he, remarkably for a schoolboy, kept her letters, unlike those which she wrote to me when I was his age. She acquired a gift for self-mockery and the mocking of others, akin to the juvenile burlesques of Jane Austen, for she found disapproval more amusing than approval, but without malice. London, apart from Leslie's tantrums, was fun; so was the country. On holiday in Huntingdonshire in 1899, she wrote to Emma Vaughan: 'I shall think it a test of friends for the future whether they can appreciate the Fen country. I want to read books about it, and to write sonnets about it all day long. It is the only place for rest of mind and body, and for contentment and creamy potatoes and all the joys of life.'

She was honing her gift for observation, and was interested not so much in the weird as in the mysteries of the normal. She scarcely needed formal education. She was her own guide through history and literature. She was learning all through her life.

Another side of her childhood was darker. Her two half-brothers, George and Gerald Duckworth, regarded Vanessa and Virginia as sexual objects, first of wonder, then of desire. Virginia recalled how once at St Ives Gerald lifted her onto a table, and out of curiosity, put his hand under her skirt and examined her private parts. To Virginia, who was always exceptionally modest about her body, this was repulsive. She never forgot it. She did not accuse Gerald of any other indiscretions. George became the monster. After Julia's death, he would enter Virginia's bedroom, fling himself onto her bed, and take her in his arms. She wrote later of his 'violent gusts of passion', and of his behaviour as 'little better than a brute's'. The suggestion was that he had committed, or at least attempted, incest with the girls, and this was Quentin Bell's belief when he first wrote of these incidents. The term 'incestuous relationship' is how he summarized them in the index to the first volume of his Life of his aunt. Other biographers took up the theme. George's behaviour was said to have been responsible for Virginia's sexual timidity and even contributive to her periodic fits of insanity. Louise de Salvo, the American Woolf scholar, has claimed that 'sexual abuse was probably the central and most formative feature of her early life', and she alleges that 'virtually every male member of the Stephen household was engaged in this behaviour'. She uses the term incest without qualification.

The allegation is far-fetched. Soon after Quentin Bell's book was published, I visited George Duckworth's son Henry in his Sussex house to enquire whether his father had kept any letters from Virginia that might throw more light on the matter. Appalled by Bell's innuendoes, he gave me five letters with permission to publish them, because he believed that they would prove beyond doubt that the relationship between George and his half-sisters stopped short of any reasonable reproach. He argued that it was almost inconceivable that a girl who had been subjected to such brutal treatment could address her seducer as 'My dear old Bar' and 'My dearest George', or that Vanessa, the other victim of his endearments, would have gone happily to Paris with him in 1900 and two years later to Rome. Quentin Bell, in his last book, *Elders and Betters*, modified his censure of the Duckworth brothers. He concluded that whatever George's lust may have been, he never carried it to the extent of rape. Nasty erotic fumblings are the most we need suppose. George's instinct was no doubt incestuous, but his practice was not. So conventional a man would never have run the risk of an incestuous and illegitimate child. In recollection, Virginia made more of a drama of the affair than the facts justify.

George's attempt to introduce the sisters to polite London society ended in failure. He himself was handsome and socially ambitious, and no doubt sought to magnify his popularity by association with two exceptionally attractive girls. He assumed the role of their dead mother. To him every party was a challenge to Virginia's and Vanessa's marriageability. He could not understand why they were so ungrateful. He was proud of their beauty: should they not be proud of his? But they refused to act the part he planned for them. 'We are failures really', Virginia wrote to Emma Vaughan. 'We can't shine in society. I don't know how it's done. We ain't popular. We sit in corners and look like mutes who are longing for a funeral.' When they were taken as guests to country houses, it was no better. At Corby Castle, which belonged to Jack Hills's father, 'it was very dismal and strange. Everything is very stately and uncomfortable. I wish to goodness I could find myself at home.' This was written to Thoby.

Then Leslie fell ill with abdominal cancer, and took two years to die. The course of his decline was described by Virginia in almost daily bulletins to her new confidante, Violet Dickinson, who had been Stella's friend, and although she was seventeen years older, Virginia conceived for her an almost passionate affection, writing to her letters that startle us by their frankness: 'It is astonishing what depths – hot volcanic depths – your finger has stirred in Sparroy [her name for herself when writing to Violet], hitherto entirely quiescent.' Their flirtation was carried on step by step with Leslie's decline. Virginia was not heartless, but she could not help revealing to Violet her impatience for his death. On Christmas Day 1903 she wrote, 'If only it could be quicker', but she meant it as much for Leslie's sake as for her own. He died two months later, on 22 February 1904, when Virginia was just twenty-two. She wrote to Janet Case next day, 'Father died very peacefully, as we sat by him. I know it was what he wanted most. All these years we have hardly been apart and I want him every moment of the day. But we still have each other – Nessa and Thoby and Adrian and I, and when we are together, he and Mother do not seem far off.' There was no room for the Duckworths in their little world. Orphaned, they moved as a group, Vanessa taking the lead.

II

A FEW DAYS after Leslie's cremation they went to Manorbier in south Wales, and Violet Dickinson joined them there. It was empty country, between moor and sea, and Virginia walked alone along the cliffs, meditating on her future. In 1922 she recorded in her diary that it was during these walks that the vision of what she wanted to write focussed clearly in her mind, but at the time she made no mention of it in her letters, which dwelt, as so often when a parent dies, on what more she should have done for her father, and her regret that he never knew how much she loved him. Vanessa was harsher. Many years later she confided to her son that Leslie's death had come as a relief. 'It was impossible not to be glad', she said. 'He had been ill for so long, and we had for so long been expecting it, and it was of course in many ways convenient', by which she meant that the four of them could escape from the Duckworths and the stuffy gentility of Hyde Park Gate.

They would find a house for themselves, if possible in Bloomsbury.

Before taking this important step in their lives, the four of them, as if in need of a further purging of the past, went to Italy. It was Virginia's first visit abroad apart from a childhood jaunt to Boulogne, but the holiday was not well managed. Nobody had bothered to book rooms in Venice, and their first gondola trips were in search of lodgings, and when they found them, they were so cramped that they were obliged to move into an expensive hotel which they could ill afford. Only then could Virginia 'wander about open-mouthed', but she was never an avid sightseer, preferring people and pictures to palaces and churches. The party continued to Florence, where they met English friends and were pestered by begging children. Virginia did not think well of the Italians, of whose language she could not speak a word. She thought the country beautiful but its people degenerate. 'Thank God', she wrote to Emma Vaughan, 'that I was born an Englishwoman'. All her life she remained a partial xenophobe.

In Paris, on their way home, they were more fortunate. They found Clive Bell, whom Virginia had met once before in Thoby's rooms at Cambridge, and he took them to visit Auguste Rodin in his studio. Clive was the first non-Duckworth man in Virginia's life, and she loved him for his joviality, intellectual adventurousness and a constant undercurrent of flirtatiousness. She was half amused, half scared, and their friendship would have developed rapidly had she not succumbed, on the day after their return from Paris, to a severe mental breakdown.

'All that summer she was mad', wrote Quentin Bell, and his words were borrowed in 1981 for the title of a book by Dr

Stephen Trombley which set out to prove them unjustified. She was not mad in the technical sense, nor even manic depressive, the looser term often employed by people unqualified to make a judgment. Dr Trombley proposed a more scientific diagnosis: 'She suffered from a complex somatic reaction to a series of difficult personal situations'. But 'mad' was the word employed by Virginia's family and by herself, in faint derision of her condition, because they knew that it would pass, and once passed, her mind would be clarified by it, as a storm clarifies the sky. 'The insane view of life has much to be said for it', she told Emma Vaughan, meaning that imagination is let loose, and some of her best ideas came to her when was in no fit state to record them. But at the time, it was no joke to her family and friends. Once before, following the death of her mother, Virginia had acted very strangely, fainting without reason, blushing when spoken to, and subject to bouts of insomnia and headache, but this second attack, in May–August 1904, was more serious. She refused to eat. She insulted her closest friends. The birds were talking Greek, and Edward VII was yelling obscenities in the shrubbery. Like Septimus Warren Smith in *Mrs Dalloway* she threw herself from a window in attempted suicide, but it failed because the window was too close to the ground. All this time she was staying with Violet Dickinson in Hertfordshire, under the care of three nurses and the eminent nerve specialist George Savage, who had little idea how to treat her dementia or its cause. If this was not madness, it was something akin to it. 'The Goat's mad', her siblings would remark cheerfully, using her childhood nickname. They were not unsympathetic, but busy in arranging the move from Hyde Park Gate to Bloomsbury.

When Virginia recovered, she spent some weeks at Cambridge with her Quaker aunt, Emelia Stephen, who bored her with trivial chatter and tedious benignity, and she busied herself by helping Frederic Maitland with his life of Leslie Stephen, to which she contributed a passage about Leslie as a father. Then, as a further instalment of the convalescence planned for her, she was sent to stay in Yorkshire with her cousin William Vaughan, headmaster of Giggleswick School, and his wife Madge. Life in a headmaster's house was no rest-cure. She was involved in constant meetings with other masters, tea parties with their wives, and compulsory attendance at chapel. She pitied Madge, a woman of stature and literary ambitions, now condemned to intellectual penury. Virginia was well looked after. She was given a large well-windowed bedroom, in which I once spent a night as the guest of a later headmaster, and she could escape from the school to wander on the moors.

Giggleswick also gave her the chance to resume her writing, and for the first time to publish what she wrote. She turned from private journal-keeping to journalism. Violet had introduced her to Mrs Arthur Lyttelton, editor of the Women's Supplement to *The Guardian*, an Anglo-Catholic clerical weekly, and Virginia begged her for work. Her first essay to be published was a description of her visit to Haworth Parsonage, the Brontës' old house. 'There is a knack of writing for newspapers which has to be learnt, and is quite independent of literary merits', she told Violet with the temerity of a first-time journalist. She needed the money after the heavy expenses of her three-month illness, and she invited criticism from her friends, by which she meant praise. Quite soon her gratitude to Margaret Lyttelton changed to indignation that her copy was subjected to minor cuts and alterations. *The Guardian*, which was intended for nuns and clerics, was an absurd medium for a young writer bursting with new ideas. But it was a start. Before long she was invited to contribute reviews to the more prestigious *Times Literary Supplement* and *The National Review.*

Virginia was not the solitary, secretive writer that she later became, hugging her conception to herself like a mother her unborn child. Always relating fact to fancy, she began to define character by body language, clothes and tone of voice, and landscape by the centuries of toil that had created it. Her letters matched her youthful exuberance. When she returned on holiday to Giggleswick, but this time staying in lodgings, liberated from the routines of school life, she wrote to Violet: 'You can imagine that I never wash, or do my hair, but stride with gigantic strides over the wild moorside, shouting Odes of Pindar, as I leap from crag to crag, and exulting in the air which buffets me and caresses me, like a stern but affectionate parent. That is Stephen Brontëised.' Sometimes in writing to Madge Vaughan, who at that period was her literary confidante, she experimented in fumbling terms with a new view of literature, 'a vague and dreamlike world, without love, or heart, or passion, or sex. ... For though they are dreams to you, and I can't express them at all adequately, these things are perfectly real to me.' She might have been defining *The Waves.*

The Stephen family held together for two years after Leslie's death, years that Virginia described as 'a burst of splendour'. Vanessa organized the move to 46 Gordon Square, Bloomsbury, George Duckworth conveniently married, and his brother Gerald became a publisher, drifting apart from them, so that the Stephens were free to lead their lives untrammelled and unsupervised. They could dress as they wished, eat when and how they wanted, and felt no need to retain friendships imposed on them in their adolescence. Vanessa later wrote, 'It was as if one had stepped suddenly into daylight from darkness'. But their elders saw it as the opposite. Even Henry James was shocked by their disavowal of conventional etiquette. Virginia exulted that at one stroke they abolished the napkin as a symbol of correctness. But there were limits. Vanessa was still addressing Clive, the most intimate of her friends, as 'Dear Mr Bell'.

Bloomsbury itself was symptomatic of their quiet rebelliousness. It was a district of London that in spite of the elegance of its Georgian squares was considered by Kensington to be faintly decadent, the resort of raffish divorcees and indolent students, loose in its morals and behaviour. The Stephens' circumstances matched their income. Leslie Stephen had left property valued at about £15,000, a substantial sum, equivalent to about £350,000 today, and the freehold of Hyde Park Gate, which they chose to lease, not sell, and while neither Thoby nor Adrian earned any money, their sisters were already professionals, Vanessa as a painter (her first paid commission was a portrait of Lady Robert Cecil), and Virginia as a journalist. They could afford to employ two servants, and to take holidays together or separately. Virginia and Adrian went by sea to Portugal and Spain, and all four spent two months in Cornwall and two more in a rented manor house in Norfolk. But it was London that established the pattern of their lives.

First Virginia engaged herself to teach in Morley College in south London, where the poor were offered education after school-age. Her decision was a strange one, possibly inspired by lingering Victorian guilt towards people born without middle-class advantages, or maybe simply from curiosity about other people's lives. For two years she stuck doggedly to this task, teaching English composition, history and literature to classes that could number as few as two students. She was touched by their enthusiasm, but it often waned under pressure, for she started from an utterly different base, and although she tried to simplify her lectures, writing them out beforehand, her audience was apt to dwindle or miss the point. Once, when she had been talking about the Italian Renaissance, the only question was, 'Please, Miss, did the beds in Venice have fleas?'

More important was the slow gathering of like-minded young people at Gordon Square, again on Vanessa's initiative, and the guests, all in their mid-twenties, were mostly Thoby's friends from Cambridge. She formed two weekly soirées, Thursday Evenings and the Friday Club, the latter mainly devoted to the discussion of the arts, but the company on both occasions was interchangeable, apart from Vanessa's girlfriends from the Slade. Among the regular attenders were Lytton Strachey, Clive Bell, Saxon Sydney-Turner, Walter Lamb and Desmond MacCarthy, and a little later, Duncan Grant, Roger Fry and Leonard Woolf, but Leonard for only a single evening before he left to govern part of Ceylon as a colonial civil servant. He was to remain there for seven years.

They were a serious group of young men, and their symposiums in Bloomsbury were at first extensions of their seminars at Cambridge. They read papers to each other and discussed abstract ideas like truth and beauty, fuelled by nothing more than cocoa and a tot of whisky, which was all they could afford. The difference from Cambridge was the presence of the two girls. At the University no girls had been admitted to their society, for although they were known to exist in colleges in the outer suburbs, they were regarded in the same way that monks might regard nuns, unavailable and therefore undesirable. In consequence most of them were homosexual, but not irremediably. Now they were confronted by two young women who not only matched them in intelligence but, as Leonard recalled, were astonishingly beautiful. He later wrote, 'It was almost impossible for a young man not to fall in love with them.' But for the moment, only Clive Bell, the least solemn of the group, dared express his admiration. He proposed to Vanessa, and was refused.

They were dedicated, as Quentin Bell has described, 'to a new honesty and a new charity in personal relations', but one must not imagine that their conversation was always scintillating. Virginia was often in despair at her failure to strike a spark. Though at that stage of her life she was both eager and reserved, like Rachel Vinrace in *The Voyage Out*, she did not take immediately to Thoby's friends. Duncan Grant remembered that she was a little aloof, never addressing the company at large, only individuals. Even that could be tough going. When Sydney-Turner and Strachey joined them for a few days in Cornwall in September 1905, she wrote to Violet: 'They are a great trial. They sit silent, absolutely silent, all the time; occasionally they escape to a corner and chuckle over a Latin joke. Perhaps they are falling in love with Nessa; who knows? It would be a silent and very learned process. However, I don't think they are robust enough to feel very much. Oh, women are my line, and not these inanimate creatures.' She was exaggerating. If these parties were truly so melancholy, she would not have repeated them year after year. These 'inanimate creatures' were to become her most intimate friends and shared with her the 'burst of splendour' that followed her escape from Kensington. But apart from Clive they seemed to lack her vitality. There was no Byron or Trelawny among them. They were embarrassed by their friend's sisters. It was not until they came to discard their Cambridge asceticism that their company was enjoyable. Even Leonard struck Virginia at their first meeting as 'a violent, trembling, misanthropic Jew'. She remained devoted to her few women friends, and only once did she consent to attend a party in the smart world that she had renounced. 'I went to a dance last night', she told Violet, 'and found a dim corner where I sat and read *In Memoriam*, while Nessa danced every dance till 2.30.' Vanessa, who was to become the more exclusive and reclusive of the sisters, was now the more audacious. 'She has volcanoes under her sedate manner', Virginia wrote about her, and to her, 'You are the most complete human being of us all.'

In September 1906 the quartet went to Greece, and then onwards to Turkey. It was the only holiday that Virginia took outside Europe, and had it not been that illness spoiled its last stages, it was for her an unforgettable experience. Drenched in classical history and literature (she carried the *Odyssey* in her handbag), her only regret was that the 5th century BC was succeeded by civilizations that could not match it for originality and zest, and she cared little for their monuments.

She and Vanessa, with Violet Dickinson, travelled by train through France and Italy, and by sea from Brindisi to Patras, from where it was but a short step to the classic site of Olympia. There they were joined by Thoby and Adrian, who had sailed down the Dalmatian coast and took horse through Montenegro. Their reunion was followed by visits to Corinth and Nauplia. At Mycenae they stayed in the inn named after Helen of Troy, where thirty years later I found their signatures in the visitors' book. Virginia kept a careful journal of their travels, which was edited in 1990 by Mitchell Leaska. Her description of Mycenae contains the sentence, 'I conceived that here was a single spot of intense and brilliantly painted life, girt in by great wastes of desert land'. She was never a guidebook addict: she wrote her own. As Leaska commented, 'Something new and different was finding its way into her style. … Her imagery was becoming more impressionistic, ambiguous, and therefore more resonant, in sound and meaning', a quality that was to distinguish all her writing.

At Athens Vanessa fell ill, and was cared for by Violet while the others visited friends in Euboea. She recovered sufficiently to continue to Constantinople with all of them except Thoby, who returned to London. Virginia was impressed by the Turks. Religion was a natural part of their daily life: they could turn to their devotions as easily as to their ledgers. Many of the women walked without covering their faces, and she wondered why it had ever been necessary to hide the face 'of a benevolent spinster, with gold rims to her spectacles, trotting out to buy a fowl for dinner. What danger has she got to hide from?'

Vanessa was still unwell, and they thought it would be wiser to cut short their holiday and travel home by the Orient Express. At Dover, Violet, too, was taken ill, and they were met by the news that Thoby was in bed with a high fever. They had succumbed to what was at first assumed by the doctors to be malaria, but was then diagnosed as acute typhoid. Thoby and Violet lay scarcely a mile apart, desperately ill. She recovered, but Thoby died on 20 November 1906, aged twenty-six.

His death was shocking to his friends. He was in the prime of life, handsome, attractive, vivacious. He was Virginia's idolized brother. She had loved him as a schoolboy, worshipped him as an undergraduate. Adrian was no substitute. His daughter later admitted, 'The wrong brother died', and though Virginia and Vanessa never said this, they felt it. Adrian was a good, clever, affectionate man, but Virginia still thought of him as a 'poor little boy' when he was aged twenty-three and 6 ft. 5 in. tall. She felt Thoby's death so acutely that she concealed it for nearly a month from Violet, even inventing bulletins of his recovery long after he had died, in case the shock should kill her too. She reserved the expression of her grief for *Jacob's Room*, where Jacob is a recognizable portrait of Thoby, and his journey through Greece was almost mile by mile the one they had taken together.

Then, in scarcely less dramatic circumstances, Virginia lost her sister too. Two days after Thoby's death ('indecently soon', Virginia felt), Clive Bell proposed to Vanessa a second time, and she accepted him. He was Thoby's closest friend, in some ways his *alter ego*, but Vanessa was not in love with him, merely grateful for his kindness to her during Thoby's illness, and happy that he loved art and possessed the gift of making other people happy. Both were highly sensual. I remember a discussion at a men's dining club about the most important discoveries of the twentieth century. Some people nominated the telephone, the aeroplane, the radio. 'What do you think, Clive?', one of us asked. 'The most important discovery of the century', he replied, 'is that women like it too.'

Clive took his fiancée – the word seemed ludicrous to them, but there was no other – to meet his parents in their house in Wiltshire, and foolishly invited Virginia to join them. While Vanessa was obliged to express some pleasure in the visit, Virginia was under no such obligation, and all her contempt for middle-class respectability spilled into her letter to Violet Dickinson: 'The thickness of this nib and the luxury of this paper will show you that I am in a rich and illiterate house, set in its own grounds, gothic, barbaric. I dip my pen into the hoof of an old hunter.' Clive's mother was a 'little rabbit-faced woman, with wisps of white hair', his father 'an obvious country gentleman', and their daughters 'exactly what one would have guessed. They play hockey and beagle, and laugh at Adrian's jokes and come down to dinner in pale blue satin with satin bows in their hair.' She found it difficult to believe that Clive had remained unaffected by this background. She pitied her sister.

This was a very temporary phase of jealousy, for soon after Vanessa's marriage in February 1907, Virginia found in Clive a correspondent in whom she could confide and a friend who shared her dislike of domesticity which the birth of her son Julian forced on Vanessa. Virginia could tolerate children for short periods, but fled from babies. 'I doubt that I shall ever have a baby', she wrote to Violet from Cornwall, where she, the baby and its parents were on holiday. 'Its voice is too terrible, a senseless scream like an ill-omened cat. Nobody could pretend that it was a human being.' Clive refused to cuddle it. It leaked unpleasantly from every orifice. So Clive and Virginia were thrown together by this infant, and they found in each other an escape. Quentin Bell, Vanessa's second son, has called it more than a flirtation. He claimed that

Virginia's motive was 'to break down that charmed circle within which Vanessa and Clive were so happy, and by which she was so cruelly excluded'. Her behaviour, like Clive's, was inexcusable. She set out to detach her sister from him, while he by his response to her showed how shallow was his love for Vanessa. Frances Spalding, Vanessa's biographer, has summed up the affair (Virginia's own term for it) as 'more a game of wits than a matter of passion, but this did not lessen the outrage'. Virginia soon came to regret her treachery, and for the rest of her life treated her sister with loving caution, to which Vanessa, the stronger character of the two, did not always respond. Clive, on the other hand, showed no symptom of remorse, and his relations with Virginia were undamaged. She found him the most sympathetic and intelligent of all those whom she consulted on the topic that meant most to her, her writing. Indeed he was the only person to whom she ever showed a book in draft, her first, *Melymbrosia*, which she began to write in 1907 and published eight years later under the title *The Voyage Out*.

The original Hyde Park Gate family of ten was now reduced to two, Virginia and Adrian. Julia, Stella, Leslie and Thoby were dead, George and Vanessa married, Gerald a publisher, Laura locked up mad. As it was clearly impossible for Virginia and Adrian to share Gordon Square with their married sister, they searched Bloomsbury for another house, and eventually found 29 Fitzroy Square, only a few blocks away, thus initiating those moves from square to square that continued throughout the next three decades, like a game of chess, but never overstepping the boundaries of the board that was Bloomsbury.

Having established themselves so agreeably, Virginia and

her brother were continually travelling. Fundamentally she was an urban woman: she needed the society of friends, and ready access to libraries, picture galleries, theatres and concert halls. But she was rural too. She loved long and solitary country walks, and although she had no knowledge of horticulture, agriculture or wild animals, she enjoyed the queer shapes and sounds of the countryside, the flight of birds and a fox's bark. Thus we find her and Adrian spending the Christmas of 1906 in a cottage in the New Forest, the following summer in a rented house at Rye in Sussex, and in 1908 she took lodgings by herself at Wells in Somerset and revisited Manorbier in Wales.

She kept in touch by letter-writing. Even after the telephone became easily available, the letter was her medium. She would write several on most days, of which about a fifth have survived, and I, who edited them in six volumes with Joanne Trautmann, have been rereading them with renewed astonishment at their versatility. She might write three long letters to different correspondents in an evening without repeating a single phrase from one into another. They vary in depth and speed, like a stream now running fast over pebbles, now settling into pools. Their mood is almost invariably cheerful, merry, solicitous. When she gossiped (which was frequently) it was not with malice, but as a caricature. Take, for example, her famous description of her meeting with Henry James in Rye:

> He fixed me with his staring blank eye – it is like a child's marble – and said, 'My dear Virginia, they tell me – they tell me – they tell me – that you – as indeed being your father's daughter nay your grandfather's grandchild – the descendant I may say of a

century – of a century – of quill pens and ink – ink – ink pots, yes, yes, yes, they tell me – ahm m m – that you, that you, that you *write* in short.' This went on in the public street, while we all waited, as farmers wait for a hen to lay an egg – do they? – nervous, polite, and now on this foot now on that. I felt like a condemned person, who sees the knife drop and stick and drop again.

Virginia was not then the alarming person that she became, unintentionally but inevitably, when she was famous. Meeting her for the first time you might have considered her timid, shy. Such an encounter was recorded by Arnold Bennett when he met her in a Paris café in April 1907: 'Young Bell [Clive] was there with his wife, who is a daughter of Leslie Stephen. Another daughter [Virginia] and a son [Adrian] came in. Bell's wife was slightly attractive; the other daughter not – I mean physically. All seemed very decent, quiet young people, carrying very well the weight of their name', when that was the very weight that they had succeeded in shaking off. As for their appearance, Bennett's judgment is contradicted by every contemporary compliment and photograph. He was expecting two pretty girls. He met two sophisticated young women.

Two men fell seriously in love with Virginia. One was Walter Headlam, a lecturer in classics at King's College, Cambridge, whom she liked well enough to lend him her manuscripts for criticism, but he was old enough to be her father and died quite suddenly in 1908. The other was Hilton Young, the assistant editor of *The Economist* and an habitué of Thursday Evenings. Virginia played him like a fish, dangling herself like a bait before him, and then withdrawing. Eventually he proposed to her, and she refused him, saying that she could marry nobody but Lytton Strachey. But when Lytton did propose to her in February 1909, she changed her mind twenty-four hours after accepting him, to the evident relief of both of them. 'He's perfect as a friend', she told Molly MacCarthy, 'but he's a female friend.'

III

IN SPITE OF these distractions, the ten years before the outbreak of war marked the full flowering of Bloomsbury. In 1982 I lectured about this celebrated group of friends at Austin, Texas, and warned my academic audience that there was a danger that in America they might be overestimating, and we in Britain underestimating, their influence and achievement. Our Virginia, I said, had become their Woolf, and they were not the same person. While for American scholars Bloomsbury still bulks large in the development of twentieth-century ideas on feminism, socialism and pacifism, the British are more cautious, less exclamatory, sometimes downright hostile, looking for the pioneers of these movements more to the Fabians, the Webbs, Wells, Shaw, Marie Stopes, Ethel Smyth, Emmeline Pankhurst and Millicent Fawcett, who were contemporaries of the Bloomsbury group but by no possible definition members of it. Americans, I said, may inadvertently be moulding the Bloomsberries into their preconceived notions of them, and putting into their mouths things that they wish they had said and meant, but didn't actually say or mean, while we may be dismissing important things that they did say as plagiarisms or platitudes.

If it can be said that a Group exists and has an identity, it must hold certain ideas in common and a wish to propagate them. In Bloomsbury I find it hard to define what those ideas were, beyond claiming in the loosest sense that they were more liberated than their predecessors, expressed themselves more frankly, treated women as equals to men and had a respect for intellectual excellence. But that does not amount to a doctrine. Michael Holroyd has pointed out that it is quite untrue that they shared a philosophy or a system of aesthetics, and those who claim that they did, 'understand next to nothing of the isolated way in which a work of art is evolved'. Forster's novels owed nothing to Virginia's, Strachey's theory of civilization little to Clive Bell's. Or take Leonard Woolf's thinking on international relations, and Keynes's on economics: in no way could it be said that it was a Bloomsbury way of thinking. There was a little more community of taste in art and music, and negatively they were linked by their indifference to science and religion, as well as by their pacifism in the First World War. Their socialism was tepid: it assumed the perpetuity of the capitalist system and the subordination of the servant class. Virginia's championship of women's rights did not extend far down the social scale. She never protested that it was the lot of most women to remain at home and cook their husbands' dinners. She was anxious that more women of her own class should have the opportunity to become doctors, lawyers, teachers, writers, but she felt no need to argue that secretaries should become directors of their companies if they were clever enough, or that cleaning ladies might by their own efforts rise to become ladies for whom other ladies cleaned.

That is the negative side. More positively it should be emphasized that this small group of men and women exerted in several directions a beneficent influence of which we are the inheritors. Each in his or her own way was attempting the most difficult feat that a man or woman can undertake – to give an art or a doctrine a new shape which survives challenge and ridicule to be accepted as non-controversial decades later. Virginia Woolf and E.M. Forster achieved this by their novels; Duncan Grant, Vanessa Bell and Roger Fry by their own paintings and advocacy of the French. Lytton Strachey revolutionized biography; T.S. Eliot, poetry; Desmond MacCarthy, literary criticism; Leonard Woolf, international affairs (he wrote the first draft of the Charter of the League of Nations); Keynes, economics. And all of them by their conduct can teach us how to live, how to allocate our time, how to be happy, how to love.

The fascination that these people still exert is partly due to the vast amount of information we have about them. The discovery of their intimacies, the cat's cradle of their correspondence, generates a vicarious excitement in all who study their works and days. We are privileged to know more about them than any of them knew about the others. They were the first to regard homosexuality as normal: it was a joyful consequence of friendship. If they were unfaithful to each other, their infidelities tended to be permanent and only temporarily resented. Bloomsbury's greatest legacy, indeed, was their concept of friendship. Nothing – not age, nor success, nor rivalry in art or love, nor different careers and branching intimacies, nor separation for long periods by war, travel or occupation – ever parted these people who first came together when they were young.

There is no doubt that their society was exclusive and alarming. I can just remember what it was like, because once, when I was aged about twelve, I was taken by my mother to a Bloomsbury party. The room was large, smoky and warmed more by excitement than by artificial means. There were divans and carpets, walls painted gaudily like a seraglio, gramophone records on trays and books everywhere. People were sitting on the floor at other people's feet, and there was much noise and laughter, high-pitched and faintly neighing, which ceased suddenly on the arrival of people like us. My mother and I found a corner where we could sit more or less unobserved, and I was given a tomato sandwich. People were jumping up all the time, reaching for a book, peering at a picture. There was an undercurrent of competitiveness, as if everyone had to justify their presence each time afresh. On one such occasion, when Virginia had told one of her funniest stories and the laughter had died down, she turned to a girl of eighteen and said, 'Now you tell us a story'. Of course it wasn't kind. It was not intended to be. Bloomsbury demanded that you catch the ball when it was thrown in your direction and if you missed it, you were not invited again, and didn't wish to be.

In his diary, quoted by his nephew Quentin in his biography of Virginia, Adrian Stephen recorded an incident that must have been typical. It was at an impromptu party in July 1909 at Fitzroy Square. People slowly drifted in, uninvited:

Saxon Sydney-Turner, Lytton Strachey and his brother James came first; then Clive, Vanessa, Duncan Grant and Henry Lamb.

'The conversation', wrote Adrian, 'kept up a good flow, though it was not very interesting, until at about half-past eleven Miss Cole arrived. She went and sat in the long wicker chair with Virginia and Clive on the floor beside her. Virginia began in her usual tone of frank admiration to compliment her on her appearance: "Of course you, Miss Cole, are always dressed so exquisitely. You look so original, so like a seashell. There is something so refined about you coming in among our muddy boots and pipe smoke, dressed in your exquisite creations". Clive chimed in with more heavy compliments, and then began asking her why she disliked him so much, saying how any other young lady would have been much pleased with all the nice things he had been saying, but she treated him so sharply. At this Virginia interrupted with, "I think Miss Cole has a very strong character", and so on. ... The poor woman was the centre of all our gaze, and did not know what to do with herself.'

Now, Annie Cole was no mouse. Two years later she married Neville Chamberlain, and when he became Prime Minister, she took on an important part in international politics.

Virginia's conduct on this occasion was her mordant side. When friends fell ill, or were bereaved, or long absent abroad, or crossed in love, she could show great sympathy. But she never hesitated to lampoon them, put them at jumps which she knew they could not clear, and invent for them situations ('I know what you have been doing this morning: you have been riding a white horse down Piccadilly') which exposed them to ridicule. Her chaff was not confined to outsiders like Miss Cole. Members of Bloomsbury were ruthless in criticism of each other's books, pictures and attitudes. The most false of all legends about them is that they were a mutual admiration society. On the contrary, they set themselves standards of integrity and originality so high that they constantly fell short of them, and they said so, without malice, in speech or a flurry of letters. Sometimes their mock insults were direct. Virginia could write to Violet Dickinson, 'Adrian thinks he met you today. The lady smiled — was it you or a prostitute?', and Violet was supposed not to mind. They were so keen to amuse each other that they exaggerated their friends' failings and misfortunes, magnified their own small adventures, and gilded every lily richly. It was an abrasive society, highly stimulating. It was said that the difference between Blooms-bury and Cambridge was that at Cambridge nothing witty was said unless it was also profound, and in Bloomsbury nothing profound was said unless it was also witty. Virginia was largely responsible for this change in mood.

In August 1909 she went with Adrian and Saxon Sydney-Turner to Bayreuth and Dresden, and relieved her boredom by writing acerbic letters to Vanessa. *Parsifal* was a tedious opera, she thought, 'weak and vague stuff', and Saxon 'rather peevish. He hops along humming like a stridulous grass-hopper. He clenches his fists, scowls, and stops at once if you look at him.' As for the natives, her xenophobia surfaced again: 'I haven't seen one German woman who has a face; they are puddings of red dough.'

In 1910 Virginia made two political gestures. She was per-suaded by Janet Case to join the Women's Suffrage Move-ment, and while she could in no way be described as a militant, she spent hours in the movement's offices addressing envelopes to indifferent politicians. The campaign had been gaining popular support for years, but the Prime Minister, Asquith, was a strong opponent, and his refusal to grant the vote to women led to increasing protests and violence. The outbreak of war in 1914 halted the campaign but gained its object. Most women were granted the vote in 1918. Virginia took no further part in the movement, regarding political agitation as foolish, even when she sympathized with its causes and benefited from its results.

It is therefore all the more surprising that she allowed herself to be drawn into the Dreadnought Hoax in February 1910. The details have been well recorded by Adrian and Virginia herself, and amplified by their biographers. It was the event that first drew attention to Bloomsbury. Their success in hoodwinking the Royal Navy shocked and amused the public, but few people realized that the hoax was not just the prank of a few mischievous young men and women, but a political and pacifist statement.

The plan was the joint concept of Adrian and his friend Horace Cole (a brother of Annie), who was renowned for his practical jokes. They proposed to expose the Navy to ridicule by staging a formal visit by 'the Emperor of Abyssinia' to the fleet's newest and most prestigious battleship, the *Dreadnought*, then moored in Weymouth harbour. They sent a telegram to the commander-in-chief, purporting to come from the Foreign Office, instructing him to receive the Emperor and his suite with honour. The conspirators then hired a theatrical costumier to dress them appropriately, Adrian as the British interpreter and Cole as the Foreign Office official. All the others blackened their faces and wore heavy disguise. Duncan and Virginia were both in robes, turbans and false moustaches. They had themselves photographed, and set off by train for Weymouth, practising *en route* a fictional language that they hoped would be taken for something faintly aboriginal.

There are two unexplained puzzles. Why did Virginia consent to take part in this escapade? She was not by nature a practical joker. She had no acting ability. She hardly knew Cole, and Adrian had little influence on her. Vanessa strongly discouraged her. At that stage of her life she had given little thought to the iniquities of armies and navies. But she never regretted taking part, and as late as 1940 lectured on the hoax with amusement and a certain pride. It was a successful lark, and in later life she attributed to it a moral motive that can scarcely have occurred to her at the time.

The second puzzle is why the Navy was taken in. The authenticity of the Foreign Office telegram was never checked, the disguises never penetrated. The party were given a red-carpet welcome at Weymouth, and conducted by launch to the *Dreadnought*, where the Admiral received them on the quarterdeck with his flag-Commander, William Fisher, Virginia's cousin (who might well have recognized her and Adrian), and they were shown round the most modern and secret of Britain's warships. They were offered refreshments, which they declined on religious grounds, but in reality for fear that their makeup might run, and a twenty-one-gun salute, which they generously declared to be unnecessary. Then they returned to London.

Cole, delighted with the success of the hoax, leaked the story to the newspapers. Indeed, there would have been no purpose in it unless it was to become public knowledge.

Questions were asked in Parliament, but the fuss was minimal compared to what it would have been today. The most severe punishment suffered by the conspirators was a ceremonial tap on Cole's and Duncan's bottoms, inflicted by young officers to restore the Navy's honour. Cole consented to this chastisement on condition that he could tap them back. The only older people to be outraged by the incident were members of the Stephen family and the Fishers.

This incident was in no way responsible for Virginia's mental breakdown later in that year. She suffered from headaches and insomnia, and seemed once again on the verge of insanity. Visits to Cornwall, Dorset and a rented house near Canterbury failed to restore her. In late June 1910 Dr Savage advised her to enter a mental nursing home for six weeks, but her condition was not serious enough to prevent her mocking it in letters to Vanessa and her friends. She showed great fortitude, shut up with mad women in a hideous house, while she herself was not mad enough to be unaware of their madness. 'I feel my brains, like a pear', she wrote from her prison, 'to see if it's ripe: it will be exquisite by September.'

After a convalescence in Cornwall and Dorset, it was. She was able to resume work on *Melymbrosia*, her novel, and give a little time to Women's Suffrage. But the main excitement of the autumn, and Bloomsbury's major pre-war claim to fame, was the First Post-Impressionist Exhibition. The guiding inspiration was Roger Fry's. The Bells had first met him early in the year, and he was captivated by Bloomsbury, as Bloomsbury was by him. He determined to confront English society with the paintings and sculpture of modern French artists, whose very names – Cézanne, Van Gogh, Matisse, Picasso – were almost unknown in Britain, and with

Desmond MacCarthy as his adjutant, he ransacked the studios and galleries of Paris to bring back examples of their work and present them to the public in the Grafton Galleries. The exhibition caused a sensation. The pictures were reviled even by innovative British painters like Walter Sickert. They were called 'pornographic', 'the work of madmen'. Laughter mingled with pretended revulsion.

Virginia had little to do with mounting the exhibition, and supported it hesitantly from the sidelines, but it affected her strongly. What the artists were doing in paint (disdaining what Vanessa called the 'fatal prettiness' of conventional British art), she intended to pioneer in prose, giving the essence of a person or a place without describing it precisely. As Desmond MacCarthy put it in his Introduction to the catalogue, 'A good rocking horse has often more of the true horse about it than an instantaneous photograph of a Derby winner'. 'Art', said Fry, 'is significant deformity.' For example, Duncan Grant's portrait of Virginia painted at this time, and now in the Metropolitan Museum, New York, is unrecognizable as her – it might be a fishwife – but it reflects Virginia's brooding contemplation, while in Vanessa's portrait of her, painted in the next year, her left eye is entirely missing. Virginia made no protest. It was a breaking of convention. The fashionable world did not see it like this. The suffragettes, the Dreadnought Hoax, and now this exhibition, were all part of a deplorable attack on taste and good manners. When Virginia and Vanessa appeared at the Post-Impressionist Ball dressed in gaudy draperies and very little underneath, it was taken as further proof that the younger generation were inebriated by a passing French fashion.

In April 1911 Vanessa, Clive, Roger Fry and Harry Norton

went to Turkey on holiday, and while there, Vanessa fell seriously ill after a miscarriage. Virginia, intensely worried by rumours of her condition, hastened to join them – it was her second visit to Turkey – and brought her sister back by train. Her help was scarcely needed. Fry, not Clive, took control. He was solicitous and amazingly competent. In the process, he fell in love with Vanessa, and she with him. From that moment the Bell marriage was transformed into what her son Quentin has called a 'union of friendship'.

Virginia had no lover and no wish for one, and turned down two further offers of marriage, one from Walter Lamb (Henry's brother), the other from the diplomatist, Sydney Waterlow, who was divorcing his wife in the hope of marrying her. In writing to Sydney, Virginia was kind ('I don't think I shall ever feel for you what I must feel for the man I marry'), but in writing about him, she did not spare him her sharpest ridicule. She needed solitude to complete her book, and bought one half of a Victorian house at Firle, her first venture into the part of east Sussex which was to be her country retreat for the rest of her life. She agreed that 'the cottage' was in fact 'a hideous suburban villa', the only ugly house in a pretty village, but that didn't matter, because when you are inside, you can forget the outside. It was also a good base for walking on the Downs. Here she remained for much of the summer of 1911, revising her novel, and broke off only to stay with Ottoline Morrell, and go camping in Devon with Rupert Brooke, his lover Ka Cox, and Maynard Keynes.

Virginia painted in 1911–12 by her sister Vanessa Bell, a portrait now in the National Portrait Gallery. The portrait soon followed the Post-Impressionist Exhibition, which strongly influenced Vanessa's art, and indirectly Virginia's writing. 'Her left eye is entirely missing, but she made no protest.'

IV

LEONARD WOOLF RETURNED on leave from Ceylon determined to marry Virginia. Although they had not once corresponded during his seven-year absence, he was encouraged by Lytton Strachey's letters to think that she might accept him. They met several times after his return, and she was happy to notice that he was unchanged by 'shooting tigers, hanging natives and ruling a province the size of Wales', as she chose to imagine his life of exile, and he slipped back easily into Bloomsbury moods and manners. He did not have the wit of Lytton Strachey, the sparkle of Roger Fry nor the geniality of Clive Bell, but he had an exceptionally fertile and original mind, and Virginia already loved him because he had loved Thoby. The only permanent mark left on his character by his colonial career, as he admitted in his autobiography, was, 'I was a stickler for what was officially right and proper'. I remember him as kind but rather formidable. His awkwardness with children made us awkward too. His hands trembled all the time. He could not lift a cup of tea without spilling it. That fascinated us. In her diary, twenty-five years later, Virginia speculated that this trembling, which had persisted since infancy, may have 'moulded his life wrongly. All his shyness, his suffering from society, his sharpness and definiteness, might have been smoothed' had it not been for this affliction. To think of this gaunt man in his ill-fitting suit as an ardent lover strains the imagination, but he was.

Virginia invited him to stay several times at Firle, and on

one of their walks over the Downs they discovered Asheham, a pretty Regency house, of which Virginia took a joint lease with Vanessa, and they moved there from Firle at the end of 1911. At about the same time, the lease of Fitzroy Square ran out, and she rented 38 Brunswick Square, a large Bloomsbury house which she shared with Adrian, Maynard Keynes and Duncan Grant. In December they were joined there by Leonard Woolf. It was the first of their houses to be equipped with a telephone, and Virginia accepted the device without excitement, still relying on letters as the civilized way for friends to communicate when apart. In consequence we can know a great deal about the progress of Leonard's courtship.

The intimacy between them grew fast. He first proposed to her in January 1912, and she gently repulsed him. She hesitated again in May when he renewed his appeal, and gave him her reasons candidly. Her mind was unstable, she said: she might become a burden to him. Then, 'I feel angry sometimes at the strength of your desire', which she might be unable to reciprocate. Next, 'possibly your being a Jew comes in also at this point'. This was not too serious an objection, but Virginia had inherited a certain anti-Semitic prejudice from her father. Her letters are speckled with evidence of it. 'There are a great many Portuguese Jews on board and other repulsive objects', she had written to Violet Dickinson in 1905 when she was on her way to Spain. She wrote again to her in 1910, 'I sat on a platform next to Portuguese Jews, whose sweat ran into powder, caked and blew off.' As late as 1933, she described the eminent philosopher, Isaiah Berlin, on first meeting him, as 'a Portuguese Jew, by the look of him' (why always Portuguese?). She came to boast of Leonard's Jewishness as if it was to her credit that she married him in spite of it. In 1930 she told Ethel Smyth, 'How I hated marrying a Jew – how I hated their nasal voices, and their oriental jewellery, and their noses and their wattles – what a snob I was, for they have immense vitality.' She was not alone in thinking this. In *The Years* (1937) one hears the voice of her class and generation:

'Was someone coming in?' Her eyes were on the door.

'The Jew', she murmured.

'The Jew', he said.

They listened. He could hear quite distinctly now. Somebody was turning on taps; somebody was having a bath in the room opposite.

'The Jew having a bath', she said.

'The Jew having a bath', he repeated.

'And tomorrow there'll be a line of grease round the bath', she said.

'Damn the Jew!', he exclaimed.

Hermione Lee has pointed out in her biography of Virginia Woolf that anti-Semitism in upper-class England persisted well into the inter-war period. We must not make too much of it in Virginia's case, because she didn't; but it was unpleasant.

Leonard sensed that her reservations about marrying him amounted to consent. Vanessa encouraged him ('You are the only person I know whom I can imagine as her husband'), and Virginia showed no resentment of his eagerness. So he took the risk of resigning from the Colonial Service, and waited. Then, quite suddenly, on 29 May, after they had been lunching together in Brunswick Square, she told him that she loved him and would marry him. They went rowing on the

Leonard Woolf by Vanessa Bell. 'To think of this gaunt man in his ill-fitting suit as an ardent lover strains the imagination, but he was.'

Thames to calm down. She broke the news to all her friends (to Janet Case she wrote, 'I am going to marry Leonard Wolf [sic] – he is a penniless Jew'), and was introduced by Leonard to his mother at her house in Putney. It was not a success. Mrs Woolf, to her understandable distress, was not invited to her son's wedding. It took place on 10 August 1912 at St Pancras Registry Office in London, in the presence of Vanessa, the Duckworth brothers, Duncan Grant, Roger Fry and one or two others. Clive gave them lunch in Gordon Square. So they were married. Virginia was thirty, Leonard thirty-one.

If a honeymoon is the first test of a couple's compatibility, it can be said that in all but one sense theirs was a success. After one night at Asheham, they spent nearly a week in the Plough Inn at Holford in Somerset, where their love-making must have been disturbed by the rowdiness at the bar below that continues to this day, and then they went for six weeks to France, Spain and Italy, recording their adventures in letters that lost nothing in frankness. Bloomsbury was agog to know how the wife, as virginal as her name, had coped with her husband's legitimate desire. She did not cope well. From Saragossa she wrote to Ka Cox, 'Why do you think that people make such a fuss about marriage and copulation? I certainly find the climax immensely exaggerated.' Leonard confessed to Vanessa that Virginia's performance, from his point of view, had been most unsatisfactory. Vanessa suggested that he might try a whip. However, this was not the end of their sexual experiments. For several more months they shared a bed, for several years a bedroom, and it was not until Leonard was advised by her doctors that Virginia was too delicate in mind and body to bear a child, and that sexual excitement might trigger off a new attack of madness, that they decided to give up. Thereafter, though they almost always slept under the same roof, it was rarely under the same ceiling. But they continued to kiss and cuddle. Once I applied the word 'frigid' to Virginia's sexuality. It was mistaken. Her letters to Leonard, and his to her, on the rare occasions when they were apart, are full of ardour. In April 1916, for example, she wrote to him, 'There's no doubt that I'm terribly in love with you. I keep thinking what you're doing, and have to stop – it makes me want to kiss you so.' Their correspondence makes it almost certain that for the thirty years of their marriage, Leonard remained in effect chaste, sublimating by his work the passionate love that Virginia denied him.

If their honeymoon had failed to conceive a child, they returned with the literary equivalent – the revised manuscripts of twin novels, one by each of them. Leonard's was *The Village in the Jungle*, based on his experiences in Ceylon; Virginia's was *Melymbrosia*, now renamed *The Voyage Out*, on which she had been working for the same seven years that Leonard had been abroad. His book was published soon after their return. Virginia's was further delayed by her dissatisfaction with it (after five drafts!), and it was only in March 1913 that she delivered the typescript to the only publisher she knew, her half-brother, Gerald Duckworth. For a month she anxiously awaited the verdict of a man whom she despised. Gerald accepted it, but again there was a long delay due to Virginia's recurring illnesses. *The Voyage Out* was not published until March 1915, by which time she was once again insane.

It was mainly the strain of finishing and revising the book, 'with a kind of tortured intensity' as Leonard observed, that caused her breakdown, but there were other stresses too – the punishing schedules that they imposed on themselves, and in August 1914, the outbreak of war. At first they divided their time between lodgings in London's legal district and Asheham. Leonard began to involve himself deeply in politics and journalism, specially in connection with the Cooperative Movement in the Midlands and the north as far as Glasgow, where Virginia accompanied him, bemused by people and causes quite alien to Bloomsbury, but she remained complacent out of loyalty to Leonard. They were obliged to earn money. One cannot claim that they were desperately poor. Virginia had inherited her share of her father's, Stella's, Thoby's and Aunt Emelia's legacies, about £9,000, which, when invested, gave them an income of £400. Leonard had no fixed job, and capital of only £500, the balance of the £690 he had won in a sweepstake. It was not enough. What with the expense of two houses, travel between them, servants in each place, entertainment and books, they needed an income double what their capital could provide. They could not live by novel-writing. In fifteen years *The Voyage Out* earned Virginia less than £120. So Leonard worked doggedly as a political journalist, and she resumed her articles and reviews for the *Times Literary Supplement* until the strain became too great for her, and she collapsed.

Her strong intellect matched her soaring imagination, and her imagination sometimes took control. She talked wildly, suffered from acute headaches, heard strange voices, and could not sleep and would not eat. For three months in 1913 her condition deteriorated to such an extent that there was talk of certifying her insane, and Leonard thought it wise to send her back to the nursing-home in Twickenham where she had been two years earlier. She made hardly any protest, writing to him touchingly affectionate letters ('I got up and dressed last night after you were gone, wanting to come back to you. You do represent all that's best, and I lie here thinking of you'). After two weeks under care, she was well enough to return to Asheham, but there her mind deteriorated once more. On the doctor's strange advice, Leonard took her to the very inn at Holford where they had spent part of their honeymoon. It did no good. She was still hearing voices. So they returned to London, staying with Adrian in Brunswick Square, and there, for the second time in her life, Virginia attempted suicide. Leonard had left unlocked a phial of veronal tablets which he had given her from time to time to help her sleep. While he was out of the house, she swallowed a hundred of them, and sank immediately into a coma. Fortunately, Geoffrey Keynes, Maynard's brother and a surgeon at St Bartholomew's Hospital, who was sharing Adrian's rooms, realized at once that she was on the point of death, and drove her at speed through the streets, shouting at the police, 'Doctor, doctor! Urgent, urgent!', and managed to reach the hospital in time to apply a stomach pump which saved her life. It was two days before she recovered consciousness.

Asheham was not large enough to accommodate the nurses she now needed, and they accepted the offer of her half-brother, George Duckworth, to loan them his Sussex mansion, Dalingridge Hall, complete with servants and every luxury. There they stayed for two months. In the summer of 1914 they moved back to Asheham, and were there when war broke out in August. They saw no reason to cancel a holiday they had planned in Northumberland, and on their return looked for new lodgings. After spending two months on The

Green in Richmond, one of the loveliest parts of London before parked cars destroyed its serenity, they found an idyllic place with a hundred-foot garden, Hogarth House, also in Richmond, which they managed to rent. How their straitened finances and their battered furniture stood up to these constant moves is unexplained.

It was while Leonard was negotiating the lease of Hogarth House in February 1915 that Virginia suffered yet another mental breakdown, her worst. Leonard described her condition as 'a nightmare world of frenzy, despair and violence'. It was not, as previously, simply a matter of insomnia and refusal to eat. She had crossed the borderline between a mental illness of which she was fully conscious to a state of garrulous insanity, speaking incoherently and without pause, sometimes for hours on end until she lost consciousness. Leonard could do nothing for her. She would seldom speak to him except to abuse him, but it was due to his presence that she survived.

They moved her to Hogarth House while she was still insane, and somehow found the wages for four living-in nurses. It was not until September 1915 that she could return to Asheham, still with a nurse, and began that slow process of rehabilitation that restored her to sanity for the next twenty-five years.

V

SO TRAUMATIC HAD been these experiences that Leonard, now a leading expert on international affairs, had barely noticed the outbreak of the European war. He was exempt from military service by the constant trembling of his hands. If he could not lift a cup without spilling it, a loaded rifle would have been more dangerous to his comrades than to the enemy. He was grateful for this relief, for to abandon Virginia would almost certainly have led her to fresh attempts at suicide, and in any case, he was half won over by the pacifist arguments of his friends. All Bloomsbury were conscientious objectors, on moral more than political grounds. When hauled before tribunals to affirm their motives, they would say that they totally disapproved of war as an instrument of policy, except Keynes, who considered that as the war was now a fact of life, it should be run as efficiently as possible. Clive Bell published a pamphlet called *Peace at Once*, which was destroyed on orders of the Lord Mayor of London for the defeatist arguments it proclaimed. Clive took a logical position: better surrender than allow the carnage to continue. Leonard did not go so far. While maintaining that it was a 'senseless and useless war', he hoped that we would win it. But he expressed no admiration for the soldiers who alone could win it, and broke completely with friends like Rupert Brooke, who went off to the Dardanelles with a song in his heart, writing to Violet Asquith, 'Oh Violet, I could not imagine that fate could be so benign. Oh God, I have never been quite so happy in my life.'

Virginia's attitude was different from Leonard's. She made no attempt to argue her case. To her the greatest war in history which killed ten million young men was an irrelevance. It simply confirmed her suspicion of a man-dominated society. It was 'a preposterous masculine fiction'; patriotism was 'a base emotion'. Let them fight if they must, but they were behaving 'like some curious tribe in central Africa'. When one of Leonard's brothers was killed and another severely wounded, all she wrote in her diary was, 'On Sunday we heard of Cecil's death and Philip's wounds', without a word of the pity she undoubtedly felt. She slept night after night in the cellar of Hogarth House, sheltering from the air raids, and although she mentioned these events in her diary, she never commented on them. She maintained an attitude to the war of complete indifference. Having no role in it herself, she would not bother to record it. Of the great battles in France – the very sound of the gunfire penetrated to Asheham – of America's entry into the war and the Russian Revolution, she wrote nothing in her letters or diary. But the war left an impact on her. In Virginia's later books, *Jacob's Room* and *The Years*, there are images of war, just as we can hear the distant boom of naval bombardment in Jane Austen's *Persuasion*.

Bloomsbury took to farming in the war, as the only alternative to fighting acceptable to the authorities and themselves. Ottoline Morrell provided such a refuge at Garsington for Lytton Strachey and Clive among others, with minimal labour attached. Duncan Grant, who had replaced Roger Fry in Vanessa's affections, and David ('Bunny') Garnett, who was in love with Duncan, worked at first on a fruit farm in Suffolk, until Virginia made a move on their behalf which changed their lives. She discovered Charleston. It was a roomy

Sussex farmhouse lying on the north side of the Downs near Firle, and she persuaded Vanessa to take a long lease of it. The two men could work out their war service in the local farm. The trio, with Vanessa's two sons, moved there in October 1916, and Clive, as titular husband and father, was treated as a welcome guest and had his permanent rooms there. Roger Fry wrote of this strange ménage, 'It really is almost an ideal family, based as it is on adultery and mutual forebearance, with Clive the deceived husband and me the abandoned lover. It really is rather a triumph of reasonableness over the conventions.' Charleston remained Vanessa's and Duncan's house until they died, and has since become the most enduring memorial of Bloomsbury's art, energy, relationships and taste.

Nearly three years had been taken out of Virginia's and Leonard's lives by her illnesses, and they emerged chastened, poor and eager for fresh enterprise. Their resilience was remarkable. She resumed her journalism, and Leonard was increasingly involved in Fabian and Labour Party politics. They alternated between Asheham and London, where Virginia took lessons in Italian and kept in touch with her friends, of whom the one who came to mean most to her was Lytton Strachey. She wrote of him in her diary, 'He is the most sympathetic and understanding friend to talk to. . . . If one adds his peculiar flavour of mind, his wit and infinite intelligence, he is a figure not to be replaced.' Wartime duties had dispersed Bloomsbury (Virginia was now regularly using the term as a collective noun), but a nucleus remained in the Omega Workshop, which Roger Fry had founded to give employment to young artists and to experiment with the decorative arts, ranging from simple boxes to entire rooms.

Leonard's interests were not Virginia's, but from time to time she accompanied him on his political excursions, which were not always to her taste. Of Mrs Sidney Webb, the Fabian Socialist, she wrote, 'She pounces on one, rather like a moulting eagle, with a bald neck and bloodstained beak.' When Leonard became Secretary to the Labour Party's Committees on International and Imperial Affairs, and a deeply committed Socialist, she thought it behoved her to contribute some of her own ideas. 'V. said we ought to give up all our capital', he noted in his diary. 'I said it was nonsense.' Undismayed, she took the chair of the Richmond Branch of the Women's Cooperative Guild, and held monthly meetings at which lectures were given by her friends to audiences which often numbered as few as twelve. It was like Morley College again, but with a change of subject. When she proposed a lecture on venereal disease, her women were deeply shocked. Virginia persisted with the chore for two years. There was no doubting the genuineness of her wish to understand the mentality of the working class, nor the nobility of her failure, but it could not be an activity central to her life. She had already embarked on her second novel, *Night and Day.*

In his autobiography, Leonard described how profoundly she immersed herself in her work, and the passage is worth quoting, for nobody knew better than him what her writing cost her in mental stress:

I have never known anyone work with more intense, more indefatigable, concentration than Virginia. This was particularly the case when she was writing a novel. The novel became part of her, and she herself was absorbed into the novel. She wrote only in the morning from 10 till 1, and usually she typed out in the afternoon what she had written by hand in the morning, but all day long, when she was walking through London streets or on the Sussex Downs, the book would be moving subconsciously in her mind, or she herself would be moving in a dreamlike way through the book. It was this intense absorption which made writing so mentally exhausting for her.

Leonard decided, with her full agreement, that Virginia needed a diversion, apart from walks and parties. Instead of proposing gardening or knitting, he revived an earlier idea to buy a printing press. 'It would take her mind completely off her work', he considered. He intended it not so much as therapy, to avert another mental attack, but as a recreation. They both thought of it that way, but as they decided that they would print and sell booklets, it was a more ambitious venture than a hobby, though Virginia once used that word to describe it. They were amateurs at the trade, but dedicated. They taught themselves, with the aid of a brochure and a friendly printer at Richmond Green, how to operate the handpress which they bought in April 1917 and put in the drawing-room at Hogarth House. After much labour, they issued their first booklet, *Two Stories*, of which one was by Leonard, and the other, *The Mark on the Wall*, by Virginia, illustrated with woodcuts by the Slade student, Dora Carrington, and sold it to their friends under their own imprint, the Hogarth Press, for one shilling and sixpence a copy. They printed 150 copies, and when twenty-seven were left, Leonard upped the price to two shillings. He intended to be not only a printer-publisher, but a businessman. Clive gave a copy to my mother before she had ever met Virginia. I treasured it after Vita's death, but was foolish enough to boast to a group of tourists that a copy had recently been sold at auction for £8,500. Two days later it was missing from Vita's bookshelves. I never saw it again.

Their difficulties were formidable. Leonard had chosen an occupation which required the handling of very small pieces of metal, a task impossible for a man whose hands trembled so violently, and he allotted it to Virginia, for whom it was certainly no rest-cure. She stood for hours sorting out the 'm's from 'n's, and arranged them on a printer's rule letter by letter, line by line, and when she had completed five lines, she handed them to Leonard who imposed them on his little machine. They could not print more than two pages at a time because they must reuse the type, being unable to afford to buy more. Virginia would take the text to pieces, inky though it was, and distribute the letters into their proper slots so that the process could be started all over again. Their earliest products were disfigured by incompetence. The typography was ugly, the printing and inking unequal, and the paper jackets often fell apart.

Unpredictably, Virginia enjoyed it. 'You can't think how exciting, soothing, ennobling and satisfying it is', she wrote to Margaret Llewelyn-Davies, and the adjectives were well chosen. It was not only the printing but the binding, of which she had had some practice as a child, that delighted her. For Leonard there was the additional pleasure of mastering a technique and organizing a business. He prided himself justifiably on having started the enterprise on a capital of only £20 (the cost of the handpress, type and essential tools) and sustained it for years on no further injection of money than was generated by sales. They had next to no overheads because their office was their house, they took no salaries for themselves, and when they began to employ assistants like Barbara Hiles and Ralph Partridge, they paid them a minimum wage. From the very start the Hogarth Press made a nominal profit.

Equally novel was their decision to publish poems and pamphlets that no commercial publisher would touch, and sell them exclusively by subscription. Leonard hoped to find a market for a new generation of writers, as Fry had fostered young artists by founding the Omega Workshop. The Woolfs could also publish their own books without having to endure the comments of outsiders like Gerald Duckworth. The third book issued by the Press was Katherine Mansfield's sixty-eight-page story *Prelude*, the fourth was T.S. Eliot's *Poems*, the fifth Virginia's *Kew Gardens*, and in 1920 E.M. Forster's *The Story of the Siren*. They limited themselves at first to two books a year, and when these were modestly successful, in 1921 they bought, at second-hand, a much larger press, a Minerva platen machine, operated by a foot-treadle. On this they printed Eliot's *The Waste Land*, 'which had a greater influence on English poetry,' Leonard remarked, 'indeed upon English literature, than any other book in the 20th century'. Virginia set the whole poem with her own hands, and Leonard printed it. At first it did not do well. Six months after publication, it had sold only 330 copies, on which the Press made a profit of £21 and Eliot earned £7. It was on this modest scale that it all began. Nobody knows what happened to the original handpress. It may have been thrown away. After printing a score more books on the platen machine, Leonard sold it to my mother in 1930, and it still stands, an inert chunk of metal like a medieval instrument of torture, in the oasthouse at Sissinghurst.

I must not exaggerate the pleasure that the Woolfs derived from the Press. It is true that its success is one of the legends of publishing. From its amateurish start it developed into a professional publishing firm which survives to this day. But instead of giving them an amusing recreation, like the flute-playing of Frederick the Great, it imposed on them endless chores. Virginia was obliged to spend hours of her time distributing and setting type, and reading other people's manuscripts when she longed to be writing her own, and there were inevitable misunderstandings with authors and artists. More than once they considered abandoning it ('It's worse than six children at the breast simultaneously', Virginia wrote in a moment of despair), but they never did.

Before acquiring *The Waste Land* they were offered James Joyce's *Ulysses*, its equal in audacity, but turned it down, partly because it would have taken them two years to set the type at their snail's pace and Leonard could find no commercial printer willing to risk prosecution for obscenity, and partly because Virginia herself found it distasteful. She thought it 'interesting as an experiment', but as she wrote to Nick Bagenal, 'I should hesitate to put it into the hands of Barbara [his wife] even though she is a married woman. The directness of the language and the choice of incidents . . . have raised a blush even upon such a cheek as mine.' It is the only recorded occasion when Virginia admitted that a book was more scatological than she could stomach. It has been said that she changed her mind on rereading it. I can find no evidence of this. In 1922 she wrote to Lytton, 'Never did I read such tosh. As for the first two chapters we will let them pass, but the 3rd, 4th, 5th, 6th – merely the scratching of pimples on the body of the bootboy at Claridges'. The book that the

Hogarth Press was never offered, and would most have liked, was Strachey's own *Eminent Victorians*, published in May 1918, which surprisingly made acceptable to a wide public Bloomsbury's deflationary attitude to pre-war heroes.

From Virginia's diaries and letters we can know what she was doing almost every day. The diary was to her like a hammock, for contemplation; the letters were like a trampoline, for literary exercise and gossip. The dominant tone of the diary was melancholy; of the letters, provocation and delight. She showed the diary to no one, and many of the letters must have been put away after a single reading. They are evidence of how extraordinarily full her life had become in the closing years of the war. She was busy with the Cooperatives, and constantly entertaining and being entertained. She was writing the last chapters of *Night and Day* without any of the labour and self-distrust that had brought her first novel to birth. She thought it 'a much more mature and finished and satisfactory book' than *The Voyage Out*, but later told Leonard that she wrote it 'as a kind of exercise', to show that she could write a traditional novel before experimenting with *Jacob's Room*. She said, 'I've never enjoyed any writing so much as I did the last half of *Night and Day*', but she barely mentioned it in her diary and almost never in her letters while she was writing it. One is given an occasional hint. On Armistice Day, 11 November 1918, she wrote to Vanessa, 'How am I to write my last chapter with all this shindy', the shindy being Richmond's victory celebrations outside Hogarth House. Most of her correspondence is about who has married, or is likely to marry, the beauty of the Sussex Downs, or descriptions of parties in the 1917 Club where left-wing politicians met young artists and intellectuals, or abuse of friends, affectionately or semi-maliciously, like her description of Will Arnold-Forster, whom she was determined to dislike because he had married Ka Cox, 'His mongrel cur's body, his face which appears powdered and painted like a very refined old suburban harlot's.' Or take this account of dining alone with Ottoline Morrell:

> It was a frigid success. The poor woman has broken out into eruptions which she tries to make dramatic by pasting pieces of black plaster on them – but they exude at the edges. It is a terrific business whipping her into life now. One has to bow and scrape and do all sorts of antics. ... When she said that I dressed so beautifully that I made her feel older and uglier than ever, I said, 'My dear Ottoline, like the Lombardy poplar you have only to stand up naked to put us all to shame.' She liked that.

These sallies were unkind. But they were written to amuse Vanessa for half a minute, not generations of scholars for a century.

It was to Vanessa that she most frequently wrote at this period, although for weeks at a time they lived only four miles apart. There was a certain defensiveness in Virginia's fencing with her sister, as if she was nervous of losing her. They had had a slight tiff over the reproduction of her woodcuts in *Kew Gardens*, and Vanessa had said that she wondered whether the Hogarth Press should not be given up; professional printers produced books so much better. This hurt Virginia. To her

Vanessa Bell in 1918 by Duncan Grant. To Virginia, 'Vanessa was a goddess, pagan "but with a natural piety", a madonna capable of bawdiness, sometimes mysteriously withdrawn, but vigorous, competent, serene.' National Portrait Gallery.

Vanessa was a goddess, pagan but 'with a natural piety', a madonna capable of bawdiness, sometimes mysteriously withdrawn but vigorous, competent, serene. She was valiant and strong, a magnet to attract the few she loved and to repel the many she found wanting. And she was a mother, now threefold. On Christmas Day 1918, a daughter was born to her at Charleston, to be named Angelica. She was not Clive's child, but Duncan's, as all Bloomsbury knew or surmised, except Angelica herself, who was not told the truth about her paternity until she was seventeen. In later life she wrote of her mother, 'Even if she said little, there emanated from her an enormous power, a pungency like the smell of crushed sage.'

It is something of a mystery how the Woolfs managed to spend so much money while earning so little. Leonard was now a prolific writer on international affairs and for some time he edited *The International Review*, but his fees and salary were exiguous. *Night and Day*, although it received excellent reviews, earned more for its publisher, Gerald Duckworth, than for its author. Her journalism brought in annually about £100. In its first four years the Hogarth Press's total net profit was £90. A little more was added by interest on Virginia's investments. But how did they manage on this income to keep two houses going in London and the country? That was not all. They rented for £15 a year three cottages in Cornwall which D.H. Lawrence had occupied during the war, and Leonard bought the freehold of Hogarth House and the house adjoining it for £1,950. Asheham was required by its landlord to house his bailiff, and they were obliged to give up the tenancy. Virginia, on impulse, bought the Round House (the stump of a windmill) in central Lewes for £300. There is no evidence that they ever spent a night in it, nor in the Cornish cottages, because in June 1919 they discovered Monk's House in the village of Rodmell, five miles from Lewes. They sold the Round House at a small profit, and bid successfully for Monk's House at the auction. It cost them £700.

Monk's House, and Charleston, its sister-house, have become more closely identified with Bloomsbury than any other buildings that survive. Vanessa and Duncan lived at Charleston until their deaths, while Monk's was Virginia's country home for the rest of her life, and Leonard's until he died in 1969. Both houses have been restored to more or less the condition that they knew, Charleston retaining many of its original decorations and paintings and Monk's its furniture. It was there, alternating with London, that Virginia wrote all her novels except the first two, and the simplicity of it is an indication of her taste and character.

It was not a beautiful house, and very uncomfortable. When they moved in from Asheham in September 1919, loading their books and furniture on two farm carts, like the Brontës on moving from Thornton to Haworth, there was no running water, no electricity, no bath, an evil-smelling earth-closet in the loft and only an oil stove to cook upon. The house had no extensive views from its windows, and its garden was a jungle. But it was the potential beauty of the orchard that made the greatest appeal to both of them, and the lawn from which they could look across the valley of the Ouse to the Downs. It was the last house on the lane that led down to the river. They could work undisturbed except for the tolling of the church bell and the shouts of small children in the school.

Very cautiously they made improvements, and risked

friendships by inviting guests to stay a night before the improvements were ready, but it was one of the pleasantest characteristics of Bloomsbury that they never craved luxury or complained of discomfort. Monk's House would never rate more than one star for bed and breakfast. I remember it in the Woolfs' days as a simple place, rather larger than a cottage, rather smaller than a house, not shabby exactly, but untidy, with saucers of pet food left on the floor and books on each tread of the narrow staircase. When they began to make money by Virginia's books, they added some amenities (the water-closet was named after Mrs Dalloway), but Leonard was no architect, and when *Orlando* made possible an annexe for Virginia's bedroom, he built it with no direct access from the house, no bathroom and no lavatory, and the gardener would gaze at her through the window as she lay in bed. They both lacked visual taste. The only objects to please the eye were chairs and tables from Omega and Vanessa's tiles around the fireplaces. Even the garden, which was Leonard's delight, was conceived by him on too grand a scale, with ornamental pools, urns and statues. Virginia once asked my mother what she thought of it, and Vita rather hesitantly replied, 'You can't recreate Versailles on a quarter-acre of Sussex. It just cannot be done.' Virginia acquired a wooden hut and put it in a corner of the garden from where she had a view of Mount Caburn. There she wrote her books during the summer months. After her death it was doubled in size for a studio. It should be halved again, to restore its shape and character.

In April 1920 she began to write her third novel, *Jacob's Room*, her first truly experimental book. It was 'the things one doesn't say', the art of suggesting important truths by deviousness, that she now began to explore, the delineation of character not by direct description but by the behaviour of other people around them. She wrote to a new friend, Gerald Brenan, in one of the few letters where she discussed her work, 'The human soul, it seems to me, orientates itself afresh every now and then. It is doing so now. No one can see it whole, therefore. The best of us catch a glimpse of a nose, a shoulder, something turning away, always in movement. Still, it seems better to me to catch this glimpse, than to sit down with Hugh Walpole, Wells etc etc, and make large oil paintings of fabulous fleshy monsters complete from top to toe.' Other writers were too conventional or too frivolous, even Lytton Strachey, whose *Queen Victoria* she admired with reservations. 'I think one is a little conscious of being entertained', she wrote to him. 'It's a little too luxurious reading – I mean, one is willing perhaps to take more pains than you allow.' She had put her finger on the spot, gently, and then lifted it again. When Lytton asked if he might dedicate the book to her, she agreed, insisting on 'Virginia Woolf', not just 'V.W.', in case some Victoria Worms or Vincent Woodhouse would snatch the compliment from her.

The only writer for whom she felt acute jealousy was Katherine Mansfield. They were attempting to transform fiction in the same sort of way, and Virginia sometimes suspected that Katherine was the more successful. In character, they were opposites. Katherine, a New Zealander, six years younger than Virginia, was abrasive more than provocative, sexually more audacious, less anxious to impress and please, alarming, vulgar even. While Virginia was capable of hurting people's feelings and then regretted it, Katherine didn't care:

she would do it again. She could be as envious of Virginia as Virginia was of her. While courteous to each other when they met, they were highly critical when apart. In reviewing *Night and Day*, Katherine called it 'old-fashioned', 'reeking with snobbery', which deeply hurt Virginia, and she decided, but only in the privacy of her diary, that their friendship 'was almost entirely founded on quicksands'. She admitted her jealousy ('the more she is praised, the more I am convinced that she is bad'), but when Katherine died of tuberculosis in 1923, aged thirty-four, Virginia wrote movingly about her, expressing relief that she had 'a rival the less', but, 'it seemed to me that there is no point in writing: Katherine won't read it'. They had stimulated, angered, each other, flint against stone. When Joanne Trautmann and I were editing Virginia's letters, we searched despairingly for her letters to Katherine, as their correspondence would probably be the most important in both their lives, but we found only one letter of three lines, a false note of congratulations on Katherine's *Bliss*. When Professor Trautmann was editing the one-volume edition of the letters, which she called *Congenial Spirits*, she was able to include one other, much longer letter, in which Virginia complimented Katherine on her style: 'You seem to me to go so straightly and directly – all clear as glass – refined, spiritual', while to Janet Case, a year later, she castigated it: 'I read *Bliss*, and it was so brilliant – so hard, and so shallow, and so sentimental that I had to rush to the bookcase for something to drink', by which she meant Shakespeare. It was a difficult relationship, with love and envy on both sides.

In these post-war years Bloomsbury gathered itself together again. Thirteen of them formed a society called the Memoir Club, which endured until 1956, the younger members replacing those who died. Its purpose was strange: to read to each other recollections of their youth. The papers were written to entertain, and truth was frequently sacrificed to fantasy. When some of them were published many years later, the qualifications and note of ribaldry were missing. Virginia's unkind account of George Duckworth, for example, has ever since stained the reputation of that conventional but fundamentally decent man. In public Bloomsbury had much to be reticent about, though certainly not ashamed. They had settled into separate but intercommunicating pools. There were the Woolfs at Rodmell, so happy together that Virginia considered that there was no more contented couple in the country. There was Garsington, where Ottoline Morrell offered Bloomsberries generous hospitality, only to be rewarded by their ridicule, though Virginia, who was not slow to join in, would admit to Ottoline's 'fundamental integrity' and 'an element of the superb'. There was the Mill at Tidmarsh, where Lytton Strachey cohabited with Carrington, who loved him, while he loved Ralph Partridge, who was to marry her. And there was Charleston, the hub of the entire circuit, where Vanessa presided with her lover Duncan Grant and David Garnett. It was when a cousin, Dorothea Stephen, expressed disapproval of Vanessa's morals and hesitated to meet her, that Virginia discarded her pen for a flame-thrower: 'I could not let you come here without saying that I entirely sympathise with Vanessa's view and conduct'. It was not just loyalty to a sister. It was confirmation that Bloomsbury people could live with whomever they chose, whatever their sex, because they loved them, and that was more moral than continuing for propriety's sake to live with someone whom you had ceased to love in any meaningful way.

From time to time Virginia was too ill to work. In the summer of 1921 she was so often bedridden with fluctuating headaches and sleeplessness, symptoms of an approaching breakdown, that she sometimes feared that she had not long to live. When she recovered from these spasms, she usually convalesced in Cornwall, and on returning to London would immediately resume her social life. She never moped. She expressed self-distrust but never self-pity. Much as she loved the quietness of Rodmell, she enticed her friends to visit her there, and in London scarcely had a meal alone with Leonard. When invited out, her defiance of convention was forgiven for the sake of the brilliance of her talk. Dining with Nellie Cecil, 'I said all the most impossible things in a very loud voice ... abused Lady Glenconner, and then attacked Rupert Brooke: but at my age and with my habits, how conform to the way of the world? Hairpins dropped steadily into my soup-plate: I gave them a lick, and put them in again.' When she chose, she could be decorous, and rather enjoyed high society, but it was at supper in Hogarth House with Eliot or Strachey when she felt most content.

She was a generous person, not so much with money, for she had little to spare, but with her time and patience. She wrote long letters to Jacques Raverat because he was dying of multiple sclerosis. She did her utmost to save T.S. Eliot from the drudgery of working in a bank when he could be writing immortal poetry. With Ezra Pound and Ottoline Morrell she organized an Eliot Fund, appealing to her friends to donate £10 a year towards his upkeep, but Bloomsbury was poor, and suspected that Pound might spend their £10 on drink, so that the fund never topped £100, and Eliot, squirming with embarrassment, suddenly declared that he must be guaranteed £500 a year for five years before he could consider leaving the bank. Virginia's campaign had been heroic. She disliked asking friends for money as much as he disliked receiving it, and she confessed in her diary that she wished Eliot had more spunk in him. They wound up the fund, giving him a paltry £50, but that was not the limit of Virginia's efforts on his behalf. She tried to persuade Maynard Keynes, who had taken control of the *Nation*, the highbrow weekly, to offer Eliot the literary editorship, but after much shilly-shallying he refused it, and the job was given, to their surprise, to Leonard.

The Woolfs' careers were now in full spate. Leonard stood for Parliament, and to their joint relief failed to be elected. The Hogarth Press never wavered in its ascent from obscurity. When Ralph Partridge was eased out by Leonard for insufficient dedication to the Press, they hired George (Dadie) Rylands to take his place, but the work imposed on the two founders was still crushing. Having spent most afternoons setting type and machining it, they would set out for the bookshops, attempting to sell their wares to a mostly indifferent trade, and even toyed with the idea of opening a bookshop or picture gallery of their own.

Their most provocative new publication was Virginia's *Jacob's Room*. It puzzled the literary world. Its treatment of fiction was so original that critics hesitated to abuse it for fear that they might be overlooking a masterpiece. It was not a consecutive narrative, but more like a shuffled pack of cards or slides for a lecture arranged in no logical order. Virginia explained that it was an 'experiment', which she intended to develop in her next book, and before long she started to write *Mrs Dalloway*, finding it immensely difficult, and to put in order some of her past essays for *The Common Reader*.

Her concentration on her own work never dulled her interest in other people's. She was teaching herself Russian in order to help Samuel Koteliansky with his translations of Tolstoy's love letters. She continued to study Homer. She discovered the novels of Rebecca West, whom she had never met, 'a brave, clever woman', she decided, 'who sometimes writes a few words very nicely', which from Virginia was high praise. Proust, whose great work she was steadily absorbing, left her 'in a state of amazement, as if a miracle were being done before my eyes. One has to put the book down and gasp.' She thought Anthony Trollope's *The Small House at Allington* 'perhaps the most perfect of English novels'. She even found time for the Old Testament, but it could not compete with Proust. 'I don't think God comes well out of it', was her comment on the Book of Job.

In April 1923 they went abroad for the first time since their honeymoon in 1912. They travelled through France and Spain to Madrid and Granada, and continued by bus and mule to Yegen, a remote village in the Sierra Nevada where Gerald Brenan, ex-soldier and romantic, had isolated himself in a small cottage to study great works of literature, and, if possible, add to them himself. Out of friendship for him, Ralph Partridge had induced Lytton to visit him in the previous year, and Carrington, now Ralph's wife, went with them. No man was less suited to arduous travel than Lytton Strachey. He suffered terribly. The oil-soaked Spanish food upset his stomach. Their journey, at first by bus, then by cart, finally by mules zigzagging up the mountain tracks or wallowing belly-deep in swollen rivers, utterly exhausted him. When they finally reached Brenan's cottage, he found that the only lavatory was a board with a hole in it poised over the chicken-run. Then Carrington and Brenan fell in love. It was too much. All this he related to Virginia as a warning, but it did not deter her. Everyone considered her too fragile to attempt such an ordeal, but she loved it. Unhappily, her diary of the expedition is lost, but we have Brenan's tribute in his book *South from Granada* that 'though quiet, she was as excited as a schoolgirl'. She spent ten days with him, and three days in Paris on their return. She spared her friends any account of her achievement. 'How dull travellers' stories are!', she wrote to Molly MacCarthy as a caution to all of us. 'I omit all about the adventures, with the mule, the vulture, and the wolf. Your imagination can play freely upon them.'

VI

FROM MURCIA IN Spain Virginia wrote to Vita Sackville-West, my mother. They had met for the first time only a few months before. Her letter was to refuse Vita's suggestion that Virginia might care to join the PEN Club, an international literary society which discussed not so much literature as authors. Virginia's letter was kindly expressed but in effect it was a snub. Vita had misunderstood her character. She thought that because Bloomsbury was a sort of society, Virginia must be clubbable, and would enjoy discussing with other writers, most of whom would be strangers to her, the difficulties of their trade. It was a curious mistake for Vita to have made, because she herself was equally secretive about her writing. It seemed that her bloomer would put an end to their friendship scarcely before it had begun.

They had met in December 1922, dining with Clive Bell, and four days later Vita invited her to dinner with Clive and Desmond MacCarthy. From Vita's point of view, the party was a great success. She wrote to my father, 'I simply adore Virginia Woolf, and so would you. You would fall quite flat before her charm and personality. She is utterly unaffected. She dresses quite atrociously. I've rarely taken such a fancy to anyone.' Virginia's account of Vita in her diary was less flattering: 'Not much to my severer taste – florid, moustached, parakeet coloured, with all the supple ease of the aristocracy, but not the wit of the artist.' All the same, she invited Vita to Hogarth House, and their friendship, if not their intimacy, grew: 'Dined with Virginia at Richmond. She is as delicious as ever.' 'Lunched with her in Tavistock Square, where she had just arrived. Went on to see Mama [Lady Sackville], my head swimming with Virginia.' Her admiration was not yet reciprocated, and then came the PEN episode, which nearly put a stop to it.

They were reaching out to touch with fingertips what can only be grasped by the whole hand, leaving time and space for retreat if either of them came to regret it. It took two years

Vita Sackville-West, a photograph by Lenare taken in 1927 during her short affair with Virginia. 'Here we have Vita, exceedingly bold at one moment, and exceedingly shy at the next, falling in love with Virginia, ten years older than herself, and scared of her.'

70

for their friendship to develop into intimacy, and three for intimacy to be acknowledged on both sides as love. It was so unlikely a friendship that their biographers have all reached different interpretations of it. Here we have Vita, exceedingly bold at one moment and exceedingly shy at the next, falling in love with Virginia, ten years older than herself, and scared of her. Bloomsbury was too clever for her, and deliberately alarming to strangers. 'Ever heard of Moore?', Virginia asked Vita. 'You mean George Moore, the novelist?' 'No, no, no – G.E. Moore, the philosopher', of whom Vita had never heard. Early in their relationship, Vita and my father were invited to dine in Gordon Square with Virginia, Leonard, Vanessa, Duncan Grant, Clive and Lytton Strachey. It was all too obviously designed as an occasion to inspect Virginia's new friend. Lytton sneered at my father's life of Tennyson (published on that very day), and Harold, recoiling from his contempt, relapsed into silence. In sympathy, so did Vita. Two days later Virginia wrote in her diary, 'It was a rocky steep evening. ... We judged them both incurably stupid.'

Harold was not a stupid man, but Vita, when ill at ease, could be slow-witted. When she was at her writing-table, ideas pullulated from her brain as if from a cornucopia, but in company with more than one or two people, her conversation was apt to be halting. She lacked the gift of repartee: she could not turn a challenging question to her own advantage, an art at which Bloomsbury excelled. What's more, in their eyes she was old-fashioned. Her pastoral poem *The Land* was contrasted with *The Waste Land* (the very titles pointing up the difference) and found wanting. She had no taste for classical music, and thought Duncan's and Vanessa's panels in Tavistock Square 'of inconceivable hideousness'. It is not surprising that Vanessa considered Vita 'an unnecessary importation into our society', and was astonished by Virginia's growing intimacy with her, if not actually jealous. 'Has your Vita gone?', she once wrote to her sister. 'Don't expend all your energies on writing to her. I consider that I have first claim.'

What, then, caused this uneasy relationship to develop into a love-affair? What was Vita's attraction for Virginia? In the first place, Vita had had a fruitier past. There was her ancestry, and the Sackvilles' great house, Knole, which aroused Virginia's historical senses like the smell of pot-pourri in an antique bowl, but not, I think, her snobbishness, since she had no use for the aristocracy unless, like David Cecil, they also possessed the qualities she sought in other people. Vita herself had reacted against her family's traditions, while honouring them. It was her *Knole and the Sackvilles* that had first caught Virginia's attention. But Vita refused to play the role expected of the only child of so great a dynasty. From the age of fourteen, without any encouragement from her parents, she had written plays and full-length romances with astonishing exuberance, some of them in French and Italian, which she spoke fluently. She was indifferent to the playmates whom her mother enticed to Knole for tea parties: she locked them up in the toolshed, and stifled their cries of protest by stuffing their noses with putty. As she grew to débutante age, she was very beautiful, dark and lustrous, and was courted by 'every little dancing thing in London', as she described them. She could have been châtelaine of Belvoir or Harewood, houses as famous as Knole itself, but she chose to marry Harold Nicolson, a penniless third secretary in the Foreign Office.

That was not all. While still an adolescent, she recognized

in herself an attraction towards her own sex rather than to boys and men. She had a sentimental love-affair with a foolish girl called Rosamund Grosvenor, and then dropped her for Violet Trefusis, daughter of Alice Keppel, Edward VII's mistress. Only a year or two before she met Virginia she eloped with Violet to France, to be retrieved by their two husbands in a dramatic scene at Amiens which has become, in print and film, a notorious incident in the history of the British upper classes.

All this Virginia knew, and was impressed by it. There was the further attraction that Vita was also a writer, better-known in 1922 than Virginia herself, for besides her early novels, she was a poet too, and a critic good enough to be judged by Leonard worthy to contribute regular book reviews to the *Nation*. They could discuss literature together not on equal terms, for Vita acknowledged Virginia's superior gift, which Virginia did not trouble to deny, but with a common background in the literature of the past, and they corresponded endlessly. The letters of one took fire from the other's. How much more entertaining were Virginia's letters to Vita than those she had written to Violet Dickinson, and Vita's to Virginia than those to another Violet. There were occasions when Virginia could not suppress admiration for Vita's writing. 'A pen of brass', was her dismissive verdict to Jacques Raverat, which is often quoted to indicate her contempt, but it was not typical. She saw in *The Land* a talent of which she was incapable, in *Seducers in Ecuador* (which she published) a cleverness which she could hardly have suspected from Vita's conversation, and of *Passenger to Teheran* she wrote to Vita, 'Yes – I think it is awfully good. I didn't know the extent of your subtleties', and meant it. Vita, she discovered, had a 'rich, dusky attic of a mind'. In Victoria Glendinning's phrase about *Seducers*, Vita had 'out-Bloomsburied Bloomsbury'. In the same issue of the *New York Evening Post* it was reviewed jointly with *Mrs Dalloway*, but it was *Seducers* that headed the column with high commendation, while Virginia's book was considered more shortly as 'a fog of words'.

It was said that Vita was like a mother to Virginia, but I can find no evidence of this. Their relationship, though tentative at first, was always on the level, protective, perhaps, on Vita's side, but not maternal, nor submissive on Virginia's. They were mutually solicitous and provocative. Vita seemed astonished that Virginia should love her carnally (Virginia's word), and when in December 1925 they first slept together at Long Barn, Vita's house near Knole, it seems to have been as much on Virginia's initiative as on the more experienced Vita's. As Mitchell Leaska has astutely commented, 'Vita seemed forever fanning the embers of passion yet forever stepping back from its blaze.' She was flattered, naturally, but fearful of arousing in Virginia passions that might ignite a fresh attack of madness. 'For heaven's sake be careful', Harold warned her when she confessed to him. 'It's not merely playing with fire; it's playing with gelignite.' He need not have worried. Their affair continued, on and off, for about three years, without damaging either of them.

More puzzling is Virginia's attitude. She was not a deeply sensual woman. Her affection for Violet Dickinson and Madge Vaughan had been more sentimental than physical, but she confessed to herself that women attracted her more than men. Towards the end of 1924, when her friendship with Vita was intensifying, she wrote in her diary, 'If one could be friendly with women, what a pleasure – the relationship so secret and private compared with relations with men!' But when, a year later, after the Vita affair had begun, she asked herself who were essential to her happiness, she named six people – Leonard, Vanessa, Duncan, Clive, Lytton and E.M. Forster – only one of whom was a woman, and Vita was not mentioned at all. She expressed no fear, and no shame, in undertaking at the age of forty-three the only love-affair of her life. Rather, she was curious about her own reaction to it, as Vanessa was when Virginia told her about it one day when they were shopping, and Vanessa asked her how one woman could make love to another. Virginia did not record her reply, and worded her account of what was happening ambiguously, even in her diary. 'These Sapphists', she wrote, as if she were not one herself, 'love women. Friendship is never untinged with amorosity.' She found homosexual relations between men distasteful. 'Have you any views on loving one's own sex?', she asked Raverat. 'All the young men are so inclined, and I can't help finding it mildly foolish, though I have no particular reason. For one thing they all tend to the pretty and ladylike. They paint and powder. ... Then the ladies, either in self-protection, or in imitation or genuinely, are given to their sex too', and then follows a fanciful account of Vita's elopement with Violet, not to either woman's credit.

Does all this covering-up indicate that Virginia considered that she was doing wrong, or was it an attempt to minimize scandal about her and Vita? Undoubtedly she was anxious not to distress Leonard. When he heard of the affair, she laughed it off and told him not to worry. Their marriage was not threatened by it. If Harold did not mind (in fact he thought it would do Vita much good), nor should Leonard.

But the two marriages, though similar in several ways, were not identical. Leonard was not a homosexual like Harold, and he spent almost every day with Virginia, while Harold at the beginning and height of the affair was in Teheran at the British Legation. Vita wrote to him an almost daily commentary on it, telling him, 'One's love for Virginia is a very different thing, a mental thing, a spiritual thing if you like, an intellectual thing, and she inspires a feeling of tenderness which I suppose is because of the funny mixture of hardness and softness. . . . Also she loves me, which flatters and pleases me.' Then she added, 'I am scared to death of arousing physical feelings in her because of the madness'. Presumably Leonard cautioned Virginia too, but he seemed to be more bored than worried. It is not surprising that Vita saw Leonard as 'a funny, grim, solitary creature' in contrast to Virginia, who was an angel of wit and intelligence.

It was at this period that I first came to know her. In 1924 I was seven years old, and my brother Ben was nine. She often came to Long Barn for a night or two, and we greatly looked forward to her visits, being ignorant of their cause. (A woman, who should have known better, once said to me, 'You realise that Virginia loves your mother', to which I innocently replied, 'Yes, of course she does: we all do.') Virginia was not particularly fond of children apart from Vanessa's, and except for James in *To the Lighthouse*, they do not figure largely in her novels. But she was interested in us, because children, like eccentrics, are unusual people, and under the guise of amusing us she would amuse herself: 'Tell me, what have you done this morning?' 'Well, nothing much.' 'No, no, that won't do. What woke you up?' 'The sun, coming through our bedroom window.' 'Was it a happy sun or an angry sun?' We answered that somehow, and then it was dressing: 'Which sock did you put on first, right or left?' And breakfast, and so on, right up to the moment when we came to find her. It was a lesson in observation, but it was also a hint: 'Unless you catch ideas on the wing and nail them down, you will soon cease to have any.' It was advice that I was to remember all my life.

We did not think of her as famous: indeed, when we first knew her, she wasn't. She was more like a favourite aunt who brightened our simple lives with unexpected questions: 'What is the French mistress like? What sort of shoes does she wear? Can you smell her scent when she comes into the classroom?' Apart from the butterfly-hunting, she seemed to us an indoor person, autumnal more than summery, happiest when warming her hands at a log fire, and talking, talking, talking, in a deep, slightly sing-song voice, teasing, provocative, drawing back her hair from her forehead as if to clear her mind. It is with Long Barn that I mainly associate her, but we would often go to Knole, where she would lean S-curved against a doorway, finger to her chin, contemplative, amused. I do not remember thinking her beautiful, but children's taste is for prettiness not beauty. Although Vita exaggerated in saying that she dressed 'atrociously,' she cared little for her appearance, hating make-up and being fitted by shop assistants, and bought loose, unemphatic clothes off the peg, which draped around her like folded wings.

Occasionally Vita would take one of us to Monk's House when she was not staying the night there, and one incident remains very clearly in my memory. Besides Virginia and Leonard, the only people present were Keynes and his wife Lydia Lopokova, the ballerina. We sat in the larger of the two sitting-rooms, and the discussion (I forget what it was about)

Nigel (left) and Ben Nicolson with Virginia Woolf at Knole in 1928, when she was writing *Orlando*. 'She would lean S-curved against a doorway, finger to her chin, contemplative, amused.'

grew animated. Virginia, standing by the fireplace, was arguing excitedly, when Leonard slowly rose from his chair and gently touched her on the shoulder. Without enquiry or protest, she followed him from the room, and they were absent for about a quarter of an hour. Nobody made any comment when they returned, since everyone except myself knew exactly what had happened. In her excitement, Virginia might overstep the bounds of sanity, and Leonard, observing her closely, took her away to calm down. When I read in some feminist accounts of their relationship allegations that Leonard neglected her, even drove her to suicide, I think of that incident. The gesture with which he touched her on the shoulder was almost biblical in its tenderness, and her submission to him indicated a trust that she awarded to no other person.

VII

IN MARCH 1924 they left Richmond for 52 Tavistock Square in Bloomsbury, dragging the Hogarth Press with them. The move was dictated by Leonard's desire to live closer to his work, and Virginia's for the society of her friends. Hogarth House was too remote. But their new house lacked the calm of Richmond. It was a sandwich, the Woolfs occupying the two top floors and the Press the basement, the offices of a solicitor lying between them. Virginia chose to write in a back room next to the Press, sitting in a moulting armchair with a board on her knee, and as it was also the stockroom, she was constantly interrupted by the assistants, who succeeded each other in quick rotation, such was Leonard's severity as an employer and so poor the pay. Even Dadie Rylands, whom they both liked, fled back to Cambridge after a few months.

It was in these conditions that Virginia finished *Mrs Dalloway*. It made great demands on her, particularly when she was describing the madness and suicide of Septimus Warren Smith. It was published in April 1925, a few weeks after *The Common Reader*. The two books were inevitably contrasted by the critics, the novel arousing bewilderment for its deliberate mistiness, 'the half-light of experience', the essays praise for their lucidity and wit. Vita, not wishing to offend or to be considered stupid, settled for 'will-of-the-wisp' for *Mrs Dalloway* and 'a guide, philosopher and friend' for *The Common Reader*. Virginia considered that hardly anyone had grasped her intention, 'but that's the penalty we pay for breaking with tradition'. Lytton Strachey thought the novel flawed, and Virginia, always vulnerable to criticism, felt more inclined to trust his judgment than Clive Bell's, who declared it to be a masterpiece, as did E.M. Forster and Jacques Raverat, who read the proofs as he lay dying, and dictated to his wife a letter which gave Virginia 'one of the happiest days of my life'. For many readers *Mrs Dalloway* meant too much hard work. Arnold Bennett admitted in a review, 'It beat me; I could not finish it'. In her famous essay, 'Mr Bennett and Mrs Brown', which she adapted as a lecture to a Cambridge literary society, Virginia answered him, explaining that she had hoped to change the whole direction of fiction-writing. She had already written in her diary: 'The method of writing smooth narrative can't be right. Things don't happen in one's mind like that. We experience, all the time, an overlapping of images and ideas, and modern novels should convey our mental confusion instead of neatly rearranging it. The reader must sort it out.' Less sophisticated readers were unconvinced. In reply to Violet Dickinson's letter of despair, Virginia advised her to give it up, and that was the end of that relationship.

She made new friends warily: Raymond Mortimer, Hugh Walpole, Vita's first cousin Edward Sackville-West. She could find little to admire in young men: she thought them insipid. Young women like Janet Vaughan, Rose Macaulay, Frances Marshall (Partridge to be), Carrington and Rebecca West had more spunk in them, more pride, and were less anxious to please. She and Leonard were increasingly reluctant to spend weekends away from home. They found it disagreeable to be under the constraint of other people's habits and hospitality, and to be forced to mix cordially with their neighbours. After one such winter visit to the Arnold-Forsters in Cornwall, Virginia thought it necessary, like many another weekend guest, to simulate the pleasure she had not felt. To Ka, her hostess, she wrote, 'I can't think how you manage such comfort and warmth in that howling blizzard': but to Vanessa, 'We fled from Zennor a day early, unable to stand the perishing cold'.

Monk's House was little better, but it was slowly acquiring the basic conveniences that they had lacked for seven years. 'Mrs Dalloway's lavatory' and hot water on tap were operating in time to comfort Virginia when she was obliged, once more, to spend months in bed with recurrent headaches. Her illnesses alternated with moves to London and back again, at the very period when she was longing to make progress with *To the Lighthouse*. When she was well enough to write, it came easily to her. 'I am now writing as fast and freely as I have written in the whole of my life', she confided to her diary when she was at Rodmell, but it was not the same in Tavistock Square. 'To write a novel in the heart of London', she told Vita, 'is next to an impossibility. I feel as if I were nailing a flag to the top of a mast in a raging gale.'

Vita was in Persia. In the years 1926 and 1927 she made two visits there, to join Harold in Teheran for a month or two, and her correspondence with Virginia gained on both sides a new intensity. They were not explicitly love-letters, for discretion's sake, but they were by implication. Virginia to Vita: 'No letter from you. Why not? Only a scrap from Dover, and a wild melancholy adorable moan from Trieste. No photograph either. Goodbye, dearest shaggy creature.' Vita to Virginia: 'It's incredible how essential to me you have become. Damn you, spoilt creature. I shan't make you love me any the more by giving myself away like this. But you have broken down my defences.' That was all very well. Vita was accompanied on both her journeys to the East by Dorothy Wellesley, another lover, and was writing ahead to Harold in Teheran letters as ardent as those she was writing back to Virginia in London. She did not consider it deceitful. She was simply sharing her affections between them. When she reached Teheran, having dumped Dorothy in India, she hardly mentioned her husband in her letters. She exchanged with Virginia common distastes, hers for smart diplomatic parties, Virginia's for their London equivalents, 'those damned people sitting smug round their urn, their fire, their tea-table. ... I felt inclined to leave them all alone, for ever and ever, these tea-parties, these Ottolines, these mumbling sodomitical old maids.'

Such moods were frequent with her. Once she was persuaded by Leonard to spend a day with his brother Herbert and his wife, who lived at Cookham in Berkshire. Herbert was a stockbroker, lacking all intellectual interests, and Virginia, instead of ridiculing them as was her custom, reflected how comforting it would be never to have heard of Roger, or Clive, or Duncan, or Lytton. 'Oh this is life, I kept saying to myself; and what is Bloomsbury, or Long Barn either, but a contortion, a temporary knot;' she wrote to Vita, 'and why do I pity and deride the human race, when its lot is profoundly peaceful and happy? They have nothing to wish for. They are entirely simple and sane.'

It is doubtful whether Herbert mentioned the Stock Exchange or Leonard the problems of the Hogarth Press, for shop talk, by common convention, was taboo. Yet the Press was causing them much worry. They were still printing and binding pamphlets like Laura Riding's *Voltaire* and Robert Trevelyan's *Poems*. Longer books, like Virginia's own novels and Vita's *Passenger to Teheran*, they delegated to commercial printers, but their time, which Leonard would have preferred to devote to journalism, books and politics, and Virginia to her novels, was eroded by their mechanical tasks, packing parcels and interviewing booksellers and salesman. Was it worth this incessant drudgery? In 1927 their net profit was only £27. But they persisted. They considered buying David Garnett's bookshop, and publishing the works of Freud in translation. They abandoned Garnett, but Freud they carried through, though it is doubtful whether Virginia read a word of him.

The General Strike of May 1926 was more of an excitement than a diversion. The Hogarth Press was only marginally affected by it, because their sole employees, Angus Davidson and a secretary, did not strike, and printing by outside firms was interrupted only for the nine days that the strike lasted.

Leonard and Virginia Woolf at Monk's House in 1926, with Pinka (Flush) in the foreground. A photograph taken by Vita.

The main public services were kept going by volunteers. Buses, underground trains and taxis no longer ran, but London's traffic was sustained by bicycle and its communications by telephone and the radio. The strike obliged Virginia to take political sides. Hitherto she had been lukewarm. Now, in support of Leonard, she stood by the strikers, if not as valiantly as he did. 'If ever a general strike was justified', he wrote in his Memoirs, 'it was in 1926', and he organized in their support a petition by leading intellectuals which only Galsworthy refused to sign. The strike was suddenly settled, to the disadvantage of the miners who had started it. 'Everyone is jubilant', Virginia reported to Vanessa. 'We are going to have a strike dinner, and drink champagne with Clive, the Frys, and other spirits.' Her support for the strikers was couched in terms of dislike for authority, including the Prime Minister, Stanley Baldwin, whose radio appeal she thought ridiculous. She did not explain her reasons, not even in *A Room of One's Own*, where she quoted Baldwin's broadcast. She was as uncertain in her political judgments as Leonard was firm in his.

It was in the middle of this shindy that she wrote the magical chapter in *To the Lighthouse*, 'Time Passes'. On Vita's return from her first journey to Persia, their love-affair continued intermittently with exchange visits to Rodmell and Long Barn. Virginia was at heart more passionate, Vita on paper more outspoken. While Virginia could write in her diary, 'It is a spirited, creditable affair, I think innocent (spiritually) and all gain I think, rather a bore for Leonard, but not enough to worry him', there was no 'I think' in Vita's replies from Persia on her second visit in 1927: 'I always get devastated when I hear from you. God, I do love you. You say I use no endearments. That strikes me as funny, when I wake in the Persian dawn, and say to myself, "Virginia, Virginia" '.

After two months in Teheran ('God, the people here!', by whom she meant not the Persians but the diplomatists and their wives), she embarked with Harold and two friends on an arduous crossing of the Bakhtiari mountains to the Persian Gulf, the subject of her second book of Persian travels, *Twelve Days*. At the same time Virginia and Leonard were in Italy, loving it so much ('We found wild cyclamen and marble lapped by the water') that they thought of taking a villa in Rome's Campagna. Vita and Virginia reunited in May, exhilarated by work and travel. Each was buoyed up by success. *The Land* won the Hawthornden Prize, and *To the Lighthouse*, the Femina Prize, England's two most prestigious literary awards. The reviews of Virginia's book were favourable but cautious, as if the critics felt themselves to be on trial as much as the author, Arnold Bennett acknowledging that it was 'an improvement' on *Mrs Dalloway*, but he was still disconcerted by her fragmentary style, as was Aldous Huxley, who wrote that she had lost touch with the real world. Edwin Muir wrote of 'Time Passes', 'For imagination and beauty of writing it is probably not surpassed in contemporary prose'. But the verdict which Virginia most anxiously awaited was Vanessa's. The book was written in recollection of their childhood holidays in Cornwall. Mr Ramsay was a portrait of Leslie Stephen, Mrs Ramsay of their mother, and 'James' of their brother Adrian. The lighthouse was not in the Hebrides as she pretended, but at Godrevy, across the bay from St Ives. She need not have worried. Vanessa wrote her a long letter of gratitude: 'You have given a portrait of mother which is more like her to me than anything I could have conceived of as possible. It is almost painful to have her so raised from the dead.' The book sold well in England and America, and with the profits, the Woolfs bought their first car, a second-hand Singer, which Virginia never learnt to drive.

Vita's return from the Bakhtiari was followed by two overnight expeditions. She went to Oxford to hear Virginia lecture to undergraduates on Poetry and Fiction, and on 28–9 June 1927, with Harold, Leonard, Quentin and Edward Sackville-West, they took the night train to Yorkshire to view the total eclipse of the sun in a cloudy dawn. I have photographs of the occasion. The party looks dismally cold and unbreakfasted. Virginia wrote in her diary, 'Then it was all over till 1999'. It was startling to find her reaching so far into the future to nominate the very year (in fact the actual day, 11 August 1999, on which I was writing these lines) when to English observers the sun would next be extinguished by the moon. She recalled the whole episode in the final pages of *The Waves*.

VIII

THEN CAME *Orlando*. *Mrs Dalloway* had made Virginia known. *To the Lighthouse* made her well known. *Orlando* made her famous.

She was anxious to start on *The Waves* as soon as she had finished 'Phases of Fiction', which she planned as a short history of English literature, but she put both aside when an idea flashed into her mind. She wrote to Vita:

Yesterday morning I was in despair. . . . I couldn't screw a word from me; and at last dropped my head in my hands, dipped my pen in the ink, and wrote these words, as if automatically, on a clean sheet: Orlando: a Biography. No sooner had I done this than my body was flooded with rapture and my brain with ideas. I wrote rapidly till 12. . . . But listen: suppose Orlando turns out to be Vita; and it's all about you and the lusts of your flesh and the lure of your mind (heart you have none, who go gallivanting down the lanes with Campbell) . . . shall you mind?

Vita did not in the least mind. She was enchanted. But when she came to quote this letter in a broadcast many years after Virginia's death, she omitted the words 'lusts of your flesh' and the reference to Campbell, because the book, although in one sense it was a hymn of gratitude for all the happiness that Vita had given her, in another it was a reproach for deserting her for Mary Campbell, Vita's new lover. Campbell might be younger and more luscious, but Virginia had the better mind. She would recapture Vita by writing a book about her, so ingenious, so affectionate that Vita would be unable to resist its appeal.

Mary Campbell was the wife of the South African poet Roy Campbell. They had come to live in Vita's village, and when she discovered them, she invited them to move into the cottage (*our* cottage, when we were at boarding school), where they could live rent-free and Mary could easily slip down the garden path to the main house where Vita lived. She had fallen deeply in love with Mary. In a single night, when Mary was away, she wrote twelve sonnets to her, some of which the Hogarth Press later published. Roy found out about the affair and was furious. Kitchen knives were brandished. Then he threatened to commit suicide. Vita rushed to Virginia and sobbed her heart out. *Orlando* was one result.

There were other family links. Harold Nicolson had just published *Some People*, a collection of stories which he had written during lonely evenings in Teheran, developing a new form of fiction, half true, half fantasy, in which real people like Harold himself were put in imaginary situations, and imaginary people in real situations. Virginia was impressed by Harold's book: he was not as stupid as she once thought. She reviewed it in the *New York Herald Tribune* under the heading, 'The New Biography', and something of its manner crept into *Orlando*, elaborating his fact-cum-fiction into an elegant arabesque. She would turn Orlando from man into woman halfway through the book, to suggest that human nature, especially Vita's, is androgynous, 'that a woman could be as tolerant and free-spoken as a man, and a man as strange and subtle as a woman', as she expressed it in the book itself. Orlando does not change her nature when she changes sex. All the time she is curiously like Vanessa – competent, audacious, stand-offish, often tongue-tied. Virginia also determined to identify Vita with Knole for ever, in compensation for losing it. In January 1928, when Virginia was writing the book, Vita's father, Lord Sackville, died, and it turned into a memorial mass for him and for Vita's double loss. As a girl, his only child, she could not inherit the house, which she had loved as profoundly as she had loved her father. It passed, with the Sackville title, to her uncle Charles. *Orlando* would be her consolation. It had turned into something much more than the joke Virginia had first intended.

There was another ingredient to this complex story. Virginia used it as a medium to explore English history and literature. Therefore it must extend over several centuries, beginning with Vita (as a boy) in the reign of Queen Elizabeth I and ending with Vita (as a woman) in 1928, the year of publication. She ages twenty years in 350. Virginia did not intend her history or her geography to be taken seriously. St Paul's Cathedral is given a dome before the Great Fire of London destroyed its spire; there is no mention whatever of vast events like the Civil War or the American Revolution; the mountains of Wales are visible from the park at Knole. But she made no attempt to conceal the identity of her central character. The book was dedicated to Vita; it contained photographs of her in different guises; and it is full of sly allusions to their personal lives. Orlando drives a four-in-hand as boldly as in real life Vita drove a Ford; Violet Trefusis is reincarnated as a Russian princess, and they meet at the ice carnival on the Thames in 1608 (a scene brilliantly imagined by Sally Potter in her film of the book in 1993); Vita's rejected lover, Lord Lascelles, becomes inexplicably the Archduchess Harriet; and she discovers Shakespeare sitting with a tankard of beer and a pen in his hands, in the servants' hall at Knole.

It is a fantasy. It is Vita-in-Wonderland. It is an impressionist picture – you must stand back from it to grasp its meaning. But it was rooted in Knole, where the manuscript is now on public display. While Virginia was writing it, my brother and I went with her more than once to pace the long galleries, and she would ask us, pointing at a picture, 'Who's that? What was she like?', and as we never knew, she would invent a name and a character on the spot, so that we came to guess something of her intention. Nobody, not even Vita, read a word of it until it was in print. Even when they spent a week together in Burgundy shortly before publication, they scarcely mentioned it. Then, on 11 October 1928 (which are also the last words of the book), Vita received her specially bound copy. She was almost incoherent with astonishment and delight. *Orlando* celebrated their love-affair – and defused it.

IX

WHILE THE BOOK was still simmering in the literary journals, they went to Cambridge together. Virginia was giving at Girton College the second of two lectures which she turned into *A Room of One's Own*. It was overtly feminist, and it became for a time, specially for Americans, the bible of the feminist movement. It stated the case with overwhelming force, grace and humour. Since the book originated as lectures, its style was conversational, more like her letters than her diary. As Quentin Bell said of it, 'In *A Room* one can hear her speaking. In her novels she is thinking'. But, strangely, he thought her tone too mild, too conciliatory, while to me it is fierce beyond reasonableness. She upbraids the male sex for their love of war and making money. She dwells on the disadvantages that women have endured, particularly as writers. They did not have a chance. If Shakespeare had had an equally brilliant sister, not a word of what she wrote would have survived – if she had been allowed by her parents or husband to write any words at all. Even Jane Austen was obliged to hide her manuscripts from prying eyes: 'There was something discreditable in writing *Pride and Prejudice*', Virginia said, ignoring the fact that Jane's father had urged her to publish it. If she covered up her manuscript when someone entered the room, so did Virginia, because until a book is published, it is the most intimate of secrets. Was it really necessary for a woman to have a room of her own before she could write a line? Virginia herself chose the busy stockroom in Tavistock Square, when the upper floors of the house contained several rooms where she could have found peace. Her claim that in the nineteenth century women of genius were stifled by men sits oddly beside the achievements of Austen, the Brontës, Gaskell and George Eliot, and even in Shakespeare's day they were not hammered into insignificance, if we take Portia, Olivia and Desdemona as representatives of contemporary women of mettle.

A Room of One's Own was in part a polemic, in part a fantasy. The mood of *Orlando* was still upon her. She was having fun, but the fun was soured by a note of real bitterness. 'Why did men drink wine and women water?', she asked again. In Bloomsbury both sexes drank wine. And was not Virginia herself, by her conduct and achievements, proof that women of her class were already emancipated? She was not thinking of classes other than her own. Among her friends, only Ethel Smyth considered that her career had been thwarted by masculine presumption. When, a few years later, Virginia wrote an introduction to a collection of reminiscences by working women (*Life As We Have Known It*), she was appalled by their conventionality. They thought it vulgar for a woman to smoke a pipe or read detective novels. 'I don't think they will be poets or novelists for another hundred years or so', she told Margaret Llewellyn-Davies.

Vita was at a loss how to deal with the book in one of her broadcasts on current literature, for she disliked its stridency as much as she disliked *Three Guineas* ten years later for the same reason. She commended *A Room* to her listeners for its 'common sense', when common sense was the last quality that Virginia had envisaged. It was not her style. What can Vita have thought, sitting in the lecture hall at Girton, when she heard Virginia declare, 'Women have had less intellectual freedom than the sons of Athenian slaves', as if there had been no improvement since then, no Acts of Parliament giving women political equality with men, and, for that matter, no Girton? She made great play, in the most famous passage of the book, with the contrast between men's and women's colleges. At King's she had lunched superbly off sole, partridge and a sugary confection, flavoured with red wine and white. At Newnham (another women's college) the menu for supper was soup, beef, prunes and custard, and for drink, 'the water-jug was liberally passed round'. How could conversation flourish, how could genius take root, on such a diet? She did not mention that the lunch was given in his own rooms at King's by one of the Fellows, George Rylands, and at Newnham the supper was in hall with the students. It was undergraduate fare.

Two incidents occurred at this time to test Virginia's beliefs. First there was *The Well of Loneliness*, a novel by Radclyffe Hall which dealt openly with the subject of lesbianism. As soon as it was published, the press attacked it for indecency. The editor of the *Sunday Express* wrote, 'I would rather give a healthy boy or a healthy girl a phial of prussic acid than this novel'. The publisher, Jonathan Cape, voluntarily submitted it to the judgment of the Home Secretary, who declared it obscene, and it was withdrawn from circulation. This act of censorship aroused the fury of Bloomsbury, although their common opinion was that the book was bad and its author conceited. E.M. Forster took the lead in organizing a petition to reverse the Home Secretary's ban, and persuaded Virginia to sign a letter to the *Nation* pleading that, although lesbianism was 'uninteresting and repellent to the majority', it was a fact of life and therefore a legitimate subject for literature. Forster was himself homosexual, but during a visit to the Woolfs in Sussex he declared, according to Virginia's diary, that 'he thought Sapphism disgusting: partly from convention, partly because he disliked that women should be independent of men'. She seems to have taken this provocative statement calmly. She continued to support Forster and Hall, and offered to give evidence, presumably of literary merit, on behalf of the book, though Leonard advised her not to become personally involved, in case she came to be regarded as a mouthpiece for lesbianism and blacken the fair name of Bloomsbury. She persisted, attending the court with a galaxy of other intellectuals, but their claim that *The Well of Loneliness* was a serious work of art was declared irrelevant by the magistrate, and the novel remained on the index of banned books till 1949.

Virginia had done her best for a woman-writer whom she did not much like. Then another situation arose which concerned her more personally. Vita had acquired a new lover after Mary Campbell. She was Hilda Matheson, talks director of the BBC. They had gone on a walking tour in France, and Virginia was openly jealous, accusing Vita, with some justice, of having concealed this holiday from her. It was not simply that Hilda seemed to have supplanted her: Virginia disliked her for other reasons. She was a woman of real ability and determination. She had gained a high position in the BBC, and had persuaded eminent men and women, including Wells and Shaw, to broadcast on subjects of their own choice. Virginia herself had contributed to a discussion with Leonard, but the experience only added to her dislike of Hilda. She had never met a woman like her before. She thought her pushing. 'Her earnest aspiring competent wooden face appears before me,' she wrote in her diary. 'A queer trait in Vita – a passion for the earnest middle-class intellectual, however drab and dreary.' This description of Hilda was unfair. She fought valiantly for high standards in broadcasting which are still valid today. As her biographer, Michael Carney, has written, 'She was a genuine creative spirit, an administrator and programme-maker of genius'. But Virginia could not bring herself to admire an ambitious woman who fought her corner in a man's world. She had as instinctive a dislike for organizing women as she had for organizing men. She told Vita that Hilda 'affects me as a strong purge, as a hair-shirt, as a foggy day, as a cold in the head'. When Hilda Matheson died in 1940, she was still unreconciled: 'I didn't get on with her: she seemed so dried, so official', but that was not true of Hilda, whom I had come to know well and love.

The Matheson affair marked a decline in the Virginia–Vita relationship. They remained friends until Virginia's death, and in the early years of World War II something of their early intimacy revived. But when in January 1929 they met in Berlin, where Harold was now Counsellor in the British Embassy, the visit was a failure. Leonard refused to attend a lunch party of German politicians which Harold had arranged in his honour, and Virginia, hating Berlin and the trappings of diplomacy as much as Vita did, was miserable. One day, when they lunched alone together, Virginia attempted to restore their old relationship only to be met with unexpected coolness. Then there was an incident that involved myself. The party, which included Vanessa and Duncan, went to a controversial film titled *Sturm über Asien*, and I, aged eleven, was refused admission. Vita was enraged by this display of pre-Hitler puritanism, and took me back to my father's flat through snow-slushed streets. I remember the gloom of the occasion, the anger, the incompatibility, which Vanessa's contempt for Vita's distress did nothing to allay.

Virginia returned from Berlin in a state of collapse, due partly to the 'rackety' life she had endured there, and partly to a pill which upset her more than the seasickness it was intended to cure. She was bedridden for a month. Her main correspondent was still Vita ('Have you any love for me, or only the appreciation which one member of the PEN has for another?'), and when she recovered, her time was occupied by two major novels, Vita's *The Edwardians*, which the Hogarth Press published, and her own masterpiece, *The Waves*.

The Edwardians, like *Orlando*, was about Knole and the Sackville family. It was a romantic story – and Vita could tell a story well – in which she tried to reconcile her love of tradition with her conviction that the values of Edwardian society were false. It was a best-seller, the choice of the Book Societies both in Britain and America, and the Hogarth Press, with its wholly inadequate staff, handled the rush of business with success, as they did with Vita's next book, *All Passion Spent*, which was also a best-seller. It was Vita's finest novel, the reflections of an old woman, Lady Slane, on how convention had denied her any freedom of action or expression.

Virginia liked it more than *The Edwardians*, and was impressed by Vita's declaration that she didn't care a scrap for her novels. She wished to be remembered as a poet. She wrote fiction only in order to pay the school bills for Ben and me. She had written them at speed.

The Waves, on the other hand, was the product of intense thought and labour. It was so original a book that only a few grasped its purpose. In outline, it was the outcome ('story' is not a word that one can use in this connection) of six friends soliloquizing about their lives from childhood to middle age. Their individual contributions were separated by lyrical passages describing the rising and setting of the sun over the sea. When she began it in 1929, she told her nephew Quentin that it was to be 'an entirely new kind of book', and when it was published in 1931, she replied to an ecstatic letter from Goldsworthy Lowes Dickinson, 'I did mean that in some vague way we are the same person, and not separate people. The six characters are supposed to be one.' This gives an indication of the complexity of the book. It was a rainbow of different colours forming a single arc, the most poetic of her novels. It made every reader feel inadequate. Yet it sold 6,500 copies in three weeks.

Never had she concentrated so hard over a book. The history of its composition is amazing. She wrote it in manuscript twice over, the second version bearing little relation to the first. We can follow its progress in her diary. It began to torment her. 'I write variations of every sentence; compromises; bad shots; possibilities. . . . I wish I enjoyed it more.' She fell ill, but the book continued to ferment like wine in the cask. Each afternoon she typed out what she had written in the morning, altering as she went, and then she had it retyped professionally, and further revised it, then again slightly in proof. 'Never', she wrote, 'have I screwed my brain so tight over a book.' She barely mentioned the struggle in her letters. It was an intensely private labour, the printed book the only public declaration of her intent. Years later she wrote to Edward Sackville-West, 'It's the only one of my books that I can sometimes read with pleasure. Not that I wrote it with pleasure, but in a kind of trance into which I suppose I shall never sink again.'

Her distractions were many, because except when she was ill, she never relaxed for a moment her busy social life, her manifold correspondence, or her work for the Hogarth Press reading innumerable manuscripts and 'travelling' their books with Leonard to the West Country as far as Penzance. There is something touching about the picture of these two middle-aged intellectuals trying to persuade indifferent, and sometimes downright insulting, booksellers to take their highbrow publications. 'It's becoming too much', Virginia confessed to Vanessa. But instead of giving up, they enlisted John Lehmann as manager, with the intention of making him a partner after an eight-month trial. He was much more than a manager. He brought them young authors like Stephen Spender, W.H. Auden and Cecil Day-Lewis.

Another person entered Virginia's life contemporary with her writing of *The Waves*, who to some extent took Vita's place as her confidante and correspondent-in-chief for the next ten years, but without reciprocated love. Although Ethel Smyth undoubtedly loved Virginia with a sick passion, Virginia tolerated her, rather as she tolerated the Hogarth Press, as a diversion, and then a burden which she could not easily shake off. They had many friends in common, Vita among them, and each had long been interested in the other's books. It was *A Room of One's Own* which compelled Ethel to seek a meeting, since Virginia had expressed precisely the grievance that Ethel had nursed for three decades, the unequal struggle of women artists to win recognition in a man's world. Ethel, now seventy-three years old, was a composer who imagined that only male prejudice had prevented the performance of her works, when in fact it was the other way round. A woman composer was so rare that her very existence excited wonder, and a woman who had added to her reputation in many other ways – by her autobiographies, her friends in high places, her two-month imprisonment as a suffragette – was regarded as a national phenomenon, and her music, like her opera *The Wreckers*, was performed not only because it was fresh and vigorous, but because it was by Ethel Smyth.

Her pursuit of Virginia soon ran into trouble. 'It is like being caught by a giant crab', she complained to Quentin, but Ethel's persistence paid off. This is how I described their relationship in the Introduction to the fourth volume of Virginia's letters, of which 130 were written to Ethel herself:

Virginia was half-amused, half-defensive, referring to 'this curious unnatural friendship', fearing ridicule, fearing too deep an involvement. She was wary of her. They had both voyaged too far before berthing in the same dock. Ethel took the initiative with a volley of questions to which she seldom awaited the replies even if she could hear them [she was very deaf] but they could be repeated in Virginia's letters. Reading them, one hears their talk, the gradual unloading of all that cargo, more reticent on Virginia's side than on Ethel's, but gradually, under pressure, she yielded, and wrote to Ethel about matters that hitherto she had scarcely mentioned to anyone – her madness ['It's terrific, I can assure you'], her feelings about sex ['I was always cowardly'] and even her thoughts of suicide that she had confessed to Leonard ['If you weren't here, I would kill myself']. She began to teach Ethel the benefits of patience and humility, and Ethel became a little calmer, a little less prone to beat the cymbals. Virginia enjoyed the combat, admired her, respected her. She was a gadfly, and paradoxically a solace.

I just remember Ethel. She often came to Long Barn, dressed like a coachman in cloak and tricorn hat, and she was vigorous in a way that didn't frighten children, bursting through the weeks like paper hoops, a woman whose pertinacity was irresistible. Deafness, which can make people tedious to their friends, was for Ethel an asset. She told us to yell at her, and we yelled with an exuberance unequalled when talking to normal people. Once she insisted, when sitting on our terrace at Long Barn, on hearing a nightingale. A bird sang its heart out in the garden, but not a note penetrated to Ethel until it obligingly perched on the table in front of her and gave her a solo performance. How we cheered! How we adored her!

X

IN THE EARLY 1930s the Woolfs went on annual holidays abroad. Now that Virginia's books were earning a higher income, they could afford to travel, and there was always the lure of Vanessa who spent much of the year with Duncan and her children at Cassis in the south of France. They often went further afield, Leonard driving their brand-new Lanchester car over the almost empty roads of France. He wrote that Virginia had a passion for travelling, 'a mixture of exhilaration and relaxation', which refreshed her mind with new sights, sounds and smells. She tolerated discomfort, and was never impatient for quicker progress. It was the journey, not the arrival, that mattered, the slower the better. There were stepping-stones on which they could pause awhile – Montaigne's tower, Joan of Arc's castle – but they rarely visited a museum and scarcely spoke to anyone but servants in the inns, because Virginia was uncertain of her French, and there was no need.

She enjoyed most the countryside and life of the small towns, the scenes that Baedeker leaves out, the smell of aromatic plants on low hills, 'where no one has ever been before', picnicking under cypresses and olive trees, and always the delicious release from London, the joy of being unavailable.

Her excellence as a traveller is best displayed in the letters and diaries she wrote on a tour of Greece in April 1932. She and Leonard were accompanied by Roger Fry and his sister Margery, the one an authority on classical and Byzantine art,

Ethel Smyth in about 1930, when she first came to know Virginia, who
was 'half-amused, half-defensive, referring to "this curious unnatural
friendship"... But she enjoyed the combat, admired her, respected her.
She was a gadfly, and paradoxically a solace.'

the other on the wild flowers. For Virginia it was her second visit. A quarter of a century earlier she had toured many of the same sites – Athens, Nauplia, Mycenae, Corinth – and Greece was little changed. The country roads were so abominable, often as pitted as torrent beds, that few tourists ventured far from Athens. The emptiness of the mountains and the coast gave Virginia infinite delight. It was like Chaucer's England, she said, even Homer's Greece. Her letters and her diary (hardly a phrase repeated from one into the other) were not about the temples and the churches, but about the country and its people. In the diary she made verbal notes, much as a painter might sketch a scene from which to make a finished picture in his studio ('how lovely the pure lip of the sea touching a wild shore, with hills behind, and green plains and red rocks'), but in her letters she took flight, fitting words to images with unequalled virtuosity. To Vita: 'We saw the Greek shepherds' huts in a wood near Marathon, and a lovely dark-olive, red-lipped, pink-shawled girl wandering and spinning thread from a lump of wool.' To Vanessa: 'If ever I had a turn towards Sapphism, it would be revived by the carts of young peasant women in lemon, red and blue handkerchiefs, and the donkeys and the kids and the general fecundity and bareness; and the sea; and the cypresses.' To Ottoline Morrell: 'Not a bungalow, not a kennel, not a teashop. Pure sea water on pure sand is almost the loveliest thing in the world.' It was a lesson in how to travel, how to observe, and how to describe what you observe, as different from the style of her novels as a Cotman is from a Cézanne. She called it the best holiday of her life, and one reason was that it was arduous. She was blistered by the sun and exhausted by the roads, but her endurance was rewarded by the remoteness of the places they visited. She was moved by their stark simplicity. 'I could love Greece as an old woman [she was only fifty] as I once loved Cornwall as a child.'

Another spring holiday, in 1935, was of a very different nature. They drove through Holland, Germany and Austria to Florence and Rome. Leonard had been warned by the Foreign Office that it was inadvisable for a Jew to visit Germany, and they found every town placarded with anti-Semitic posters. But nowhere were they molested, although in the neighbourhood of Bonn they coincided with a visit to the city by Goering, and security was very tight. What might have been ominous attention by the Stormtroopers to Leonard's unmistakable Hebraic features was diverted by Mitz, his marmoset, who was travelling with them. I remember Mitz. The Woolfs brought him to lunch at Sissinghurst, the house to which we had recently moved from Long Barn, and my father, who had a horror of rodents, was amazed that Leonard could endure the pawing of this rat-like creature round his face and neck. Mitz ruined our lunch party. But the Germans adored him, and they were waved through every barrier with blessings and applause.

Virginia never travelled outside western and southern Europe, apart from her two short visits to northern Turkey before her marriage. Her only interest in the Far East was prompted by Arthur Waley's translations from the Chinese. She never visited any part of Africa, never flew in an aeroplane, and never crossed the Atlantic. Although she had two or three invitations to visit America, she never did. She remained as prejudiced against the United States as she would have been against Liberia. Three of her friends were born Americans, Tom Eliot, Logan Pearsall Smith and Ethel Sands, but she counted them as British, unless she was cross with them, when they became Americans again, with all the failings that she associated with that race. 'So ugly, so dusty, so dull', she wrote of two visitors from San Francisco whom she was about to meet for the first time, and when she was introduced to Blanche Knopf, the publisher, all that she could subsequently remember about her were her eyebrows, 'picked out so that one pencil of hair remains in the middle of her forehead: the effect is one of perpetual surprise, and to me unpleasing'. May Sarton, the poet and novelist, was 'that goose – a pale, pretty Shelley-imitation American girl'. New York meant little more to her than the address of her publisher, Harcourt Brace, and the magazines *Vogue* and *Harper's Bazaar*, the generosity of whose cheques she much appreciated. Yale University was only the *Yale Review*, which in 1932 published her *Letter to a Young Poet*, but outside the northeast coast she had little conception what America was really like. When in 1933 Vita and Harold went on a lecture tour of the United States, Virginia wrote to her:

> I imagine you sitting on a tight plush seat in a car, with views of the Middle West – an unattractive land, largely sprinkled with old tin kettles – racing across vast slabs of plate glass. The negroes are spitting in the carriage next door, and after 25 more hours, the train will stop at a town like Peacehaven, only 75 times larger, called Balmoralville, where you will get out, and after a brief snack off clams and iced pear-drops with the Mayor, who is called, I should think, Cyrus K. Hinks, you will go to a large Baptist hall and deliver a lecture on Rimbaud.

Her vision of California was equally fantastic. Writing to

Hugh Walpole, who was in Hollywood, she imagined: 'You are sitting with vast blue plains rolling round you: a virgin forest at your back; a marble city gleaming at your feet; and people so new, so brave, so beautiful and utterly uncontaminated by civilisation, popping in and out of booths and theatres with pistols in their hands and aeroplanes soaring over their heads.' It was as if she considered that an ancient place like Greece must be more virtuous, more estimable, because of its antiquity, than America, which must be brash, unlovable and deficient in all the qualities that she held most dear, just because it was new. She allowed their people no worthwhile literature, no physical evidence of a long tradition, because all these desirable attributes can only be acquired by centuries of effort and suffering. She could fancy herself living in Tuscany, the Dordogne, the Morea, but not conceivably in Maine. It lacked Bloomsbury's patina.

She told an American student who was writing a thesis about her that the name 'Bloomsbury Group ' was 'merely a journalistic phrase which had no meaning', and that was becoming increasingly true. Bloomsbury was unravelling. Vanessa considered that it had died with the outbreak of the First World War. Its membership bifurcated, like a river approaching its delta. They now had different careers, different lovers. Keynes was a senior economist, Duncan Grant and Vanessa fashionable painters and decorators, Roger Fry Slade Professor at Cambridge, Desmond MacCarthy the leading literary critic of his day, Eliot Professor of Poetry at Harvard, Strachey a best-seller, Virginia a genius. Moreover, the Bloomsbury attitudes that had once made them notorious had become commonplace. Women had votes and entered the professions; homosexual love and sex before marriage were tolerated if not yet condoned; censorship of literature was thought old-fashioned; socialism was practised; the League of Nations existed; the Impressionists were accepted, and Diaghilev was the rage. In fact, as Quentin Bell observed in his book about Bloomsbury, 'the audacities of one age became the platitudes of the next'. Only their pacifism was not in general found acceptable, and Bloomsbury itself was fast abandoning it as a creed.

They did not correspond or meet as regularly as in the past, but there was still the Memoir Club, and odd meals and visits which reunited individuals for an hour or a day. Monk's House, for all its discomforts, was a favourite resort, and it was at Charleston that Strachey read aloud the first chapters of *Eminent Victorians* and Keynes composed his *Economic Consequences of the Peace* before he moved with his wife to Tilton House, only half a mile away. For Virginia these friendships formed the core of her life. When Lytton died of stomach cancer in 1932, aged only fifty-two, she wrote to Ottoline, 'I have got a queer feeling that I'm hearing him talk in the next room – the talk I always want to go on with. I have a million things to tell him, and never shall.' His death was followed within a few weeks by Carrington's suicide. She thought life unbearable without him. The day after Leonard and Virginia had visited her at Ham Spray, she borrowed a rifle, ostensibly to shoot rabbits, and shot herself. She took six hours to die. Leonard thought her act histrionic, but later generations have come to regard her death as Bloomsbury's finest gesture, a symbol of their incandescent gift for friendship. Then Roger Fry died, in 1934, two years after his journey to Greece with the Woolfs, and Virginia wrote of him in her diary, 'Dignified and honest and large – something ripe and musical about him – and then the fun, and the fact that he had lived with such variety and generosity and curiosity'. She called him 'the most intelligent of my friends, profusely, ridiculously, perpetually creative'.

She had diversions to console her for these losses, and some new pleasures   a camera, an inflatable canoe in which she paddled down the Ouse, another pool for Leonard's garden, a Frigidaire for Monk's kitchen, Orlando's new bedroom for herself, learning Italian once more. The literary world wondered what she would write next. Would *The Waves* be followed by another novel in the same elusive style? She published several essays in a second series of *The Common Reader*, and then surprised everyone by writing a short novel about a dog. *Flush* was the title of the book and the name of the dog, which had belonged to Elizabeth Barrett Browning. No topic is more prone to sentimentality than dog and cat stories. People remembered *Where's Master?*, a best-selling novel, ostensibly written by Caesar, Edward VII's dog, which had followed the King's coffin to the grave. Virginia's book never pretended that Flush could talk or even think like a human being: but he could observe, and Mrs Browning would do the talking for him. The book was poetic. Through Flush's eyes she retold the story of Elizabeth's elopement with Robert Browning. It was the only work of which Virginia gave me a copy, possibly because it was the only one which a child could be expected to understand. She was not pleased with it. She had started it 'to let my brain cool' after *The Waves*. It was 'easy indolent writing'. But as she finished her 30,000 words, she regretted the time she had spent writing them. She told Vita that it was 'a foolish, witless joke', and herself that it was 'silly', at one moment too slight, at the next too serious. Nevertheless, it was a great success, the Book Society choice in England and America. Virginia despised the critics who praised it and the public who bought it, but when Rebecca West called it 'a family joke', she was upset, because she agreed. Her mind was on something larger, *The Pargiters*, which came to birth four years later as *The Years*.

Her fame was becoming more of a disability than a reward. It meant constant interruptions – letters from strangers, requests for interviews, photographs, autographs, the tedium, as she expressed it, of 'seeing and being seen'. She did not resent visits from friends old and new (Elizabeth Bowen, William Plomer) who understood a writer's need for solitude, so much as visits from friends of friends who did not. Even Peter Quennell, a poet, critic and biographer of intelligence and merit, was lambasted by Virginia as 'a pushing and at the same time wriggling eel', just because the Woolfs were landed with him as a weekend guest. When Ethel Smyth begged her to come to Woking and meet some of Ethel's neighbours, Virginia turned on her with a machine-gun. How could Ethel imagine for a moment that she had time to spare for 'admirers', that she was flattered by the invitation? 'You've been thinking I'm that sort of person – that's how I spend my time, in a rose-coloured teagown, signing autographs.'

Ethel was capable of rallying from a snub in a way that Vita never could, and continued to exert a pressure to which Virginia unexpectedly succumbed, for she was fond of Ethel, and admired her pertinacity even when she was the victim of it. Vita, shyer, more reticent in public, and reluctant to intrude on Virginia's privacy now that she had lost her love, withdrew to Sissinghurst, cultivated her garden, and moved into a new phase of her life, reflecting on the nature of religion, as her poems *Solitude* and *Sissinghurst* (the latter dedicated to Virginia) excellently reveal. They were followed by her biographies of Joan of Arc and St Teresa of Avila. Virginia came three or four times to Sissinghurst with Leonard, but spent only a single night there, in Harold's bedroom when he was away. Her affection for Vita was summed up in a phrase: 'I can't deny that I have a sort of dying ember in my heart for you.'

Virginia was indifferent to honours. She had accepted the Femina Prize for *To the Lighthouse*, possibly because she was then relatively unknown. But now that her name was widely canvassed as the protagonist of a new type of fiction, public tributes were thrust upon her and she refused them all. She would not accept from the Crown the Companion of Honour (which Vita did accept for herself), the most enviable award for the arts after the Order of Merit. She refused an honorary degree from Manchester University, writing to the Vice-Chancellor a letter that started, 'I need not say how deeply I am honoured ...', but in her diary she described it as 'all that humbug'. More surprising was her refusal to give the Clark Lectures at Cambridge. It was a highly prestigious invitation. Her own father had given the first lectures in 1883, and Virginia was the first woman to be invited to succeed him. Would it not advance the cause of women to accept? But no. Her formal reason for declining was that she had no time: it would take at least a year to prepare the six lectures, and she was anxious to make progress with her novel. But her private reasons were that she considered university lectures 'an obsolete practice inherited from the Middle Ages when books were scarce. Students should read, not listen. To swallow instruction from a lectern is like sipping English literature through a straw. Lectures, she was to proclaim in *Three Guineas*, only pander to the vanity of the lecturer and stimulate conflict between academics. What's more, there would probably be a reception after each lecture. Sherry and cocktails would be served, which seemed to her even less palatable than the prunes and custard at Newnham. 'It is a vain and vicious system', she declared, but she knew that to utter such heresies at Cambridge would be an intolerable breach of manners. So she refused.

When Walter Sickert asked her to write about his paintings, she consented with misgivings. She was no art critic. Her letters to Vanessa on the subject were full of love and admiration, as were Vanessa's to her about her novels, but each was wary of the other, fearing to write something inadvertently wounding or foolish. In criticizing the Pre-Raphaelites, companions of her father, Virginia was outspokenly hostile. On an exhibition of Edward Burne-Jones's paintings, she wrote, 'The suavity, the sinuosity, the way the private parts are merely clouded – it's all a romantic dream, which makes me think of Hyde Park Gate.' With Sickert it was a different matter. She had genuinely admired his pictures, but when she met him face to face, she was put off by his vanity and weariness, 'his hard little eyes, very old [he was seventy-three], no illusion about his own greatness'. Still, she was committed, and urged by Vanessa, she wrote a brilliant essay comparing portraiture to biography, and coming to the conclusion that painting was the more truthful, although 'we cannot penetrate the zone of silence in the middle of every art'. Sickert was delighted. He told her that it was the only criticism of his work worth having. Not surprisingly, said Virginia to herself, as she had praised him throughout. Fry's and Clive's verdicts on her essay were more astringent.

It is an example of Virginia's courtesy and kindness. Although her letters often crossed the borderline, they pricked more than gashed. It was the custom of Bloomsbury to tease. They were all guilty of ridiculing each other. But if someone were in serious trouble, or unlikely to respond to teasing with the tolerance of Ethel Smyth, Virginia would be endearingly sympathetic. An instance is her reply to an American, John Nef, who sent her his two-volume work *The Rise of the British Coal Industry.* Instead of answering that she greatly looked forward to reading it (the formula recommended by Harold Macmillan, the statesman-publisher), she read it, and thanked him for his 'delightful present. ... I am enjoying your coal much more than all the manuscripts which I should be reading'. The deceit (if it was one) was legitimate. But with her intimates there was no need. She could scold, but more often she encouraged, particularly Vanessa's children. She sat through Angelica's interminable school play; she applauded Julian for writing a dissertation on 'The Good' in the hope of a Fellowship at King's College, Cambridge; and with Quentin she carried on a merry typewritten correspondence, the speed of her typing keeping pace with the cataract of her ideas.

There was still the problem of being over-visited. Typical of her despair and the humour with which she controlled it was this letter to Ethel Smyth:

Tom Eliot for twenty-four hours solid talk yesterday; Rosamond Lehmann now coming for lunch; Oliver Strachey, tea; Lady Colefax I have refused; must go to London to write about 12th Night. Must write journalism. Must see friends. Have therefore decided from today to give up all other writing in order to see there's beef for lunch and cakes for tea. Am going to spend all my money on clothes, face powder. . . . Fingers to be red. Toes to be silver. Face to be lifted, nose to be filled with wax. [Signed] V., who gave up literature at the command of her friends.

There can be no doubt that she resented interruptions, but she spent hours describing them for her friends, perhaps as a warning to them, perhaps as a diversion, more likely as a conductor for her wrath. 'I like it when people actually come, but I love it when they go', was the most charitable of her complaints.

It was untypical of her to wail in public. But she wrote to the *New Statesman* a letter which might have been written today on behalf of all celebrities:

Open the dailies and the weeklies. Among the pictures of Atlantic flyers and murderers you will find portraits of well-known people, and by no means all of them public people, but private people, musicians, writers, painters, artists of all kinds. Their homes are photographed, their families, their gardens, their studios, their bedrooms and their writing-tables. Interviews appear: their opinions on every sort of subject are broadcast.

She admitted that the celebrities often succumbed to this treatment out of kindness to a friend. Can she have been so innocent as to imagine that they all disliked it? Ethel, for one, revelled in public attention. Fame is desirable for those without it, not always detestable to those with it. Virginia was quite capable of mocking her own modesty. At the height of her fame she read a paper to the Memoir Club entitled, 'Am

I a Snob?'. She confessed that Society fascinated her. She would leave a coroneted letter on top of the pile in the hope that visitors would notice it. She cultivated the aristocracy because they behaved 'more naturally' than most people, and she knew that they cultivated her because she was famous. Lady Oxford (Margot Asquith) asked her to write her obituary for *The Times* because 'you are the greatest female writer living'. She did not expect such people to test her intellectually: that was Bloomsbury's function. 'If you ask me would I rather meet Einstein or the Prince of Wales', she wrote in her Memoir, 'I plump for the Prince without hesitation.' The type of person she most disliked were climbers. The snobs who look up are even worse than the snobs who look down. As she was neither, she decided that she was not a snob at all. She was simply curious. She liked nailing people down as specimens, like butterflies. Stephen Spender, aged twenty-four, 'is a nice poetic youth, big-nosed, bright-eyed, like a giant thrush'. Noël Coward 'called me darling, and gave me his glass to drink out of'. Then she would turn suddenly fierce, as when defending Strachey against a man who had called him heartless, 'Lytton had more love in his little finger than that castrated cat in the whole of his mangy stringy partless gutless tailless body.' She knew how to be formidable when she chose.

An excellent example of her reaction to new people and new places is provided by her visit to Ireland in 1934 to stay with Elizabeth Bowen. Virginia had first met her with Lady Ottoline two years before, and did not immediately take to her. She was awkward, she stammered, and was married to the Education Officer for the City of Oxford, Alan Cameron, which was no commendation to Virginia who distrusted officials of all kinds; and she suspected that Elizabeth had modelled her novels on her own. Later, her attitude changed. After the Camerons had moved from Oxford to London, Elizabeth became her literary confidante. Virginia liked *The House in Paris* (1935) very much indeed, and told her so. It was the start of Virginia's most successful literary friendship. Unlike Katherine Mansfield, Elizabeth provoked no jealousy. And unlike Ethel Smyth, she was neither exclamatory nor an intruder.

It was the Woolfs' first visit to Ireland, and their curiosity to see the country was greater than their curiosity to see the Camerons, with whom they stayed but a single night. Virginia disliked their house, Bowen's Court. She called it 'pompous and pretentious and imitative and ruined – a great barrack of grey stone, four storeys and basements, like a town-house, high empty rooms'. That was the verdict she entrusted to her diary. In writing to Vanessa she went further: 'It's a great stone box, but full of Italian mantelpieces and decayed 18th-century furniture, and carpets all in holes. However, they insisted on keeping up a ramshackle kind of state, dressing for dinner and so on.' Worst of all, they found as fellow-guests Cyril Connolly and his wife, to whom Virginia took an instant dislike: 'A less appetising pair I have never seen out of the zoo'. The house and the company had such a depressing effect on her that she descended to ridicule in order to brighten the conversation. According to Connolly's account of their miserable evening, 'she asked Elizabeth Bowen what "unnatural vice" was, and what acts constituted it, and I sensed that she was a virginal and shy character', when she was neither.

On escaping from Bowen's Court they travelled quite extensively through Ireland, and Virginia was entranced by the beauty of the country, its emptiness, its simplicity. She thought it a mixture of Greece, Italy and Cornwall, and, as always, considered buying a small house there, but the idea was short-lived: the landscape was suffused in melancholy, and the houses were either ruined mansions or horrid Victorian cottages. She liked the people. They had a genius for talk. 'I can give no notion of the flowing yet formed sentences, the richness and ease of the language. ... Why aren't these people the greatest novelists in the world?'

However, when they reached Dublin, she spared no thought for James Joyce, and unexpectedly did not find the city beautiful, when it is one of the loveliest capitals in Europe. Her taste had never been for urban or Palladian architecture. She thought Dublin's wonderful squares poor replicas of Bloomsbury's, and its population unsettled, feverish. This was not, as one might expect, due to the rise of the Fianna Fáil under de Valera, but to their poverty and lack of spirit – 'no luxury, no creation, no stir, only the dregs of London, rather wishy-washy, as if suburbanised'. 'No', she concluded in her diary, 'it wouldn't do, living in Ireland, in spite of the rocks and the desolate bays. It would lower the pulse of the heart.'

She returned to England with a dose of flu which added to her melancholy, but one should not think of her as normally morose or disapproving. Her usual expression was contemplative, not, like Leonard's, severe, and when she looked up, it was with a smile brimming with new ideas and phrases. She enjoyed provoking people, but not aggressively. As boys we felt ourselves under observation, but not under scrutiny. Her manner was more courteous than polite. By her laughter she would arouse the laughter of other people, and if she did not thrust herself forward in conversation, nor did she shrink. She wanted people to display their best in her company: innkeepers must be welcoming, intellectuals entertaining, children eager. And she would poke at our silences. When we were throwing fragments of bread to the ducks one day, she said, 'How would you describe the noise that the bread makes when it hits the water?' 'Splash?', we suggested. 'No.' 'Splosh?' 'No, no.' 'Then what?' 'Umph', she said. 'But there's no such word!' 'There is now.'

Once I travelled up to London alone with her by train. As we drew out of our local station, she whispered to me:

'You see that man in the corner?'

'Yes.'

'He's a bus conductor from Leeds. He's been on holiday with his uncle, who has a farm near here.'

'But, Virginia, how can you possibly know that? You've never seen him before.'

'No question about it.'

And then she told me, during the whole half-hour that the journey took, the life story of this man, who remained, puffing at his pipe, totally unaware that he was now a figure in twentieth-century literature.

XI

THE WOOLFS CONTINUED to alternate between Monk's House and Tavistock Square, a week or two at a time in each. In the country Virginia would walk the Downs, and cook a little (she baked good bread), and play skilfully with bowls on the lawn. She also took lessons to improve her French, and opened an exhibition of Roger Fry's paintings. She wrote, and she read. Her reading was prodigious. Most authors, when deeply engaged in writing a new book, as she was with *The Pargiters*, rarely give themselves time to read anything not related to it. But Virginia on returning from a long walk would take up *Timon of Athens*, the biography of an eighteenth century parson, *David Copperfield* for the sixth time, or the Bible, for its language, not its doctrine. In addition to the manuscripts submitted to the Hogarth Press, there were books by friends like Ethel Smyth or Stephen Spender, on which she would comment candidly, and usually end with the propitiatory sentence, 'But pay no attention to this', knowing that they always would. She found it difficult to judge contemporaries. They were like people singing in the next room, too loud, too near. 'Hence my unfairness to [D.H.] Lawrence', she wrote. 'How can you put him into the very great? To me he's like an express train running through a tunnel – one shriek, sparks, smoke and gone.' Nor did T.S. Eliot escape her censure. The Woolfs went to a performance of *Murder in the Cathedral*: 'I had almost to carry Leonard out, shrieking.'

For Angelica's birthday in 1935 she staged the only performance of her only play, *Freshwater*, a comedy about Mrs Cameron, the photographer, and her friends in the Isle of Wight. She had first drafted it in 1923, and now wrote a second version, which was performed in Vanessa's studio in Fitzroy Square to an audience of eighty friends. Julia Cameron's role was taken by Vanessa, her husband's by Leonard, and Ellen Terry's by Angelica. Other parts were allotted to Duncan Grant, Adrian Stephen and Julian Bell. Virginia was the producer and prompter.

Further interruptions were caused by political tensions at home and abroad. Hitler was now the German Chancellor, and had murdered some of his closest associates. Mussolini invaded Abyssinia. The Labour Party was split on what attitude to take. Virginia attended, as a reluctant and scornful spectator, its annual conference at Brighton, where the pacifist George Lansbury was squashed by Ernest Bevin, 'like a snake who's swallowed a toad'. She could not bring herself to think that these people or their debates could add an ounce to human happiness, but there was no avoiding them, now that Leonard was deeply involved. Kingsley Martin (editor of the left-wing *New Statesman*) was a constant self-invited guest, and the radio in London and in the country was tuned to every news bulletin. To please Leonard, she canvassed support for an anti-Fascist exhibition, probably unaware that it was Communist-inspired, and even wrote an article for the Marxist *Daily Worker*. But when she was approached to succeed H.G. Wells as President of PEN, the international society of authors which was much concerned with human rights, she exploded: 'I flicked my hand, as a Greek woman flicks a bug off her child's head', she wrote to Ethel. 'Conceive their damned insolence! Ten dinners a year, and I to sit at the head of this puling company of back-scratchers, and administer balm!'

Pinka died, the spaniel immortalized as Flush, but Mitz the marmoset lived on. With Vanessa spending half the year at Cassis, and her son Julian teaching in a remote university in China, it was to those two that Virginia addressed her most entertaining gossip, hopping from twig to twig like Jane Austen in her letters to her sister Cassandra. She resembled a pianist, playing with her right hand the lighter notes (her letters) and with her left the more sombre (her diary), and it is by means of this antiphony that we can follow with unparalleled intimacy the progress of *The Years*. In the letters she described her struggle as if it were little more than an irritating cough that she could not shake off: in her diary, she was a woman in labour.

She had begun the book, when it was called *The Pargiters*, in 1932, and in nine weeks wrote 60,000 words, every one of which she scrapped. She was alternately elated and profoundly depressed. At one moment her brain felt like 'a Rolls Royce engine, purring its 70 miles an hour', and at the next she was writing 'feeble twaddle'. Typical diary entries were: 10 June 1935: 'Working very hard. I think I shall rush these scenes off.' 11 June: 'Yet I cannot write this morning.' 12 September: 'Never have I had such a hot balloon in my head as re-writing *The Years* because it's so long and the pressure is so terrific. But I will use all my art to keep my head sane.' She was fifty-three, the year of her menopause, and Leonard was anxious. In March 1936 she wrote, again in her diary: 'I must very nearly verge on insanity. I think I get so deep in this book I don't know what I am doing. Find myself walking along the Strand talking aloud.' And about the book itself:

'Such twilight gossip, it seemed, such a show-up of my own decrepitude.' Next morning, it seemed not quite so bad: 'On the contrary, a full bustling-like book'. Weeks later, 'I have never suffered, since *The Voyage Out*, such acute despair on re-reading.' In April 1936 Leonard feared that she might suffer a complete mental collapse and took her to Cornwall for a fortnight. Virginia put the proofs aside for two months before starting to correct them, and then she cut out 'enormous chunks', amounting to 250 pages. Even after such drastic surgery, it was still the longest of her books.

So much for her private ordeal. The 'sickle side of the moon' (words that we adapted for the title of the fifth volume of her letters) was her social and family life which she never neglected even when her spirits were lowest. She did not conceal from her friends the suffering that the book caused her, but her hints were self-reproachful, never self-pitying. To Dadie Rylands, 'It is wholly worthless'. To Ethel, 'a hopeless bad book. Verbose, foolish.' To Vanessa, 'this long weary dreary book'. To Ottoline, 'long and dreary'. To Ethel again, 'I don't know or care if it's the worst book or the best'. To Janet Case, 'very bad'. And to Vita. 'I should be delighted to tie a stone to it, and drop it into the Atlantic.'

She was steeling herself to accept the criticism she expected by anticipating it herself. Nobody, surely, could think quite so badly of it as she did. Then came the moment when she must show it to Leonard. As always, he must be her first reader. She relied entirely on his judgement whether to publish the book or scrap it. In her diary for 3 November 1936 she described the scene:

On Sunday I started to read the proofs. When I had read to the end of the first section, I was in despair: stony but convinced despair. I said, This is happily so bad that there can be no question about it. I must carry the proofs, like a dead cat, to Leonard and tell him to burn them unread. This I did. [She then goes for a short walk through Holborn.] I was no longer Virginia, the genius, but only a perfectly insignificant yet content – shall I call it spirit? a body? And very tired, Very old. [Various social engagements intervene]. We went home, and L. read and read and said nothing. I began to feel acutely depressed. . . . Suddenly L. put down his proof and said he thought it extraordinarily good – as good as any of them

Two days later he finished it. 'L. put down his last sheet about 12 last night, and could not speak. He was in tears. He says it is "a most remarkable book" – he likes it better than *The Waves*, and has not a spark of doubt that it must be published. The moment of relief was divine.'

In fact, Leonard was exaggerating. In one of his auto-biographical volumes, *Downhill All the Way*, he confessed: 'I knew that unless I could give a completely favourable verdict, she would be in despair and would have a very serious break-down. . . . The verdict which I gave her was not absolutely and completely what I thought about it. I praised the book more than I should have done if she had been well.' He does not say why he found it disappointing. His imprimatur was sufficient. She returned to the proofs, revised them exten-sively once more, and three weeks later was still confident: 'It seems to me to come off at the end. Anyhow to be a taut real strenuous book: with some beauty and poetry too. A full packed book. Feel a little exalted. Nor need I care much what people say.'

The Years was published in March 1937, five years after its conception. The days of waiting were dull, cold torture to her, but all except very few of the reviews were superlative. She was not, as she had expected, ridiculed. On reading Basil de Selincourt's review in *The Observer*, she thought, with delight, of other people reading it. She was not a failure. People would talk about her book, praise it, buy it. She was as happy as a first novelist who buys the *Evening Standard*, opens it in the Underground, and finds her book glowing on an inner page. Then she could be cast down by a single mildly hostile notice like Edwin Muir's in *The Listener*, 'All the lights sank', she wrote on perusing it, 'my reed bent to the ground. Dead and disappointing – so I am found out, and that odious rice-pudding of a book is what I thought it – a dank failure.'

She had been nervous that people would expect another cloudy, lyrical book like *The Waves*, and would be disappointed that the narrative of *The Years* was more conventional, direct. She told Stephen Spender that this time she wanted to catch the attention of the general reader. But nobody could have written *The Years*, as de Selincourt said, who had not already written *The Waves*. Ostensibly it was about a family, the Pargiters, who began in a Victorian house like Hyde Park Gate in the 1880s, and we follow their branching, fraying lives until the year of the book's publication. It is in part autobiographical. We are given a taste of Virginia's experience in the First World War, under bombardment in London, and of the major themes which concerned her, like the subordination of women and her agnosticism. Take this passage describing the funeral of Mrs Pargiter, as her daughter listens to the vicar pronouncing a benediction over the open grave:

'We give thee hearty, thanks', said the voice, 'for that it has pleased thee to deliver this our sister out of the miseries of this sinful world'. 'What a lie!', she cried to herself. 'What a damnable lie!' He had robbed her of the one feeling that was genuine.

That was the defiant Virginia speaking. We also hear Virginia the poet. She, who had never written a line of poetry in her life, could devote an entire page of her novel to rain, not as Hardy would have done it, expositorily, but like Spenser, evocatively. There is a touch of Bloomsbury too. The second-generation Pargiters are unafraid to discuss sex, war, cruelty, the poor, the rich, youth contrasted with age, permanence with change, but they were less adventurous than Bloomsbury. They did not voyage out.

Although it was more clairvoyance than simple narrative, the book was an immediate success with a public who had come to regard Virginia Woolf's novels with the same awe that the next generation paid to Henry Moore's sculptures. In England its sales restored the Woolfs' finances, which, after the long interval since the success of *Flush,* had started to wobble again. In America, as a reward for Donald Brace's infinite patience with Virginia's constant postponements, it sold 25,000 copies in two months, and for weeks remained top of the fiction best-seller list. As Mitchell Leaska, himself an American, has remarked, 'She was left with the grotesque fact that her most certain failure had become her greatest popular success.'

The long process of correcting the proofs of *The Years* coincided with the start of two other major projects in Virginia's literary life – her biography of Roger Fry, which his sisters had begged her to undertake, and her polemic, *Three*

Guineas. She enjoyed the polemic, for which she had begun to collect material, more than the biography, since there was no restriction on what she wanted to say about men and war, but with Fry there were personal problems of discretion: he had been Vanessa's lover; Clive had been accused of pla-giarizing his ideas. And the amount of information about him was overwhelming. 'You can cut a novel by 250 pages, but how do you cut a life?' 'The facts', she wailed to Vita, 'the swarm of facts. How can anyone lift a pen among them!' But she was committed by her promise to the sisters. Somehow she would have to indicate his love-affairs without stressing them, for even Bloomsbury would not accept a treatment of sex in biography which became customary forty years later. To Ethel she wrote, 'How does one square the relatives? How does one euphemise 20 different mistresses? But Roger every day turns out more miraculous.'

She slowly recovered her health after the ordeal of *The Years*, and was able to alternate her literary work with other obligations, just as Leonard managed to combine progress with his magnum opus *After the Deluge* with control of the Hogarth Press. When Margaret West, the most satisfactory of their managers, died in 1937, their burden was doubled. Virginia was still the main reader of manuscripts submitted to them, and travelled their books on publication. As the Press became better known, and Virginia herself its star author, inevitably the flood of unsolicited prose and poetry increased. 'Every boy and girl who can buy a fountain pen and a ream of paper', she told Janet Case, 'instantly writes a novel, ties it up and sends it to us.' But she found time to write articles for the weekly journals, and gave one broadcast in the BBC series 'Words Fail Me'. The tape of her talk, which she called

Craftsmanship, is the only substantial recording of her voice that survives. It had a sing-song quality, a rise and fall in intonation, with emphasis placed in unexpected places, as in 'c*i*vili*z*ation'. It was known as the Bloomsbury voice.

The abdication of Edward VIII in December 1936, before he had even been crowned, thrust aside for a few days every other consideration, personal and public. Virginia was excited to be living through an event which would be discussed for centuries to come. She did not much care for the monarchy. As a girl, she had stood in the street while Queen Victoria's carriage rolled by, but that was her nearest encounter with royalty. When George V died, she thought the public's grief 'for a very commonplace man' excessive. To her it was a curious survival of 'barbarism, emotionalism, heraldry, ecclesiasticism, sheer sentimentality and snobbery'. Of Edward VIII she wrote, from hearsay, that he was 'a cheap second-rate little bounder, whose only good points are that he keeps two mistresses and likes dropping into tea with the wives of miners', when there was only one current mistress, Wallis Simpson, and only one cup of tea with a miner's wife.

When the King's affair became public knowledge, Bloomsbury's attitude was one of liberal indifference. Why shouldn't he marry anyone he wants? But when they realized that the very existence of the monarchy, not just the fate of one monarch, was involved, they slightly changed their tune. This 'insignificant little man' was moving a pebble that could precipitate an avalanche. So let him keep Wallis as his mistress, and when he tires of her, take another. 'But apparently', Virginia noted in her diary, 'the King's little bourgeois demented mind sticks fast to the marriage service', in order to make

Wallis respectable at the cost of losing his throne.

On Abdication Day, 10 December 1936, she took a bus to Whitehall, where a shuffling crowd awaited the news. By chance she met Lady Ottoline there, and, inspired by the same reflections, they looked up at the window from which Charles I had stepped onto the scaffold. 'I felt I was walking in the 17th century with one of the courtiers, and she was lamenting not the abdication of Edward but the execution of Charles.' They hailed a taxi. The driver said, 'We don't want a woman that's already had two husbands, and an American, when there are so many good English girls.' *Vox populi.* Then they saw a newspaper van drive past bearing on its poster the one word ABDICATION.

XII

LIFE FOR THE WOOLFS returned to normal at the start of 1937, but international tensions were disturbing it. Leonard held constant meetings in Tavistock Square for politicians and journalists, from which, as far as she could manage, Virginia stood aloof. 'The bray and drone of those tortured voices almost sent me crazy', she wrote to Ethel, and having been persuaded to join a Committee of anti-Fascist intellectuals called Vigilance, she resigned, feeling that she had nothing to contribute. Leonard could speak for both of them. People were always asking her what she thought was happening in Abyssinia, in Poland, in Spain. She had no idea. 'Why does everyone bother me about politics?', she moaned to Ethel. 'Do you also have to trump up this meaningless nonsense, sign books, sign letters perpetually?' She was reserving her fire for *Three Guineas.*

Then something happened which forced her to pay attention. Julian Bell was killed in the Spanish Civil War.

Virginia was devoted to him and had come to admire him for his sterling character, and because they shared Vanessa between them. After his death she wrote privately, 'Our relationship was secure because it was founded on our passion – not too strong a word for either of us – for Nessa.' She liked his strong, masculine, adventurous style. He reminded her in some ways of her brother Thoby, who died at about the same age. They were both intellectuals in the sense that they were interested in ideas and the clear expression of them, but Thoby had been more mature in his thinking and writing than Julian, who 'never quite grew up', wrote Leonard. His life, like his writing, was never co-ordinated, although in love and politics he had lived it to the full. He had no profession, and no real qualifications for one. He had failed to gain a Fellowship at King's. The Hogarth Press had rejected his Memoir of Roger Fry, and T.S. Eliot (for Faber's) a collection of his essays. On his return from China in March 1937 Virginia saw in him a new maturity. He was well able to hold his own in political debate with Leonard and his father, but he was still excitable, clumsy (Keynes's word), undisciplined, though immensely likeable, combining in his character qualities inherited from both his parents, Clive's rumbustiousness, Vanessa's integrity. In looks he was a young Achilles.

Why did he decide, against the advice of his friends and

the entreaties of Vanessa and Virginia, to fight on the Republican side against Franco? Many of his contemporaries saw in the Spanish Civil War the stage on which the major political struggle of the period was being enacted, Communism versus Fascism. Julian was not a Communist. Surprisingly, indeed, he was not much interested in the ideological conflict. A friend, Richard Rees, who was in Spain with him, testified that 'political subtleties and allegiances did not overly concern him'. He was more attracted by the opportunity to experience war, to be 'in the thick of things', to prove his manhood, to strengthen his hold on life. After a somewhat fluttering youth, he yearned for excitement, perhaps glory. Virginia explained it as 'a fever in the blood'. It was also in reaction to Bloomsbury's pacifism. He would not be content to sit comfortably at Cambridge waging the intellectual battle when the only activity that mattered was at the front. But knowing how greatly he was distressing his mother, he agreed to compromise. He would not enlist as a soldier in the International Brigade. He would join a British unit, known as Spanish Medical Aid, as a non-combatant, and drive an ambulance. This would satisfy Bloomsbury's pacifism without allaying their fears for his safety.

He joined the unit in July on the eve of a major Republican offensive to relieve Franco's investment of Madrid. His role was to ferry casualties from the battlefield to two hospitals established in Philip II's great palace of the Escorial. Though his task was passive, it was highly dangerous. He was constantly under fire. Half the British medical unit were killed in the battle. On 18 July 1937 Julian himself was killed by a shell-splinter plunging deep into his chest. He was taken to the Escorial and died there six hours later. His last words were,

'Well, I always wanted a mistress and a chance to go to war, and now I've had both.'

The news reached England two days later, and for the next few weeks Virginia was constantly at her sister's side, first in London and then at Charleston, and she wrote to her every day when they were apart. It was not simply consolation that she offered, but her presence. She could not tell her sister what she thought, that Julian's death was a 'complete waste', as she said to others, and endeavoured to invest it with a certain grandeur. He had died doing what he wanted. It cannot have been easy for her. Her intimacy with Vanessa had never, since childhood, been fully reciprocated. 'When she is demonstrating I always shrink away', Vanessa once confessed. Now that an event so terrible, so deeply personal, had brought them closely together again, Virginia found not only words of sympathy which must soon have been exhausted, but an attitude, often expressed by silence, and then, as the pain lessened, by shared memories and jokes, which Vanessa could accept from no other person, least of all from Julian's father, Clive. Years later, after Virginia's death, she wrote to my mother, 'I remember all those days after I heard about Julian, lying in an unreal state and hearing her voice going on and on, keeping life going when otherwise it would have stopped.' At the time she found it impossible to express her gratitude to her sister. She asked Vita, whom she scarcely knew and did not much like, to express it for her. 'I cannot ever say how Virginia has helped me. Perhaps some day, not now, you will be able to tell her.' Vita passed on the message.

Julian's death coincided with Virginia's immersion in *Three Guineas*, a condemnation of war and of men who wage war.

To her it was agonizing that the young man of whom she was most deeply fond had thrown away his life in the manner that she most deeply deplored. She did not mention his fate to fortify her argument – indeed, there is nothing in any way autobiographical in the book – but 'I was always thinking of Julian when I wrote'. She was determined to expose the folly of resisting evil by a greater evil. It was a pacifist's statement, but it was something more. She wished to lay the blame for war on men and their treatment of women. She came near to saying that if women had a greater influence in the state, there would be no wars. They were denied that influence. They were poorly educated, excluded from the professions, and even given a subordinate place in the home. Women should protest, not militantly like Ethel Smyth, but passively. They should have no share in male arrogance and ambition. They must declare themselves 'outsiders', even to the extent of abrogating their nationality. 'If you insist on fighting to protect me or "our country"', she wrote, 'let it be understood soberly and rationally between us, that you are fighting to gratify a sex instinct which I cannot share; to procure benefits which I have not shared and probably will not share.' No appeal could be made to women to contribute to their country's defence, as their country had done nothing for them. The outsider will say, 'in fact, as a woman, I have no country. I want no country. As a woman my country is the whole world.' That was the pith of her argument. It was neither sober nor rational.

I find myself in some difficulty. I am writing the life of a woman for whom I had great affection and whom I much admired. I am obliged to argue against her profoundest convictions on a subject central to her life. In the Introductions to Volumes 5 and 6 of her Letters I stated my reasons, and find little need to alter them. Hermione Lee in her biography of Virginia said that I and others like me, including Quentin Bell, misunderstood and undervalued Virginia's attitude. She was tapping a deep well of feminine grievance in a profound and very vivid way. While *A Room of One's Own* had stated the case for women's rights charmingly, wittily, *Three Guineas* was angry. Much of it was written with a stridency that I do not recognize in any of her other books, her diary, her letters or her conversation. She considered that she had the right to be angry. It was her duty to exploit her fame as a vehicle for her protest. She was living in very dangerous times. They were dangerous, she thought, because men were instinctively bellicose. Men liked conflict: women didn't.

Nobody denies her right to say this, but her reasoning must be open to challenge. As Quentin Bell put it, 'It was wrong to involve a discussion of women's rights with the far more agonising and immediate question: What we were to do in order to meet the evergrowing menace of Fascism and war.' The two controversies had little in common. Nor was it true that women in general were more pacifist than men: from Helen of Troy to Margaret Thatcher they have encouraged war as an instrument of policy, and to demonstrate men's hardihood and pride. It was not other men in the First World War who distributed white feathers to supposed malingerers, but women. They admired the brave, despised the cowardly, and in later wars were proud to share its hazards with men. If Virginia was right, why were women not all pacifist? Why did they not use their new-won votes to overthrow any government that advocated war? And how did she propose to overcome Fascism, which she hated, except by military preparations to fight it?

It could be argued that as a pamphleteer – and she called *Three Guineas* 'my war pamphlet' – one should not expect from her a scholar's fidelity to logic and sources. She was not a politician. Leonard remarked in his autobiography that she was the most unpolitical person since Aristotle invented the term. But in *Three Guineas* she was using the weapons of political invective and the scholarly apparatus of quotation and extensive footnotes. She wished to be taken seriously, particularly on the theme which she had prefaced in *A Room of One's Own*, that women had always been disadvantaged by men, and still were. She was not complaining of her own fate, for the flowering of her genius had in no way been thwarted by ill-treatment or convention. It is true that she had been deprived of a university education, but that meant only that she had never experienced the intellectual discipline that might have saved her from the hyperbole of *Three Guineas*. As in *A Room* she was speaking only of women of her own class and cultural background, a tiny minority who had little cause for complaint. As I summed up my criticism of her argument in 1979: 'Today the newspapers print every day the obituaries of women who began distinguished careers at the very time when Virginia was protesting that few opportunities existed for them. She drew most of her examples from the past, but presented them in such a way as to suggest that they were still relevant. She was describing a world that had evaporated, but which to her was still real. She, who had won free from it so young, so defiantly, so successfully, was almost alone in imagining that nothing had basically changed.'

Three Guineas was published in June 1938, and was given a warm but not rapturous reception by the critics. Graham Greene and Basil de Selincourt were friendly, if a little puzzled, perhaps feeling nervous that if they picked holes in her arguments, they would be confirming everything that Virginia had written about male arrogance. Women were more outspoken. Theodora Bosanquet wrote in *Time and Tide*, 'I do not suppose that Mrs Woolf would sustain in the teeth of much evidence that jealousy, vanity, greed and possessiveness are found only in public life and exhibited almost exclusively by the male sex', and Queenie Leavis said in a long article which Virginia did not even bother to read to the end, that 'this book is not merely silly and ill-informed, but contains self-indulgent sex-hostility'.

At first Virginia did not mind these attacks. She expected them. She was proud of what she had done. 'I thought I would raise their hackles – poor old strumpets', she wrote in her diary after reading the first reviews. 'I have already gained my point, I am taken seriously, not dismissed as a charming prattler as I feared.' Nelly Cecil, Lady Rhondda (an ardent feminist), Naomi Mitchison, Emmeline Pethick Lawrence (the doyenne of the Women's Suffrage Movement) and of course Ethel Smyth ('Your book is so splendid that it makes me hot'), wrote her letters of gratitude for what she had done for their cause. Bloomsbury were slightly embarrassed by it. Keynes called it 'a silly argument, and not very well written', a verdict of which the first part could be defended but not the second, since it was eloquent and elegant in style and muscular in treatment. When Leonard first read it, 'he gravely approves' (Virginia's diary), and thinks it 'an extremely clear analysis', but that this was not his true opinion was revealed two months later when she noted, 'I didn't get so much praise from L. as I hoped', and significantly he made no comment on it in his Memoirs. As late as December 1938 she recorded, 'Not one of my friends has mentioned it' (not true), 'My wide circle has widened, but I am altogether in the dark as to the true merits of the book.'

Curiously it was Vita who aroused her to protest. She had written to Virginia, 'You are a tantalising writer because at one moment you enchant one with your lovely prose and next moment exasperate one with your misleading arguments. I read you with delight, even though I wanted to exclaim, "Oh but Virginia", on 50 per cent of your pages.' Virginia replied, 'When you say that you are exasperated by my "misleading arguments", I ask, What do you mean? If I said, I don't agree with your conception of Joan of Arc's character [in Vita's recent book about her], that's one thing. But if I said, Your arguments about her are "misleading", shouldn't I mean, Vita has cooked the facts in a dishonest way in order to produce an effect which she knows to be untrue?' Unfortunately that came close to expressing exactly what Vita did mean, as is shown by her own copy of *Three Guineas*, which is scored with exclamation marks and hostile annotations. But she replied 'I never for a moment questioned your facts, but only disagreed in some places with the deductions you drew from them. ... To take an example, you suggest that fighting is a sex characteristic which women cannot share, but is it not true that many women are extremely bellicose and urge their men to fight?' Virginia did not reply to this. It was her only quarrel with Vita, and it left no permanent scar.

XIII

THE HOGARTH PRESS was still extending its scope without growing to a size that would have monopolized their time or exposed it to a takeover bid from larger publishers. In 1938 John Lehmann, after a brief absence, became an equal partner with Leonard, buying out Virginia's half-share for £3,000 and bringing with him the literary miscellany *New Writing* which he had founded and edited and was ideally suited to the Press's tradition. At first the partnership was an uneasy one. When the agreement was signed, Lehmann proposed that they should celebrate the event by drinking a toast, but Leonard grimly replied that he had only cold water in which to drink it. Then Virginia turned down Lehmann's own novel, and they disagreed about the memorial volume of Julian's poetry and essays which Quentin was editing. No wonder that Virginia complained to Vanessa, 'John is as touchy as a very old spinster whose one evening dress has a hole in the behind', but it was as much Leonard's reluctance to share control as John's touchiness which caused the trouble. However, Lehmann remained Leonard's partner until 1946, when he left to found his own publishing firm.

Looking back, the Hogarth Press had been a great success. Its history has been admirably written by Professor J.H. Willis of William and Mary College, Williamsburg, and in his concluding chapter he draws up a balance sheet, regarding it first as a business, then as a contribution to English culture. It was not until 1928, when they published thirty-six titles, that the annual profit exceeded £100. It rose to a peak in 1930 with

£2,373 (*The Edwardians* year) and to £2,442 in 1937 with *The Years*. Virginia and Vita, and Sigmund Freud, were undoubtedly the main money-spinners. As for the quality of its output, Willis is fully justified in concluding that 'Virginia Woolf's nine major works of fiction and non-fiction, T.S. Eliot's two volumes of poetry, translations of Freud's eight best-known books and the translations of Rilke's poetry in five volumes would make the Hogarth Press an important publisher even if it published nothing else.' In Virginia's lifetime they published 474 volumes, an impressive contribution to the intellectual life of England between the wars, but surprisingly they had not been able to attract the major Bloomsbury authors apart from Virginia herself. Forster, Strachey, Keynes and Fry were under contract to larger publishers, and Eliot and Plomer abandoned them once the Woolfs had made them famous. It was only out of loyalty to Leonard that Virginia played so large a part for so long, and the emergence of John Lehmann as a partner was a great relief to them both.

Two months after his appointment, they went on holiday to Scotland. It was Virginia's only visit there apart from a brief trip to Glasgow in 1913. On their drive north they discovered parts of England which she imagined they were the first people ever to explore, particularly the more desolate parts of Northumberland where Hadrian's Wall runs across the moors. 'What the Romans saw, I see', she wrote, 'miles and miles of lavender-covered loneliness.' In the Highlands she was impressed, as she had been in Ireland, by the emptiness of the land and the poverty of the people, and sudden glimpses of Landseer scenes: 'There was one lake, with trees reflected, which I think carried beauty to the extreme point: whether it is expressible, that rapture, I doubt', but she was writing to Ethel. When writing to Vanessa she curbed expressions of her delight, thinking that Vanessa's tastes had far surpassed Landseers and that ecstasy of this sort would bore her.

On their return to Sussex, Virginia was involved in the continuing repercussions of *Three Guineas*, and she again took up, simultaneously, her two new books, the life of Roger Fry and *Pointz Hall* (published as *Between the Acts*.) She found the novel more enjoyable work than the biography, switching from 'assiduous truth' (Fry) to 'wild ideas' (*Pointz*). She was still worried how to deal with Fry's wife Helen, who was locked up mad, and his love-affair with Vanessa. 'What am I to say about you?', she asked her. Should she come out with the truth, or compromise? 'Do give me some views: how to deal with love so that we're not all blushing.' Vanessa replied, 'I hope you won't mind making us all blush. It won't do any harm, and anyhow, no one's blushes last long. ... The only important thing is to tell the truth, for the sake of the younger generation.' Despite this unexceptionable Bloomsbury declaration, Virginia did compromise. In the book she primly referred to the Vanessa–Roger relationship as 'their friendship'.

It was like handling three saucepans on the stove simultaneously. Fry and *Pointz* were alternately brought to the boil, while *Three Guineas* was left to simmer. It was the latter that caused her most trouble, both for the flood of reviews and letters that it provoked, and because actuality caught up with theory: how was she to respond to the imminence of another European war?

In 1936 she had allowed herself to become involved in a movement called 'For Intellectual Liberty', or FIL. Its membership was very select (Huxley, Wells, Forster, G.E. Moore, Gilbert Murray, Leonard Woolf), but its aims were uncertain, for it proclaimed 'the need for united action in defence of peace, liberty and culture', without agreeing on what that action should be beyond a vague appeal to governments to disarm and sign a universal treaty of peace. In face of Mussolini's conquest of Abyssinia and Hitler's occupation of the Rhineland and Austria, and the involvement of both dictators in the Spanish Civil War, such high-minded manifestos seemed an inadequate response. Were Britain and France to arm or disarm? Resist the dictators or surrender to them? Aldous Huxley, the President of FIL and an outright pacifist, resigned with the excuse that he intended to live in America, and Leonard, his deputy, was on the point of resignation for the opposite reason, that he was unable to persuade FIL or the Labour Party – he was still Secretary to its International Committee – to support rearmament as the only reaction that would make the dictators pause. 'Until the hawk actually has its beak in their flesh', he groaned, 'they will not face them.' The Tories were even worse. 'They do a dirty deal with Musso, and call it peace', he had written to Julian Bell in his most Tacitean manner. We should revert to rapid rearmament and a broad anti-Fascist alliance, including an Anglo-Soviet military pact. The great powers must unite to protect the smaller powers. This was Leonard's constant theme in the later 1930s and the message of his book *The Barbarians at the Gate*. It consorted ill with *Three Guineas*, where Virginia had declared herself an outsider who would have nothing to do with this masculine folly.

It was a difficult situation for her. The two main interests in her life – support for Leonard, and opposition to his most cherished beliefs – had come into conflict. She co-signed a letter to *The Times* appealing for 'sympathetic benevolence' towards the Spanish democrats, and a FIL telegram to the Prime Minister, Neville Chamberlain, which read, 'Profoundly deplore rapprochement Mussolini before his troops leave Spain'. This was safe enough. Neither sentiment involved rearmament. Her true feelings were expressed in a letter to Janet Case written from Monk's House on Christmas Eve 1936:

> I'm sitting over a log fire with Leonard reading history for his book [*After the Deluge*], and the black and white spaniel is in its basket beside him. I'm glad to hoick him away from his eternal meetings – Labour Party, Fabian Research, Intellectual Liberty, Spanish Medical Aid – oh dear, how they poach on him – what hours he spends with dirty, unkempt, ardent, ugly, entirely unpractical but no doubt well meaning philanthropists at whom I should throw the coal-scuttle after 10 minutes if I were in his place.

Franco's victory in Spain effectively put an end to FIL, and Virginia tried to face realities. At first she passed Hitler off as 'a ridiculous little man', and his speeches, which resounded by radio through the garden at Rodmell, as the ravings of a lunatic. Then the Munich Pact caught her in a dilemma. 'If it is war, then every country joins in: chaos. But it's a hopeless war this – when we know winning means nothing' (diary). But a week later: 'All Europe in Hitler's keeping. What'll he gobble next?' Like the great majority of her countrymen and women, she was ambivalent. How resist evil except by a greater evil? If Britain and France go to war to save

Czechoslovakia, would we carry our people with us? Would we win? Even Kingsley Martin, who almost camped on the Woolfs' doorstep during the crisis, came to the conclusion, 'the strategic value of the Bohemian frontier should not be made the occasion of a world war'. So the inglorious pact signed at Munich, which gave Hitler almost all he wanted (he took the rest), came as an intense relief. Virginia's letters to Vanessa, who was in France, described the sand-bagging, the trench-digging, the issue of gas masks, the plans to evacuate children from London, with a mixture of excitement and despair. When it was all over, she summed up her emotions for Ethel Smyth as a 'residue of anger and shame, on top of sheer cowardly relief'. Leonard considered that Munich meant 'peace without honour for six months'. It is not unfair to Virginia to conclude that she never clarified her mind. Pacifism, and with it the central argument of *Three Guineas*, had been overtaken by events. When war came a year later, and she expressed her horror, Leonard replied, 'Yes, but now it's come, it's better to win the war than lose it', to which Virginia had no reply. Wars can only be won by fighting.

Many friends and relations were dying before war added to their number. After Lytton, Carrington and Roger Fry, she lost George Duckworth, Ka Arnold-Forster, Janet Case, Charles Sanger, Mark Gertler (suicide), Leonard's mother, Jack Hills and (on the same day) Mitz the marmoset. She still needed the excitements of London. From time to time she complained of the 'frizz and fritter' of social life, but even lunch with Lady Colefax could be enjoyable. Colefax was ruthless in her head-hunting and earned the ridicule of her guests, but her parties were carefully composed, to the extent of excluding spouses whom she found uninteresting. On one

Roger Fry, a self-portrait now in the National Portrait Gallery. Virginia loved him for the three qualities that she emphasised in her biography of him, 'his charm, his intelligence, and his persistence, which in combination made him a major influence on his generation. He lifted people's spirits.'

such occasion, in November 1938, Virginia found herself in company with Max Beerbohm, Somerset Maugham and Christopher Isherwood, and she was careful to record her impressions of them, first in her diary, and then, sharpened, for Vanessa. Beerbohm was 'a charmer, rubicund, gay, apparently innocent but in fact very astute and full of airy fantasies'. Maugham was 'a grim figure, rat-eyed, dead-man cheeked, unshaven, a criminal I should have said had I met him in a bus'. Isherwood 'seemed all agog with amusement, but is a shifty, quick-silver little slip of a creature – very nimble and rather inscrutable and on his guard'. On leaving, Maugham said to her, indicating Isherwood, 'that young man holds the future of the English novel in his hands', a somewhat tactless statement that Virginia seems not to have taken amiss.

She also met Sigmund Freud. The Hogarth Press had been his British publishers since 1924, and now he was a refugee from Austria, living in Hampstead where the Woolfs called on him for tea in January 1939. The visit was not a great success. Virginia described him as 'a screwed up, shrunk, very old man [only 82], with a monkey's light eyes, paralysed spasmodic movements, inarticulate, alert'. He had an old-world courtesy (he solemnly presented Virginia with a narcissus), and Leonard's impression was of 'great gentleness, but behind the gentleness, great strength'. They never saw him again. He died from cancer eight months later.

Bloomsbury was diminishing in importance in Virginia's life. Her main correspondents were still Ethel Smyth, Vanessa and Vita, and it was curiously Vita's elder son, Ben, who after the outbreak of war caused her to write him a careful retrospect of its significance. Ben had rather foolishly attacked Bloomsbury, and Fry in particular, for its ineffectual stance against Fascism and social injustice. They had been living in 'a fool's paradise', he wrote to Virginia. She was fond of Ben, and had asked him to sort out some of Fry's papers. She answered him in two long letters, for one of which she made a rare draft that also survives, protesting that Bloomsbury had done its best. Keynes had written *The Economic Consequences of the Peace*; Leonard had alerted us for years to the menace of the dictators; she herself had worked at Morley College and for Women's Suffrage, and had written *Three Guineas*. What more could they have done? Lytton by his books, Duncan and Vanessa by their paintings, Roger by his lectures, had opened people's eyes to new ideas and roused them from cultural apathy. Should they have become active politicians? What was Ben himself doing about it? He was an art historian, and Deputy Surveyor of the Kings's Pictures under Kenneth Clark. Was his occupation any less ivory-tower than Fry's had been? Artists do not, cannot, influence events, she said. They must use their gifts to widen understanding and appreciation of the arts. But what's the use of telling people who left school at the age of fourteen that they ought to enjoy Shakespeare? She had just been lecturing to a working-class audience at Brighton, and sensed a gulf that was almost unbridgeable, but it was not for that reason a matter for shame. Her replies to Ben were more tolerant and logical than his attack, though clearly she was indignant. It was typical of her to end her letter by inviting him to spend his leave at Rodmell.

Her main defence of Bloomsbury and its values was her biography of Roger Fry, published in July 1940. She had not enjoyed the heavy breathing of the Fry family down her neck as she was writing it, and she was not practised in biography.

Nor did she enjoy the advantages enjoyed by the biographer of, say, Virginia Woolf, for whom the main work has already been done by others, the diaries annotated, the letters collected, the arguments for and against astutely marshalled. But she had known her subject intimately, been intimate with his intimates, and had loved him for the three qualities that she chose to emphasize, his charm, his intelligence and his persistence, which in combination had made him a major influence on his generation. Virginia quoted with approval Julian Bell's comment, 'He made one share his pleasure in thinking', which might be taken as a tribute to Bloomsbury as a whole. He lifted people's spirits, as when he persuaded businessmen to accept Omega products, telling them, 'It is time that the spirit of fun was introduced into furniture and fabrics. We have suffered too long from the dull and the stupidly serious', or when addressing a wider public at the time of the Post-Impressionist exhibitions, he said, according to Virginia, that 'he feared that the art of painting was circling purposelessly among frivolities and was at a dead end. Now he was convinced that it was alive, and that a great age was at hand.' Virginia's description of Fry's personality and life, sometimes introducing her own memories of him, but only in the third person ('a friend', 'an admirer'), was alternately taut with meaning or running fresh with pleasure. The review of the book that she most appreciated was by J.T. Sheppard, where he said that Roger Fry was there and not Virginia Woolf. But Leonard was frankly critical. The book was too impersonal, he told her: 'It's merely analysis, not history'. It was the first time that he had ever directly criticized her work. In moments of depression, she considered that it was not a book at all, but 'cabinet making'.

XIV

THE WOOLFS NEVER denied themselves an annual holiday however pressing their work, and in June 1939 they toured Normandy and Brittany by car, finding renewed pleasure in non-English sights like a pale farmhouse disguised as a château or a bishop blessing a fishing-boat. On their return to London they were obliged to leave 52 Tavistock Square, where they had lived for fifteen years, because it was due to be demolished (a fate anticipated in 1940 by German bombs), and move to a flat in 37 Mecklenburgh Square, only a few blocks away, taking the Hogarth Press and its files with them. The move was not completed until after the outbreak of war, which considerably hampered it, and they were not able to occupy even a single room until October.

Virginia was completing her revision of *Roger Fry* at the same time as Leonard published the second volume of his *After the Deluge*, and she was also writing articles and stories for American magazines, including one of her best-known, 'Lappin and Lapinova'. Although they were by now quite comfortably off, the Woolfs were nervous about overspending on small luxuries ('Should I spend 1/8 on scissors?', Virginia asked herself) or on loans to other people. It was this constant need to top up their income – for Leonard earned very little – that accounts for Virginia's remarkable output of journalism. One tends to think of her as a novelist who published a new book once every four or five years, but her critical essays filled three posthumous volumes, apart from *The Common Reader*, First and Second Series published in her lifetime, and her shorter fiction occupies a stout volume. In addition, the Hogarth Press issued in the autumn of 1939 her pamphlet *Reviewing*, and having refused the prestigious Clark lectures at Cambridge, she spent weeks preparing for the Brighton branch of the Workers' Educational Association a lecture on modern literature, later published as 'The Leaning Tower'. *Pointz Hall*, for the moment, was set aside. She also began to write her Memoirs, but they made little progress before she died.

Britain and France declared war on Germany on 3 September 1939, when they were at Monk's House, and they remained there for most of the winter, one of the coldest on record, with occasional trips to London. At first Virginia felt only 'dumb rage' at being 'fought for by young people whom one wants to see making love'. Although the war entered an inactive phase between the conquest of Poland and the German invasion of Norway in April 1940, she was unable to isolate herself from it. London children and pregnant mothers were evacuated to Rodmell (but not to Monk's House), clerks from the Hogarth Press took it in turn to spend quiet weekends there, the village windows were blacked out to hide from German pilots signs of inhabited places, and there were weekly meetings of the Labour Party to discuss the latest events. It seemed at times, as Virginia wrote to Ethel Smyth, that 'there's a peace in the country which surrounds me as a mouse is surrounded by cheese' but in London, she recorded in her diary, 'You never escape the war. Very few buses. Tubes closed. No children. No loitering. Everyone humped with a gas-mask. Strain and grimness. At night it's so verdurous and gloomy that one expects a badger or a fox to prowl along the pavement. A reversion to the middle ages with all the space and silence of the country set in this forest of black houses.'

There was scarcely a single air raid during that first winter of war, and no fighting on land. Virginia wrote to Vita, 'Of course I'm not in the least patriotic', but she let drop phrases to other people which indicated that she was not in the least indifferent either. To Eddy Sackville-West, for example, she wrote of 'the obvious horror we all feel for war; but then, with a solid block of unbaked barbarians in Germany, what's the good of our being comparatively civilised?'; and to Judith Stephen, Adrian's young daughter, 'I'm more and more convinced that it is our duty to catch Hitler in his home haunts and prod him if even with only the end of an old inky pen.' The pen was hers; but the 'catching' could only be by air attack. Bloomsbury was no longer pacifist. Even Clive Bell patrolled the South Downs with a slung rifle. Only Ham Spray, where Frances Partridge kept the flag of pacifism flying with her husband Ralph, was faithful to the cause, and this was all the more remarkable, because Ralph had fought with the utmost gallantry in the First War. His experience was his main reason for thinking its successor ethically unjustifiable.

When a significant event occurred in the outside world, like the sinking of a great ship or the Russian invasion of Finland, Virginia mentioned it casually in her diary after noting that she had seen a kingfisher on her walk. Her mood was melancholy and subdued, further depressed by an acute attack of influenza in March. Then in May 1940 it was no longer possible for anyone to lead a sheltered life. The German army swept through France, the British escaped without their weapons from Dunkirk, and were evicted from Norway. In

her diary of 25 May she made a rare strategic judgment, not far short of the truth: 'The Germans seem youthful, fresh, inventive. We plod behind.' In her letters she barely referred to these disasters, just as Jane Austen, writing to her sister from their brother's house near Canterbury, never mentioned Napoleon's army poised for invasion from Boulogne. But in her diary she kept an almost day-by-day record of her experiences and reactions, and it is interesting to see how her mood varied with the intensity of the crisis. In July she wrote, 'I don't like any of the feelings that war breeds: patriotism; all sentimental and emotional parodies of real feelings', and when she saw soldiers passing through Sussex after escaping from France, she thought it absurd to describe them as heroes. But during the air battles over south-east England, of which she was often a direct witness – even falling flat on her face in the garden of Monk's House when German planes flew so low that she could see the swastika painted on their tail fins – she felt a stirring of hatred for them. Watching a squadron of British fighters flying out to sea to intercept a Luftwaffe raid, she wrote, 'I almost instinctively wished them luck', as if surprised by her emotion. At that moment, she was glad that she was of the same race as them. For Churchill she could not suppress a certain admiration. 'A clear, measured, robust speech', she commented when he spoke of the imminence of invasion. It was natural for her to identify love of the Sussex

Virginia Woolf in 1939, a photograph taken, much against her will, by Gisèle Freund. She wrote to Vita: 'I'm in a rage. That devil woman Giselle [sic] Freund calmly tells me that she's showing those d—d photographs – and I made it a condition she shouldn't. I loathe being hoisted about on top of a stick for anyone to stare at.' In fact, it is the best photograph ever taken of her.

countryside with love of England, and to that extent she reversed what she had told Vita, that she had not a grain of patriotism in her. London, too, raked her heart. 'Have you that feeling for certain alleys and little courts between Chancery Lane and the City?', she asked Ethel. 'I walked to the Tower the other day by way of caressing my love of all that.' She felt for ordinary people an affinity that she had scarcely acknowledged before. In September 1940 she wrote, again to Ethel:

When I see a great smash like a crushed matchbox where an old house stood, I wave my hand to London. What I'm finding odd and agreeable and unwonted is the admiration this war creates – for every sort of person: chars, shopkeepers, even much more remarkably, for politicians – Winston at least – and the tweed-wearing, sterling, dull women here [Rodmell], with their grim good sense. ... I'd almost lost faith in human beings, partly owing to my immersion in the dirty water of artists' envies and vanities while I worked at Roger. Now hope revives again.

At the height of the invasion threat, the Woolfs moved regularly between London and the country. Rodmell was only three miles from Newhaven, one of the south-coast ports where British Intelligence expected the Germans to land (correctly – it was the *Schwerpunkt* of their 9th Army, and paratroops would have dropped on the Downs), and Leonard, knowing that if they were captured, they would both be proscribed by the Gestapo for his Jewishness and prominent anti-Nazi activities, carried a lethal dose of morphine for both of them and kept enough petrol in his garage to asphyxiate themselves if the Germans landed. Yet they remained remarkably cool. Leonard wrote in his auto-biography, 'I never myself felt, or saw anyone else feeling, fear', and although I, who lived through the same period, find this statement scarcely credible, it is true that Virginia saw some beauty and excitement in the air battles overhead. 'It's rather lovely', she wrote to John Lehmann, 'to see the [search] lights stalking the Germans over the marshes', and when bombs breached the banks of the River Ouse, allowing the flood water to spread as far as Monk's House itself, she did not speculate that this would make invasion at this point less likely, but was reminded by it of William Morris's poem 'The Haystack in the Floods'. When four bombs flowered like ruby tulips in the nearby fields, she boasted that Vanessa, immune at Charleston, would be jealous.

It was during that long spring and summer of 1940 that *Roger Fry* was published, and it sold slowly, the military crisis making men like Fry seem somehow irrelevant. Virginia resumed her work on *Pointz Hall*, which at one moment she described as 'so much more of a strain than Roger', but on finishing it in November, she wrote in her diary, 'I've enjoyed writing almost every page'. There had been nothing to match the stress of *The Years*. She even found domestic chores enjoyable. Having lost her only live-in maid, she discovered for the first time the freedom that came from being unmolested by servants, and began to cook their meagre rations, helped by a village woman, Louie Everest, who remained with Leonard years after Virginia's death. She also joined the village Women's Institute and became its treasurer. It was a curiously pleasant existence, varied only by occasional visits to London and expeditions like that with Vita to Penshurst Place on the day when Paris fell. Sometimes visitors came for the night –

the MacCarthys, G.E. Moore, Elizabeth Bowen.

While Mecklenburgh Square was still intact, it was possible for them to stay there for a night or two. In September a bomb shattered a house across the street from their own, and another, unexploded, prevented them from approaching it. When it went off ten days later, the ceilings of No. 37 fell in, and the flat was uninhabitable. In October it was the turn of 52 Tavistock Square. It was flattened, Duncan's murals hanging over a smoking gap, but this was no cause for added distress, since they had failed to sublet the house and were still paying rent for it. Now it was impossible to charge for a house that did not exist. 'With a sigh of relief', wrote Virginia, 'we saw a heap of ruins.'

With the greatest difficulty they moved their belongings from Mecklenburgh to the country, climbing over the fallen plaster to retrieve their sodden books and papers, and they rented some rooms in Rodmell where they could temporarily store them. John Lehmann moved the Hogarth Press and its staff to Letchworth in Hertfordshire, where the Woolfs visited him in February 1941. But it was at Monk's House that Virginia spent the remaining months of her life, and they were the months when the German *Blitzkrieg* slackened. They lived in comparative peace. Virginia's feminist instincts resurfaced. In a lecture to the village branch of the Labour Party on Women and War, she argued that wars derived from 'manliness' and manliness bred 'womanliness' – 'both so hateful', she wrote to Lady Simon, 'but I was scowled at as a prostitute'.

Those same village people, in disguise, were the characters in *Pointz Hall*, which she renamed in the last stages of revision as *Between the Acts*. In the novel she attempted to mingle history with reality, the events occupying a single day as in

Mrs Dalloway but reaching back for centuries as in *Orlando.* This device was made possible by making a village pageant the central episode of the book, with scenes acted by the villagers. In amateurish make-believe they depicted the English character from the time of Queen Elizabeth to the present day. The novel was as ambitious as the pageant itself. It was the only time when Virginia attempted to mingle ancient forms of dialogue with modern rustic speech, and to portray the interpenetration of classes from the owners of Pointz Hall, where the pageant was staged, to the village idiot. The novel had a deeper meaning too. She was exploring the spiritual significance of life, and how it came about that civilization had been created by such trivial characters as ourselves. Her message was as puzzling to her readers as the pageant was to its audience. Perhaps Virginia was aware of this. It is known that she intended to revise it further. Conceivably she might have toned down the comedy to reveal the tragedy more clearly, and made more obvious when her characters were speaking as themselves or as symbols. We cannot be sure. The book was published by Leonard after her death with the cautious note: 'She would not, I believe, have made any large or material alterations.'

XV

ON 25 JANUARY 1941 Virginia Woolf reached the age of fifty-nine. She did not suffer from the usual infirmities of advancing age, like deafness or loss of memory, and although she told several people that her hands had begun to tremble, there is no sign of this in her manuscripts, which remained clear and distinguished till the end. Her letters were cheerful, and those she wrote to Vita were specially affectionate, as if she was appealing for a renewal of their love: 'How I long to hear from your own lips what's been worrying you – for you'll never shake me off – no!' 'How much I depend on you, and should mind any word that annoyed or hurt you.' Again: 'What can one say – except that I love you, and I've got to live through this strange quiet evening thinking of you sitting alone.' They were reunited by the experience of the war, their neighbour-counties, Sussex and Kent, being the most vulnerable to invasion and the skies above them scarred by the same planes in combat. Vita once managed to make the journey to Rodmell in spite of petrol rationing. On 17 February she spent a night there, and lectured to the village Women's Institute on her journeys to Persia. It was the last time that the two women met.

Almost to the end Virginia was capable of much enjoyment and intensive work. After her death Leonard discovered as many as eight drafts of a review she had written of a biography of Mrs Thrale, her last piece of criticism, and while revising *Between the Acts*, she was also toying with *Anon*, her history of literature. She was enjoying her household chores – making butter, beating carpets, arranging books – and visitors saw little change in her manner. This was Elizabeth Bowen's recollection of a two-night visit in February: 'I remember her kneeling back on the floor – we were tacking away, mending a torn Spanish curtain in the house – and she sat back on her heels, and put her head back in a patch of sun, early spring sun. Then she laughed in this consuming, choking, delightful, hooting way. That is what has remained with me.'

Her diary offers some more sombre clues. On 26 January she wrote that she was 'in a trough of despair', but it seemed short lived; and on 8 March she wrote of 'my despondency', but 'I shall conquer this mood, and I will go down with flying colours'. Various things contributed to her depression. The war, of course, and the renewed threat of invasion in the spring; the destruction of her two London homes; the rationing of basic foods; the difficulty of travel; Angelica's love-affair with David Garnett (whom she later married), which Virginia considered 'grotesque' given their disparity in age. More important was her fear of failure as a writer. Leonard's criticism of *Roger Fry* may still have rankled, but it was mainly *Between the Acts* that worried her. She thought it foolish, not worth publishing. She told her new doctor, Octavia Wilberforce, at the end of December that it was 'a completely worthless book', and her disappointment with it never left her during the remaining months of her life. Although Leonard genuinely praised the book, thinking it 'better than anything she has written', as he told her American publisher, Donald Brace, Virginia was insistent that it needed extensive revision, if not cancelling altogether. This was not merely her usual reaction on finishing a book. It was something more terrible. She sensed a decline in her creative energy. 'I've lost all power over words', she told Dr Wilberforce, 'can't do a thing with them.' What was the point of living if she was never again to understand the shape of the world around her, or be able to describe it? In any case, who cared about books in wartime? 'It's difficult, I find, to write', she told another friend. 'No audience. No private stimulus, only this outer roar.' To end her life at this point was like ending a book: it had a certain artistic integrity.

It is only in retrospect that her intimates recognized the signs of approaching disaster. Vanessa 'never suspected the danger'. Vita and Ethel Smyth thought her no more affected by the war than they all were, and her letters gave them no other clue. Leonard in his autobiography said that he 'had no foreboding until the beginning of 1941', and that it was not until 25 January that she showed the 'first symptoms of serious mental disturbance'. She had begun to hear voices. She ate but little. She was advised by Dr Wilberforce, who had become her closest confidante, that she should stop working for a space: she needed rest, and as far as wartime rationing allowed, a proper diet. Virginia would not heed these warnings. She sensed that she was going mad again, and although she well knew that rest had cured her before, she was convinced that she would never recover this time. It was better to die while she was sane than linger on as a burden to others. But there was nobody with whom she could discuss it. If she opened her heart to Leonard, Vanessa or even Wilberforce, they would put her under constraints to prevent her harming herself. She must escape them, and face them with the accomplished fact.

She left three suicide notes behind her. Joanne Trautmann and I brooded over them for a long time (the originals are in the British Library), and came to a conclusion different from Leonard's and Quentin Bell's, who believed that she had written all three on the day of her suicide. We concluded from the evidence of the letters themselves that she had first attempted to kill herself on 18 March 1941. She arrived back at Monk's House dripping wet, and told Leonard that she had fallen by accident into a water-filled ditch. He had not found the letter that she had left for him, and suspected nothing. It was the most significant of the three, and I give it in full:

Tuesday

Dearest, I feel certain that I am going mad again: I feel we cant go through another of those terrible times. And I shant recover this time. I begin to hear voices, and cant concentrate. So I am doing what seems the best thing to do. You have given me the greatest possible happiness. You have been in every way all that anyone could be. I dont think two people could have been happier till this terrible disease came. I cant fight it any longer, I know that I am spoiling your life, that without me you could work. And you will I know. You see I cant even write this properly. I cant read. What I want to say is that I owe all the happiness of my life to you. You have been entirely patient with me and incredibly good. I want to say that – everybody knows it. If anybody could have saved me it would have been you. Everything has gone from me but the certainty of your goodness. I cant go on spoiling your life any longer.

I dont think two people could have been happier than we have been.

After writing this letter, she lived another ten days. In her diary, which she continued to write until 24 March, there was no hint of what she had done or intended to do. She wrote a similar letter to Vanessa, but hid it with her first letter to Leonard, and simulated calm. Although Leonard was aware that she might be on the verge of a major breakdown, he reasoned that if he bothered her, or appeared to be monitoring her every movement, he might drive her to take the very action that non-interference might avert. He did, however, persuade her, much against her will, to visit Dr Wilberforce in Brighton on 27 March, but nothing much resulted from the consultation. Wilberforce said afterwards that she foresaw no immediate danger and counselled Virginia, once again, to rest. On the same day Virginia wrote to John Lehmann telling him not to publish *Between the Acts*: 'it's too silly and trivial'.

Next morning, Friday 28 March 1941, she went as usual to her garden lodge, and having spent some time there alone, she wrote a second, shorter, letter to Leonard, repeating the sense of the first. Leaving it in the lodge, she took her two earlier letters into the house and put them where Leonard would find them. Then, about midday, she walked the half-mile to the River Ouse, and thrusting a large stone into the pocket of her fur coat, she threw herself into the water. Although she could swim, she forced herself to drown. It must have been a terrifying death.

Leonard, on discovering her notes, searched the river bank and saw her walking-stick floating on the surface, but no sign of her. There was little doubt what had happened. He told Vanessa, who by chance called at Monk's House that afternoon, and wrote one letter, to Vita: 'I do not want you to see in the paper or hear possibly on the wireless the terrible thing that has happened to Virginia...'.

Vita hoped that they would never find her body: 'I hope that it will be carried out to sea.' But three weeks later it was found by some children who thought it was a floating log washed up by the bridge at Southease, not far from the place where she had drowned herself. After the inquest, she was cremated at Brighton, with only Leonard as a witness, and her ashes were interred in the garden at Rodmell, with the last words of *The Waves* as her epitaph:

> Against you I will fling myself unvanquished
> and unyielding, O Death

SHORT BIBLIOGRAPHY

Books by Virginia Woolf

The Voyage Out. 1915
Night and Day. 1919
Jacob's Room. 1922
Mrs Dalloway. 1925
The Common Reader (First Series). 1925
To the Lighthouse. 1927
Orlando: A Biography. 1928
A Room Of One's Own. 1929
The Waves. 1931
The Common Reader (Second Series). 1932
Flush: A Biography. 1933
The Years. 1937
Three Guineas. 1938
Roger Fry: A Biography. 1940
Between the Acts. 1941, posthumously

All of the above titles, except the first two, published by the Hogarth Press. *The Voyage Out* and *Night and Day* published by Duckworth's.

The Diary of Virginia Woolf, edited in five volumes by Anne Olivier Bell, assisted by Andrew McNeillie. 1977–84, Hogarth Press

The Letters of Virginia Woolf, edited in six volumes by Nigel Nicolson and Joanne Trautmann. 1975–80, Hogarth Press

Congenial Spirits. The Selected Letters of Virginia Woolf, edited by Joanne Trautmann Banks. 1989, Hogarth Press

A Passionate Apprentice. The Early Journals 1897–1909, edited by Mitchell A. Leaska. 1990, Hogarth Press

Autobiography by Leonard Woolf, in five volumes (differently titled). 1960–69, Hogarth Press

Letters of Leonard Woolf, edited by Frederic Spotts. 1989, Weidenfeld & Nicolson

Moments of Being, edited by Jeanne Schulkind (memoirs by Virginia Woolf). 1985, Sussex University Press

Bell, Quentin: *Virginia Woolf, A Biography*, in two volumes. 1972, Hogarth Press *Elders and Betters*. 1995, John Murray

Bell, Vanessa: *Selected Letters*, edited by Regina Marler. 1993, Bloomsbury

Holroyd, Michael: *Lytton Strachey: The New Biography*. 1994, Chatto & Windus

Leaska, Mitchell A.: *Granite and Rainbow: The Hidden Life of Virginia Woolf*. 1998, Picador

Lee, Hermione: *Virginia Woolf*. 1996, Chatto & Windus

Lehmann, John: *Thrown to the Woolfs*. 1978, Weidenfeld & Nicolson

Sackville-West, Vita: *Letters to Virginia Woolf*, edited by Mitchell A. Leaska and Louise de Salvo. 1992, Hutchinson

Spalding, Frances: *Vanessa Bell.* 1983, Weidenfeld & Nicolson
Duncan Grant. 1997, Chatto & Windus

Shone, Richard: *Bloomsbury Portraits.* 1976 and 1993, Phaidon
Press *The Art of Bloomsbury.* 1999, Tate Gallery

Willis, J.H.: *Leonard and Virginia Woolf as Publishers.* 1992,
University Press of Virginia

· LIVES · LIVES · LIVES · L